Dear Readers,

Many years ago, when I was a kid, my father said to me, "Bill, it doesn't really matter what you do in life. What's important is to be the *best* William Johnstone you can be."

I've never forgotten those words. And now, many years and almost 200 books later, I like to think that I am still trying to be the best William Johnstone I can be. Whether it's Ben Raines in the Ashes series, or Frank Morgan, the last gunfighter, or Smoke Jensen, our intrepid mountain man, or John Barrone and his hard-working crew keeping America safe from terrorist lowlifes in the Code Name series, I want to make each new book better than the last and deliver powerful storytelling.

Equally important, I try to create the kinds of believable characters that we can all identify with, real people who face tough challenges. When one of my creations blasts an enemy into the middle of next week, you can be damn sure he had a good reason.

As a storyteller, my job is to entertain you, my readers, and to make sure that you get plenty of enjoyment from my books for your hard-earned money. This is not a job I take lightly. And I greatly appreciate your feedback— you are my gold, and your opinions *do* count. So please keep the letters and e-mails coming.

Respectfully yours,

WILLIAM W. JOHNSTONE

CUNNING OF THE MOUNTAIN MAN

POWER OF THE MOUNTAIN MAN

PINNACLE BOOKS
Kensington Publishing Corp.
http://www.kensingtonbooks.com

PINNACLE BOOKS are published by

Kensington Publishing Corp.
850 Third Avenue
New York, NY 10022

All Kensington Titles, Imprints, and Distributed Lines are available at
special quantity discounts for bulk purchases for sales promotions, pre-
miums, fund-raising, and educational or institutional use. Special book
excerpts or customized printings can also be created to fit specific needs.
For details, write or phone the office of the Kensington special sales
manager: Kensington Publishing Corp., 850 Third Avenue, New York,
NY 10022, attn: Special Sales Department, Phone: 1-800-221-2647.

Pinnacle and the P logo Reg. U.S. Pat. & TM Off.

First Pinnacle Books Printing: February 2006

10 9 8 7 6 5 4 3 2 1

Printed in the United States of America

CUNNING OF THE MOUNTAIN MAN

1

Sound came to him first. It might be the buzz of an insect, only faint and teasingly erratic. Feeling slowly returned in the form of a throbbing stab of pain in his head. Light registered in a dimly perceived slash of pale gray rectangle, intersected by dark lines. Last to return was memory. Fragile and incomplete, it at least gave him a name, an identity. Jensen. Smoke Jensen.

For many, that name conjured images of a larger-than-life hero, as featured in over a hundred penny dreadfuls and dime novels. Legend had indeed drawn Smoke Jensen larger than his six-foot-two, although broad shoulders, a thick, muscular neck, big hands, and tree-trunk legs left him lacking in nothing when it came to physical prowess. He could truly be considered of heroic proportions.

In the opinion of others, Smoke Jensen was a killer and an outlaw. Some claimed he had killed three hundred men, not counting Indians and Mexicans. The truth was closer to a third of that. And, there was no back-down in Smoke Jensen. He had shot it out with the fastest, fought the toughest, outrode the swiftest. Now he found himself helpless as a kitten.

With an effort that nearly failed to overcome the pulses of misery-laden blackness, Smoke Jensen forced himself up on his elbows. The back of his head felt like he had been kicked by a mule. Where was he? With the fuzziness of a swimmer emerging from murky water, his vision managed to focus on the gray smudge above his head.

A window . . . a barred window. How had he gotten here?

Slowly, scraps of memory began to solidify. "Yes," said Smoke Jensen in a whisper to himself. "I am—or was—in Socorro, New Mexico."

He had been on his way back to the Sugarloaf from selling a string of horses to the Arizona Rangers. They had been fine animals, big-chested and full of stamina. The Rangers wanted some sturdy, mountain-bred mounts for the detachment patrolling the areas around Flagstaff, Globe, and Show Low. Smoke's animals, raised in a high valley deep in the Rockies, answered their needs perfectly. The sale had been arranged through an old friend, Jeff York, now a Ranger captain. His recollection gave Smoke a sensation of warmth and contentment. Even though he was in jail, the money he had received would be safe. It had been forwarded to Big Rock, Colorado, by telegraph bank draft.

None of this told him why he had awakened with a gut-wrenching headache in a jail cell.

A new scrap of memory made itself known. He had three hands along. Where were they? Sitting up proved even more agonizing than rising to his elbows. For a moment the brick walls and bars swam in giddy disorder. Gradually the surge of nausea receded, and his eyes cleared. Full lips in a grim slash, Smoke Jensen examined his surroundings.

He soon discovered that outside of himself—and two drunks sleeping it off in adjacent cells—the jail was empty. The snores of one of the inebriates had provided the insect noises he had first heard. Again he asked himself what had gotten him in jail. Another wave of discomfort sent a big hand to the back of his head.

Gingerly, Smoke Jensen inspected the lump he found there. It was the size of a goose egg and crusted with dried blood. At least it indicated that he didn't have a hangover. Smoke then tried to focus his thoughts on the past few hours. All his effort produced another blank. Suddenly, a door of flat iron straps banged open down the corridor from Smoke's cell. Two men entered, both with empty holsters. Obviously the jailers, Smoke reasoned. At least now he would have some answers.

In the lead came a slob whose belly slopped over a wide, thick leather belt to the point of obscuring his groin. He waddled on hamlike thighs and oddly skinny, undersized calves. His face was a bloated moon, with large, jiggly jowls; the lard of his cheeks all but buried his small, pig eyes. He carried a ring of keys and a ladle.

Behind him came a smaller man lugging a heavy kettle, filled with steaming liquid. Shorter by a head than the fat one, by comparison he managed to look frail and undernourished. His protuberant buck teeth and thin, pencil-line mustache, above an almost lipless mouth, gave him a rodent's appearance. In a giddy moment, Smoke Jensen thought the man would be more suited to be jailer in Raton, New Mexico. Their presence roused one of the drunks.

"Hey, Ferdie, what you got for breakfast?"

Ferdinand "Ferdie" Biggs worked his small, wet, red mouth and spoke in a surprisingly high, waspish tone. "Ain't gonna be any breakfast for you, Eckers. I ain't gonna have you go an' puke it up . . . an' me have to clean up the cell! Got some coffee, though, if you can call this crap coffee."

"How 'bout me, Ferdie Biggs?" whined the other boozer. "You know I don't spew up what I eat after a good drunk."

"It's a waste of the county's money feedin' you, Smithers. If you want som'thin' to fill your belly, suck yer thumb."

Smithers's face flushed, and he gripped the bars of his cell door as though he might rip them out. "Damn you, Biggs. If you didn't have these bars to protect you, I'd beat the livin' hell out of you."

"Says you," Biggs responded. By then he and his companion had reached the neighboring cells. Biggs turned and dipped the ladle into the light brown liquid and poured a tin cup half-full. "Since you gave me so much lip, you get only half a cup, Smithers."

"I'm ravin' hungry," Smithers protested.

Biggs gave him a cold, hard stare. "You want to be wearin' this?" Smithers subsided, and Biggs shoved the cup through the access slot cut in the bars above the lock case. He served Eckers next. Three steps brought him to the cell occupied by Smoke Jensen. He paused there, his small mouth working in a habitual chewing motion. When he took in Smoke's shaky condition, Biggs produced a wide grin that revealed crooked, yellowed teeth.

"You're gonna hang, Jensen. You killed Mr. Tucker in cold blood, and they're gonna string you up for it."

Smoke nodded dumbly. Murder called for a hanging, he silently agreed.

Who is Mr. Tucker?

Martha Tucker sat on the old horsehide sofa in the parlor. Head bowed, hands covering her face, she sobbed out her wretchedness. Larry gone, dead, murdered, they had told her. She vaguely recalled hearing the name Smoke Jensen, who, the sheriff had informed her, had killed Lawrence Tucker. Only her abysmal grief kept her from now recalling who or what Smoke Jensen was. What was she going to do?

What about the children? What about the ranch? Could she legally claim it? Most states, like her native Ohio, considered women mere chattel—property like a man's house, horse, or furniture. At least New Mexico was still a territory and under federal law. That might offer some hope. Martha's shoulders shook with greater violence as each pointed question came to her. For that matter, would the hands stay on with Larry gone? She knew with bitter certainty that no one who considered himself a "real" man would willingly work for a woman. Martha broke off her lamentations at the sound of soft, hesitant footsteps on the large, hooked rug in the center of the parlor floor.

She dabbed at her eyes with a damp kerchief and looked up to see her eldest child, Jimmy. At thirteen, albeit small for his age, he had that gangly, stretched-out appearance of the onset of puberty. His cottony hair had a shaggy look to it; Larry was going to take him into town Saturday for a visit to the barber. Oh, God, who would do it now?

"Mother . . . Mommy? Please—please, don't cry so. Rose and Tommy are real scared." The freckles scattered across his nose and high cheekbones stood out against the pallor of his usually lightly tanned face.

For his part, Jimmy had never seen his mother like this. Her ash-blond hair was always meticulously in place, except for a stray strand that would escape to hang down in a curl on her forehead when she baked. She was so young, and the most beautiful woman Jimmy had ever seen. His heart ached for her, so much so that it pushed aside the deep grief he felt for his father's death.

"Jimmy . . ." Anguish crumpled Martha's face. "Oh, my dearest child, what are we . . . what *can* we do?"

At only thirteen, Jimmy Tucker lacked any wise adult suggestions to offer. All he could do was at last give vent to the sorrow that ate at him, and let large, silent tears course down his boyish cheeks.

Quint Stalker sat his horse in the saddle notch of a low ridge. A big man, with thick, broad shoulders, short neck, and a large head, Stalker held a pair of field glasses to his eyes; bushy, black brows seemed to sprout from above the hooded lenses. Down below, to Quint Stalker's rear, in a cactus-bristling gulch, were the seven men who would be going with him. His attention centered on a small, flat-roofed structure with a tall, tin stove pipe towering above its pole roof at the bottom of the slope.

Old Zeke Dillon had run the trading post beyond the crest for most of his life, Quint reflected. You'd think a feller in his late sixties would be glad to get away from all that hard work and take some good money along, too. But not Zeke.

Bullheaded, was Zeke. A stubborn, old coot who insisted on hanging on to his quarter-section homestead until he dropped dead behind the plank counter of his mercantile, where he traded goods for turquoise and blankets with the Hopi and Zuni. Well, today he'd get an offer he could not turn down.

It just happened that Zeke Dillon's trading post occupied ground far more valuable than he knew. But Quint Stalker's bosses knew. That's why they had sent Quint to obtain title to the 160 acres of sand and prickly pear, road-runners and cactus wrens. Quint lowered the field glasses, satisfied that Zeke, and no one else, occupied the pole-roofed building half a mile from his present position. He raised a gloved hand and signaled his men.

Twenty minutes later, Quint and his henchmen rode up to the front of the trading post. Dust hazed the air around them for a while, before an oven-breath of breeze hustled it away. Quint Stalker and three of his men had dismounted by the time Zeke Dillon came to the door. He stood there, squinted a moment in hopes of recognizing the visitors, and rubbed wet hands on a stained white apron.

"Howdy, boys. Step down and bide a spell. There's cool water an' lemonade inside, whiskey, too, if you ain't Injun."

"Whiskey and lemonade sound good, old-timer," Quint Stalker responded.

Zeke brightened. "Like in one o' them fancy cocktails I been hearin' about out San Francisco way, eh?"

With a nod, Quint shoved past the old man. "Sort of, old-timer." Inside, he let his eyes adjust to the dimness, his sun-burnished skin grateful for the coolness. Then he turned on Zeke Dillon. "Business first, then we'll get to the pleasure."

"How's that?"

"Before we leave here this afternoon, you're gonna sell us your trading post."

"Nope. Never on yer life. I've done turned down better offers than the likes of you can make."

Suddenly a .44 Merwin and Hulbert appeared in Quint Stalker's hand. "What if I were to say you'd sign a bill of sale and take what we offer, or I'll blow your damned brains out?"

Zeke Dillon swallowed hard, blinked, gulped again, and kept his eyes fixed on the gray lead blobs that showed in the open chambers of the cylinder. Tears of regret and humiliation filled his eyes. Not ten years ago, he'd have beaten this two-bit gunney to the draw, and seen him laid out cold on the floor with a bullet in his heart. But not now. Not ever again. With a soft, choked-off sob, Zeke said goodbye to his beloved way of life of the past fifty years.

Quint Stalker produced a filled-out bill of sale and a proper transfer of title form, and handed a steel-nibbed pen to the thoroughly intimidated old man. With a sinking heart, Zeke Dillon dipped the pen in an inkwell on the counter and affixed his signature to both. Then, sighing, he turned to Stalker.

"All right, you lowlife bastard. When do I get my money?"

"Right now," Quint Stalker replied evenly, as he shot Zeke Dillon through the heart.

Sheriff Jake Reno, of Socorro County, New Mexico, who looked every bit an older—but less sloppily fat—version of his chief jailer, stepped into the hall from an office above the Cattlemen's Union Bank in Socorro. He gleefully counted the large sheaf of bills, using a splayed, wet thumb. Nice doing business with fellers like that, he concluded.

All he had to do is see that one Mr. Smoke Jensen gets hanged all right and proper, and he'd get another payment of the same amount. Not bad for a couple of days' work. Given the sheriff's nature, he didn't even bother to wonder why it was that these "business men," as they called themselves, were so set on disposing of Smoke Jensen.

God, the man was a legend in his own time, a dozen times over. Sheriff Reno knew *who* Smoke Jensen was, and a thousand dollars went a long way to ensuring he didn't give a damn why those fancy-talking men—clearly the one with a hyphen in his name sounded like an Englishman— wanted Smoke Jensen sent off to his eternal reward; it was none of the sheriff's business. Time, Sheriff Reno decided, to celebrate his good fortune.

Down on the street, he walked the short block and a half to the Hang Dog Saloon. The building front featured a large, scalloped marquee, heavy with red and gold paint, lettered in bold black. It had a big, ornately bordered oval painting in the middle, which showed a dog, hanging upside down, one foot caught by a strand of barbed wire. It served as a point of amusement for some of the town wags. For others, more involved with the war against the "wicked wire," it represented a political statement. For still others, the sign pointed out man's indifference to cruelty to animals.

Sheriff Reno entered through tall, glass-filled wooden doors. He waved to several cronies and headed directly to the bar, where he greeted the proprietor and bartender, Morton Plummer.

"Howdy, Mort. A shot and a beer."

"Sort of early for you, ain't it, Sheriff?"

Reno gave Plummer a frown. "I'm in a mood to celebrate."

"Celebrate what, Jake?" Morton Plummer asked as he poured a shot of rye.

"I got me a notorious killer locked up in my jail. And enough evidence to hang him for the murder of one of our more prominent citizens."

"I heard something about that," Mort offered, a bit more coolly than usual. "D'you really believe a gunfighter as famous as Smoke Jensen would do something so dumb as let himself get knocked out right beside a man he'd just killed?"

Jake Reno's face pinched and his eyes narrowed. "Who told you that, Mort?"

"Hal Eckers was in for his usual morning bracer a while ago. Said he was locked up acrost from Smoke Jensen most of the night. Ferdie Biggs was shootin' his mouth off about the killin'."

An angry scowl replaced the closed expression on the face of Sheriff Reno. "Damn that Ferdie. Don't he know that even a drunk like Eckers remembers what he hears. Especial, about someone as famous as Smoke Jensen. Might be some smart-ass lawyer"—he pronounced it *liar*—"got ahold of that and could twist it to get Jensen off."

Reno downed his shot and sucked the top third off his schooner of beer. What he had just said set him to thinking. To aid the process, he signaled for another shot of rye. With that one safely cozied down with the other to warm his belly, he saw the problem with clarity. It might be he could use some insurance to see that he collected that other five hundred dollars. Slurping up the last of his beer, Jake Reno signaled Mort Plummer for refills and sauntered down the mahogany to where Payne Finney stood doing serious damage to a bottle of Waterfill-Frazier.

"Is Quint Stalker in town?"

Payne Finney gave the sheriff a cold, gimlet stare. "I wouldn't know."

"I find that odd, considerin' you're his—ah—foreman, so's to speak."

"I've got me a terrible mem'ry, when it comes to talkin' with lawdogs."

Sheriff Reno gave a friendly pat to Finney's shoulder. "Come now, Finney, we're workin' on the same side, as of . . . uh . . ."—he consulted the big, white face with the black Roman numerals in the hexagonal, wooden case of the Regulator pendulum clock over the bar—"ten minutes ago."

Finney's cool gaze turned to fishy disbelief. "That so, huh? Name me some names."

Jake Reno bent close to Payne Finney's ear and lowered his voice. The names came out in the softest of whispers. Finney heard them well enough and nodded.

"I guess you wouldn't know them, if you weren't mixed up in it. What is it you want?"

Sheriff Reno spoke in a hearty fashion after gulping his whiskey. "Thing is, of late, I've come to not trust the justice system to always function in the desired way."

"That a fact, Sheriff?" Finney shot back, toying with the lawman. "And you such a fine, upstanding pillar of the law. Now, what is it you don't trust about the way justice is done in the Territory?"

"Well, there's more of these smooth-talking lawyers comin' out here from back East. They got silver tongues that all too often win freedom for men who should damn-well hang."

"You may have a point," Finney allowed cautiously.

"Of course, I do. An' it's time something was done about it."

"Such as what?"

"Well, you take that jasper I've got locked up right now. Think how it would distress that poor Widow Tucker if some oily haired, silver-tongued devil twisted the facts an' got him off scot-free? It'd vex her mightily, you can be sure."

"What are you suggesting?" Finney pressed, certain he would enjoy the answer.

"Depends on whether you think you're the man to be up to it. For my part, I'd sleep a lot better knowin' some alternative means had been thought up to see that Smoke Jensen gets the rope he deserves."

2

Ranch hands, local idlers, and a scattering of strangers crowded into the two saloons closest to the Socorro jail by midafternoon. Talk centered on only one topic—the killer the sheriff had locked up in the hoosegow.

"That back-shooter's needin' some frontier justice, you ask me," a florid-faced, paunchy man in a brocaded red vest and striped pants declared hotly from the front of the bar in the Hang Dog Saloon.

"Damn right, Hub," the man on his left agreed.

Several angry, whiskey-tinged voices rose in furtherance of this outcome. Payne Finney kept the fires stoked as he flitted from group to group in the barroom. "This Smoke Jensen is a crazy man. He's killed more'n three hunnerd men, shot most in the back, like poor Lawrence Tucker."

Finney added to his lies as he joined a trio of wranglers at the back end of the bar. "Remember when it was in the papers how he killed Rebel Tyree?" He put an elbow to the ribs of one cowhand and winked. "In the back. Not like the paper said, but in the back."

"Hell, I didn't even know you could read, Payne."

"Shut up, Tom. You never got past the fourth grade, nohow. I tell you, this Jensen is as bloodthirsty as Billy Bonney."

"Bite yer tongue, Finney," Tom snapped. "Billy Bonney is much favored in these parts. He done right by avengin' Mr. Tunstill."

Payne Finney gave Tom Granger a fish eye. "And who's gonna avenge Mr. Lawrence Tucker?"

"Why, the law'll see to that."

"An' pigs fly, Tom. You can take my word for it, somethin' ought to be done."

"You talkin' lynch law, Payne?" The question came from a big, quiet man standing at a table in the middle of the room.

Turning to him, Payne Finney blinked. Maybe, he considered, he'd pushed it a bit too far. "Gotta give them the idea they thunked it up on their own." That's what Quint Stalker had taught him. Payne silently wished that Stalker was there with him now. He had no desire to get on the wrong side of Clay Unger, this big, soft-spoken man who had a reputation with a gun that even Quint Stalker respected. He raised both hands, opened them, palms up, in a deprecating gesture.

"Now, Clay, I was just sayin' what if . . . ? You know a lot more about how the law works than I do—no offense," Payne hastened to add. "But from what little I do know, it seems any man with a bit of money can get off scot-free."

"And you were only speculating out loud as to, what if it happened to Smoke Jensen?"

"Yeah . . . that's about it."

Clay Unger raised a huge hand and pointed his trigger finger at Payne Finney. It aimed right between his eyes. "Don't you think the time to worry about that is after it's happened?"

"Ummm. Ah—I suppose you're right, there, Clay."

Finney made his way hastily to the doors and raised puffs of dust from his bootheels as he ankled down the street to Donahue's. There he set to embellishing his tales of Smoke Jensen's bloody career. His words fell on curious ears and fertile minds. He bought a round of drinks and, when he left an hour later, he felt confident the seeds of his plan would germinate.

* * *

After Clay Unger and his friends had left the Hang Dog, two hard-faced, squint-eyed wranglers at the bar took up Payne Finney's theme. They quickly found ready agreement among the other occupants.

"What would it take to get that feller out of the jail and swing him from a rope, Ralph?"

Through a snicker, Ralph answered, "If you mean co—oper—ation, not a whole lot. Ol' Ferdie over there surely enjoys a good hangin'. Especially one where the boy's neck don't break like it oughta. Ferdie likes to see 'em twitch and gag. Might be, he'd even hand that Jensen over to us."

"'Us,' Ralph?" a more sober imbiber asked pointedly.

Ralph's mouth worked, trying to come up with words his limited intellect denied him. "I was just talkin'—ah—sorta hy-hypo—awh, talkin' like let's pretend."

"You mean hypothetically?" Ralph's detractor prodded.

"Yeah . . . that's it. Heard the word onest, about a thang like this."

Right then the batwings, inset from the tall, glass-paneled front doors, swung inward, and Payne Finney strode in. "What's that yer talkin' about, Ralph?"

Puppy-dog eagerness lighted Ralph's face. "Good to see you, Payne. I was jist sayin' that it should be easy to get that Jensen outta the jail and string him up."

Finney crossed to the bar and gave Ralph a firm clap on one shoulder. "Words to my likin', Ralph. Tell me more."

Seated in a far corner, at a round table, three men did not share the bloodthirsty excitement. They cast worried gazes around the saloon, marked the men who seemed most enthused by the prospect of a lynching. Ripley Banning ran short, thick fingers, creased and cracked by hard work and calluses, through his carroty hair. His light complexion flushed pink as he leaned forward and spoke quietly to his companions.

"I don't like the sound of this one bit." He cut sea-green eyes to Tyrell Hardy on his right.

Ty Hardy flashed a nervous grin, and stretched his lean, lanky body in the confines of the captain's chair. "Nor me, Rip. Ain't a hell of a lot three of us can do about it, though."

From his right, Walt Reardon added a soft question. "How's that, Ty? Seems a determined show of force could defuse this right fast."

Tyrell Hardy cut his pale blue eyes to Walt Reardon. He knew the older man to be a reformed gunfighter. Walt's fulsome mane of curly black hair, and heavy, bushy brows, gave his face a mean look to those who did not know him. And, truth to tell, Ty admitted, the potential for violence remained not too far under the surface. He flashed a fleeting smile and shook his head, which set his longish, nearly white hair to swaying.

"You've got a good point, Walt. But, given the odds, I'd allow as how one of us might get killed, if we mixed in."

"There's someone sure's hell gonna get killed, if this gets ugly," Rip Banning riposted. "What'er you sayin', Walt?"

Walt's dark brown eyes glowed with inner fire, and his tanned, leather face worked in a way that set his brush of mustache to waggling. "Might be that we should keep ourselves aware of what's going on. If this gets out of hand, a sudden surprise could go a long way to puttin' an end to it."

Martha Tucker went about her daily tasks mechanically. All of the spirit, the verve of life, had fled from her. She cooked for her children and herself, but hardly touched the food, didn't taste what she did consume. She had sat in stricken immobility for more than two hours, after word had been brought of Lawrence's death. Now, anger began to boil up to replace the grief.

It allowed her to set herself to doing something her late husband had often done to burn off anger he dared not let explode. Her hair awry, her face shiny in the afternoon light, an axe in both hands, Martha set about splitting firewood for the kitchen stove. With each solid smack, a small grunt escaped her lips, carrying with it a fleck of her outrage.

She cared not that at least a full week's supply already had been stacked under the lean-to that abutted the house, beside the kitchen door. Neither did Martha have the words or knowledge to call her strenuous activity therapy; neither she, nor anyone in her world, knew the word "catharsis." She merely accepted that with each yielding of a billet of piñon, she felt a scrap of the burden lift, if only for a moment.

"Mother," Jimmy Tucker called from the corner of the house.

He had to call twice more, before his voice cut into Martha's consciousness.

"What is it, son?"

Jimmy's bare feet set up puffs of dust as he scampered to his mother's side. "There's a man coming, Maw."

Cold fear stabbed at Martha's breast. "Who . . . is it?"

"I dunno. He don't . . . look mean."

"Go in the house, Jimmy, and get me the rifle. Then round up your sister and brother and go to the root cellar."

"Think it's Apaches?"

"Not around here, son. I don't know what to think."

Jimmy's eyes narrowed. "I had better stay with you, Maw."

"No, Jimmy. It's best you are safe . . . just in case."

"If it's that Smoke Jensen, I'll shoot his eyes out," Jimmy said tightly.

A new fear washed over Martha. "You hush that kind of talk, you hear? If I had time, I'd wash your mouth with soap."

Almost a whine, Jimmy's voice came out painfully. "I didn't cuss, Maw."

In spite of the potential danger of the moment, Martha could not suppress a flicker of a smile. Since the first time, at age four, that Jimmy had used the *s*-word, a bar of lye soap had been the answer, rather than his father's razor strap. Oh, how Jimmy hated it.

"Go along, son, do as I say," Martha relented with a pat on the top of Jimmy's head, something else he had come to find uncomfortable of late.

In less than a minute, Jimmy returned with the big old Spencer rifle that had belonged to his father. One pocket of his corduroy trousers, cut off and frayed below the knees, bulged with bright brass cartridges. Martha took the weapon from her son and loaded a round. She held it, muzzle pointed to the ground, when the stranger rode around into the barnyard two minutes later.

"Howdy there," he sang out. "I'm friendly. Come to give you the news from town."

"And what might that be?" Martha challenged.

"Well, ma'am, it looks like it's makin' up for a hangin' for that Smoke Jensen feller. Folks is mighty riled about what happened to your husband."

Unaccountably, the words burst out before she had time to consider them. "Is it certain that he is the guilty party?"

The young wrangler did a double take. "Pardon, ma'am? I figgered you'd consider that good news."

Committed already, her second question boiled out over the first. "They've held a trial so soon?"

A sheepish expression remolded the cowboy's face. "In a way. Sort of, I mean, ma'am. In the—in the saloons. The boys ain't happy, an' they're fixin' to string that feller up."

"Good lord, that's—*barbaric.*"

Self-confidence recovered, the ranch hand responded laconically. "There's some who might consider what he done to your husband to be that, too, ma'am."

"You're not a part of this?"

"No, ma'am. I just rode out to bring you the word."

"Then—then ride fast, find the sheriff, and have him bring an end to it. I don't want another monstrous crime to happen on top of the first."

"You don't mind my sayin' it, that's a mighty odd attitude, ma'am."

"No, it's not. Now you get back to town fast and get the sheriff."

"I say now's the time, boys!" Payne Finney shouted over the buzz of angry conversation in the Hang Dog. "Somebody go out and get a rope. Do it quick, while we still got the chance."

"Damn right!"

"I'll go over to Rutherford's; they got some good half-inch manila."

"No, a lariat will do," Forrest Gore sniggered. "Cut into his neck some that way."

"We'd best be making time, then," another man suggested. "Who all is with us?"

Twenty-five voices shouted allegiance.

"I'll go wind up the fellers at Donahue's," Finney informed them. "Take about half an hour, I'd say. Then we do it."

Covered by the shouts of approval, Ty Hardy leaned toward his companions. "Oh-oh, it looks like the boil's comin' to a head."

"Best we think fast about some way to lance it," Walt Reardon prompted.

"Yeah, an' quick," Rip Banning urged.

Long, gold shafts of late afternoon sunlight slanted into the office above the Cattlemen's Union Bank. Dust motes rose as a strong breeze battered the desert-shrunken window sashes and found the way inside. Crystal decanters sat squat on a mahogany sideboard; glasses had been positioned precisely in front of the three very different men who sat around the rectangular table. Seated at one end, head cocked to the side, listening to the growing uproar from the saloons down the street, Geoffrey Benton-

Howell pursed his thin lips in appreciation. Tufts of gray hair sprouted at each temple, creating a halo effect in the sunbeams; the rest of the tight helmet remained a lustrous medium brown. Long, pale, aristocratic fingers curled around the crystal glass, and he raised it to his lips.

Smacking them in appreciation, he spoke into what had become a long silence. "It appears that our designs prosper." Geoffrey's accent, although modulated by years in the American West, retained a flavor of the Midlands of England. "Miguel, you were wise indeed to suggest we take the sheriff into our confidence. It sounds to me that he is an inventive fellow."

Miguel Selleres glowed in the warm light of this praise. "*Gracias, Don Geoffrey. Mi amigos,* I would safely suggest that we have killed two birds, so to speak, with a single stone."

Although not quite as much the dandy as Benton-Howell, Selleres dressed expensively and had the air of a Mexican grandee. Short of stature, at five feet and six inches, he had the grace and build of a matador. Age had not told on him, though already in his mid-forties; he seemed every bit at home in this rough frontier town as in the salon of a stately hacienda. One side of his short-waisted, deep russet coat bulged with the .45 Mendoza copy of the Colt Peacemaker, which he wore concealed.

"*Señor* Selleres," the third man at the table said, pronouncing the name in the Spanish manner: *Say-yer-res.* "What, exactly, are you getting at?"

"May I answer that, Miguel?" Benton-Howell interrupted when he saw his partner's danger signal, a writhing of his pencil-line mustache.

"Go right ahead, *Señor* Geoffrey," Selleres grunted, containing his anger.

"What he's getting at, Dalton, is that Tucker is out of our way, with the perfect man to pin it on."

"Umm. You do make things so much clearer, Geoff," Dalton Wade said with a lip curl, to make clear his attitude toward Miguel Selleres.

Miguel Selleres cut his jet-black eyes from one partner to the other. He saw affability in the expensive clothing and impeccable manners of Geoffrey Benton-Howell, whom he had referred to as *Sir* Geoffrey. His obvious affluence radiated security to their ambitious goals.

Across the table from him sat a man Miguel thought ill-suited to their company. Although he masked it with sugared words and no overt insult, Dalton Wade's intense dislike of anyone or anything Mexican radiated from his pig face in waves of almost physical force. His swelling paunch matched his heavy jowls, and emphasized his porcine appearance. Wade dressed in the tacky manner of a local banker—which he was—in a rumpled suit of dark blue with too-wide pinstripes. Miguel Selleres felt a genuine wave of revulsion rise within himself. Like a seller of secondhand buggies, Miguel thought with a conscious effort to throttle his rising gorge. It further angered him to acknowledge that he was the youngest of this unholy trio.

"In light of our obvious success, I'd suggest that you contact Quint Stalker and ensure that he moves with dispatch on the properties we desire," Selleres said to Wade.

"It has already been done," Wade snapped, barely in the boundaries of civility.

Benton-Howell stepped in to keep the peace. "Let me expand on that. As we speak, Stalker and some of his men should be acquiring the trading post at Twin Mesas. When that is accomplished, they will move on to the next post, and the next. So there is little left we must address today. However, I have come upon a third benefit we can count as ours in this affair."

"Oh, really? What's that?" Dalton Wade remained cool, even to the man to whom he was beholden for being included in the grand design.

"Why, the most obvious of all, gentlemen. I propose a toast to us—the men who are about to put an end to Smoke Jensen."

3

Sheriff Jake Reno eased his belly through the doorway to his office in the Socorro jail. His small, dusty boots made a soft pattering on the floorboards, as he crossed to a tiny cubicle set in the wall that divided the office from the cellblock. He poked his head in the open doorway and grunted at a snoozing Ferdie Biggs.

"Open up, Ferdie. I want to talk with that back-shooter."

A line of drool glistened on Ferdie's ratlike face. It flashed as he wobbled the sleep out of his head and came to his boots. "Sure 'nuff, Boss. You gonna give him what for?"

"Do you mean beat hell out of him? No. No entertainment for you this afternoon, Ferdie. I only want to talk to him."

Disappointment drooped Ferdie Biggs's face. He reached for a ring of keys and unlocked the laced strap iron door that opened the cellblock for the sheriff. Reno stalked along the corridor, until he reached the cell that held Smoke Jensen.

Smoke reclined on his bunk, head propped up by both forearms. He didn't even open an eye at the sound of the lawman's approach. Heedless of possible damage to the weapon, Reno banged a couple of bars with the barrel of his Merwin and Hulbert. When the bell tone faded, Smoke opened one eye.

"What?" he asked with flat, hard menace.

"I come to get a confession out of you, Jensen."

"Fat chance. I didn't do anything."

"Sure of that, are you?" Reno probed.

"Yes. I'm sure I didn't back-shoot that man."

"You don't sound all that positive to me."

"Sheriff, I'm not sure about what exactly happened to me, how I got here, or when, but I *do* know that I have never deliberately back-shot a man in my life."

"Smoke Jensen, gunfighter and outlaw, and he's never shot a man in the back before? I find that hard to believe. You're pretending, Jensen. I know it and so do you."

"Humor me, Sheriff. Tell me about it."

Taken aback, Sheriff Jake Reno gulped a deep breath. "All right. If it will help you see the light and give me a confession. It happened last night, about ten-thirty. Some shots were heard by customers in the Hang Dog Saloon. They rushed out to find out what was going on. In the alley at the edge of town, they came upon a body lying on the ground, and you.

"You were cold as a blowed-out lamp. The body was dead," Reno explained further.

"Mr. Tucker?"

Reno brightened. "Then you do admit knowing him?"

"No. Your jailer gave me the name early this morning."

"That idiot. Handed you a way out on a platter, didn't he? I'll fix his wagon later. Yes, it was Mister Lawrence Tucker, a highly popular and respected local rancher. He'd been shot. You were laying not far from him, with a .45 in your hand."

"I don't carry a .45," Smoke began to protest.

"You had it in your hand, damnit," Reno snapped. Then he drew a deep breath to regain his composure. "It had been fired twice. There were two bullet holes in Mister Tucker's back. End of case."

"That's ridiculous, Sheriff."

"Oh, yeah?"

"Yes. I normally carry a .44. Two of them, in fact."

"Don't matter, Jensen. No .44s were found anywhere around you, or on Mister Tucker, and no double rig. Your cartridge belt had a pocket for only one iron, and that .45 fit in it like in a glove."

"Did you or anyone recognize the gun and belt, Sheriff? Ever see it before?"

But Reno had already turned away. Over a shoulder he softly purred his last words for Smoke Jensen. "I'd like to stay and chat, Jensen, but I have important business outside town. You all just sit tight, an' we'll get you hanged all legal and proper."

Hank Yates turned from the batwings of the Hang Dog Saloon. "He's ridin' out of town now."

A wide grin turned the cruel, thin line of Payne Finney's mouth into something close to happy. Leave it to Jake Reno to cover himself. "Good. Now, boys, we can really get to work. Some of you go out the back way and wait in the alley between here an' the saddler's. The rest come with me. Spread out across the street and hold yer place, while I go get the fellers from Donahue's."

"You really think we can just walk down there and take Jensen out?" Yates asked, doubtful.

Finney started for the door as he spoke. "Matter of fact, I know we can."

With a surge of action, the men in the saloon obeyed Finney's commands. For a moment, their alcoholic confusion marred any smooth departure, as men aimed in opposite directions bumped into one another. They ironed it out quickly enough and left the barroom almost empty. All except for three men at the corner table they had occupied since the establishment opened.

"I think we'd best stay here awhile," Walt Reardon suggested.

"We've gotta do something to help," Rip Banning urged, his face nearly the color of his flaming hair.

"We will. In due time."

"Dangit, Walt, every second means more danger."

"Relax, Rip. Those boys have got to get all fired up with more whiskey and brave words, before they do anything drastic. Believe me, I know. I've been on the receiving end of more'n one lynch mob."

Neither Ty nor Rip wanted to dispute Walt over that. Rip eased back in his chair and stared balefully at the front doors. Ty examined his empty beer schooner. Walt eyed the Regulator clock on the wall above the bar. Sounds exploded inside the barroom, as boot heels drummed on the planks of the porch outside.

Two rough-looking characters burst in, demanding bottles of whiskey. They took no note of the trio in the corner. After they left, Walt and the other two waited ten long, tense minutes. Then Walt eased his six-gun from leather and put the hammer on half-cock. He rotated the cylinder to the empty chamber and inserted another cartridge. Then he closed the loading gate and returned his weapon to the holster.

"Rip, you go fetch our gear, an' go saddle up the horses."

Rip nodded and departed. Then Walt turned to Tyrell Hardy. "Ty, why don't you slip out the back door and go to the hotel. Bring our long guns back with you."

"Sure, Walt, right away." Ty Hardy was gone faster than his words.

Smoke Jensen heard the ruckus coming from the saloons and correctly interpreted its meaning. He needed to find some way out of this, before they drank enough liquid courage to come and do what they wanted to do. He had to think. He had to find out what had happened after the middle of the previous afternoon, when he and his hands arrived in Socorro.

"We checked into a hotel," Smoke muttered softly to himself. "Got our gear settled in the rooms, then stopped off at a saloon for a drink before supper." It felt like invisible hands were ringing his mind like a washcloth. "What did we eat? Where?"

The silence of the jail and in his mind mocked him. Smoke came up on his boots and paced the small space allowed in his tiny cell. "Something Mexican," he spoke to the wall. "Stringy beef, cooked in tomatoes, onions, and chili peppers. *Bisték ranchero,* that's it."

A loud shout interrupted his train of thought. One voice rose above the others, clear though distant; the cadence was that of someone making a speech. It floated on the hot Socorro air through the small window high in his cell.

"I knew Lawrence Tucker for fifteen years. From when he first moved to these parts. He was a good man. Tough as nails when he had to be, but a good father and husband. Know his wife, too. An' those kids, why they're the most polite, hardworking, reverent younguns you'd ever want to know."

"Yeah, that's right," another voice joined the first. "Larry smoked cigars, like y'all know. Right fancy ones, from a place called Havana. Now, I'll tell you what. I'll buy a box of those special cigars for the first man who fits a rope around the neck of Smoke Jensen!"

Loud cheering rose like a tidal wave. Smoke Jensen stared unbelievingly at the stone wall and gritted his teeth. The testimonials went on, and Smoke could visualize the bottles being passed from hand to hand. In his mind he could see the faces, flushed with whiskey and blood-lust, growing shiny with sweat, as the crowd became a mob.

"In the fifteen years Lawrence Tucker has been here,"

the first orator went on, "he never done a mean or vicious thing. Oh, he shot him a few Apaches, and potted a couple of lobo wolves who wandered down from the San Cristobals, but he never traded shots with another man, white or Mezkin. Didn't hardly ever even raise his voice. Yet, he was respected, and his hands obeyed him. If it wasn't for havin' to tend the stock and protect the ranch, they'd be here now, you can count on that. And they'd be shoutin' loudest of any to hang that back-shooting sumbitch."

More cheers. The whiskey, and the rhetoric, were doing their job.

Smoke Jensen climbed on the edge of the bunk and stretched to see beyond the walls of his prison. It did him little good. He found that his cell fronted on the brick wall of a two-story bakery. It had been the source of the tormenting aromas since his awakening. So far he had received not one scrap of food—only that swill laughingly called coffee, shortly after first light.

Never one to worship food, Smoke's belly cramped constantly now at the yeasty scent of baking bread and sugary accompaniment of pies and cakes. No doubt, the sadistic Biggs had placed him in this cell deliberately, and denied him anything to eat. For a moment it had taken his mind off his very real danger.

More shouts from the distant street soon reminded him. "What're we waitin' for?"

"The fellers at Donahue's are fixin' to join us," Payne Finney bellowed. "Y'all stay here, I'll hurry them on."

Smoke Jensen knew he had to do something before they got the sand to carry out their threats. To do that, he needed help. The question of getting it still nagged him. What *had* happened to the hands he had with him?

Three men sat on their lathered horses under a gnarled, aged paloverde tree that topped a large, red-orange mound overlooking the Tucker ranch. The one in the middle pulled a dust-blurred, black Montana Peak Stetson from his balding head, and mopped his brow with a blue gingham bandanna. He puckered thick lips and spat a stream of tobacco juice that struck an industrious dung beetle, which agitatedly rolled his latest prize back toward the hole it called home.

"That woman down there," he said to his companions. "She's got lots of grit. Say that for her. Wonder what the Big Boss will have to come up with to get her off that place?"

A soft grunt came from the thick-necked man on his right. "I say we jist ride down there, give her what her old man got, an' take over the spread."

Contempt curled the bald man's lips. "Idiot! You'd kill a woman? That's why you take orders from me, and I take 'em from Quint Stalker. It's gotta be all proper and legal, idjit."

"Didn't used to be that way," the bellicose one complained.

"Right you are. But ever since ol' Lew Wallace was territorial governor, we've had an extra large helpin' of law and order."

"You tell me? I done three years, breakin' rocks, because of him."

"Then don't open that grub hole of yours and spout such stupid ideas, or you'll do more than that."

"Sure, Rufe, sure. But I still say it would be the easiest way."

"All we're here to do is drop in and scare her a little."

"Then why don't we get on with it?"

They came down in a thunder of hooves. Dust boiled from under their horses, which rutched and groaned at the effort, adding to the eerie howls made by the men who rode them. Quint Stalker had sent only three men because it was such an easy assignment. In less than two minutes, the overconfident hard cases learned how badly their boss had read the situation.

A skinny, undersized boy with snowy hair popped up out of a haystack and slid down its side, yelling as he went. "Mom! Mom! Hey, they're comin' again!" The callused soles of his bare feet pounded clouds from the dry soil.

He cut left and right, zigzagging toward the house. A woman's figure appeared in one window. Rufe and his henchmen had no time to take note of that. With a whoop, the bald one bore down on the lad and bowled him over with the churning shoulder of his mount. A wild squawk burst from Jimmy Tucker, as he went tail over top and rolled like a ball. He bit down hard, teeth grinding, and cast a prayerful glance toward his mother.

In a flash, that became the last bit of scaring they did.

A puff of smoke preceded the crack of a .56 caliber slug that cut the hat from bald Rufe's head. He let out a squall of his own and grabbed uselessly at the flying Montana Peak, then set to cursing. Another bullet forced his companions to veer to the side and put some distance between them.

"Git back here! It's only a damn woman," Rufe bellowed.

Martha Tucker refined her aim some, her left elbow braced on the windowsill, tapered fingers holding the forestock. Calmly she squeezed off another shot from the Spencer. Her third round smacked meatily into Rufe's right shoulder, and exploded terrible pain through his chest. It also convinced him that this was no simple damn woman.

He'd had enough. He, too, reined to his left and put spurs to the flanks of his horse. Another shot sounded behind him and sped all three on their way.

It started with a sound like an avalanche. A low, primal growl that swelled as it advanced, metamorphosing into the roar of a tidal bore, bent on smashing up an estuary and inundating everything along the river. Although coming from a distance, the angry bellow echoed from the brick wall of the bakery. It made the hairs on the nape of Smoke Jensen's neck rise and vibrate.

They were coming.

How many? Would they get in? Smoke Jensen had been scared in his life many times before. Yet nothing compared to what he experienced now—not the grizzly that had nearly taken off his face before he killed it with a Greenriver knife . . . not the dozen Blackfeet warriors who had surrounded him, alone in camp, with Preacher out running traps . . . not when he faced down a dozen hardened killers in the street of Banning. None of them compared. This absolutely paralyzed him for the moment. He was so helpless, vulnerable. Death rode the mob like a single steed, a hound out of Hell, and it made Smoke reexamine his own fragile mortality. How easily they could take him.

NO! He could find a way to get out of this. Somehow, he could hold off the mob. Think, damnit!

The rattle, squeak, and clang of the cellblock door interrupted Smoke Jensen's fevered speculation as it slammed open. He left the window at once, pressed his cheek to the corridor bars, and looked along the narrow walkway. Waddling toward him, Smoke saw the fat figure of Ferdie Biggs. The keys jangled musically in one pudgy paw.

"Turn around and back up against the bars, Jensen."

"You're taking me out of here?"

"Yep. Jist do as I say."

Smoke turned around and put his hands through the space between two bars. Biggs reached him a moment later, puffing and gasping. Cold bands of steel closed around the wrists of Smoke Jensen. A key turned in the small locks.

"Now step back. All the way to the wall."

"Am I being taken to some safer place?" Smoke asked, his expectations rising.

"Get back, I said." Biggs snarled the words as he reached behind his back and drew a .44 Smith and Wesson from his waistband. He stepped to the door and turned a large key in the lockcase. The bar gave noisily, and the jailer swung the barrier wide. He motioned to Smoke with the muzzle of the Smith, and a nasty smirk spread on his moon face. "Naw. I'm gonna give you over to those good ol' boys out there."

4

Ferdie Biggs prodded Smoke Jensen ahead of him along the cellblock corridor. At the latticework door he passed on through without closing it. He had done the same with the cell, the keys hanging in the lock. The sudden rush of adrenaline had cleared the fuzziness from Smoke's head. He realized that for all of Biggs's slovenly appearance and illiterate speech, he was at least clever enough to lay the groundwork for it to appear the mob had overwhelmed him and broke into the jail.

"You're not smart enough to fake a forced entry, Ferdie," Smoke taunted him. "You're going to get caught."

Biggs gave him a rough shove that propelled Smoke across the room to the sheriff's desk. The narrow edge of the top dug into his thighs. Bright pinpoints of pain further cleared Smoke's thinking. He was ready, then, when Biggs barked his next command.

"Turn around, I wanna have some fun, bust you up some, before I let the boys in."

Smoke turned and kept swinging his right leg. The toe of his boot connected with the hand that held the six-gun and knocked it flying. It discharged a round that cut a hot trail past Smoke's rib cage, and smashed a blue granite coffeepot on a small, Acme two-burner wood stove in the corner. Biggs bellowed in pain and surprise, a moment before Smoke reversed the leg and planted his boot heel in the jailer's doughy middle.

Ferdie Biggs bent double, the air *whoosh*ing out from his lungs. Meanwhile Smoke Jensen recovered his balance and used his other foot to plant a solid kick to the side of Ferdie Biggs's head. From where it made contact came a ripe melon *plop!*, and Ferdie went to his knees.

"The keys, Ferdie," Smoke rasped out. "Give me the keys to these handcuffs."

"Ain't . . . gonna . . . do it."

Smoke kicked him again, a sharp boot toe in the chest. Ferdie gulped and sputtered, one hand clawed at his throat in an effort to suck in air. He turned deep-set, piggish eyes on Smoke Jensen in pleading. Smoke belted him again, from the side. A thin wail came from far down Ferdie's throat—he'd been able to gulp some breath.

"I keep kicking until I get the keys."

Smoke's hard, flat, unemotional voice reached Ferdie in a way nothing else might. One trembling hand delved into a side pocket of his vest. Shakily, he withdrew a single key on a small ring. He dropped it twice, while he knee-walked to where Smoke Jensen stood beside the desk.

"Now, reach around behind me and unlock these manacles." Smoke shoved the tip of one boot up in Ferdie's crotch. "Try anything, and you'll sing soprano for the rest of your life."

Sobbing for breath, and in desperation, Ferdie complied. It took three fumbling attempts to undo the first lock. Then Smoke took the key from Ferdie's trembling fingers and shoved the bleeding, glazed-eyed jailer back against the wall that contained a gun rack. Smoke freed his other wrist, then snapped the cuffs on Ferdie.

"Is there a back way out of here?"

Before Ferdie could answer, a loud pounding began on the closed and barred front door. "C'mon, Ferdie, open up!" a man bellowed.

"Bring him out! Bring him out! Bring him out!" the mob chanted in the background.

"Don't be a fool, Ferdie. He ain't worth gettin' hurt over."

"Your 'good ol' boys' don't seem to like you much, Ferdie," Smoke taunted. "Answer me. Is there a back way out?"

"N-no. Usedta be, but the sheriff had it bricked up."

"How brilliant of him. Nothing for it but to face them down."

Ferdie Biggs blinked incredulously. "How you gonna do that, all alone?"

"I won't be alone," Smoke advised him as he reached to the gun rack. "I'll have Mr. L. C. Smith with me."

He selected a short-barrel, 10-gauge L. C. Smith Wells Fargo gun and opened the breech. From a drawer at the bottom of the rack, he took six brass buckshot casings. Two he inserted into the shotgun. A loud crash sounded from the direction of the front door. Ferdie Biggs cringed.

"They shouldn' do that. It was all set—" He snapped rubbery lips tightly closed, and lost his porcine appearance as he realized he had said too much.

"Set up or not, it isn't going the way they expected, is it?"

A rhythmic banging sounded as four men rammed a heavy wooden bench against the outer face of the door. Ferdie worked his thick lips.

"Oh, hell. Sheriff's gonna have my butt, if that door gets broke."

"The thing you should be worried about is that I've got your butt right *now.*"

Ferdie Biggs looked at Smoke Jensen with sudden, shocked realization. "You ain't gonna shoot me, are you?"

"Not unless I have to." The door vibrated with renewed intensity, and Smoke cut his eyes to it. He saw signs of strain on the oak bar.

"Get something heavier," the mob advised.

"Hell, get some dynamite."

That sent Ferdie Biggs on a staggered course to the shuttered window. He shouted through the thick wooden covers and closed the lower sash. "Oh, Jeeezus, don't do that. I'm still in here."

"Who cares?" a laughing voice told Ferdie.

"Great friends you've got." Smoke Jensen added a cold, death-rattle laugh to increase the effect of his words.

From a drawer in the sheriff's desk, Smoke took a very familiar pair of cartridge belts. One had the pocket slung low, for a right-hand draw. The other rode high on the left, with the butt of a .44 pointing forward, canted at a sharp angle.

Smoke cut his eyes to a thoroughly shaken Ferdie. "And here the sheriff told me they found no sign of my own guns. Now they show up in his desk. Wonder how that happened."

"Don't ask me. All I saw was that old .45."

Smoke hastily strapped himself into the dual rigs. His hand had barely left the last buckle, when the door gave a hollow *boom* and the cross-bar splintered apart and fell to the floor. Another *slam* and the thick oak portal swung inward. Three men spilled into the room. The one in the lead held a rope, already tied into a hangman's knot.

To his left stood another, who looked to Smoke Jensen to be a saddle tramp. His wooden expression showed not the slightest glimmer of intelligence. The rifle he held at hip level commanded all the respect he needed. To the other side, Smoke saw a pigeon-breasted fellow, who could have been the grocery clerk at the general mercantile. Indeed, the fan of a feather duster projected from a hip pocket.

Triumph shone on their faces for only a second, until they took in the scattergun competently held in the hands of Smoke Jensen. Payne Finney reacted first. He let go of the noose and dived for the six-gun in its right-hand pocket.

"For godsake, shoot him, Gore," he yelled.

"You shoot him, Payne," came a wailed reply.

Smoke Jensen had only one chance. He swung the barrels of the L. C. Smith into position between the two gunmen, so that the shot column split its deadly load into two bodies. The deafening roar filled the room. A scream of pain came from the suddenly animated man named Gore. A cloud of gray-white powder smoke obscured the view for a moment. Smoke Jensen had already moved and gazed beyond the huge puffball.

His finger had already found the second trigger; Smoke guided the shotgun unerringly to the next largest threat. When that man made no move to carry on the fight, he sought out the two he had shot. Both lay on the floor.

Payne Finney had taken the most of the 00 pellets, and bled profusely from five wounds. Gore had at least three pellets in his side and right forearm. He lay silent and still now. Shock had knocked him unconscious. A third man, who had been unlucky enough to be in the open space between Finney and Gore, was also down, his kneecap shot away. He writhed and whined in agony. Smoke's keen sight also took in something else.

Sputtering trails of sparks arched over the heads of the mob, who stood stunned on the stoop and in the street. Instinctively, Smoke dived away from the open door, expecting a shattering blast of dynamite. Instead, the red cylinders fell among the members of the lynch mob and went off with thunderous, though relatively harmless, roars. Starbursts of red, white, and green fountained up to sting and burn the blood-hungry crowd. Immediately, three six-guns opened up from behind the startled men of Socorro. Yells of consternation rose among the would-be hangmen.

More shots put wings to the feet of the least hearty of them. Movement away from the jail accelerated when Smoke Jensen stepped into the doorway, shotgun ready. Laughing, yelling, and shooting, Smoke Jensen's three missing ranch hands, Banning, Hardy, and Reardon, dusted some boot heels with lead to speed the lynchers on their way.

"Hey, Walt," Ty Hardy shouted over the tumult. "I told you those Mezkin fireworks I bought in Ary-zona would come in handy."

Walt Reardon looked upon Smoke Jensen with a near-worshipful expression. "Kid foolishness, I called them. Reckon I was wrong. Smoke, good to see you."

"Alive, you mean," Smoke returned dryly.

Reardon brushed that aside. "What the hell happened? You disappeared, and the next thing we know, folks are sayin' you killed a man; back-shot him—which means it sure as the devil weren't you."

"What took you so long?" Smoke smiled to take the sting out of his words.

"We had to have a plan. You should have seen them. Half a hunnerd at least." Reardon tipped back the brim of his hat and wiped a sweaty brow. "What now?"

"I suggest we leave the lovely town of Socorro for better parts," Smoke advised.

"Suits," Reardon agreed. "We—ah—took the precaution to get your horse saddled and ready. It's down the block."

All four started that way. Behind them, Ferdie Biggs tottered out onto the stoop. "What about me? What's gonna happen to me?"

Smoke Jensen swiveled his head and gave Ferdie Biggs a deathly grin. "You'll have quite a story to tell the sheriff now, won't you, Ferdie?"

Through no fault of their own, Geoffrey Benton-Howell, Miguel Selleres, and Dalton Wade erroneously toasted the demise of Smoke Jensen when they heard the commotion coming from the jail. Beaming heartily, Benton-Howell refilled their glasses and raised his again.

"And here's to our prospects of becoming very wealthy men."

"Hear, hear!" Dalton Wade responded.

"I think it is fortuitous that our man found Quint Stalker so quickly," Miguel Selleres remarked. "Now that he is rounding up his men, we can put our next phase in operation."

"I'd like to see Smoke Jensen swinging from a tree." Bitterness rang in Wade's words.

Benton-Howell gave him a hard look. "It would be more politic for us to remain here, out of the sight of others. If you would be so kind, why is it you have such a hatred for Smoke Jensen?"

Dalton Wade considered a moment before answering. "Three close friends are in their graves because of that damned Smoke Jensen."

Geoffrey Benton-Howell said, "They were all good friends?"

"Yes, they were. Two of them were doing quite well, running a small town up in Montana with iron fists. Some of their henchmen stepped on the toes of someone related to Smoke Jensen. Jensen took exception to it. When Jensen finished, fifteen men were dead, another twenty-seven wounded. Among them, my friends."

"What about the third?" Benton-Howell asked.

"Jeremy and I were very close friends. He fancied himself a good hand with a gun. Fast, exceptionally fast in fact. But . . . not fast enough. He braced Smoke Jensen one day. Jensen was actually a bit slower on the draw, but oh, so much more accurate. Jeremy didn't have a chance."

"I see. So all along this has been personal with you, not just a means to an end. For my part, and Don Miguel's, when our involvement in this is known, we'll be considered clever heroes to many people. It will make what comes after . . . ah . . . more palatable to them." His smile turned nasty. "From now on, events are going to turn rather rough. It's necessary that they are blamed on a mythical Smoke Jensen gang, seeking retribution for his death."

Benton-Howell poured more brandy, and his laughter filled the room.

Sheriff Jake Reno rode into a town oddly quiet for the scene of a lynching. Socorro slumbered under the hot New

Mexico sun. A deep uneasiness grew when he saw no signs of a dead Smoke Jensen hanging from any tree on the northern edge of town. He found the jail door open, as expected, but no sign of Ferdie Biggs. He dismounted and entered.

Ferdie Biggs lay slumped on the daybed used by the night-duty jailer. He had a fist-sized lump on the side of his head—bandaged in yards of gauze—a fat, swollen lip, and more tape and bandage around his ribs.

"What the hell happened to you?" Reno blurted.

"Smoke Jensen's what happened. He kicked the crap out of me and escaped. Had three fellers with him, outside the jail when the mob came. Set off some kind of explosives, shot up the place, and they all got away."

Rage burned in the sheriff's chest as he saw his five-hundred-dollar bonus flying away. He crossed to where Biggs lay and grabbed a double handful of shirt, yanking the slovenly jailer upright. "Goddamnit, can't you do anything right?"

"Ow! Oh, damn, I hurt! I meant what I said, Jensen *kicked* me."

"I suppose because he was in handcuffs?" Reno said scornfully.

Ferdie gulped. "Yep. I had him cuffed, right enough."

"But you got too close. Pushed your luck, right?"

"Uh-huh. I wanted to punch him up a little, have some fun before they hung him. Next thing I knew, he was usin' them of his boots on me."

"Idiot. Get that lard butt of yours out there and round up some men to form a posse. We're going after Jensen." Sheriff Reno's decision came automatically, without a thought of consulting the men who had bought his cooperation.

There'd be hell to pay when they found out his means of disposing of Smoke Jensen had failed, he reckoned. Best to put that off for awhile. Chances were, he'd run Jensen to ground easily, and come back to collect his five hundred. Sure, Reno's growing self-confidence told him, Smoke

Jensen or not the man was on the run in strange territory. It would be easy.

It would take all of the cunning of the last mountain man to evade the posse Smoke knew would be sent to pursue him and his hands. Ten miles out of town, Smoke had called a halt and sincerely thanked his men for the rescue. He saw clearly now, that they had laid low in order not to become ensnared in whatever skullduggery had put him in line for a lynching. He also explained the options open to them.

". . . so that's about it. You can all take off for the Sugar-loaf, or take your chances with me."

"What do you reckon to do?" Walt Reardon asked.

"I'm going to find out who killed Tucker, and why. That should clear my name in these parts."

Reardon, used to being a wanted man, nodded soberly. "Might be a big undertakin'. I allow as how you could use some help."

"Same for me," Ty Hardy chimed in.

"I'll stick it out with you, Smoke," Rip Banning added.

"It can get rough. There's a chance some of us will draw a bullet."

"Way I see it, Smoke, that's an everyday experience. Long as it's not a stacked deck, count me in for the game."

Smoke Jensen looked hard at Walt Reardon, appreciating his staunch support and his knowledge. Smile lines crinkled around Smoke's slate-gray eyes, and he nodded curtly. "Best I could come up with is to head for the nearest mountains. Wear the posse down, confuse them. Sooner or later they'll give up and go home."

Walt grinned. "Now, that shines. I 'member the time me an' old Frisco Johnny Blue did just that up in Dakota Territory. Worked fine as frog hair. Is there . . . ah . . . somethin' else we could be doin', while givin' that posse the slip?"

"Maybe. I'll think on it. Now, let's put some distance between us and them. Next stop's the Cibola Range."

5

Sheriff Jake Reno trotted his blotched gray along the main trail leading north out of Socorro. The posse had covered eight miles at a fast trot, then slowed the pace to look for tracks. They found them easily. Reno held them to a leisurely pace from then on.

"My guess is, they'll be cuttin' west soon," he advised the man on his left.

"Why's that?" the uncomfortable store clerk asked.

"Smoke Jensen's got him a rep'tation of bein' a mountain man. The last mountain man. I reckon he'd feel more at home in the hills. Too open to keep on north toward the Rockies. Those three saddle bums is wanted for jailbreak, along with Jensen, an' you can add murder on Jensen's head. No, they won't want to run into a lot of folks."

Snorting doubt through a nose made red by whiskey, the clerk issued his own opinion. "If he wanted mountains, there's plenty around Socorro."

"But too close to town for his likin'. Smoke Jensen's nothin' if he ain't clever. If he was to sneak around outside town, we could keep resupplied forever and wear him down. Now, you be for keepin' a close eye out for where they turn off."

They almost missed it, as it was. A bare, wide slab of rock

led into the bed of an intermittent stream, presently made liquid by heavy rains in the mountains. A fresh scrape, made by the iron shoe of a heavy horse, told the story to the sheriff's favorite scout. He waved the posse down as they approached.

"They went into the water."

"Not too smart under the best of conditions," Jake Reno opined.

"It will run dry in an hour or two," the scout suggested.

"Or it'll come a flash flood gushin' down on us. We'll ride the banks, let them take the risk. Jensen and his trash friends'll come out sooner than later, I figger."

Five miles to the west, the posse came upon the spot where four horses began to walk on wet sand. Sheriff Reno halted the men and tipped back the wide brim of his hat. A blue gingham bandanna mopped at the sweat that streaked down his temples and brow.

"Yep. They're headin' into the Cibolas. Eb, you an' Sam head back for town. Get us some pack animals and lots of grub. This is gonna be a long hunt."

"Like I said, boys. This ain't like the High Lonesome, but at least it's mountains." Smoke Jensen dismounted and continued to speak his observations aloud. "I'd say the sheriff is a good ten miles behind. Time to fix up something for him to remember us by."

"How's that?"

"Walt, you were with the Sugarloaf back when those Eastern dudes tried to attack the place. Perhaps you could enlighten young Rip here."

"Sure, Smoke." Walt proceeded to tell Ripley Banning about the deadfalls, pits, and the great star-shaped log obstacles that had so befuddled the army of Eastern thugs, who had been sicked on the Sugarloaf hands only a year past. Rip started to grin early on, and his eyes danced with mischief by the time the tale had been told.

"Considerin' your fondness for ornery tricks, Walt, it couldn't be that maybe you thought up some of those nasty traps?"

Walt Reardon pulled a face. "Rip, you wound me. Though I confess, it was my idea to gather up them yeller-jacket nests in the night whilst they was restin', and flang gunnysacks full in among the sleepin' outlaws." He clapped his hands in approval. "They folks danced around right smartly."

Under the direction of Smoke and Walt, several large snares and a deadfall were rigged on the trail they left. "We'll cut south a ways now," Smoke suggested. "If I was making a way through these hills, I reckon I'd pick me a way through that pair of peaks yonder. Looks like a natural pass to me."

"You've got a hell of an eye, Smoke," said Walt admiringly.

Sheriff Jake Reno heard a faint *twang*, a second before a leafy sapling made a swishing rush through the air and cleaned two possemen off their mounts. One's boot heel caught in the stirrup, and the frightened horse he had been riding set off at a brisk run along the trail. The man's screams echoed off the high sandstone walls that surrounded them.

Not for long, though, as his head plocked against a boulder at the side of the narrow passageway, and he lost consciousness. Wide-eyed and pale, the sneering clerk lost some of his cockiness. He cut his eyes to the sheriff and worked a mouth that made no sound for a moment.

"What was that?"

"A trap, you dummy. Nobody move an inch, hear?"

The sheriff's advice proved wise indeed. The riders cut their eyes around the terrain and located two more of Smoke Jensen's surprises: a deadfall and another swing trap. Reno ordered the men to dismount and search on foot. That worked well enough, until a second *swoosh* of leaves and a startled scream froze them in place.

Jake Reno found himself looking up at a man suspended some ten feet off the ground, his ankles securely held in a rope snare. "Just like a damn rabbit," the lawman grumbled. "Some of you get him down. We'll stick to the center of the trail. Walk your mounts. And . . . keep a sharp eye, or you'll be swingin' up there next . . . or worse."

Smoke Jensen stood looking south at the summit of a natural pass through the Cibola Range, and studied the land beyond. "I figure that bought us a good three hours. It appears to me there's a small box canyon about a half hour's ride along this trail. We'll camp there for the night."

From that point on, Smoke and his wranglers took care to hide their tracks. Walt Reardon took the rear slot with a large clump of sagebrush, which he used to wipe out their prints on soft ground. They reached the overgrown entrance to the side canyon in twenty minutes. Smoke went ahead and made sure they could navigate the narrow passage without leaving obvious signs of their presence. At the back of the small gorge, they found a rock basin of water, cool and clear. Called a tank in these parts, from the original Spanish designation of *tanque,* this natural water reservoir had saved many a life on the barren deserts of the Southwest.

Some, like this one, were even big enough to swim in. Of course, Smoke advised his ranch hands, that would have to wait until they and the horses had drunk their fill, and used all they needed for cooking.

"Though I don't mind leavin' behind some dirt for the good Sheriff Reno to swallow," he concluded with a chuckle.

Ty Hardy and Walt Reardon set about locating pine cones and dry wood to make a nearly smokeless fire. Smoke figured they had a good three hours in which to prepare food for that night and the next morning. Once well accustomed to the outlaw life, Walt Reardon had prepared well, stuffing their saddlebags with coffee beans, flour, sugar, salt, side pork, and dry beans. Smoke got right down to mixing dough for skillet bread. Resembling a giant biscuit, baked over coals in a cast-iron skillet, and sealed with the lid of a Dutch oven, it was served in pie wedges. Not as tasty as the flaky biscuits Smoke's lovely wife, Sally, made, but it would serve, and could be eaten hot or cold. Rip Banning watched intently, until Smoke sent him for water for the Dutch oven to soak beans. Rip returned with a broad, boyish grin.

"Found me a bee tree. It's jam-packed with honey. Reckon it'll go good on that skillet bread."

Smoke cocked an eye on him. "How you reckon on getting that honey without having an argument with the bees?"

"Why, I'll just smoke . . . uh . . . dumb of me, huh? Can't drowse 'em out with a big ol' puff of pearly white that'd let the sheriff know where we'd gone."

"You're learnin'. We'll just have to forego the honey tonight. And," Smoke continued, "I'm appointin' you to make sure all fires are well out before sundown."

"Make the lesson stick, huh?"

"You got the right of it, Rip."

Walt returned from his last trip for wood with four plump squirrels. Excitement filled Rip Banning. "We're gonna feast. How'd you git 'em without firing a shot, Walt?"

Walt made light of it, but could not avoid a tiny brag. "I come up on them, frolickin' on the ground. So I just locked eyes and mesemer . . . mesariz . . ."

"Mesmerized," Smoke provided.

"Yeah, that's right. I done stared them down."

Rip nodded with youthful enthusiasm, then produced a frown over his green eyes. "Squirrels are hard to dress out."

Walt gestured with his russet-furred contribution to dinner. "That's why you're cleaning all of 'em."

"Awh, Walt—"

"You fixin' to sink a tooth into one of 'em, you can do the honors."

They tasted delicious, roasted over the fire, helped along with skillet bread, thick beans, wild onions, and watercress from the tank. Half an hour before sundown, Rip poured water on the fire, raked the ashes, and distributed the stones that had formed the fire ring. With muttered good-nights, Smoke and the two older hands rolled up in their blankets and fell into deep sleep. Rip, being youngest, had the first watch. He would wake Walt for second shift, who in turn would roll out Ty Hardy. Smoke took the last trick, usually the most likely for a surprise attack.

Setting down the empty tin cup, Sheriff Jake Reno wiped a drop of coffee off one thick lip and rested the hand on the swell of his belly. He was beginning to suspect that they had taken the wrong trail. This one led nowhere, if he recollected correctly. It would take them half a day to cross south over the ridges between them and the pass that led to the great inner valley of the Cibola Range. There they could get reinforcements and resupply at Datil, or further on at Horse Springs.

Provided, of course, that Smoke Jensen didn't get there first and tie up with some local guns. That could get nasty. The heavy breakfast the sheriff had eaten rumbled in his gut. Oh, lord, all he needed was to work up a burnin' stomach. Those damned traps set out by Jensen had cost them half a day. Just thinking about them put him in a stew.

"Herkermer, I want you to round up a dozen of the boys and take the shortest route to Cristoforo Pass. I got me a feelin' we're in the wrong part of the Cibolas."

"The trail led us northwest," Herkermer protested. "Besides, the shortest way is the longest. All them ridges to climb."

"You'll pick up speed goin' down the other sides," Reno snapped back.

"What'll you be doing in the meantime?"

"Look, Herkermer, I'm runnin' this posse, not you. We'll be havin' a look-see at this trail; the canyons yonder link up, make for hard goin', but a body can get through. We have to be certain which way Jensen went. Then we'll join you in Datil. I've a hunch Jensen is makin' for the main part of the range."

"He'd sure have to know a hell of a lot about the country for him to figger that out," Payne Finney said obstinately, the pain in his side making him more irritable than usual.

"What's to say he don't have a map, you ninny? Those buckshot holes is makin' you dizzy-headed. Truth to tell, you ain't in fit condition to ride with us. I think I'm goin' to send you back to Socorro with a message for some certain gentlemen."

"Our mutual employers, you mean," Payne prompted nastily. "Suits me. I ain't feelin' all that whippy, nohow."

"You tell 'em where we are and what we're doin'," was the sheriff's command.

You're splittin' the posse, an' makin' a fool of yerself, Payne Finney thought silently. He knew only too well how damned dangerous Smoke Jensen could be. *Goddamn you, Smoke Jensen,* Payne Finney vowed to himself, *I'm gonna fix your clock sure as shootin'.*

Geoffrey Benton-Howell and his partners already knew of the fiasco in the jail. Miguel Selleres and Dalton Wade fumed, while Geoffrey Benton-Howell tried to calm his partners and get some positive thoughts out of them about a bit of news just delivered. The bearer of the good tidings, Axel Gundersen, watched the two would-be tycoons vent their spleens with mild amusement. At last, he spoke into the silence after their tirade.

"*Ja,* sure, Sir Geoffrey, it's exactly like I say. The gold is there, true enough, *hufda.* Make no mistake about that.

Some of it is exposed on the surface. The problem is getting it out."

Miguel Selleres rounded on him. *"Hijo de la chingada!* Make sense, *Señor!* Didn't you just say that gold was to be found on the surface? What's to make it difficult getting it out?"

Gundersen drew a straight face and called on his ample knowledge of English idioms. "About eight hundred angry White Mountain Apache warriors, *ja*, sure."

"Ah . . . ummm, yes, Miguel. There is a small difficulty to get around the Apaches."

"What's the problem in that?" Dalton Wade snapped.

"The gold is on their land," Geoffrey Benton-Howell reminded his listeners.

"Land they've got no goddamned right to," Wade thundered. "What do those stupid savages know about gold?"

Benton-Howell tried a soft approach. "That we white men desperately want the yellow rocks, as they call the gold. That we go absolutely mad over possessing it."

Wade's lip curled downward in a parody of a pout. "There you go. To those stinking Apaches, they are just rocks. If people can't appreciate what they have on their land, it should be taken from them."

"Which we are in the process of doing. Here, take some brandy and relax. Well, Gundersen, you've done a fine job. Your compensation will be in keeping with your achievements."

"Ja, sure, I expected no less. Now all you need to do is follow through with the politicians."

During the lonely hours of his watch, Smoke Jensen had thought through the situation in which he found himself. The previous day had been given over to surviving long enough to examine conditions and options. He announced the result of his deliberations over breakfast the next morning.

"We're going to split up."

"We done anything that don't suit you?" Walt Reardon asked cautiously.

"No, nothing like that. We can stick together and run that posse ragged, but in a way, that's spinnin' a wagon wheel over a gorge. Someone needs to get word to the Sugarloaf. Ty, I'm going to leave that up to you."

"I'd rather ride beside you, Smoke."

"I know you would. But Sally has to hear about this from someone on our side. Besides, it might be we'll need help from the other hands, before this is over. Or from Monte Carson. He knows you; so does Sally. Walt, I want you and Rip to head back to Arizona. Contact Jeff York, the Ranger captain we sold those horses to. Tell him what's going on, and ask if he knows what's behind it."

"Want us to bring him here?"

"Out of his jurisdiction, Walt. But if he offers, carry him along."

"I've got the feeling there's gonna be hell to pay 'fore long."

Smoke came to his boots, put a hand on Walt's shoulder. "You're right. And I aim to see the ones payin' it are Sheriff Reno and his posse. I'm headin' on. Lead your horses up the trail a ways in the direction you're going, then wipe out every sign of this camp."

Walt nodded curtly. "Keep a wall to your back, Smoke."

"I will, whenever I can, Walt."

"Hell, this ain't gettin' us anywhere, Sheriff," a disgruntled posseman complained.

Jake Reno considered that a moment. "You're right, Jim. We ain't seen a sign of them in hours. Might be we're following the wrong trail. What we need to do is fan out, follow ev'ry game and people path heading south. I know it in my bones that Smoke Jensen is headed toward Horse

Springs. There's a telegraph there, and he can get help if he wants it."

"What would any wanted man go into a town for?" Jim asked.

"It's not like he really kilt—" Reno realized what he was about to say and bit off the words.

Two of the citizens of Socorro exchanged nervous glances. Doubt wrinkled the brows of several others.

"Now, I want you to keep this in mind. This whole affair has gone too damn far. Check out everything that moves, and if you see Jensen, shoot to kill."

6

Smoke Jensen ghosted through the trees in a low ground mist that had drifted in around three in the morning. Only his wranglers had left the northern slopes of the Cibola Range. Smoke had kept his place, expecting to catch Sheriff Jake Reno off guard. And he had.

A crackle of brush made Smoke Jensen cut his eyes to the left. Only a second passed before he heard soft, murmured words from that direction. His keen vision marked the shapes of two heads, close together. The sheriff had been smart enough to put out pickets, but he hadn't been too smart about who he had assigned the duty, Smoke reckoned. The mountain man had exchanged boots for moccasins earlier, and now moved with utter silence.

Half a dozen carefully placed strides brought him up behind the unwary pair. One of the possemen had just fished the makin's out of a vest pocket. When he started to roll a quirley, Smoke Jensen reached out with two big, hard hands to the sides of the duo's heads, and slammed them together. He made quick work of binding their hands and feet with short lengths cut from a rope he had taken off another inattentive sentry earlier.

Smoke stuffed the neckerchiefs of the unconscious men into their mouths. Satisfied with his work, he moved on. A surprisingly short distance inside the camp, he came upon a line of picketed horses. A reassuring pat on the muzzles of the critters gained their silence, while Smoke undid their reins from the tightly stretched lariat that served as an anchor. A sudden, cold thought speared at him: This was entirely too easy.

"I figgered you'd come lookin' for us. So, I left you a few tidbits to whet your appetite," said Sheriff Reno, as he clicked back the hammer of his Smith and Wesson .44 American.

Smoke Jensen turned his way and made a draw in one smooth motion. Jake Reno had never seen anything like it. One second he was looking at Smoke Jensen's back; a split-second later, Jensen faced him, the black hole of a .44 muzzle settling in on the lawman's belly. Without conscious direction, Reno's body took over, flexed at the knees, and he flew backward into the sharp thorns of a clump of blackberry bushes. Smoke's .44 roared and spat fire, before Reno could even think to trigger his.

Hot lead cut a shallow trail across the upper curve of the sheriff's buttocks. With wild squalls, the horses took off at a run, and so did Smoke Jensen.

"Goddamnit, he's shot me! Smoke Jensen's shot me," Jake Reno roared, more angry than hurt.

Bent double, the famous gunfighter streaked along, parallel to the camp and at a right angle to the direction taken by the frightened critters. From behind, Smoke heard new, painful yelps from the sheriff, who was learning why any man with good sense sent his woman and kids out to pick berries.

Sleepy cries of alarm rose from the disturbed camp. Men began to curse hotly, when they realized what the sound of pounding hooves meant. Smoke Jensen ignored them and forced his way through the underbrush to where he had left his mount. He'd give them some time to settle down, he reasoned, then hit again about midnight.

* * *

Five of Quint Stalker's gang, who had ridden with the posse, paused at the dark entrance to a side canyon. Not even the full moonlight could penetrate the gorge. Under the frosty starlight, they cut uncertain glances at one another.

"Don't know why the hell the sheriff wants us checkin' this out in the middle of the night," one complained.

"Says he's got a hunch. You ask me, it's a little indigestion proddin' his belly."

"Or his sore butt stingin'," another opined.

At the rear of the loose formation, the last man saw a brief flicker of movement right before his eyes. Then he let out a short, startled yelp, as the loop tightened and pinned his arms to his sides above the elbows. The others turned in time to see him disappear from the saddle.

"What the hell!" the nominal leader exploded. "Hub! Where the hell are you?"

But Hub wasn't saying anything. He was too busy sucking on the barrel of a .44 in the hand of Smoke Jensen. Smoke gave an unseen nod of satisfaction and bent low to whisper in Hub's ear.

"You want to stay alive, you keep real quiet." Smoke removed the steel tube from Hub's mouth at the man's energetic nod of agreement. "I'm going to tie your legs together and string you up in that tree."

"You said I could live," Hub blurted in confusion and fear.

"Upside down, idiot. And you will live, if you give me five minutes to get clear of this place. Then you can yell your fool head off."

Hub Peters had no problem believing everything Smoke Jensen told him. He felt the rope circle his ankles and the tension increase. The tight band around his chest eased off, and he swung free of the ground. His fear somewhat abated, he could again hear his companions.

"D'you see that? Where in hell did he go?"

"I don't know, but it's some more bad news from Smoke Jensen, count on it."

"We goin' in after Hub?"

"You crazy?" the leader challenged. "Want to wind up disappearin' before yer friends' eyes?"

"What about Hub?"

Hearing this, Jensen said, "Nice friends you have, Hub. If I was you, I'd light me a shuck for someplace far, far away from them." Smoke's soft chuckle faded off into the distance.

Silently, Hub Peters agreed with Smoke Jensen.

Had they been looking in the right direction, the men of the posse would have seen a telltale spurt of gray-white powder smoke, some three seconds before the blue granite coffeepot gave off a metallic clang and leaped from the fire. Boiling liquid flew everywhere, then the sound of the shot came. Three hard cases—brought by the sheriff to keep the townies in line—squawked in alarm as the hot brew scalded their flesh.

They tore at their shirts and trousers in an effort to escape their torment, unmindful of the danger. Most of the others had already bellied down in the dirt.

"Over there!" came a frightened cry as another blossom of gray rose from the hillside.

This time, one of Quint Stalker's gunnies went down with a bullet through his right thigh. He flopped and cursed and moaned in the dust, while his companions skittered off to find better cover. One outlaw hanger-on with better foresight had brought a long-range Express rifle. He unlimbered it from its scabbard, adjusted the sight, and took aim. After levering three rounds through the Winchester, he had to acknowledge that only a fool would have stuck around after the second shot. He'd wasted the ammunition.

When the sniper fire did not resume after five minutes,

the possemen picked up the remains of their breakfast and fell into their routine. A crack-whisper of sound above their heads turned faces upward, to receive a shower of shredded leaves. Right on the tail of the high round, another snapped into camp and split the cross-tree of a pack saddle.

Once more, everyone dove for cover. One pudgy townsman didn't take as much care as his comrades, and paid for it with the heel of one boot. The howl he put up might have convinced someone his foot had been shot off.

"Goddamn you, Smoke Jensen!" Sheriff Jake Reno roared, shaking a fist above the boulder behind which he sheltered. A .45-70-500 Express bullet whipped past his knuckles, close enough for him to feel its heat. He gave a little yelp and hunkered down.

This time no one moved for fifteen minutes. Two of Stalker's hard cases came out in the open first. "We'd best go look for a trail," one opined.

"What for? It'd only lead to an ambush," the other outlaw complained.

"Damn you, men, you're my deputies now, and you'll do as I say," Reno raved. "Get on your horses and go out there and hunt down Smoke Jensen."

"*Temp-orary* deputies, Sheriff," the reluctant one reminded Reno. "And, right about now, I'm figgerin' that short time has runned out."

"You're not leaving," an unbelieving Sheriff Reno gasped.

"Reckon to. I sure ain't gonna stand around and git shot at by a man who don't miss lest he wants to."

"You're cowards, that's what you are."

Eyes narrowed with sudden anger, the hard case faced off with the sheriff. "Now, I don't 'zactly take kindly to that, Sheriff. Y'all want to back up them bad-mouthin' words with gunplay?"

Ooops! Sheriff Reno suddenly realized he had gone too far. "Ah—ummm, no, not at all. I spoke out of hand, gentlemen. Go if you want. Besides, I need someone to take a message to our mutual friend."

"You mean Quint?"

Sheriff Reno winced. "Uh . . . tell him what's going on, and have him send some more men."

"Don't reckon he'll be able to do that. We've got other irons in the fire."

"Damnit, man, nothin's more important than stopping Smoke Jensen. Just carry the message, and I'll be satisfied."

"Sure 'nuff, Sheriff," the grinning hard case responded as he headed for his horse.

He made it three-quarters of the way there, before a bullet from Smoke Jensen took him in the meaty point of his left shoulder. Little pig squeals came from skinned-back lips, along with bloody froth from a punctured lung as he went to the ground.

"Oh. Sweet . . . Jesus!" Sheriff Reno shouted to the sky. And to those around him it sounded like a prayer.

Smile lines crinkled around Smoke Jensen's gray eyes, and the corners of his mouth twitched. After this, those townies would be afraid to drink anywhere in the mountains. Of course, it would be hard on anyone who happened on the stream before it washed clear.

He'd left the carcasses out to bloat and ripen in the sun for two days. They had become so potent that Smoke needed to cover his face with a wet kerchief to cut down the stench. Even then, it near to gagged him when he rigged the rope that held them in the water. He made sure it was easy to see.

A final look around the clearing by the stream, and he got ready to leave. Carefully, Smoke wiped out any sign of his presence as he departed. Within a minute, only the muted echo of a soft guffaw remained of the last mountain man.

* * *

"What's that awful smell?" a townsman asked of Sheriff Reno.

"Smells like skunk. Mighty ripe skunk," the lawman replied.

"It's coming from the crick," one of Quint Stalker's outlaws advised.

"Skunks don't take baths," another contradicted.

"Hey, there's a rope hangin' down over the water," another shop clerk deputy declared. "Somethin's on the end of it."

Three of Stalker's men rode over to investigate. One dismounted and bent over the bank. He turned back quickly enough, his face a study in queasiness.

" 'Fore God, I hate that Smoke Jensen. He's put three rotten skunks in the water."

"Three skunks?" the sheriff echoed.

"Three *rotten* skunks. Flesh all but washed off of 'em, guts all strung out."

Gagging, retching sounds came from a trio of townies. Faces sickly green, they wobbled off into the meadow to void their stomachs. One finished before the others and turned back to the sheriff, who sat his horse with a puzzled expression.

"We—we drank from that crick not half a mile back. Filled our canteens, too."

A couple of Stalker's hard cases began to puke up their guts. Those affected wasted no time in remounting. They put heels to the flanks of their animals and fogged off down the trail in the direction of Socorro. Sheriff Jake Reno remained gape-mouthed for a moment, the slight wound on his hindside stinging from the sweat that ran down his back, then bellowed in rage. "Goddamn you, Smoke Jensen! I'm gonna kill you, you hear me? I'm gonna kill you dead, dead, dead, Smoke Jensen!"

While Smoke Jensen frazzled the nerves of the posse, five hard-faced men paid a visit to the Widow Tucker and her three small children. Their leader, Forrest Gore, had been barely able to stay in the saddle on the long ride out from Socorro. Jimmy Tucker saw them first, and the smooth, hard-callused soles of his bare feet raised clouds as he darted from the barn to the rear of the house.

"Some more bad guys comin', Maw," he shouted as he banged through the back door.

Martha Tucker looked up from the pie crust she had been rolling out, and wiped a stray lock of hair from her damp forehead with the back of one hand. The effort left a white streak. "You know what to do, Jimmy."

"Yes, ma'am," the boy replied.

He stepped to the kitchen door, put his little fingers between full lips, and blew out a shrill whistle. Rose and Tommy Tucker came scampering from where they had been playing under a huge alamogordo. A stray breeze rattled the heart-shaped, pale green leaves of the old cottonwood as they deserted it.

"Into the loft," their mother instructed.

Without a protest or question, the smaller children climbed the ladder to where all three youngsters slept. Rose covered her head with a goose-down quilt. Big-eyed, Tommy watched what went on downstairs.

"Hello the house," Forrest Gore called in a bored tone. "We mean you no harm. They's five of us. May we come up and take water for our horses?"

"You can go to the barn for that," Martha said from the protection of a shuttered window.

"Thank ye, kindly. Though it's scant hospitable of ye."

"Hospitality is somewhat short around here of late. If yer of a mind to be friendly, when you come back, I'll have my son set out a jug of spring water for your own thirst, and a pan of spoon bread."

"Now, that's a whole lot nicer. We're beholden."

When the five returned, Jimmy had placed the offered refreshments on the small front porch and withdrawn behind the door. The hard-faced men ate hungrily of the slightly sweet bread, and drank down the water to the last drop. When the last crumb of spoon bread had been disposed of, Forrest Gore glanced up to the window; he knew he was being watched.

"Mighty tasty. Say, be you Miz Tucker?"

"I am." Curt answers had become stock-in-trade for Martha Tucker.

"Then I have a message for you. You've forty-eight hours to pack up and get off the place."

"I thought I'd made it plain enough before. We are not leaving."

"Oh, but you got to now, Miz Tucker. Ya see, yer late husband, rest his soul, sold the ranch the day he was murdered by that back-shootin' scum, Smoke Jensen. No doubt he was killed for the money he carried."

"I don't believe you." Martha Tucker had opened the door and stepped across the threshold.

"'Fraid you're gonna have to, Miz Tucker," Forrest Gore replied with a polite tip of his hat in acknowledgment.

"Not without proof. Lawrence didn't take the title deed with him to town. He couldn't have sold, and he didn't have any intention of doing so. Now please leave."

"Sorry you see it that way, Miz Tucker. But we got our orders. Forty-eight hours, not a second more. Pack what you can, and get out. The new owner will be movin' in direc'ly."

"We won't budge until I see the bill of sale and a transfer of title."

Gore's face stiffened woodenly and his eyes slitted. "That's mighty uppity lawyer talk, comin' from a woman. A woman's place is to do as she's told. Might be your health would remain a whole lot better, if you'd do just that."

"Meaning what?" Frost edged her words.

"Your husband's done already got hisself killed over this place. Could be it might happen to you next."

"Jimmy." Tension crackled in the single word, as Martha reached back through the open door.

Her son handed her a Greener shotgun, which she leveled on the center of Forrest Gore's chest. Deftly, she reared back both hammers. "Get the hell off our land. And tell whoever sent you that next time, I'll shoot first and ask questions after. My oldest son's a crack shot, too. So there'll be plenty of empty saddles."

Gore blanched white in mingled fear and rage. "You'll wish you'd done what's right . . . while you still had the chance." He mounted with his gaze fixed on the barrels of the scattergun. Nothing worse than a woman with a gun, he reminded himself in a sudden sweat. Astride his horse, he cut his eyes to his men. "Let's ride."

Smoke Jensen knew a man could not drive a bear. Not even a big old brown bear, if one could be found in these desert mountains. But antelope and deer could be herded, if a fellow took his time about it. Through all the days of his travels in the Cibola Range, Smoke had often caught signs of deer. Now he set out seriously to locate a suitable gathering.

His search took only three hours in the early morning. He counted some thirty adult animals, a dozen yearlings, and a scattering of fawns. They would do well for what he had in mind. Slowly he closed on the herd, got them ambling the way he wanted.

It took all the skill Smoke Jensen possessed not to spook the deer and set them off in a wild stampede. A little nudge here, another there, then ease off for a while. So long as they only felt a bit uncomfortable grazing where they stood, they would remain tractable. By noon he had them out of the small gorge where he had found them.

"Easy does it," he reminded his mount and himself.

By putting more pressure on the herd leader, he got them lined out up a sloping game trail toward the crest. That, Smoke knew, overlooked the main trail. And that's where he wanted them anytime now. The wary animals heard the approach of other humans before Smoke did.

He nudged the creatures out into a line near the top of the ridge, then left the rest in the hands of Lady Luck.

With a whoop, Smoke set the deer into a panicked run. They boiled over the rim and thundered down the reverse slope. Alerted by the pound of many small hooves, the posse halted and looked upward. Dust boiled up through the piñon boughs, and a forest of antlers jinked one way, then the other.

Before they could recover their wits, the outlaws and townsmen who made up Sheriff Reno's posse became inundated by the frightened animals. The stricken beasts bowled several men off their horses, set other mounts into terrorized flight. Four townies wailed in helpless alarm, and abandoned the search for Smoke Jensen right there and now.

"Aaaawh . . . shiiiii-it!" Sheriff Reno howled in frustration, as a huge stag fixed his antlers on the lawman's cavorting pony and made a spraddle-legged advance.

7

Sheriff Jake Reno's eyes bulged, unable to cut away from that magnificent twelve-point rack. Somehow, he knew Smoke Jensen had been behind the appearance of the deer. The grand stag pawed the ground again and snorted, hindquarters flexed for a lunge. Sensing the menace, Sheriff Reno's mount reared, forehooves lashing in defensive fury. It spilled the lawman out of the saddle.

He landed heavily on the sorest part of his posterior, and howled like a banshee. Alarmed, the stag lurched to one side and joined its harem in wild flight. An echo of mocking laughter bounded down from above. Sheriff Reno looked around to find that fully half of the remaining posse had deserted him. That left him with little choice.

He pulled in his horns.

Only eleven men remained with the posse when the corrupt lawman gave up his search for Smoke Jensen and turned back toward Socorro. Smoke watched them go. Faint signs of amusement lightened Smoke's face as he gazed down a long slope at the retreating backs. One leg cocked over the pommel of his saddle, he reached into a shirt pocket for a slender, rock-hard cigar, and struck a lucifer on the silver chasing of his saddlehorn.

A thin, blue-white stream of aromatic smoke wreathed

the head of Smoke Jensen as he puffed contentedly. Walt Reardon had thoughtfully provided the cigars among the other supplies the hands had obtained when they planned to get Smoke out of the Socorro jail. These were of Italian origin and strong enough to stagger a bull buffalo.

Not exactly Smoke's brand of choice, it would have to do, he reckoned. And he would have to make tracks soon. South and west would best suit. That would put him closer to Arizona, when Ty Hardy and Walt Reardon brought word from Jeff York.

Smoke Jensen had met Jeff York a number of years ago. The young Arizona Ranger had been working undercover against the gang and outlaw stronghold of Rex Davidson, same as Smoke. When each learned the identity of the other, they joined their lots to bring down the walls of every building in Davidson's outlaw town of Dead River, and exterminate the vermin that lived there. As he rode down out of the northern reaches of the Cibola Range, Smoke Jensen recalled that day, long past . . .

Their pockets bulging with extra cartridges, York carrying a Henry and Smoke carrying the sawed-off express gun, they looked at each other.

"You ready to strike up the band, Ranger?"

"Damn right!" York said with a grin.

"Let's do it."

The men slipped the thongs off their six-guns and eased them out of leather a time or two, making certain the oiled interiors of the holsters were free.

York eased back the hammer on his Henry, and Smoke jacked back the hammers on the express gun.

They stepped inside the noisy and beer-stinking saloon. The piano player noticed them first. He stopped playing and singing and stared at them, his face chalk-white. Then he scrambled under the lip of the piano.

"Well, well!" an outlaw said, laughing. "Would you boys just take a look at Shirley. [Smoke had been using the outrageous moniker of Shirley DeBeers, a sissified portrait

painter, for his penetration of the outlaw stronghold.]
*He's done shaven offen his beard and taken to packin' iron. Boy,
you bes' git shut of them guns, 'fore you hurt yourself."*

*Gridley stood up from a table where he'd been drinking and play-
ing poker—and losing. "Or I decide to take 'em off you and shove
'em up your butt, lead and all, pretty-boy. Matter of fact, I think I'll
jist do that, right now."*

"The name isn't pretty-boy, Gridley," Smoke informed him.

*"Oh, yeah? Well, mayhaps you right. I'll jist call you shit! How
about that?"*

*"Why don't you call him by his real name?" York said, a smile
on his lips.*

*"And what might that be, punk?" Gridley sneered the question.
"Alice?"*

*"First off," York said, "I'll tell you I'm an Arizona Ranger. Note
the badges we're wearing? And his name, you blow-holes, is Smoke
Jensen!"*

*The name dropped like a bomb. The outlaws in the room sat
stunned, their eyes finally observing the gold badges on the chests of
the men.*

*Smoke and York both knew one thing for an ironclad fact: The
men in the room might all be scoundrels and thieves and murder-
ers, and some might be bullies and cowards, but when it came down
to it, they were going to fight.*

*"Then draw, you son of a bitch!" Gridley hollered, his hands
dropping to his guns.*

*Smoke pulled the trigger on the express gun. From a distance of
no more than twenty feet, the buckshot almost tore the outlaw in two.*

*York leveled the Henry and dusted an outlaw from side to side.
Dropping to one knee, he levered the empty out and a fresh round
in, and shot a fat punk in the belly.*

*Shifting the sawed-off shotgun, Smoke blew the head off another
outlaw. The force of the buckshot lifted the headless outlaw out of
one boot and flung him to the sawdust-covered floor.*

*York and his Henry had put half a dozen outlaws on the floor,
dead, dying, or badly hurt.*

The huge saloon was filled with gunsmoke, the crying and

moaning of the wounded, and the stink of relaxed bladders from the
dead. Dark gray smoke from the black powder cartridges stung the
eyes and obscured the vision of all in the room . . .

Oh, that had been a high old time all right, Smoke reflected. But it hadn't ended there. Smoke had gone on
back to the East to reclaim his beloved wife, Sally, who was
busy being delivered of twins in the home of her parents in
Keene, New Hampshire. Jeff York and Louis Longmont
had accompanied him. And a good thing, too. Rex Davidson and his demented followers had carried the fight to
Smoke. And it finally ended in the streets of Keene, with
Rex Davidson's guts spilled on the ground.

The twins, Louis Arthur and Denise Nichole, were near
to full grown now. They lived and studied in Europe. But
that was another story, Smoke reminded himself as he
gazed upon a smoky smudge on the horizon, far out on a
wide mountain vale, vast enough to be called a plain.

Smoke Jensen rode into Horse Springs quietly. He attracted little attention from the locals, mostly simple
farmers of Mexican origin. The place had been called *Ollas*
de los Caballos, before the white man came. Near the center
of town was a rock basin, fed by cold, crystal-clear, deep
mountain springs. This natural formation provided drinking water for everyone in town. Fortunately for the farmers,
a wide, shallow stream also meandered through the valley
and allowed for irrigation of crops of corn, beans, squash,
chili peppers, and other staples.

Smoke splashed through it at a rail-guarded ford and saw
at once that it also accommodated as a place of entertainment. Small, brown-skinned boys, naked as the day they
had been born, frolicked in the water, the sun striking highlights off their wet skin. Clearly, they lacked any knowledge
of the body taboo that afflicted most whites Smoke knew.
For, when they took notice of the stranger among them,
they broke off their play to stand facing him, giggling like

a flock of magpies, and making shy, though friendly, waves of their hands.

Returning their greetings, Smoke rode on to the center of town. On the Plaza de Armas, he located what passed for a hotel in Horse Springs. *POSADA DEL NORTE*—Inn of the North—had been hand-lettered in red, now faded pink, and outlined in white and green over the arch in an adobe block wall that guarded the building's front.

He dismounted and walked his horse through the tall, double-hung, plank gates into a tree-shaded courtyard. A barefoot little lad, who most likely would have preferred to be out at the creek with his friends, took the reins and led Smoke's big-chested roan toward a stable. Smoke entered a high-ceilinged, remarkably cool hallway. To his right, a sign, likewise in Spanish, with black letters on white tile, advised: *OFICINA*.

Smoke stepped through into the office and had to work mightily to conceal his reaction. Behind a small counter he saw one of the most strikingly beautiful young women he had ever encountered. Her skin, which showed in a generous, square-cut yolk, a graceful stalk of neck and intriguing, heart-shaped face, was flawless. A light cast of olive added a healthy glow to the faintest of *café au lait* complexions. Her dress had puffy sleeves, with lace at the edges, and around the open bodice, also in tiers over her ample bosom, and in ruffled falls down to a narrow waist. There, what could be seen of the skirt flared in horizontal gathers that reminded Smoke of a cascade.

Her youthful lips had been touched with a light application of ruby rouge, and were full and promised mysteries unknown to other women. For a moment, raw desire flamed in the last mountain man. Then, reason—and his unwavering dedication to his lovely and beloved Sally—prevailed. Those sweet lips twitched in a teasing smile as the vision behind the registration desk acknowledged his admiring stare.

"¿Yes, *Señor*? Do you desire a room for the night?"

Her voice, Smoke Jensen thought, sounded like little tinkling bells in a field of daisies. "Uh . . . ummm, yes. For a week, at least."

"We are happy to be able to accommodate you, *Señor.* If you will please to sign the book?" When Smoke had done so, she continued her familiar routine of hospitality. "The rooms down here are much cooler, but the second floor offers privacy."

Accustomed to the refreshingly cool summer days in the High Lonesome, Smoke Jensen opted for a first-floor room. The beautiful desk clerk nodded approvingly and selected a key. She turned back to Smoke and extended a hand comprised of a small, childlike palm and slender, graceful fingers.

"When Felipe returns with your saddlebags, he will show you to your room."

"I think I can manage on my own."

Her smile could charm the birds from the trees. "It is a courtesy of the Posada del Norte. We wish that our guests feel they are our special friends."

"I'm sure they do. I know that I—ah—ummm—do." Silently, Smoke cursed himself for sounding like an adolescent boy in the presence of his first real woman. He was spared further awkwardness by the return of the little boy, Felipe.

"Come with me, *Señor,*" the youngster said with a dignity beyond his nine or ten years.

After Felipe had unlocked the door to No. 12 with a flourish and ushered him inside, Smoke pressed a silver dime into the boy's warm, moist palm. Although fond of children, Smoke Jensen preferred to watch them from a distance; he recalled his first impression of this little lad and curiosity prompted him to speak.

"Do you work here every day?"

"Oh, *sí, Señor,* after school is over at *media día.* It is my father's *posada.*"

"Wouldn't you rather be out swimming with your friends at the creek?"

An impish grin lighted Felipe's face. "After my early chores, I get to go for a while. Until the people come for rooms, and my father rings the bell to call me back. Sometimes . . . when I'm supposed to be cleaning the stable, I slip away and also go on adventures."

Smoke had to smile. "You remind me of my sons when they were your age."

Felipe blinked at him. "Did you run a *posada?* And were your sons Mexican?"

A chuckle rumbled in Smoke's chest. "No to both questions. But they were every bit as ornery as you. Now, get along with you."

After Smoke had settled in, he strolled out to the central courtyard. The corridor that served the second floor overhung the edges of the patio, to form alcoves where tables were being set for the evening meal. More pretty Mexican girls draped snowy linen cloths at just the proper angle, while others put in place napkins, eating utensils, and terracotta cups and goblets. Next came clay pitchers that were beaded on the outside from the chilled spring water they held, and bowls of fiery Southwestern salsa picante. Experience in Arizona, Texas, and Mexico had taught Smoke that prudent use of the condiment added a pleasant flavor to a man's food.

Beyond the alfresco dining arrangements, a fountain splashed musically in the center of the courtyard. Desert greenery had been arranged in profusion, in rock gardens that broke up the open space and gave an illusion of privacy. On the fourth side of the patio, opposite his room, Smoke found a small cantina. Tiny round tables extended onto the flagstone flooring outside its door. Smoke entered and ordered a beer.

It came in a large, cool, dark brown bottle. Smoke

flipped the hinged metal contraption that held a ceramic stopper in place, and a loud *pop* sounded. Hops-scented blue smoke rose from the interior. Smoke took his first swallow straight from the bottle, then poured the remainder into a schooner offered by the *cantinero*.

"You are new in town," the tavern keeper observed.

"Yep. Just rode in today."

"If you have been on the trail awhile, *Señor,* perhaps you are hungry for word of what is happening in the world. I will bring you a newspaper."

"Thank you," Smoke responded, surprised and pleased by this shower of conviviality.

It turned out to be a week-old copy of the Albuquerque *Territorial Sentinel.* Most of the front-page articles had to do with the financial panic in the East, and events in and around the largest city in the territory. Smoke read on. The second page provided at least part of the answer to his dilemma, although he did not realize it at the time.

SURVEYORS
TO LAY OUT
WESTWARD ROUTE

Bold black letters spelled out the caption of the story. Smoke Jensen scanned it with mild interest. It revealed that survey crews would soon arrive to begin laying out the right of way for a new spur of the Southern Pacific Railroad. It would pass through Socorro and head westward to connect with Springerville, Arizona; Winslow; and the copper smelters being built south and west of Show Low.

Interesting, Smoke considered. If one had stock in the railroad, or the right copper works. But it didn't seem nearly as relevant as the small article on the third page, which featured an artist's sketch of Smoke's own likeness, and a story about the supposed murder of Mr. Lawrence Tucker.

From it, he gleaned that Tucker had been a longtime

and respected resident of the Socorro area, with a large ranch on the eastern slopes of the Cibola foothills. He was survived by a wife, Martha, and three children, boys aged thirteen and seven and a girl nine. Tucker had been outspoken about the prospects of dry land farming, and used the techniques of the Mexican and Indian farmers, longtime residents of the area. He also advocated the protection of those fields by the use of barbed wire.

Not a very popular position for a rancher to take, Smoke mused. It had been enough to get more than half a hundred men killed over the past decade. Maybe Mr. Tucker had enemies no one knew of? Maybe someone, like Sheriff Reno, knew only too damn well who those enemies might be? Smoke put his speculations aside, along with the paper, and finished his beer. Leaving money on the mahogany for the barkeep, he left to stroll the streets and get a feel for the town.

It might be well to have a hidey-hole. The inn seemed a good one. Although, Smoke allowed, with his face in the newspapers, and no doubt on wanted posters by now, it would be better to lay low in Arizona, until he could piece together more information. He had done well to scatter that posse. And it might be necessary to go back and scatter another, if he were to have that time of peace.

Early on the afternoon of the third day in Horse Springs, Smoke began to feel uneasy. A week had gone by since they had ridden out of Socorro. By now he should have heard from Walt Reardon and Ty Hardy. He would give them a couple of more days and then head west. With that settled, he turned in through the open doorway of a squat, square building with a white-painted, stuccoed exterior.

The odor of stale beer and whiskey fumes tingled his nose. No matter where in the world, or what it was called, Smoke mused, a saloon was a saloon. A chubby, mustachioed Mexican stood behind the bar, a once-white apron tight around his appreciable girth. Two white-haired, retired caballeros sat at a table, drinking tequila and playing dominoes. Smoke Jensen relaxed in this congenial atmosphere and eased up to the bar.

"Do you have any rye?" he asked.

"Bourbon or tequila."

"Beer then."

A large, foam-capped schooner appeared before him a few seconds later. The glass felt pleasantly cool to the touch. Smoke had grown to understand the inestimable value of the icy deep rock springs the town had been named for. Smoke drank deeply of the cold beer, and a rumble from his stomach reminded him that he hadn't eaten since early that morning. He'd finish this and find a place to have a meal.

"Jeremy, you don't have the sense God gave a goose." The loud voice drew Smoke's attention to the entrance.

"There you go again, Zack, bad-mouthin' me. I tell you, that feller made it sound so downright good, I jist had to trade horses with him."

"Only it done turned out that he had *two* gray horses, the other one all swaybacked and spavined. Which he hung around your dumb neck."

"Awh, Zack, tain't fair you go bully-raggin' me about that all the time. Hell, cousin, it happened a month ago! That's old news."

"It's an old bunko game, too," Zack replied dryly.

Smoke Jensen marked them to be local range riders. But with a few differences, that could make them dangerous. For instance, the way they wore their six-guns, slung low on their legs, holsters tied down with a leather thong. The safety loops had been slipped free of the hammers. The weapons were clean and lightly oiled, all the cartridges in their loops shiny bright. No doubt, they fancied themselves good with their guns, Smoke surmised. They had silver conchos around the sweat bands of their hats, sewn on their vests, and down the outside seam of their left trouser legs.

A regretful sigh broke from Smoke's lips. Almost a uniform in the Southwest for young, tough-guy punks. Smoke faced the bar, head lowered, and tried not to draw their attention. The one called Zack looked hard at the big-shouldered man at the bar and turned away. Smoke finished his beer, the taste nowhere near as pleasant as it had been, and pushed off from the bar.

Outside, he headed toward an eatery he had seen earlier. He had noticed a sign, hand-lettered on a chalkboard, that advertised HOY CARNITAS. His limited Spanish told him that that meant they were serving carnitas today. He had become acquainted with the savory dish while in Mexico to help two of his old gunfighter friends, Miguel Martine and Esteban Carbone. Thoughts of the succulent cubes of pork shoulder, deep fried over an open, smokey fire, brightened Smoke's outlook considerably.

He had finished off a huge platter of the "little meats," with plenty of tortillas and condiments, and another beer, when he looked up from wiping the grease from his face and saw the same pair of salty young studs again. They stood in the middle of the street, hands on the butts of their six-guns, eyes fixed on the doorway of the bean emporium.

At first, Smoke didn't know if they had gotten so drunk that they couldn't figure how to get in the eatery. But when he rose from his table, paid the tab, and stepped out under the palm frond palapa that shaded the front, he soon learned that that was not to be the case.

"B'god, yer right, Zack. It's him, all right."

"Yeah, Smoke Jensen," Zack sighed out. "An' we've got us a tidy little re-ward comin', Jeremy."

8

Seems these boys had read the same newspaper he had seen, Smoke surmised. The reward was something new. Too bad about that. He spoke to them through a sigh.

"Don't believe everything you read, fellers."

"We believe this right enough. You're Smoke Jensen, and they's a thousand dollars on yer head."

"Not by the law. So there's no guarantee you'd *get* the reward, if you lived to collect it."

"What you mean by that?"

Smoke sighed again. "If I *am* Smoke Jensen, there's not the likes of you two who can take me. Not in a face-on fight."

"I ain't no back-shooter, an' I think we can," Zack blurted.

Smoke let Zack and Jeremy get their hands on their irons, before he hauled his .44 clear of leather. Jeremy's eyes widened; it caused him to falter, and he didn't have his weapon leveled when he pulled the trigger.

A spout of street mud fountained up a yard in front of Jeremy's boot toe. Although a hard, violent man when he needed to be, Smoke Jensen took pity on the young gunny. He shot him in the hip. Jeremy went down with a yowl, the streamlined Merwin and Hulbert flew from his hand, and he clutched his wound with desperation. Smoke shifted his attention to Zack.

Zack's jaw sagged in disbelief. He hadn't even seen Jensen draw, and already the gunfighter had let 'er bang. Shot Jeremy, too, and he was rattlesnake fast. His consternation held Zack for a fraction of a second, during which he saw eternity beckoning to him from the black muzzle of Smoke Jensen's Colt.

"Nooooo!" he wailed and tried feverishly to trigger a round.

For this one, Smoke Jensen had no mercy. He had taken note earlier of the notches carved in the walnut grip of Zack's six-gun. That told a lot about Zack. No real gunhawk notched his grips to keep score. Killing men was not a game. They didn't give prizes for the one with the most chips whittled out. The only thing that came from winning was the chance to live a little longer. Smoke Jensen knew that well. He'd been taught by an expert. So, he let fly with a .44 slug that punched a new belly button in Zack's vulnerable flesh.

Shock, and the impact, knocked Zack off his boots. He hit hard on his butt in the middle of the street. He had somehow managed to hold onto his Smith American, and let roar a .44 round that cracked past the left shoulder of Smoke Jensen. New pain exploded in the right side of Zack's shoulder, as Smoke answered in kind with his Peacemaker.

"Damn you to hell, Smoke Jensen." Bitter pain tears welled up in Zack's eyes and Smoke Jensen seemed to waver before him like a cattail in a stiff breeze. Supported on one elbow, he tried again to raise his weapon into position. His hand would not obey. It drooped at the wrist, the barrel of the Smith and Wesson canted toward the ground.

"Y-you done killt me, Jensen," he gasped past the agony that broiled his body.

"It was your choice, Zack."

"I—I know." Zack sucked in a deep breath and new energy surged through him.

His gun hand responded this time, and he willed his

finger to squeeze the trigger. The loud bang that followed came before his hammer had fallen. Zack couldn't figure that one out. He understood better an instant later, when incredible anguish blossomed in his chest and a huge, black cavern opened up to engulf him.

"You di'n't have to kill him," Jeremy sobbed from his place on the ground.

"The way I see it, he pushed, I pushed back." Smoke made a tight-lipped answer.

Despite his misery, Jeremy had managed to work free his sheath knife. He held it now by the blade. A quick flick of his right arm as Smoke Jensen turned in his direction, and the wicked blade sped on its way. It caught Smoke low. The tip slid through the thick leather of his cartridge belt and penetrated a stinging inch into meat. Smoke's .44 blasted reflexively.

From less than three feet away, hot lead punched a thumb-sized hole between Jeremy's eyebrows, mushroomed, and blew off the back of his head. Smoke eased up, let his shoulders sag. A sudden voice from behind him charged Smoke with new energy.

"¡Tien cuidado, Señor! They have a frien'." Black pencil line of mustache writhing on his brown upper lip, the owner and cook of the cafe where Smoke had eaten stood in the doorway. He pointed a trembling finger toward the balcony of the saloon across the street. Smoke followed the gesture and saw a man kneeling behind the big wooden sign, a rifle to his shoulder.

Fool, Smoke thought. If he thinks that sign will stop a bullet, he's in for a surprise. The Winchester cracked once, and cut the hat from Smoke's head as he returned the favor. Two fast shots from the pistol in the hand of Smoke Jensen put a small figure-eight hole in the sign and the chest of the sniper. With a clatter, the hidden assassin sprawled backward on the floor planks of the balcony.

In the silence that followed, Smoke Jensen surveyed the carnage he had created. Damnit, he didn't need to be caught knee-deep in corpses. This spelled more complications than he wanted to think about. He reloaded swiftly.

"No question of it, I'm in more trouble than before," he muttered to himself. To the Mexican cook, he added, "The law will be coming soon. Tell them the man who did this is long gone."

The smiling man shrugged. "There is very little law in this town, *Señor*. Only the *alcalde*—the mayor—who is also the *jefe*—the marshal, an' also the *juez . . . el magistrado, ¿comprende?*"

"I reckon I do. You're saying you have a one-man city administration?"

"*Seguro, sí.*" In his excitement over the confrontation in the street, the man had forgotten most of his English.

"Where do I find this feller?"

A broad, warm smile bloomed on the man's face. He tapped his chest with a brown, chili-stained finger. "It is I, *Señor.*"

That made matters considerably less complicated for Smoke Jensen. Smoke recounted where he had first seen the would-be hard cases, and gave his opinion of what had sparked the attempt on his life. The mayor/police/chief/judge—his name turned out to be Raphael Figuroa—didn't even ask if they had the right man. He looked at the human garbage in the street and shrugged.

"They are no loss. This is not the first time they have provoked trouble. Usually with tragic consequences for the other party. This is the first time they have been on the receiving end. You are free to go, or stay as long as you wish, *Señor.*"

"I'm fixin' to pull out tomorrow morning," Smoke informed him. He did not give a destination.

Forty-six miles into Arizona, Smoke Jensen discovered why he had not been joined by his companions. Walt and Ty waited for him in Show Low, along with Jeff York. Smoke and the Arizona Ranger had a rousing, back-pounding reunion, and the four men retired to the saloon made famous by the poker game that had given the new name to what had once been Copper Gulch.

A drifter had played cards all through one night with the local gambler and owner of the town. His luck had run well and, on the turn of a card in a game of Low Ball, he had won title to Copper Gulch, which he promptly renamed Show Low in honor of his accomplishment. Or so the story goes.

"What's this about you being wanted for killing a man, Smoke?" Jeff inquired, his pale bluish gray eyes alighted with interest. "Don't sound like the Smoke Jensen I know."

"It's a long story, Jeff. Just yesterday, I found out there's a price on my head. A big one." Smoke went on to explain what he faced. He concluded with, "So with a reward out, I had to figure that sheriff would be out hunting me again, and decided Arizona would be a safer place to stay while I worked it all out."

Jeff York sat in silence a moment before responding to all Smoke had told him. "I'll cover for you here in Arizona, of course. And I'd like to help. As much as I can."

"How's that? The governor got his hand cinched up to your belt?"

"Not so's it chafes. I was up this way to check out something when Walt and Ty came along. So far it's only rumors. Still an' all, the ones puttin' them around are considered reliable men. 'Pears there's some scallywags that have their eyes on a land grab on the White Mountain Apache reservation."

"Do tell," Smoke prompted.

"The word is that some high-rollers are fixin' to bring a number of the big tickets in Washington out to be wined and dined—and bribed—to get them to cut a big chunk out of the res for the benefit of those same local money men."

"Why in the world would anyone want to move in next door to the Apaches?"

Jeff gave Smoke a bleak smile. "Perhaps it's because Chief Cuchillo Negro and some of his braves have found gold on that land. And, of course, it might be that these good ol' boys has gotten a serious dose of religion, and only want to make better the lot of their less fortunate red brothers."

"I'll believe that when pigs fly," Smoke grunted.

Smoke Jensen had fought and killed any number of Indians over the years, and he was not considered one to stomp lace-edged hankies into the mud over the wretched plight of the Noble Red Men. Yet, he respected them as brave men and fierce fighters. The Apaches, most of all. He acknowledged the Indians' right to a place in this world. After all, it was Indian land before the white man came to take it away from them. Indians and the white men had different ways, neither one better than the other, to Smoke's way of seeing things. Truth to tell, he sometimes thought the Indian way came out a bit on top. They sure had more respect for nature and the land. And they used to live in harmony with all its creatures.

It wasn't the coming of the white man that spoiled all that, Smoke acknowledged. It was too *many* of them coming, too fast and too soon. Set in their own ways, and pig-head stubborn against change, they never considered the differences beyond the Big Muddy. Civilization ended at the Mississippi, and white folks stupidly refused to admit that.

Sharing that all too human trait, most of the Indians would not make any effort to accommodate to white people's ways. They preferred to fight a losing battle to preserve their way of life. Those tribes lost, too. Now only the Apaches and a passel of Sioux and Cheyenne remained any sort of threat to the tens of thousands of white men overwhelming the vast frontier. Smoke Jensen shook his head, saddened by his sour reflections. "There's six more

Rangers headed this way. I'm supposed to direct it all, and also get a man inside this consortium," Jeff went on.

"You wouldn't be electin' me to that position, would you, Jeff?"

"No," Jeff York shrugged. As tall as Smoke and nearly as broad, that gesture moved a lot of hard-muscled flesh. His big hands spread on the table, and thick fingers reached for a fish-eye whiskey glass. "I reckoned to do that myself."

"I recall the last time I knew you went undercover."

York smiled at Smoke's remark. "We sure shot hell out of Rex Davidson's Dead River, didn't we."

"And you damned near got yourself killed, before you could get to the doin'," Smoke reminded him.

"Water under the bridge. We're still here, both of us. Now, maybe I had oughta make myself useful," York changed the subject. "First off, I'll fill you in on who is who around Socorro."

"You Rangers keep an eye on folks from another territory?" Smoke asked.

"Good practice to know the influential folks. Also the bad hombres and riffraff—all part of the job."

"Then tell me about them," Smoke prompted.

"First off, there's the Culverts and the Mendozas. About the richest ranchers around. Old Myron Culvert's son is mayor." He went on to list the power structure of Socorro, New Mexico. Then Jeff's voice changed, took on a tightness. "Then there's some who are sort of on the edge. There's an Englishman; folks say he's a lord or something. They call him Sir Geoffrey Benton-Howell. He owns a couple of large ranches, two saloons, a women's millinery store, and a number of houses he rents out to the Mexican workers. He's partnered up with Miguel Selleres. Selleres looks like one of those bullfighter fellers. Neat and trim, a handsome dog. But we've heard word he's got a mean streak."

"What about hard cases?"

"Comin' to that, Smoke. Big frog in the pond over

that way is Quint Stalker. Supposed to be a gunfighter from Nevada."

"I've heard of him. He crossed my path one time. I should have killed him then."

"He's for sure bad news, then?"

"Bet on it, Jeff."

"All right. He's got a gang of maybe thirty fast guns. There's talk he takes his pay from Benton-Howell. If that's so, we could be in heavy trouble. The lord and Selleres have been buying up parcels of land in New Mexico and Arizona for some time now. Most of them are out in the middle of nowhere. With the money, land, and the guns to back them up, they could become a power to reckon with. Only, why pick such remote spots?"

Smoke recalled the article he had read about surveyors for the Southern Pacific. "Would those parcels be anywhere near the proposed right of way of the new Southern Pacific spur line?"

It was as though a lamp had been lit behind the eyes of Jeff York. "They sure would."

"Water and coaling stops make great places for towns to be built," Smoke pointed out. "The man or men who own one—or in this case, *all* of those—will get mighty rich."

"Where did you come up with that?"

"I read about it in the Albuquerque newspaper," Smoke told him. "I wonder now, if the railroad intends to cross land owned by the late Mr. Tucker?"

"I wouldn't doubt it any. I think you waiting out more developments here might be a mistake, Smoke."

"I'm way ahead of you. I reckon we should all head back to Socorro and dig into the affairs of Sir Geoffrey Benton-Howell."

"Maw, there's someone movin' around out there," Jimmy Tucker informed his mother from the small, circular window in the loft.

"Can you make out who?" Martha Tucker asked her son, as she climbed from the bed in the room off the central part of the house.

"No, ma'am." Jimmy had a cold chill down his spine, though, that told him the mysterious figures were up to no good. He had an itch, too, that made him want to snug the butt-plate of his little Stevens .30-30 up against his right shoulder.

Martha crossed the living/dining area of her home in darkness, every inch familiar to her. She took up the Greener and slung a leather bag of shot shells over one shoulder. She reached a window just as a yellow-orange brightness flared in the barnyard. Jimmy also saw it, and the mop of snowy hair fairly rose straight up on his head.

He propelled himself off the pallet that served as a bed and flew down the ladder, his bare feet flashing below the hem of his nightshirt. He, too, went unerringly to the gun-rack on the near wall. Martha saw the movement and gasped. She almost blurted out a refusal, then drew her lips into a thin line.

"You be careful, son," she urged him.

"Yes, ma'am."

Jimmy took his rifle and a spare box of shells and went back to the loft. The window that overlooked the barnyard had been installed on a pivot, with latches to both sides. Jimmy undid them and turned the sash sideways. Slowly he eased the barrel of his Stevens out into the night. Then he remembered his father's training. He stuck a small finger in the loading gate and felt the base of a cartridge. Satisfied, he slowly worked the action, to keep as quiet as he could.

Three more torches burned now, and so far none of the nightriders had noticed anything happening in the house. At a muffled grunt of command, the torchbearers started toward the barn. By the light of the firebrands, Martha and Jimmy saw that they wore hoods that covered the entire head. When they reached a point fifty feet from the barn, the shotgun boomed, with the bright crack of the Stevens right behind.

One arsonist yowled and pitched off his mount, one arm and shoulder peppered with No. 2 goose shot. Another grunted softly, swayed in his saddle a moment, then sank forward to lay along the neck of his horse. For some unexplainable reason, Jimmy Tucker found his breath awfully short and tears filled his eyes. He had to swallow hard to drive down the sour bile that rose in his throat.

He took one deep gulp of breath and levered another round into the .30-30. Good thing he did, because a second later two of the hooded thugs turned toward the house and fired at the ground-floor windows. Jimmy shot one of them through the shoulder, and heard a thin wail answer his defense. From downstairs, he heard his maw's shotgun belch in anger.

"I'm hit! Oh, God, I'm hit, Smoke," one of the outlaws sobbed.

The use of that name had been a clever contribution by Quint Stalker. He figured it would direct any suspicion away from him, and particularly his bosses. Unseen by the hard cases in the yard, it had the intended effect, as Martha Tucker's face hardened and she swiftly reloaded the shotgun.

"Burn that barn, goddamnit! You boys, go after the corral. Turn out that livestock," the leader said.

"We're bein' shot at," another thug complained.

"I'll take care of that," the leader responded.

He turned toward the house in time to catch the side edge of a column of shot in his left biceps and shoulder. Grunting, he fired his six-gun dry and wheeled away. Another man took his place and got blown out of the saddle for his determination.

Flames began to flicker in the barn.

Jimmy brushed more tears from his big, blue eyes and sighted in on another man with a torch. At the last moment, the outlaw darted forward and to his left, the

.30-30 round shattering his hand. It sent the blazing torch flying from his grasp to land harmlessly on the ground. A dozen young heifers bellowed in terror from the corral, then made thunder with their hooves as others of the nightriders swung open the gate and ran them off.

"We've done enough for now. Let's pull out," was the command.

While they raced off into the darkness, mother and son discharged several rounds each to give wings to their flight. Several ranch hands, who had been held impotent at gunpoint, rushed out and began hurling buckets of water on the blazing barn. But Martha knew it would do no good. A fine, beautiful building, destroyed by that bastard Smoke Jensen.

Then a smile broke through her outrage. At least she'd gotten some pellets in him. He'd be bandaged up after this, and not so cocky anymore. Next time she saw him, she'd kill Smoke Jensen, she swore.

9

A hot, dry wind blew steadily across the mesa even at this early hour. A low pole frame sat well back from the rim, protected from the view of unwelcome eyes. It consisted of a lattice framework covered with the thick, green leaves of the agave, what the whites called the century plant. Already five of the lesser chiefs of the White Mountain Apaches had gathered. They waited in patient silence for the arrival of their principal chief, Cuchillo Negro—Black Knife.

Long before their composure had been well tested, ten of the best warriors among the Tinde approached soundlessly from as many directions. At last, when the sun rode high overhead, Cuchillo Negro appeared. With him was Ho-tan, his most trusted advisor. He greeted the assembled council in the harsh gutturals of their language.

"Why do the white men come into our land?" Broken Horn asked of the chief.

Cuchillo Negro considered the question in silence a long time before he answered. "It is true that many *Pend-dik-olye* come to our mountains. Words spoken on the winds say that they covet what little they left to us."

"That could be true," Ho-tan mused aloud. "It is the best of any of our agencies."

"The whites, who are always greedy, must think it is too

good for us," Spirit Walker observed with tart humor. "They seek to send us back to San Carlos."

Angry mutters rose over that. Black Knife silenced them with a stern look. The breeze fluttered the long, obsidian wings of his hair, held in place by a calico headband. He rose to his moccasins from where he squatted on a blanket.

"You are right to be angry, my brothers. But we must be cautious, while we go about finding out what is behind this."

"No," Bright Lance, one of the senior warriors, growled. "I say we drive them off the agency. I say we follow those who survive and take the warpath to all whites."

"Like Geronimo?" Cuchillo Negro asked sarcastically.

They all knew the fate of the famed and feared warrior chief. He was said to be rotting in a stinking, white man's prison in a far-off land called Florida. Obsidian eyes cut from one face to another. Broken Horn rose to speak.

"I am of a mind with Bright Lance. For us to meekly let the whites push us out, to be returned to San Carlos, is to die. Sickness will waste away our women and children, and we will catch the mosquito fever and die slaving in bean fields. I hate bean fields."

A loud murmur of agreement ran through the assembled council. Cuchillo Negro made a quick evaluation of the change in heart. "No. We cannot do that. I, too, hate bean fields, my old friend," he admitted with warm humor in his voice. "We must not take the fight to the whites off the reservation. That will bring the pony soldiers as certainly as Father Sun follows the night."

Clever man that he had to be to have achieved his paramount position, Cuchillo Negro shifted gears and spoke in laudatory tones of conciliation. "Yet, our good brother, Bright Lance, has some wisdom in what he says. If we hope to keep in our beloved mountains, we must not anger the soldiers. We must not leave the agency to fight." A beaming smile lighted the face of Cuchillo Negro, and his eyes sparkled with mischief. "But Bright Lance speaks well when he says we must punish those who trespass on our land. For now, we must satisfy ourselves with that."

To his surprise and satisfaction, he had no trouble achieving a consensus. The war societies of the White Mountain Apaches would soon ride to take retribution on the interlopers.

Smoke Jensen raised a hand to signal a halt. Ahead, a huge dust cloud rose beyond a swell in the red-brown desert country. Smoke and Jeff studied it a moment.

"Think it could be a posse?" Jeff asked.

"Too much dust for men on horseback. I'd say it's a trail drive."

Jeff cut his eyes to his friend. "Here? Headed this way?"

Smoke broke a grin. "I didn't say it made sense. What say we slip over and get a look?"

After dismounting, Smoke Jensen and Jeff York advanced, crouched low to avoid showing on the skyline. Both men bellied down near the crest of the rise and removed their hats. Jeff put a brass-tubed spyglass to one eye, and Smoke studied the distance with a pair of field glasses.

In the lead were three men, coiled lariats held loosely in their right hands. Behind, blurred by the reddish haze, they made out the horns of some fifty head of cattle. Smoke and Jeff exchanged a glance.

"Looks like you were right," York acknowledged. "Only I can't figure why they're headed toward Arizona."

"Better crossing places into Mexico, I'd reckon." Smoke Jensen took another look at the slow-moving cattle. "The border is less settled in Arizona than New Mexico or Texas. Even I know that. If someone had cattle that didn't belong to him, and wanted to dispose of them at a profit, that would be the way to go about it."

Ranger York didn't buy it entirely. "You think these cattle have been rustled?"

Smoke turned his attention to the men bearing down on

them. "From the looks of those boys out there, they aren't regular hands. Not by the way they're dressed, or the way they wear their guns."

Jeff York's eyebrows rose. "If we're fixin' to do anything, we'd better know how many they have on flank and drag first."

"My thinkin' exactly," Smoke agreed. "We'll split up for awhile. You take Reardon, I'll take Hardy. Let's ride around this gather and see what we can."

They joined up half an hour later, behind the herd. Jeff York wore a scowl. "Those beeves are wearin' the Tucker brand. I recognized it right off."

"The same Tucker I'm supposed to have killed?"

"Right, Smoke. Only those drovers aren't the sort Lawrence Tucker would have hired. Funny thing is, none of their horses are wearing the Tucker brand."

"What say we swing in for a little talk?" Smoke's suggestion met with ready agreement.

One man rode around the herd, which had been turned in on itself for the night. Five more squatted around a hat-sized fire topped by a coffeepot. A larger blaze had been started to cook on. All six looked up as strangers rode toward the camp.

"Hello, the fire," Smoke hailed. "I thought I smelled coffee."

"Yep," was an answer from a thick-set man with small, piggish eyes. "But we didn't brew up any extra."

Smoke pulled a face. "Now, that's mighty inhospitable in these parts, Mister. Mind if we ride up a piece?"

The gunhawk's eyes shot anger at Smoke Jensen, which didn't match his words. "It's a free country."

Once in by the fire, Smoke and his companions dismounted. They made no move to tie the horses off to the picket line, dropping the reins to the ground. Smoke nodded to the cattle.

"You're a far piece from the Tucker spread," he observed. The proddy one's eyes narrowed. "Who says we ride for that brand? Truth is, we bought these steers off him three days ago."

"That would be kind of hard, wouldn't it? Considering that he's been dead better than a week."

Smoke's words were all it took. Without knowing who they might be facing off against, the edgy rustler dropped his hand to the gun at his side. At once, the other four did the same. Smoke, Jeff, and Walt beat them all out. For a moment, they had a standoff.

Then the herd guard, a long, lean character with frizzy yellow hair, pounded toward them, his hand clawing at the butt of a Colt on his left hip. Six against four apparently seemed mighty good odds to the argumentative one. He canted the muzzle of his six-gun downward slightly. Smoke Jensen shot him through the chest, before his hammer could fall. Startled into panic, the cattle exploded in every direction. Jeff York put a bullet through the side of another rustler.

He went down with a soft grunt, but kept hold of his revolver, which he aimed at Jeff York a moment before Walt Reardon plunked a round into the gunhawk's forehead and ended his career. Ty Hardy had joined the dance. Hot lead from his .45 Colt snatched the hat off the head of another hard case, who had made a dash to his horse. Dazed by the close brush with a bullet, the rustler fell out of his saddle and rolled into some brush.

Half a dozen head of wall-eyed steers thundered over his body and trampled him into an unrecognizable mess. Smoke Jensen had not been standing still, both literally and figuratively. He had jumped to one side and went to a knee for his second round, which trashed the kneecap of another cow thief. Squalling, the man flopped to the ground, clawed at his waistband for a second six-gun, and hauled it clear.

Jeff York was busy with another gunny, and did not see the swing of the barrel to his midsection. Smoke Jensen did, and dumped the tough shooter into hell with a fast bullet that sliced through the left collarbone, lung, and the edge of his heart. A slug cracked past Smoke's ear, and he moved again.

Snatching at the horn of one steer, Smoke used the animal as cover and transportation. He heard fat splats as bullets smacked into the slab-sided creature. It bellowed in pain and stumbled. It had served its purpose, though. Smoke Jensen let go, and lowered his feet to the ground in a shuffling run. The maneuver had put him behind the last gunhawk.

Surprise registered as the man turned to find himself facing Smoke Jensen. He eared back the hammer and let fly wildly. Smoke, always calm and cool in the heat of battle, had better aim. His bullet found a home in the right shoulder of the hard case. The six-gun he had been holding flew high and came down hard. It discharged the last round of the brief, fierce fight. Slowly, he raised his good left arm.

"Okay, okay. Ease up. I'm done. I ain't never seed anyone so almighty fast. Who are you?"

"You wouldn't want to know," Smoke Jensen told him. "Sit down over there, and I'll patch you up while the rest round up these cattle."

Jeff, Walt, and Ty set off to gather in the stampeded beeves. It was a task that would take them the rest of daylight and part of the next day. From the moment Jeff York had revealed the identity of the owner of the cattle, Smoke Jensen had an idea start to grow. It would be, he decided by the time the shooting was over, a good gesture to return the cattle to the widow of Lawrence Tucker. It might even go some way toward convincing her that he had nothing to do with the death of her husband. A few answers from the survivor of the shoot-out might prove useful, he also decided. So, while he prodded the wound, cleaned it, and poured raw, stinging horse medicine in the hole, he probed for information as well.

"I don't know why I should tell you anything," was the surly answer. "I don't even know who you are."

"I'm the man who let you live, instead of killing you like the rest."

"You gonna give 'em proper Christian burial?"

"There isn't a proper minister among us, but we'll dig a shallow hole and put some rocks on top of them."

Smoke's harsh plans for the dead outlaws seemed to upset the wounded gunman. "You're gonna put my friends in the ground all together?"

"Unless you figure on digging separate graves. Now, where were you taking those cattle?"

"Far as I can tell, it's none of your business."

"They hang cattle rustlers." Smoke's voice had a heavy tone of doom.

Ty Hardy rode up then and waved his hat over his head. "Hey, Smoke, we got twenty-three head rounded up down by the creek."

"Good. Jeff can hold them. You and Walt find the others."

Icy fear touched the voice of the wounded outlaw. "He called you Smoke. What's your other name?"

"Jensen."

"Oh, Jesus! Smoke Jensen. I heard you was fast, but that— that weren't human. You gonna kill me, Jensen?"

"If I had that in mind, you'd already be stretched out there with your friends. Let's get back to the point. What about those cows?"

"W-we were takin' them into Arizona, and then into Mexico. The boss had a buyer all lined up."

"This boss have a name?"

"Uh—sure . . . only, I'd get myself killed for sure if I gave it to you."

"Like I said, I could give you to Jeff York—he's an Arizona Ranger—and see you hang."

"Jeez, Mr. Jensen, I don't want to hang!"

"Then give."

His face a lined mask of conflicting terrors, he shook his head. "Quint Stalker. He ramrods the outfit."

"And Stalker works for Benton-Howell," Smoke related later to Jeff York.

A week and a half had passed since the morning when the terrible news of her husband's death had been brought to Martha Tucker. At the time, she believed that nothing could dampen the awful grief she felt. Then the pressure had begun to force her and the children off the land.

She could not believe Lawrence had actually sold the ranch. Adding strength to that conviction had been that none of those who came would reveal the name of the person to whom he supposedly sold. Then the veiled threats took on substance; shots in the night, the attempt to burn the barn, cattle rustled.

Oh, she had been frightened all right. Yet that only served to strengthen her determination. Now she didn't know what to make of this latest development. Part of her wanted to believe. Another portion of her mind urged caution. It could be some sort of trick. The two young men, one slightly older than the other, who stood before her, could be seeking to gain her trust, catch her off guard, drive them from the ranch entirely. She cut her sky blue eyes to her eldest son.

"I believe them, Momma," Jimmy responded, as though reading her thoughts.

The older man cleared his throat as though preparing to repeat his remarks. Martha spoke over them. "Tell me again how you came upon our cattle."

"Well, ma'am, we were ridin' this way from over in Arizona. We came upon these six men workin' some fifty or so head of cattle. One of the men with us, an Arizona Ranger, recognized your brand. Also that none of the drovers was the sort your hus—er—late husband would have hired."

"So we questioned them," Ty Hardy took up for Walt Reardon. "They lied to us, said they'd bought the cattle offin your husband only three days before that."

"How did you know that to be a lie?"

"We—ah—well, ma'am, we were over Socorro way when it happened, him gettin' shot." Ty Hardy looked uncomfortable with the situation.

"Are you men employed somewhere?" Martha asked, liking the cut of them, more than half-convinced they spoke the truth.

Walt Reardon took over. "Yes, ma'am. We are. Our boss was along with us. It was him said we should bring back your livestock."

Thinking to thank whichever of her neighbors had been so considerate, Martha asked, "Who is it you work for?"

"Well—ah—it's . . . Smoke Jensen," Walt reluctantly told her.

Fury burned in those cobalt eyes. "I don't believe it! Not that murdering, back-shooting bastard!" Face pinched with her outrage, she demanded further, "Were you with him last week when he tried to burn down our barn?"

"Ma'am, please listen to me. Mr. Smoke didn't kill your husband. He'd never shoot a man in the back, nohow. And he wasn't within thirty miles of this ranch anytime last week. We was all up in the Cibola Range, dodging a posse," Ty Hardy pressed urgently.

"Smoke Jensen is the finest man I know." Walt Reardon added his endorsement. "He—he saved me from a life of crime and evil. I swear it, ma'am. I was a gunfighter an'— and an outlaw. Smoke Jensen reformed me, an' that's God's own truth."

Doubting, but moved, Martha asked, "How'd he do that?"

A rueful grin spread Walt's lips, and he flushed with embarrassed recollection. "First he beat the livin' hell out of me. Only that wasn't enough, so later on he shot me. Said he spared my life because he saw a glimmer of good in me. So, I'm askin' you, not to think harsh of Smoke Jensen. He could never kill a man in cold blood, believe me."

Flustered by this, Martha ran the back of one hand across

her brow. "I'll consider what you've both said. The return of our cattle, I must say, adds credence to your story. I'll thank you for that again. And thank your Mr. Jensen for me, also. I'll have to think over what I have learned. Good day, gentlemen."

Sheriff Jake Reno wanted to hit the man more than he'd ever wanted to hit anyone. Mash those pursed, disapproving, aristocratic lips into bloody pulp. Who was this Fancy Dan to talk down to him. Hell, this limey-talkin' pig probably didn't even carry a gun. Fat lot he knew about facing down Smoke Jensen. The lawman turned his face away to hide the fury that burned there.

"You are to raise another posse and go back into those mountains and track down Smoke Jensen. Is that perfectly clear, Sheriff Reno?" Geoffrey Benton-Howell accentuated each word with a jab of an extended index finger.

"Who am I gonna get? Those that were with me have been talkin' around town. Not a soul will volunteer. They got the idea that Smoke Jensen is ten foot tall, can shoot a mile with his six-guns, and disappear in a cloud."

"Quint Stalker will provide you ample men, Sheriff."

Reno glowered at the expensively dressed Englishman. "Then why the hell don't he jist go out after Jensen hisself?"

"Because we want this done all legally and proper. You are a lawman. Stalker is . . . just my ranch foreman."

"He's a gunfighter and an outlaw, is more near the truth," Reno snapped.

To the lawman's surprise, Benton-Howell chuckled softly. "He is that all right." Then the ice returned to his voice. "And the reason he is not out openly hunting for Smoke Jensen is because everyone else knows it, too. So, use his men, Sheriff Reno, and bring me back the head of Smoke Jensen."

10

At first, Giuseppi Boldoni could not believe his good fortune. Only a month after he, his wife, and three children had gotten off the boat from Napoli, he had become the proud owner of a truly magnificent tract of land in the Far West. Not even the richest vine grower of his native Calabria claimed so many hectares. The nice man who had sold him the land, Dalton Wade, had also made arrangements for two wagons and all of the equipment Giuseppi would need to build his home. He had picked it up in St. Louis. All paid for, part of the—what had *Signore* Wade called it?—the package, that was it.

What Giuseppi Boldoni learned when he arrived in the White Mountains gave his shrewd Italian mind much food for thought. Small wonder the land sale presentation had offered such generous terms. No one had told Giuseppi that his neighbors would all be red Indians. From the start, they had not gotten on all that well. Now, as he faced a dozen hard-faced Apaches, every one of them abristle with weapons, Giuseppi came to the conclusion that his neighbors were downright hostile.

"You will leave our land now," the big one in the middle demanded in mangled English, which Giuseppi understood only poorly. "Take what you can put in your rolling wikiups and go."

"*Perche?*"

"It is our land." It sounded enough like "porqué," so the leader answered the "why" in Spanish, and Giuseppi could make out most of the words.

"But I bought it," Giuseppi protested in Italian.

"It was not for sale," was the Spanish answer. "Go now." The eyes turned to chips of obsidian. "Or you die."

Giuseppi went. His wife and daughter in tears, his sons blinking unspoken questions at him, they loaded the wagons and drove off with only some clothing, food, and the rifle Giuseppi had purchased in St. Louis.

The two salty prospectors danced wildly in the icy, rushing water of the stream on the White Mountain reservation. They had actually found color. And not flake gold, either. Nuggets the size of a man's thumb! Some even bigger. The man who had hired them to search had promised them a share. But what counted was who's name was on the claim form.

"We done it, Burk. We sure-nuff did. They's plenty here to share," one bearded sourdough went on. "But what says we got to divvy up with that feller with the double last name?"

"Yer right, Fred. There ain't nothin' writ on paper to say we had us a deal. We done the work, took the risk, we should get the reward."

Neither Burk nor Fred got the prize they anticipated. What they got was their last reward. An Apache arrow cut deeply into Burk's back, quickly followed by another. He hadn't even time for a scream, when the third fletched shaft was embedded in his left kidney. He sank to his knees in the stream, eyes glazing on the shocked expression of his partner.

Fred didn't fare any better. A ball from a big, old .64

caliber trade musket punched through his chest and shattered his right shoulder blade. Two arrows festooned his belly and he wobbled obscenely as he gasped for his last breath.

Cuchillo Negro and three Apache warriors appeared before Fred's dying eyes. "You steal the yellow rocks," the war chief stated flatly. "It is said they make you feel good. Let us see if you can eat them."

He motioned to two of his braves, who took Fred by the arms. Cuchillo Negro yanked on the small leather pouch around Fred's neck. He opened it and extracted two of the large nuggets. One by one he shoved them down Fred's throat. Three more followed, before the last caught and set the white prospector to choking.

"It is enough," Cuchillo Negro said in his own tongue. "Let him die like that."

Smoke Jensen and Jeff York were about to discover that Quint Stalker was nowhere to be found. To keep his face out of Socorro during this phase of the takeover, Benton-Howell had dispatched Stalker and three of the outlaw leader's men to the White Mountain reservation. Under a morning sun, already made hot by the sere desert terrain, they busily occupied themselves pounding claiming stakes into the ground.

Stalker knew enough of the general plan to understand that this land would be taken from the Apaches and given over to white settlement. The first claims filed on it would be those of his bosses. A neat little scheme, he considered it, as he began to collect stones for a boundary marker.

"Sure's hell's lonely up here, Quint," Randy Sturgis announced. "I thought there was supposed to be 'Paches around."

"They're around," his boss replied. "Only we just don't see 'em. Apaches don't usual get seen unless they wants to."

"Gol-ly, Quint, what if they's warriors?"

Stalker paused to give Randy a cold grin. "Then, I'd reckon as how we'd already be missin' our hair."

Half an hour later, Quint Stalker rounded a bend in the creek with an armload of stones for the last marker. He came face-to-face with two startled Apache boys about thirteen or fourteen years of age. The rocks clattered to the ground, and the youths bolted like frightened deer. Quint knew he dare not let the boys get back to their village with news of the presence of white men. His hand found the butt of his Merwin and Hulbert, as he shouted a warning to his followers.

"Heads up, boys. We got us a couple of rabbit-sized bucks headed your way."

A pistol shot cracked loudly a moment later, followed by a thin wail. Quint pushed himself to a lumbering run and caught up to the surviving Apache boy in time to put a bullet through the youngster's right knee. Eyes wide with pain, the youth fell down, lips closed against any show of pain. Stalker shot him in the other leg.

"Never could abide a damn Apache brat."

"Why's that, Quint?"

"They turn into growed-up Apaches, Randy."

"I can fix that quick enough," Randy offered, and shot the boy in the groin.

Intense pain and the horror caused by the nature of the wound brought a howl of agony from the little lad. "He sure ain't gonna have any git of his own," Randy laughed.

"Awh, hell, finish him off," Marv Fletcher encouraged. "Plum cruel geldin' even an Injun."

Quint Stalker turned away indifferently. "You want to do it, go ahead. I'd as leave play with him a little more."

The fatal round sounded a second later. It presented another surprise to the outlaws. A high, thin gasp, followed by a sob, drew their attention to a clump of deer berries on the bank of the creek. Quint Stalker walked to the screen of vegetation and reached in. He yanked out an Apache girl, of an age with the dead boys, her slim forearm firmly in his big-handed grasp.

"Well, lookie here," Randy Sturgis gloated, advancing on the terrified child. "We got us some rec-re-a-tion."

"I get seconds," Marv Fletcher blurted.

Sky Flower had never known such intense pain in all her life. She knew, of course, what men and women did together. Had known for a long time. Only there was no pleasure for her in what was happening. Tears streamed from her eyes, and she felt like being sick.

Her thought became the deed. It earned her a fist to the jaw, when she vomited on the bared chest of the *Pen-dik-olye* who rode her. With all the pain within her, she never noticed the new source.

"Little bitch, puked all over me," Randy complained.

"No more'n' you take a bath, we'd never notice, Randy," Quint Stalker jibed.

"Go to hell, Quint."

They had all visited her body twice. This one, called Randy by his fellows, had come back for a third encounter. It went on forever before the youthful white outlaw finished.

"Anybody else?"

"Naw," Stalker answered for the others. "Finish her off."

Sky Flower did not hear the gunshot that robbed her of her life.

Walt Reardon and Ty Hardy rode into the small valley with important news. They joined Smoke Jensen and Jeff York at a small, smokeless fire, and eagerly accepted tin cups of steaming coffee.

"The Widow Tucker was mighty grateful for the return of her cattle," Walt drawled.

"Walt told her we worked for you, Smoke. She flew off

the handle at first, but calmed down some when Walt an' me explained how you had taken the stock from rustlers and sent us to bring them back."

Walt offered a new possibility. "Way I see it, she might even be willin' to consider the chance you didn't kill her husband."

Jeff York reacted to it first. "I think that's something worth looking into, Smoke."

"When I can prove who *did* kill her husband, then I'll be glad to talk to the woman," Smoke replied stubbornly.

"Wait a minute, now," Jeff urged. "You need a secure place to operate from, right? My reading of our Sheriff Jake Reno tells me that when brains were being passed out, he was behind the door. When we start stirring things up around Socorro, there's bound to be some real serious hunting around for you. The last place Reno would think to look for you, has to be the ranch of the man you're accused of murdering."

Jeff's words received careful consideration. "You may have a point, Jeff," Smoke allowed. "At least it might be worth looking into."

"If a lawman vouches for you, and a famous Arizona Ranger at that," Jeff added with a mischievous twinkle in his eyes, "it might get the widow to see you in a different light."

"You reckon to handle this yourself?"

"Why not, Smoke? It's the strongest card we've got to play right now."

Smoke Jensen took a final sip of coffee. "Walt and Ty are going to poke around a little, see if they can get a line on Stalker. I'm headed south of Socorro. We'll meet in San Antonio three days from now. Between now and then, Jeff, see what you can set up."

Martha Tucker studied the silver badge pinned on the vest of Jeff York. He wore clothes a cut above the average range hand, was well-spoken, and no doubt was who he claimed to be. Still, she considered his proposal outlandish.

"I'm not certain I'm ready for what you have told me, Ranger York."

"Mrs. Tucker, I've known Smoke Jensen for years. In all that time I've never known him to do a dishonorable thing. What motive would he have to kill a total stranger?"

"But he was found beside my husband's bod—body."

"Unconscious, as I understand it. Tell me everything you know about . . . what happened."

For the next ten minutes, Martha Tucker related all that she had been told about her husband's death. Jeff York listened with intense interest. When she had finished, Jeff pondered for a moment before speaking.

"I was taken with what Smoke told me, there's no doubt that someone arranged things to make him look guilty. For one thing, your husband was shot with a .45. Smoke carries twin .44s. Always has."

Martha nodded. "Go on."

"Smoke was found with the single holster strapped around his waist. Yet, when he escaped from the jail, his own guns and their holsters were found in the sheriff's desk. How would you suppose they got there?"

"I have no idea." Martha sighed heavily. "It doesn't appear that the sheriff, or the man he sent out here to tell me about it, has been entirely honest with me."

Jeff grinned in anticipation of success. "Not in the least."

"But why would you come over here from Arizona to look into it?"

"Like I told you before, Mrs. Tucker, Smoke Jensen is my friend. We've fought together before. And he's always stood up for what's right. At least, couldn't you hear him out? Give him an opportunity to tell you what he knows."

Martha Tucker's face lightened, and a soft smile of acquiescence lifted the corners of her mouth. "Yes. I suppose it's the least I can do."

* * *

Cuchillo Negro's face darkened with the fury of his outrage. They had been running off the *Pen-dik-olye* for three suns now. But to come upon such a scene as this threatened to make him break his resolve to keep their actions on the reservation. Three children, killed without reason, the girl ravaged before she died. He looked up sharply as Tall Hat spoke.

"I know their village, their families."

"You will carry the message to them?"

"Yes. They will want to come and care for their children."

"We will find the white men who did this. Their end will not be easy," the war chief declared flatly.

He sent men out looking for signs. They soon found plenty in the cairns of stones and stakes that marked the boundary of a claim. At the direction of Cuchillo Negro, the warriors scattered these items over a wide area. Faint traces of shod hoofprints pointed the way the interlopers had left the creek bank.

"Follow the trail," Cuchillo Negro ordered two skilled trackers. "We will come along behind."

"If they leave the reservation?" Ho-tan asked.

Black Knife looked back at the ruined face of the little girl. "We will go after them."

The sign left by the white men meandered through the White Mountains, roughly eastward, and downhill toward the land of the Zuni and Tuwa people. Diligently, the Apaches followed. They came upon the site of a carefully disrupted night camp. When Cuchillo Negro saw it, he spoke his thoughts aloud.

"These men know us well. They took care to see that no sign of their camp could be noted. Your eyes are clever, *Waplanowi*. Now see if you can bring me to them before this day is over."

White Eagle beamed with pride at the chief's compliment. "*Zigosti* is wiser than I. He says their fire burned two sleeps ago. We will not find them before *nolcha* sleeps."

Cuchillo Negro frowned. "We travel together from now on. The *Pen-dik-olye* seem in no hurry. By tomorrow we might catch them."

Wink Winkler mopped his brow with a large bandanna. "I'm shore glad we're shut of them mountains. I began to see an Apache behind every tree."

"There ain't that many Apaches around these parts, Wink," Randy Sturgis replied. "Though I'll admit I'm glad they prob'ly not follow us into New Mexico."

The two hard cases sat on a red-orange mesa that overlooked the Rio San Francisco outside Apache Creek, New Mexico. Randy, who could read on only a third-grade level and had quit school at the age of ten, was fortunate not to know how the small community had acquired its name. If he had, he would not have been nearly so confident. Quint Stalker stood with them, giving his horse a blow and considering their remarkably good luck in escaping the Apaches, who had no doubt set out after them.

"We're not out of it yet, boys. We'd best put more miles between us and the White Mountains."

"Awh, we're safe enough here, Quint," Randy protested. "These critters is near to run into the ground. They gotta have a rest. Us, too. From up here, you can see for miles. No way any Injuns could sneak up on us."

Quint tossed that around awhile, then nodded, his mind changed. "Right. We can rest the horses and catch our breath. But no fires after dark, hear? Be sure what you do build is small and smokeless."

For all their precautions, Quint Stalker and the three members of his gang learned the extent of their error in judgment shortly before midnight. A dozen Apache warriors rose up in the darkness and fired a shower of arrows into their camp. The first volley failed to find flesh, but awakened two of the targets.

"What the hell?" Randy Sturgis blurted. Then by weak starlight, he made out the familiar silhouette of an Apache. "Ohmygod! It's Apaches, Quint, it's Injuns!"

"I know that, damnit. Make a run for the horses."

"Injuns ain't supposed to fight at night," Randy wailed.

Quint Stalker's .44 Merwin and Hulbert barked and produced a flare of yellow-orange that illuminated more of the warriors. "Someone forgot to tell that to these bucks."

By then the other pair had been roused. They added to the volume of fire and momentarily held the Apaches in check. Another volley of arrows hissed and moaned through the air. Wink Winkler howled and came to his bare feet.

"My arm! There's an arrow shot clean through it."

Quint Stalker put a bullet in the chest of the Apache nearest him, snatched up his bridle, and ran for the horses. If they lived through this, he reckoned, they'd face a lot more hell, being barefoot and without saddles, food, or a change of clothing. Another Apache materialized out of the gloom at the picket line. Quint coolly pumped a .44 round through the warrior's heart. Low, menacing whoops and the soft rustle of moccasins added haste to his fumbling efforts to slip the headstall over the twitching ears of his horse, and shove the bit between fear-clamped teeth.

Randy Sturgis appeared at his side. "Wink's bad hurt. There's three Apaches jumped him."

"I'll fix your bridle, go back and help him."

Doubt and fear registered clearly in the dim light. "That's a hell of a lot of Injuns back there."

"Do it anyway. I never leave a man who ain't dead," Stalker snarled.

"Might be that's already the case," Randy opined.

Gunfire erupted from two locations on the small mesa, which disproved for the moment Randy's expectation. A hard shove from Quint Stalker sent him back to the melee.

Halfway there, he encountered Wink Winkler and Vern Draper.

The arrow still protruded from both sides of Wink's left forearm. He had been cut across the chest and a chunk of meat was missing from his right shoulder, where a war hawk had bitten deeply. Vern cut wild, glazed eyes to Randy, and gestured over his shoulder.

"Damn near got myself punctured back there," he panted. "But I freed Randy from those devils."

"Let's make tracks," Randy urged.

Quickly they rejoined Quint Stalker. Bridles fitted in place, the outlaws made ready to mount. Randy and Vern lifted Wink astride his mount. Then Vern gave Randy a leg up. Quint Stalker got Vern Draper on his horse, then vaulted to the back of his own. By then the Apaches had maneuvered into position close enough to see their targets in the dark.

More arrows sung their deadly songs as the white men rode fearfully away toward the trail that led off the mesa. Cuchillo Negro raised his trade musket to his shoulder and squeezed off a round that ended the evil career of the first to violate little Sky Flower. The big .64 caliber ball drove a hand-width chunk of shattered spine through the lungs and heart of Randy Sturgis.

Back arched suddenly, Randy did a back flip over his mount's rump. He landed hard on the reddish soil of the nameless butte that overlooked the San Francisco River at Apache Creek.

11

Five of Quint Stalker's ne'er-do-well hard cases lounged in front of the Tio Pepe cantina in the little town of San Antonio, New Mexico. They listlessly passed a bottle of tequila from hand to hand, drank, spat tobacco juice, or rolled smokes. One of them, Charlie Bascomb, perked up somewhat when a stranger rode into town on a big-chested roan.

"Hey, don't he look like that feller we's supposed to be huntin' down?" Bascomb asked his companions.

Weak-eyed Aaron Sneed squinted and dug a grimy knuckle into one pale blue orb. "Nuh-uh. Don't think so. Last I heard, he was supposed to be up north a ways, in the Cibolas."

"I for one," barrel-chested Buck Ropon declared, "am glad to hear that, Aaron. After I heard what happened to them boys that went along with the sheriff, I'm not so certain I want to tangle with the likes of Smoke Jensen."

"Turnin' yeller, Buck?" Charlie taunted. "'Sides, them boys was alone most times. They's *five* of us. I say us five can take any Smoke Jensen, or the devil hisself if it came to that."

Unwittingly, Charlie Bascomb had cast their fate in a direction none of them would have wanted, and which none of them later liked in the least.

After the stranger entered the general mercantile across the way, Charlie kept on worrying aloud. Like a big, old tabby with a little, bitty mouse, it finally wore down the caution so wisely held by Buck Ropon. Rising to his boots, Buck adjusted the drape of his cartridge belt across the solid slab of lard on his big belly, and nodded in the direction of the general store.

"I reckon you're gonna keep on about that until we know for certain, ain'tcha?" Buck Ropon groused.

Charlie screwed his mouth into a tight pucker. "Wouldn't do no harm to get a closer look."

"Are you crazy?" a heretofore silent member of the quintet demanded. "What if it *is* Smoke Jensen?"

Charlie grinned widely, his eyebrows and ears rising with the intensity of it all. "Why, then, we've got his butt and a thousand dollars reward!"

Inside the mercantile, Smoke Jensen ducked his head to miss the hanging display of No. 4 galvanized washtubs, buckets, washboards, and various pieces of harness. A wizened old man with a monk's fringe of white hair around a large expanse of bald pate glanced up through wire-rimmed half-glasses, and peered at his customer.

"What'll it be?"

"Howdy," Smoke addressed the man. "I could use some supplies. A slab of fatback, couple of pounds each of beans, flour, sugar, a pound of coffee beans, some 'taters."

"Yessir, right away." The merchant made no move to fill the order.

"Better throw in a can of baking powder, some dry onions, and a box of Winchester .45-70-500's if you've got them."

"Ummm. That's for that new Express Rifle, ain't it? I don't have any."

In a moment of inspiration, Smoke amended his list.

"Then throw in a dozen sticks of dynamite. Sixty percent will do."

"Don't stock that, either. You'll have to go to the gunsmith. He's got a powder magazine out back of his place."

"Thank you. Uh . . . I'll take me a couple of sticks of this horehound candy," Smoke added as he reached for the jar.

"You got younguns?" the seam-faced oldster asked suspiciously.

"No Smoke replied with a smile. Truth was, Smoke Jensen had always been partial to horehound candy.

The storekeeper took in the double-gun rig: the right one slung low, butt to the rear, the left set high, canted so as to present an easy reach for the front-facing grip. A gunfighter. That fact screamed at the merchant. Hastily, to cover the tremor in his hands, he set about packaging Smoke Jensen's supplies. Smoke, meanwhile, rolled the sweets in a sheet of waxed paper and twisted the ends closed. He stuck his prize in his right shirt pocket, under his fringed leather vest.

When the small stack of purchases had been tallied, Smoke paid for them and removed a rolled-up flour sack from a hip pocket. Slowly, carefully, he put each item inside and hefted the load.

The clerk had a dozen questions forming in his mind—but caution kept him silent. He stood behind the counter and watched his customer head for the door. Then he tilted his chin and shot a glance beyond the tall, powerfully built stranger. He saw the five hard cases in the street, facing his store. He gulped forcefully and licked dry lips with a suddenly arid tongue. How he wished he had taken seriously the suggestions of steel shutters for his windows.

Smoke Jensen stepped out onto the abbreviated boardwalk that extended porchlike around one side, and along the wider front of the general mercantile. It also fronted the next building on the main street. No doubt the structures had been built at the same time, by the same man. Blazing, afternoon sun came from the right angle to blind the eyes of Smoke Jensen to all but five pairs of legs, stuffed into an equal number of boots, arranged in a semicircle that curved out into the street and blocked all avenues of egress. All that left him was a fight, or a cowardly flight back through the store and out the rear. Through the distortion of heat waves, Smoke heard a hoarse whisper.

"It's him, right enough."

"What we gonna do?"

"Well, for one thing, we won't even have to shoot him. He's got the sun in his eyes. An' he ain't got nowhere to go to get away. Let's jist jump him, boys."

Smoke Jensen sat the sack of his supplies on a bench in front of one big display window, his vision gradually clearing. He raised his left hand in a cautioning gesture.

"I think both your ideas are wrong," said Smoke blandly.

Suddenly, three of the men launched themselves at him. Smoke stepped in on one with groping arms. He grabbed a wrist and pivoted on powerful legs. His attacker spun away. When Smoke released him, he hurtled sideways into a shower of glass as a display window broke. He landed in the midst of a selection of bolts of cloth. Bleats of pain came from him, accompanied by the sustained tinkle of more falling shards. Smoke had already turned to face his next threat.

Two hard cases rammed into him at the same time. For all the tree-trunk strength of Smoke's legs, they bore him off his boots. Smoke managed to turn slightly in the air and take them with him. They toppled through the open space created by the shattered window.

"Ow! Gadang, I'm cut," one outlaw wailed, and released his hold on Smoke Jensen.

Immediately Smoke flexed his right knee and drove it into the belly of the hard case. Forcibly ejected from the display counter, he slammed painfully into a four-by-four upright of the awning over the boardwalk. His ribs could be heard breaking like dry sticks. A painful howl tore from his throat. Before Smoke could get to work on the other, hard hands clamped on his shoulders and strong arms yanked him into the store.

"You're gonna git yours, Jensen," Charlie Bascomb snarled.

"I'm gonna kill him!" the outlaw with the broken ribs shrieked. "Let me at him. I'll kill him." He stumbled through the door, fingers curled around the flashy pearl grips of his six-gun. "Get outta my way, Charlie!"

Charlie did; but before he could fully register what happened, Smoke Jensen had recovered from his manhandling, drew, and fired. Smoking lead pinwheeled the crazed gunman. He dumped over, arms flying wide. His released Colt sped from his hand and broke a glass display case. A wail of protest came from the merchant, now crouched behind his counter. He had cause for further complaint a moment later, when the thug in the window reared up and threw a wild shot at Smoke Jensen.

It spanged off the cast-iron side of a black, pot-bellied stove, ricocheted through the ceiling, and left a crack behind. Because Smoke Jensen was no longer where he had been. He moved the instant he fired. Now he swung the hot muzzle of his .44 toward the offensive gunhawk.

Smoke's six-gun spoke, and a yelp of surprise and pain came as shards of wood from the window's inner framework showered the gunhawk's face. It was not enough to incapacitate him, Smoke soon learned. Two more rounds barked from the outlaw's .45, as the remaining pair of gunslicks charged through the open doorway.

Another hasty round clipped the thug in the shoulder, a moment before the last mountain man ducked behind a floor island to escape a murderous hail of lead from the newcomers. A soft grunt told him he had scored a hit. Bullets ripped and shredded a rack of black, weather-proofed dusters, searching blindly for Smoke. He easily kept ahead of their advance, then hunkered down and duck-walked back along the section the slugs had chewed through. At the end of the island, the wounded hard case in the window spotted him and blinked in surprise.

"Nobody could live through that," he declared in astonishment a second before he died, a bullet from Smoke Jensen turning his long, sharp nose into an inverted exclamation point.

Smoke immediately reholstered his expended six-gun and cross-drew his backup. A snigger came from Charlie Bascomb. "That's five, iffin' I count right, Jensen. We're comin' after you."

Could this one they called Charlie be so stupid as to not have seen his second six-gun? Or did he forget about it? Smoke let go of the questions as quickly as he had formed them. He ducked low and spotted the boots of his taunter. The big iron barked, and Charlie shrieked as he went to the floor. He found himself staring into the steely gray gaze of Smoke Jensen.

Without visible pause, Charlie began to roll toward the door. He blubbered and sobbed as he called entreaties to his remaining sidekicks. "Go after him, boys. He's right back o' them coats."

Only Smoke was not there anymore. One outlaw ankled around the far end of the island to discover that fact. He stared disbelievingly, while his partner emptied another six-gun into the linen dusters and his companion. The thug died without Smoke firing a shot.

The man from the Sugarloaf made up for that quickly enough, though. The last of a trio of fast shots found meat. A grunt and curse preceded a stumbling bootwalk across the plank floor toward the back counter. Smoke had only a single round left. He edged along a wall of shelves loaded with boots and shoes, until he could see the counters at the rear of the store.

From his vantage point, the gunhawk saw Smoke first. He tripped his trigger on a final round, and immediately abandoned it for a large knife. When the target jinked to Smoke's right, it threw his shot off. Smoke's last slug punched through the outer wall of the store. Only then did Smoke see that the knife was not the usual hog-sticker carried by frontier hard cases. In fact, it looked more like a ground-down sword, with a two-foot blade.

While that registered on Smoke, his adversary gave a roar and leaped at him. The blade swished through the air with a vicious sound. Smoke jumped back and to the side, away from the swing. He instantly stumbled, tripped, and fell into a double row of light farm implements. Their clutter muffled his muttered curse. A second later, the knife-wielder charged Smoke again.

His own coffin-handle Bowie, formidable under any other conditions, would be of little use against this on-slaught. Smoke Jensen knew that in an instant. He bought himself some time by a quick, prone scramble down the aisle. Not quite far enough, as the two-foot blade whirred through the air and clipped a heel from Smoke's boot. While his opponent remained off balance, Smoke thrust upright. He backed away further, both hands groping among the tools.

A snarl of triumph illuminated the contorted face of Buck Ropon. He rushed after Smoke Jensen with his altered sword raised high. He had just begun the downswing— aimed to split Smoke's head from crown to chin—when Smoke's hands closed on the familiar perpendicular handle of a scythe. He tightened his grip and jumped backward.

Swiftly, Smoke swung the keen-edged blade like the Grim Reaper. The long handle easily outdistanced the reach of Buck Ropon. The big, curved blade hissed through a short arc. Shock jolted up the handle to Smoke's arms when the edge made contact. With Smoke Jensen's enormous strength, it cut clean through. Buck Ropon had just been decapitated by a scythe.

His headless body did a grotesque quick-time dance, while twin streams of crimson fountained to the ceiling.

The head, lips still skinned back in a snarl, hit and rolled on the floor. When the blood geysers diminished, the deflated corpse fell full-length. Smoke Jensen immediately recovered himself.

He set the scythe aside and started to reload both six-guns. Stunned into mindless shock, the merchant stumbled around his business, alternately sobbing and cursing. Bitterness colored his words when he was capable of comprehensible speech.

"*Mein Gott! Mein Gott!* Look at this. I'm ruined! Who will pay? Who will pay for all this damage?"

By then, Smoke Jensen had finished punching fresh cartridges into both weapons, loading six rounds in each. Seeming to ignore the distressed shopkeeper, he went from corpse to corpse, examining the contents of their pockets. He accumulated a considerable amount of paper currency and coins. Then, with the merchant looking on in horror, he stripped the boots from them and recovered even more.

It totaled about two hundred dollars and change. He handed it to the horrified man. "This should help. And that scythe is like brand new. All you need do is clean it up, and sell it to someone."

"Never! No one would want it. I'll never be able to sell it."

Smoke delved into one of his own pockets and brought out a three-dollar gold piece. "Then I'll buy it."

"That's it, *Mench*? You are going to hand me money and walk out of here like nothing happened?"

"You saw it all. You can tell the law what happened. They attacked me, right? I only protected myself."

"Wh-who . . . are you?"

"Smoke Jensen."

A sudden greenness crept into the existing pallor of the merchant's face. "*Ach du lieber Gott!*" he wailed, as he tottered toward the cash drawer with the money clutched in one hand.

Smoke Jensen retrieved his supplies and assessed his own damage. He found the worst that had happened was that his horehound candy sticks had been broken. He left San Antonio without a backward glance.

Smoke camped a hundred yards off the only road he figured Jeff and his hands would use coming to San Antonio through this sparsely settled country. Sure enough, early the next evening, while coffee brewed and he tended a hat-sized fire over which biscuits baked in a covered skillet, he heard the thunder of the hooves; he made it out to be three horses in a brisk canter. Smoke kept a careful eye to the north, as the sound grew louder. He had the polished metal shaving mirror from his personal kit cupped in one hand, and when the riders came close enough to be recognized, he signaled them by a series of flashes.

"You could have took that damn thing out of my eyes a little sooner," Jeff York complained, as he rode up to where Smoke bent over to add more fatback to a second skillet.

"Wanted to make sure you knew it was me. Might have been you Arizona boys don't know that trick," Smoke teased.

"Hell, the Apaches have been usin' mirrors to signal with since the Spanish brought them way back. That smells good."

"Step down and pour coffee. You two as well. What's the news?"

"We can't find anything of Sheriff Reno or Quint Stalker, nor any of Stalker's hard cases," Jeff declared.

"Everything is set up with the widder for two nights from now," said Walt, adding his good news.

Smoke nodded. "Small wonder you didn't see any of Stalker's men. I had a run-in with five of them yesterday in San Antonio. That's why I'm out here waiting for you."

Jeff snorted and ran a hand through his sandy blond locks. "Did you stick around to explain to the local law?"

Smoke gave him a blank look of innocence. "I didn't know there was any. Didn't overstay my welcome by finding out. Not when one of them got away. My guess: our friend Sheriff Reno is in charge around here anyway."

"Losing five of his prize possemen will sure enough make his day for him," Walt said drolly. "Uh . . . one thing we did find out: the sheriff is usin' Stalker's outlaws on the posse. There's some folk around Socorro don't take too fondly to that. Includin' the Widow Tucker."

"Then I am even more inclined to meet with the good woman." Smoke's eyes twinkled with suppressed merriment, as he continued, "I seem to recall you mentioned she was some looker, Walt. There any chance of you making a place for yourself?"

"You hurt me to the core, Smoke. You know I ride for the Sugarloaf an' no one else."

"Sometimes the heart has a way of changing the mind. Whatever," Smoke summed up, "eat hearty and sleep with a packed outfit. Tomorrow we ride to the Tucker ranch."

12

Smoke Jensen stared down into the black pool in his coffee cup. It struck him powerfully to realize how long it had been since he had last drank strong, dark brew from a delicate china cup like this. Of course, it had been back home, on the Sugarloaf. For all her ability to rough it like a man, Sally Jensen insisted on her finery in the large, log building that housed the headquarters of Smoke's horse-breeding ranch. Only there, he noted, the tension didn't grow so thick that it could be felt and tasted.

After Jeff York had made the introductions, Martha Tucker sat across from Smoke Jensen, at the core of that tension. From her viewpoint, Smoke allowed, she had ample cause to radiate so much distrust and suspicion. Might as well get on with it and see how much of that he could boil away. Sighing, Smoke cut his eyes to the woman across the table. His eyes locked with her sky blue ones. In a soft, steady voice, pitched low, Smoke described what he knew of events surrounding the death of Lawrence Tucker.

She listened, hands in her lap, palms up, like opening flowers. Her face remained impassive, until he recounted the discovery of their cattle on the trail outside of Datil. Suddenly strained muscles tightened her face into deep, shadowed lines. She drew a sharp breath, recalling when and how the livestock had been driven off the ranch.

"Those cattle were stolen more than a week ago," she stated in a hollow voice. "The men who did it called their leader Smoke."

Smoke Jensen looked sharply at her. "Someone was being cute. My guess, based on what the survivor of that encounter told us, is that Quint Stalker thought that one up." He sighed and paused. "It couldn't have been Stalker. He's not been seen around Socorro for a good two weeks."

"Where might he be?" Martha asked.

"We . . . don't know," Jeff York inserted.

"Wherever he is, he'll be up to no good, you can be sure of that."

First Smoke picked up on this change in Martha's attitude. "Pardon me, Mrs. Tucker, but could you tell us more about what has happened here, to you and your children? Jeff has filled in on part of it, though surely not everything."

Smoke's prompting opened the flood gates. "First, a man came from town, Elert Cousins it was, to tell me tha—that Lawrence had been killed. He said the sheriff had caught the man who had done it. That it was . . ." Her voice faltered, lowered, "Smoke Jensen."

"And now, maybe you're not so sure?" Smoke urged.

"You can count on what Smoke told you," Jeff York jumped in. "Like I said before, Smoke is on the right side of the law, a straight shooter." A sudden pained expression of embarrassment twisted the Arizona Ranger's handsome features. "Sorry. Poor choice of words."

"I understand," Martha said softly. Then she continued to recount the efforts to force her and the children to abandon the ranch. When she had ended her account, she added, "At first they claimed that you had taken the money and bill of sale when you killed Larry. After that, when I insisted on seeing the transfer of title and sale bill, they stopped even mentioning that.

"Lately, I've been giving it some thought," Martha continued. "Especially after talking with your hands, who were quite gentlemanly, though with a few rough edges. Then, Ranger York, who spoke on your behalf. I got to wondering how it could be that you were found unconscious, beside my hus—beside his body, and they didn't find the money and bill of sale on your person?"

Smoke Jensen studied her calm demeanor. Certainly a powerfully attractive woman. Her heart-shaped face revealed a firm, though not stern mouth, wide-set, clear, blue eyes, and a high brow. Her hands, worn by years at the washboard and cookstove, still retained a semblance of youthful elegance. Carried herself well, too. Even the hostility she had directed toward him at the outset had been muted by an inner disposition toward true justice, rather than revenge. Her children, quiet and polite, showed good upbringing. They had been clean and wore neat clothing. They had gone off to their loft beds shortly after Smoke and Jeff arrived.

Most of all, as he had just discovered, her mind worked rather well. No one else had come up with that particular question, let alone an explanation.

"Score one for the lady," Smoke announced to break his contemplation. "I asked the sheriff that very question when he came into my cell to—ah—arrange a confession. He didn't have an answer."

"Neither do I," Martha allowed. "That's what perplexes me."

Much as she disliked the direction of her thoughts, Martha Tucker had to admit that this trim-waisted, broad-shouldered man was far more handsome than either of his hands. His hair, cut a bit longish for current fashion, had a natural curl in the ends, that turned inward to brush at his earlobes. His eyes had turned a soft, comforting gray. Martha had no way of knowing that they could take on the color of glacial ice when angered. To her dismay, Martha Tucker found herself comparing him with her husband, with Smoke

Jensen coming out ahead in most attributes. She chastised herself for the strong, though unwanted attraction she felt toward the rugged mountain man/gunfighter.

Although, to give herself credit, she also felt repelled by his reputation. There! She had said it all. Yet, he seemed sincere in what he said. What with Ranger York to vouch for him, what reason did she have to distrust Smoke Jensen? She suddenly realized that she had been asked a question, when Smoke repeated it.

"How do you mean, Miz Tucker?"

"Why, simply that there have been rumors about our Sheriff Reno. It's said that he's lazy, which I can vouch for. Also that to make work easy, he's sent more than one innocent man to the gallows."

"That's not true, ma'am," Jeff York interjected. "The law don't have anything to do with convictions and sentencing. That's up to the judge and jury."

Martha's eyes held a heretofore unseen twinkle. "Don't their decisions rely a great deal on a lawman's evidence and testimony?"

Jeff knew when he had been bested. A light pink flush colored his fair cheeks. "You got me there, ma'am."

"I see that I haven't been entirely clear. What I was getting at, is that Sheriff Reno is supposed to have created evidence out of whole cloth several times before, also withheld evidence or suppressed testimony that would have favored the accused person."

"Fits with the way he handled this case," Smoke Jensen provided. "Last thing I remember, I was wearing my own guns. Then they showed up in Reno's desk drawer. And I was supposed to be packin' some hand-me-down, cast-off, conversion Remington. And if I had the money I was supposed to have taken, he would have bragged that up to me, too."

Martha, who had cast a nervous glance up at the loft, cut her eyes back to Smoke. "Of course, it would be argued that the sheriff, or that sticky-fingered jailer of his, could have relieved you of it while you were unconscious. For my part,

I think there never was any money. Because I know that Larry had no intention of ever selling this ranch."

"So then, that's what led you to believe me?" Smoke prodded.

Martha took a deep breath, sighed it out. "Yes. At least enough to ask you, What do you intend to do about it?"

"I intend to find the one who did it and why. That'll clear my name."

"Then the next question has to be, What can I do to help?" It had taken Martha considerable effort to frame those words, yet the strain did not show on her lovely face.

Smoke and Jeff exchanged smiles. "Well, Miz Tucker, I need a place to operate out of. Somewhere the sheriff and Quint Stalker's men would never believe me to be."

"I can let you and your two hands and Ranger York move onto the ranch. They've tried so hard to make me believe you are guilty, no one would ever suspect you to be here."

Smoke beamed at her. "We'll be settled in by morning. Then I'll come let you know where we set up."

"Why, in the bunkhouse, of course. I read somewhere that if one wanted to hide something important, the best place would be in plain sight."

"Poe, I think," Smoke offered. "*The Purloined Letter.*"

More of her heavy mood sloughed off, and Martha clapped her hands together in delight. "I am impressed, Mr. Jensen. I never expected—"

"A gunfighter to be well read? I had a good teacher."

"Who was that, Mr. Jensen?"

"A man they called Preacher. He raised me up from about the age of your oldest. Taught me things that would astound a body. Some of 'em I never believed until I'd gotten around a bit. Walt and Ty are close at hand. We should be moved into the bunkhouse before midnight."

"Fine." Martha rose, extended a hand in courteous fashion. "Then I'll see you for breakfast at first light. We can start laying plans on how to expose the truth."

* * *

Geoffrey Benton-Howell set aside the sheet of thick, creamy, off-white linen stationery. He could not restrain the smile of triumph that lighted his face, all except his malevolent, deep-set, blue eyes. He rose to his highly polished boots from behind the cherry wood secretary desk, and crossed the room to the tall, drape-framed window that overlooked the main street of Socorro. Backlighted by the searing sun, he struck a familiar pose, proud of his lean, hard body for all his fifty-one years.

"They will be here, as expected. Train to Albuquerque, then on by carriage. I suggest we send one of ours. It will make a good impression. These politicians of yours seem to dote on such privileges."

Miguel Selleres took a deep sip from a glass of excellent port wine. "They are not *my* politicians, my friend. I am a citizen of Mexico."

"New Mexico, to be precise," Benton-Howell thrust a sharp barb. "The country of your adopted nationality lost this territory to the United States in the Treaty of Guadalupe Hidalgo. That was long before you were born."

"No, *amigo,* I was born in this part of Mexico in 1845, and to me and my family, the distinction of which country has claim to it on paper is not in dispute. It is a part of Mexico. It always will be. The day will come when we cast off the foreign occupation of our lands."

Lordy, Quint Stalker thought as he stared at Miguel Selleres in disbelief, this boy's wagon's got a busted wheel. One good thing—so far no one had asked him why they had come runnin' back to Socorro with their tails between their legs. A moment later Benton-Howell destroyed Stalker's sense of relief.

"They will be entertained as planned. Now, tell me, Stalker, what brings you so hastily back to Socorro?"

A pained expression preceded Stalker's words. "Truth to

tell, Mr. Benton-Howell, the Apaches runned us clear the hell an' gone out of them mountains."

Benton-Howell's tone mirrored his disbelief. "A few scruffy savages with bows and arrows? Surely you had enough firepower?"

"Not for more 'an a dozen of them. Those Apaches is tough fighters, Sir Geoffrey." Try a little flattery, Stalker told himself.

"Perhaps your men have lost their *cojones—¿es verdad?*" Miguel Selleres sneered.

"Don't you get on my case, *Señor.*" Quint pronounced it *sayn-yor.* "What is it your people call them?"

"Ah, yes," Selleres replied, recalling. *"La raza bronce que sabe morir.* The bronze race that knows how to die. But they *do* die."

"Eventual." To Benton-Howell, Stalker explained, "Often-times, their raiding parties are no more than five, six men. But they can tie up a platoon-sized army patrol for weeks at a time. All the while, they're killin', burnin', an' running off stock. Those stinkin' Injuns kilt one of my boys, stuck arrows in three more. We was lucky to get out of it with our hair."

"Yes, I can appreciate that. The fact remains that we must keep control of those claims. I want you to gather in all of your men and head back to the White Mountains. This time, make certain you can hold off every red nigger there, man or boy."

"Mr. Benton—Sir Geoffrey," Stalker protested through a series of gulps. "Thing is, we take in too many, and it attracts the attention of the soldier-boys an' the Arizona Rangers. We can't fight all of that at once. Besides, I need to leave a few men here, keep a lid on things."

"Very well, those who are out with Sheriff Reno on the posse can remain here to handle local matters. Take the rest and leave by noon tomorrow."

Chastened, Quint Stalker came to his boots, his head hung, and started for the door. "Yes, sir, if that's what you want." At the door he asked, "Does that mean you're givin' up the hunt for Smoke Jensen?"

"Oh, no, my dear boy. Not at all. We have some other plans for your Mr. Smoke Jensen. Plans I'm sure he will find most unpleasant."

They had left the Tucker ranch after this admonition: "Jeff, I want you and Walt to ride into Socorro. Hang around the saloons, the barbershop, and livery. I'm sure you know why," he added, cutting his eyes to Jeff.

"Any lawman knows that's where you hear all the gossip," Jeff replied with a grin.

"Right. Go soak up all you can get on Quint Stalker, this Benton-Howell you mentioned in Show Low, and his partner, Selleres. Find out about the sheriff, too."

Jeff and Walt reached town as the swampers were dumping their mop buckets and tossing out the dirty sawdust from the previous day. Jeff, who sported a clean-shaven face and fresh haircut, opted for the livery. Walt ambled his mount down the street to the barbershop.

He entered and settled himself in a chair. "Trim and shave. Trim the mustache, too."

"Right away, sir," a mousey, pigeon-breasted individual with a pince-nez squeaked.

"Hear there's been some excitement in town since I left?" Walt probed gently.

"Oh, yes, yes indeed. Were you here when Mr. Lawrence Tucker was murdered?"

"Yep. Rode out the next day."

"Well, then, you don't know about the jailbreak!"

"What jailbreak?"

"Three desperadoes broke that Smoke Jensen out of the jail."

Walt noted that the barber—Tweedy was the name on the fancy diploma above the sideboard, bevel-edged mirror—omitted to mention the lynch mob in his colorful rendition of Smoke's escape. When he at last wound down, Walt remarked dryly, "That sounds like quite a tale, right enough. Are you sure those desperadoes weren't part of the Stalker gang?"

"Oh, no, not at all. Mr. Stalker lent his foreman and some of his hands to the posse the sheriff took out. He's got more out with him now."

"Then . . . this Jensen is still on the loose?"

"From what we've heard. Hold still now, I have to shear over your ears."

Scissorlike sounds came from the mechanical clippers in the hand of Tweedy. He shaped and trimmed in silence for a while, then bent Walt's head the other direction. "One more now, and we're almost through."

Two men entered and peered curiously at Walt. Under normal circumstances this constituted a serious insult to any man on the frontier. Well accustomed by his years on the dodge, Walt Reardon showed not a flicker of annoyance at the scrutiny. As it continued, though, another idea occurred to him.

"You—ah—lookin' for somebody you know, Mister?" he said, in a gravelly voice, to the nearer of the pair.

"No—no, just thought I'd seen you around."

"Maybe you have, but what business is it of yours?"

Tweedy, a nervous, flighty type, dithered in agitation. "Now, now, gentlemen. I'm sure these fellows meant no disrespect, sir."

"I ain't heard from the other one yet," Walt growled.

A long second ticked by; then the smaller of the pair cut his eyes away from Walt Reardon's riveting stare. "No offense, Mister. We was lookin' for a friend."

"That's right," the other one blurted hastily, suddenly nervously conscious of the miles-long, gunfighter stare of Walt Reardon. "We expected him to be here ahead of us."

Walt sensed a pair of easy marks here, and produced a smile. "No offense taken, then. Tell you what. I'll buy you a drink when we get through."

"That's mighty white of you, Mister—ah?"

"Walt—" He cut it off, well aware that the name Reardon still meant gunfighter to many. "Kruger."

"I'm Sam Furgeson. This is Gus Ehrhardt. We'll just take you up on that drink, Walt. Say at the Hang Dog?"

"I know where it is. I'll be waitin' for you there."

Hands still shaking, barber Tweedy knicked Walt's left cheek with the straight razor. Wincing as though he had cut himself, the short, slender tonsorialist quickly dabbed with a towel and applied a piece of tissue paper to the tiny wound. "Sorry, there. Just a little slip."

"Make certain you don't slip like that when you get to my neck."

"Oh, no! Why, I'd never—" Tweedy caught a glimpse of those gunfighter eyes in the mirror, and choked off his protest.

Three riders, looking the part of ranch hands, rode into the livery stable shortly after Jeff York arrived there. Jeff knew they were not wranglers when they turned their mounts into nearby stalls and called to the old codger who ran the place to take care of them, then walked down the alternating stretches of boardwalk and hard-pounded path-way into the center of town. A lifetime of observation had told Jeff York that *real* cowboys would never walk anywhere. They would straddle their horses to go from one saloon to another, even if only two doors apart.

Jeff stood in the shade of the big livery barn and watched them ankle down the street. He marked the saloon they en-tered, then turned back to the liveryman. "They come in often?" he asked.

"Right as rain." He added a wink, a nod, and a sharp elbow in Jeff's ribs. "Some of Quint Stalker's randy crew. Real hard cases. Looks like they don't bother you none."

"Oh, they do. It's just I don't show it all that much," Jeff told him lightly.

"There's some things a feller could say about them, sure enough. The breed, if not them in partic'lar."

"Oh?" Jeff prompted gently.

"Them three do their best work on wimmin an' kids, way I hear it. Right tough hombres, when it comes to scarin' the bejazus outta some ten-year-old."

"Sounds like you don't hold them in great esteem?"

"Nawsir. They're lowlife trash, an' that's for sure."

Jeff gathered a few more tidbits and then made his way to the saloon the men had entered. The Blue Lantern turned out to be a dive, hardly more than a road ranch. Jeff York evaluated it, as he pushed through the hanging glass bead curtain that screened the interior from passersby. He had barely turned left toward the bar, when one of the trio spun around, his fingers closed on the butt of a big Colt in a left-hand holster.

"You followin' us, Mister?" Apparently with odds of three to one, they had no qualms about bracing a full-grown man.

"No, not at all," Jeff responded in his calming voice. "I only got in town a bit ahead of you."

"An' waited all this time to come in here, huh?" The taunting tone turned to vicious challenge. "I say you're snoopin' around where you don't belong. You smell of lawdog to me. You want to prove otherwise, you'll have to do it with an iron in your hand."

Well, crap, Jeff York thought. Not in town a quarter hour, and already he had a gunfight on his hands.

13

In the split second that passed after Jeff York's recognition of the situation facing him, he made a quick decision to follow a maxim of Smoke Jensen. "Let speed work for you, but remain in control," the savvy gunfighter had advised Jeff during their sojourn in Mexico with Carbone and Martin. So, Jeff followed that suggestion now.

Jeff's Colt appeared in his hand in a blur. The sound of the hammer ratcheting back made a loud metallic clatter. Jaws sagged on the three gunnies, which drew their mouths into gaping ovals. They had not even made a move. The one with his hand on the grip of his six-gun released his hold instantly, his arm rising up and away from his body.

"Did any of you ever see a lawdog haul iron that fast?" Jeff asked in a sneer.

All three shook their heads in a negative gesture. Then the mouthy one recovered enough aplomb to get in a word or two. "Well, there is Elfego Baca."

"He don't count," one of his companions nervously blurted. "He's over Texas way right now. Besides, Baca's about half-outlaw anyway."

"Right. An' Sheriff Reno runned him out of town after that dustup with McCarty an' his crew down in Frisco," the third hard case added.

"So what will it be, fellers?" Jeff demanded.

"Awh, hell, we was just a little proddy. We been out chasin' some jackass who killed a rancher hereabout."

Jeff recalled that Stalker's men were serving with the posse. If he could completely defuse this situation, he might learn something useful, he surmised. "All right by me. I'm just gonna ease this hammer back down, and then I'll join you for a drink."

"Shore enough, Mister. Say, you got a name?"

"It's Jeff."

"Good enough for me." He made the introductions of his companions and the palpable tension in the room bled off in a relieved sigh from the bartender.

Walt Reardon had gone on ahead to the Hang Dog Saloon, where the two rough-edged wranglers from the barbershop joined him half an hour later. A short while before they arrived, a conversation at the bar drew his interest.

"Say, I sure wouldn't mind workin' for the B-Bar-H right about now," one obvious cowhand advised his friends.

"Why's that?" one of the latter asked.

"Ain't you heard, Yancy? That English feller that owns the place is fixin' to throw a real fiesta. Gonna be the get-together of the season, from what some of his hands have been sayin'."

"What's the occasion? He gettin' hitched?" another one asked.

"Maybe he found a place to sell beeves for more than twenty dollars a head," suggested a third with a snorting laugh.

"Way I got it, this here Benton-Howell is doin' it to honor some big-shot politicians from Washington."

Mighty interesting, Walt thought to himself as he took another swig of beer. Might be we'll hear more about that, he speculated hopefully. The gossipy one continued.

"Gonna be in three days. Even the hands is invited. At

least after the high mucky-mucks git their fill of vittles. They're roastin' a whole steer, doin' some *cabrito*, too. There'll be likker and music and dancing. Those are lucky boys to be workin' for that English dude."

Yancy had another question. "What's these politicians done to be honored for, Hank?"

Hank smirked. "Don't mean they done anything . . . yet. The way it is, politicians are always lookin' for a little somethin' extra, if you get my drift. So, it don't harm nothin' to have 'em in yer pocket, *before* you want a favor done."

Walt's new, slightly nervous friends banged through the door at that point, and the interesting revelations got tuned out.

Smoke Jensen spent the day in a fruitless search for any sign that could lead him to the men who had been pestering the Tucker family. From the confession he had gotten out of the wounded rustler, he knew that Quint Stalker and his gang were involved in that job. Could he be responsible for all the other harassment?

More than likely, Smoke considered as he headed his big roan back to the ranch headquarters. Ty Hardy cut his trail some ten minutes later.

"What did you find?" Hardy asked Smoke.

"From the look on your face, the same as you."

Hardy grunted. "A whole lot of nothin'."

"Too much time has gone by. We can't sift any strange tracks from those of the hands. I've been hearin' about a lot of little incidents around the valley from Mar—ah—Miz Tucker. One of them is a trading post owner who got himself killed back a couple of weeks. From what I figure, it happened the same day I got away from that lynch mob. I know this might be just chasin' another whirlwind, but I'd like you to ride over that way and find out what you can."

The younger man nodded. "I can do that, Smoke. What was the man's name, and where do I find this trading post?"

"Ezekial Dillon. He ran his outpost at the far side of the valley, north and east of Socorro."

"I'll set off first thing in the morning."

When they returned to the barnyard, Jimmy Tucker met them with an enthusiastic welcome. "Mom says we got fried chicken, smashed taters an' gravy, an' cole slaw for supper. An' a pie. She also said that if it holds off hot like this after, Tommy an' me can go down to the crick for a swim. You want to come along?"

Grinning in recollection of his own sons' boyish exuberance, Smoke Jensen declined. Still close enough in age to be vulnerable to the call of such youthful enticements, Ty Hardy agreed to accompany the boys.

After a sumptuous spread of savory food, Smoke Jensen took his last cup of coffee out onto the porch and lit up a cigar. Pale, blue-white spirals rose from the glowing tip. The rich tobacco perfumed the air. Sniffing appreciatively, Martha Tucker joined him a short while later.

"My father smoked cigars. I always liked the aroma. I suppose that's one reason I married a cigar smoker," she informed Smoke in an unexpected burst of candor. "Have you been married long, Mr. Jensen?"

Smoke flushed slightly. "Many years," he answered. "How'd you reckon I was a married man?"

Martha did not need to think about her answer. "The way you are with the children; affectionate, but not over-bearing. Also, I might add, the remarkable restraint you show in my presence." She blushed furiously.

Half-amused, and uncomfortably aware of her alluring presence, Smoke answered with some evasion. "Not long ago you believed I had murdered your husband. But, I'll thank you for considering a more noble motive. Yes, Sally has been my treasure for most of my grown life. We have a daughter of marrying age and three younger."

"You must miss them?"

"I do. This is a far piece from the High Lonesome," Smoke admitted.

"The High—? Oh, I understand," Martha went on quickly. "Your hands said your ranch was in the heart of the Rockies. It must be beautiful. So much variety, compared to the desert sameness everywhere one looks around here."

"You're right about that." Smoke took a long draw on the dark brown tobacco roll.

For all her determination, and her grief, Martha could not help herself, she realized. She found herself strongly attracted to the big, handsome, soft-spoken man from the mountains. *He's as closemouthed as he is strong,* she mused, then put her thoughts to words.

"You're not very talkative, Mr. Jensen. Don't take that as a criticism. What I mean is, that you may not say a lot, but your words are filled with meaning. It takes a wise man to conduct himself like that."

"I'm flattered," Smoke said, finishing his coffee. He came to his boots. "I'll be headin' to the bunkhouse now. Ty's headin' out early in the morning, and I want a few words with him before he turns in. Provided, of course, your boys don't drown him down there at the creek."

Martha laughed with an ease that surprised her. "Goodnight, Mr. Jensen."

By nightfall, liquor had loosened plenty of tongues in the saloons of Socorro. Jeff York and Walt Reardon had each obtained several independent confirmations of the big fiesta to be held at the B-Bar-H. When they met in the *Comidas La Jolla* for a meal of *carne con chili verde,* they quickly discovered this.

"I'd say Smoke would be mighty interested," Walt opined after they had exchanged information.

"What I think he'd be most likely to want to know, is what's behind the festivities. I'm going to try to wangle you and me an invitation."

"You think you can do it?" Walt sounded doubtful.

"Should be easy. A rich, Arizona cattleman, interested in

buying the seed bull I saw advertised at the feed mill. In-
quiries to be addressed to Mr. Geoffrey Benton-Howell, of
the B-Bar-H."

Walt Reardon gave him a blank look. "I'll be damned. I
missed that one entire."

Jeff York gave him a friendly chuckle. "You've got to have
a lawman's eye for small details, Walt. We'd best head for
the Tucker place and fill in Smoke. Then I'll outfit myself
in expensive clothes, do up a flash-roll of currency, and
head for the office of Benton-Howell. Might be we'll find
out what's behind all this without any effort at all."

Late the next afternoon, Geoffrey Benton-Howell effu-
sively welcomed Steven J. York, of Flagstaff, Arizona, into his
office. He ushered his visitor to a plush chair beside the
huge cherrywood desk, and crossed to a sideboard where
he poured brandy for two.

"This is the first personal inquiry I've received from such
a distance," the Englishman informed Jeff in dulcet tones.
"May I ask what excited you sufficiently about Herefordshire Grand Expositor to pay me this visit?"

Jeff York leaned back in the chair with a comfortable
slouch, conveying his ease to an attentive Geoffrey Benton-
Howell. "I know it's common practice, and I don't want you
to take offense," he drawled. "But I've learned that in horse
trading and cattle buying, it's best not to purchase sight
unseen." He chuckled softly and sipped the brandy to
soften the implication of distrust.

"A wise man, indeed," Benton-Howell responded as he
clapped one big hand on a thigh. "Of course, before any
transaction was completed, I would urge the buyer to make
a personal inspection of Expositor. He's a fine Hereford
bull, and I'm justifiably proud of him."

He studied his visitor, while the Arizona cattleman
framed a response. Geoffrey saw a well-dressed man,
turned out in dustless boots. A hand-tooled, concho-

decorated cartridge belt, of Mexican origin no doubt, fitted snugly around a lean waist. A shaft of magenta sunlight put a soft glow to well-cared-for gun metal in the leather pocket. The suit had a flavor of Mexico in its cut, sort of the *haciendado* style favored by Miguel Selleres. The flat-crowned Cordovan sombrero clinched it for Benton-Howell. He bought the man as genuine.

"I've heard good things about crossing these new, shorthorn, polled Herefords with range cattle. Improves the stock remarkably," Jeff spieled off from memory of conversations with the more progressive ranchers in Arizona Territory.

"More meat, more pounds, with less size. They're all the rage back East."

"Not many willin' to take the risk out here, I'll bet."

Benton-Howell nodded agreeably. "Not so far. Tunstil tried it, and some say that's what got him in the Lincoln County War. Some people are slow to accept any change. Take barbed wire."

Jeff made the expected nasty face at mention of the often lethal barriers. That encouraged Benton-Howell to risk planting yet another false lead to Smoke Jensen. "We had a fellow around here who loudly advocated the use of barbed wire. Said all the small Mexican farmers around Socorro needed it, to keep range cattle out of their fields. There's some say that's why a gunfighter named Smoke Jensen was hired to get rid of him."

"Smoke . . . Jensen? I've heard of him. Did this happen recently?"

"Only a couple of weeks ago. Rancher's name was Lawrence Tucker. He was thrown out of the Cattlemen's Association because of his stand on barbed wire." Benton-Howell chuckled lightly and took Jeff's glass for a refill. "Might be someone took the whole matter a bit more personally than others. For my own part, I say live and let live. God knows there's plenty of rocks around here. If the Mexicans want to protect their fields, let them busy themselves building stone walls. They've worked well enough in jolly old England, I daresay."

"Quite," Jeff responded, well aware of the irony of his sally. "Aah, thank you," he remarked on the excellent brandy handed to him. "Now, when can I get to examine Expositor?"

"How long did you intend to stay in Socorro?" Benton-Howell inquired.

"Two or three days. As long as it took to see this championship animal of yours."

Benton-Howell thought for a long moment. "I'm having a rather gala soirée at the ranch two days hence. I would be honored, if you would attend. You can see Expositor, and I can introduce you to some gentlemen who might be of some benefit to you over in Arizona."

"Sounds good to me. I've always liked nice parties—enjoy good grub, good whiskey, and interesting company." Jeff was enjoying himself, playing the role to the hilt.

"You're staying at the hotel?" At Jeff's nod, Benton-Howell went on. "I'll have one of my hands meet you there tomorrow, escort you to the ranch."

"Much obliged, Mr. Benton-Howell. It's sure nice doin' business with a gentleman like yourself." Jeff finished off the brandy and rose to his boots to leave. "Oh, I have my foreman along with me. He's a better judge of prime cattle than I am. Would you mind, if I bring him along?"

"Oh, not at all. He'll be most welcome. Until tomorrow, then, Mr. York?"

"Hasta la vista."

Down on the street, as Jeff York strode away from the brick bank building, he congratulated himself on catching a mighty big fish. That, or he'd gotten himself into one damn dangerous situation.

Out at the Tucker ranch, Smoke Jensen made his own plans for the day of Benton-Howell's big fiesta. He wanted to be on hand to inspect the layout firsthand. To do so, he would have to scout the place. And that night seemed ideally suited to his needs. He asked Martha Tucker for directions and rode out an hour before sundown.

While midnight beckoned with stygian darkness, Smoke Jensen crested a piñon-studded ridge and started down the back slope. Only the scant, frosty light of stars illuminated his surroundings. Well and good, Smoke thought to himself. If Benton-Howell had night riders posted, he had a better chance of eluding them this night. What he had in mind could all go up in a flash, if some nighthawk stumbled on him prematurely.

Might be he was overcautious, Smoke decided, as he descended the eastern grade that formed the bowl valley which housed the B-Bar-H. The thicket of trees grew denser, the further he drifted toward the distant ranch house. He wanted to check out sites within long-rifle range of the area where the fiesta would be held, in the event he needed to make use of them.

Smoke had used this tactic with telling effect in earlier confrontations with some of the evil trash that infested the frontier. Not one to discard a useful strategy, he always considered employing it when presented the opportunity. Preacher had seen to it that a much younger Smoke Jensen had learned to be an effective fighter, even when entirely alone. Yet, he didn't like being out of contact with Jeff York. No idea what might develop there. He had to live with it, though.

The widespread nature of this sinister business made it necessary to go at it from more than one direction at a time. He recalled situations in the past when it would have been convenient to be able to divide himself in two or even three parts. A sudden flare of yellow light alerted Smoke that Benton-Howell had put out sentries.

Not very smart ones, at that. The flare of a match not only gave away the position of a guard, but destroyed his night vision long enough for him to lose his hair, if there were Indians about. One of the first lessons Preacher had taught him, Smoke thought grimly. Now he would have to find out how many there might be, and where.

Smoke combined his missions. He worked his way with great caution around the crescent face of the ridge through the long hours of early morning. A thin line of gray brightened the eastern horizon when he finished scouting the ranch. Another hour on foot took him away from the area far enough so that he could risk mounting and riding off toward the Tucker spread.

It would take some doing, but he could spoil Benton-Howell's little party right easily. "And that's the way I like it," Smoke said aloud to himself.

"Viejo Dillon come to these mountains long time ago," the wrinkle-faced, Tuwa grandfather related to Ty Hardy, both men seated outside his summer brush lodge.

"I hear he was killed recently," Ty prodded.

A curt nod answered him. The old man looked off a moment, then spoke in his lilting manner. "It's supposed to look like a thief took things. But this one's eyes saw the men who came."

"Do you know them?" Ty hadn't thought of getting this much so fast.

"Oh, yes. Very bad men—*malos hombres.* The big one . . . their chief . . . this one has seen him before. He is called Stalker."

Ty's eyes widened, and he fought to keep his expression calm. "You are sure of this? Did you tell the law about it?"

The Tuwa shrugged. "Why do this? This Stalker and the *Jefe* Reno are like two beans in a pod, this one is thinking."

How many other unexposed secrets lay buried in this old gray head? And those of others like him. Ty had learned much about respect for Indians from Smoke Jensen. And, Ty considered, the old man sure had the sheriff down right.

"Thank you, Hears Wind. I will hold your words close to me."

"You tell the *Jefe* Reno?" Anxiety lighted the obsidian eyes.

"I don't think so. I work for another man. Smoke Jensen."

Hear Wind's expression changed to one of pleasure. "His name is known to our people. That one walks tall with honor. You are fortunate to be one of his warriors. Go with the sun at your back."

Ty Hardy left with the certain knowledge that he had learned something important, and also that he had been honored simply for being one of Smoke Jensen's hands. Powerful medicine, as the Injuns said.

14

Still done up as a wealthy rancher, Jeff York, along with Walt Reardon, arrived at the B-Bar-H at mid-afternoon the next day. Not a lot of originality in that name, Jeff thought for the tenth time since discovering the notice of sale in the feed mill office. He was greeted by Geoffrey Benton-Howell in person; he had come out the day of their meeting to oversee final preparations.

"Glad you came," the Englishman remarked abruptly. "I'll introduce you to some of the other guests who journeyed out early. Then I'll show you Expositor."

"That's my main interest," Jeff replied.

On a wide, flagstone veranda, several portly men, dressed in the typical garb of Washington politicians, lounged in large wicker chairs. All had drinks in their hands, and it was obvious to Jeff York that these were not their first for the day.

Benton-Howell ushered Jeff and Walt from one to the next, making acquaintances. Uniformly, their handshakes were weak, soft, and insincere. Not a one of them has done a day's work in his life, thought the Arizona Ranger. A white-jacketed servant shoved a cut crystal glass of bourbon into Jeff's hand, and he took an obligatory pull.

After their first drinks had been drained, Walt acknowledged a signal from Jeff and excused himself. He wanted a good look around the ranch. Most of the next half-hour's conversation centered around competing accounts of the importance of each man to the smooth functioning of the federal government. Jeff York endured it with less than complete patience. He felt genuine relief and expectation, when Benton-Howell announced that he intended to show off his prize stud bull.

"What do you think of them?" the corrupt rancher asked, once he and Jeff were out of earshot of the guests.

"They're not long on sparkling conversation," Jeff replied cautiously.

"Boors, the lot of them. Boobies, too," Benton-Howell snapped. "Although, quite necessary, if one is to operate unhindered in your territory or mine. Well, then, here we are," he concluded, directing Jeff into a small barn that contained a single stall.

Expositor had a slat-level back, his face, neck, and chest a creamy white mass of tight curly hair. The rest of him, except for the tip of his tail, was a dark red-brown with similar woolly appearance. The bull had one slab side turned toward them, and he regarded them over a front shoulder with a big, brown eye. Although a lawman, rather than a stockman, Jeff considered him to be a magnificent animal, and said so.

"I thought you'd be impressed. He's barely four years old, and he's already topped over three hundred heifers and cows."

Jeff chuckled. "Wonder he isn't worn down to a nubbin'."

Geoffrey Benton-Howell had been away from England, and on the frontier, long enough to understand. "Oh, there's nothing wrong with his equipment. Far from it. If I had a cow in season, I'd show you."

They talked of the animal's performances for a while, then Jeff moved in close to look at the confirmation of the huge beast. "He's certainly blocky," Jeff observed.

"That's how you get the weight-to-size ratio to work out," Benton-Howell advised. "The bloodline came originally from Herefordshire." Benton-Howell pronounced the county name *Hair-ford-sure*. "They've revolutionized live-stock raising back East. Even a man with a small farm can pasture thirty or forty head. Not like out here, where one needs a thousand acres for fifty head."

For a moment, Jeff began to doubt Benton-Howell's involvement in the murder of Lawrence Tucker, or anything else not aboveboard. The man's expert knowledge of animal husbandry, and his obvious rapt interest in it, argued that it must be his main concern. Yet, why the obvious allusions to bribing or otherwise obtaining a favorable connection with the slippery striped-trouser crowd? Jeff would have to wait and see if something important came out at the fiesta the next day.

"What time does this shindig start tomorrow?"

"When the heat breaks over. About four o'clock, I would imagine," Jeff's host responded genially. Then he changed the subject. "Are you ready to buy Expositor right now?"

"He's a handsome critter, I'll allow. A lot bigger than I'd expected from the breed. I'd like to think on it awhile."

Benton-Howell clapped a hard hand on Jeff's firm shoulder. "Sleep on it, if you want. Enjoy what the ranch has for diversions tomorrow, and then give me your answer at the fiesta."

A festive atmosphere prevailed over the ranch headquarters the next morning from early on. Two huge, stone-lined pits had been stoked with wood long before dawn. With the contents reduced to glowing coals, half a steer turned slowly over each of them. Whole goats revolved on smaller spits on fires of their own. Ranch hands worked clumsily at unfamiliar tasks, erecting striped canvas awnings to provide shade and a pretense of coolness, setting up tables under them and laying out tableware and napkins. More guests began arriving shortly after an early breakfast. Jeff York took careful note of the occupants of each buggy, and consigned to memory the name and position of each visitor.

"And this is Senator Claypoole," Benton-Howell introduced yet another to York. "He's on the committee for Indian Affairs. Steven York from Arizona," he concluded.

Claypoole had a politician's, glad-hander shake, pale blue eyes dancing with merriment. "A pleasure, sir. Are you a cattle breeder, too?"

"No. I raise cattle for market."

"I see." The good senator cooled off, wondering why a common rancher had been invited. "Sparse vegetation over Arizona way, I'm told. How many hundred head can you feed?"

"Not hundreds," Jeff exaggerated wildly, "thousands. I run five thousand head this time of year. And I hold most of the mountain pasture from Flagstaff to Globe in the Tonto Range."

Claypoole warmed immediately. This was a big rancher. "I—ah—stand corrected. How do you manage such a vast area? Aren't the Indians a constant threat?"

Jeff gave him a warm smile. "Not really. If all the Indians killed in the dime novels had been for real, there wouldn't be an Apache left alive. I've found that the Eastern journalists tend to embellish the truth."

Another carriage, a mud-wagon stagecoach hired for the occasion, rumbled in with more politicians. That ended the exchange between Jeff York and Senator Claypoole, much to Jeff's relief. Benton-Howell took him in tow and made him acquainted with the newcomers. From the corner of one eye, Jeff noted that Claypoole made directly for the heavily laden liquor table.

The heavy drinking began around ten-thirty. Jeff held on to a single tumbler of whiskey and took sparing sips from it. He began to wonder what Smoke Jensen had in mind for this gala party. Knowing the gunfighter as he did, Jeff could not see Smoke passing up such an opportunity.

Noontime came, and still no sign of the fine hand of Smoke Jensen. Many of the ranch hands drifted in during the next hour. They all had the look of second-rate gunhawks to Jeff. The rich aromas of cooking meat and pots of beans, field corn, and other delights filled the air. Jeff had emptied his glass and had turned back to the beverage table, when he found himself face-to-face with a man he knew only too well.

"What the hell you doin' here, Ranger?" Concho Jim Packard growled in a low, menacing voice.

"Excuse me? You've got me mixed up with someone else," Jeff tried hard to misdirect the desperado.

"Not a chance. No gawdamned Arizona Ranger kills three of my best friends and I don't remember him." Packard turned to search the crowd for his employer. "Hey, Boss," he shouted over the buzz of conversation. "You done brought a rattlesnake into your nest."

Geoffrey Benton-Howell came over at once. "What are you talking about?"

"This one," Concho Jim snarled, pointing at Jeff.

"Why, Mr. York's my guest. He's come to buy Expositor," Benton-Howell spluttered.

"He has like hell! His name's York, right enough, but it's Jeff York, Arizona Ranger," Concho Jim grated out.

Strong hands closed on Jeff York's arms before he could react or try to make a break. Benton-Howell gave him a disbelieving look, then cut his eyes to Concho Jim. "You're sure of this?"

"Damn right I am. He got me locked up in the territorial prison for six years, killed three of my partners, too."

Unseen, but witnessing it all, Walt Reardon made a quick evaluation of the situation. Two guns against all those present made for poor odds. Better that he get away from here and find Smoke Jensen. He edged his way out of the crowd and made for the livery barn and his horse.

Frowning, Benton-Howell lowered his voice and addressed the gunhands holding Jeff. "Let's not make a spectacle of this. Take him away quietly. Lock him in the tool shed. We'll deal with our spy later, after our distinguished guests have eaten and drunk enough to forget about it."

Careful to create the least disturbance possible, the hard cases lifted Jeff York clear of the ground and carried him to a shed out of the direct sight of the partying politicians. There they disarmed him and threw him inside. A drop bar slammed down, and Jeff heard the snick of a padlock.

By three o'clock that afternoon, most of the guests of Geoffrey Benton-Howell had forgotten the small disturbance in the side yard of the ranch house. Great mounds of barbecued beef and goat *(cabrito)* filled the serving tables, where a splendid buffet had been laid out. Laughing and talking familiarly, as colleagues do, they lined up to pile Benton-Howell's largess on their plates. Some tapped a toe to unfamiliar strains of music.

Mariachi musicians played their bass, tenor, and alto guitars, Jaliscan harp, and trumpets with gusto. Songs such as *La Golandrina, Jalisco, Cielo de Sonora,* and *El Niño Perdido,* won applause and praise from the visitors from Washington. Three white-aproned cooks toiled over the pots of beans, bowls of salsa, skillets of rice, platters of corn boiled in its shucks, and, of course, the savory meat, as they ladled and served the festive crowd. Beer, whiskey, and brandy had flowed freely since mid-morning. It kept everyone in a jolly mood.

Yes, his fiesta was going exceedingly well, Geoffrey Benton-Howell thought to himself as he gazed on this industrious activity. It continued to go well until a whole watermelon, taken from among half a dozen of its twins in a tub of icy deep well water, exploded with a wild crack, and showered everyone in the vicinity with sticky, red pulp.

* * *

Smoke Jensen shifted his point of aim and destroyed a line of liquor-filled decanters in a shower of crystal shards that cut and stung the now terrified guests. He levered another .45-70-500 round into the chamber, and blasted a round into a large terracotta bowl of beans, showering more of the politicians with scalding *frijoles*. That made it time to move on to the next position.

Two hours earlier Smoke had met with Walt Reardon. The ex-gunfighter had come upon Smoke with the news of Jeff York's unmasking and capture. Quickly he panted out his account of events. He concluded with, "They put him in a little shed out of the way of the party."

"With the right distraction, do you think you could get in there and get Jeff out?"

Walt grinned. He had a fair idea of what Smoke Jensen considered the "right distraction."

"Damn right."

"Then, let's ride."

They made it back unseen to the ridge overlooking the B-Bar-H headquarters. Walt ambled his mount down a covered route back to the party. He soon found he had not been missed. No one, in fact, paid him the least attention. He took up a position close to the toolshed and waited for Smoke to join the dance.

Smoke Jensen had a clear field of fire over the whole ranch yard. He used it to good advantage, firing four more rounds, then reloading the Express rifle on the move to another choice location. Two of Benton-Howell's hard cases had more of their wits about them than the others. They grabbed up rifles and began firing back.

Their spent rounds kicked up turf a good two hundred yards short of Smoke's last position. Smoke knelt and shouldered the .45-70-500 Express, and squeezed off another shot. The bullet made a meaty smack when it plowed into the chest of one rifleman. The dead man's Winchester went flying, as he catapulted backward and flopped and twitched on the ground. His cohort made a hasty retreat. Then Smoke went to work on the nearest buffet table.

A stack of china plates became a mound of shards as Smoke's rifle spoke again. A short, stout congressman from Maine yelped, and popped up from the far side of the table like a jack-in-the-box. He lost his expensive bowler hat to Smoke's next round. With a banshee wail, the portly politician ran blindly away from the killing ground.

He crashed headlong into a Territorial Federal judge. They rebounded off one another, and the little man wound up on his butt. "I say, Judge, someone is trying to kill us," he bleated.

"Congressman Ives, you are an ass," the judge thundered. "If whoever is out there wanted to kill us, we'd be dead. Like that outlaw thug who returned fire. Now, get ahold of yourself, man, before someone thinks you're a coward."

When another watermelon showered those nearby with wet shrapnel, Walt Reardon considered the confusion to be at maximum. Lips set in a thin, grim line, he made his move. He approached the shed from the rear. Rounding one side Walt placed himself behind a guard posted by Benton-Howell. With a swift, sure move, Walt drew his six-gun and screwed the muzzle into the sentry's right ear.

"I'll have the key to that lock, if you don't mind," Walt growled.

"What the hell—!"

"Do it now, or I'll put your brains all on one side of your head."

"You son of a bitch, you don't have a chance," the gun-hawk said with the last of his rapidly waning bravado.

"I'm talking the outside," Walt snarled, and gave his Colt a nudge.

It took less than a second for the thoroughly cowed hard case to fish a brass key from his vest pocket. His hand trembled, when he raised it above his shoulder. Walt Reardon snatched the key with his left hand.

"Thanks, buddy," he told his prisoner a moment before he clubbed him senseless with the barrel of the Peacemaker.

Walt bent to the lock on the door of the shed, as Smoke shifted his aim to the house. Smoke had already made the striped-pants politicians scatter in utter panic. Some had fled to the carriages that had brought them, and driven off in reckless abandon. Others dived into corrals, Smoke noted with amusement, where fresh, still-warm cow pies awaited them.

Now the last mountain man listened to the satisfying tinkle of glass, as he shot out windows and trashed the interior of one room after another. A sudden gout of black soot from a chimney told Smoke a ricochet had hit a stove pipe. Half a dozen females—painted ladies provided by Benton-Howell to entertain the politicians—came shrieking out every door visible from Smoke's position.

While he kept up this long-range destruction, Smoke kept an eye on an unpainted shed, its boards faded gray by the intense New Mexico sun and desiccating effects of the desert. It was there, Walt Reardon had told him, that Geoffrey Benton-Howell had confined Jeff York. Smoke saw the guard stiffen, and a hand appear with a six-gun poked in the hapless fellow's ear. Good work, Smoke mentally complimented Walt. Now it's time to make a stir down there.

When Walt opened the door and Jeff came stumbling out into the light, Smoke shifted his aim once more. Two of the outlaw trash Benton-Howell hired walked rapidly toward Walt, each with a hand on a gun. The third mother of pearl button on one hard case centered on the top of the front post of Smoke's Express rifle. The weapon slammed reassuringly into his shoulder, and a cloud of powder smoke obscured the view. A stiff northwesterly breeze cleared it away in time for Smoke Jensen to see the impact.

Shirt fabric, blood, and tissue flew from the front of the gunhawk's chest in a crimson cloud. It slammed him off his boots, and he hit the ground first with the back of his head.

No headache for him, Smoke thought. He shifted his sights to the second saddle tramp in time to see him jackknife over his cartridge belt and pitch headlong into hell. Smoke cut his eyes to where he had last seen Jeff and Walt.

A thread of blue-white smoke streamed from the muzzle of Walt's six-gun. He and Jeff advanced on their challengers, and Jeff stooped to retrieve both of their weapons. Smoke took advantage of the lull to shove more fat rounds in the loading gate of the Winchester Express. Time to move, he decided.

From his fourth location, Smoke had a clear view of the other side of the headquarters house. The windows quickly disappeared in a series of tinkling, sun ray–sparkling showers. Faintly, Smoke Jensen made out the rage-ragged bellow of Benton-Howell.

"Goddamn you, Smoke Jensen!"

At least he knew who had paid him a visit, Smoke allowed with a smile. From his final position, where he had left his roan stallion tied off to a ground anchor, Smoke Jensen gave covering fire, while Walt Reardon and Jeff York burned ground out of the B-Bar-H compound. Smoke chuckled as he mounted and set off obliquely to join them, well out of range and sight of the terrorized mass of milling men below.

"Smoke Jensen?" The name echoed through the raddled politicos after Geoffrey Benton-Howell's furious bellow.

Livid with outrage, their host stomped around the flagstone veranda of his house, looking bleakly at the broken windows, shredded curtains, the bullet holes in the interior walls. He cursed blackly and balled his fists in impotent wrath.

"Everything is under control, gentlemen. Don't let this act of a madman interrupt our celebration today. Come, fill your plates, get something to drink. You there, strike up the music." Then Benton-Howell turned away and hid his bitter anger from the still-shaken politicians. "I know it was him," he shouted to the skies as though challenging the Almighty. "It was Smoke Jensen. Somehow . . . he's . . . found . . . out."

Most of those present had no idea of what he meant. Miguel Selleres, who had taken a slight nick in the left shoulder, knew only too well. He hastened to the side of his co-conspirator. "Softly, *amigo,* softly! It would not do to bring up such unpleasant matters in the presence of our guests. You have suffered enough loss today."

"How do you mean?" Benton-Howell demanded.

"When the shooting stopped, all but two of your working hands rolled their blankets and departed. They don't like being shot at."

Benton-Howell blanched. "Damn them! Cowards, the lot. Oh, well, they were only fit for nursing cows anyway."

"One does not run a ranch without someone to nurse the cows—¿*como no*?" Selleres softened his chiding tone to add, "I can lend you some men, until you can hire more. Or clear up this difficulty with Smoke Jensen."

"Thank you, my friend." Benton-Howell clapped Selleres on his uninjured shoulder. "Now, I want the—ah—other hands to assemble outside the bunkhouse. Tell those hired guns of Quint Stalker's to hunt down Smoke Jensen and *kill* him, or don't come back for their pay!"

15

Much to his discomfort, Forrest Gore had to deliver orders to the hard cases hired on to do Benton-Howell's dirty work. With the boss gone, leadership devolved on Payne Finney, who had sent him out to take over the boys in the field. Finney was making slow progress in his recovery from the pellet wounds given him by Smoke Jensen. If he could speak honestly, Finney would prefer to have nothing further to do with Smoke Jensen. Absolute candor would reveal that he feared the man terribly.

With good cause, too, Payne Finney told himself as he sat in the study of the B-Bar-H, covering ground already talked out with Geoffrey Benton-Howell. He had never seen a man so skillful that he could divide a shot column between two targets. Benton-Howell's next words jolted him.

"I don't care if you have to use a buggy. I want you out there looking for Smoke Jensen." Half of the influential men he had gathered at the ranch had failed to return after the shooting ended. It put a damper on the conviviality of those who remained. He hadn't even been able to broach the subject of cutting away a portion of the White Mountain Apache reservation.

"I take my orders from Quint, the same as all the others,"

Payne began to protest. "I'm still weak from being shot. I doubt the men would do what I told them."

Benton-Howell's fist hit the tabletop like a rifle shot. "They had damned well better! Stalker isn't here now. You give the orders; I'll see they are obeyed."

Payne Finney winced at the pain that shot from the knitting holes in his lower belly as he came to his boots. He accepted the finality of it with bitterness. "I'll do my best."

Half an hour later, Payne Finney rode out of the B-Bar-H on the seat of a buckboard. His face burned with the humiliation of being reduced to such a means of transportation, and for being talked down to like some lackey on the mighty lord's tenant farm. His saddle rested in the back, along with supplies he carried for the men searching for Smoke Jensen. His favorite horse trailed behind, reins tied to the tailgate. With effort, he banished his resentment and thought of other things.

If Finney had his way, Smoke Jensen would be run to ground in no more than two days. After all, the man was flesh and blood, not a ghost. He had to eat and sleep and eliminate like any other man. And Payne Finney had brought along the means of ensuring that Smoke Jensen would be found.

Seated right behind him, tongue lolling, was a big, dark brindle bloodhound. All they would have to do is find a single place Smoke Jensen had made camp, and put the beast on his trail. That's why Finney gave the ambitious estimate of two days. He raised himself slightly off the seat, and his right hand caressed the grip of his .44 Smith and Wesson American.

"Goodbye, Smoke Jensen, your butt is mine," he said aloud to the twitching ears of the horses drawing the wagon.

Forrest Gore had his own ideas about finding Smoke Jensen. "It's goddamned impossible," he declared to the five men gathered around a small pond in the Cibola Range.

"Smoke Jensen camped here last night. We all know that," Gore lectured to his men. "Then he rode out to the west early this morning."

He was wrong, but he didn't know it yet. Ty Hardy had spent the night there, and ridden back to the Tucker Ranch shortly before first light. Two of the hard cases, suspecting that they chased the wrong will-o'-the-wisp, muttered behind gloved hands. A minute later, Smoke Jensen proved them right.

With startling effect, a bullet cracked over their heads and sent down a shower of leaves. Forrest Gore jumped upright and hugged the bole of a tree, putting its bulk between him and the direction from which the slug came. Then the sound of the shot rippled over the mountain slopes.

"We been set up," another gunhawk announced unnecessarily. "That's Smoke Jensen out there, and he's got us cold."

"I'm gettin' out of here," the fourth man announced.

"No! Wait," Forrest Gore urged. "Keep a sharp eye. When he fires again, we can spot where he is, split up, and close in on him."

Vern Draper snorted in derision. "By the time we get there, he'll be gone."

"Yeah, an' firin' at us from some other place," Pearly Cousins added.

Forrest Gore gave their words careful consideration. They had been hunting Smoke Jensen for the better part of two weeks now. With always the same results. The bastard was never seen, and they got shot at. Maybe it wasn't Smoke Jensen at all? With a troubled frown, Gore worked his idea over out loud.

"What if that's not Jensen at all? What if it's one of those hands of his, who broke up the lynch mob? It ain't possible that he was down in San Antonio and leadin' you fellers around by the nose up here in the Cibolas at the same time."

"I don't think it was him down there," Cousins opined.

"Who else could do in four of our guys, and send Charlie Bascomb runnin' with his tail 'twixt his legs?" Gore challenged. "I say we're lookin' in the wrong place. I say we leave whoever it is up here to hisself, and head south."

"You better clear that with Quint," Vern Draper suggested pointedly.

"Quint's busy elsewhere. Payne sent me out here to help you find Smoke Jensen. I think he's clean out of the area. So, we go where he is."

Another round from the Express rifle of Smoke Jensen convinced the others to follow the rather indistinct orders of Forrest Gore.

Later that day, Smoke Jensen met with Jeff York and the hands from the Sugarloaf. They sat around a table in the bunkhouse at the Tucker ranch, cleaning their weapons and drinking coffee. Smoke made an announcement that caught their immediate attention.

"Looks like the searchers are being pulled out of the mountains. I think it's time to pay another visit to the B-Bar-H."

Jeff produced a broad grin. "I sorta hoped you'd do that. I want to pay my respects to Sir Mucky-muck."

They rode out half an hour later. Ty and Walt went deeper into the Cibolas, to track and harass the hard cases with Gore. Also to determine where they might be headed. Smoke and Jeff covered ground at a steady pace.

An hour before nightfall, they reached the tall, stone columns with the proud sign above that declared this to be the B-Bar-H. Smoke studied the fancy letters a moment. Then he cut his eyes to Jeff.

"I think this is a good place to start," Smoke declared.

He loosed a rope from his saddle, and Jeff did the same.

It took them only a minute to climb the stone pillars and affix their lariats to the edges of the sign. Back in the saddle, they made solid dallies around the horns, and walked away from the gateway. When the ropes went taut, the metal frame began to creak and groan. Smoke Jensen touched blunt spurs to the flanks of his roan stallion, and the animal set its haunches and strained forward.

Jeff York did the same, with immediate results. A loud crash signaled the fall of the wrought-iron letters. Badly bent and twisted, the B-Bar-H banner lay in a cloud of dust, blocking the entrance road. Smoke and Jeff retrieved their lassos and chuckled at their mischief, as they cantered off over the lush pasture grass. The rest of Smoke Jensen's plans contained nothing so lighthearted.

Geoffrey Benton-Howell had learned one thing from the attack on his headquarters. Smoke Jensen located the first night guard while a magenta band still lay on the mountains to the west. He signaled Jeff to ride on to their chosen spot, and put a gloved index finger to one eye to sign to keep a lookout for more sentries. Then he walked his roan right up to the guard.

"Who are you?" the surly hard case asked, a moment before Smoke Jensen drew with blinding speed and smacked the hapless man in the side of his head.

Well, perhaps they weren't all that much smarter than those he had encountered before. At least this one recognized a stranger when he saw one. Smoke dragged the unconscious outlaw from the saddle and trussed him up. He pulled the man's boots off and stuffed a smelly sock in a sagging mouth. Then, with the empty boots fastened in the stirrups, he smacked the rump of the gunhawk's mount and sent it off away from the house.

A short distance further, he found another one, similarly done up by Jeff York. Smoke smiled grimly and rode on. A roving patrol of two came into sight next. Smoke Jensen eased himself out of the saddle and slid through the tall grass. When the horsemen drew nearer, Smoke rose to the side of one silent as a wraith. Sudden movement showed him Jeff York likewise engaged.

One startled yelp came from an unhorsed hard case before Jeff had him on the ground and thoroughly throttled. Smoke's man made not a sound. Smoke came to his boots after tying the sentry, and waggled a finger at Jeff.

"Sloppy. He made a noise."

"Sorry, teacher," Jeff jibed back. "I'll do better next time."

"Might not be a next time before we're in position. I'd like to put them all down, before we start shooting."

"That'll take some time," Jeff observed.

"That's why we came early."

Smoke drifted off to recover his horse. Jeff York swore to himself that he had not even seen his friend start away. For a moment he had a flash of pity for the men they would encounter this night. Then he said softly to himself, "Nawh."

A quarter hour went by before Smoke found another night guard. The man sat with his back to a tree, eyes fixed on the higher ground away from the ranch house. Somewhat brighter than the others, Smoke reasoned. He had no reason to suspect someone coming from behind him. Too bad.

Easing up to the tree, Smoke bent around its rough bark and popped the unaware sentry on the head with a revolver barrel. It took only seconds to secure tight bonds. Then Smoke Jensen slipped on through the night. There would be a moon tonight. Smoke had taken that into consideration.

He and Jeff would fire and move, fire and move, until each had exhausted a full magazine load. Then time to leave, before the silver light of the late-rising half-moon made them too easy to see. All in all, he anticipated making life even more miserable for Geoffrey Benton-Howell.

* * *

Windows had been reglazed in most of the downstairs portion of the two-story frame house. Yellow lamplight spilled from one, as Smoke Jensen eased into a prone firing position on the slope above. He sighted in carefully, with the bright blue-white line of the burning wick resting on the top of his front sight. Slowly he drew a deep breath, let out half, and squeezed the trigger.

With a strong jolt, the steel butt-plate shoved his shoulder as the Winchester Express went off. While Smoke came to his boots, he listened for the tinkle of glass. It came seconds later, followed at once by sudden darkness within the house as the lamp exploded into fragments. An outraged voice wailed after it.

"Goddamnit! Jensen's back," Geoffrey Benton-Howell raged in the darkness.

While Smoke moved to his second location, Jeff let off a round from the opposite side of the house. Yells of consternation came from the bunkhouse, as the thin wall gave little resistance to a .44-40 slug. Grinning in the starlit night, Smoke dropped into a kneeling stance.

"Get in here, somebody! Damnit, this place is on fire," yelped a now frightened Benton-Howell.

"Tien paciencia, amigo," Miguel Selleres called out.

"Have patience, hell! I'll burn up in here."

An eerie new light glowed in the ruined window. It flickered and grew in intensity as Smoke Jensen sighted in once more, this time on the door across the room. He put a round about chest-high through the oak partition. A muffled scream came from the hall beyond. It served to notify Benton-Howell that he had a fat chance of getting out that way.

Smoke Jensen was already at a steady lope through the trees, when the remaining glass in the sash tinkled and Geoffrey Benton-Howell dived through to escape the flames. Smoke stopped abruptly and fired a round into the pool of darkness directly below the window. A howl that blended into a string of curses told him he had come close, but not close enough. Jeff York shot twice this time, and dumped a man in the doorway of the bunkhouse with a bullet in one leg.

"Don't get overconfident, Jeff," Smoke whispered to himself.

From the position he had selected earlier, Smoke put a .45-70-500 round through a second floor window. At once, he heard the alarmed bellow of a man, nearly drowned out by the terrified shriek of a woman. His shoulder had begun to tingle. He knew from experience that it didn't take too many cartridges run through the big Winchester, to change that sensation to one of numbness. Three rounds left in the magazine tube.

Smoke wanted to make them count, so he swiftly changed positions. On an off chance, he put the next bullet through the outhouse at about what he estimated would be an inch or two above head high on an average man. He was rewarded with a howl of sheer terror as a man burst out the front of the chicksale, his trousers at half-mast. Legs churning, the Levis tripped the hard case and sent him sprawling. Two cartridges to go, then Smoke would meet Jeff where they had left their horses.

Unexpectedly a target presented itself in Smoke's field of fire. A huge man, barrel-chested, thick-shouldered, arms like most men's thighs, hands like hams, barreled around the corner of the house and snapped a Winchester to his shoulder. He fired blindly, the slug nowhere near Smoke Jensen or Jeff York. Cursing, he worked the lever rapidly and expended all eleven .44-40 rounds.

Sprayed across the hillside, the next to the last found meat in horseflesh. Jeff York's mount squealed in pain and fright, reared, and fell over dead on its side. Anger clouded Smoke Jensen's face.

"Damn, I hate a man who'd needlessly kill a horse," Smoke grunted.

He took aim and, as the last bullet sped from the Winchester in the giant's hand, discharged a 500 grain slug that pinwheeled the shooter and burst his heart. Only twenty yards from his horse, Smoke put out another light in a downstairs window and hurried to the nervous roan.

Jeff York joined him a moment later, and began to strip the saddle off his dead mount. Smoke had the bridle and reins in one hand. "We'll double up," he informed Jeff.

"Make it easier to track and catch us," Jeff complained. "I'll walk out."

"No. I brought you here; I'll get you back. They aren't going anywhere for a while."

Jeff looked back toward the house. A bucket brigade had formed to douse the flames that roared from two rooms of the ranch house. With a whinny, a horse-drawn, two-wheel hand-pumper rolled up from a small carriage house next to the barn. A pair of hard cases ran with a canvas hose to the creek bank, and plunged the screened end into the water. At once four volunteers began to swing the walking arms up and down. An unsteady stream spurted from the nozzle.

"No, I guess you're right," he told Smoke.

Even so, Smoke Jensen wasted no time, nor spared any caution in departing from the B-Bar-H. He left behind a cursing, shrieking, livid Geoffrey Benton-Howell.

After the large number of recent disasters, Benton-Howell had been forced to send for reinforcements. The nine men who had been patrolling the slope behind the house on the previous night had quit first thing after being found the next morning. Smoke Jensen had nearly succeeded in burning down his house. His study was a ruin. All meals were being prepared in the bunkhouse; the kitchen had burned out completely. Now he confronted one of the men he considered responsible for his current calamity.

Sheriff Jake Reno stood across the cherry wood desk in Benton-Howell's office above the bank. With him was the mayor of Socorro. Both wore sheepish expressions. Benton-Howell had poured copious amounts of his deep-seated vitriol over them. Only now had he begun to wind down.

"I didn't spend the money to get you two elected to hear a constant stream of reports of failure. I expected competence. I expected success. Now, I'm going to get it. I want your full cooperation. No complaints, no excuses, no lectures on why it can't be done. I'm putting out the word for every available gunhand in the Southwest, to come here to put an end to Smoke Jensen."

"I thought you wanted it all done legally," the sheriff protested.

"I wanted results!" Benton-Howell snapped.

Mayor Ruggles looked stricken. "You'll fill the streets of Socorro with saddle tramps and every two-bit gunslick around," he whined. "Think of the good people of the community."

"I am thinking of the good people—Miguel Selleres and myself."

"Why don't you simply offer a larger reward?" Jake Reno suggested.

Too tightfisted to raise the ante on Smoke Jensen's head, Geoffrey Benton-Howell spluttered a minute, then focused his disarrayed thoughts on a new proposition. "Without gunmen to collect it, that would only tie up more of my money. What's going to happen, is that the city is going to add a thousand dollars to the reward."

"What?" the mayor and sheriff echoed together.

"If you think it such a good idea for me to put out more funds for the purpose, then surely it behooves you to do it." To Mayor Ruggles he added, with a roguish wink, "Sort of putting your money where your mouth is, eh, old boy?"

In that quick, pointed thrust, Mayor Ruggles lost his head of steam. "If that's what you want, we'll see about it right away. Only let me appeal to you to keep the gun trash out of town."

"It's your posterior they'll be saving, as well as mine. You

16

Socorro became a busy place as the word went out for fast guns. Mayor Ruggles stewed and dithered, his anxious eyes scanning the rough-edged characters who swarmed the streets. The new posters came out with the wording: "$2000 Reward Offered for Capture Dead or Alive of the Killer of Lawrence Tucker." No mention was made of Smoke Jensen. It sounded good that way, all agreed.

Some of the gunfighters and wannabes who came to Socorro to search for the "killer," left suddenly when they learned the identity of the accused. Sheriff Jake Reno noted with some smugness that eleven no-reputation young pretenders departed in a group shortly after the mention of the name Smoke Jensen.

"Perhaps they decided that it was safer to travel in numbers," he confided to Morton Plummer at the Hang Dog shortly after they blew out of town.

"Considerin' who it is they were expected to run to ground, I'd say they're right smart fellers," Mort responded with a grin. He loved to tweak this pompous ass of a sheriff.

Reno scowled. "Watch that lip, Mort." He quickly downed his shot and beer and stormed out of the saloon.

Being on the payroll of Benton-Howell and Selleres had other drawbacks, Sheriff Jake Reno considered as he directed his boots toward the jail. Those politicos who remained behind had been frightened almost witless by that second visit from Smoke Jensen. Only an hour ago, Benton-Howell had summoned him to the office to demand that he put men on the ranch to keep the politicians there, until an agreement could be reached on his White Mountain project.

"Like he'd bought all my deputies, too," Reno complained aloud, as he hurried to round up men to guard the B-Bar-H.

He returned to the world around him in time to meet the cold, hard stare of one of a pair of gaunt- and narrow-faced men with the look of gunfighters about them. Their square chins jutted high in arrogance, and the mean curl of their lips had to come from hours of practice before a mirror. The one with black leather gloves folded over his cartridge belt spoke, revealing yellowed, crooked teeth.

"Sheriff. Just the man we wanted to see. How are we supposed to find this feller done killed your Mr. Tucker, if we don't know his name? Who is he, or do you know?"

"Oh, I know all right. The name is Smoke Jensen."

"Not *the* Smoke Jensen?" the sneering one blurted as his face grew pale.

"The only Smoke Jensen I know," Sheriff Reno replied, as he laughed inwardly at the discomfort his words sparked.

The sneer gone from his face, the gunhawk cut his eyes to his partner. They appeared to reach wordless agreement that concluded with a nod. "Do you happen to have any idea where he might be found?" The question seemed to lack conviction of being acted upon.

"Yep. He's hangin' out in the Cibolas, last I heard."

"Why ain't you got a posse out?" the taller of the two challenged.

"I already lost a dozen good men to that bastard. I don't reckon to reduce the whole population of Socorro to bring him outta there." It was a lie. Smoke Jensen had killed only three of the posse, wounded six or seven more. Also some

twenty had quit all together. What Sheriff Reno wouldn't
admit was that he couldn't get anyone to go after Smoke
Jensen. Not even Quint Stalker's men.

"Bein' we're from Texas, which way is these Cibolas?"

Suspecting what would come next, Sheriff Reno waved
his arm expansively. "All around here. To the east, north,
and mostly to the west. That's where Smoke Jensen can be
found, west of here, I'm certain of it."

"Thank you kindly, Sheriff," the tall one replied.

Together they crossed the boardwalk and mounted their
horses, while Sheriff Reno watched in silence. They
touched reins to necks and pointed the animals south. Face
alight with quivering amusement, Sheriff Reno pointed out
their error.

"West's that way, fellers."

"We know it," the second-string hard case with the black
gloves replied in a low, gruff voice.

They barely cleared the business district of Socorro,
down in its canyonlike draw, before they fogged out of town
in a lather. Behind them, Sheriff Jake Reno bent double
with a torrent of laughter that rose from deep within. He
kept on until the tears ran, then laughed even more . . .
until he counted score and realized that that made a record
of twenty-two for one day, and left him with that many less
to stand between him and Smoke Jensen.

Senator Claypoole examined the certificate authorizing
him to draw on the Philadelphia mint for the sum of twenty
thousand dollars in gold bullion. Carefully he folded it and
placed it reverently in an inside coat pocket. He gave a beatific smile to Geoffrey Benton-Howell, and patted over the
spot where he had deposited the draft.

"You are a gentleman and a scholar, Sir Geoffrey. Likewise a man of his word. Nice, anonymous gold has always
appealed to me. It can be used anywhere."

Benton-Howell pushed back his castored desk chair and

lit a fat cigar. The rich aroma of a Havana Corona-Corona filled the study at the B-Bar-H. "I daresay, if you fail to use your usual, impeccable, diplomatic skill in this, you might have need of somewhere else to spend that."

"I know. My colleagues and I shall invent some sort of reason why that land has to be separated from the reservation. Heaven forbid that we ever mention gold being found there. Too many others would want a piece of the pie, and spoil your project all together."

"You understand only too well, Chester. Now, then, I suggest a small tot of brandy to seal the bargain, and then I have others to see."

"Certainly."

Ten minutes later, Chester Claypoole had departed, and the leather chair opposite Benton-Howell had been occupied by His Honor, Judge Henry Thackery of the Federal District Court for the Territory of Arizona. His Honor didn't seem the least bit pleased. A heavy scowl furrowed his high, shiny forehead.

"You've handled this Smoke Jensen affair miserably, Geoff," he snapped, accustomed to being the ranking person in any gathering.

"I will admit to having erred slightly in regard to the security of my ranch headquarters," Benton-Howell answered with some asperity.

"It's a great deal more than that, Geoff. If it ever comes out that your man, Quint Stalker, arranged the scene of the crime to indicate the guilt of Smoke Jensen, you may find yourself seeking the life of a grandee down in Mexico, or even South America. Or worse still, standing on the gallows in Santa Fe. I certainly do not intend to be there beside you."

Benton-Howell fought to recover some of his sense of well-being. "And you shall not be, my friend. Judge, everything is arranged as you asked. Seven thousand, five hundred in gold coin, mostly fifties and twenties. It is right there in my safe. A like amount to be paid, whenever you are called upon to hear any challenge to our claim of the White Mountain reservation land."

Judge Thackery pondered a moment, pushed thin lips in and out to aid his musing. "That's satisfactory. However, Geoff, I must caution you. Smoke Jensen has to be dealt with swiftly and finally . . . or the consequences will fall on you."

Jeff York and Walt Reardon rode into Socorro with Smoke Jensen. They had come for supplies for the Tucker ranch. Martha's idea of hiding in plain sight seemed to have worked so far. Recently, Smoke began chafing at the inactivity, and expressed a willingness to test how anonymous he had become. Walt halted the buckboard at the rear loading dock of the general mercantile, and dismounted.

"Jeff and I are going to amble over and visit with Mort Plummer at the Hang Dog, while the order is filled."

"Fine with me. I'll meet you there when it's loaded," Smoke replied.

"We'll be waitin', Kirby," Jeff drawled, a light of mischief in his eyes.

Being a purloined letter did not include speaking Smoke's name in public. Jeff had wormed Smoke's given name out of him for just such events as this. From the pained expression on the face of the gunfighter, Jeff gathered that Kirby was not Smoke's favorite handle. Walt untied his saddle horse from the tailgate of the wagon, and stepped into a stirrup. Together, he and Jeff rode to the mouth of the alley and turned left on the main street.

Business was sparse in the saloon at this early hour. Only a handful of barflies lined the mahogany, shaky hands grasping the first eye-opener of the day. Walt and Jeff ordered beers and settled at a table near the banked and cold potbelly stove. Walt started a hand of patience.

"You ever play two-handed pitch?" he asked Jeff.

"Yeah. About as exciting as watching grass grow."

"Now, I don't know about that," Walt defended the game. "If it's four-point, a feller's got a whole lot of guessin' to do to figure out what his opponent is holdin'."

"For me, I like to have all the cards out. Seven players is my sort of game."

"What about that fancy game all the hoity-toity Eastern dudes play—whist?"

"Not for me," Jeff declined. "I'm a five-card-stud man myself."

Walt chuckled. "Now yer talkin'. I ain't had a good hand of poker for nigh onto six months. Nobody on the Sugarloaf will play with me anymore."

"You win too much?"

"You got it, Jeff. And honest, too. No dealing seconds or off the bottom, either. Never stacked a deck in my life."

Two young wranglers stomped into the saloon. They turned to the bar at once, and did not take notice of the pair in conversation at the table. Jeff York had a good look at them, though. He grew visibly tense and sat quite still.

When they had sipped off their first shots and chased them with beer, the tall, lanky blond turned from the bar and peered into the shadowed corner that contained Jeff York and Walt Reardon. His face took on an expression of extreme distaste.

"I'll be goll-damned, Sully. It's that no-account Ranger from back home."

"You're seein' things, Rip. We's in New Mexico now."

"Nawh, I'm right. Turn around an' see for yourself. I know an asshole, when I see one."

Walt Reardon cut his eyes to Jeff York's muscle-tightened face. Jeff knows this pair, that's a fact, he reasoned. This could get deadly in about a split second. He scooted back his chair, came to his boots, and started for the rear.

"Got to hit the outhouse," he announced to Jeff, but cut his eyes toward the location of the general store. Jeff nodded.

"Hey, Rip, you're right," Sully declared as he turned to

look Jeff's way. "It's the same lawdog that locked us away in Yuma prison for three years. Like to have kilt me, heavin' all them big rocks onto the levee. Bit far from your stompin' grounds, ain'tcha, Ranger?"

"You're making a mistake, Sullivan," Jeff grated out.

"Nope. Way I sees it, it's you've made a big mistake. They's two of us . . . and this time our backs ain't turned."

Jeff rose slowly, shook his head in sad recollection. "Never could abide a liar, Sully. You two were facing me that day in Tombstone. Didn't either one of you clear leather before I had you cold. I did it then, I can do it now."

"You've got older now, slower, Sergeant York."

"No. It's Captain now, and I'm not getting older . . . only better."

Two more second-rate fast guns stepped through the batwings and took in the action. "Sully, Rip, you got some fun lined up?" the chubby one asked.

"That we have, Pete. Just funnin' with an old acquaintance from Arizona. Ain't that right, Ranger York?"

"Can we get a piece of him, too, Sully?" the skinny teen next to Pete asked eagerly.

"Sorry, Lenny. When I get through, I don't reckon there'll be enough left to go around," Sully said in refusing the offer, a sneer aimed at Jeff York.

"You're forgetting the Ranger here has a friend along," Mort Plummer said from behind the bar. He hoped to delay the inevitable. To at least get the killing started out in the street, not in his bar.

"He run out at the git-go. Plumb yellow," Sully brayed.

"I don't think so," the bar owner countered. "I sort of recognize him from a while back. Never asked him personal, understand? But I figger him to be Walt Reardon, the gunfighter from Montana."

"No wonder he ran. I hear he lost his belly a long while ago."

"Not so's you'd notice," Walt Reardon announced, as he

pushed his way between Pete and Lenny. He was followed a second later by Smoke Jensen.

"I'm gonna go get the rest," Lenny declared, as he moved his boots quickly through the door.

Mort Plummer chose that moment to avoid damage to his property. "Get out. The bar's closed."

Sully turned back to him. "I don't think so. Pour me another shot, and set up the boys, too, when they come."

"Get out of my saloon."

"You pushin' for a bullet all your own, barkeep?"

Mort Plummer tried to stare Sully down, but it was Smoke Jensen who answered. "You've got a nasty mouth. Too bad you don't have a brain to go with it."

Two of the town drunks, who blearily recognized Smoke Jensen from the day of the lynch mob, beat a hasty retreat. One literally dived through the space below the spring-hinged batwings. He collided with the legs of five proddy outlaw trash. Lenny led the way as they entered. Mort Plummer had gone white with fear. The hard case quintet spread out and faced off against three coldly professional guns. Eight to three. Pretty good odds, the way Sully figured it.

"You boys have no part of this," Jeff told the newcomers. "Walk out now, and no harm will come of it."

Sully's eyes never left Jeff. "You boys have a drink on me, then I'll open this dance."

"No. I will," Smoke Jensen contradicted. Smoke's .44 leaped into his hand, leveled at Sully's belt buckle, before the wannabe gunhawk's hand could even reach his. Smoke forced a sneer to his lips. "You're too easy."

The humiliation of having been tossed back, like an undersized fish, pushed Sully to unwise desperation. He foolishly completed his draw.

"Goddamn ya, I'll kill ya all."

Smoke Jensen didn't even bother with him. Jeff York had iron in motion, and completed the life of the petty outlaw with a round to the heart. Sullivan never even fired a shot. Three of the gang of outlaws turned bounty hunters had their own six-guns in play. Smoke shot one of them in the upper right chest, and put another down with a .44 slug in the thigh.

When that one went down, three of the remaining shooters pounded boots on the floor in an effort to widen the space between them all. Walt Reardon tracked one, and took him off his boots with a bullet in the side. Jeff accounted for another. But the third had disappeared. Sudden motion behind Smoke Jensen's back ripped a warning from Mort Plummer, who had ducked below the thick front of his bar and had seen the reflection in the mirror.

"Look out, Smoke!"

"Smoke Jensen!" Pete and Rip yelled at the same time.

"Oh, my God! I give up," Lenny wailed. "Don't shoot me, Mr. Jensen, please. Ranger," he appealed to Jeff, "I give up." He raised his arms skyward, the Smith American dangling from one finger by the trigger guard.

"Yeller belly," Rip growled at Lenny as he swung his six-gun on Smoke Jensen. "Kiss your butt good—"

Smoke Jensen drove the last word back down Rip's throat with a sizzling .44 slug. Mort Plummer moaned in anguish. Glass exploded outward in a musical shower from one of the paint-decorated front windows, as two of the remaining hard cases dived through it to escape certain death.

Pete found himself alone, facing the guns of Smoke Jensen, Jeff York, and Walt Reardon. Pete's momma had always considered him a bright little boy. He proved her right when his Colt thudded in the sawdust that covered the plank floor. He raised trembling hands above his head.

"All righty, I call it quits. After all, Sully said we was only funnin' with y'all."

Smoke cut his eyes to Jeff. "Do you want him, or shall I?"

"My pleasure," Jeff York announced as he reholstered his .45 Colt.

He took a pair of thin, pigskin leather gloves from his hip pocket and slid them on his hands, his eyes never off of

Pete for a second. Slowly he advanced on the frightened two-bit gunhawk.

"Eight to three. Is that the way you boys usually play it? Now it's just one-on-one," Jeff taunted. "You got a choice. You can pick up that gun on the floor and try me . . . or you can use your fists."

"I ain't got no quarrel with you, Ranger. Ain't no fight in me," Pete pleaded.

"No backbone, either," Jeff retorted. "Do something, even if it's wrong. I'm getting tired of waiting."

Pete's eyes widened suddenly, then swiftly narrowed. He lunged at Jeff with a knife that seemed to spring from behind his back. Jeff popped Pete solidly in the mouth. Lips mashed and split, Pete's face sprayed blood in a rosy halo.

Jeff sidestepped the blade and grabbed the wrist and upper arm of the knife hand. He brought it down, as he quickly raised a knee. The elbow broke with an audible pop. Pete went down, to howl his agony in a fetal position in the spit-and-beer-stained sawdust. Jeff silenced him with a solid kick to the head.

"Sneaky bastard, wasn't he?" Jeff rhetorically asked the silent room.

"The supplies are loaded," Smoke Jensen said dryly.

"Then I suppose we're through in town," Jeff said in an equal tone.

"You weren't never here, Mr. Jensen," Mort Plummer swore from behind his bar. "Wouldn't do to confuse our good sheriff as to who shot up my place."

"Take whatever you can find in their jeans to cover your loss," Smoke suggested.

"Right. And I've never seen you in my borned days. Good luck."

"We'll need that," Smoke advised him. "Used up a bit here today."

17

He didn't like going to Arizona to take charge of the turnover of the White Mountain land. He felt even worse when the lacquered carriage he rode in jolted to an unexpected halt.

"Woah up, Mabel, woah, Henry, hold in," the driver crooned to his team. "What the hell do we have here?" he asked next.

"Yes," Miguel Selleres called from the interior of the coach. "What do we have? Why did you stop out here in the middle of nowhere?"

"It's—it's . . . I think it's Quint Stalker and some of his boys."

"They are supposed to be in Arizona," Selleres shot back.

"Well, we're here," spoke the familiar voice of Quint Stalker, noticeably weakened.

Selleres poked a head out of the curtained window. Four men, without horses, all wounded, all dirty and powder-grimed, stood at the side of the road. Astonishment painted Selleres's face. He had never seen the proud, gamecock Stalker so bedraggled. "How did this happen?" Selleres demanded. "Why are you not in Arizona?"

"We were headed there," Stalker related glumly. "Those

damned Apaches waited around and hit us a second time. Killed all but us four. And we're all wearin' fresh wounds."

"You have had a hard time. There are some tanques not far ahead. Climb on the top and we'll ride there. After you've cleaned up, you can ride inside with me," Selleres told them grandly.

"Well, thanks so damned much, *Señor* Selleres," the aching Quint Stalker replied sarcastically. "Only we ain't gonna go back out there. No way, nohow."

"Oh, I disagree, *Señor* Stalker."

His patience tried beyond any semblance of his usual cool nature, Miguel Selleres reached under his coat and drew out a Mendoza copy of the .45 Colt Peacemaker. Slowly he racked back the hammer, as he leveled the weapon on the tip of Quint Stalker's nose. "You will go back to that Apache reservation with me, or I will shoot you down for the cowardly dog you are."

Nervously, Quint cut his eyes to his three remaining men. Slowly he shrugged and outstretched both hands, palms up. "Who can argue with such logic?"

Martha Tucker looked at the mound of supplies being carted into the kitchen and the bunkhouse with eyes that shined. The ranch had run dangerously low of nearly everything in the three weeks since her husband's murder. She clapped her hands in delight, and made much of the small, tin cylinder cans of cinnamon, ground cloves, allspice, and black pepper.

"Now I can bake pies again! What would you like?" That she directed to Smoke Jensen.

"Anything would be fine. I'm pleased you approve of my shopping. It's not often I do such domestic chores."

"And I'll bet your Sally doesn't have to send along a list," Martha praised him delightedly.

Color rose in the cheeks of Smoke Jensen. "No, Mrs.

Tucker, but then, Sally usually comes along with me. Watchin' her is how I learned to pick the best."

They had ambled off during this exchange. Horizontal purple bars filled the western quarter of the sky, layered with pink, orange, and pale blue. At this altitude, stars already twinkled faintly in the east. Martha Tucker led the way to a circular bench, built around the bole of a huge, old cottonwood. There she turned to face Smoke Jensen.

"I feel that Mr. Jensen and Mrs. Tucker are rather stiff after so much time. May I call you Smoke?"

"If you wish, Martha." Smoke produced a rueful grin. "You know, it's funny, but I've been thinking of you by your given name for several days now."

They sat, and each resisted the urge to take the other by the hand. "I don't wish to seem prying, but could you tell me about your life before now," Martha urged.

Smoke sat silent for a while, then sighed, and laced his fingers around his right knee, crossed over the left. "I ran away . . . ah, that's not quite true. My home ran away from me, when I was twelve. I wandered some, and wound up out on the plains. I was about to get my hair lifted by some Pawnee, when this woolly-looking critter out of hell rose up from the tall grass and shot two braves off their horses with a double-shot Hawken rifle. Dumped two more with another of the same, then banged away with a pair of pistols, which I later learned were sixty caliber Prentiss percussion guns, made in Waterbury, Connecticut. That's how I met Preacher."

Smoke went on to relate some of the milder adventures he had encountered as a youth in the keeping of Preacher. Martha listened with rapt attention. When words ran dry for Smoke, she told of her life back East, before she married Lawrence Tucker.

"We had a fine place, right outside Charleston, South Carolina. The War ruined all that, though. I was not yet eighteen, when I met Lawrence. He had come down with the occupation forces of Reconstruction. Like a proper young Southern lady, I hated all Yankees. Yet, Lawrence seemed somehow different.

"He had genuine concern for the well-being of white Southerners. He treated whites and darkies with the same reserve and respect. And I found out later that he didn't profit a penny's worth out of the false tax attachment schemes that deprived so many of their land and property."

"Given the circumstances, I'm surprised you ever got together," Smoke prompted.

"I had little choice. Lawrence and his staff occupied our plantation house. Daddy had lost a leg at Chancellorsville, and been invalided out of the service. Lawrence insisted from the first day his carpetbaggers moved into the main house, that rent be paid. Only, it was him paying that rent.

"He was young, and a lawyer. He'd only served the last year of the War with the Bluebellies." Smoke smiled at the use of that term, while Martha paused to order her recollections. "One night at the dinner table, he absolutely astonished the whole family by stating forcefully that the War had been fought for economic reasons and politics, and had nothing whatsoever to do with slavery."

"Not a popular opinion among our brethren to the north," Smoke observed.

"I'll say not. He and Daddy got along famously after that. One day, one of the vilest of carpetbaggers showed up with those falsified documents about back taxes on Crestmar. Lawrence produced a stack of paid receipts, and said those taxes were not due anymore." A tinkle of laughter brightened her story. "He even threatened to have the man run off the plantation by our darkies, who were working then for wages. They were armed with some shotguns and a few Enfield muskets left over from the War. We whites were not permitted to carry arms, even for self-protection, although General Grant said we could."

A profound change had come over Martha Tucker. She talked like a young girl, when she recalled her life in the South. Her mannerisms also revealed the stereotypical

Southern belle. Smoke noted this with not a little discomfort. He saw it as though she were two different persons, the lighthearted one hidden under the burdens of the other. He wondered if it was good for her. To make matters worse, he received a strong impression that she was flirting with him.

"I've enjoyed this talk of old times, Martha. No offense, but right now, my stomach thinks my throat's been cut."

"Oh, my! What a ninny," Martha babbled, the Old South sloughing off her speech as she rose. "I'll see to supper right away. The children will be starved, too. And thank you for confiding in me about your past life."

Smoke Jensen heaved a long sigh of relief as Martha Tucker headed toward the kitchen. A soft chuckle came from the far side of the tree trunk, and Jeff York stepped into view. "That one's fallin' in love."

"You can go straight to hell, Jeff York," Smoke growled as he came to his boots.

Awakening at the palest of dawn light, Miguel Selleres drew a deep breath, redolent with sage and yucca blooms. He immediately understood why Benton-Howell coveted this land so much. Very like the valleys of the Sierra Madre Occidental, where he had grown up. A moment later he received a lesson in why it was not wise for white-eyes to desire this vista of piñon-shrouded mesas.

Some twenty-seven Apache warriors—in varying sizes from short and squat to tall and square, painted for war— rose up to fire a volley of arrows into the camp erected by the seven men who had accompanied Miguel Selleres and Quint Stalker's survivors. The whirring messengers of death had barely begun to descend on the unsuspecting white interlopers, when a ragged fusillade of rifle fire erupted, shattering the quiet of early morning.

With grim silence, the Apaches swarmed down into camp on the tail of their surprise opening. Shouts of confusion and alarm came from the sleep-dulled outlaws. Only their leader had the presence of mind to make a positive move. Miguel Selleres unlimbered his Mendoza .45, and shot the nearest Apache through the breastbone. He then came to his boots and made directly for his carriage.

Unlike most of its contemporaries, fashioned by the skilled wainwrights of Durango, it did not have sides and a roof of thick oak planking. Sandwiched between layers of veneer, strong sheets of steel—fashioned from the boiler plates of a wrecked locomotive on the *Ferocarril de Zacatecas*—made it nearly impregnable. Even the curtained windows had bulletproof shutters. Miguel Selleres reached his goal, along with Quint Stalker, who knew about the construction of the coach. They entered, secured the doors and shutters, and began to pick targets among the attacking Indians.

Durango's coach makers had provided firing ports, not so much for fighting off Apaches, but for driving away bandits. They well knew the requirements of the rich and powerful in their own country. The armored vehicle withstood assaults from arrow, lance, ball, and stone war club. Many who attacked it died for their efforts. A growing volume of firepower drove off the Apaches after a closely fought five minutes.

"Did you think to bring some water and grub?" Quint asked anxiously, when the shooting dwindled to long-range sniping.

"Under the seat. There's extra ammunition, *también*."

"You think of everything, *Señor* Selleres."

"Not everything, or I would not be in here, with those cursed devils outside."

Quint Stalker actually cracked a smile, and his troubled countenance brightened. "That shines! I like a man with a sense of humor in tough situations."

"You flatter me. Help yourself to my humble repast."

Stalker dug into the wicker hamper inside the hinged

rear seat. He pulled out a cloth bag of *machaca*—shredded dry beef, Mexican style—another of parched corn, a tin can of bean paste, and another of peaches. "We're gonna feast like kings," he exclaimed with delight.

"The men won't fare so well, unless they gather up what the *indios* failed to destroy. I suggest you order them to bring everything they can, and form defenses around my carriage. We could use two more guns in here. The rest can form barricades from rocks, saddles, and . . ." Selleres winced, "dead horses."

Mid-morning came and the situation had changed little. It had grown blood-boilingly hot inside the coach. Great wet patches showed under the arms of the occupants and along their spines. Several of the hard-bitten outlaws had managed to round up enough horses to harness the carriage and provide transportation for the survivors, if some rode double. Miguel Selleres noted that spirits had risen considerably. Then Fate struck them cruelly again.

This time, when the Apaches charged, the solid drum of shod hooves joined in the whisper rush of moccasin soles. A dozen Arizona Rangers, led by Tallpockets Granger, stormed the mesa top and the desperate hard cases who had been trapped there. A steady swath of bullets made a drum of the inside of the carriage.

Desperation added its own brand of discipline to the forlorn outlaw band. When the Apaches crashed into the improvised barricades, the white vermin reversed their rifles and used them for clubs. Winchesters bashed Apache heads, broke ribs, slowed the advance, and low-held six-guns blazed a clear path through the throng.

Miguel Selleres spotted it first. The reins of the team had been threaded through a narrow, hinged slot near the roof of the coach. Selleres handed them to one hard case and shouted through a riskily opened window.

"Get this team going. Surround the coach and ride for it. That's our only chance."

"That was damned Arizona Rangers out there fightin'

alongside the Apaches," Quint Stalker observed in a wounded tone. "What they takin' the redskins' side for?"

Miguel Selleres gave him a droll look. "Perhaps our bought politicians have not been able to accomplish all they promised. Or they aren't honest."

"What's a honest politician?" Quint asked, never having known of one.

"One who, when he's been bought, stays bought by the same people," Selleres answered glibly.

"Oooh, hell, here they come again," Stalker groaned as he slammed the shutters tight.

At once the two outlaws at the lead team spurred their mounts and got the armored vehicle in motion. Firing to their sides, they fought clear of the horde that rushed at them. Driving blind, the border trash who held the reins expected at any instant for the carriage to turn over. Bouncing and swaying, he kept erect as the seconds, then the minutes, passed.

"Ohmygod!" he gulped in a rush, as the coach canted downward onto the trail off the mesa.

"I think . . . we have . . . made it," Quint Stalker muttered in wonder.

"*¡Gracias a Dios!* I do believe we have," Miguel Selleres breathed out softly.

Tallpockets Granger watched the heavy carriage lumber down the steeply inclined trail and called in his detachment of Rangers. Most of the tough, Arizona-wise lawmen cautiously eyed the charged-up Apaches, who also broke off pursuit. An explosive situation could erupt at any second, Tallpockets knew, yet he had to fight an amused smirk as he made known his plan. Using the Tinde language, which he had learned as a child, he made a stunning announcement to Cuchillo Negro and his warriors.

"Black Knife, I want you and your braves to raise their right hands. Yeah, that's the one. Good. Now, do you swear to uphold the laws of the Territory of Arizona, obey the orders of the law chief over you, and keep the peace as directed? Answer, *enju*."

"*Wadest*, what is this you are doing, *shee-kizzen*?" Cuchillo Negro asked, calling Tallpockets White Clay—the name he had earned as a boy when his father was agent to the White Mountain people—and calling him blood brother.

"Why, I'm making you my deputies, *shee-kizzen*."

Black Knife's reaction began as a grin, grew into a broad smile, and ended in a deep belly laugh. "*Enju-enju*—yes, yes," he responded. "I never believed I'd live to see this day."

Tallpockets, who at six-foot-five truly fit the name, pulled a perplexed expression. "General Crook organized two companies of Apache scouts for the Army, so why can't the Rangers take you on?"

"For what purpose?"

"To track down those white lice and squash them," the long-faced Tallpockets stated levelly, his one brown and one blue eye glinting with his anger. He had heard of what had been done to the Tinde children.

Tension evaporated as the rest of the Tinde offered their oaths and went among the Rangers clasping forearms in the Apache fashion. Tallpockets stood beside his blood brother and accepted the fealty of the warriors, all the while glancing at the fading streamer of dust that marked the course of the outlaws. At last his patience wore thin.

"Let's mount up and go after that slime."

Sir Geoffrey Benton-Howell received two pieces of extremely bad news at the same time. The rider from town brought him word of the shoot-out in the Hang Dog, and a telegram, sent in haste from Springerville, Arizona Territory. He listened in a growing storm of rage.

"It was Smoke Jensen, right enough. Enough folks recognized him while the shootin' was goin' on, and when he rode out of town. He was with a buckboard from the Tucker ranch."

"*WHAT?*" Benton-Howell bellowed.

"He was with some riders who drove a Tucker ranch buckboard."

"I heard what you said, fellow, I just could not believe it. We worked so hard to convince that foolish woman that Smoke Jensen had killed her husband. How could she do this?"

"He didn't kill Tucker?"

"Of course not, you lout," Benton-Howell snapped, his control rapidly slipping. "One of Quint Stalker's men, Forrest Gore, did the job, and bungled it mightily, I might add. Wait here while I read this, then I will have some instructions for you."

Benton-Howell slit the yellow envelope and pulled the message form. His face went crimson with each word that leaped from the page. Miguel Selleres defeated and put to route by a band of Apaches and the Arizona Rangers? His mind refused to accept it. The Arizona Rangers? Impossible. That made it even more important to end this matter with the Tucker woman at once.

"Rocky, I want you to round up five or six men, and ride over to keep a watch on the Tucker ranch. Better take enough to send messages back, for that matter. What you will be looking for is the next time Smoke Jensen leaves there. You are to send word to me, and then go in and apprehend the widow and her children. We're going to make them disappear from the face of the earth, and then take that ranch."

18

Smoke Jensen turned away from the window that overlooked the dooryard of the Tucker ranch. "I'm not satisfied with the results of the visits to Benton-Howell's ranch. We need to take the fight to what's left of Stalker's men around Socorro. The four of us can get them mightily stirred up."

"How you figure to work it?" Jeff York asked.

"We'll split up, cover more area that way. You and Walt, Ty Hardy and I."

"Must you do this?" Martha Tucker asked with almost wifely concern as she entered the room.

"I'm afraid so. I don't figure this Englishman for being stupid. His partner's smart enough from what I've heard," Smoke explained. "They'll figure out sooner or later that the only place we can be is here. I want to keep the fighting away from you and your youngsters."

"I'm grateful for that, Smoke, but the risk . . . ?"

Smoke gave her a smile just short of indulgent. "I've taken risks before and come out all right." He didn't mention the scars that crisscrossed his body, or the eyes swollen shut and blackened by hard knuckles, the loose teeth and split lips. "We'll head out in half an hour," he told Jeff.

Not unexpectedly, Jimmy Tucker wanted to ride along. When the four gunfighters—Ty Hardy just a beginner—

had mounted up, Jimmy came to them and blurted out his wishes. Smoke Jensen looked down at the lad long and hard.

"That's not possible, Jimmy. Although they're hardly the best of a sorry lot, it's no place for you to be. You're good enough with a gun to protect your mother and the other kids, so your place is to stay here and do just that."

Jimmy made a face like he might cry, then turned away. "Awh . . . hell, I never get to do anything," he muttered.

Smoke Jensen withheld his sympathetic chuckle until they had ridden away from the ranch headquarters. When he looked back at the crest of a low rise, Martha and Jimmy were waving at them with equal enthusiasm.

Forrest Gore slid the brass telescope closed and slipped it in the case hung from his saddle horn. "They're long gone, and nothing's stirring around the bunkhouse or corrals. You boys spread out, take your time, so's we can hit them from all sides at once. Today's washday, so the woman'll be out in the yard. If we cut her off from the house, we won't have any troubles at all."

For once it worked exactly like Gore wanted it. He and seven men swarmed down on the Tucker ranch, and caught Martha Tucker at the clothesline. Arms above her head, a sheet flapping in the breeze, she did not have a chance to reach for the rifle that leaned against one upright of the drying rack. Two men literally plucked her off the ground and rode away.

After her first, startled yelp, Martha shouted desperately, "Run, Jimmy!"

Only Jimmy Tucker did not obey. He dived for his own rifle and came up with the lever action cycling. The other five men, led by Forrest Gore, closed in on the children. A slug cracked over Gore's head, close enough to make him cringe. He still smarted from the pellet wounds given him by Smoke Jensen. Three of the Tucker hands got into the fight a moment later.

Outnumbered by the outlaws, one went down almost at once, as Marv Fletcher blasted him in the center of his chest. A second gunhand took a bullet in the leg and lay helplessly under the guns of the Stalker gang. The third hunkered down behind a large water tank and fired at those surrounding his friend.

After Vern Fletcher took a slug in his shoulder, Arlan Grubbs got around behind the wrangler and shot him in the back. Jimmy got off another round before the broad chest of a lathered horse knocked him off his bare feet.

Forrest Gore dismounted swiftly and wrestled the rifle from the boy's grasp. Then he backhanded Jimmy hard enough to loosen teeth. Quickly he tied the boy's hands and feet. With a grunt of effort, he booted the dazed lad onto the crupper of his saddle. Shrieks of fear from Rose and Tommy Tucker cut through the rumble of hooves. Dust swirled in the abandoned yard, as the outlaws rode off with their prisoners.

"What do we do with 'em?" a snaggle-toothed hard case asked.

"We're to take them to the B-Bar-H. Sir Geoffrey wants to entertain them for a while," Forrest Gore replied with a lustful leer.

Jeff York pointed ahead to what Smoke Jensen had already seen. "Someone's sure foggin' the road this way," the Arizona Ranger told him, stating the obvious.

"Must have come from a long way off," Smoke stated flatly. "I've been watching the dust rise for a good twenty minutes."

"Carbone said you had the eyes of a *halcon*—a hawk," Jeff said softly. "Now I believe him. Who do you think it could be?"

Smoke studied the growing column of red-brown dust,

and the thin line far behind. "Not someone we're going to enjoy meeting."

"Quint Stalker and his gang?" Jeff suggested.

"It could be, Jeff. Right funny if we set out hunting them and they find us first."

"I'd maybe see the fun in it, if we still had Walt and Ty along," was Jeff's glum reply.

Smoke looked around the barren desert terrain. "There's nowhere to hide out here."

"There'd be plenty, if you were an Apache."

Smoke cut his eyes sharply to Jeff. "Think like an Indian. That's a shinin' idea, Jeff. Let's get busy."

A quick coursing of the ground located a shallow gully. Smoke and Jeff rode into it and dismounted. At Smoke's direction, they stripped the saddlebags from their mounts and put the animals down on their sides. With stones from the bottom of the wash, they reinforced the lip of the draw in two places and set out rifles and ammunition.

"Nothing left to do but wait," Jeff said out of nervousness.

"Not for long, either." Smoke had already picked up the distant, growing rumble of wheels that moved fast and carried a heavy burden.

They had a good view down the reverse slope of the elongated ridge where they had found the gully. Only thing, the road curved out of sight against the swell of the land, a scant three hundred yards away. Outriders came into view first.

Smoke caught sight of the heads of their horses, then the forward-bent outlines of three men, riding abreast. Behind them came a six-up team, hauling a lumbering coach. The men to the rear of the carriage had their weapons out and ready, and kept casting glances behind them.

"Whoever it is, looks like they're in some sort of trouble."

"I reckon, Jeff. Only, which side do we pick?" At Jeff's droll expression, Smoke went on. "Reckon we let them get in close enough to see if we recognize any of them."

"Not too close, I hope," Jeff suggested. "I count nine men, plus whoever is in that coach."

"Funny there's no one up on that box to drive." Jeff nodded understanding at Smoke's observation.

By then the lead riders had come well within field glass range. Smoke studied the faces, and his full lips thinned into a grim line. He put the binoculars aside and levered a round into the chamber of his Winchester.

"One of them is Quint Stalker," Jeff advised a moment later.

"Well, we know which side we're on," Smoke tossed back as he made ready for a fight.

Quint Stalker had obtained a horse at the first homestead they came upon after escaping from the White Mountains. He used the simple expedient of stealing it. He had so far ridden two mounts into the ground, and the team hauling that armor-plated carriage had been replaced three times. The cause of their unseemly haste hovered tauntingly on the western horizon.

Contrary to the assurances of Miguel Selleres, the Apaches had continued in pursuit, and by all appearances, the Arizona Rangers rode with them. Try as he might, Quint Stalker could not visualize those two traditional enemies as allies. Yet they had joined against him and the eight men who remained. That conclusion had been reached in the moment Quint swerved his mount to the left to avoid a large rock in the trail.

That movement put the bullet meant for his heart in the eye of his horse, and killed the animal instantly. When the dead beast's foreknees hit the hard, red-brown soil, Quint Stalker catapulted out of the saddle. He hit hard, the air driven from his lungs, and rolled along in the sharp-edged gravel that lay in his path.

His chin took a lot of punishment, and wound up bleeding profusely when he sprawled to a halt. What the hell?

Those Injuns couldn't have gotten ahead of them. After his ordeal, thoughts didn't stick too well in Quint's mind. He tried to see to his left, from where the shot came, only everything looked fuzzy. Then his blood turned to ice.

From behind, he heard the coach bearing down on him. He'd be squashed into a red pulp by two dozen hooves. To say nothing of those wheels! Squalling, Quint lurched upward and threw himself to one side. He could see the hooves of the horses up close, and feel the heat of their bodies as they thundered past. The swaying carriage halted directly beside him.

"Get in here, you idiot!" Miguel Selleres growled from the open doorway.

Grateful for the protection of those armored walls, Quint Stalker did so with alacrity. Once secure, he found himself the target of unanswerable questions.

"What happened out there?"

Quint Stalker gaped at Miguel Selleres. "I . . . don't know. Someone shot my horse out from under me."

"Who? How many? I don't see anyone," Selleres rattled off, while squinting out the firing loop of one window. "It can't be *los indios*," he added to himself.

"That's what I thought, and you're right. It can't be."

"Then who?"

Stalker's first attempt at an answer got drowned out by the loud slam of bullets into the side of the coach. In a brief lull, he tried again. "Smoke Jensen."

"*¡Bastante, no más!*" Selleres barked. "We have enough men to finish him for all time."

He came to his feet and leaned over the seated outlaw. A hinged panel in the back of the coach opened, and Selleres shouted through it. "Get over there and find who's shooting at us."

At once the gunmen spread out, and jumped their horses toward the lip of the ravine. Withering fire challenged them, yet they pushed on. One hard case yowled and clutched at his arm, where a bloodstain began to spread. Another doubled over, lips to the neck of his mount, as though kissing it. The remainder drew off, seeking cover behind the carriage.

"¡Cobardes! ¡Pendejos! Get out there and kill those men! I see only two guns against you. ¡Adalante, pronto!"

With obvious reluctance, the outlaws charged again. This time they fired steadily at the noted gun positions. Their heavy volume of fire forced Smoke and Jeff to pull down below the lip of the bank. Selleres watched with growing satisfaction. The riders reached the edge of the gully.

Then a gunhawk from Albuquerque threw up his hands and fell backward off his horse. Smoke Jensen had switched to his .44 and blasted upward into the man's face. Jeff York opened up also. Bullets gouged the ground and cracked through the air. Another gunhawk grunted in pain, as one of Smoke's slugs pierced his left leg, front to rear, right below the knee. Suddenly they had had enough.

Huddling behind the armored coach, they heard a muffled string of curses from inside. The shutters opened on one window, and they saw the face of Quint Stalker. "Get over there and finish it, you sonsabitches."

"Give us some covering fire, damn you," Charlie Bascomb snarled.

"Yeah—yeah, good idea. Spread out, hit them from two sides. We'll keep their heads down."

It worked even better than Miguel Selleres expected from the thoroughly demoralized gunmen. He and Quint Stalker opened fire first, the riders charged out from behind the carriage, and streaked for the arroyo ahead of and behind the position of the ambushers. Victory lay only fractions of a second away.

Then Selleres and Stalker learned how deceptive the desert terrain could be to eyes accustomed to a fifteen-mile horizon. Around the bend in the road that masked the back trail, some twenty Apache warriors swarmed with a dozen Arizona Rangers. Rapidly closing ground, they opened fire immediately. Miguel Selleres weighed the outcome quickly and accurately.

"Get us out of here," he snapped to the driver at his side.

Tallpockets Granger saw the coach stopped in the road ahead. A dead horse lay on its side behind the armor-plated vehicle. Someone had ambushed them. He knew that someone had to be Capt. Jeff York. At once he turned in the saddle, waved an arm over his head, and pointed forward.

"Unlimber your irons, boys. It looks like ol' Jeff's bit a bear in the butt."

They crashed into the nearer trio of outlaws with rifles and six-guns blazing. One man fell without a sound, shot through the head. Another took two bullets in his side and dropped from the saddle. The last threw up his hands. The Apaches accompanying the Rangers streamed on by, intent on taking on the child-killers beyond the coach. Suddenly the vehicle bolted forward, the horses straining to pull the heavy load.

Terror blanched the faces of the *Pen-dik-olye* as Cuchillo Negro and his warriors raced toward them. One had self-control enough to steady his mount and take careful aim. Smoke Jensen rose up slightly and put a slug through his chest. The gunhawk made a gurgling cry as he fell sideways off his saddle.

His companions started dying seconds later, hard and slowly, as the Apaches swarmed over them. It took some time to stop them. While the Rangers did what they could to drag the vengeful warriors off the outlaws, Tallpockets Granger pounded boots to the edge of the draw.

"Thought it might be you, Cap'n," he drawled through a grin. A nod toward Smoke. "Mr. Jensen, good to see you again. Them horses you brought us worked real good. Let us run the hell out of those *ladrónes*."

Smoke came up onto the level. "Glad you like them. What brings you over this way?"

"We decided to wipe out that Stalker gang once and for all. Besides, I sort of figgered ol' Jeff here might need some help."

"And the Apaches?" Jeff asked with a nod toward Cuchillo Negro.

"They're my deputies." At Jeff's astonished gape, he added, "We're after the same enemy, Cap'n."

Smoke clapped a hand on one shoulder of Granger. "Then they are as welcome as can be. Only thing that bothers me, is that coach got away. I thought we'd shot it to doll rags."

"Wouldn't have done no good," Tallpockets informed Smoke. "That belongs to Miguel Selleres. It's all made of boiler plate under thin wood."

"That ties everything together," Smoke allowed, after hearing an account of the battle in the White Mountains. "I think the time has come to move directly on Benton-Howell and his partner."

Tallpockets Granger volunteered his posse of deputy Arizona Rangers. That gave them an effective force of fifteen. To Smoke's surprise, the Apaches led by Cuchillo Negro offered to continue as deputies to Tallpockets. At the suggestion of Smoke Jensen, they rode first to the Tucker ranch to enlist any others who wanted to join the fight.

"A good place to start is in Socorro. We can clean out the trash that Benton-Howell has been gathering, then close in on the ranch," Smoke declared.

When they reached the Tucker ranch two hours later, a wounded hand, Sean Quade, gave them the bad news. "They killed Hub and Carter," he concluded, "and took Miz Tucker and the kids."

"Who?"

"Don't know all of them. Some of the trash that's been showin' up in town. Forrest Gore led them. I saw him clear."

"Which way did they go?" Smoke asked with winter in his voice.

Quade scratched an isolated circle of sandy hair that hung down his forehead. "Southwest, toward Socorro."

Shock at learning of the abduction had turned to cold, controlled anger in Smoke Jensen. "Then that's the way we're going. We'll send a doctor out to take care of that leg, Sean," Smoke advised the wounded man.

"Damned right," Jeff agreed.

"I'm goin', too," Sean Quade stated flatly.

Jeff York tried to reason with Quade. "You wouldn't be much use with a bullet in your leg."

"I can sit on my butt in a buckboard, and use a shotgun," Sean defended his decision.

"You've lost a lot of blood," Smoke Jensen told the man. "The ride in could knock you out, or worse."

Quade could not argue with that. "All right. I'll stay here and wait for the doc. Good luck . . . and keep your heads down."

19

Socorro literally burst at the seams with gunfighters and wannabes. From beyond rifle range, Smoke Jensen studied the crowded streets through field glasses. When he had worked out in his mind how it should be done, he turned to Cuchillo Negro and spoke, with Tallpockets translating.

"I want to save you as a nasty surprise for the gunhawks in there."

The Apache chief pulled his full lips into a grim smile. "These white men will have no heart for the fight when we attack."

"That's what I'm thinking. They won't think much of the rest of us riding in. We can take a few by surprise. But the best of them will fort up somewhere. When that happens, and we get bogged down, you hit them from the far side of town."

Cuchillo Negro cut his eyes to Tallpockets. "This one thinks like a Tinde."

Tallpockets rendered it in English. Smoke nodded in acceptance of the compliment. "I learned most of my fighting skills from a man named Preacher."

Eyes widened, Cuchillo Negro grunted harshly. "My father knew such a man and spoke of him often. We Tinde called him Gray Wolf. No other man could move so silently, or fight so ferociously. I do not say that lightly."

"He'd be proud to know you folks thought so highly of him," Smoke returned.

Black Knife smiled around his eyes. "Many Chiricahua, Mescaleros, and Tinde died before we learned to respect him."

That could go on Preacher's headstone, if he had one, Smoke thought. "They had plenty company," he told the Apache chief.

A second later, the Apaches left for their position. They seemed to dissolve into the empty terrain. One moment they were in plain view; the next, only faint puffs of dust showed where their horses had walked. And *they* had this great respect for his mentor. For perhaps the thousandth time, Smoke saw Preacher in yet a new light.

"We'll give them half an hour, then ride in," Smoke informed the others.

Two second-rate hard cases sat their horses at a point where wood rail fences and a cattle guard kept livestock from wandering the streets of Socorro. One of them jolted out of a doze at the sound of approaching riders. He tipped up the brim of his hat and peered into the wavery heat shimmer of midday.

"More guns on the way," he remarked to his companion. "You'd think we were going after an army."

"Hell, Mike, for twenty dollars a day I'd take on ol' Gen'ral Sherman hisself."

"No denyin' the money's good." Suddenly Mike's spine stiffened him upright, and his hand went to his gun.

"Damn! That one in front's Smoke Jensen!"

"Yer seein' things," his partner contradicted. He just knew Smoke Jensen would never be within ten miles of Socorro.

Mike whipped his six-gun clear of leather. In the time it

took for him to reach the hammer, his intended target had spoken and drawn his gun.

"Your friend's right, you know."

"Awh, hell."

The last thing Mike saw was the beginning of a spurt of smoke from the barrel of the .44 aimed at him. He died so quickly, he didn't fall off his horse. Smoke Jensen's second bullet hit the other would-be gunfighter somewhat lower. It ruined his liver and spine on the way out. He pitched to one side and landed with a heavy *plop*.

"So much for taking anyone by surprise," Smoke complained, as he and the Rangers rode past the dead men.

Halfway down the block, a trio of lean, gaunt-faced men stepped into the street to block the way. "That something personal between you an' Mike?" the one in the middle asked. Then he saw the silver badge on the vest of Jeff York. "Awh, damnitall," he bemoaned his fate as he drew against the Arizona Ranger.

Jeff shot him with the Winchester in his right hand. The other two scattered. They threw wild rounds behind them, as they made for the nearest saloon. Jeff grunted and put his free hand to his left shoulder. It came away bloody-fingered. Jeff brought the rifle to his right shoulder then, and took careful aim. His bullet shattered the offender's ankle and put him on the ground.

Smoke's second slug shattered a kerosene lamp beside the door through which the last gunman dodged. The Rangers spread out, weapons at the ready. Smoke and Jeff continued toward the barroom. Jeff York stuffed a neckerchief under his shirt front, to sop up the blood from the deep gouge cut in the meat of his shoulder point. Glass crunched under their boot soles, when they dismounted and stepped up on the boardwalk. Smoke and Jeff entered through the batwings together. They found themselves facing nine outlaw guns.

Five of those roared at once. Showers of splinters

erupted from the door frame and lintel. One bullet went by so close to the ear of Smoke Jensen, that it made more of a hum than a crack. Smoke already had one of the shooters on the floor, doubled over the hole in his belly. Jeff York had a second gunhand down, crying really sincere tears over his ruined left hip. Then the remaining four six-guns exploded into life.

Smoke Jensen had dived to one side and flattened a felt-covered poker table, scattering chips, cards, and players in all directions. He did a forward roll before the table came to rest, then bounced to one knee, flame spitting from the muzzle of his six-gun. At short range, a .44 slug does truly awful damage to human flesh. Smoke's round hit a thick, hard-muscled belly, with a *splat* like a baseball bat striking a whole ham.

His target gave a hard grunt and looked down stupidly at the hole where his fifth shirt button used to be. "Jeez, Mister, who is it killed me?" he asked weakly.

"Smoke Jensen," the owner of the name told him.

Then Smoke was on the move again. He jumped over a man who had only then come off the sawdust from his upset chair. The move saved his life. The hard case they had chased into the saloon leveled a round at where Smoke had knelt. All it killed was a fly on the faded, pale green wall. The gunhawk gaped at his act of minor mayhem, and paid for it with his life as Jeff York shot him down.

One of his comrades in murder reeled backward into the bar, blood gushing from a neck wound he had received courtesy of Smoke Jensen. The bodies continued to pile up at an incredible rate, the bartender, Diego Sanchez, noted. He sat on the floor behind two full beer barrels, and watched the slaughter in reverse through the mirror. It was a technique barkeeps learned early on in their profession, or they didn't have long careers.

A stray slug shattered a decanter and sent shards of thick crystal shrapnel flying. They in turn broke half a dozen cheaper bottles, and inundated the bartender's apron with bourbon, rye, and tequila. Taking a bath in booze came with the territory also, Diego Sanchez knew from experience. *¡Por Dios!* His Conchita would make him sleep in the hammock between the palo verdes again.

Suddenly it got eerily silent in the saloon. Not a boot sole scraped the floor. No one could be heard breathing. No glass shards tinkled. Even the echoes of gunshots had died out. Slowly, Diego Sanchez sucked in air. He raised himself slowly until his eyeballs came above the top of the bar. Four men faced one another from opposite ends of the mahogany. Two he knew: Logan and Sloane, gunfighter trash that had drifted into town three days ago. The other pair wore badges, a U.S. Marshal and an Arizona Ranger.

"It's your choice," the Marshal said tightly.

Jesus, Maria y Jóse, he was a big one. Diego moved back from the bar, until he pressed against the shelf behind.

"You ran that thing dry," Logan drawled nastily. "Now I'm gonna ventilate that tin star of yours."

"You know, I think you're right," Smoke Jensen told him, as he threw the .44 in the air and instantly snatched the second one from its left-hand holster. The hammer dropped on the primer before Logan could react and yank his trigger. Smoke caught the flying six-gun left-handed, at the same moment his bullet punched a hole through Logan's chest. The gun in the Ranger's hand blasted a second later and downed his man.

"Jesus, Smoke, I didn't think anyone could do that," Jeff York said in awed tones.

Smoke? Smoke Jensen? Diego Sanchez sucked in air and crossed himself. Then he slowly lowered his head below the bar. As though spoken from far away, his words reached the ears of Smoke Jensen.

"*Vereso nada, Señor Jensen.*"

"He said, 'I saw nothing,'" Jeff translated.

"Yeah. I caught that. I think we're through here, Jeff." Then, with a chuckle, "Adios, *Señor cantinero*."

"*Conosco nada, nada,*" was the weak reply.

Diego Sanchez might have been willing to see and know nothing, but that didn't go for the swarm of hard cases and two-bit gunslingers who thronged the streets of town. They damn well wanted to know what was going on in the *Cantina La Merced*. They didn't like what they found when the batwings swung outward. Smoke Jensen and Jeff York had reloaded, and met the gathered gunslicks with six-guns roaring.

"This town is out of bounds for your kind from this minute on," Jeff York bellowed over the sound of gunmen panicking. Half a dozen of them were foolhardy enough to resist. Two of them died instantly. One of them shot the hat off Smoke Jensen's head and bought an early grave for his efforts.

"On the balcony over there, Smoke," Jeff shouted.

Smoke pivoted to his left and sent another wannabe gun-fighter off to hell. The gunman staggered forward and tripped over the railing. He did a perfect roll in the air on the way down. The other lawmen had spread out along the main street, and began herding surprised hard cases off benches and out of saloons, prodding them toward the jail. By that time, Jeff had drilled a second resister in the shoulder.

"Jeff, drop!" Smoke shouted the warning as a gunhand popped up from behind a rail barrel and aimed at Jeff York's back.

Jeff went down, and the bullet fanned air where he had been standing. A fraction of a second later, a .44 slug from Smoke Jensen's iron flattened the back-shooter against the wall of the Mercy Cantina. The corpse left a long, red smear down the whitewashed stucco, as he slumped beside a cactus in a large terracotta pot.

Hot lead cracked through the air around Smoke then. He moved swiftly across the street, charging the shooter instead of fleeing. The mountain man's six-gun bucked one. The gunslinger stiffened, then his knees buckled. Smoke had already turned away.

None of the original, six foolish gunslingers remained on their feet. Smoke cut his eyes to Jeff and nodded down the block to where the volume of fire had increased noticeably. "I think Tallpockets and the boys could use some help," Smoke suggested.

"Then, let's go see," Jeff agreed, shoving fresh cartridges into his still-hot Colt.

Some twenty gunfighters and assorted saddle trash had banded together and taken over a bank building. Its thick fieldstone walls made it into a fortress. The structure stood alone, an island at an intersection, which allowed the Rangers to completely surround it. When Smoke Jensen and Jeff York arrived, the occupants hotly exchanged shots with those outside.

"I reckon they have the Tuckers in there," Smoke allowed.

"Won't they be in danger?" Jeff asked.

"Most likely they'll be somewhere safe. Probably in the cellar, if there is one. Dead hostages don't make good bargaining chips."

On the roof, the head and shoulders of a hard case appeared. He apparently wore all black, and had a full-flowing walrus mustache in matching color. He put a Ranger down with a bullet in the side. While he ducked down behind the stone verge and cycled the action of his rifle, Smoke Jensen didn't even break stride. His hand dropped smoothly to the .44 at his side, which came free of leather with a soft whisper. When his left boot sole next struck the street, the weapon barked in Smoke's hand.

Above, behind the low stone parapet, the gunman's hat took sudden flight, along with a gout of blood and brains. Jeff York stared at his friend in open amazement. Smoke pointed with the smoking barrel of his Peacemaker.

"There's a narrow crack right . . . there. I just waited until his black hat blotted out the light."

"That was one steady-handed shot," Jeff complimented. Smoke merely shrugged and sought another target. When the volume of fire increased even more, Jeff looked toward the north end of town. "Anytime now," he observed.

"Them damn Rangers ain't even supposed to be over here," one lanky gunfighter from Arizona declared, as he fired an unaimed shot into the street. "They ain't got no juri—jures—they ain't the law in New Mexico!"

"You see that slowin' down the lead they're punching at us?" growled an exceptionally short, bushy-headed gunslick with thick, gold-rimmed glasses.

"Shut up, Bob," the Arizonan snapped.

Glass tinkled like chimes as more windows took fire from the Rangers. Gradually, over the roar of gunfire from both sides, the men inside the bank heard the rumble of hooves and thin, high-pitched yelps. Bob cut his eyes upward at the slender Arizonan.

"What the hell's that?"

"Sounds . . ." The gunfighter cocked his head and concentrated. "Sounds like Injuns."

"What Injuns would that be?" Bob challenged.

"By god, it sounds like Apaches. I've heard enough of them to last a lifetime."

"What are *they* doing over here?" Bob gulped. "Are they attacking the town?"

Arizona Slim edged to a window on the north side of the bank lobby and peered out. "No. Oh, hell no! I can't believe this. They—they've joined the damned Rangers. They're comin' after us!"

Outside, the Rangers checked their fire as the Apaches swarmed through their cordon and flung themselves directly at the shot-out windows of the bank. The Arizona lawmen began reloading, while the men led by Cuchillo Negro raced closer, firing while bent low over the necks of their mounts. Three dived through shattered sashes with stone-headed war clubs held high.

Muffled gunshots came from inside, and the screams of dying men. A second wave hit the stone building, and a lance hurtled through an opening to pin Bob to a desktop; bloody froth accompanied his screech of agony. With the Apaches rampaging inside, the Arizona Rangers charged the building.

Once the lawmen got in close and mixed it up with the gunhawks, all resistance ended quickly. When the survivors had been rounded up and secured in manacles, Smoke Jensen and Jeff York made a thorough search of the cellar. They came up with no sign of the Tucker family. But Smoke did find Payne Finney, hiding in a coal bunker.

"The Tuckers? Where are they?" he demanded of the thoroughly demoralized Finney.

"They aren't here. Never have been. I don't know where Stalker told Gore to take them," Finney lied smoothly.

Smoke clasped Finney by one shoulder, his thumb boring into the entry wound from a .44-40 round. Finney squirmed and grunted. "You wouldn't figure to try to run a lie past me now, would you?" he asked Finney in a calm, level tone.

"No—no. I'm serious. I don't know where they took them. I've been here all the time."

"He's right," a surly member of the Stalker gang supported Finney. "He's been in town like the rest of us. We never heard anything about the Tuckers."

Smoke cut his eyes from Payne Finney to Jeff York. "Case of the right hand not lettin' the left know?" he asked.

"Could be. Where do we start from here?"

"Back at the ranch." Jeff groaned as Smoke went on. "The trackers I set out should have something by now. It's not your fault, Jeff. I figured, too, that they'd want to take 'em to some neutral ground to arrange terms."

Jeff brightened. "There's only one place makes sense. We can save a lot of time, if we ride direct for the B-Bar-H."

"That fits. But I want to hear what the trackers say first. And we do have these prisoners to take care of. After that, we'll ride."

20

Half a dozen hard cases had ridden out of Socorro as the Rangers thundered into town. From a safe distance they had watched the roundup develop, heard the gunfire raise to a crescendo, and then watched in horror as a horde of Apaches swarmed into town. Then they lit out for the B-Bar-H.

They arrived on lathered, winded horses that trembled and walked weak-kneed to turns at the water trough. Charlie Bascomb, the nominal leader of the contingent that had escaped, reported to Quint Stalker and Geoffrey Benton-Howell. What he had to tell them did not get a warm reception.

"It's the truth, Sir Geoffrey. I tell ya, the Apaches sided with those Arizona lawmen. My guess is, they'll be headed this way before long."

Quint Stalker swore and smacked a balled fist into the opposite palm. "That's the same lawmen that came after us. But they ain't got authority in New Mexico."

Frowning, Benton-Howell answered him, "I'm afraid they do. It's called hot pursuit. If you are right, then they can keep coming until you are caught."

"You ain't gonna let them, are you?" Stalker all but pleaded.

"Of course not. You've served me well and faithfully—ah—with a few recent exceptions. I think it expedient to bid my friends from Washington and Santa Fe a fond *adieu*. We can hold off any force here, until the governor learns of my plight. I'm sure he can get the interloping Arizona lawmen out of his territory."

"Hummm. That could be," Stalker caught at the thin strand of hope.

"Meanwhile, I want you to organize the men we have here. Fortify the headquarters, and prepare to stand off a siege."

"Do we got supplies for that?"

"Oh, my, yes. Ample food and ammunition, even some dynamite. Water might become a problem, if this becomes protracted."

Stalker raised a brow. He knew the absolute importance of water in a desert. "Like how long?"

"Four or five days. All of the wells are out in the open. A marksman's delight, don't you know?"

"What about the Tucker woman? Can't we use her and the brats to bargain with?"

Benton-Howell considered Stalker's words a moment. "That was my intention, if the situation required it. More to the point, I want her signature on a bill of sale. That must come first. I'm going to see her now. See to the preparations."

Martha Tucker looked up from her dark contemplations when Geoffrey Benton-Howell entered the small, bare pantry in which she had been confined. She had been separated from her children the moment they arrived at the ranch. That troubled her a good deal more than the constant insistence that she sign the ranch over to the Englishman. Jimmy would be all right, she felt certain, but little Rose and Tommy could be easily frightened. When her eyes fixed on her visitor's face, she noted at once that something seemed to have ruffled his usual icy composure.

"Mrs. Tucker, I'm afraid I really must insist on you signing the quit claim deed form I provided. Time is—ah—running short."

"For you or for me?"

"For both of us, I regret to say."

Again, Martha noted a flash of distress, and seized upon it at once. "What is it, Mr. Benton-Howell? Is Smoke Jensen closing in on you?"

Damn the woman, Benton-Howell thought furiously. Had she heard anything, even locked away here? He fought to retain his calm demeanor. "Smoke Jensen has nothing to do with the business between us. What I want is your ranch."

"Smoke Jensen has *everything* to do with it," Martha surprised herself by saying. "I see it now. You tried to frame Mr. Jensen for the murder of my husband."

"Damnit, madam, I'll not have that sort of talk from you. I had nothing whatever to do with that sorry incident." He omitted mentioning Miguel Selleres and Quint Stalker. "The matter is plain and clear. I—want—that—ranch."

"How much are you offering for it?"

Benton-Howell pinned her with icy eyes. "Your life, and the lives of your children."

"I have had better offers than that," Martha snapped.

"Which you chose to spurn. My patience is growing short. Perhaps I should have one of the youngsters brought here. I assure you my men have ways that are most persuasive when dealing with a child."

Martha paled, then red fury shot through her cheeks. "You'd not dare harm one of them."

"Ah, but I would, indeed. If my wishes are not acceded to. The form is on the counter there, and pen and ink. I recommend you sign now."

"Why do you want our ranch so badly?"

"That's none of your affair. Sign that paper, madam."

"Or else?"

Benton-Howell thought a moment. "That younger boy of yours, ah, Tommy, I believe. Is he a good scholar?"

"He does very well in school."

A smirk twisted Benton-Howell's aristocratic visage into a mask of ugliness. "He wouldn't do so well missing a couple of fingers, would he?"

Outrage and horror choked Martha Tucker. She made no sound as she leaped to her feet. Her fingernails flashed like the talons of an eagle, as she raked them down the face of her tormentor. Benton-Howell cried out in an almost feminine shriek, and he pushed her roughly away. He stormed to the door and hurled his last threat over one shoulder.

"Sign it or suffer the consequences."

By late afternoon, half a dozen hard-faced men had ridden in and tied horses at the Socorro livery. Smoke Jensen observed to Jeff York that there must be an inexhaustible supply of second-rate gunhawks in New Mexico. They decided to delay their departure from town. One of the hands who had volunteered to help was sent back to the Tucker spread to make contact with the trackers, and bring their discoveries to Smoke. Now, with twenty gunmen locked in jail, more than half of them wounded, the town began to fill up with more of the same.

"By this time tomorrow, it'll be every bit as bad as it was when we rode in," Jeff stated in disgust, as he sipped at a beer in the Hang Dog.

"Too bad we couldn't keep the Apaches in town," Smoke observed.

"The good people of Socorro would have died of heart failure left and right. Some of my own men were concerned about how Black Knife's bucks would behave when they got the killin' hunger on them."

"They're damn good fighters," Smoke said tightly.

"They're that. They're also savages. No different from any other tribe. They got their ways; we've got ours. There isn't often that the two meet and work well together, like we did here yesterday."

Smoke lifted the corners of his mouth in a hint of a smile. "It worked well enough, I'd say. Of course, we had common cause. Some of those men you chased down were responsible for killing those Apache kids. I'll give you that if we go into their country next week, there's no guarantee they won't lift our hair. Like Preacher used to say, 'Injuns is changeable.'"

Boots clumped importantly on the porch outside. Sheriff Jake Reno bustled through the doorway and came directly to Jeff York. "I see you are still in town, Ranger. Maybe that's a good thing. There's more of that border trash drifting in every hour. I'm danged if I know what got them stirred up."

Jeff York put on a big grin and hooked a thumb in Smoke Jensen's direction. "Maybe it's that big reward you put out on my friend here."

Sheriff Reno turned to see whom the Arizona lawman meant. He came face-to-face with Smoke Jensen. His jaw sagged, and the color drained from his cheeks. He staggered back a few small steps. At first, no sound came. Then, a wheeze and squeak slid past rigid lips. A moment later, he found full voice, and bellowed, albeit with a quake.

"Goddamnit! It's Smoke Jensen!"

"In person, Sheriff. How's tricks?" Smoke asked with a mischievous twinkle in his eyes.

Sheriff Reno choked over the words that rushed to spew from his lips. He reached for his Smith American and handcuffs at the same time. "S—sta—stand ri-right there, Jensen. You're under arrest. Give up, or by God, I'm gonna gun you down right here."

Smoke Jensen backhanded Jake Reno so swiftly, the sheriff never saw Smoke's big hand. The impact sounded like a shot. "You're not arresting anyone, Sheriff," Smoke told him in a flat, deadly tone.

No small man, Jake Reno balled huge, ham fists and swung at the taunting man before him. Smoke easily slipped the first blow and caught the second on the point of one shoulder. He brought his hands up and worked on the sheriff's soft middle. The fat yielded easily and, to his surprise, Smoke found a hard slab of muscle beneath. Reno grunted and punched Smoke in the face.

Smoke's head snapped back and heat flared in his eyes, as he drove a hard left to the side of Reno's jaw. Jake Reno backpedaled rapidly until he struck the bar. Smoke followed with hard rights and lefts to the sheriff's ribs. He felt bone give under his pounding, and shifted to Reno's gut. Stale whiskey breath gusted from behind yellowed teeth.

A hard right from Smoke stopped that when it cracked three of Reno's teeth and mashed his lips. Blood flew through the room when Sheriff Reno shook his head violently in an effort to clear his fogged mind. He managed to get his guard up in time to parry two more solid swings, then Smoke broke through and did more damage to Reno's mouth.

Jake Reno sagged slowly, desperately seeking his second wind. It came gradually as his vision dimmed. With a blink of his eyes, he saw everything clearly again. He lunged awkwardly for Smoke Jensen and planted a left on the gunfighter's cheek. Smoke took it without a flinch. Smoke's own knuckles stung—he had not had time to put on his gloves before handing out this lesson in restraint. He ignored it and planted another fist in Reno's face.

Reno countered with a vicious kick aimed at Smoke's crotch. With a slight bob, Smoke slapped the booted foot away and then yanked upward on it. A startled *whoop* came from Jake Reno as he fell flat on his butt. Smoke closed in and stood over the seated man, to pound blow after blow onto the top of Reno's head. Reno began to gag and spit up blood. He must have bitten his tongue, Smoke considered.

With what would prove to be his final defiance, Jake Reno reached out with both arms and encircled Smoke Jensen's legs. He hauled with rapidly dwindling strength. When he put a little shoulder in it, he dislodged Smoke's boots from the plank floor and toppled the mountain man.

Smoke recovered quickly though, and popped Reno on one ear with a stinging open palm. It had the effect of a gun going off beside the sheriff's head. Through the ringing, with eyes tearing, Jake Reno pawed uselessly at Smoke Jensen's torso while Smoke drove hard, punishing blows into already weakened ribs. Without warning, Jake Reno uttered a small, shrill cry, arched his back, and fell over backward. His head thudded in the sawdust.

Panting, blood dripping from the cut under his left eye, Smoke Jensen came slowly to his feet. He reached gratefully for the schooner of beer Jeff York offered him. He rinsed his mouth and spat pinkish foam into a brass gobboon.

"We've got enough evidence on the good sheriff to lock him up, don't we, Jeff?"

"I'd say so. It'll be up to the prosecutor if he's tried for anything."

"Then get this trash out of here. Put him in his own jail, and make sure he stays there."

"We found sign about three miles from the ranch," one of the trackers Smoke Jensen had sent out reported late the next day. "The Tuckers were taken to the B-Bar-H, sure enough. The closer they got, the less careful they were about covering their trail. An' something else, Mr. Jensen. That place is being turned into a fort. Armed riders everywhere, fence lines are being raised higher, the windows of the main house are boarded up."

Smoke considered this report while he sipped coffee.

"Kevin, how many men do you figure are siding with Benton-Howell and Selleres?"

Kevin Noonan evaluated the quality of the gunmen they had seen. "I'd say twenty-five to thirty of them are average to good. They stay off the ridge lines, keep to the trees where they can, most don't smoke at night. There's another twenty or so who just don't measure up; trash with a gun strapped on. And there's more driftin' in all the time, five to ten a day."

Those numbers didn't appeal to Smoke Jensen. Even a poor shot could hit someone sometime. He simply didn't have enough men for a head-on fight. "It sounds like they're getting ready to stand off an army."

"Could be that this Englishman is trying to buy time," Walt Reardon suggested.

"For what purpose?" Jeff York asked.

Smoke Jensen picked it up from there. "He did have all those politicians out there for a big party. While you were there, did you gather that they were being paid for favors already done?"

"More like Benton-Howell was courting them," Jeff recalled. "It could be that they haven't come through so far."

"Yes. So he has to stall us, until whatever he is doing becomes legal," Smoke completed the thought. "Which means we should do a little pushing right soon. We have to force the issue *before* he can get whatever he's after out of the politicians."

"How soon?" Walt Reardon asked.

Smoke thought on it. "In a day or two. First we have to make Socorro unpopular with the sort Benton-Howell is attracting to town."

Walt Reardon lightly touched the grips of his six-gun. "We'd best do that before the place fills up again."

"Right about now should be a good time to start," Smoke announced, rising to his boots.

* * *

Orin Banning turned away from the lace curtains that covered the window of the parlor in Fanny Mae's Residence for Refined Young Women. "I never saw a town with so many badge-toters in it," he grumbled.

Beyond him, in the street, Arizona Rangers busily nailed up small, neat posters. One of the six men who had ridden with Banning to Socorro to answer the call put out by Benton-Howell made his way toward the brothel, eyes fixed on the industrious lawmen. After one had fastened a notice to a lamppost, he ripped it down and made his way quickly to the front door.

"Hey, Orin, lookie at this. We're being posted out of town."

"You mean *us?*" the would-be gang leader demanded.

"Well, yeah. Us an' everybody else. It says here that, 'Everyone not a resident of Socorro, New Mexico Territory or its environs'—whatever that means—'is hereby ordered to be out of town by noon Tuesday.' That's tomorrow."

"Who is going to be doin' the throwin'?"

"Them Rangers, I reckon. Oh, an' I heard a funny thing down at the Hang Dog. A feller said Smoke Jensen was in town."

Banning frowned. "Jensen would never mix into something like this. Thinks he's too damned good to work for another man."

"Maybe so, maybe not," the gunslick opined. "Anyway, what'er we gonna do?"

"For starters, we're not going to leave," Banning told him firmly.

By late afternoon, some of the least confident among the gunmen began to drift out of town. A few more joined them the next morning. Many hung around though, to see how this hand would be played. Some soon learned, when the Rangers—and some local residents who had been deputized—began to make sweeps of the streets.

"You ride for one of the ranches around here?" Tallpockets Granger asked a pair of wannabe gunhawks lounging outside the barbershop.

"Nope."

"Then fork them scruffy mounts of yours and blow on out of here."

"What if we don't want to?"

Tallpockets's eyes turned to ice. "Then you'll be in jail faster than you can whistle the first two bars of 'Dixie.'"

From down the block, a voice of authority made a hard demand. "Move along. You don't have business in this town anymore. I'd make it fast, if I was you."

Three Arizona Rangers filled an intersection off the main street and began to walk along the dirt track. Every time they looked at a man, the subject of their scrutiny shied his eyes away and silently mounted up to ride out. Slowly, the crowd of low-grade gunfighters began to thin noticeably. Most of them knew who was hiring and how much would be paid, Smoke Jensen believed, and many even knew how to find the B-Bar-H. No doubt they'd be heading that way.

He had to admit to Jeff and Walt that there was little they could do about it. They had spoken on the matter only a minute before one of Granger's men approached. "There's some hard cases over at Fanny Mae's parlor house say they're comin' out shootin'. One of them with a big mouth told us that they'd take on all comers at that windmill in the center of town."

Jeff and Walt cut their eyes to Smoke. The legendary gunfighter quirked his lips in a hint of a smile, and hitched up his cartridge belt. "Then I guess we'd better get down to the *Plaza de Armas*. This might get interesting after all."

That didn't seem to faze Banning, but he paled slightly when Walt said, "Walt Reardon. No doubt you've heard of me."

"Y-yeah. Can't believe you've turned lawdog. How about you," he directed at Smoke.

"Smoke Jensen."

Right then Orin Banning did a right peculiar thing, considering he faced three of the best gunfighters on the frontier. He gave his sidemen the signal and went for his gun. Most of them didn't clear leather before Smoke, Jeff, and Walt fired their first rounds.

One of the outlaws went down gagging, a hand clutching his belly. Another spun sideways, then turned back to the action with a vengeance. He put a bullet through Walt's left arm a moment before he died of .44 caliber poisoning from the pistol in the hand of Smoke Jensen.

Bullets zipped through the small garden of the *Plaza de Armas* as Smoke sought another target. He soon found one. A hard case from the short-lived Banning gang crouched behind the edge of the pedestal of the unknown Spanish don. He rested the barrel of a Winchester on the smoothed surface of granite. Smoke put stone chips in the man's eyes with a quick round. The shooter fell back screaming. A hearty boom came from the barrel of the short-barreled L.C. Smith double ten that Walt Reardon had swung up from behind his back, after he emptied his six-gun.

The shot column of 00 Buck lifted a short, squat gunslick off his boots and planted him in the water tank. He went under without so much as a second splash. Walt cut his eyes to Smoke, then Jeff, to make sure of their whereabouts, then swung the shotgun toward a new target. The wound in his arm bled profusely. Smoke Jensen headed his way, when he saw Walt Reardon's knees start to buckle.

"Hang on, old friend," Smoke encouraged. "We've got to stop the bleeding."

"In the middle of a shoot-out?" Walt asked wonderingly.

"Damn betcha," said Smoke as he forced a grin.

Bullets cracked overhead and to both sides, as Smoke quickly bound Walt's arm. He helped Walt to the edge of the artificial pond created by the water tank, and eased the younger man to the ground.

"You can cover us from here." To Jeff, "Time to clean out the rest of this vermin."

"I'm with you," Jeff agreed.

They faced only three living enemies. Orin Banning would have been fortunate to have died first. That way he wouldn't have had to see the destruction of his gang. Smoke gave that passing thought as he darted between the neatly trimmed clumps of hedge that defined walkways through the plaza. He saw a flicker of movement to his left and spun on one heel.

Gunfire had attracted more of the ne'er-do-wells, like vultures to carrion. The newcomer had only a brief instant to see the badge on the chest of Smoke Jensen before the famous gunfighter busted a cap and sent the gunhawk off to join Orin Banning's men in Hell.

"Awh, damn," Smoke grumbled, as two more took the dying one's place.

Wildcat Wally Holt could not remember a time when he didn't have a gun in the waistband of his trousers or on his hip. He'd killed his first man at the age of eleven; shot him in the back. He had killed a dozen more since. At nineteen, Wildcat Wally saw himself as one of the best gunfighters in New Mexico Territory. Why, he had even been so bold as to compare himself with Billy Bonny. In less than thirty seconds, he was about to learn that he had nowhere near the speed, accuracy, or determination of Billy the Kid, let alone the man he suddenly found himself facing.

"You gonna use that thing, or sit on it?" Smoke Jensen asked of him as the youthful tough skidded into the center of the gunfight on the plaza.

"Yeeeaaaaah!" Wildcat Wally roared as he drew his Colt.

Or at least he tried to draw it. Suddenly his right arm would not obey him. Immense pain radiated from his shoulder through his chest and neck. Wildcat Wally jolted backward a few wobbly steps, and again tried to raise his six-gun. Nothing happened. Swiftly he made a grab for the Peacemaker on his left hip. He had it clear of leather when some unseen force punched him solidly in the center of his body, right below his ribs. A splash of crimson droplets rose before his eyes, as they started dimming.

Wildcat Wally next discovered that he could not breathe. He willed himself to draw deeply, yet his chest never moved. Slowly he dropped to his knees, an unbelieving expression on his face.

He worked his mouth. "Wh—who are you, Marshal?"

"Smoke Jensen."

"Go—good. At least it took the best to do me in." So saying, Wildcat Wally Holt lost all his wildness and slipped into the long slumber of death.

"Smoke, behind you!" Walt Reardon shouted from the water tank.

A Winchester gave its familiar .44-40 bark and Smoke Jensen felt a tug and fiery burning sensation along the right side of his ribs. He had dodged and started to turn at Walt's shout, which had saved his life. Now he faced the back-shooter and watched fear drain the smirk of triumph off the coward's face. Blood ran freely down Smoke's right side as he raised his gun and put a .44 period right between the would-be killer's running lights. The back of his head left with the gunman's hat, and he did a high kick backward into oblivion.

"Thanks, Walt."

"Anytime, Smoke."

Three more hard cases, lured by the sound of action, dashed onto the plaza, weapons at the ready. Walt cut the legs out from under one of them with a load of buckshot. The other two turned in his direction to see the double zeroes of the L. C. Smith pointed their way. They also saw Smoke Jensen off to the right. The wounded man managed to fish his six-gun out from under him, and died instantly from a gunshot wound delivered by Jeff York, whom they had not seen off to their left.

Made desperate by the sudden confrontation, the remaining pair swung weapons toward Smoke and Walt. The scattergun ripped one's chest apart. Smoke pumped a round into the last man, who draped himself over the back of a wooden bench. A dozen others, wishing to have no part of these deadly gunfighters, gave up a bad cause.

It was then that Orin Banning reared up from behind a low hedge and, screaming defiance, emptied his six-gun in wild, stray rounds that hit no one. He jammed the smoking weapon in his waistband and hauled another six-gun from his left-hand holster.

"Smoke Jensen, you baaastard!" he yelled as he opened fire.

Smoke dodged the first bullet, then returned fire. Banning grunted and staggered to one side. He got off another round, which plowed the ground between Smoke's legs. Then Smoke's second slug caught Banning full in the chest. That dropped him at last, amid the useless dregs of human garbage that had formed his gang. All at once the shooting stopped.

"Lay down your weapons and put hands in the air," Smoke Jensen demanded.

"What are you goin' to do to us?" one bleated.

"You're going to jail. When we have time to sort you all out, we'll send you home," Jeff York added.

A straggly parade of glum, disgruntled would-be gun-hawks wound along the way to the jail. Inside, Ferdie Biggs had been talking with Sheriff Reno. When the prisoners trooped in, led by Jeff York, Ferdie cut his eyes to the disgraced sheriff. He received a slight nod in response.

"Lock 'em up yourself," he grumbled to Jeff York.

Jeff took the keys from Ferdie as the latter pushed past

him. A moment later, Ferdie Biggs reached the office section. Smoke Jensen bent over a seated Walt Reardon. He changed the makeshift bandage and again insisted that Walt see a doctor. With Smoke's back turned, Ferdie had all the encouragement he needed. His six-gun had already cleared leather with a soft, wicked whisper.

Before Ferdie Biggs could ear back the hammer, Smoke Jensen turned in an eye blink, his right fist filled with a big .45 Colt. Transfixed by surprise, Ferdie stupidly tried to continue. Smoke shot him twice before Ferdie could squeeze his trigger.

Ferdie's legs reflexed violently and catapulted him over the former sheriff's desk. He sprawled on the floor behind, twitched and shuddered, then sighed out his life.

"Damn, how'd you know?" Walt Reardon gulped out.

"I saw your eyes narrow," Smoke answered.

"I was going to call a warning to you."

"Ferdie didn't give you enough time, Walt. But that squint did enough to tip me off."

"What now?"

"We drag that garbage out of here, and get on with it," Smoke answered with a glance at the corpse.

With their assorted wounds properly tended to, Smoke Jensen, Jeff York, and half of the Rangers with Tallpockets rode directly toward the B-Bar-H. Walt Reardon stayed behind to hold the jail. Even as they rode past the town limits, more fast-gun types drifted into Socorro.

"We're mighty short on numbers," Jeff observed tight-lipped.

"I thought about that before we left." Smoke flashed a white-toothed grin. "So I brought along enough dynamite to lower the odds a little."

Jeff let out a low whistle. "Reckon this is the last go-round."

"It had better be."

They rode on in silence for a while. By late afternoon they reached the boundary of Benton-Howell's ranch. Smoke noticed it first. The split-rail fences had been filled in with rocks and dirt, to form parapets; behind them stood some twenty rifle-toting gunhawks, lured by the high money paid and a chance to test themselves against Smoke Jensen. Smoke and his men reined in just out of range.

"We aren't going through there, even with dynamite," Jeff opined.

"Don't go off too sudden, Jeff. What we need to do is look around a little more. We'll ride around the whole spread, and see how much is done up like this."

They made it only halfway around the ten sections controlled by Benton-Howell by nightfall. So far it appeared that only a half-section, some three-hundred-twenty acres, had been sealed off. Not all the approaches were covered by so many men. Smoke had led them out of sight of those guarding the road and gate, when they had been able to cross over onto the ranch property. Well-accustomed to the rigors of man-hunting, the Rangers made a cold camp.

Smoke sat, chewing on a strip of jerky, and took counsel from the stars. After a while, he rose to his boots and walked over to where Jeff York had already bedded down for the night. He squatted beside his friend and spoke softly.

"I've made up my mind. Come first light, we'll ride back to the Tucker place and send for the rest of Tallpockets's men. Then I'm going to fix up something that will get us through all those defenses."

"What do you have in mind, Smoke?"

"The dynamite got me to thinking on it. That and the wide gaps along this side that aren't being watched. You'll see what I'm doing when we get to working on it."

Smoke Jensen had added to the mystery by instructing the young Ranger headed for Socorro, "Bring the wainwright from town out here, when you come back."

Now, two days later, with night on the sawtooth ridges to the east, the curious among the Arizona Rangers stood around, watching while the wagon builder rigged an unusual attachment to a buckboard which Smoke Jensen had purchased from Martha Tucker. One of the older—which meant a man in his late twenties—Rangers scratched at a growing bald spot in his sandy hair, and worked his lips up for a good spit.

"Now, what the heck kind of thing do you call that?"

Laughing at something said inside, Smoke Jensen stepped out of the house and walked directly to the curious lawman. "That's a quick release lynchpin, to let the team get away from the wagon in time."

"Time for what?" the sandy-haired peace officer fired back.

"Come along with me and you'll see," Smoke promised.

At the rear of the buckboard, eleven wooden cases of dynamite, from Lawrence Tucker's private powder magazine, were being carefully loaded into the wagon. Baskets and barrels of scrap metal from the blacksmithy and sheds of the ranch were being emptied around and over the explosives, except for the one in the middle. It had its top off, and several sticks of sixty percent dynamite were missing.

"You buildin' a bombshell?" the seasoned Ranger asked.

"I thought you'd figure it out right quick," Smoke praised him. "When we get done, this will be like the largest exploding cannon shell in the world."

"How come that one case is open?"

"We get to that one last. After the wagon is in position for what I want it to do. That's the primer that's going to set off all the rest."

"Gol-ly, Mr. Jensen, I ain't never seen anythin' quite like this."

"Those on the receiving end will wish they had never seen this one."

"I want everyone to get a good night's rest," Jeff announced as he joined Smoke at the wagon. "We leave for the B-Bar-H at first light." To Smoke, he said, "Time for another cup of coffee?"

Smoke Jensen cut his eyes skyward. "If I do, my eyes will turn brown. I'm going to grab a few winks."

"Sleep well," Jeff offered.

"You know it's funny, but I never do the night before a big fight," Smoke responded on his way to the bunkhouse.

22

Smoke Jensen saw at once that the time they had taken to prepare for the attack on the B-Bar-H had a double edge. It had given Benton-Howell the opportunity to strengthen his defenses. Instead of penetrating the outer ring of hastily made revetments on the north, they had to go around to the east, because of reinforcements who now patrolled where none had been before. It took some doing, and cost several hours to move slowly enough not to reveal the presence of their force of some twenty-five men and the wagon. Smoke oversaw the operation with patience and good humor.

"Look at it this way," he advised a grumbling ranch hand from the Tucker spread. "The longer goes by without an attack on the B-Bar-H, the more restless and bored those second- and third-rate gunhands are going to get. When we do hit, it will shock them right out of their boots."

"When do we hit them, then?"

"Tonight, well after dark, when all of them are relaxed and off their edge. The big thing is to get a hole cut in the outer defenses, wide enough to drive the wagon through without being detected."

"We have enough shovels along," Jeff York added, as he

rode up beside the buckboard being driven by Smoke Jensen. "Should go fast."

"That is if they aren't as thick around there as on the north," a gloomy Ranger commented.

"Ralph, you always look on the dark side," Jeff snapped.

"He has a point," Smoke Jensen injected. "Even if Benton-Howell doesn't have enough reinforcements now to cover the whole perimeter, we'll have to get rid of those on the east without making a sound. Knives and 'hawks if you've got them," he concluded through the scant opening between grimly straight lips.

Darkness had come an hour before and Pearly Cousins had given strict instructions to the gunmen who had accompanied him not to light up a smoke during their time on watch. It was hard enough seeing before the moon rose, let alone to be blinded by the flare of a lucifer. He yawned and stirred in his saddle. Pearly had been up late the night before, and had only five hours' sleep in the past two days. We're stretched too thin, Pearly thought to himself. Best be checking on the lookouts along the east side of the wall. Some of them aren't wrapped all too tight.

Pearly didn't find the rider at the northeast corner. "Must be patrollin'," he muttered aloud. He turned south.

Close to where he expected to find two of the eight men guarding this side of the defenses jawing instead of doing their work, he came upon a riderless horse. That was something Pearly hadn't expected. It ignited the first suspicions.

"Lupe, you takin' a leak, or what?" Pearly asked in a muted voice.

When he received no answer, Pearly edged his horse forward and caught up the reins of the abandoned mount. Then he started inward to seek the negligent sentry. He did not go far before he dimly saw a huddled form on the ground. The black silhouette of a big Mexican sombrero two feet from the body identified it as Lupe. His alarms jangling now, Pearly dismounted and crouched beside the unmoving man.

Pearly rolled Lupe onto his back. Pearly saw that Lupe's throat had been slit from ear to ear. Stealthy motion caught Pearly's eyes, as a huge human figure rose from the brush directly in front of him. He heard a soft *swish* a moment before the tomahawk in the hand of Smoke Jensen split Pearly's skull to his jawbone.

Smoke wrenched his 'hawk free and cleaned it on the dead outlaw's shirt front. He tucked it back behind his belt, and set off for the spot he judged to be directly in line with the ranch house. When he reached the place, he found the other night stalkers there ahead of him.

"Had an extra one to take care of," he explained. "We had better get started."

Taking turns at the dirt barrier, the lawmen spent only half an hour opening a space wide enough to admit the buckboard. Smoke drove, while Jeff led the mountain man's roan stallion. The Arizona Rangers and ranch hands formed a crescent-shaped line to right and left.

A mile inside the outer defenses, Smoke called a halt. "Time to set the primer charge," he announced tightly.

With that accomplished, the posse started up again. Smoke had allowed enough fuse for what he thought approximated twenty minutes. He would light it a moment before they topped the rise to the east of the house. Then he would set the team in a gallop, and make ready for the rest of the plan. If it didn't work the way he expected, if the fuse burned too quickly, then he would never know it.

"Good luck," Jeff York said tightly thirty minutes later, as the lawmen dropped back to let the wagon take the lead.

Smoke Jensen lit the fuse, and slapped the reins lightly on the rumps of the wheelers. The team dug in, the sixteen hooves of the draft animals pounded the ground with increasing speed. They crested the steep swale, and the velocity increased. Smoke snapped the reins again. He stood upright now, a small rope wrapped around his gloved left hand. The rumbling of the buckboard's wheels drowned out the sound of the mounts of the lawmen with him.

Closer loomed the mounded dirt that formed the inner fortifications. Smoke Jensen drove straight at the parapet. Flame lanced at the wagon from half a dozen places. Still Smoke remained upright, swaying with the erratic motion of the heavily laden buckboard. The vehicle careened onward. Closer, ever closer . . . the blackness of the hastily erected defenses filled Smoke's field of vision. He pulled slightly on the cord in his left hand, felt the lynchpin loosen. Anytime now . . . any . . .

NOW!

Smoke dropped the reins and yanked the lynchpin. It came free, and the horses, undirected now, curved from the mass before them, the tongue carried between their churning bodies. Smoke jumped free and rolled in the tall grass. Suddenly Jeff York swerved in close at the side of Smoke Jensen. He trailed the reins of Smoke's roan. Without breaking stride, Jeff flashed past. Smoke readied himself and leaped for the saddle horn. He caught it and swung atop his rutching stallion.

Immediately they all curved away and outward from the barrier. Five seconds later, the wagon struck the solid wall of dirt with a thunderous crash. A heartbeat later it exploded with a roar that came from the end of the world.

Waiting for an attack that might or might not come had started to get on his nerves. Geoffrey Benton-Howell paced the thick oriental rug in his study, hands clasped behind his back. His eyes cut frequently to the crystal decanter of brandy on the sideboard that formed part of a wall of bookshelves. No, that wouldn't do, he thought forcefully.

This was no night to get lost in the heady fumes of the grape. Not any night was fit for tippling until that offensive son of a bitch, Smoke Jensen, had been hunted down and eliminated. Nearly a week had passed since Jensen and the Rangers had cleared out Socorro. It did little to improve his outlook to know that the town had filled up once again with eager fast guns. Most of the Rangers had disappeared, and the remainder had forted up in the jail. He needed to get those new men involved in a search for Jensen. Benton-Howell sighed heavily, almost a gasp, and crossed to the door.

He leaned through the opening and called down the hall to the large sitting room. "Miguel, I need you in here for a moment."

When Miguel Selleres entered the paneled study, Benton-Howell had arranged his thoughts in order. Selleres likewise declined any liquor. He seated himself in a large, horsehair-stuffed leather chair and rested elbows on the arms. He steepled his long fingers and spoke over them.

"So, you have grown tired of waiting, *amigo?*"

"Just so. I want you to take two of the better gunmen and ride into Socorro. Organize that rabble, and set them off hunting for Smoke Jensen."

"I thought we had agreed to make him come to us here."

"We did. Only I don't think it is working."

Suddenly, as though to put the lie to Benton-Howell's pronouncement, a ragged volley of gunfire broke out at the dirt barricade that surrounded the house and barn. There followed a moment of silence, then a violent crash of splintering wood. Then the darkness washed away in a wall of sheer whiteness. The sound of the explosion, like a thunderclap directly overhead, came a second later. The shockwave blew every window on that side of the building inward.

It knocked books from the shelves and set the brandy decanter to dancing. Stunned to immobility, the two plotters stared at each other. Fighting for words, Benton-Howell got control of his voice first.

"They're attacking! Take charge of the men. There's no time to head for town. We have to stop them."

"Someone else can go, Stalker perhaps, and bring the others back. They could hit the Rangers in the rear."

"It's half a day in and the same back," Benton-Howell reminded. "By then we could all be dead."

"Or worse, on the way to jail," Miguel Selleres riposted.

Shuddering, Benton-Howell dismissed such weakening visions and began to organize the defenses. "Get torches lit; the men can't see which way to shoot. Are the sandbags in place around the outer walls?"

"Yes, since yesterday. Both floors."

"Have men at every window. Bolt the doors."

Sparks from the fuses in single sticks of dynamite began to make twinkling trails through the black of night. The blasts began to rout men caught in the open yard. Some bolted for the covered passageway that led to the well nearest the house. They made it without incident, only to be forced to cringe on the ground when holes began to appear in the wooden walls, as hot lead cracked through at chest level.

Sharp blasts illuminated the yard, as the dynamite began to explode. Their flashes strobed the action of the disoriented outlaws in the ranch yard. Two went down, shot through the chest, and a screech of agony came from another who had caught a short round in the groin. With a muffled curse, Miguel Selleres rushed from the room to bring order out of the chaos.

Fully a third of the defenders had been knocked off their feet by the tremendous explosion, Smoke Jensen noted as he and Jeff rode through the breach created in the parapet. Dust and the acrid odor of dynamite smoke still hung in the air. Jeff pointed to the rubble of scattered earth.

"If they'd used gabions, that wouldn't have worked," the Arizona Ranger said.

"What are those?"

"Sort of tubelike baskets, made of reeds or thin tree

branches; they're used in building fortifications." Jeff looked sort of embarrassed. "I learned that from General Crook, when I scouted for the army."

Smoke grunted. "Good thing the one who built this didn't know it."

Bullets cracked past Smoke and Jeff, and they saw that some of those not affected by the blast had recovered enough to offer resistance. One of the Tucker hands yelped, and clapped a hand to a profusely bleeding wound in his right arm. The shooter didn't have time to celebrate his victory. Smoke Jensen put a .44 round in his ear, and sent him, brainless, onto the outlaw level of Hell.

Suddenly a pack of dogs charged into the yard from a run behind the house. One launched itself and sank fangs into the leg of an Arizona Ranger. The lawman screamed as the teeth savaged him. He swung with the barrel of his revolver. It made a hollow sound when it struck the flat, triangular head of the bristling mastiff.

That had no effect on his grip though. He hung on, his body weight sagging downward, ripping his fangs through tender flesh. Tallpockets Granger whirled in his saddle and shot the vicious monster through the head. It fell away with a whimper and twitched violently on the ground. Another of the beasts, crazed by the explosive blasts, leaped on the back of one of the hired guns. His shrieks could be heard until the huge dog reached his throat.

"Keep clear of them," Smoke called out. "They'll do us more good than harm."

Smoke pulled a fused stick of dynamite from his saddlebag and lit it from a cigar clinched in his teeth. He hurled it toward the house. It hit the window frame and bounced off. A moment later it went off with a blinding flash and roar.

More quickly followed from the Arizona Rangers. Two more of the savage dogs died in attempts to attack strangers among the outlaw defenders. Smoke rounded the house and found himself facing two hard cases with six-guns cocked and ready. His right hand dropped to the curved butt-grips of his .44 Colt. One of the gunslingers fired before Smoke finished his draw.

His bullet cut a hot trail along Smoke's left side, below the rib cage. Then Smoke had his Peacemaker clear and in action. It bucked sharply, and he emptied the saddle of the second outlaw. Hammer back and another sharp recoil as the .44 belched. It spat hot lead that ended the ambitions of a would-be giant-killer. Smoke chucked another stick of explosives through a window and spun away.

The blast, muffled somewhat, blew out two walls of the kitchen. Plaster dust and powder smoke made a heavy fog that was all too easy for the hard-pressed gunhawks to hide in. Smoke knew that the noise they had made would soon attract the larger portion of the gunslick army from their outer defenses. He had taken that into consideration in his plans. Now, he decided, would be the time to pull out. He worked the thin leather glove off his right hand and put thumb and forefinger between his lips.

He whistled shrilly and headed at once for the gap blown in the defenses. The Arizona Rangers and Tucker ranch hands streamed behind him. Only a few random shots followed them. That and the shrill, patently hysterical curses of Geoffrey Benton-Howell.

In the cold, hard light of dawn, Geoffrey Benton-Howell and Miguel Selleres surveyed the damage. Every window in the house had been blown out again. Two walls of the kitchen had been scattered over the ranch yard, and the second-floor extension sagged precariously over what remained. Food had to be prepared in the bunkhouse and the outdoor rock-lined fire pits. Those of the hired guns who remained, shivered in the chill, early morning air as they waited in line for coffee, beans, and fatback.

Half an hour later, as the partners accepted plates of food from the grizzled range cook, a patrol sent out at first light returned.

"Then Rangers blew holes in the barricades in half a dozen places on their way out," Charlie Bascomb, who had led them, reported. "Anytime they want, they can pour through on us like water through a sieve."

"Damn him to eternal hell!" Benton-Howell blurted. "It's the doing of Smoke Jensen, you can be certain of that."

"¡Oye, amigo! No te dejes poner los verdes. He is only a man," Miguel Selleres jokingly told his partner.

"I am *not* letting him pull the wool over my eyes," Benton-Howell snapped angrily. "You know as well as I what that man has done to us. It's not natural, not . . . human! We started this project off with him waiting a lynch mob in the Socorro jail. Now he has nearly destroyed my home."

"What do you propose?" Selleres prompted.

Benton-Howell considered that a while. "It's obvious that the ranch is not secure enough. There are ample gunmen waiting in Socorro to assist us. If we move the Tuckers into town, Smoke Jensen will hear of it. We can draw him out and make him fight on ground of our choosing."

Selleres played the devil's advocate. "What if he's waiting for us on the way?"

Benton-Howell shaped his plan aloud. "We'll take everyone from here, form a screen of protection around us and our hostages. Once we reach town, we'll be safe enough. You'll see."

Walt Reardon met the raiding party when Smoke Jensen brought the men back to the Tucker ranch. His grim expression alerted Smoke to possible new problems. He and Jeff met with the ex-gunfighter in the kitchen over coffee and sweet rolls.

Walt chomped on a yeasty cinnamon roll, and washed it down with a long swallow of Arbuckle's Arabica before revealing what brought him to the ranch. "Something big is building up in town." Walt cut his eyes to Jeff. "The Rangers you left me have been overpowered one by one, and completely disappeared. Socorro's runnin' chock-a-block with ne'er-do-wells and gunslingers. Somethin' big's cookin', I can feel it in my bones."

"Any ideas?" Smoke prompted. "We did a fair job of rattling Benton-Howell and his gunhands on the ranch." He looked at the table, chagrined by the admission he had to make. "We were too outnumbered to make a push to get the Tuckers out."

Walt shook his head. "I got this feelin' somethin' big is comin' on. If nothin' else, we need to find those missing Rangers."

Smoke Jensen came to his boots, thumbs hooked in the front of his cartridge belt. "I agree. Cuchillo Negro's warriors are needed to guard the ranch, so I suggest we take the Rangers we have on hand, any hands who volunteer, and head for Socorro."

23

Clear, sharp eyes, undimmed by long afternoons and nights of drinking and carousing in the saloons of Socorro, first spotted the large plume of dust that rose from the horses of the Rangers and ranch hands. It took little time to realize that trouble rode toward town. Even so, the alert gunhawk placed on lookout on the north edge of Socorro waited until he could count heads, make certain who and how much trouble was headed his way. Then he sent one of the hungover wannabes to report his findings.

"Go to the Exchange Hotel and tell Mr. Benton-Howell that twenty-three men are headed this way. Tell him Smoke Jensen and that Ranger are in the lead."

The two-bit gunslick ambled away, while he held his head with one hand and licked dry lips, wishing for a little hair of the dog—no, wolf—that had bit him the night before. He found the lordly Englishman in the saloon of the Exchange, which gave him an excuse to get a drink.

First he had to report, which he did, cringing a little from the expression of wrath that grew on Benton-Howell's face. When he delivered the message, he turned toward the bar. "No drinking. Not today," Benton-Howell declared imperiously. "Every man must be sober for what is sure to come." He turned to Quint Stalker, who sat at a table drinking coffee, which he had surreptitiously laced with rum in defiance of the orders of the big boss.

"Quinten, I want you to deliver a message to Smoke Jensen. Under a flag of truce, naturally."

"Sure, Boss. What do you want to say?"

Benton-Howell told him and sent the gang leader on his way. On the slow ride to the edge of town, Quint Stalker tied a strip of white petticoat to the barrel of his Winchester. He had torn it from the undergarment of a soiled dove he had encountered on the street. He reached the city limits only a minute before Smoke and the posse thundered up to the wooden bridge that crossed the dry creek. Quint hoisted his white flag, and showed himself in the middle of the road.

"I got a message for Smoke Jensen," he called out.

Smoke edged forward on his roan stallion. "Spit it out."

"Mr. Benton-Howell done told me to tell you that he's turned Miz Tucker an' her brats over to Miguel Selleres. *Señor* Selleres has orders to kill them slowly, starting with the youngest kid, if you don't give yourself up within one hour."

Anger flared in Smoke's chest. He dared not risk the lives of the Tuckers further, yet he had no intention of providing target practice for a bunch of second-rate *pistoleros*. He had to buy some time.

"Do you know what happened in the Middle Ages when a messenger brought bad news?" he asked Stalker.

"No, what?"

"They killed him."

Stalker blanched. "Now, look, I'm under a flag of truce. You got no call to kill me. It ain't fair," he ended with a nervous titter.

"Very little is in this life," Smoke returned.

Stalker knew enough about the gunfighter business to know Jensen wanted something, a deal, a way out. "You got that right. What are you after, Jensen?"

A bleak smile answered him for a long moment, and Quint Stalker felt a chill as the icy gray eyes of Smoke

Jensen bored into him. "Time. I didn't expect to find the Tuckers here. I need to rethink things."

Sensing he had regained the upper hand, Stalker snapped, "You've got an hour, that's what The Man said."

"I need more than that. Make it two hours. Tell Benton-Howell that if I see the Tucker family, alive and well, after that, I'll come in alone."

"No tricks?"

"Your boss has all the aces, Stalker," Smoke Jensen replied in a disarming tone.

"I'll see what I can do." Smirking, Stalker turned on one boot heel. Then he threw over his shoulder, "If you hear a gunshot an hour from now, you'll know Mr. Benton-Howell has rejected your terms."

"Damn! What do we do now?" Jeff York exploded.

"It's a rigged deck, the way I see it," Smoke told him bluntly. "It's too obvious to mention what will happen, if I go in there alone. If I don't go in, the Tuckers will die. Benton-Howell is a desperate man."

"I can believe that," Jeff allowed. "He has to see that his scheme is falling apart. Even if he gets you, there's no way he can bring it off."

"My thoughts, too, Jeff. So, here's what we'll do," Smoke offered. Without hesitation he laid out his plans.

Ten minutes went by before Tallpockets Granger walked his mount down the main street of Socorro, a white shirt tied to the muzzle of his rifle. He stopped outside the Exchange Hotel and called out for Quint Stalker. When Quint appeared, Tallpockets waved the white flag over his head to make it clear that he was under truce. Then he leaned forward and spoke eye to eye with Stalker.

"Smoke Jensen wants to talk to you again. He says he wants to spell out the manner of his surrender."

"I'll be right with you." Stalker returned to the hotel, and walked back out in less than half a minute. "The Boss says that's all right with him."

They rode together to the edge of town. There, Stalker threw a look of contempt at Smoke Jensen and spoke in a crisp tone of command. "Mr. Benton-Howell said you were in no position to set terms. But he agreed to listen this time. What is it you have in mind?"

"I've decided to turn myself in. Provided that the Tuckers are unharmed. And I want to see them riding away from town, alone, or no deal. They go free before I reach the center of town. And no back-shooting, or the rest of my friends here will take Socorro apart, regardless of what happens to me or the Tuckers. Benton-Howell and Selleres will hang, and there won't be a one of those two-bit *pistoleros* left alive."

Anger rose to choke Stalker, so that he spluttered when he snapped, "That's bluster, Jensen, and you know it. You must be gettin' old. Old and yellow, deep down in your core, or you'd not be runnin' yer mouth instead of your gun."

Fire replaced the ice in the eyes of Smoke Jensen. "You want to try me now?"

Quint Stalker hesitated a moment, and Smoke Jensen thought, *Gotcha!* "Another time. I'll take what you said to the Boss, and we'll see." He turned his mount and rode away.

Fifteen minutes later, he returned. "Mr. Benton-Howell agrees," Quint Stalker shouted across the dry creek. "I'm to accompany you to the jail to see there are no tricks . . . from either side."

"How noble of you," Smoke responded sarcastically.

Stalker looked hurt. "I insisted on it. I admire you for this, Jensen, and I wanted to make sure there was no hanky-panky on either side."

Quint Stalker's words raised Jensen's assessment of the outlaw leader. He shrugged and cut his eyes to Jeff, "You know what to do." To Stalker, "Let's get on with it." Smoke eased his roan onto the bridge.

From that first step, Smoke felt his gut tighten with sour tension. At each step the horses took, a spot between his shoulder blades grew warmer and tingled with anticipation of a bullet to rend and tear his flesh and end his life. Not one to fear death, the mountain man still had a healthy regard for living. By the end of the first block, with not a hard case in sight, Smoke began to gauge each building as the possible spot from which the assassin's bullet would come.

Beside him, Quint Stalker appeared to be equally apprehensive. His eyes cut from side to side, suspicion deeply planted on his face. Sweat popped out on his brow, and he licked his lips continuously. Smoke suspicioned that Stalker's palms oozed moisture inside the black leather gloves.

"Don't you trust your masters?" Smoke taunted, partly to break his own chain of anxiety.

"Of course—come to think of it, not a hell of a lot. It's me that's the target out here, not them."

"Good thinking, Stalker."

Another block further along, Stalker nodded toward the balcony of the Exchange Hotel. "Over there."

Smoke cut his eyes to three tiny figures standing there. Jimmy, Rose, and Tommy Tucker huddled close together, the older boy's arms protectively around the shoulders of his siblings. They had all been crying, and began again at the sight of Smoke Jensen riding in a prisoner.

"Don't let 'em do it to you, Smoke," Jimmy's high, thin voice cut through the dust haze to Smoke's ears.

Smoke gave the boy a short, friendly wave. Lace curtains at a second-floor front window fluttered and drew apart. A Mexican *pistolero* stood beside Martha Tucker, a wicked grin whitening his face under a thick, drooping mustache. Smoke reined in. He jabbed a finger at the hostages and spoke harshly.

"Bring them down here. Now."

Quint Stalker sighed heavily and shrugged. "This is the part makes me uneasy. They don't get loose, until you're locked in jail. The Boss ordered it that way."

Smoke Jensen started a curse, broke if off, knowing it to be futile. If the shooting started now, the Tuckers would die for certain. "Never could abide two-faced bastards like your Benton-Howell," he growled bitterly.

"Truth to tell, I ain't too fond of him, myself," Stalker muttered.

Smoke eyed him thoughtfully. "Ever think of changing sides?" From the light that glowed in Stalker's eyes, Smoke knew that he had planted a seed in fertile soil. "Let's get on with it."

At the jail, without a shot fired, Stalker dismounted, tied off his horse, then drew his six-gun. He covered Smoke while Jensen climbed from the saddle and let himself be led into the office. With Ferdie Biggs no longer among the living, a new jailer had been selected. His smirking grin revealed a missing front tooth and the yellow stain of an inveterate tobacco chewer. Quint Stalker removed Smoke's cartridge belt and twin .44s and tossed them on the desk. Then the jailer revealed his nature to be much like his predecessor.

He took two quick steps forward and solidly punched Smoke Jensen in the ribs. Pain shot through Smoke from the bullet scrapes on both sides, as he rocked with the blows. He caught another pair in the gut, and fought the urge to double over from the effect. Carefully he sucked in fresh air.

"Are you any relation to Ferdie Biggs?" Smoke asked in as calm a voice as he could manage.

"Naw, I ain't no kin of his."

"Funny, there's such a resemblance," Smoke taunted.

Smoke's taunt had the desired effect. With a roar the lout lunged forward again without any caution. Smoke's hard, looping left caught him on the point of his protruding jaw;

the gunfighter put all his body behind it. He had the satisfaction of hearing a loud snap and feeling the loose wobble of bone before the jailer dropped like a stone.

"Gawdamn!" Stalker blurted.

"He needed that."

Awe filled the eyes of Quint Stalker, as he nodded his head in agreement. "I still gotta lock you up. You know the way."

Down the corridor of the cellblock, Smoke found three of the missing Rangers, locked together in one large cell. No doubt the holding tank for drunks. They all had depression written on their faces.

"In you go," Quint Stalker said with a wink.

He opened the cage, and Smoke joined his three allies. Without further comment, Stalker left the cellblock and the jail and returned to the Exchange Hotel.

Deft, brown fingers worked at the fastenings of the wire basket that enclosed the cork. With it pried open and removed, two thumbs pried the cork until it popped loudly and flew to the ceiling of the men's bar in the Exchange Hotel. A shower of bubbles followed. Laughing, Miguel Selleres turned to the four other men in the room.

"We have much to celebrate, *Señores*. Our good friend, Sheriff Reno, is out of jail and . . . Smoke Jensen is inside!"

"Not to mention, we still have the hostages, old boy," Geof-frey Benton-Howell chortled as he presented his glass to be filled.

"More important, the Tuckers will not be released until the ranch is signed over to the three of us," Dalton Wade crowed.

"They'll not be released even then," Benton-Howell stated quietly, instantly drawing the attention of Sheriff Reno, Dalton Wade, and Miguel Selleres.

"Whatever do you mean by that, Sir Geoffrey?" Dalton Wade asked, concern creasing his brow.

"There's no percentage in leaving behind any living witnesses. Surely you see the wisdom of that, Dalton."

"My word. I'd never given that problem any consideration. Isn't it a bit savage to take the lives of women and children?"

Benton-Howell peered at his partner over the rim of his champagne glass. "We live in brutal times, my friend. We cannot afford to have anyone—outside of ourselves—left to bear tales of how we obtained all this property and the wealth of that goldfield in the White Mountains. Oh, yes, I have been assured the transfer will take place as promised. You can see the importance now, can you not? Not even these troublesome Arizona Rangers must escape our little cleanup."

"Yes," Selleres agreed. "Which brings us to what means to use to dispose of Smoke Jensen."

All four men remained silent with their thoughts a moment. Then a beatific smile spread on the face of Benton-Howell.

"I think the most demeaning, humiliating, degrading form of death should be applied to Smoke Jensen. Unfortunately, there is not a single guillotine to be had in this forsaken country. So, I suggest we hang him. How ignoble."

Soft applause came from Dalton Wade and Miguel Selleres. Sheriff Reno nodded approval. As did Quint Stalker, who had to fight to keep his face rigidly devoid of any expression. The plotters were convinced of the complete defeat of Smoke Jensen, only the outlaw leader felt no surprise when a cacophony of sound blasted into the elegant barroom, followed by the crumbling of stone and brickwork from the direction of the jail.

Following Smoke Jensen's instructions, the Rangers watched until he disappeared into the jail, then drifted off in groups of threes and fours. They made their way out of sight of town at the slow pace of men who had reluctantly admitted their cause to be lost, yet were unwilling to leave in a body. The ruse worked, Jeff York realized half an hour later when no pursuit had begun against them.

At that point, Geoffrey Benton-Howell had as yet to pronounce their death sentences along with the rest. After the Rangers departed, Quint Stalker had withdrawn the lookouts, leaving only some of the hungover dregs to keep watch, so that his men could join in the celebration. Before he had returned to the hotel, he noted a number of those who had come bounty hunting had drifted off toward more promising fields. He would soon regret that.

Jeff York and six men had no difficulty in slipping unobserved into Socorro. They went directly to the jail, located the cell holding Smoke Jensen and the missing Rangers. They cut short any reunion for the business at hand.

"Get mattresses," Jeff instructed curtly. "Sit down clear of this wall, cover yourselves, and hold your ears."

"Awh, crap, Jeff, you ain't gonna blow us outta here, are you?" one lanky, horse-faced Ranger complained.

"Come up with a better way, and I won't have to," Jeff quipped.

While he spoke, Jeff rigged a bundle of dynamite sticks to the wall, close to the small window, which he figured for the weakest point. With everything in readiness, he lit the fuse and cleared out with his Rangers. The blast reverberated all over town, bounced off the steep walls of the gorge in which the village had been built, punished ears for a quarter mile, and set dogs to howling hysterically.

It didn't do too much for the men in the cell, for that matter. The brick wall within the native fieldstone one pummeled them with chunks that would leave bruises the next day. Even with fingers in ears and mouths open, the pressure was enormous. Two Rangers lost consciousness, and Smoke Jensen discovered he had a bloody nose. A tad bit more dynamite, and they'd all be playing harps for St. Peter, he thought dazedly as the caustic fumes and mortar dust swirled around him. Only indistinctly did he hear the pounding of hooves, as Jeff and his volunteers rushed back to extricate them from the jail.

Upright beside Jeff York, Smoke Jensen gestured to the ruined building they had just exited. "We have to get our weapons."

"Already taken care of."

Smoke frowned as the import of that struck him. "Then why in Billy blue hell did you try to turn us into red mush?"

"Thought it might scare hell out of some of these tender-feet gunhawks."

"You did a fair job of that on us." Jeff gave a shrug, so Smoke continued, "Give me my rig, and let's go get these bastards who hide behind women and children."

24

Geoffrey Benton-Howell had no doubt as to the source of the explosion. He immediately sent Quint Stalker to organize the horde of gunslingers who milled about the streets of Socorro, most of them confused as to what was going on. Miguel Selleres went upstairs at once, to make sure the Tuckers remained secure in the Exchange Hotel. He spoke urgently to the guards outside the door to the room that held the children.

"No one gets in there, none of our own or any lawmen."

"Sí, Señor Selleres," one Sonoran *pistolero* responded respectfully. "Not a soul will get past us."

"See to it." Selleres went on down the hall to where Mrs. Tucker was being kept. "Unlock it," he demanded. Inside, he crossed to a small table where Martha Tucker sat taking her evening meal. He shaped his features to show pleading. "*Señora*, there is going to be a great deal of bloodshed. You can prevent it. Simply sign the ranch over to us . . ." Selleres ended with hands outstretched, palms up in silent appeal.

"I do not believe in fairy-tales, *Señor* Selleres. The moment I sign those papers, myself and my children are dead. On the other hand, I can trust that for now, no stray bullet will strike any of us."

Selleres hardened his face. "Can you trust that we will not

kill you outright, rather than let you fall into the hands of Smoke Jensen?"

A chill ran along Martha's spine. She girded herself for the answer she knew she had to make. "If you are that thoroughly reprehensible, then I can only place my trust in the Lord . . . and Smoke Jensen."

A burst of gunfire from down the street interrupted the hot retort that started from the lips of Miguel Selleres. He turned on one boot heel and started for the door.

Two gun-toting henchmen appeared high up in the windows of the feed mill. The tinkle of broken glass alerted those below. Smoke Jensen went to one knee and snugged the Winchester .44 carbine to his shoulder in one smooth motion. Jeff York raised his Colt, and put a .45 round through the corrugated metal skin of the grain elevator.

It expanded as it went its way, and slammed into flesh an inch above the buckle on the cartridge belt of one hard case. He jolted forward in reaction to his wound, and lurched through the window sash. His startled companion had only a moment to hear the agonized scream, as Smoke Jensen put out his lights for all time with a hot lead snuffer. The sniper's body jerked backward and out of view.

"That was close," Jeff observed.

"They never got off a shot," Smoke reminded him.

Halfway down the next block, four men ranged across the street. They had a variety of mismatched weapons, which spoke for their lack of expertise. What they lacked in knowledge they made up for in courage—or foolishness. All four entered the dance with blazing six-guns.

Smoke Jensen downed one easily, and heard the nearby crack of a bullet that sailed past his head. He lined his sights on another as two more weapons opened up through windows on the second floor above the general mercantile. He made a quick shot at his target, missed, and swung the muzzle of the Winchester upward. Three rounds levered through the Winchester silenced one of the hidden assassins. From behind Smoke the six-gun of Tallpockets roared and spat flame.

"They ain't gonna do any back-shootin'," the lanky Arizona Ranger remarked casually.

"We have to get to the Exchange Hotel fast," Smoke urged. "Every minute puts the Tuckers in more danger."

"Was I doin' it," Tallpockets drawled, "I'd get me away from here an' come at 'em from behind. Let me an' the boys take care of Main Street."

Smoke smiled broadly. "I appreciate the offer, Tallpockets. And I'll take you up on it. Jeff, Walt, and I will take this alley and come at the hotel from the back door."

"Three of you gonna be enough?" Tallpockets asked, then he looked over the trio indicated, grunted, and answered his own question. "I reckon so."

The street fighting grew fiercer as the outlaw scum and bounty-hungry drifters realized a major push was on against them. The way they saw it, they had to stand their ground; they simply had no way to go and no money to take them there. While they hotted up the battle, Smoke, Jeff, and Walt darted down an alleyway and turned into the one that paralleled the main street. Three blocks to the hotel, and no way of knowing how many of Benton-Howell's gunhands they would encounter.

They made it only a block, and ran into half a dozen desperate men forted up in the rear of the saddler's shop. Lead flew thick and fast. Smoke Jensen felt a searing pain just below the point of his right shoulder, and cut his eyes to a ragged tear in the cloth of his shirt. Another fraction of an inch, and he'd be dripping blood again. Suddenly one of the defenders showed enough head for a clear shot.

Smoke took it with his old .44. The hat of the hard case flew off as his head snapped back. His eyes glazed as he sagged to the floor. A pair of boot heels could be heard pounding on the floorboards, headed for the front. That slackened the fire enough for Jeff York to dart along the alley, past the shop. From that angle, he poured fire into the back of the saddlery. Smoke and Walt did the same.

A couple of yowls of pain came from the interior. Then the firing lessened. A table, hastily put in place to barricade the back door, slid noisily across the floor. Nervous sounding, a voice called to them.

"That does it. We give up! We're coming out."

Smoke Jensen knew the darkness served as an ally to the dangerous men inside. He set himself and responded, "Come out one at a time. Hands in sight."

"Sure—sure. Don't shoot us, huh?"

A moment later the door opened, and a man's silhouette appeared in the frame. He advanced, hands at shoulder height, palms forward. So far, so good. Another man followed a moment later. When the body of the first to surrender blocked the view, the second man reached forward and yanked a hidden six-gun from the small of his partner's back. He threw a shot in the general direction of Smoke Jensen.

And died for his treachery. Smoke drilled him through the left eye. Bleating his nonexistent innocence, the first man went to his knees. The three lawmen ignored him for the moment, and concentrated on the others. A trio of rounds sped through the doorway, and the others came out so docile that one would think they were in church.

"That's more like it," Jeff York growled.

They quickly trussed up their prisoners and left them for the other Rangers to tend to. Of one accord, Smoke and his companions started off toward the hotel. Smoke found the back door first. He tried it, found it latched, and pondered their problem.

"This isn't going to be as easy as we thought," he advised the others. "If we make any noise going in there, they just might kill Martha and the children."

* * *

Whether by chance or design, the beleaguered gunfighters in the streets of Socorro drew back on the Exchange Hotel and the few buildings immediately around it. There they rallied and put up a determined resistance. Without a foolish risk of life, the Arizona Rangers could not expose themselves to make a frontal assault. Gradually it became obvious to everyone that the battle had degenerated into a standoff.

By one-thirty in the morning, only a few of the more aggressive individuals took potshots at their counterparts. Another problem presented itself, brought to the attention of Smoke Jensen by Walt Reardon.

"We've got more prisoners than places to put them. Blowin' out that wall weren't such a good idea. That drunk tank could hold an easy twenty, twenty-five."

Smoke thought a moment. "Go to the Tinto Range Supply. There should be some barbed wire there. Use all you need to crisscross that opening like a spiderweb. Then put some men to guarding it. Some of the Tucker hands should be fine for that. They aren't getting paid to be shot at. Jeff and I will hold the fort here."

"Mighty interestin' idea. Just might work." Walt scooted out of there.

Within half an hour, prisoners had begun to be shifted from the grain bins of the livery into the holding cell of the jail. The first ones inside stared in stunned disbelief at what appeared to be a gaping hole in the wall.

"C'mon, boys, let's make a break for it," Wink Winkler muttered to those nearest to him. He made a dash for the opening, only to be caught in midair on the all but invisible strands of barbed wire. He howled in agony and thrashed a while, until he realized he only made it worse.

"Never did like that damned stuff," one hard-faced gunman remarked.

"Been more than one war fought over it," another agreed.

"Git me down offa here," Winkler wailed.

"Sure, but it'll smart some."

"You get close to that wire, and I'll blow your head off," a voice from outside said.

"Do something, get me off of here!" Wink Winkler wailed on the verge of hysteria.

"Reckon I could shoot you, to put you out of your misery," the Tucker wrangler suggested.

Morning brought no change in the stalemate. It also did not provide any easy access into the hotel. Smoke Jensen left Jeff York and three Arizona Rangers to watch the back exit to the Exchange Hotel, while he scouted for ideas. He found a possible solution within a block of the two-story structure.

He also received some bad news. Simms, one of the Rangers, came upon Smoke while he was trying to drag a tall ladder out of a litter of barrels and boxes outside the back of a store. The bantam rooster of a lawman announced that he sought Jeff York.

"Jeff's at the Exchange Hotel back door."

"We've got more troubles," Simms replied. "Durin' the night, more of this border scum drifted into town. Seems as how they got us caught between the ones we've corralled, and themselves."

Smoke Jensen gave it only a moment's thought. Using the ladder to scale to the second floor windows at the back of the hotel would have to wait. "When you're surrounded, there's only one thing to do."

"Surrender?" Simms asked doubtfully.

"Where've you been all your life? What we're going to do is attack in both directions at once." Smoke set off immediately to inform Jeff.

Eyes glazed with blood lust, the newcomers to Socorro sensed an easy kill. They moved in on the thin line of

Rangers with weapons in hand. Their shock was complete then, when half of the lawmen turned on them and opened fire, while the remainder yelled chillingly and charged buildings to either side of a large hotel. The rapid-fire crackle of rifles and six-guns drowned out the exclamations of consternation.

Three of the hard cases went down in a hail of bullets. Two ran toward the partial shelter of an alleyway, only to be met with the flat report of a shotgun. A scythe of buckshot kicked them off their boots. Writhing in the dirt, their multiple wounds gradually went numb.

Few among their fellow gunfighters took notice, as the downed gunhawks lost their struggle to hold on to life. After a moment of stunned inactivity, the remaining fast guns released a ragged volley of their own. By then the astonished defenders inside the buildings nearest the Exchange Hotel found themselves overwhelmed by the surprise assault. Smoke Jensen led the way into the dry goods store.

Smoke's .44 barked with authority, as he jumped through a shattered window and pushed aside a mannequin in the display case. It bounced off a rack of dresses, and a member of Quint Stalker's gang used its distracting motion to cover his move to get Smoke Jensen.

Rising up, he swung the muzzle of his Colt into line with Smoke, only to find himself staring down a long, black tunnel to the afterworld. Smoke Jensen fired first. Hot lead released a thunderous pain in the chest of the outlaw, who slammed backward to upend over an island of discounted women's shoes. High-top button creations in uniform black flew in three directions.

When the powder smoke cleared, Smoke Jensen saw his man lying still in death. "Put some men in place to hold this window," Smoke told the nearest Ranger.

Numbers began to tell. Doing the unexpected had gained the Rangers the dubious shelter of two wooden frame buildings, only to be pinned down by concentrated fire from outside. Several of the lawmen gave fleeting thought to how Benton-Howell's defenders in the hotel must have felt. Smoke Jensen took a quick mental inventory.

It didn't look good. Not counting those who broke through the ring of guns in the hands of the newly arrived hard cases, he could account for only some seven men not wounded or dead among the Rangers. They still faced some thirty or more guns. He had to find a way into the hotel. In memory, the ladder beckoned.

"Can you hold them here?" Smoke asked of Tallpockets.

He received a curt nod. "Don't know how long, but we'll do our best. Jeff an' the other boys should be hittin' 'em from behind soon. What'er you gonna do?"

"Get in that hotel." Not waiting for a response from the Arizona Ranger, Smoke headed for the rear of the shop.

A small loading dock behind the dry goods store could be accessed by three heavy plank steps. Smoke Jensen didn't waste time on them. A small shock ran up his legs when his boots hit the ground. He turned right and soon located the ladder. Fighting a sense of being too late, he lugged the heavy wooden object back to the hotel. Smoke leaned it against the clapboard siding of the hotel under a window. Colt in one hand, he started upward.

When he reached a position below the sash, Smoke Jensen crouched and removed his hat. He held it in his left hand, while he raised his head and six-gun to peer inside. The room was empty. Smoke suddenly realized that he had been holding his breath. Stale air gusted out of his lungs, and he drew in a fresh draught. He tried the window, but it had been secured by a slide latch.

No time for finesse. Smoke cracked the lower center pane of glass, and reached through to slide the bar out of place. Then he raised up the lower half of the sash. He climbed into the room without incident. He crossed the room in four long strides, and paused at the door.

Smoke strained his keen hearing to gauge the unknown surroundings outside. At first he heard nothing, yet caution urged him to open the door only a crack. His first glance of the hallway showed him some ten gunmen lounging around, worried looks on their faces. Then all hell broke out on the street in front of the hotel.

25

Jeff York levered rounds through the Winchester in a blur of speed, as he advanced on the hard cases milling in the street. One of the steadier of the band of thugs placed a round close enough to put Jeff down behind a full watering trough. He hunched forward on his elbows and took aim at one gunhawk's left kneecap. The Winchester bucked, and the man screamed as he went down.

But he was not out of the fight. His six-gun cracked and brought a shower of splinters from the trough. Stinging pinpricks on his face told Jeff that the man could definitely shoot. His next round ended the contest with the border ruffian doubled over his perforated intestines. Jeff sought another target.

He had all too many, Jeff reflected on the situation. Enough that they were no longer intimidated by gunfire from the Rangers. They gathered their ranks and actually began to advance. A shirtless ruffian bounded out of the barbershop two doors down from Jeff, and raised a Smith and Wesson American to blast the life from the Arizona Ranger.

Jeff saw him first and put the last round from his Winchester through the small white button, third down on the front of the thug's red, longhandle underwear top. His mouth formed a black oval in his shaving cream–lathered face, and he did a pratfall on the boardwalk. His weapon discharged upward and shattered one square pane of glass in a streetlight. Dead already, he didn't feel the shards that pierced his scalp and chest. Three more popped up seemingly out of nowhere.

Screams of rage reached Jeff's ears a moment before he heard the distinctive yowl of a coyote. The voices of several desert birds joined, then came the thunder of hooves. Jeff York looked behind him to see seven riders, hugging low on the necks of their horses, rumbling toward the center of the fight.

Bands of red and yellow cloth fluttered from the forestocks of three rifles, and he saw the sharp curve of a bow a moment before an arrow flashed overhead and buried its point in the stomach of a would-be gunfighter not five feet from where Jeff lay.

Cuchillo Negro and six of his warriors had come through at a crucial time. They pounded down on the suddenly disorganized outlaws, and brought swift death with them. Several of the wiser among the hirelings of Benton-Howell took off running toward the nearest empty saddle. They took flight in utter panic, leaving all possessions behind. Others chose to fight it out.

They got a poor bargain for it. Hot lead laced the street from both Ranger positions. Black Knife operated his trapdoor Spencer with cool, smooth expertise. Round after round of lethal .56 caliber slugs smacked into flesh. One gunhawk went down with two Apaches swarming over him, knives flashing silver, then crimson in the sunlight.

In that mad, swirling instant, what had been certain defeat for the Arizona Rangers turned into a promise of victory.

Boot heels thumped along the carpeted upstairs hall in reaction to the rattle of gunfire. Smoke Jensen watched the retreating backs of the hard cases, as they responded to the increased fighting outside. When all but two started down the wide staircase, Smoke Jensen stepped out of the room he had entered moments before and took stock.

A pair of men stood at the door to each of two rooms. Guarding the bosses? Smoke pondered a moment. At the far end, one gunhand was mostly out the door of the balcony that fronted the establishment. Another waited his turn. That meant five guns against Smoke. Six in the worst case. An arrow thudded into the wooden panel of the balcony door with enough force to wrest it from the hand of the youthful outlaw. A moment later he went to his knees, hands clutched to the shaft of the projectile that protruded from his chest.

Only five guns now. Considering who Smoke Jensen suspected had been confined behind those guarded portals, he could not simply leave well enough alone. When he opened up on the gunmen below, they would no doubt kill the hostages at once. He walked up to the Anglo pair guarding the center door.

"Benton-Howell said for me to relieve you two. He needs more guns in the fight downstairs."

Suspicion shined in the eyes of the nearer outlaw. "How'd he tell you that with you up here?"

"Don't you know anything about this place? There's a brass speaker from the desk connected to every room." Smoke had noticed the device beside the door as he had exited, and took the chance that everyone was aware of them. "He just blew into it, and it whistled in my room. I answered and got told what to do."

"Yeah. I guess I did see them things. Looked like a pipe organ behind the counter."

"That's the one. Now go on, before those damned Rangers get inside the building."

They turned away with a dubious look, then joined the third white man at the top of the stairs. "I ain't gonna go out there. Damn Injuns have ridden in," he told them. "I'll go with you boys."

Once the three were out of sight, Smoke turned his attention to the two sombrero-wearing *bandidos* at the other door. He walked up to them, displaying a casual manner. A smile and his poor and rusty Spanish should help put them off guard, Smoke reckoned.

"*Oye*, my Spanish she is not so good," Smoke greeted in mixed language. "Your *jefe*, he says for me to tell you that they need more guns—*más pistolas*—downstairs. You are to go at once."

"Don Miguel ordered us to stay here, not to leave unless he told us," the burlier of the pair protested in rapid-fire Spanish.

"*¿Como?* You speak too fast for me."

"Not too fast for me," a heavy voice rumbled from the head of the stairs.

A sharp crack of a .44 round from his Merwin and Hulbert punctuated Quint Stalker's statement. The bullet burned along the meaty portion of the small of Smoke Jensen's back. Smoke sprang across the hallway, out of reach of the two Mexican bandits, and spun to face Stalker.

"I see you got out of jail."

"Damn right, Jensen. You an' me got a score to settle."

"Words are cheap. Let's get to it," Smoke grated, hand on the grip of his pistol.

"I don't think so. Ramon, Xavier, grab him."

For all the girth of Xavier, he moved like a startled cat. As his ham hands closed on the arm of Smoke Jensen, he left his ample belly open to ready attack. Smoke did not overlook it. He drove two hard, fast rights into the swell of gut before him. Xavier grunted and yanked Smoke toward him. By then, Ramon had Smoke's other arm. Smirking, Quint Stalker advanced along the hall. The Merwin and Hulbert drooped indolently in his gunhand, but even with his victim held captive, he took no chances with Smoke Jensen.

When he reached an arm's length from Smoke, Stalker cocked a solid left and drove knuckles into Jensen's face. "Hold him up," Stalker commanded. Another punch to the cheek, and Smoke Jensen went slack in their grasp.

Quint Stalker leered at the apparently dazed Smoke Jensen. "I'm gonna make this last, Jensen. Go real slow, give you a lot of pain . . . before I kill you."

Smoke gasped as he imperceptibly tightened his muscles, positioned now with his weight supported by the Mexican outlaws. His ears caught a distinct sound from outside. "You . . . may not . . . have time, Stalker. Those Apaches still want to get their hands on you."

The word "Apaches" galvanized Quint Stalker. He turned his attention away from his intended victim to listen to the war whoops that drifted through the open doorway. Then he saw the dying hard case with the arrow in his chest. Time to move, Smoke Jensen judged. Swiftly shifting his weight, Smoke drove the pointed toe of his boot into Stalker's groin.

A banshee shriek ripped from the throat of Quint Stalker. Following it came a wet, sucking sound, as the hurting outlaw leader fought to pull air into his body and stop the misery. He doubled over until his chin touched his knees. Before the Mexican bandits could react, Smoke kicked Stalker in the face. Then, his feet planted firmly on the carpet runner in the hall, Smoke Jensen flexed powerful muscles in his shoulders and slammed Ramon and Xavier together face to face.

Their foreheads met with a *klonk!*, and Ramon went slack-legged to the floor. Quint Stalker lay twitching on the carpet strip. Smoke Jensen had no desire to trade punches with Quint Stalker, let alone the massive Xavier. He had his .44 halfway out of the holster when Xavier spotted the motion and, still dazed by the ramming, groped for his Mendoza .45 copy. He freed it and fired too soon. The slug zipped between the legs of Smoke Jensen and ploughed into a floorboard. Vibration from the hammer blow partly revived Quint Stalker.

He squinted and blinked his eyes to fuzzily see that Smoke Jensen had his Colt leveled. Smoke fired while Xavier tried desperately to cock his six-gun again. The slug slammed into Xavier's hip; he staggered and finished cocking. Eyes tearing in pain, he sought to sight in on the insubstantial target of Smoke Jensen.

Eyes fixed on Xavier, Smoke brought his pistol to bear and tripped the trigger. Ramon's hand closed on Smoke's ankle, and he yanked as the hammer fell. The .44 bullet went wide of its intended mark. With his attention now divided between the Mexican bandits, Smoke did not notice Stalker's stealthy, crablike crawl away from the conflict.

His strength rapidly waning, Xavier sent a round over Smoke's left shoulder. Smoke Jensen had had enough of this. His next round shattered Ramon's shoulder, and the grip on his leg released at once. He turned back to Xavier, as the pudgy Sonoran went white-faced and sagged back against the opposite wall. Internal bleeding had sapped him of all his strength. He slithered to a sitting position and sighed regretfully before he passed out.

That's when Quint Stalker regained reason enough to take a shot.

Quint Stalker's bullet cracked past Smoke Jensen's head close enough for the gunfighter to feel its hot breath. One thing he knew for certain: he did not want Stalker to reach the ground floor and bring the news of Smoke's presence in the hotel. Far too many guns awaited him down there, and what little element of surprise remained was all Smoke had going for his plan to free the Tuckers. Quint Stalker had already negotiated the top three treads, his weight borne by the banister, over which the outlaw leader had draped himself heavily.

A quick memory check told Smoke that he had emptied

his right-hand gun. He holstered it and went for his second .44. The time lapse got Stalker to the upper landing, where he paused, gasped, and looked upward. He was out of sight of Smoke Jensen and glad of it. Determined not to let Stalker get away, Smoke advanced down the hallway toward the head of the stairs.

When he reached his goal, the wooden ball on top of the newel post exploded in a shower of splinters. Several stung and bit into Smoke's cheeks. Ignoring them, he threw a quick shot down the stairwell. Hot lead brought forth a yelp of alarm, when it tugged at the shoulder piece of Stalker's vest. At once, Smoke bounded down four steps.

Stalker fired again and, with his strength returning, retreated downward before he could check the results. There were none, except for a hole in the plaster high over Smoke Jensen's right shoulder. Smoke came after him at once. At the central landing, feet planted squarely on the level, Quint Stalker's bullet caused Smoke Jensen to dive to one side to avoid a mortal wound.

Crying out at this near-triumph, Stalker started off down the final flight of stairs. Smoke Jensen reached the platform seconds behind Quint Stalker. He steadied his arm and took aim. Stalker looked back, spun on a boot heel, and tried again to blast Smoke out of existence. Smoke Jensen fired first.

Smoke's slug took Quint in the chest, to the right of his sternum. The outlaw boss rose on tiptoe and a thin whine came through his lips. He tried to raise his gun barrel . . . and failed. Smoke's shot hit in the center of the chest.

Stalker teetered backward and cartwheeled down four treads. His body went slack, and he rolled the rest of the way to the bottom of the staircase. Smoke Jensen was already heading upward. He took the steps two at a time. Excited voices followed him.

"Have the savages gotten in?" Benton-Howell's English accent floated upward.

"Someone has," another voice answered, as he spotted the body of Quint Stalker.

"Then go after them," Benton-Howell commanded.

Half a dozen hard cases started for the stairway. At the same moment, chunks of plaster showered into the room from the wall dividing the hotel from the dry goods store. Another crash drove the heavy metal base of a display rack through the lath. The barrels of rifles and shotguns followed.

A few of the hired guns made instant response, only to be cut down in a hail of lead. Not bound by years of loyalty, the majority saw the inevitable end for their kind, and deserted the cause. They rushed out into the street to surrender, hope filling them that the Indians had ridden on to other depredations.

There the Arizona Rangers began to disarm and handcuff the demoralized mob of shootists. Jeff York detached himself from his men and made for the hotel. Upstairs, Smoke Jensen caught a glimpse of a flat-crowned Cordovan sombrero disappearing down the back stairway. Suspecting defeat, he hurried to the first of the two rooms that had been guarded.

He threw open the door . . . and found the stark cubicle empty.

"Selleres has them," Smoke Jensen shouted to Jeff York, when the Arizona Ranger's head topped the stairs. "He went down the back."

Jeff didn't waste time asking if Smoke was sure. Smoke Jensen rarely made such a statement if he didn't know for certain. Instead, Jeff strode rapidly to where Smoke stood at the top of the back staircase. As he did, Jeff passed two open doors, the rooms behind them gaping emptily.

"We're going after them?" Jeff asked.

"Just you and me. I don't want to frighten Selleres into killing any of them."

They started down, only to find the way blocked by three of Quint Stalker's loyalest men: Vern Draper, Marv Fletcher, and Charlie Bascomb. Bascomb fired first. His bullet cut the air between Smoke and Jeff. Smoke got a slug into the leg of the young gunslinger, and sent him tumbling back down the stairs. That bought Smoke and Jeff half the flight, before a muzzle appeared around the corner of the hallway and sent a bullet winging upward.

Hunkered down, Smoke and Jeff duck-walked uncomfortably down the next five treads. A six-gun blazed in their direction, and Smoke put a round through the wall. A soft grunt answered him. No more shots came, and they made it to the bottom. A quick look showed Charlie Bascomb sprawled on the floorboards of the rear hallway in a pool of blood. He wouldn't be holding them up anymore.

"Out back," Smoke prompted.

He made his way cautiously to the open back door. The moment Smoke Jensen's head appeared around the jamb, Vern Draper and Marv Fletcher opened up. Smoke jerked back in time. The slugs whistled down the corridor. Smoke saw that Jeff had wisely flattened himself against the far wall, out of the line of fire.

"We'll lose too much time going around the long way," Smoke figured aloud. "Nothing for it but to rush them." At that moment he would have given anything for Walt Reardon's 10 gauge L. C. Smith.

Both he and Jeff took time to reload. Then, with a six-gun in each hand—something Preacher had told Smoke never, ever to do—he crouched low and went through the doorway, his matched pistols leading him. They blasted alternately in a steady rhythm. From behind he heard Jeff York join the dance. Marv Fletcher cried out and spun to one side, hit by two slugs at the same time. He fell like wet wash. That left only one.

Vern Draper backed up in the direction obviously taken by the fleeing Miguel Selleres and the hostages. He fired repeatedly as he gained what speed he could in his ungainly

walk. Beyond him, near the mouth to the alley farthest
from the activity around the hotel, Smoke caught sight of
Jimmy Tucker's towhead flashing white in a ray of sunlight.
Geoffrey Benton-Howell yanked the boy by his collar. Another man, whose identity Smoke Jensen did not know,
dragged the other children along. Miguel Selleres roughly
shoved Martha Tucker in the desired direction.

Unwilling to risk their lives, Smoke Jensen holstered his
right-hand .44 and drew his coffin-handle Bowie. He hefted
it and closed fingers around the grips. A swift up and down
motion of his arm, and he released the blade. It turned one
full time in the air, and buried half its length in the chest of
a surprised Vern Draper.

The six-gun fell from numbed fingers, and Vern's eyes
bugged at the enormous, hot pain in his chest. Draper went
rubber-legged and staggered to one side. Smoke Jensen
pushed past him, and only faintly heard the thump of Jeff
York's six-gun when it ended the life of the snaggle-toothed
outlaw. Smoke started running, with Jeff pounding along
behind.

Beyond the fleeing conspirators and their captives, a
coach had rumbled into place. The armored carriage of
Miguel Selleres.

At the direction of the corrupt *haciendado,* three burly
Mexican bandits, who had accompanied the coach,
stepped between their leader and the two lawmen. Each
wore the wide, floppy sombrero of a *charro,* with bandoliers
of ammunition crossed over their chests. Beneath the cartridge belts they wore short, open bolero jackets, white
shirts with string ties and lots of lace ruffles. They were large
men, but not with puffy fat, yet their bellies protruded over
the belts that supported their holsters.

Each had a brace of Mendoza .45s, canted forward so as
to provide easy reach to a man in the saddle. Their tight
trousers, the outer seams trimmed with silver conchos,

pegged down to slender tubes where they met the tall boots. They all sported flowing, long, thick mustaches that drooped to their jawlines. Without comment, they swiftly drew their weapons.

Jeff York killed the one opposite him before the *bandido* could squeeze his trigger. Beside him, he heard the steady bang of Smoke's .44. Jeff's target flopped on the ground and raised a cloud of dust. The two Smoke had shot staggered forward a step, fired wildly in the general direction of the lawmen they faced, and then took another bullet each.

Impact turned them inward, facing each other, their foreheads rebounded off one another, and they spun away, arms hooked together in a macabre do-si-do. Meanwhile, Benton-Howell energetically shoved Jimmy Tucker into the coach. He gestured impatiently to his second partner, Dalton Wade, to pass him the other two children.

By then, Selleres' three bandits had been dispatched. Slowly, the cloud of expended powder began to clear. Miguel Selleres found himself facing Smoke Jensen and Jeff York, smoking Colts in their hands.

"It's over, Selleres. Let your hostages go," Smoke Jensen demanded.

Swiftly, Selleres grabbed Martha Tucker under one arm and laid his wrist tightly across her throat, the muzzle of his Mendoza pressed to the soft flesh behind her chin. "Put up your *pistolas, Señores,* or I will kill her before your eyes."

26

The sneer on Miguel Selleres's face portrayed more fear than contempt. "We are leaving here. All is lost—¿como no? We'll take the woman and these brats for safe passage. Do not come after us."

"Why not? You'll kill them eventually," Smoke challenged.

Selleres shrugged. *"Que obvio. Pero no es importante para té."*

"It's sure as hell important to the woman and her kids," Jeff York growled.

"Holster your guns or she dies," said Selleres coldly.

Jeff York cut his eyes to Smoke Jensen. Smoke considered only for a brief second, then gave a small nod. Both lawmen slid iron into leather. Miguel Selleres began to back toward the armored coach.

Madness glittered in his eyes. "We're leaving now. But we'll be back. Everyone will be made to pay for what they've done to us. The whole damned world will tremble before us!"

At that moment, Martha Tucker managed to dip her chin low enough to get a mouthful of the arm holding her. She sank her teeth in and ground them.

With a howl of anguish, Miguel Selleres jerked his head upward in reflexive response to the pain. His grip loosened,

Martha opened her mouth and fell to one side. Smoke Jensen drew his left-hand .44

"No, we won't," Smoke Jensen barked, as his bullet popped a hole in the forehead of Miguel Selleres.

The Mendoza Colt dropped from a lifeless hand. Selleres had overlooked one vital requirement. He had not cocked his weapon. Driven by desperation, Dalton Wade made the terrible mistake of unlimbering the age-worn, 5-shot Herington and Richards .38 from its long, soft pouch holster. To do so, he had to release the hand of Tommy Tucker. It did him no good, though. A bullet each from Smoke Jensen and Jeff York struck his chest at the same moment. Screaming, Rose Tucker ran after her little brother. A major transformation had come over Benton-Howell. He sank to his knees, hands upraised in supplication, tears streaming down his full cheeks, face ruddy.

"Please, don't kill me. I don't want to die. None of this was my idea. You—you can't kill me," a sudden hope rising in his quaking body. "I'm a peer of the realm! And, after all, no one important got hurt."

Smoke Jensen turned an icy gaze of utter contempt upon the groveling Englishman. "We'll save you, all right, *Sir* Geoffrey . . . for the hangman. Jeff, go after the Tucker kids."

Once they had been restored to their mother, who wept copiously in relief over the safe resolution of their dangerous situation, Smoke Jensen turned his attention back to Benton-Howell.

"*Sir Geoffrey?*" His lips curled with contempt. "Well, you're sure not a gentleman, let alone a knightly one. You're a coward, a murderer, and a thief. You're so low and corrupt, you'd have to reach up to scratch a snake's belly. I said we'd save you for a date with the hangman, but I didn't promise what condition you'd be in for the trial." Smoke undid his cartridge belt. "Put up your hands and defend yourself."

Benton-Howell began to splutter. "Bu—but, I'm—I'm your prisoner, sir. You cannot strike me."

In an eye blink, Smoke Jensen hit him with a right and left to either side of the jaw. Benton-Howell sagged and raised a futile left arm in an attempt to block the next solid punch, which whistled in as a sizzling right jab. He gulped and backpedaled. His shoulders slammed against the heavy side of the coach. Jimmy Tucker's head popped out the door.

"Yaaah-hooo! Kick him between the legs, Smoke."

"*James Lee Tucker,*" Martha admonished, scandalized by her son. "Such language. For shame."

Jimmy didn't look the least repentant. "I mean it, too, Mom."

Left arm still up, Benton-Howell darted his right in under its concealing position. Suddenly Smoke Jensen was there. One hand clinched a lapel as Smoke spun Benton-Howell around. Smoke pulled down the frock coat to reveal a concealed shoulder holster that held a short-barreled .44 Colt Lightning. Jeff stepped in and plucked the weapon from its holster. Smoke swung the frothing-mouthed Benton-Howell around and slammed his head into the armored side of the carriage. It made a solid *thunk.*

Smoke brought his dazed opponent face to face, and went to work on the midsection. Feebly Benton-Howell tried to fend off the blows. Clearly this was not a fight, it was a beating, plain and simple. Every bit of the outrage and frustration of the last mountain man poured out on the source of it all. Benton-Howell doubled over, his air exhausted, and Smoke Jensen straightened him up with a hard left.

The Englishman's knees buckled and his head drooped. Still Smoke bore in. Blood ran from a cut on the cheek of Benton-Howell, from the corner of his mouth, and the corner of an eye swollen shut by severe battering. At last, Smoke Jensen took control of his anger and eased off. When the red haze left his eyes, he found Benton-Howell on his knees, thoroughly battered and defeated.

Disgust plain on her face at having witnessed the savaging of Benton-Howell, Martha Tucker hugged her children to her and spoke with unaccustomed chill to Smoke Jensen. "It's over then?"

"Yes. All but the roundup of the trash and, of course, the trial. I've no doubt Benton-Howell will be convicted of ordering your husband's murder. And he *will* hang."

"Yes . . . of course," she responded stiffly. "At least that way it will be done according to law."

Her sudden, inexplicable disapproval stung Smoke Jensen. He started to make some sort of reply, thought better of it, and shrugged. He retrieved his hat from the ground, dusted it off, and indicated the way back toward the hotel with it. Without further comment, Martha Tucker followed, her children clustered at either side.

They had progressed only a third of the way down the alley, when a shot crashed overloud in the confined space, and little Tommy Tucker slammed forward out of the protective circle of his mother's arm. Martha took one stunned look at the spreading red stain on the boy's back, and began to wail hysterically. Young Rose Tucker screamed and dissolved into tears. Jimmy hit the ground.

Smoke Jensen reacted quickly also. He jumped to one side and looked beyond the frozen tableau of the Tuckers to where a wooden-faced Forrest Gore worked the lever of his Winchester in a frantic effort to chamber another round. Smoke's hand dropped to the butt of his .44, and he freed it before the bolt closed on Gore's rifle.

Smoke's arm rose with equal swiftness and steadied only a fraction of a second to allow the hammer to drop. Quickly he slip-thumbed three more rounds. All four struck Forrest Gore in the chest and belly. The Winchester flew to the sky, and Gore jerked and writhed with each impact. A cloud of cloth bits, flesh, and blood made a crimson haze that circled his body. Jeff York turned in time to plunk two more slugs into the child-killer. Then he spun, pistol still smoking, toward Benton-Howell.

"That does it! No waiting for the hangman, damn you. It's your scheming that brought it to this. Now you pay."

"No, Jeff!" Smoke Jensen barked harshly. "Let him sit and sweat and wait for that rope to be put around his neck. That way he'll die a thousand times over."

Jeff York's shoulders sagged. "You're right, Smoke. Sorry, I lost it for a moment."

Martha Tucker drew out of her grief long enough to look up with a face drawn with anguish, and addressed Smoke Jensen with some of her former warmth. "Thank you, Smoke Jensen. Thank you for saving a fine lawman's career and self-esteem. And thank you for avenging my husband and my—my son."

All at once, Smoke Jensen felt as though he had been the one to take a beating. "I did what I had to do, Martha. Now, we have a lot yet to accomplish."

Martha Tucker had been restored to her ranch. A week had gone by since the Arizona Rangers had cleared the streets of Socorro of saddle tramps and low-class gunfighters. They had ridden away after little Tommy Tucker's funeral. Each one had expressed their deep sympathy for the courageous woman who had lost a husband and son within a month's time. Even Cuchillo Negro and his Apache warriors left small, feather-decorated gifts on the raw earth of the grave. Then they, too, rode off to the west.

That left Smoke Jensen alone at the ranch. He recalled the tension and black grief at the burial of the small boy, and a sensation of relief flooded him as he watched Martha Tucker step from the kitchen, smiling and brushing at the swatch of flour on her forehead in a familiar gesture. She smiled up at him as she approached where he stood with his saddled roan.

"I've put a pie on. I—I sort of hoped that you would stay on, if not with your hands, at least yourself, for a while."

"I really can't, Martha. I'm long overdue in returning to my ranch."

"With it in the capable hands of men like Walt and Ty, I see no reason why a few days more would matter."

Smoke sighed. "Truth is, I miss 'em. The High Lonesome, the Sugarloaf, and . . . my wife. It's time I got back to them. Goodbye, and bless you, Martha Tucker. You're a strong woman. Strong even if you were a man."

"Why, I—I take that as the supreme compliment," she said, clearly flustered. Then Martha rose on tiptoe and kissed Smoke lightly on one cheek. "Goodbye, Smoke Jensen. You'll be missed . . . awfully."

Jimmy Tucker rushed forward and hugged Smoke Jensen around the waist. He was too deeply moved for words, but his silent tears spoke it all. That made it even more difficult for Smoke Jensen to take his leave, but he did.

Prying the lad's arms from around him and giving a final tip of his hat to Martha, Smoke swung into the saddle and rode off. He didn't look back until he reached the top of the ridge to the northeast. The backward glance did not last long, for his thoughts had already spanned the miles ahead to his secure nook in the Shining Mountains, the cozy log and stone home on the Sugarloaf, and his beloved Sally.

POWER OF THE
MOUNTAIN MAN

1

Winter had poised to blow its way across the High Lonesome. Most of the aspens had lost their leaves. Those that remained glowed in a riot of yellow and red. The maples and scrub oak resisted stubbornly, greenness proclaiming their independence dotted in among the less hearty trees. Smoke Jensen took a draw on the flavorful cigar and sent his gray gaze out across the vista of his beloved Sugarloaf Ranch while the white ribbons rose from around the stogie.

It wouldn't be long, he mused, before a thick blanket of snow covered everything in sight. Which reminded him of the letter he held in his hand. It had come from San Francisco that morning, brought by a ranch hand who had gone to Big Rock for the weekly mail run. Smoke cut his eyes to the brief message, only a single line.

"Come at once. Meet me at Francie's." It was signed simply with a bold L.

Because of where they were to meet and of whom he suspected as the sender, Smoke refrained from mentioning the cryptic message to his wife Sally. That he would go went without question. Despite the harsh winter looming over them, he would not suggest that his lovely wife accompany him to the more hospitable clime. He sighed gustily and ran long, strong fingers through his hair, pleased to reflect that only thin threads of gray showed at his temples. As to breaking the news of his departure, he had better get to that right away.

Smoke Jensen lifted himself out of the cane-bottom chair he had tilted back against the outer wall of his home on the Sugarloaf. Once a tight, square cabin of fir logs, it now sprawled with the additions brought on by a large family. He crossed to the door and entered. At once his nostrils twitched and swelled to the delicious scent of a pie baking. Drawn by that tempting aroma, he gained the kitchen with a broad grin on his face, his unpleasant mission forgotten for the moment. He negotiated the floor on cat feet and caught Sally with both big hands around her still-trim waist. She gave only the slightest of starts at the contact, then looked over her shoulder, long curls dancing.

"It's the last of the blackberries. I thought you'd like it."

"I know *I* will," young Bobby Jensen chirped from the big, round oak table in the center of the expanded room.

Smoke turned to the boy, surprise written on his face. "I thought you were out with the hands."

"I woulda been, but . . ." Bobby elevated a bare foot, a strip of white rag tied around his big toe. "I got this big ol' splinter when I went to wash up this morning."

"You'll live," Smoke told him with a grin.

Smoke and Sally had adopted Bobby Harris several years ago, after Smoke had been forced to kill the boy's abusive father. The elder Harris had been a brute, a drunk who'd tormented both people and animals. He had gone after Smoke Jensen with a pitchfork while Smoke's back had been turned. Bobby's shout of alarm had saved Smoke's life.

On an important mission to help old friends in Mexico, Smoke had sent the orphaned lad to the Sugarloaf and put him in Sally's charge. What had forged that decision had been Bobby's revelation that Harris, Sr., had killed the lad's mother some months previous. For all his reputation as a deadly gunfighter—the best ever, many maintained—his past did not harden Smoke from compassion for the boy. Sally would take care of Bobby, since there was no way he could go where Smoke was headed. Bobby's sunny smile recalled Smoke to the kitchen. By God, the lad would soon be thirteen.

"Oh, I know that. It just stings, and my toe swelled up too much to put in a boot."

Sally recognized the distracted expression Smoke wore and came right to the point. "There's something in that letter I don't know about," she challenged.

"I was coming to tell you. Maybe you ought to check on that pie and then get a cup of coffee and come sit at the table."

Sally frowned. "Bad news." Then she added, "As always." She complied, however, and when seated, Smoke revealed the summons to San Francisco. When he concluded, Sally fought back her disappointment and provided, "You're going, of course."

"I have to, Sally. You know as well as I who probably sent that."

Sally's scowl deepened. "I've no doubt. And that always spells danger."

"Danger for who?" Bobby piped up.

Smoke and Sally shot him a look. "For *whom*," she corrected automatically, then answered his question. "Smoke, of course," she advised him. "But mostly for anyone who gets in his way."

That made Bobby's day. His face lit up with expectation. "You're goin' gunnin' for someone, huh, Smoke?"

Smoke Jensen sighed wearily and shook his head. "Not if I can help it. I really don't know what to expect. But I'll be leaving early in the morning. Sally, make sure there's plenty of firewood and supplies laid in, who knows when I'll be back?" He shrugged. "Then all I can think of is that you all bundle up tight for the winter."

* * *

Shortly after sunrise, Smoke Jensen fastened the last strap on his saddlebags and swung atop his 'Palouse stallion, Thunder. He had kissed Sally goodbye minutes earlier and had left her at the kitchen table, her eyes bright with suppressed tears. Now, as he turned his mount south, toward the main gate of the ranch and the town of Big Rock beyond, Sally came from the back door, a shawl over her shoulders to stave off the morning chill.

She hurried to his side, calling his name. Smoke turned and bent low as Sally reached him and stood on tiptoe, arms out to embrace the man she loved with all her heart. Deeply moved by her affection, Smoke kissed her ardently. When their embrace ended, he spoke gruffly.

"Always did have to have the last word, woman."

"Goodbye, Smoke, dearest. Be careful."

"You, too. And keep your friend close at hand."

"I will." Sally turned away so as not to have to witness the actual moment of Smoke's departure. When Thunder's hoofbeats faded down the lane to the ranch, she turned to wave at Smoke's back.

Mountain man instincts, imbued in him by his mentor, Preacher—who some were starting to call, rightly or not, the First Mountain Man—alerted Smoke Jensen to the presence of others even before Thunder twitched his big, black ears and swiveled them forward to listen down the trail. The stallion's spotted gray rump hide rippled in anticipation. Always cautious, even in this settled country, Smoke drifted off the trail, thankful that snow had not yet fallen. He dismounted and put a big, hard hand over Thunder's muzzle to prevent an unwanted greeting to others of the stallion's kind. Five minutes later, two young men rode into view.

They had the look about them of ranch hands and an air of that wandering fraternity loosely described as drifters. Smoke Jensen noted that their clothing was a cut above average. They wore their hats at a jaunty angle and rode easy in the saddle. Their conversation, when it reached his ears, convinced Smoke of the accuracy of his surmise.

"It's gettin' close to winter, Buck."

"Sure is, Jason. I sure hope there's a spread out here somewhere that'll take us on for the winter. Be dang cold tryin' to get by on our own."

"No foolin', Buck. But you know, I hear there's old cabins hereabouts, shanties put up by the fur traders. We could settle down in one of them."

"What are we gonna use to buy supplies?" Buck challenged.

Jason considered it in silence as they approached the spot where Smoke Jensen had concealed himself off the trail. "I reckon that's why we should find us a place to earn some cash money."

"Don't no moss grow on you, Jase."

That decided Smoke. He led Thunder by the headstall onto the trail. Startled, the riders reined abruptly, then raised their hands, eyes wide. "You ain't gonna rob us, is you, Mister?"

Smoke chuckled. "No—nothing like that. I overheard you talking about looking for work. As it happens, I could use a couple of hands right now." Smoke took stock of their location. Less than three miles from Big Rock. Couldn't take them back. "I can't take you there and introduce you around. I'll write you a note. Take it to Cole Travis, my winter foreman, and to my wife, Sally."

"Why, that's mighty generous of you, Mister . . . ?"

"The name's Jensen."

"Right, Mr. Jensen," Buck said. "We're obliged. I'm Buck Jarvis, an' this is Jason Rucker. We'll work hard for you, that I promise."

"I know you will, boys." Smoke's steely gray eyes told them why he did. "The Sugarloaf is ten miles up this trail, in a large highland valley. You'll make it about in time for dinner. Walk your horses slow. Takes time to accustom them to the altitude."

"Thank you, Mr. Jensen. You'll not regret this."

"Fine, boys. Let me do that note." Smoke delved in a shirt pocket for a scrap of paper and a stub of pencil.

After Smoke had parted from Buck and Jason, the young drifters pondered over the name. "Jensen, huh?" Buck intoned. "I wonder if he's any relation to you know who?"

"Naw, he couldn't be. That Smoke Jensen's a gunfighter and a cold-blooded killer. Ain't no way a man that nice would be related," Jason assured his partner.

In Big Rock, Smoke Jensen had a three hour wait for the D&RG daily train north to the Union Pacific junction. He left Thunder to be loaded on a stock car and walked down Main Street to the sheriff's office. Although Smoke was a skilled woodsman, the horse was an integral part of the life of a mountain man as in later years it became for the Texas cowboys. Old Preacher always grumbled when put to walking.

When Smoke had met Preacher, his life changed forever.

Mountain men invented rugged individualism. They personified self-reliance. And the man known to all as Preacher outdid them all. Preacher had named him Smoke the first day they'd met.

And "Smoke" he became from that day. Now, walking along the muddy, rutted central avenue in Big Rock, Smoke Jensen savored all that. Yet he missed Thunder's slab flanks between his legs more than he would admit, even to himself. Gratitude flooded him as he reached the open doorway to the sheriff's office.

"Don't you ever do any work?" Smoke bellowed at the man behind the desk inside, whose newspaper concealed his face, and whose ubiquitous black hat topped a thick mane of silver hair.

The boots came down from the desk with a thud and the copy of the Denver *Post* fluttered to the desk top. "Dang it now, Smoke Jensen. What the devil you mean, sneakin' up on a body like that?"

"Monte, you never change. I'm on my way to San Francisco, thought I'd stop by and let you know I'd be gone from the Sugarloaf."

"Glad you did. I've been hopin' for an excuse to go after a cup of coffee with a shot of rye in it. Let's go down to the Gold Field."

"Might as well. I've got a three-hour wait."

Out of doors again, the two old friends ambled down the street, lawman fashion—out in the middle, where no one could come at them suddenly from a doorway. Smoke Jensen had often trod both sides of the law. Yet he had always returned, passionately, to the side of decency. The main thing that had kept him from settling down and accepting a permanent badge, as Monte had done, was all the infernal walking a man had to do in the job. One could not rattle doorknobs from horseback. Of course, the deputy U.S. marshal's badge he carried in the fold of his wallet was another matter entirely.

None of the mundane details of a peace officer's routine stifled his freedom of movement or action. Smoke rarely used it, and he thought of it even less. Yet it was a comfort, given the reputation he had acquired, much of it the fanciful blathering of the authors of the penny dreadfuls and dime novels. More than once, his marshal's badge had gotten him out of tight spots. In the last few years he had not needed to resort to it often.

Perhaps the world had indeed passed him by while he'd languished in the beautiful valley that housed his ranch. He banished such thoughts when he realized Monte had been talking to him for some while.

". . . Like I said, this country is getting downright tame."

"Uh—yep. Funny thing, I was just thinking the same thing," Smoke responded.

"Used to be, it was wild fights. Now, I don't bust the head of more than one rowdy drunk a week."

Smoke gave his friend a puzzled look. "You're complaining, Monte?"

Monte sucked his cheeks hollow as he contemplated that. "Well, now, I 'm not sayin' that I object all that much. Bruises take longer to heal at my age. I caught me a winner of a shiner three weeks ago. The last of the yaller an' green faded out yesterday."

Smoke joined him in a hearty laugh. Abruptly, new voices, harsh and slurred by whiskey, interrupted their camaraderie. "What we got here?"

"Couple of old farts hoggin' the street, I'd say."

"You be right, Rupe. Hey, Grandpa, ain't you got horses? Or cain't you git up in the saddle anymore?"

"That's the ticket, Bri. You geezers get over on that boardwalk. The street is for *men*."

Brian's fourth companion joined in. "That big 'un's packin' iron, boys. S'pose he knows how to use it?"

The menace in his words froze Smoke Jensen and Monte Carson in their steps. Slowly, they turned as one to face their drunken tormentors. Arctic glaciers covered Smoke's words. "If you are looking for a lesson, I would be glad to oblige."

Monte laid a hand on Smoke's forearm. "No need for that, ol' hoss. Remember, you have a train to catch in less than three hours."

Brian got back into it. "D'ya hear that, Casey? This doddering idiot is calling you out."

Rupe got his two cents in, as well. "Fin, you think we oughta back up ol' Casey? That feller looks mighty mean."

Truth to tell, the years had been kind to Smoke Jensen. He still retained the barrel chest and large, powerful muscles of his youth. His face was creased, but with the squint lines of an outdoorsman. Only the faintest traces of gray could be seen at his temples. Those, and the streak of pure white where a bullet had once gouged his scalp, provided the only indications that he was not a man in his early thirties. The legendary speed of his draw had not diminished a jot. Still, he had no quarrel with these intoxicated louts. Smoke raised a hand in a gesture of peace.

"There'll be no gunfighting," he declared, in as soft a tone as he could manage.

With a skin full of liquor, Fin just had to push it. "Oh, yeah? You insulted my friends, and I'm not going to let you get away with it, old man."

Smoke cut his eyes to Monte and sighed heavily. "I don't see as how there's much you can do about it. My friend and I simply will not draw on you."

Swinging a leg over his mount, Brian issued a new challenge. "Then, what say we step down and pound you into the ground like a fence post?"

Smoke Jensen had run out of all his nice guy attitude. His eyes turned a dangerous ice-gray and narrowed while he drew on a pair of thin black leather gloves he carried folded over his cartridge belt. "If you try it, I'll have to kick your butt up between your shoulder blades."

That did it. Fin, Rupe, Brian, and Casey cleared their saddles and rushed at Smoke Jensen and Monte Carson. Brian swung a hard fist that did not connect. With surprising speed, Smoke had stepped back. Confused, Brian hesitated. Which gave Smoke time to set himself for a hog-stopper of a punch. A blissful smile lighted his face as he rapped Brian solidly in the teeth.

Blood flew from one tooth that broke off. Brian rocked back on his feet and shook his head. A red haze misted his eyes. To his left, Fin threw a punch that landed hard against Smoke's ribs. Without taking his gaze from Brian, Smoke snapped a sharp sideways right that landed in the center of

2

Brian came at him like a furious bull. The punches he had gleefully planned a moment before did not land. Smoke Jensen received the young bully with a series of stinging, punishing blows to the face, left . . . right . . . left . . . right . . . left. A cut opened above Brian's left eye that sent a sheet of blood to blind him. His nose smashed, more crimson fountains joined the flow. Already damaged lips grew fatter and scarlet ribbons of tinted saliva hung in long strands. Brian's knees buckled when the hard leather-encased knuckles of Smoke Jensen crashed solidly against his jaw.

Taking a step back as Brian toppled, Smoke brought up a knee with blurring speed. It cracked under the point of Brian's chin. He went to the ground twitching and unconscious. That didn't slow Fin any. He had recovered enough to fly at Smoke, arms held wide, to grab the older man around the waist. They crashed to the dirt of the street together. Fin's arms tightened, squeezing Smoke's intestines painfully. Air gushed from his lungs. Dark dots danced before Smoke's eyes. Fin drove a shoulder into Smoke's gut.

Sharp agony shot through Smoke's liver. Smoke rolled slowly to the side until Fin was on top. Then he drove a fist into Fin's right kidney. It brought forth a grunt and a howl. A second hammer blow brought another grunt and a loosening of Fin's grip. Smoke smacked him soundly on the top of the head. Fin's arms fell away. Smoke grabbed Fin by the chin and the back of his head. His slackened neck muscles gave little resistance as Smoke twisted violently to his right. Just short of breaking Fin's neck, he let off pressure.

Fin began to twitch and jerk like a demented marionette. Arms and legs flew akimbo as he did a crab scuttle in the dust. In the next second, Smoke Jensen turned to aid his older friend. Monte Carson had one of the punks bent over a tie-rail, pounding the exposed, taut belly of Rupe like a drum. Clutching an abandoned length of two-by-four, Casey began a swing at Monte's head.

Smoke got to him first. Before Casey could launch his attack, Smoke grabbed the chunk of lumber and yanked backward. Casey went off his feet. He struck the ground on his shoulders. Give him credit, Smoke thought, he bounded right back. Snarling, the bully swung the board at Smoke. The last mountain man anticipated that and dodged. With his opponent off balance, Smoke kicked him in the knee. Wobbly, Casey doubled over, to catch a fist in his face. He backpedaled two painful steps and then sat down. Hands at the ready, Smoke Jensen surveyed their accomplishments.

Fin still jittered on the street, his face in a pile of horse dung. A groggy Brian tried to regain his feet. His face a mass of red gore, he shook his head, which released a shower of droplets. Bleary-eyed, he located his enemy and stumbled toward Smoke Jensen. His arms weighed a ton each. In aching slow motion, he raised his fists and set himself for a punch.

It came not from Brian, but from Smoke. Brian's head snapped back, his knees buckled and he toppled like a fallen tree. Smoke stepped in to finish him. Monte Carson released the drunken lout he had been pounding and turned to Smoke Jensen.

"That's enough, Smoke."

"Whaaa?" Rupe bleated. Clutching his badly pounded belly, Rupe looked up as though from a deep bow. "What'd you call him?"

"Smoke," Monte answered simply. "His name is Smoke Jensen."

"Aaah, gaaad!" Rupe wailed. "Please, Mr. Jensen, please don't kill us."

Smoke turned to the youth. "I didn't start this."

"I know—I know," Rupe babbled. "Only we was just funnin'. Please spare us, Mr. Jensen. I—I know who you are."

"Obviously," Smoke replied icily. "Too bad you didn't before you started this."

Fin had stopped twitching and now came to all fours with a groan. "Didn't mean no harm, Mr. Jensen," he whined, whey-faced.

Smoke glowered at them. "It sure as thunder didn't look like it."

"I should lock the four of you up until you get sober."

"Who are you? The marshal?"

"No. I'm Sheriff Monte Carson."

"Oh, Jesus, now I know we're dead," Rupe sobbed.

"Like I said, I *should* lock you up, but I figure you've had enough punishment for one day. Now, get your partners on their horses and get the hell out of Big Rock. You have a quarter hour."

"Yes, sir—yes, sir, oh, yessir!" Rupe gobbled in terror and relief.

They managed it in less than five. Their humiliation-reddened ears still rang with the sound of hearty laughter from Smoke Jensen and Monte Carson as they cleared the city limit.

Out in California, in the goldfields on the Sacramento River, a miner worked his claim alone under the shade of huge, ancient live oaks. A crafty man and a proficient prospector, Ray Wagner had forged higher up the river than those who had been attracted by the magnet of the Sutter's Mill discovery more than thirty years before. Logic and a basic knowledge of physics told him that the gold found farther down had to have a source higher up. As a result, he had a prosperous claim that produced threefold what the next most productive outfit took from the river. He had just dumped a shovel-load of mud and gravel into his riffle-box sluice when he sensed the presence of others.

Always a cautious man, Wagner had a bulky, superbly made 10mm Mauser tucked in the waistband of his trousers. He set the shovel aside, and instead of reaching for the gold pan to work the finings, he put his long, strong fingers around the parrot-bill butt of the revolver. Then he turned to confront his uninvited guests.

"Won't be no need for that, Mister," a runty, bow-legged specimen, who had Cornish miner written all over him, declared in a crusty voice.

Level nut-brown eyes fixed on the intruder. "I didn't hear you howdy m' claim," Ray Wagner challenged tightly.

"Well, we did. Likely you didn't hear us for the water rushing through that sluice. If you be Raymond Wagner, we have something important for you.

"Yeah, I am," Wagner replied.

The runty one produced a sheaf of documents in a stiff, blue paper legal binder. "These are for you. All you need do is sign where the *x*-marks are."

Suspicious, Wagner did not reach for the papers, but kept his grip on his Mauser. "What is it I'm signing?"

"No need to read through 'em. Just sign."

Wagner's eyes narrowed and he shook his head. "I never sign anything I haven't read."

"All right," was the testy response. "Take 'em and read."

Wagner reached left-handed and took the documents. He quickly learned that they were a quit-claim deed and transfer of title for his claim. His thin lips hardened into a stubborn line. Tethering his anger, he pushed the papers back toward the former Cornishman.

"I will not sign these. I do not wish to leave this place, or give up my gold find."

Meanness revealed itself in the runt's face and he and his companions spread out, away from their horses. "You really don't have a choice. Now, sign them like a good boy, pack up, and be on your way."

"And what am I to be paid for my claim?"

"Paid?" the runt repeated. "Why, with the enjoyment of the rest of your life."

That brought the Mauser out with respectable speed. *"Unglücklicher Bastarben!* Get off my claim, you miserable bastards,"* Wagner repeated his curse in English. "I will give you two minutes to get out of sight."

Shaking with rage, the runty one stalked to his horse and mounted. "We'll be back. And when we come, you will regret this."

"I think not," Wagner countered. "Now, move, or be buried here."

Smoke Jensen got up from the table considerably better off than when he had taken a seat some two hours earlier. "Thank you, gentlemen, for an entertaining evening."

With that, he departed the smoking car of the Union Pacific *Daylight Flyer,* westbound for California. Two men, modest winners in their own right, left behind him. The carriage was provided for the convenience of gentlemen who wished to indulge in tobacco or spirits, or both, while making the long journey from their homes to their distant destinations. Three round baize-covered tables also accommodated those who wished to wager on a game of skill. In this case, poker, to be exact. Over the time Smoke had been in the game, the fortunes of those in the game had declined steadily, for three of them quite sharply. One of the heavy losers spoke bitterly, his tone one of whining complaint.

"I still say he cheated."

"No," an older man said. "Only a matter of real skill, I would say."

"But, it ain't fair; he took all of me an' Billy's money," the complainer sniveled.

"Teddy's right," a pouting Billy added to the whining. "He done cleaned us out, near on eight hundred dollars. Money we earned fair and square." Earned in this case by driving cattle to market and selling them. *Other people's* cattle.

Smarting from his own substantial loss, the elder man could bear their childish petulance no further. "If you really feel that way, why don't you go take it away from him?" he asked sarcastically.

Billy and Teddy exchanged surprised glances. They hadn't thought of that. Now, with Smoke out of the room, the sheer size and latent menace forgotten, the idea presented enormous appeal. A wicked light of cupidity shone in Billy's eyes as he cut them to the older man.

"You're a smart man, Mr. Rankin. We'd of never thought of that. What say, Teddy? You game for it?"

Teddy was already out of his chair. "You bet I am. Let's git on with it."

A teasing light of cynicism flickered in Rankin's eyes. "Of course, you'll replace my losses in return for finding the solution?"

"Oh, sure, Mr. Rankin. You can count on that," Teddy burbled.

When pigs start to fly, Rankin thought. But, never mind; he had his own idea of how to retrieve his portion, and with considerable interest. He wished the youthful rustlers well and watched them on their way.

Billy and Teddy caught up with Smoke Jensen on the platform between the parlor car behind the smoker and the Pullman beyond that. Through the beveled glass lattice window of the car door they saw him crossing over to the far platform, hand out to grasp the brass latch lever. Teddy was slobbering in eagerness, his hand on the grip of the underpowered Colt .38 Model '77 Lightning in the Furstnow/Zimmerman "Texas" style shoulder holster in his left armpit. When Billy yanked open the door on their side, he also drew his .44 Colt.

Yelling to be heard over the rattle and clatter of the steel-wheeled trucks, he called to Smoke, "Hold it right there, Jensen!"

Smoke risked a quick look over one shoulder and noted that both had weapons in hand. "What seems to be the problem?"

"You cheated, and we want our money back," Teddy enlightened him.

"Sorry. I don't cheat and you don't get anything back."

"You think because we're young, we'll bluff easy," Teddy snarled. "You don't even know who we are."

"Two boys in way over their heads, I'd say," Smoke said.

"We're *danger*. We're the biggest, meanest, smartest rustler gang in Wyoming, Colorado, and Kansas, that's who we are."

Smoke had all he could take of this pair. "Frankly, I think you are full of crap. Grow up, Sonny and take your loss like a man."

"Then we'll take it from you if we have to kill you to do it," Billy railed.

"You'll never make it, Sonny."

"Goddamn you, Jensen!" Billy shrieked.

Smoke could not hear the sear notches on Billy's six-gun ratchet to full-cock over the noise of the train, but he knew it happened. He flexed his knees and pivoted on his left boot heel. His .45 Colt Peacemaker appeared in his right fist as though by magic. Even with their six-guns at the ready, Smoke's prediction came true. He put his first bullet into Teddy's shoulder. His second took Billy in the gut.

Teddy dropped his Lightning and began to scream and cry like a girl. For all the speed of the double-action revolver, he had not been able to get it in play. Billy tried to raise his Colt again and Smoke shot him a second time. An expression of surprised disbelief fixed his features in a pinched, puckered mouth and blankly staring eyes. Slowly he sagged to his knees, then toppled sideways. His six-gun forgotten, he began to writhe in agony. Smoke stepped quickly across and kicked the revolver away from the young thug. Suddenly the door behind Billy flew open and Rankin appeared in the entrance, backlighted by the yellow glow of kerosene lamps. The blue steel barrel of the Merwin and Hulbert .44 in his left hand glittered wickedly.

Before Smoke Jensen could react, Rankin's weapon barked. The slug cracked loudly past Smoke's head an instant before Smoke obliged Rankin with a slug in the brain. Rankin went down in a rubber-limbed heap. Half a heartbeat later, the wide-eyed, badly shaken conductor arrived.

"Oh m'god, what happened here?"

"These three tried to kill me," Smoke answered.

Crouched by the corpse of Rankin, the conductor gaped up at Smoke. "But, why?"

"They figured to rob me."

Indignation rang in the supervisor's voice. "Not on *my* train."

Smoke lifted the corners of his mouth in a fleeting smile. "That's how I saw it, too."

"This is terrible, simply terrible. All this mess. And the passengers. What will we do about them?"

"Well, we could spare them the awful sight."

"How's that?"

"We could simply dump this garbage off the train."

The round eyes went wider. "Oh, no, we could never do that. There will have to be an inquiry into the shooting," the conductor insisted.

Right then, Billy ceased his groans and gasps. With a little shudder, he stopped writhing. The trainman eyed the newly made corpse and the other, and the wailing youth with the bloody shoulder. Then he looked back at Smoke and correctly read the steely gray eyes. He swallowed hard to get his words past the hard lump in his throat.

"Well," he said meekly, "if Mr. Smoke Jensen will say nothing about the incident, I certainly won't." To his surprise, Smoke frowned and pointed at the wounded Teddy.

"One's still alive."

"D-do you want that taken care of?"

"*Noo,*" Smoke drawled. "We'll stop off at the county seat and have that little inquiry."

Relieved, the conductor sighed deeply. "I'll go make arrangements to have the bodies wrapped up and moved to the baggage car."

Early morning reached San Francisco in a pink haze. Starlings twittered in the cornices of the public buildings off Market Street. Pigeons cooed indignantly at this invasion by their smaller, sleek cousins. On the wide front porch of his splendid home on Nob Hill, Cyrus Murchison gave his wife a buss on her peaches-and-cream cheek.

"I'll be late tonight, Agatha, my dear."

"Oh, Cyrus, you've been working so hard lately. Can't anyone else run that railroad of yours?"

"Yes. And there are a lot of them doing that day and night," the portly Murchison assured her. "This is . . . other business."

Agatha frowned. "You're seeing Titus and Gaylord again" —came out as a statement.

Abashed, Murchison sputtered his reply. "But they're my friends. They are also my only peers in commerce and industry."

"Empire building, you mean," Agatha charged pettishly.

Murchison brushed vacantly at the thick gold watch chain that hung in twin loops from the pockets of his dark navy pinstriped vest. Grown portly from good living, he had the florid face to go with the rich diet and ample spirits he consumed. In his early fifties, he had a layer of fat right under his skin that gave him the youthful appearance of a man ten years his junior. Often hailed in the pages of the San Francisco *Chronicle* as a "captain of industry," Murchison had reached the pinnacle of his enterprise through hard, if often dishonest, effort. His sole weakness was his relationship with his wife.

Put frankly, Agatha terrified him. One of her looks, a gesture, or a soft, deprecating word could swiftly unman him. While he was a tyrant to every subordinate and lived life like an autocrat, Cyrus Murchison quailed at the mildest rebuke from the woman he adored above all things save power. Now he shot a quick look over his shoulder. His carriage, complete with liveried driver, waited to take him to his office.

"Be that as it may, my dear. But this meeting is important. Tell cook not to hold supper."

He bent to give her another quick peck, then put his hat firmly on his head and turned to negotiate the steps. He strolled briskly down the flagstone walk to a gate in the white-painted, wrought-iron picket fence. The driver opened the carriage door and touched fingers to the brim of his hat.

Seated in the brougham, Cyrus Murchison mentally reviewed the events of the past few days. Gaylord Huntley was a fool to believe they could use those people and get out of it unaffected; they'd invented the squeeze. He sighed heavily. But they need them. Not all of the employees in their various enterprises could be corrupted. Another thing rankled even more. So they let that sourdough run them off, eh? One man against three, and not a one had had forethought or fortitude enough to force him to sign? Next time, it might be well to have Tyrone Beal take charge of gaining that mining property.

Stubborn man, that Raymond Wagner. A German, and blockheaded. Titus Hobson simply had no idea of how to properly delegate authority. He made his way to the top in the goldfields by himself, and never learned how to rely on the judgment and performance of other men. On the other hand, Murchison mused, he had learned that lesson early in the building of his California Central railroad empire. He would have some hot words for his companions that evening. Something he felt certain they would not like to hear.

An early riser by habit from his time in the goldfields of Central California, Titus Hobson already sat at his desk. Although he was a good five years older than Cyrus Murchison, he retained powerful shoulders and arms from his years of working at mining and prospecting. Every bit as rich as Murchison, he remained a bit rough around the edges. His clothes might be of the best cloth and perfectly fitted, but they lost their luster on his burly frame. He eased himself forward in the leatherbound swivel chair to gaze down on San Francisco from his office on the fourth floor of the Flatiron Building. His eyes settled on the oddly peaked roofs of Chinatown. A smile played across his craggy face and set his bushy brows to waggling.

This thing with the Chinese—he liked it. Yes, let those little yellow devils take the lumps, if indeed any were to be handed out. But would they take orders from a white man? They should; thousands of them had labored on Cyrus's railroad. They would settle the Chinese question tonight. Cyrus still had to be brought around. Gaylord had convinced him yesterday. It was up to the two of them to sway Cyrus. He smacked a hard hand on the glowing mahogany desktop.

"Hell, we should be able to handle this ourselves," he said aloud, startling himself. To cover speaking to an empty room, he called out to his male secretary, "Alex, bring me a cup of coffee."

"Right away, Mr. Hobson."

Hobson picked up the report once more. Neat rows of numbers ran down the page in columns. Looking at them irritated him. He could read and write; he'd taught himself after he'd made that big strike on Rush's Mountain. He could do his figures right enough, too. Only, this many numbers tended to blend together into a single indecipherable mass. If this accountant of Cyrus's was right, they were all going to become a whole lot richer than their wildest dreams. That comforting thought made his belly rumble. He always had a little snack at mid-morning. Why not a little early?

"Oh, and Alex, bring me a piece of that cream cake."

Gaylord Huntley stepped catfooted up to the bull-necked bruiser who stood defiantly in the gateway of pier 7. The gigantic longshoreman held a cargo hook in one huge fist and a wicked filleting knife in the other. He seemed not the least intimidated by the presence of the overlord of all San Francisco dockworkers.

"When I say you don't work these docks," Huntley growled, "I mean you are out, even in times of emergency. Now, get your butt out of my sight."

"You're not throwing me out, Huntley. I come to work, and I aim to finish it."

Lightning fast, Huntley's ham fist flashed from his side and cracked into the center of the longshoreman's chest. The dockworker's eyes crossed and air gushed out of him. Huntley followed up with a left to the jaw, then reversed to backhand the hook out of his way. Half a dozen onlookers remained frozen in place.

To them it appeared Huntley had forgotten the knife. He hadn't. As it flashed forward, his right hand filled with the parrot-bill grip of a .44 Colt Lightning, which he snapped free of a high hip holster and squeezed through the double-action trigger to send a round square into the

belligerent longshoreman's heart. He fell dead at Huntley's feet.

"Dump this trash in the bay," he commanded his other
workers.

"Yes, sir, Mr. Huntley," one blurted.

All of them had long ago been intimidated by this ferret-
faced man with the bulging shoulders and arms of their
trade. Gaylord Huntley's oily black hair, slicked straight
back on his elongated head, added to the ratlike visage created by black, close-set eyes and protruding yellowed teeth.
Seen from behind, Huntley's stature was laughable.

Some few had made the mistake of laughing. His oversized upper torso dwindled rapidly to a narrow waist and
short legs planted on small feet. It gave him the appearance
of a soaked wharf rat. Those who had sniggered at that
sight had paid for it . . . painfully. Not a few had paid with
their lives. Huntley did not waste time on watching the disposal. He reholstered his Colt and turned from the dock.
His mind went at once to the meeting with Cyrus and Titus.

Over dinner, they would settle the idea of using the Chinese instead of his longshoremen or Cyrus's railroad
detectives to enforce their will. It had been his idea. He considered himself to be a remarkable judge of the abilities
and the reliability of other men. He found Xiang Lee to be
capable and trustworthy, if a little full of himself. He believed he had sold Titus on it the previous day. Only
Murchison objected strongly. Perhaps that could be
changed. He smiled in anticipation as he entered his office.

"Ah, my dear Millie," he greeted the young woman
seated in a comfortable chair beside a large potted palm.
"Won't you come in, please? I have need of your special tal-
ents." Killing always made him hunger for a woman's
charms.

3

At Rock Springs, the county seat of Sweetwater County, Wyoming, the train pulled to its scheduled stop and Smoke Jensen readied himself for the inevitable questions he had encountered so many times before. The conductor, a man named Ames, had arranged for the sheriff and the doctor who served as coroner to come aboard the train to conduct their inquiry.

That gave Smoke a little more confidence. The railroad would back him. Unfortunately, some bogus Wanted posters might still circulate in Wyoming. That harkened back to the time when dark forces had combined to have him marked as a man wanted for murder. It had brought him literally years of grief. He looked up now as the train-man and the law returned to the baggage car.

"I know you," the sheriff growled, his eyes narrowing as he entered.

"I don't know you," Smoke quipped back.

"Sheriff Harvey Lane. You're a wanted man, Smoke Jensen."

Smoke answered simply, "No, I'm not."

"I have a wanted flyer . . ." Lane began, to be cut off by a raised hand and a sharp bark from Smoke.

"It's all crap, Sheriff. You should know that by now. Those

were fraudulent when they were printed and they were re-called a month after being issued. Let's get on to this shooting."

"Why did you kill them?" Lane quickly changed gears.

"Like I told Mr. Ames here, they were trying to kill me."

Lane spoke dryly. "Of course there could be no possible reason for that?"

"I had just finished nearly cleaning them out at poker. The punk kids turned out to be part of a rustling gang. The whole gang, I suspect."

"You have any proof of that?"

"Ask our boy Teddy. He's locked up in the strong room," Smoke snapped.

Sheriff Lane cut a sharp eye to the conductor, who nodded. "Yep. Once I got him away from Smoke—er—Mr. Jensen, he wouldn't stop babbling. Confessed to all sorts of things. Claimed the dead boy, Billy, forced him to participate. Said they'd rustled cattle in five states."

"Well, well," Lane mused aloud. "There anyone else I can ask?"

"The other players in the poker game," Smoke suggested.

Wrath darkened the lawman's hawklike visage. "Now I got a gunfighter and killer tellin' me my business."

Tired from the fight the previous day and strained to the limit by the attempt on his life, Smoke Jensen had absorbed all of this he could. "No," Smoke countered as he produced his wallet and badge. "You have a deputy U.S. marshal telling you your business."

Lane's jaw sagged. "Well, I'll . . . be . . . damned. You working on somethin' now, Marshal Jensen?"

Amazing, how his tone changed, Smoke mused. "If I am, it does not involve your jurisdiction. I'm sure Mr. Ames has told you I am ticketed through to San Francisco."

"I think I am beginning to see. Well, then, I'm off to talk to those players and this yonker rustler. Enjoy your journey, Marshal Jensen."

After the sheriff left the car, Ames looked blankly at Smoke. "What was that all about?"

"I ask you," Smoke shot back.

Three men met the eleven o'clock local of the California Central when it rolled into Parkerville, California. Their leader, the bandy-legged one who had confronted Ray Wagner, wore a surly expression and spoke with false bravado.

"Whoever the boss is sending had better be in the mood to take orders."

"But didn't the telegram from San Francisco say he was to be in charge?" one of his henchmen asked ingenuously.

"Button that lip, Quint. *I'm* the boss around here. And this sissy city dude had better know it."

With a final hiss, screech, and groan, the train came to a stop. The first to bound down the folding iron steps was a huge, burly man with flame-red hair and a big walrus mustache that drooped around thick, tobacco-stained lips. He had a saddle slung over one massive shoulder that made the rig look tiny. It became obvious he could not be someone for whom any of the delicate women and small children waited. He made a quick study of those on the platform and walked directly to the trio.

"You must be Spencer. I'm Beal. Get me a horse," he commanded the erstwhile leader.

Swallowing with difficulty, the bowlegged hard case surrendered his captaincy and responded humbly. "Yes, sir. Right away."

Tyrone Beal had arrived.

Cyrus Murchison had chosen well. Beal led a company of twenty-five railroad detectives, under the direct order of his boss, Hector Grange, Chief of Railroad Police for the California Central. Always big for his age, Beal had killed his first man at the age of thirteen, beaten him to death with his fists. The man was his stepfather, a brute and drunk who alternately beat his stepchildren and his wife. The authorities sent Tyrone Beal to a school for errant boys for six months while the family moved to another county, and then Beal was released.

Since that time, he had never let anyone back him down. Never. No two-bit gold chaser was about to be the first. He had heard of the failure of Spencer and his underlings. They should have taken ax handles to the stupid German and beaten some sense into him. He privately gave himself ten minutes to convince Wagner. He dismissed this as he studied the two henchmen who accompanied Spencer.

"Can either of you count to twenty without taking off your boots?" he growled.

They exchanged puzzled glances. "Uh—what's that mean?" one asked.

Beal gave them a contemptuous sneer. "I gather that means no. Now, get this straight, I don't like to repeat myself. You are going to take me out to this Wagner claim and we are going to get his signature. There will be no failure. Clear?"

They nodded their heads dumbly. Spencer returned then and took in the display. Anger rose again. He stomped over and put his face up in that of Tyrone Beal. "Those are my men. They take their orders from me."

Beal's answer came back heavy with menace. "Not . . . any . . . more. Now, saddle my horse and let's head for that claim."

The humiliation of that was more than Spencer could bear. "You can go to hell. C'mon, boys, we're out of this. Let the *big man* handle it himself."

Beal's right ham fist came up with a blur of speed. He mushed Spencer's mouth and knocked the smaller man on his butt. "When I give an order, it is obeyed."

He turned on one heel and started for the tie-rail at one end of the station. Spencer's underlings followed him, gaping.

* * *

Sally Jensen stood in the shade of the porch roof. Small fists on hips, she looked across the yard at the hands gathered near the breaking corral. Young Bobby had crowded in among them. Ordinarily, that would not trouble her. But of late, the boy had taken to the newcomers as his idols. It wasn't often that Sally questioned the judgment of her husband.

In his life of enforced caution, Smoke sometimes made bad judgments about people. Sally had recently begun to hold a mild distrust toward the drifters Smoke had sent with that note. At least, he would be in San Francisco the next day and she would know where to contact him. Only thing, would she pass on her distress to worry him? He would think her taken with old maidish vapors, she scoffed at herself. A loud shout drew her attention closer to the ranch hands.

At the urging of Buck Jarvis and Jason Rucker, the new hands, Bobby Jensen had climbed over the top rail and made for a particularly fractious young stallion who stood splay-legged at the tie-rail. Foam flecked its black lips and hung in strings nearly to the ground. Its buckskin hide glistened with sweat and its bellows chest heaved from exertion. So far he had dumped three hands. A sharp pang of concern shot through Sally and she hoisted her skirts to make room for her boots to fly faster.

Running brokenly, Sally streaked toward the corral. "Bobby!" she yelled. "Bobby, don't you dare get on that horse."

Most of the hands, the old-timers, turned to look and said nothing. Buck and Jase sneered and Buck turned his head to shout encouragement to the boy. "Go on, Bobby. You know you can do it.

"That's enough!" Sally commanded. "If that boy gets on that horse, you can pick up your time as of now."

"Awh, come on, Miz Jensen. You're gonna make a sissy out of him," Jason Rucker brushed off the threat.

"Cole, you hear me?" Sally called to their winter foreman, Cole Travis.

"Sure do, Miss Sally," Travis responded, a tight smile on his face.

"I mean what I say. If Bobby gets on that horse, you throw them off the Sugarloaf."

An uncomfortable silence followed in which Sally reached the cluster of hands at the corral. Buck would not meet her eye. Jase turned his back insolently. Sally marched to the gate, slid the bar, and entered. She raised an imperious hand toward the lad who stood before her, the pain of humiliation written on his face.

"Come on out of here, Bobby," she ordered quietly.

"But I *can* ride him. I know I can."

"I'm not going to argue with you. Come with me."

"Please? He's worn down some now. At least let me try?"

"Not another word. Come along."

Outside the corral again, with Bobby in tow, Sally had the first pang of regret as she looked at his miserable expression. Huge, fat tears welled up and threatened to spill down his face. She knew she had done right! Then another part of her mind mocked her: *How would Smoke have handled it?*

"*Saaan Fraaaan-cisssco. Last stop. Saaan Fraaan-ciiisssco!*" the conductor brayed as he passed through the cars of the *Daylight Express.*

Smoke Jensen, who had been snoozing, tipped up the brim of his hat and gazed out the window of the Pullman car. A row of weathered gray shanties—shacks, actually— lined the twin tracks. A gaggle of barefoot, shirtless boys of roughly eight to ten years old made impudent gestures to the passengers as the train rolled past their squalid homes. How different from youngsters in the High Lonesome, Smoke mused. There they would be clean as Sunday-to-meeting clothes, bundled up to their ears in coats and scarves and in rabbit-fur-lined moccasins or boots to protect them from the cold. Already the car felt warm, after their descent from the low coastal range. Gradually the speed drained off the creaking, swaying coaches.

Now grim factories and warehouses took the place of the shacks. No doubt those youngsters' fathers toiled in these places, Smoke reasoned. How could any man labor day after day with the only light from windows too high up to see out of and only dingy inner walls to look at. How could they stand it? He wondered again if Thunder had received proper care.

His twice-daily visits to the stock car had not provided time enough to make a thorough check. Smoke had acquired the 'Palouse stallion from an old Arapaho horse trader to add new vitality to the bloodline of his prize horses. The Arapaho had obtained Thunder from the Nez Perce who had raised him from a colt and gently broken him. The beast proved to be better as a saddle horse than as a breeder. Accordingly, Smoke had ridden him for more than three years now. A sturdy mountain horse, Thunder could cover ground with the best of them. For years Smoke had worn smooth-knob cavalry spurs out of respect for his horses. As a result, not a scar showed on Thunder's flanks. A huge rush of steam and a jolt of compressing couplers announced the arrival at the depot as the locomotive braked to a stop.

Smoke roused himself and retrieved his saddlebags from a rack overhead. At night, the same rack served as frame for the fold-down bed that he had occupied for two nights. Not the most comfortable arrangement, Smoke acknowledged, but it beat the daylights out of a chair car. A trip back East with Sally several years ago had spoiled him. They had ridden in luxury in the private car of the president of the Denver and Rio Grande.

They had their own room, and a big, soft bed that did not even creak when they made love. Now, *that* was the way

to travel. Until man learned to fly—a foolish notion!—
Smoke would prefer the pleasures of a private car for
long-distance journeys. When the Pullman finally came to
a jerking halt, Smoke walked down the aisle to the open
vestibule door and outside, to descend from the train.

He had a short wait while the crew positioned a ramp
and opened the stock car. A vague hunger gnawed him, so
Smoke availed himself of a large, fat tamale from a vendor
with a large white box fitted on the front of a bicycle. The
thick cornmeal roll was stuffed with a generous portion of
shredded beef and lots of spices, including chili peppers,
Smoke soon found out. Mouth afire, Smoke rigidly controlled his reaction, determined not to give the Mexican
peddler the satisfaction of seeing a *gringo* suffer.

Ten minutes later, as Smoke finished the last bite of the
savory treat, a trainman walked Thunder down the ramp.
Smoke hastened forward, but not fast enough. Typically,
Thunder, like most 'Palouse horses, liked to nip. With a jubilant forward thrust of his long, powerful neck, Thunder
sank his teeth into the shoulder of the crewman in a shallow bite.

A bellow resulted. "Tarnation, you damn nag!" the han-
dler roared, as he broke free and turned to drive a clinched
fist into the soft nose of the stallion.

Smoke Jensen's big hand closed on the offended shoulder in an iron clamp. "Don't hit my horse," he rumbled.

"I'll hit any damn' animal that bites me," the man
snarled. Then he whirled and got a look at Smoke's expression. *Jeez!* It looked as though *he'd* bite him, too.
"Uh—er—sorry, Mister. Here, you hold him an' I'll go
fetch your saddle."

Somewhat mollified, Smoke accepted the reins from the
trainman and walked Thunder down off the ramp onto the
firm ground. Fine-grained, the soil held thousands of
broken bits of seashell. Smoke studied the curiosity. The station was some distance from the bay and even further from
the ocean. Could it be that this area had once been under

water? He ceased his speculation, rubbed Thunder's nose, and slipped the big animal a pair of sugar cubes.

Crunching them noisily and with great relish, Thunder rolled his big, blue eyes. The pink of his muzzle felt silken to Smoke's touch. The 'Palouse flared black nostrils and whuffled his gratitude for the treat. Shortly the trainman returned with the saddle and blanket, which he fitted to Thunder's back with inexpert skill. Amused, Smoke wondered how someone could get through life without acquiring the ability to properly saddle a horse. He took over when the man bent to fasten the cinch.

"Here, I'll do that. You hold him."

With a dubious look at Thunder, the man hesitated. "You sure he won't bite me again?"

"Positive. I gave him some sugar cubes."

"That's all it takes?"

Smoke chuckled. "That's all it will take this time."

He tightened the cinch strap and adjusted his saddlebags, tying them in place with latigo strips. Then he swung into the saddle and rode off toward the far side of town.

Narrow, steep streets thronged with people made up the hilly city of San Francisco. Horse-drawn streetcars clanged noisily to scatter pedestrians from the center of the thoroughfares. Smoke Jensen steered his mount though the crowds with a calming hand ready to pat the trembling neck that denoted the creature's dislike of close places and milling, noisy humanity.

"Easy, boy, use your best manners," he murmured. "We'll be out of here soon."

The center of town consisted of tall buildings, four and five stories each, like red-brick and wooden canyon walls. Even Smoke Jensen felt hemmed in. Too many people in far too little space. He passed the opera house, its marquee emblazoned with bold, black letters.

TONIGHT!
MADAME SCHUMAN-HINKE

Whoever she was, she must be important, Smoke thought. Those letters were *big*. Beyond the commercial district, which appeared to be growing with all the frenzy of a drowned-out anthill, tenements stood in rows, rising to small duplexes and single-family dwellings. Smoke found the street he sought and began to climb another hill. This one was wider, and led to a promontory that overlooked the bay. The higher he went, the better the quality of the houses.

At last he came to an opulent residence that had a spectacular view of the Golden Gate, as the harbor was being called lately. Tall masts billowed with white bellies, a stately, swift clipper ship sailed toward port, a snowy bone in her teeth so large it could be seen from Smoke's vantage point. He watched her for a while, captivated by her grace. Then he nudged Thunder and rode on to his destination.

When he got there, his instincts kicked in and his hackles rose. Smoke cast a guarded gaze from side to side and along the street. What roused his sixth sense was the sight of a black mourning wreath that hung below the oval etched-glass portion of the large front door of the stately mansion. He slowed Thunder and eased off the safety thong on the hammer of his right-hand Colt.

When he reached the wide, curving drive, he halted and looked all around. Not even a bird twittered. Smoke could feel eyes on him—some from inside the mansion, others from hidden places along the avenue. A cast-iron statue of a uniformed jockey stood at the edge of a portico. Smoke reined in there, dismounted, and looped his reins through the ring in the metallic boy's upraised hand. Four long strides brought him to the door. A brass knocker shone from the right-hand panel. Smoke had barely reached for it when the door opened.

A large, portly black woman, dressed in the black-and-white uniform and apron of a housekeeper, gave him a hard, distrustful look. "We's closed. Cain't you see the wreath?"

"I'm not a—ah—client. I'm Smoke Jensen. Here to see Miss Francie."

Suddenly the stern visage crumpled and large tears welled in the eyes. "Miss Francie, she dead, suh."

"What?" Smoke blurted. "When? What happened?"

"We's ain't supposed to talk about it, the po-lice said. Miss Lucy, she in charge now. Do you wish to talk to her?"

"Yes, of course."

He followed her into the unfamiliar hallway. Although Smoke had known of the place, and known Francie Delong for years, he had never visited the extravagant bordello. The housekeeper directed the way to a large, airy room, darkened now by the drawn drapes. A large bar occupied one long wall, a cut-crystal mirror behind it. Comfortable chairs in burgundy velvet upholstery surrounded small white tables.

"Wait here, if you will, Mr. Jensen. Miss Lucy will join you shortly."

"Thank you." Hat in hand, Smoke waited.

Lucy arrived a few minutes later. She wore a high-necked black dress set off with a modest display of fine white lace. Her eyes, red and puffy from crying, went wide when she took in the visitor. "You have to be Smoke Jensen. Francie speaks—spoke—so highly of you." The tears came again.

"Miss Lucy, I'm sorry. I didn't know something had happened to Francie. Was she sick for long?"

"It—wasn't sickness. She was—she was run down by a stolen carriage." An expression of horror crossed her face and she covered it with both hands, sobbing softly.

So that's why the police said not to discuss it. Lips tight, Smoke laid his hat on the bar and stepped to Lucy, putting a big hand on her shaking shoulder. "It must have been terrible for you. For all the girls," Smoke said helplessly, unaccustomed to words of condolence. "When did it happen?"

"Three days ago. It was a foggy day. Francie went out to see her banker. She never came back." Lucy drew a deep breath and shuddered out a sigh in an effort to regain control.

"I received a note saying someone would meet me here."

"I don't know anything about that. I'm sorry."

"We'll wait here a while, then."

"Oh, we cannot. There's to be a reading of Francie's will at half past noon. I am to be there, and you are expected, too." She looked confused. "I sent you a telegram when I learned. We barely have time to get there as it is."

"I still want to confirm who wrote me to meet him here."

"I'll leave word with Ophilia as to where we'll be."

"Your housekeeper?"

"Yes. All the girls are to be at the reading of the will."

"All right. Let me write a little note."

Lucy took paper, a pen, and an inkwell from behind the bar. Smoke wrote briefly. He gave it to Ophilia and turned to Lucy. "How are you getting to this?"

"We have a carriage. You're welcome to come along."

"I have my horse outside. I'll accompany you."

"I'll be relieved if you do." She frowned slightly, her eyes gone distant. "Something doesn't seem . . . right about the way Francie died. It will feel nice to have a strong man around. We will meet you on the drive."

Raymond Wagner looked up from his study of the flake gold and several rice-sized nuggets he had retrieved from his sluice. The splash and rumble of water racing down the riffles and screens of his sluice box had masked the sound of hoofbeats. He stared into the ugly, impassive faces of the three men whom he had run off his claim not four days ago. They had another one with them.

This time it was he who came forward and thrust the deed for him to sign. "Sign this," Tyrone Beal demanded.

"I told them fellers I would not and I say the same to you. Get off my claim."

"Sign it and save us all a lot of trouble."

"Gehen Sie zu Hölle!" a red-faced Wagner snarled in German.

Beal sighed. "Go to hell, huh? Well, I tried to be nice."

With that, he whipped the pick handle off his left shoulder and swung it at Wagner's head. The prospector ducked and lashed out a hard fist that caught an off-balance Beal in the chest. He staggered backward, recovered, and waded in on his victim. Another swing broke the bone in Wagner's upper left arm. Beal rammed him in the gut, then the chest, and cracked the dancing tip off the stout German's chin. Teeth flew.

Wagner had not a chance. Methodically, Beal beat him with the hickory cudgel. Driven to his knees, Wagner feebly raised his arms to shield his head. Beal broke three of Wagner's ribs with the next blow. Then came a merciful pause while Beal looked over his shoulder at the others.

"Don't just stand there. Give him a good lesson."

Kicks and punches pounded Raymond Wagner into a bleeding hulk curled on the ground in an attempt to protect his vital spots. The pick handle in Beal's hands made a wet smack against Wagner's back and the prospector rolled over to face upward. His eyes had swollen shut and a flap of loose skin hung down over his left eye. His mouth was ruined and large lumps had distorted his forehead. Beal prodded him with the bloody end of the handle.

"We'll be back when you've healed enough to sign this deed."

Without another word, they left. Raymond Wagner lay on his side again and shivered in agony. Slowly the world dimmed around him.

4

Buck Jarvis and Jason Rocker looked up from the generous slabs of pie on their noon dinner plates. They fixed long, hungry, speculative looks on Sally Jensen as she distributed more of one of her famous pastries to the other hands. Only four days and Sally had grown to dislike them intensely. Forcing herself to ignore their lascivious stares, she turned away.

Jason leaned toward Buck and whispered softly into his ear, "Wonder what her body looks like under that dress?"

"I wonder what it would look like *without* a dress," Buck responded.

"I bet them legs go on forever," Jason stated wistfully.

"Shoot, man, she's too old for you."

Jason thrust out his chin. "I'm willin' to find out. Some of them older wimmin is the best ride you can get. They appreciate it more."

"You be blowin' smoke, Jason."

"Am not. My pappy tole me that when I was a youngin.'"

Buck sighed regretfully. "Well, neither one of us will get a chance to find out, you can be sure of that."

"Don't count on it, Buck. I reckon her man is gonna be gone a long time. Wimmin get to needin' things, know what I mean?"

* * *

Smoke Jensen had half the hall yet to cover when a loud pounding came on the door. Ophilia materialized out of a small drawing room and beat Smoke to the entrance. She opened the portal to reveal six tough-looking men.

"I wanna see whoever's runnin' this fancy bawdy house," a wart-faced man at the center of the first rank demanded.

"I'm sorry, we are not receiving clients at this time. There's been a death."

"Yeah. We know. An' we're here to throw you soiled doves out. This place don't belong to you."

Icily Ophilia defied them, drawing up her ample girth like a fusty old hen. "That is to be determined at the reading of Miss Francie's will this afternoon. Until then, no one is going anywhere."

"I have the say on that, Mammy," the unpleasant man barked, as he pushed past the housekeeper.

"I think not," Smoke Jensen's voice cracked in the quiet of the hall.

"Who the hell are you?"

"A man who does not like rude louts." Smoke advanced and the intruder retreated.

Back on the porch, the knobby-faced man regained his belligerence. "We come to evict them whores and we're gonna do it," he snarled.

"Who do you work for?" Smoke demanded.

"That's none of your business."

Smoke bunched the man's shirt in his big left fist and hauled him an inch off the ground. "I think it is. Is it the city? If so, by what right do they say these ladies must leave?"

A carriage had pulled around from the stable behind the house and nine lovely young women peered out with surprise at the scene before them. Lucy dismounted and stormed across the lawn and drive to the front steps. Hands on hips, she confronted the six unwelcome visitors.

"What exactly is going on here?"

"You're out in the street. My boss is taking over this place."

"Who is your boss?"

"Gargantua here asked me the same thing. I didn't tell him and I won't tell you."

Smoke Jensen shook him like a terrier with a rat. "You do a lot of talking to say so little. Maybe I should loosen your jaw a little and rattle something out of you."

The thug turned nasty. "Put me down or I'll blow a hole clear through you."

If only to better get to his six-gun, Smoke set the man on his feet again. At once, the ruffian, a head shorter than Smoke Jensen, shot out a hand and pushed Smoke in the chest. Smoke popped him back, then two more of the evictors jumped him.

Smoke planted an elbow in the gut of one and rolled a shoulder in the way of the other so that he punched his boss instead of Smoke. He took in the remaining three standing in place on the bottom step, staring. That wouldn't last long, Smoke rightly assumed. Time to give them something to worry about.

Smoke Jensen spun to his left and drove a hard, straight right to the chest of the bruiser who kept punching him. He followed with a left, then swung his right arm in a wide arc to sweep the smaller man on that side off his feet. By then, their leader had recovered himself enough to return to the scuffle. He lowered his head and came at Smoke with a roar.

Roaring back, Smoke met him with a kick to one knee. Something made a loud pop and the thug howled in pain and abruptly sat down. Smoke returned his attention to the last upright opponent. He moved in obliquely, confusing the brawler as to his intent. The man learned quickly enough what Smoke had in mind when big, powerful hands closed into fists thudded into his chest and gut. Wind whistled out of his lungs and black spots danced before his eyes. Wobble-legged, he tried to defend himself, only to be driven to his knees. Smoke finished him with a smash to the top of his bowed head. The other three, Smoke noted, had been suitably impressed.

They remained where they had been, eyes wide and mouths agape. Not so their leader. Unwilling to face that barrage of fists again, he decided to up the ante. A big, wicked knife appeared in his hand from under his coat. Sunlight struck gold off the keen edge as he forced himself upright, wincing at the pain in his leg. He took a wild swipe at Smoke Jensen, expecting to see his intended victim back up in fright.

Smoke obliged him instead with a swift draw of his .45 Peacemaker and quick discharge of a cartridge. The bullet shattered the thug's right shoulder joint.

"D'ja see that?" one of the less belligerent ones croaked. "Let's get out of here."

"Help me, you idiots!" their wounded leader bellowed. "Get me away from here."

They moved with alacrity, eyes fixed on the menace of the six-gun in Smoke's hand. Ignoring the continued yelps of discomfort, they dragged their leader away. With order restored, Smoke Jensen reholstered his revolver and tipped his hat to the soiled doves in the carriage.

"I apologize for the unpleasantness, ladies," he told them politely.

"Quite all right," Lucy replied. "I enjoy seeing scum like that get their come-uppance. We'll lead the way to Lawyer Pullen's office."

Brian Pullen had his office over the Bank of Commerce on Republic Street. Smoke Jensen was able to tie up at a public water trough, which Thunder appreciated. The ladies had to place their oversized vehicle in a lot next door to the bank. Smoke walked there and escorted them to the outside staircase that led to the lawyer's office. The sight of all those painted ladies turned more than a few heads.

Rising from behind a cluttered desk, Brian Pullen extended a hand in greeting. "You must be Mr. Jensen. Lucy—uh—ladies, I'll send my law clerk for more chairs. Please, make yourselves at home."

The lawyer turned out to be younger than Smoke had expected. His well-made and stylishly cut suit showed his prosperity without being ostentatious. Pullen wore his sandy-blond hair in a part down the middle. Not one to make snap judgments, Smoke Jensen found himself liking the youthful attorney. Chairs began to arrive and with a twitter of feminine voices the soiled doves seated themselves.

Smoke noted that Pullen had mild gray-green eyes, which he imagined could become glacial when arguing before a jury, against a prosecutor in defense of a client. He spoke precisely, addressing them in an off-hand manner.

"There is another gentleman expected, though he appears to be late. We'll give him until one o'clock."

They passed the time in small talk. Pullen made an effort to draw Smoke out about his circumstances. "I understand you are in ranching?"

"Horse breeding. I have a good, strong line of quarter horses and another of 'Palouse horses."

"Weren't they first bred by Indians?"

"Yes, Mr. Pullen. The Nez Perce," Smoke answered precisely.

"Please, call me Brian. I'm not old enough to be *Mister* Pullen. You are in Montana, or Colorado, is it?"

"Colorado, Brian," Smoke replied.

Pullen frowned and checked his big turnip watch. These short answers weren't getting him anywhere. If only the other man would arrive so they could get on with the reading of the will. He'd give it one more try.

"You've been a lawman, is that right?"

"Yes. Off and on."

"On the frontier?"

"Of course."

Brian sighed. "I suppose you have some exciting tales to tell."

"Nothin' much to tell. At least, not in mixed company. Blood and violence tends to upset the ladies." Smoke gave Lucy a mischievous wink.

Another look at the watch. "Well, it's the witching hour, you might say. I don't believe we can delay any longer. Very well, then, let's proceed. We are here for the reading of the last will and testament of Frances Delong. As her attorney, I am well aware of the contents, and feel she exercised excellent judgment in the disposal of her estate."

He paused and opened a folded document. From a vest pocket, he produced a pair of half-glasses and perched them on his generous patrician nose. Then he began to read in a formal tone. "'I, Frances Delong, being of sound mind and body, do hereby bequeath all my worldly possessions as follows: to my dear friends at the San Francisco Home for Abandoned Cats, the sum of one thousand dollars. To my faithful employees,'"—here, Brian Pullen read off the names—"'I leave the sum of five hundred dollars each. To my ever faithful assistant, Lucy Glover, I leave in perpetuity the revenue from the saloon bar at my establishment. All my other property, liquid assets, and worldly goods I leave to the man who once saved my life, Kirby Jensen.' This was dated and signed six months ago," Brian added.

Smoke had always hated his first name and had not used it except under the utmost necessity for many years, so the shocking import of what the lawyer read did not strike him at once—not until the door opened and a jocular voice advised him, "What do you think of being the proprietor of the most elaborate sporting house in San Francisco, *mon ami?*"

Just as he had expected. Louis Longmont, his old friend and fellow gunfighter, stood in the doorframe with a broad grin on his face. Smoke came to his boots quickly and crossed the short space. Both men gave one another a back-slapping embrace.

"I thought it was you who sent me that mysterious message. Now, tell me about it."

"I will, *mon ami,* but not here or now. We need some place to be alone for what I have to say."

Sally Jensen stood over the boy seated at the kitchen table. Bobby had his face turned up to hers, though he would not meet her eyes. Not ten minutes ago Sally had caught the twelve-year-old behind the big hay barn, a hand-made quirley in his lips, head wreathed in white tobacco smoke. Now, rather than the hangdog expression of shame, his face registered defiance. His explanation of the smoking incident had shocked and angered her.

"Buck made it for me. Jason said I was big enough to take up smokin'."

She hadn't liked the looks of them when they'd first arrived, and she hadn't grown any fonder of them since. This was just about the last straw.

This morning, they had both remained in the bunkhouse, claiming sickness, when the hands had ridden out to check the prize horses on graze in the west pasture. Not long ago they had come out and moseyed around the barnyard. Bobby, who had been laid up with his bunged-up toe since three days ago, had joined them. The three of them had gone around behind the barn.

Sally, at work at the kitchen sink, had kept an eye on the barn, wondering what they might be doing. When enough time had passed to arouse her suspicions, she wiped her hands on her apron and walked out to check on them. She had found Bobby alone, smoking a cigarette. She descended on him in a rush and snatched the weed from his mouth. Crushing it with a slender boot toe, she had demanded to know what he thought he was doing. His explanation only increased her pique.

"Well, Buck Jarvis and Jason Rucker are neither your mother nor your father. Smoke would have a fit if he knew what you've done. Come with me to the kitchen."

Seated now, with Sally over him, Bobby said, "Does it mean you are not going to tell Smoke? You know? What you said? That he would have a fit if he *knew* what I had done?"

"I'm disappointed in you, Bobby. I don't know now if I will tell Smoke or not. But you are staying inside for the rest of the day, young man."

"Awh, Miss Sal—Mom, I feel okay now. No more sore toe. Please let me eat with the hands. It's goin' on noon anyhow."

Sally considered it. "All right. But you stay away from Buck and Jason, hear?"

"Yes, ma'am."

"You may go to your room now."

"Yes, ma'am." Feet dragging, Bobby headed for the staircase that led to the second-floor bedrooms.

Although he ordinarily slept in the bunkhouse with the hands, since the arrival of Buck and Jason, Sally had insisted that Bobby return to his room in the main house. Something about them made her mighty uncomfortable.

She had good reason to recall that when the hands arrived at noon, Buck and Jason joined them. The two drifters stuffed themselves, then begged off work on the pretext that they still ailed a mite. After the hands rode off and Bobby came back inside, they lounged around on a bench outside the bunkhouse. When she went outside to hang up a small wash, they gave her decidedly lascivious looks.

Aware of that, Sally thought to herself it was a good thing she was not entirely alone.

Dinner for Smoke Jensen and Louis Longmont was at the Chez Paris on the waterfront, near the huge pier that people were already calling Fishermen's Wharf. The fancy eating place catered to San Francisco's wealthy and near-wealthy. White linen cloths covered the tables, their snowy expanse covered with matching napkins in silver rings, heavy silverware, and tall, sparkling candleholders, complete with chalky candles. Thick maroon velvet drapes framed the tall windows, each foot-square pane sparkling from frequent cleaning. Paintings adorned the walls, along with sconces with more tapers flickering in the current sent up by scurrying waiters.

The staff wore black trousers and short white jackets over brilliant lace-fronted shirts and obsidian bow ties. The maitre d' was formally attired in tails. He led Smoke and the New Orleans gunfighter to a table in an alcove. Seated, they ordered good rye. While it was being fetched, Louis perused the menu.

"I'll order for us both, if you don't mind, Smoke," he offered with a fleeting smile. The menu was in French.

Smoke took a glance and smiled back. "Yes, that would be fine."

When the waiter returned with their drinks on a silver tray, Louis was ready to order. "We'll start with the escargots. Then . . ." He went on to order a regular feast. He added appropriate wines for each course and sat back to enjoy his whiskey.

After an appreciative sip, he inclined his long, slim torso toward Smoke, seated across from him. "You are no doubt wondering why I so summarily summoned you here, *non?*"

Smoke pulled a droll expression. "I will admit to some curiosity."

Louis pursed his lips and launched into his explanation. "Francie was still alive when I sent that letter. It is not about her rather—unusual—demise. Something is afoot among the big power brokers of Northern and Central California. There are rumors of a secret cabal recently formed that includes Cyrus Murchison, the railroad mogul, Titus

Hobson, the mining magnate, and Gaylord Huntley, the shipping king."

"Hummm. That's some big guns, right enough. Murchison is the biggest fish, of course. Even in Colorado we have read of his doings in the newspapers."

"Well, yes. Word is that they are out to establish a monopoly on all transportation and gold mining. But, that's not all, *mon ami.* Phase two of their scheme, I have learned since coming to San Francisco, is to then go after title to all of the land in private hands.

"They will strangle out all the small farmers and shop owners with outrageous shipping rates by rail, water, or freighting company." Louis paused and nodded sagely. "Part of it, too, is to take control of all forms of entertainment: theaters, saloons, and bordellos."

"Not too unusual for captains of commerce," Smoke observed dryly. "A bit ambitious, but I'd wager any group of powerful men might seek to eliminate competition."

"Quite true," Louis agreed. "Yet this is no ordinary power play. The cabal is supposed to have made an unholy alliance, which has prompted me to seek your help. Murchison and company are believed to have made an accommodation with the dreaded Triad Society." At Smoke's quizzical expression, he explained, "The Tongs of Chinatown."

Smoke raised an eyebrow and his eyes widened. A certain darkness colored his gray gaze. "Of course I'll help, Louis. I think I've already had an encounter with some of the cabal's henchmen." He went on to describe the incident at Francie's.

Louis listened with interest and nodded frequently. "That sounds like their methods, all right. Must be the railroad police."

"Are you staying at Francie's?" Smoke asked, as the waiter arrived with their succulent, garlicky-smelling snails. Smoke took one look and made a face.

"Try them. You'll like them."

"I don't eat anything that crawls on its belly and leaves a trail of slime behind."

"Smoke, my friend, you must become more worldly. Escargots are a delicacy."

"Sally squashes them when they show up in her garden."

"These are raised on clean sand and fed only the best lettuce and other vegetable tops."

"They are still snails."

"Suit yourself," Louis said, as he picked up the tongs and fastened them onto one of the green-brown shells.

With a tiny silver fork he plucked the mollusk from its shelter and smacked his lips in appreciation. His hazel eyes twinkled in anticipation as he popped the snail onto his tongue. His eyes closed as he chewed on it thoughtfully. Smoke made a face and sipped from the glass of sherry the waiter had poured. Not bad. The aroma of the escargots reached his nostrils and they flared. His stomach rumbled. He had not eaten since the depot cafe that morning, he recalled. Tentatively, he reached for the tongs and clamped them on a snail shell.

"Aha! You have joined the sophisticates. Enjoy. Now, in answer to your question, no. I am staying at Ralston's Palace."

"I haven't taken a room. But I think one of us should stay at Francie's. The trash that showed up might come back."

"Since you own it now, it sounds reasonable to me that it is you who stays there, *mon ami*. I'll meet you there in the morning."

"Make it early. The way I see it, we have a lot to accomplish."

When they had finished the lemon *gelato,* Louis Longmont offered to accompany Smoke Jensen back to the bordello. Smoke gladly accepted; he enjoyed the company of his friend. Their route took them past the pagoda gateway that marked the entrance to Chinatown. Beyond it, a dark alley mouth loomed. They had barely passed it when the men in black pajama-like clothes attacked.

Tong hatchets whirred in the moonlight, striking a myriad of colors from the cheerful lanterns bobbing in the light onshore breeze behind Smoke and Louis. Both gunfighters had been walking their horses and now mounted swiftly. A man on horseback had it all over one afoot. With eight Oriental thugs rushing at them, it became even more critical.

In the lead, one snarling, flat-faced Tong soldier swelled rapidly. Smoke reared Thunder and prodded with a single spur in a trained command. The black cap flew one way and the cue flung backward as Thunder flicked out a hoof and flattened the Tong face. Then the others swarmed down on Smoke and Louis.

5

The Chinese gangsters soon discovered that their Tong hatchets might well strike terror into the merchants of Chinatown, but they proved no match for blazing six-guns in the hands of the two best gunfighters in the West. Smoke Jensen and Louis Longmont opened up simultaneously with their .45 Colts. Hot lead zipped through the air. Louis's first round rang noisily off the blade of a hatchet descending on the head of his horse.

Its owner howled in pain and dropped the weapon. Smoke put a bullet through the hollow of another Tong soldier's throat and blew out a chunk of his spine. Suddenly limp, the Asian thug went down to jerk and twitch his life away. Louis fired again. Another Tong fight master screamed and clutched his belly in a desperate attempt to keep his intestines from squirting through the nasty hole in his side where the slug had exited. Alarmed, others shrank back momentarily.

"Where did they come from, Smoke?" Louis asked cheerily, as he lined his sights on another enemy.

"I'd say that alley behind us." Smoke paused as Louis fired again. "I believe we can safely say you heard the right of it about the Tongs."

"Why is that?"

Smoke Jensen loosed a round at a squat Chinese who had recovered his nerve enough to foolishly charge the two gunfighters. "They don't even know I'm in town. You're the one who has been asking questions around San Francisco."

"I see what you mean, *mon ami*. Smoke, we had better make this fast, *non?*"

"Absolutely," Smoke agreed, as he dropped another hatchet shaker.

Wisely, the surviving pair, one of them wounded, turned and ran. The wide street held a litter of bodies and a sea of blood. Longmont's horse flexed nostrils and whuffled softly, uneasy over the blood smell. Both men reloaded in silence.

"Shall we go on to Francie's?" Smoke asked lightly.

"Hadn't we better report this to the police?" Louis asked.

"If the police haven't showed by now, I imagine they already know and don't want to get involved. We'll leave these here for whoever wants them."

Freshly ground Arabica beans usually made the day for Cyrus Murchison. This morning, his coffee tasted bitter in his mouth. The reason was the presence of Titus Hobson and Gaylord Huntley in his breakfast room—that, and the news they brought. The news came in the form of Xiang Wai Lee. The slight-statured Chinese could barely suppress his fury.

"The first time we are to perform a service for you, we are sent out against men of inhuman capability." His queue of long black hair bobbed in agitation as he hissed at Murchison. "You told us that Louis Longmont was a fop, a dandy, a gambler, an easy target. Not so," Lee informed the wealthy conspirators. "Then there was the other man with him. Such speed and accuracy with a firearm."

"Who was that?" Murchison demanded.

"What does it matter?" Xiang snapped. "Only two of the

men sent after Longmont and his companion survived the encounter."

"That doesn't answer my question. Who is this other man?" Ordinarily, this Oriental would not be in this part of his house. Would not even gain access, except by the servants' entrance to the back hallway and pantry. Murchison took his presence as an insult.

"My two soldiers who lived informed me that Longmont used the word 'smoke' as though it was a name."

Hobson paled and gasped. "He can't still be alive."

"Who?" Murchison barked.

"Smoke Jensen," Hobson named him. "He is reputed to be the best gunfighter who ever lived. If he still is alive, we have a major problem on our hands."

"Preposterous," Murchison dismissed.

Hobson would not let it go. "He has killed more men and maimed many more than any other three shootists you can name. His name is legend in Colorado. When I was there last, Smoke Jensen had devastated a force of forty men who hunted him through the mountains for a month. It was they who died, not Jensen. He has been an outlaw and a lawman.

"There are some who say he has back-shot many men he has killed." Hobson paused to catch his breath. "Personally, I don't believe that. I have also heard that to say so to his face is to get yourself dead rather quickly. He is mean and wild and totally savage. He's lived with the Indians. He was raised by another total barbarian, a mountain man named Preacher. The pair struck terror into the hearts of the men in the mountains for years."

Murchison snorted derisively, totally unimpressed. "What impact can a couple of aging gunfighters have on our project?" His small, deep-set blue eyes glittered malevolently in his florid face as he cut his gaze to Xiang. "If your men cannot handle this, Tyrone Beal and his railroad detectives can take care of a mere two men, no matter that they are good with their guns. Now, get out of here, all of you, and let me finish my breakfast."

Smoke Jensen punched back his chair from the round oak table in the breakfast nook of the Delong mansion. Frilly lace curtains hung over the panes of the bay window, with plump cushions on the bench seats under them. This excess of the feminine touch made Smoke a bit uneasy. If he kept the place, there would have to be some changes. No. That was out of the question. Sally would be bound to find out. When she did, she would skin him alive.

Amusement touched his lips as he recalled the time Sally had herself inherited a bordello from a favored aunt who had passed away. That and a big ranch that stood in the way of the ambitions of powerful, greedy men who needed some lessons in manners. Smoke Jensen had given those lessons, with fatal results. No, Sally would never favor him owning a bawdy house. Lucy Clover's entrance banished the images of the past.

"Mr. Longmont is here, Smoke."

"Thank you, Lucy. Have Ophilia show him in. Join us— we have a little strategy to discuss."

"Oh?"

"Yes. About protection for this establishment, among other things," Smoke informed her.

Lucy left him alone to return with Louis Longmont. *"Bonjour, mon ami,"* Louis greeted.

"Oui, c'est tres bon," Smoke answered back with almost his entire French vocabulary.

Louis chuckled. "They must have fed you well. What is in order for today?"

"First, we must make provisions for someone to protect this place." He paused to sip the marvelous coffee.

"You think there will be trouble?" Lucy asked anxiously.

"Those louts who came yesterday will be back, count on

it. And we can't stay here all the time. Now that I own the place, I want to make sure all of you are safe."

"You make it sound ominous," a pale-faced Lucy observed.

Smoke was disinclined to play it down. "Believe me, it is."

Ophilia appeared in the doorway. "Those nasty gentlemen from yesterday are here again, Miss Lucy. And they brung friends."

Smoke's lips tightened. "How many?"

"They's about a dozen, Mister Smoke."

Smoke came to his boots. Louis started to rise. "I'll take care of it, Louis."

"If you say so, *mon ami*," he answered with a shrug.

"This way, Mister Smoke," Ophilia directed. Although richer by $500, thanks to Francie, she still performed her duties as housekeeper flawlessly.

At the door, Smoke quickly counted the twelve men standing in a semicircle at the foot of the porch steps in three ranks. Several of them held stout hickory pick handles. Tyrone Beal, who had returned only that morning on the early train, acted as spokesman this time.

"Tell those girls that they are to be out of here within half an hour. This place has been sold for back taxes and the new owner, the California Central Railroad, wants immediate occupancy."

After seeing all the books and ledgers on Francie's establishment the previous day in Pullen's office, Smoke knew that there were no back taxes. "I have some bad news for you, whoever you are."

Beal drew himself up. "Captain Tyrone Beal of the Railroad Police. I'm not interested in any news you might have. I said out they go, and that's what I mean."

"The bad news, *Captain* Beal," and Smoke put a sneer on the title, "is that you are a liar. All taxes have been paid up through next year. I'm the owner now, so you had best back off so no one gets hurt."

Goaded by the insult, Beal launched himself at Smoke.

Jensen waited for him to the precise second, then powered a hard right into the face of the railroad detective. Beal, his feet off the ground, flew down the steps faster than he had ascended them. His pick handle clattered after him. The others similarly armed, pressed forward, dire intent written on their faces.

Smoke turned slightly and called over his shoulder, "Louis, would you like to join the dance?"

"I would be delighted," Louis said from the doorway, where Smoke had anticipated he would be.

Back-to-back, they met the railroad thugs. The first to attack came at Smoke. When he swung his pick handle, Smoke ducked and kicked him in the gut. The billet of wood went flying. Smoke finished him with a left-right combination to the right side of his head and jaw. He fell like a rumpled pile of clothes. Another stick-wielder went for Louis.

The New Orleans gunhand gave his hapless assailant a quick lesson in the French art of *la Savate*. He kicked the brawler three times before the man could get set to swing his hickory club. His swing disturbed, he staggered drunkenly when he missed. Louis kicked him twice in the back, once in each kidney. Grunting in misery, he went to his knees, one hand on the tender flesh at the small of his back. Louis swung sideways and put the toe of his boot to the bully's temple. He went down like a stone.

Smoke popped a hard right to the mouth of an ox of a man who only shook his head and pressed his attack. Smoke went to work on the protruding beer gut. His hard fists buried to the wrists in blubber. Still he failed to faze his opponent. Instead, he launched a looping left that caught Smoke alongside his ear. Birdies twittered and chimes tinkled in the head of Smoke Jensen. He shook his head to clear it and received a stinging blow to his left cheek that would produce a nasty yellow, purple, and green bruise.

Another pick handle whizzed past his head and pain exploded down his back when it struck the meaty portion at the base of his neck. Left arm numbed, he cleared tear-blurred eyes and snapped a solid right boot toe to the inner side of his attacker's thigh. A squeal of pain erupted from thick, pouting lips. Smoke sucked in air and stepped close.

With a sizzling right, he pulped those flabby lips. The blow had enough heft behind it to produce the tips of three broken teeth. *Finish him fast,* thought Smoke, as feeling returned to his left arm. Two powerful punches to the gut brought the man's guard, and the gandy stick, down. Smoke felt the cheekbone give under the terrible left he delivered below the man's eye. His right found the vulnerable cluster of nerves under the hinge of the jaw and the man went to sleep in an instant.

Louis had four men down in front of him and worked furiously on a fifth. Not bad, Smoke thought. He sought his fourth. The sucker came willingly to the slaughter. Wide-eyed and yelling, he rushed directly at Smoke. The last mountain man sidestepped him at the proper moment and clipped him with a rabbit punch at the base of his skull. His jaw cracked when he struck the lowest marble step. Suddenly Smoke had no more enemies. The remaining three thugs hung back, uncertain, and decidedly impressed by what these two men could do. Smoke gestured to the fallen men.

"Drag this trash off my property and don't bother to come back," he commanded hotly.

Satisfied with the results, he and Louis turned to walk back in the mansion. Enraged at this ignominious defeat, Tyrone Beal wouldn't leave it alone. Mouth frothing with foam, he shrieked at his henchmen. "What's the matter with you three? Finish them off. Kill the bastards!"

Six-guns exploded to life and a bullet took the hat off Louis Longmont's head. Instantly the two gunfighters turned to meet the threat. Crouched, they spun and drew at the same time. Smoke's .45 Colt spoke first. He pinwheeled the middle hard case, who did a little jig with the devil and expired on his face in the grass. Louis took his man in the stomach, doubling him over with a pitiful groan. Smoke's Peacemaker barked again.

The slug burned a mortal trail through the lower left portion of the railroad policeman's chest and burst his heart. He tried to keep upright, but failed. Slowly he sank into a blood-soaked heap. Powder smoke still curling from the muzzle of his Colt, Smoke Jensen addressed Tyrone Beal.

"Take this garbage out of here. You would be smart not to report this to the police. We have a building full of witnesses who saw what happened. If your boss wants to verify what I said about the taxes and owning this place, he can check with Lawyer Pullen." He turned away, then paused and spoke over his shoulder. "Oh, and don't bother coming back."

Up on the porch, Louis Longmont opened the loading gate on his revolver and began to extract expended cartridges. "Now that we have finished our post-breakfast exercise, what's next?"

"Easy," Smoke said with a slow grin. "We look into this Tong business from last night and find some reliable men to guard this place while we are gone."

"They did it again," Sally Jensen testily said.

Both of those saddle tramps, as she now saw Buck and Jason, remained behind, professing illness again. She looked up sharply from the elbows-deep soap suds when their coarse laughter reached her in the wash house attached to the outer kitchen wall. Through the small, square window she saw them lolling around, obviously in perfect health. She had sent Bobby out with the hands today. Now she was thankful she had. While she watched, Buck and Jason drew their lanky frames upright and ambled in the direction of the bunkhouse well pump. She gave her washing an angry drubbing on the washboard and abandoned it.

Wiping her arms, she headed to the kitchen. She had pies in the oven, and biscuits yet to do. When she stepped out of the wash house, Buck and Jason were nowhere in sight.

"What are they up to now?" she asked herself, mildly disturbed by this disappearance.

In the kitchen she pulled the four large deep-dish pies from the oven and slid in two big pans of biscuits. That accomplished, she dusted her hands together in satisfaction. Now, she had better cut vegetables for the stew. She strode to the sink and pumped water into a granite pan. Bending down, she pulled carrots, potatoes, turnips, and onions from their storage bins. As she came upright, her eye caught movement through the window.

Buck and Jason were back. The two young saddle tramps were headed directly toward the kitchen.

Tyrone Beal and his battered henchmen sat nursing their wounds in a saloon on Beacon Street. After they'd downed several shots of liquid anesthetic, their bravado found new life.

"We're not gonna let two country hicks get the best of us, are we, Boss?" Ned Parker growled.

"Not on your ass," Tyrone Beal growled.

Parker poured another shot from the bottle. "I want a piece of that Frenchie bastard."

"Me, too," Earl Rankin piped up.

"Sam's got a busted jaw," Beal reminded them.

"They say only sissies fight with their feet," Monk Diller observed.

"Maybe so, but that Longmont broke five of Ham's ribs with a kick," Beal said, continuing to list their injuries.

"'Twern't nothin' compared to what the big guy with him did to the boys," Ned Parker summed up.

Tyrone Beal had enough of this. "No, boys, we're not

going to let them get away with it. We'll get 'em both, even if we have to shoot them in the back."

Monk Diller's tone came out surly. "You tried that. There's three of us dead for it."

Tyrone Beal wanted to keep them on the subject. "What's done is done. The thing is, we drop everything else until we can fix their wagon."

Beal had no idea of how soon the opportunity would come. Even while he detailed a plan for ambushing Smoke Jensen and Louis Longmont separately, a young Chinese entered the saloon. The bartender noticed at once.

"Get out. We don't allow your kind in here."

"I got message for thisee gentleman, Bossee," he singsonged in pidgin, pointing to Tyrone Beal.

"Okay. Deliver your message and get out."

Walking softly in his quilted shoes, the Chinese youth approached the table. "Arrogant qua'lo disgust me," he muttered in perfect English, as he came before the railroad detective.

"What was that?"

"I said bigots like that bartender make me angry. I have a message for you from Xiang Lee. Here it is." He offered a scrap of rice paper.

Beal opened the folded page and read carefully. *"Smoke Jensen and Louis Longmont are strolling around Chinatown bold as brass dragons. It is an insult to the Triad. The Tong leaders have met and consider it wise, and more convenient, if other qua'lo take care of them. You and your railroad police are to come at once. The messenger who brought this will lead you to your quarry. Xiang."*

Boyle looked up at the young Chinese. "This says you can take us to some men we want rather badly. Is that so?"

"Oh, yes."

"Then do so," he rumbled as he rose, and adjusted the hang of his six-gun.

* * *

The door to the Jensen kitchen flew open and the two young drifters swaggered in. Sally looked askance at them from where she stood washing vegetables. She dropped the paring knife in the bowl and rubbed her arms furiously on her apron. Nursing her rising anger, she turned to them with a stony face.

"What is the meaning of this?" she demanded harshly.

Buck Jarvis cut his eyes to Jason Rucker. Then they both ogled her boldly, slowly, up and down in an insolent, lewd manner. "We're here to get some of what you must have under that dress," the smirking lout nearest to Sally brayed.

Sally took two purposeful steps to the table and picked up her clutch purse. Men had seen the expression in her eyes and known fear. This pair hadn't a clue. Her scorn aimed directly at Jason, she calmed herself as she shoved a hand into the open purse. Her voice remained level when she answered his insolence.

"No, you're not."

Buck, the bolder of the two, reached for her. His eyes, slitted with lust, widened to white fear and disbelief when the bottom of the purse erupted outward toward him, a long lance of flame behind the shattered material. An unseen fist slammed into Buck's gut an inch above his navel and an instant of hot, soul-shriveling pain raked his nerves raw. He doubled over so rapidly that Sally's second round, double-actioned from her Model '77 Colt Lightning .44, smacked into the top of his head.

A giant starburst went off in the brain of Buck Jarvis and he fell dead at her feet.

White men alone on the streets of Chinatown stood out markedly in the daytime. Particularly ones as big, strong, and purposeful as Smoke Jensen and Louis Longmont. The denizens of the Chinese quarter gave them blank, impassive faces. The few who would talk to them, or even acknowledge they understood English, made uniformly unsatisfactory replies.

"So solly, no Tongs in San Francisco," one old man told Smoke, his face set in lined sincerity. He was lying through his wispy mustache and Smoke knew it.

"I know nothing of such things, gentlemen," a portly merchant in a flowing silk robe stated blandly. "The Triads did not come with us from China."

More horse crap, Smoke and Louis agreed. They moved on, creating a wake behind them. More questions and more denials. One young woman in a store that sold delicate, ornately decorated china did register definite fear in her eyes when Smoke mentioned the Tongs. Like the rest, though, she denied their existence in San Francisco.

"This is getting nowhere," Louis complained. "We waste our time and make a spectacle of ourselves, *mon ami.*"

"We'll give it another quarter hour, then try the local police," Smoke insisted.

When the quarter hour ended, they had come to the conclusion it would be a good idea to give it up. They had turned on the sidewalk to retrace their steps when Tyrone Beal and his black-and-blue henchmen located them.

"There they are! Let's get 'em!" Beal shouted. This time they had the forethought to bring along guns. A shot blasted the stately murmur of commerce in Chinatown. A piercing scream quickly followed.

6

Hot lead whipped past the head of Smoke Jensen. More screams joined the first as women, clad in the traditional Chinese costume of black or gray pegged-skirt dresses that extended to their ankles, awkwardly ran in terror from the center of violence. Louis Longmont overturned a vendor's cart heaped high with dried herbs and spices. A sputtering curse in Cantonese assailed him. Bullets slammed into the floor of the hand cart and silenced its owner.

"Smoke, on your left!" Louis shouted as he triggered a round in the direction of the shooter who riddled his temporary, and terribly insubstantial, cover.

Smoke Jensen reacted instantly, swiveled at the hips, and pumped a slug into the protruding belly of Ned Parker. Parker's mouth formed an "O," though he did not go down. He raised the Smith American in his left hand and triggered another shot at Smoke Jensen. Another miss. Smoke didn't.

His second bullet shattered Parker's sternum and blasted the life from the corrupt railroad policeman. "We've got to move, pard," he advised Louis. "There's too many of them."

"Exactement," Louis shouted back over the pandemo-

nium that had boiled along the street in the wake of the first shots.

With targets so plentiful, they had no problem with downing more of Beal's men as they emptied the cylinders of their six-guns. More Chinese women and children ran shrieking as havoc overtook their usually peaceful streets. Bent low, Smoke and Louis sprinted from cart to cart. They reloaded on the run. Chinese merchants yelled imprecations after them. Blundering along behind, the furious railroad police overturned carts of produce and dried fish. Smoke spotted a dark opening and darted into a pavilioned stall to replace the last cartridge in his .45 Colt.

A squint-eyed hard case saw Smoke duck out of sight and came in after him—his mistake. His first wild shot cut through the cloth of the left shoulder of Smoke's suit coat, not even breaking skin. Facing him, his face a cloud of fury, Smoke pumped lead into the chest of the slightly built gunman. Flung backward by impact and reflex, the dying man catapulted himself through the canvas side of the vendor's stall. The material tore noisily as the already cooling corpse sagged to the ground, partway into the street. It forced Smoke Jensen to abandon his refuge, though.

"He's over there," voices shouted from outside.

Smoke slid his keen-edged Green River knife from its sheath and cut his way to freedom through the back of the stall. The Chinese owner gobbled curses after him, his upraised fist and his long black pigtail shaking in rhythm. Smoke moved on. Then, from behind him, he heard yelps of pain and surprised curses. A quick glance over his shoulder showed him the cause.

Wielding a long, thick staff, the irate merchant took out his frustration on the rush of thugs who poured into his establishment. He struck them swiftly on shoulder points, legs, and heads. Two went down, knocked unconscious. Smoke produced a grim smile and moved on.

* * *

Tyrone Beal looked on in disbelief as his magnificent plan began to disintegrate. How could two lone men create such havoc among his men? Granted they were a wild, wooly lot, but he had managed to instill enough discipline in them that they fought together, as a unit. Yet here and now they seemed to forget all they had learned.

"Get them, you stumbling idiots!" he railed at his men, who darted around the central market square of Chinatown in confusion. "They went down the main street."

Five or six obeyed at once. Others continued to mill around. They poked six-guns into the faces of the frightened Chinese and overturned their displays of goods. "You'll not find them that way, you worthless curs," he bellowed at them.

He had sent to the railroad yards for reinforcements. It looked to Beal as though the stupidest of the lot had responded to the summons. He had no time to stay here and reorganize this mob-gone-wild. He headed along the central artery that led to this marketplace. Ahead he saw three of his better men closing in on the one called Longmont. Well and good. Put an end to him, and then go after Jensen.

Louis Longmont had a revolver in each hand; in the left one a double-action Smith and Wesson Russian .44. He crouched, eyes cutting from one hard case to the other. Only one of them had a firearm. The other two wielded knives and pick handles. One of those lunged at Louis and he leaped catlike to the side and discharged his right-hand Colt. The roar of the .45 battered at him from the wall to his left. His target fared far worse.

Shot through the hand, the bullet lodged in his shoulder, the railroad thug howled in agony and pawed at the splinters from the hickory handle that stuck in his face. On weakened legs he tottered to the side and sat down heavily on a doorstep. Believing Louis to be distracted by this, the remaining pair moved as one.

First to act, the gunman raised his weapon for a clear shot. He never got the sights aligned. Louis shot him in the forehead with the .44 Russian in his left hand. Automatically he had eared back the hammer on the .45 Peacemaker in his right and tripped the trigger a split second later. The fat slug punched into the belly of the other thug. Before he plopped on the street, Louis went into rapid motion.

A rickety cart piled high with racks of delicate bone china loomed in his vision. Louis jinxed to avoid it, only to feel the hot path of a slug burn along the outside of his left arm. That threw him off balance enough that he crashed into the mountain of tablewear. Cascading down, the fragile pieces gave off a tinkling chorus as they collided and rained onto the cobblestones to shatter into a million fragments.

"Go, qua'lo!" the owner shouted after Louis, uselessly shaking a fist. Then he repeated his insult as two of the railroad thugs blundered through the ruin. "Barbarian dog!"

Warned by this renewed outburst, Louis turned at the hips and fired behind him. The sprint of one of the hard cases turned into a stumbling shamble that sent him into the window of a shop that dispensed Chinese medicinal herbs. Shards of glass flew in sparkling array. The largest piece fell last and decapitated the already dying man. His companions hung back, mouths agape, while Louis disappeared from their view.

Slowly Smoke Jensen began to notice a change in the people of Chinatown. When they had recovered enough composure to look at the men being pursued and their pursuers, they recognized old enemies. Shouts of encouragement came from a trio of elderly men on one street corner when Smoke plunked a slug smack in the middle of one thug's chest. He had shot his one Colt dry and now used the one from the left-hand holster, worn at a slant at belt level, butt forward. Singly and in pairs, Smoke noticed, he and Louis were gunning down the trash sent to kill them.

A volley of praise in Cantonese rose when Smoke shot a stupidly grinning hard case off the top of a Moon gate. The volume of gunfire had diminished considerably. Smoke found he had to look for targets. Unfazed by this, he continued on his way toward the main entrance to Chinatown.

"Impossible!" Tyrone Beal shouted to himself. It was all over. He could see that clearly. Only five of his men remained upright, and three of them had been wounded.

Self-preservation dictated that he get the hell out of there—and fast. He didn't delay. He would report to Heck Grange; Heck would know what to do. These two were inhuman. Nobody was that good. But his eyes told him differently. Quickly, Tyrone Beal turned away from the scene of carnage and broke into a trot, departing Chinatown by the shortest route.

His course took him to the railyard of the California Central. There he banged in the office of his superior, Chief of Railroad Police Hector Grange. "Heck, God damn it, we got wiped out."

Heck Grange looked up sharply, startled by this outburst. "Did the Chinks turn on you?"

"Some of them did, near the end. But it was Longmont and Jensen. I saw it with my own eyes. We've got to do something to stop them."

Heck considered that a moment. "We can start by filing a complaint with the city police."

"What good will that do?" Beal protested.

"You've got cotton between your ears?" Heck brayed. "Mr. Murchison is a pillar of the community, right? He owns the mayor, the police, the city fathers, even the judges. So you put together a story as to how these two troublemakers, wanted for crimes against the railroad, were located by some of your men. They opened fire without warning and killed our policemen. You follow so far?"

A light of understanding glowed in Beal's eyes. "Yeah, yeah. I think I do. We put the blame on them, send the regular police after them."

"And when we get them in court, they get convicted and hanged. End of problem. Now, get on it."

Inspired by Heck's confidence, Beal departed faster than he'd arrived.

"Stay on your knees, if you want to live," Sally Jensen coldly told Jase, the would-be rapist.

The instant Buck Jarvis had fallen dead to the kitchen floor, Jason Rucker had gone alabaster white and dropped to his knees, his hands out in appeal, and begun to beg for his life. Sally had been sufficiently aroused by their brazen attempt that she had yet to simmer down enough to ensure that this worthless piece of human debris *did* survive.

"Oh, please, please, don't hurt me. We didn't mean nothin'."

The former schoolteacher in Sally Jensen made her wonder if Jase understood the meaning of a double negative. The wife of Smoke Jensen in her made her wonder why she had not already shot him. Driven by a full head of steam, she formed her answer from her outrage.

"If I turn you over to the sheriff, you will most likely hang. Why not take the easier way out with a bullet?" she coldly told him.

Jase cut his eyes to his partner, lying dead on the floor. *"Please!"* he begged in desperation, "please. I'll do anything, take any chances with the law. Just—don't—shoot—me."

Sally considered that a moment, eyes narrowed, then told him, "Drag that filth out of my kitchen and clean up the mess while I think about it."

Gulping back his terror, he hastily crawled on hands and knees to comply.

* * *

Slowly at first, the solemn-faced residents of Chinatown came forward. Stooped with age, one frail man with a wispy, two-strand beard and long, drooping mustache approached Smoke Jensen.

"You were acting in defense of your life, honored sir," he said softly. "The damage done is inconsequential. I am Fong Jai. It shames me that our own people have not stood up to these *qua'lo* bandits like you have done."

"I am called Smoke Jensen, and this is Louis Longmont," Smoke introduced the two of them. "You know them, then?"

"Ah, yes. To my regret, we of Chinatown know them all too well. I recognized the one who led them. He is called Tyrone Beal. He is an enforcer for the greedy *qua'lo* who owns the California Central Railroad . . . and, regrettably, most of the land in Chinatown. He and his villainous rabble have broken legs and made people disappear for a long time."

Smoke gave him his level gray gaze. "Then I am doubly glad we could be of service."

Fong Jai folded his hands into the voluminous sleeves of his mandarin gown and bowed low. "It is we who have a debt to you. Earlier you asked about the Triad Society. We behaved badly toward one who is a friend. If you wish to confront the Tongs, the name to use is Xiang Wai Lee."

Smoke and Louis repeated the name several times, committing it to memory. It turned out Fong had more to say. "I would urge that you use that name cautiously. These Tong hatchet men are very dangerous."

"Thank you, Fong Jai," Smoke offered sincerely. He gestured around him. "You can see how we handle danger."

Fong smiled fleetingly and bowed low again. "It is the Tongs, I think, who should take caution if they rain trouble down on your heads. But my warning comes from another case. It is rumored that the Triad has made an arrangement with the villains of Murchison and his two devil allies, Hobson and Huntley. If that is the case, you will encounter them again."

Smoke placed a friendly hand on Fong's shoulder. "My friend, I—we—have every intention of doing so."

"Our great philosopher Confucius said, 'A wise bird never leaves its droppings in its own nest.' By arousing your wrath, I believe that the Triad should consider that carefully. Go in peace, Smoke Jensen, Louis Longmont. Ask what questions you wish. You will get answers."

It took them less than half an hour to learn all they could about the Tongs. Most people remained frightened of the Chinese gangsters and gave scant aid, and none claimed to know where Xiang could be found. When they had what could be gotten out of the residents of Chinatown, Smoke halted Louis on the street with a word.

"We have our name now, and some idea of how the Tongs work," he declared. "Now to get those bouncers for Fran—er—my new place."

"Where to, *mon ami?*"

"Why, to the dockyards, of course. There are always out-of-work longshoremen aplenty."

Tyrone Beal stood in the opulently furnished office he had never before visited. He held his hat in his hands, his head bowed, shame flaming on his cheeks as he repeated the account of his ignominious defeat at the hands of Smoke Jensen and Louis Longmont. Behind the huge desk centered between two tall, wide windows, Cyrus Murchison grew livid as each sentence tumbled out.

"You mean to tell me that twenty men could not stop those two?" Murchison roared. His thick-fingered fist pounded out each word on the desktop.

"Yes, sir. I'm sorry, sir."

"You will be sorrier if you fail again. You behaved stupidly in the matter involving Wagner. You should not have beaten him so badly he could not sign. And now this. Disgusting." He paused, poured a crystal glass full of water, and drank deeply. It successfully masked his ruminations over how to deal with Tyrone Beal. "I'm going to give you a chance to redeem yourself. You will return to the goldfields. Get me Wagner's signature on that deed. You do that, and all will be forgiven."

Relief flooded through Tyrone Beal. He had visions of ending up at the bottom of the bay, wrapped in anchor chain. "Yes, sir. Thank you, sir. I won't mess this one up. I promise you that."

Ice glittered in the deep-set eyes of Cyrus Murchison and his stunning shock of white hair shook violently. "See that you do."

With that dismissal, Tyrone Beal exited the office. When the huge door closed softly behind him, Murchison sighed heavily. "Now, we have to deal with these two gunfighters," he addressed Heck Granger. I want you to drop everything else you're working on. Find a sketchmaker who can draw likenesses of Longmont and Jensen. Go to our company printing plant and have engravings made and flyers printed. I want them by tomorrow morning. Then," Murchison went on, ticking off his points on his stubby fingers, "circulate them to every employee, every informant you've developed among the low-lives of this town, every barkeep—flood the entire city with them." He paused, anger once more flushing his face. He poured and drank off more water and licked his lips fastidiously. "Anyone who finds them is to report directly to you. Then I want you to file a complaint with the police. I'll contact the chief personally, and get them looking for Jensen and Longmont."

"A tall order, sir. But, I am pleased you approve of my idea of bringing in the regular police."

"Harrumph! The idea occurred to me before that idiot Beal got the first two sentences out of his mouth," he said, dismissing the contribution of his Chief of Railroad Police. "Now, as far as your men are concerned, they are to have orders to shoot to kill Jensen and Longmont on sight. Finally, there are some dirt-scratching farmers in the Central Valley who need convincing that selling to the railroad or to Hobson's Empire Mining and Metal would be good for their health. Send some of Huntley's dockwallopers out there to impress it on them. See to all of it," Murchison commanded. "Jensen and Longmont first."

"This is going to be harder than I thought," Smoke Jensen admitted after their fourth profane refusal.

"It is strange that men out of work, waiting in a hiring hall, would refuse an offer so generous in nature," Louis Longmont agreed.

They had spent the past half hour along the harbor. With scant results, for all that. So far, only a single man had taken up the offer. A burly man with bulging forearms, bulldog face, and thick, bowed legs ambled along a careful two paces behind Smoke and Louis. He had a knit sailor's cap on his huge head, canvas trousers, and a blue-and-white-striped V-neck pullover. Smoke privately suspected he was not a longshoreman, but that he had recently jumped ship. He would do, though.

"Over there," Louis pointed out. Two men sat astraddle a bench, a checkerboard between them. As Smoke approached, one picked up a black playing piece and made a triple jump.

"You're cheatin', Luke," his opponent growled. "I don't know how, but I know you are."

"No, I ain't," Luke responded. "You just make too many mistakes."

"I don't make mistakes."

"Yes, you do."

"No, I don't."

"Do."

"Don't."

"Now, boys," Smoke addressed them, in a tone he often heard Sally use on their children when they squabbled.

It brought up the both of them, red-faced, their disagreement forgotten. Luke gestured to the playing board. "Doin' nothin' for days on end gets to a feller," he apologized for them both.

"Out of work?" Smoke suggested.

"Sure am. We refused to turn back half our pay to the hall boss."

"Would you like to take a job?"

Luke studied the blue sky above. His eyes wandered to a wheeling dove. "Sure, if we get to keep what we earn and it ain't again' the law."

"It's not, I assure you," Louis Longmont added.

"So, what is this work you have? Cargo to unload? Sure. Warehouse to clean out? Sure. We can do anything."

"Speak for yourself, Luke," his companion snipped.

"This job does entail some danger. You may have to fight to preserve the peace."

"You ain't offering us a place with the police, are you?" Luke objected.

"Far from it," Smoke Jensen assured him. "I have recently inherited a famous sporting house in San Francisco. I need some strong, honest men to keep order. I know nothing about running such a place, but there is a nice young lady who is in charge. She can explain your routine duties to you. As for the other, there are some interests in town who don't want me to keep the place."

Louis joined the outline of what might be expected. "We will not be able to be there all the time. It would then be up to you to eject any of their convincers who happened around."

Luke squared his shoulders and gave them a roll suggestive of readiness. "A bouncer, eh? I've been one before. What's it pay?"

"Right now, fifty dollars a week."

Luke's jaw sagged. "I don't believe you. That's more than a month's wages."

"It is quite correct," Louis said sincerely.

"Why, sure, Mister," Luke addressed Smoke. "Far's I'm concerned, you got yourself another bouncer." He looked beyond Smoke to the big man who intently took in their conversation to illustrate his meaning.

"Count me out," Luke's surly friend stated flatly.

"That's two," Smoke agreed, lightly. "What we need is about six more."

Louis rolled his eyes.

Outside the next hiring hall, Smoke Jensen and his companions came face-to-face with a large group of longshoremen. Smoke noted their mood to be surly at best, if not downright hostile. A barrel-chested inverted wedge of a man stepped forward, a hand raised in a sign to stop.

"That's far enough. You fellers have been pokin' around here long enough. It's time for you to get yourselves out of here. And you, too," he gestured to Luke and the other dockworker. "You ain't workin' for them nohow. Come over here with us."

"Sorry," Smoke answered lightly. "Can't do that. I need about six more good men to work for me."

"Well, you can't have 'em," the spokesman snapped.

Smoke was quickly getting riled. First the running gunfight with the railway thugs in Chinatown, and now this. "By whose authority?" he asked with deadly calm.

Pointing to the sign over the doorway to the hiring hall, the aggressive longshoreman bit off his words. "D'you see that sign? This here's the North Star Shipping Company. Mr. Huntley heard what you two were up to and told me special to see you got run off from the docks. So take a hike."

Sharp-edged menace covered every word Smoke Jensen spoke. "I don't think so."

"Then we'll have to remove you."

Luke stepped forward and spoke uneasily in Smoke's ear. "What are we gonna do? They got us outnumbered five-to-one."

A taunting grin lighted Smoke's face. "Simple. We surround them."

No stranger to street fighting, Luke understood immediately. "Sure. We spread out and hit them from four places at once. But that don't make the numbers any less."

"I think we have the advantage," Smoke spoke from the corner of his mouth. "I failed to introduce myself and my friend. I'm Smoke Jensen. He's Louis Longmont."

"*The* Smoke Jensen?" Luke asked in an awe-filled tone.

"There's only one I know of."

"I've heard of you. Read about your doin's in the far mountains. Read about Mr. Longmont, too. The fast gun from New Orleans. I'm honored to be in such famous company." Luke dusted his hands together in eagerness. "We'd better get at it, right?"

"Yes. Before they take it on themselves to start the dance," Smoke agreed.

"Take 'em, boys," Huntley's lead henchman commanded.

At once, the phalanx of longshoremen surged forward. Smoke and company separated. Before the dockworkers realized it, they had been flanked by the two most deadly gunfighters in the nation. Two of them turned to face Smoke Jensen. He stepped in and swiftly punched the nearest one in the mouth.

Shaking his head, the hard case threw a right at Smoke, which the last mountain man took on the point of his shoulder. He rolled with it and went to work on the mouth again. Lips split under a left-right combination. Blood began to flow in a torrent when Smoke hooked a right into the damaged area. His opponent tried for an uppercut and failed to land it. Smoke took him by the upthrust arm and threw him into his companion.

A quick glance told Smoke the other three had their hands full, though they managed to deal with it. Then two more came at him. As they closed in, Smoke extended his arms widely and jumped into the air.

Eager for a quick end to it, the thugs closed in, shoulder to shoulder. Smoke Jensen clapped his hands together, one to the opposite side of each of his attackers' heads. He slammed their noggins together and they went down groggy and aching. Louis had two longshoremen at his feet, out of the battle. Luke had accounted for one and had another in an arm lock around his head. Methodically Luke pounded the man in the face.

Enough of that, the gang of thugs seemed to conclude at once. Fists rapidly filled with cargo hooks and knives.

7

One pug-faced grappler lunged at Smoke Jensen with a wicked long-bladed pig-sticker. Swiftly Smoke filled his hand with a .45 Colt Peacemaker. The hammer fell and brought a roar of exploding gunpowder. The longshoreman went off to meet his maker. Smoke reckoned the meeting would not be a friendly one. He took note that Louis had his own six-gun in action. While those menacing him backpedaled, confused by this sudden turn of events, Smoke reached left-handed for his second revolver and freed it from leather.

A line of fire blew across Smoke's left forearm. He pivoted in that direction and jammed the muzzle of his right-hand Colt up under the knife-wielder's rib cage and squeezed the trigger. Hot gases shredded the thug's intestines, while the bullet punched through his diaphragm and exploded his heart before exiting his body behind his right collarbone.

"Luke!" he barked in warning as he tossed the Colt to the young dockworker.

Facing three men armed with deadly six-guns changed the outlook of the dock brawlers. Few of them owned a firearm, and fewer had ever been in a gunfight. With a curse, the leader called his men off. They fled down the bayside street. The fight ended as quickly as it had begun. Smoke Jensen had a shallow slash on his left forearm. Louis Longmont was bent slightly, one hand clutching at a ragged tear at the point of one shoulder, which he had received from a cargo hook. His remark showed he felt little of it.

"It is nothing, *mon ami*. A big steak and a shot of brandy will make everything right again."

"Wonder why they didn't stay around?" Smoke asked jokingly. "Let me wrap up that arm for you, Louis. And then it's time for us to find six more good men."

Smoke Jensen and Louis Longmont returned to Francie's with six big, capable men, two less than Smoke had wanted, yet enough, he felt sure, to do the job. He gathered them in the spacious former ballroom, which had been converted into a saloon. Lucy joined Smoke and Louis there. Smoke introduced her and began to outline their duties to the collection of seamen and dockworkers.

"Two of you will be on watch in alternating four-hour shifts, day and night. You are to hold this place against anyone who comes here fixing to throw the ladies out. The weakest places are the back door to the kitchen and the French doors to the drawing room. A twelve-year-old could knock them down. I suggest you put some heavy furniture in front of them. The kitchen door can be blocked with that butcher's block in the middle of the room when needed. No drinking on duty, and only two drinks while off. When the emergency is over, we'll have a rip-roaring party that will be the talk of the town. Until then, I want you all sober.

"In the event someone tries to break in, everyone will respond. You will all be given a rifle or shotgun. Make good use of them, if need be." He paused. "Any questions?"

"Why's someone want to take over this place?"

Smoke smiled at him. "It makes a lot of money. That's not all of it. There are some powerful men who aim to take over every saloon and bawdy house in town. I learned yesterday that they intended to start with this one. I also discovered that Miss Francie refused to sell at a piddling price. Later she was run down by a freight wagon no one saw. I own it now and I don't intend to let these ladies be turned into virtual slaves by anyone."

"Who are these men?" Luke asked.

"Cyrus Murchison, Titus Hobson, and Gaylord Huntley."

Luke's eyes narrowed at the list of names and he gave a slight start. "That's why Huntley's dockyard trash set on us, right?"

"We don't know that for sure," Smoke advised him. "Another thing—don't wear yourselves out on off-duty time. In other words, no sampling of the wares."

That brought six loud groans. Smoke suppressed a smile. He had chosen well, he concluded. "Any other questions?"

"Where will you be while we watch over these pretty doves?" a man called Ox asked.

"Louis and I will be out finding a way to put an end to this cabal's schemes."

"Sure you won't need some help?" Ox asked.

Luke answered for Smoke. "Ox, I know you saw how four of us took care of twenty of Huntley's bully-boys. What do you think?"

Ox produced a gap-toothed grin, the absent teeth the result of more than one brawl. "I think we'll be missing out on a lot of fun."

None of the newly hired protectors had more questions. Smoke Jensen released them to their tasks and strolled to the front door with Louis Longmont. "Old friend, we're going back to Chinatown. I want to get those Tong thugs off our back before we go after Murchison and company."

Monte Carson, hat in hand, stood on the porch of Smoke Jensen's home on the Sugarloaf. Earlier in the afternoon, Sally Jensen had sent a hand to town to summon the lawman. Now he listened to Sally's account of what had happened. His frown deepened and a flush rose to color his face darkly.

"Why, them rotten damn polecats!" he growled, then flushed deeper. "Pardon my language, Miss Sally. I can't help it. You say one's dead and the other is waiting for me inside? How'd that happen?"

"I shot Buck when he made lewd suggestions and took a grab for me."

"Good for you, I don't doubt he deserved it."

"It was not . . . pleasant, Monte."

"I understand. Well," he went on, gesturing to his deputy still astride his lathered mount at the tie-rail, "best put the other one in shackles and get him out of here."

Monte's deputy came forward with an armful of leg irons, chains, and handcuffs. He and Monte entered the house. Sally remained on the porch, preferring not to observe the conclusion of this affair. When the sheriff and his deputy returned, a crestfallen Jason Rucker accompanied them. His appearance shocked Sally.

Leg irons enclosed his ankles, a chain running from the midpoint to another set of links around his waist. His wrists were restrained by thick steel cuffs, and again extended from the coupling bar to his waist. Tear tracks streaked his sallow cheeks, the usual tan faded to a sickly yellow. The corpse of Buck Jarvis had been wrapped in a tarp and draped over his horse by Jason Rucker. The morgan stood knock-kneed at the tie-rail, its loose hide rippling nervously in the presence of death. Monte paused beside Sally while his deputy frog-marched Jase to his waiting mount. She wondered how she could explain all this to Bobby.

"What will happen to him now, Monte?"

Monte Carson paused, weighing how to tell her. "He'll be tried, of course. Most likely he'll hang."

Sally lowered her eyes. "I'm . . . sorry. Oh, not that he will be punished. But I am sorry that this happened in the first place. It seems that there is something terribly wrong with a lot of the younger people these days."

Monte scratched his graying head. "Don't I know it. Well, we'd best be movin' on. It's a long way to Big Rock. And, stop frettin' yourself, Miss Sally. You'll be safe enough."

"Oh, I have no doubt of that, Monte. Though I will need a new purse."

Tyrone Beal arrived in Parkerville on the late train. He located the incompetent henchmen in the nearest saloon. He accepted that philosophically. They could sober up on the ride to the Wagner claim. He'd be damned if he failed again.

"Why'er we goin' now?" Spencer demanded with a drunken slur.

"Because I say we are," Beal barked.

"It'll be dark before we get there," Quint objected with beery breath.

"That's why we're going now. We didn't do too well in daylight, did we?" Beal taunted.

"Bet your ass," Spencer muttered sullenly.

They rode out ten minutes later. Beal took the lead, the route burned into his mind. They began the climb into the foothills along the Sacramento River as the sun sank below the coastal range. That still left ample light, the afterglow would last for a good two hours. Grumbles came to Beal's ears from the whiskey-soaked hard cases behind him. He kept a strict silence, letting his irritation with these incompetents feed his anger.

That was the good part. Spencer had informed him that Wagner had taken on a partner, a man reputed to be good with a gun. That didn't set too well with Beal. It had caused him to make changes in his plan. He knew what he would do now. It varied little from his original. Of course, that could be a little rough on Wagner.

* * *

Ray Wagner had returned to his claim the previous day. Some of the bruises had faded slightly, and he wore his left arm, broken in two places, in a sling. His ribs had been tightly bound and he moved like an arthritic old man. He had taken the precaution to bring along a burly miner friend of his as a minority partner. Let them come again, he thought. Eli Colter had a small reputation as a shootist. He wore a six-gun slung low on his right hip, another tucked into the waistband of his trousers on the left. And he could use them.

Ray had seen Eli face down three rowdy highwaymen who'd tried to rob him. He had killed two of them and wounded the third. Not a one of the robbers had gotten off a shot. He mused on this fact as he added another stick of firewood to the cookfire in a ring of stones. Above him, blue slowly faded into gray, and the first stars twinkled in the black velvet of the east.

A cloud of sparks ascended as he released the piece of firewood. He froze a second when his ears picked out the distinctive sound of a hoof striking a small rock. Slowly he uncoiled his body and came upright. A quick glance located Eli Colter.

"Eli," he cautioned tense and low. "I think we are about to have visitors. Be ready."

A gravelly voice answered him. "No problem, Ray."

"This ought to hold the fire until morning," Ray speculated, as he added another stick. When he came upright again, he directed his hand to the butt of the finely made Mauser revolver in a flap holster at his hip. Constantly alert, he went about preparing to roll up in his blankets.

He glanced away from the treeline for only a moment to do so, yet when he looked back, four men, led by Tyrone Beal, appeared as if by magic at the edge of the firelight. Wagner braced himself, certain a showdown was in the offing. Beal dismounted and came forward. Without a word, he thrust the quit-claim deed at Wagner.

"I told you I would never sign. You are trespassing. Get off my claim or I will bury you here."

Beal sighed gustily. "You failed to profit from my previous lesson, I see. You are feeling very cocky, eh, Fritzie?"

"I will not sign," Wagner ground out in a hard, flat voice, and went for his gun.

Eli Colter slapped leather a split second later. He never got off a shot. Two of the hard cases with Beal gunned him down before the muzzle could clear leather.

"You don't have a chance," Beal warned. "Sign it and be damned."

Raising his Mauser 10mm revolver to chest level, Wagner shook his head in the negative. "I will not."

At once, all four hard cases tore into him with hot lead. When they finished, eleven bullets had struck Ray Wagner. He lay at Beal's feet, quivering on the threshold of death. Tyrone Beal coldly stepped close to the dead man and rolled him over with the toe of one boot. He looked down at the deed in his other hand, shrugged, and signed it himself.

"Got that signed at last," he commented flatly as he walked away. "Mount up. We've got a long ride in the dark."

Smoke Jensen and Louis Longmont spent a fruitless afternoon and evening in Chinatown. They picked up Louis's belongings at the Palace Hotel and he moved into the bordello. Morning found them at the breakfast table. Louis took another long draw on his cup of coffee and smacked his lips.

"This is excellent coffee," he remarked.

"They're the same Colombian Arabica beans Cyrus Murchison prefers," Lucy Glover informed him.

That raised some eyebrows. "Murchison? How did Francie get her hands on anything he fancied?" Smoke asked.

"The captain of the ship that brings them to San Francisco was a great admirer of Francie's. He always saw to it that at least one full bag got delivered here. Murchison has never known."

Smoke joined Louis in laughter. When they subsided, Louis asked Smoke the key question. "What do we do today?"

"Go back and try to find a lead to Xiang Lee."

Louis made a face. Before he could make a response, Ophilia came to the doorway to the breakfast room. "Mistah Smoke, they's two po-lice here askin' for you."

Smoke and Louis exchanged glances. "We are not at home, Ophilia."

Eyes twinkling with approval for Smoke, Ophilia left to deliver this message to the lawmen. She liked a man with spunk. This would sure put those officious policemen in their place. Her enjoyment was dampened somewhat by their reaction.

"I'm not sure we believe that. You could be charged with harboring fugitives."

Ophilia controlled herself enough to not show any reaction to that. "What you callin' them gentlemen fugitives for?"

"They are wanted for the murder of fifteen railroad police officers and other crimes."

Ophilia let her outrage flow over. "That ain't true. No, suh, not one bit of it. I don' believe a word you said. Now, you get your flat feet off my porch before I throw you off." She turned her ample back on him and slammed the door.

When they learned the purpose of the visit by the police, Smoke Jensen produced a frown. This could complicate matters considerably. "Murchison is a powerful man. I reckon he's got some higher-ups in the police in his pocket. We'll have to be mighty careful going around outside here."

Louis nodded his understanding. "Perhaps a change of costume is in order," he suggested in a glance at Smoke's buckskin hunting shirt and trousers.

"Umm. I see what you mean. Sorta stands out around here, doesn't it? I don't cotton to the idea of fighting in fancy clothes, but the situation suggests I not look like myself."

"I, too, shall change my appearance," Louis offered. "Perhaps the clothing of a longshoreman would be advisable."

"What?" Smoke jibed. "And give up those fancy shirts you like so much?"

"It was Shakespeare who said, 'All the world's a stage.' In this case the actors must blend with the audience."

Smoke quipped back, "'Faith, that's as well said, as if I had said it myself.'"

Delighted amusement lighted the face of Louis Longmont. "Jonathan Swift. *Polite Conversations,* I believe. From Dialogue Two?"

"Yes," Smoke said with sudden discomfort. "Sally made me read a lot of Swift."

"And for good reason, I would say. His characters and you have a lot in common. Especially in *Gulliver's Travels.*"

"Are you comparing me to a giant among the Lilliputs? Don't wax too literary, old friend. It's too early in the morning." They shared a laugh, and Smoke went on. "Seriously, we're going to find ourselves with our tails in a wringer if the police get too involved in this."

"Why not talk to Lawyer Brian?" Lucy suggested, then flushed furiously.

Louis picked up on it at once. "Aha! So it's *Brian* now, eh?"

"He's been advising me on managing the—ah—business."

"And you have grown close? No doubt," Louis went on gallantly. "You're a lovely woman, *ma cherie.*"

Lucy hastened to protest. "It isn't—I'm just a client. He doesn't even look on me as a woman, let alone have a romantic interest."

Louis cocked an eyebrow and shaped a teasing expression. "Time for our friend Shakespeare again. 'Methinks the lady doth protest too much.' Yet it's entirely understandable, given the circumstances. What do you say, Smoke, my friend?"

"I think they deserve a tad bit less prying. Louis, can't you be serious for two minutes at a time? Lucy, I agree that maybe Pullen can help. I'd be obliged if you'd go see him about all this. As a lawyer, he can look into it, find out what the police have."

Lucy pushed back from the breakfast table, her meal forgotten. "I'll go right away."

"Finish your breakfast first," Smoke urged.

"But those policemen might come back. And they might bring more with them."

"It's a thought, Lucy. Though by then, Louis and I really will not be here."

Liam Quinn had been working for the California Central Railroad since he was a boy—first as a cook's helper and scullion, then as a switchman and telegrapher, and finally as a locomotive engineer. He was enjoying a day off with his buxom wife, Bridget, and their five dark-haired children. A small park, soon to be converted into office buildings and shops, stood across from the entrance to Chinatown. Bridget had packed a huge picnic basket, with cold fried chicken, a small joint of ham, cheese, pickled herring, cold boiled potatoes, and hard-cooked eggs. Liam had sent his eldest, eleven-year-old Sean, for a bucket of beer.

Savoring the arrival of the cool, frothy brew, Liam tore off a hunk of sourdough bread and munched contentedly, a chicken wing in the other hand. Two men, quite tall, caught his attention across the street. Lord, they moved like panthers. A full head above other white men, head and shoulders topping the Chinese who milled about near the large Moon gate, they had an air about them that riveted Liam's attention. Something about them set off an alarm in his head.

Yes, that was it. Those men had the moves of gunfighters

Liam had read of in the penny dreadfuls. And, yes, on those flyers that he had seen circulated early this morning when he had checked in at the yard office to be sure he could take the day off. These two sure resembled them. He studied them further, noting the rough dress of the bearded one and the somber cut of the other's suit. Certainty bloomed in Liam's brain.

"That's them, by St. Fiona!" Liam shouted. There was a reward offered, Liam recalled. A fat bounty on those particular gentlemen, sure and wasn't it? He must get the word to Captain Beal or Chief Grange. "Sure an' then that gold will jingle in me pocket," he muttered gleefully.

His beer would have to wait. Nothing for it, though. He had to be the first to report them and where they might be found. Liam tossed a hasty word of explanation to his wife and promised to rejoin them within the hour, then hurried off down the street.

Smoke Jensen and Louis Longmont resumed their search for the elusive Xiang Wai Lee on one of the many bustling new side streets of Chinatown. One shopkeeper, fear clearly written in his seamed old face and tired, ancient eyes, spoke with them while he cast worried glances at the front of the shop.

"Nothing good can come of your search. You are not *Han*. You have no idea with what, and whom, you are dealing."

"Then the Tongs are here?" Smoke pressed.

"Heyi! Take care in what you say," the frightened elder warned. "They have ears and eyes everywhere. I do not want a hatchet painted on my door. You should not want one on yours, gentlemen."

"I agree," Louis hastened to put in. "What can you tell us of Xiang Wai Lee?"

Eyes wide with fear, the old man blanched so thoroughly that his complexion took on a waxen color. *"Buddah nee joochung!*" he wailed. "To speak the name is to ask for death. Buddha, fortify me," he moaned again.

Smoke Jensen found his patience wearing thin. "Look, this is getting us nowhere. You saw what happened yesterday?" Slowly the aged Chinese nodded. "Then I reckon you should rely upon us to protect you, instead of this Buddha feller. If you know anything at all, tell us how we can find Xiang Lee."

Drawing a shuddering breath, the old merchant stared at a spot above and beyond the shoulder of Smoke Jensen, while he spoke in quiet, broken words. "It is said that there is a secret place, near the opera house."

"The San Francisco Opera?" Smoke asked impatiently.

"No—no, the Chinese opera. It is that large building near the south end of Chinatown. You see it easy, big pagoda, with many peaks and dragon carvings. Near it, it is said, the Triads hold secret meetings. Some say underground. I not know more."

Smoke gave him a warm smile. "You've done enough, old-timer. More than you think. Thank you."

Outside the shop, Louis asked the question that had been troubling Smoke. "Shall we go there straightaway?"

"Don't reckon to. We need to know a lot more about the Tongs. How many are they, for one thing. We don't want to stumble into some nest of wasps. I've been thinking, maybe we're goin' at this the wrong way. There must be some whites who know something about the Tongs. What say we head for those offices built into the wall that runs along Chinatown?"

Louis shrugged. "It's worth a try."

Again, they drew blanks. Not until the fifth small, narrow office did Smoke and Louis come upon anyone with specific knowledge. The sign on the outside identified it as an import broker's office. Inside, dusty chairs were littered about and a large, desk-like table had been heaped with invoices and bills of lading. Seated at a cluttered rolltop desk, a slender, bookish young man in shirt sleeves and garters glanced up, his features shadowed by a green eyeshade.

"You here to pick up the shipment of spices? The paperwork's not done yet," he added without waiting for verification.

"No. Actually, we stopped in to ask you a little something about dealing with the folks of Chinatown," Smoke Jensen advised him.

Smoke kept his questions to generalities until the man had relaxed. At that point he directed their conversation toward the area of interest. "Tell me, when you bring in things from the Orient, China in particular, do you have to deal through—ah—shall we say—out-of-the-ordinary agents among the Chinese?"

"Exactly what do you mean?"

"Do you have to make payoffs to one or more of the Tongs?" Smoke asked bluntly.

The broker did not even blink. "Yes. Anyone dealing with Chinatown has to make their—ah—contributions. It's the way they do business. Even though I am not Chinese, I am not exempt from that rule. Tell me, why are you so interested in the Tongs?"

"Idle curiosity? No, you'd never believe that," Smoke went on, as though thinking out loud. "Actually, we need to talk to Xiang Lee."

Blinking, the import broker pushed up his eyeshade and removed his hexagonal spectacles. He wiped the lenses industriously as he spoke. "Whatever for?"

"We have good reason to believe that the Tong hatchetmen are bent upon killing us," Louis informed him.

"Then the last thing you want to do is get anywhere near Xiang Lee. He's the most bloodthirsty of them all. Xiang Wai Lee is a deadly, silent reptile who gives no warning before he strikes. You wouldn't stand a chance."

"Perhaps. Though I would reserve judgment, were I you," Louis Longmont advised.

They got a little more out of the broker. Not enough,

and no confirmation of the location of Xiang's lair. Back on the street, they headed again for Chinatown, armed with new facts to prod those they questioned. To appear to be armed with more knowledge than one had often resulted in gaining what one sought, Louis reminded Smoke. They had come abreast of the small park across the street when a shout thrust them into quick action.

"Jehosephat! There they are! There's the men I told you about," a voice, thick with Irish accent, shouted.

Smoke and Louis looked that way to see a burly black-haired man. He stood at the curb, pointing directly at them. Half a dozen railroad police gathered behind him. Two of them carried carbine-length Winchesters, which they swiftly brought to their shoulders. The discharge of the rifles made a *crack-crack* sound. Before they heard the muzzle roar, the deadly bullets passed close enough beside the heads of Smoke Jensen and Louis Longmont that they felt the heat of the lead. It answered one question. These men had been ordered to shoot to kill.

8

Ten more of the railroad thugs swarmed out of the park. That put Smoke Jensen and Louis Longmont in considerable jeopardy. A quick evaluation of the situation decided Smoke on their wisest course of action.

"Let's get out of here," he said tightly.

With Murchison's hirelings streaming after them, Smoke and Louis bolted into Chinatown. The pursuers rapidly lost ground. Once they entered the throng of Chinese, the two with Winchesters did not fire again. Smoke led the way toward the central marketplace. He noted with satisfaction that many of the residents of the Chinese quarter bustled themselves into the street in a manner that would block the passage of the railroad detectives.

Cursing and shoving their way through the throng, the hired guns fell further behind. Finally the first one broke free of the obstacles and threw a shot in the direction of Smoke and Louis. His bullet passed the gunfighter pair far enough away not to be heard. Two more guns joined the fusillade. Smoke and Louis led them by a block. It forced their attackers to halt to take aim.

Now the slugs cracked past uncomfortably close. One round kicked up rock chips from the cobbles beside Smoke's boots. He drew his Colt Peacemaker and returned fire. His target emitted a weak cry and pitched forward onto his face. It gave those behind him pause. Smoke pounded boot soles on the street as he led the way at a diagonal across the market square. Louis followed. In less than five strides, Smoke and Louis found themselves in even more trouble.

Another ten railroad thugs appeared on their left. They had even less distance to cover than those coming from behind. In the blink of an eye, they had their six-guns in action. Before flame lanced from their muzzles, Smoke and Louis responded.

Smoke's .45 roared and sent a slug into the pudgy belly of a buck-toothed hard case who wore the round blue billcap and silver badge of a railroad policeman. He went down in a groaning heap of aching flesh. Smoke cycled the cylinder again and sought another target.

Louis already had his. He put out the lights for a red-faced gunman who bellowed defiance at the formidable pair facing him. He stopped in mid-bellow when Louis's bullet punched a neat hole half an inch below his nose. There was more hell to pay for the "detectives" as they closed on Smoke and Louis from two directions.

Smoke blasted a round into the chest of another of them who had ventured too close. He screamed horribly and flung his Smith and Wesson American high in the air. Beside him, a startled thug triggered a hasty, unaimed round. He did well enough, though, as his slug gouged a shallow trough along the left side of Smoke's rib cage. It burned like the fires of hell. All it did was serve to heighten Smoke's anger.

By then, so many of the hunters had weapons in action, it sounded like the Battle of Gettysburg. A Chinese woman screamed shrilly as a slug from one of the hard cases struck her in the chest. An angry mutter rose among the fright-paralyzed onlookers. A quick glance indicated to Smoke that they had only one way out. A small pagoda fronted on the west side of a small park south of the market square. It rested in stately composure atop a gentle, grassy slope. Smoke touched Louis lightly on one sleeve and nodded toward the religious shrine. Louis understood at once.

Ducking low, the dauntless pair sprinted among the vendors' carts toward their only hope. Two bullets cut holes in the sailor's jacket worn by Louis Longmont and smacked into a cart wall. The pungent odor of spicy Szechuan food filled the air as the contents of a barrel inside poured onto the ground.

Once free of the closing ring of hard cases, Smoke settled in to pick individual targets while Louis dashed forward a quarter block. Smoke zeroed in on a florid face and squeezed off a round. The thug went down with a hole in his forehead and the back of his head blown off. Those around him ducked for cover. At once, Smoke set off to close the distance between himself and Louis.

Louis sighted on one of the more daring among the throng of hoodlums and sent his target off to pay for his sins. Smoke joined him a moment later. "Take off, Louis," Smoke panted.

Longmont left without a remark. Smoke turned at once to face their enemies. He had little time to wait for a new target. Two men loomed close at hand. The first shouted an alarm too late. Smoke pinwheeled the other railroad detective and spilled him over backward. Sweat stung the raw wound along Smoke's ribs.

No time to think about that. He banished the discomfort from his consciousness. Halfway to their goal, Louis Longmont took cover behind a cart piled with what looked like small gray-brown stones. A stack had been made on a counter outside one of the barrels from which they had come. Louis opened up on the charging gunmen and immediately Smoke Jensen made a dash to join his companion. Return fire shattered several of the stones and released an abominable odor.

Smoke's nostrils flared at the scent of sulfur and sea salt. He swiveled at the hips and fired almost point blank into the chest of his closest pursuer. The man's arms flung wide and his legs could no longer support him. He hit the ground in a skid. Two more long strides and Smoke rounded the odorous cart. More of the objects had been broken open by gunfire and three of the barrels oozed a malevolent ichor.

Through the distaste in his expression, Smoke asked Louis about them. "What are those?"

"Hundred-year-old eggs," Louis enlightened him. "They are not really a hundred years old, merely duck eggs preserved in sea salt and brine."

Before Louis started off on the next leg of their retreat, Smoke asked, "What are they for?"

"The Chinese eat them," Louis answered and began his sprint.

Left behind to hold off the hoodlums, Smoke could only repeat the last part of Louis's sentence: *"Eat them?"*

Without pausing to consider that, Smoke had his hands full of burly railroad detectives and uniformed yard police. He had emptied his Peacemaker and now used the left-hand Colt to hold them at bay. A well-placed round took down a skinny thug with a huge overbite that made him look like a rabbit. That scattered the two who had been beside him. One of the nearer hard cases caught a whiff of the broken eggs.

"Gawd, that's awful. What is that stink?"

"Them things there," a comrade answered. "Let's get away from here."

"Can't. That's where they're hold up."

"Only one of them, an' you're welcome to him," the disgruntled gunhawk offered. "That stuff would gag a maggot."

Louis had reached his latest shelter and taken the time to reload his six-gun. Now he opened up. Instantly, Smoke was on the run. He concentrated on their goal and found a final dash would make it. He advised Louis of that fact when he skidded to a halt behind a stone lion carved in the Chinese style.

"I figured it that way, too, my friend. Shall I give you time to reload?"

"It would be a good idea. I don't hanker to have them follow us into that place with my iron dry."

Swiftly, without a tremble to his hands, Smoke Jensen reloaded both revolvers. Louis kept up a steady fusillade until he had emptied his own, then ran for the beckoning archway that formed the entrance to the temple. Smoke laid down covering fire, and as soon as he glanced at the pagoda and saw Louis no longer in sight, he made his own hurried rush to the promised safety. Louis blasted two more thugs into perdition while he backed up Smoke. When the last mountain man disappeared into the shrine, a jubilant shout rose from their hunters.

"We got 'em trapped, boys!" Mick Taggart yelled gleefully.

"How's that, Mick?" one of his underlings asked.

"That Chinee church ain't got no back door, that's how," Taggart told him angrily. He had lost too many men, too many good men at that.

Not all had died, though enough had to make him fume inside. He had heard of Louis Longmont; he was supposed to be a hotshot gunfighter from New Orleans. Well, he sure as hell proved that to be true. The other one really bothered him. Smoke Jensen. How many times had he read of that one's exploits? It was unnerving to see the fabled Smoke Jensen in action.

There had been a time when Mick Taggart had fancied himself good enough to go up against any gunhand west of the Mississippi—and where else were they?—then he had come across an account of Smoke Jensen. Overwhelming pride and self-confidence are necessities for a gunfighter, and Taggart had his full share. Yet he recognized that if even half of what had been written about Smoke Jensen and his fight against the Montana ranching trust was true, he didn't stand a chance. Too late to worry about that secret knowledge.

Now he faced the only man he considered his better. Think fast, he admonished himself. "Pass the word to the rest," he told Opie Engles. "We'll rush that place in a bunch. No way they can get away from us."

"When do we do it, Mick?"

"When you get back, you and me will open up. That'll be the signal."

It worked exactly as Mick Taggart had planned it. Opie returned to tell him the boys were ready. Then Taggart and Engles opened fire on the entrance to the pagoda. The entire force of railroad detectives and police charged as one toward the besieged building. To Taggart and his crew of hard cases and thugs, the shrine held no religious significance. What did it matter if they brought violence and death to its interior? They stormed through the gateway with a shout.

In no time they swarmed into the sanctuary and spread out. They ran and fired as they went. Then Mick Taggart skidded to a stop in the middle of the lacquered floor. A quick glance around verified his suspicion.

Only a smiling-faced Buddha witnessed their assault. Smoke Jensen and Louis Longmont had completely disappeared.

Jason Rucker looked up disbelievingly at his visitor to the cell in the Big Rock jail. Dressed in the height of fashion, Sally Jensen cut quite a figure in the dingy corridor of the cellblock. She wore a high-necked, full-skirted dress of deep maroon, edged with black ostrich feathers. A matching hat, small and with only a hint of veil, sat perkily on her head, cocked forward in the latest style.

"Monte told me you were convicted. I—had no reason to stay for the rest of the trial."

"Yep. They're goin' to hang me," Jason said, without even a hint of self-pity.

"That's too bad. You know, this whole thing has broken a small boy's heart?"

Jase brightened, then his lips curled down in genuine sadness. "Bobby? He's a kid with a lot of spunk. He's got sand, that he does. How's it broke his heart?"

Sally hesitated, then forged ahead. "He hasn't spoken to me since he learned about the shooting. He won't even look at me, except with a sulky pout and eyes narrowed with hate."

"That's too bad," Jason said through a sigh. "We weren't neither of us worth that."

Sally's misery wedded the pent-up anger in her heart. "Why did you have to take him into your lives?"

Jason made a helpless gesture. "I ain't sure. It was Buck that shined up to the boy. Said it reminded him of himself at that age."

"Good Lord!" Sally expelled in a rush. "And he wanted to remake Bobby in his likeness?"

"I couldn't say . . . though I suspect you've got the right of it." Suddenly he wanted to change the subject. "You know, your husband is a good man, Miz Jensen. But, he ought to be more careful who he takes on as help. It could get him bad-hurt sometime."

"I think not. Do you know who he is, Jason?" Sally responded.

"Just Mr. Jensen, I suppose."

Sadly, Sally shook her head. Maybe if Smoke did not cherish his privacy so much and had told the two of them his first name, none of what had followed would have happened. "His first name is Kirby, but everyone calls him Smoke."

"Oh, my God!" Jase paled and swallowed hard. "That's how come you shoot so good. Honest truth, Miz Jensen, I reckon it's a mercy I'll face the hangman, instead of your—Smoke Jensen."

Sally thought on it a long, silent minute. Slowly, she fixed her features into a mask of genuine concern. "You really regret what was done, don't you, Jason?"

Head hanging, he nodded in agreement. "Yes. Yes, I do."

"Well, then, there's something I must do. Your concern over Bobby and your show of remorse have convinced me that you deserve a second chance. Mind, I'm not promising anything. Nor am I given to feeling sorry for criminals. But you're young, with apparently a will of your own, although it has been long in the shadow of Buck Jarvis, I wager. I'll have a talk with Monte Carson and the judge. Perhaps we can get your sentence commuted to prison time only. Don't get your hopes up, but I will try. Goodbye, Jason."

Jason choked out a farewell through the flood of relieved tears that streamed down his suddenly gaunt cheeks.

"Come this way," a small, old monk in a saffron robe summoned Smoke Jensen and Louis Longmont when they dashed into the center of a large square area with wood floor, red lacquered walls picked out with gold leaf, and a blue domed ceiling.

They cut their eyes to the frail figure, his hands hidden within the voluminous sleeves of a plain yellow silk robe. Twin, wispy hanks of white hair sprouted from his chin to mid-chest, matched by a ghost of mustache the same color and thinness. When they hesitated, he withdrew one skeletal hand, parchmented with age, from the folds of his sleeve and beckoned.

"Come this way," he repeated.

Smoke and Louis shifted their gaze to the seemingly solid wall behind the old man. What good would it do to be against that wall, as opposed to any other? Impatiently the old monk gestured again.

"Hurry, there is little time."

"I'm willing," Smoke Jensen told him. "But I sure hanker to know what good it will do."

"I will take you out of the shrine to safety."

That was good enough for Smoke. He and Louis crossed the expanse of floor, their boot heels clicking on the high-gloss floorboards. When they neared the monk, he stepped away in the direction of a fat statue of a smiling Buddha. There, he pressed a spot on the wall that looked like any other.

A hidden panel swung open in the side wall of the pagoda. The priest-monk waited until they reached the opening and nodded to indicate they should enter. Smoke remembered the .45 Colt in his hand and thought well of keeping it there. With a small gasp of impatience at their hesitation, their host preceded them into a dark passageway.

There he used a lucifer to light a torch and return it to its wall sconce. Smoke and Louis stepped through into what they soon saw to be a tunnel. Behind them, the secret panel clicked back into place. Smoke tightened his grip on the plowhandle butt grip of his Peacemaker. The monk advanced down the tunnel, igniting more torches. When he had three burning brightly, he waited for his unexpected guests.

"I am Tai Chiu. I am the abbot of this temple. We have taken notice of your activities in the past few days. It became obvious that you are fighting the evil ones. When they outnumbered you, you took sanctuary in our humble shrine. It is our duty to protect you." He motioned with the same thin, frail hand he had used to summon them to the hidden passage. "Follow in my steps. I will take you to a hidden place and heal your wounds."

Smoke Jensen again became aware of the gouge along his ribs. The bleeding had slowed, but it still oozed his life's fluid. A quick glance apprised him that his wound did not show.

"How did you know we had been shot?"

"I . . . felt your agony. Please to come this way. Those who seek you will be befuddled."

Cyrus Murchison pushed back the picked-clean carcass of the half duck he had enjoyed for his noon meal. Silver bowls held the remains of orange sauce, fluffy mashed potatoes, thick, dark gravy, and wilted salad greens. Beyond this gastronomic phalanx sat a silver platter filled with melting ice and a pile of oyster shells, all that remained of a dozen tasty mollusks on the half-shell. Murchison hid a polite belch behind the back of his hand and dabbed at his thick lips with a white napkin.

"Well, then Judge Batey, did you enjoy your *canard à l'orange?*"

A similar array of plates and utensils covered the tablecloth in front of the judge. He patted a protruding belly and nodded approvingly. "Most excellent, my dear Cyrus. I always look forward to dining with you. Do you eat this well at night?"

Murchison produced a fleeting frown. "Alas, I have been constrained by my stomach, as well as my doctor, to curtail my epicurean adventures in the evening. A chop, a boiled potato, and some fruit and cheese is my limit of late. But I sorely miss the pig's knuckles, sauerkraut, and beer, or roasted venison with *pommes frites,* and strawberries in cream that I used to indulge in."

Judge Batey chuckled softly. "I know whereof you speak. Though I fear we digress."

"Oh? How's that?"

"You are not known to wine and dine persons of influence without some ulterior motive. What is it I can help you with this time?"

"Right to the point, eh? Your courtroom reputation has preceded you. That is why I dismissed the servants. We'll not be imposed upon." He paused, steepled his thick fingers, and belched again before launching into his proposition. "There are going to be some transfer deeds coming before your court in the near future. Some of them will no doubt be contested. I trust that you can recognize the genuineness of these instruments merely by examining them?"

Judge Batey nodded solemnly. "Is that all? Surely those excellent ducks will have gone begging for so small a favor."

Murchison wheezed stout laughter. "You're the fox, right enough, Judge. You'll be hearing a criminal matter soon— two men charged with murder of railroad police and some of Hector Grange's detectives. The culprits are named Louis Longmont and Smoke Jensen. To be quite up front with you, Judge, I want to see them hanged."

Batey hesitated only a fraction of a second. "That will depend a lot upon the evidence."

A frown flickered on the broad forehead of Cyrus Murchison. "It need not. In order to provide binding evidence, some things might come out that would prove deleterious to the California Central. We like to keep a— uh—low profile. You understand?"

"Quite so." Judge Batey pursed his lips. "That is asking quite a lot, Cyrus." He raised a hand to stave off a protest. "Not that it is impossible. I shall have to examine the circumstances and evidence and perhaps find a way to accommodate you. Whatever the case, I will do my best."

"Fine, fine. Now, help yourself to some of that chocolate cream cake."

9

Tai Chiu led Smoke Jensen and Louis Longmont down a long incline that Smoke soon judged put them well below street level. The Chinese priest remained silent, husbanding his thoughts. As he progressed, he paused at regular intervals to light another torch. The flambeaus flickered and wavered, as though in a breeze. Yet the air still smelled dank and musty. Their steps set off echoes as they advanced over the cobblestone flooring of the shaft. When they reached a level space, they had only hard-packed earth beneath them. Their course took them through a twisting, turning labyrinth of intersecting tunnels. Even with his superb sense of direction, Smoke Jensen had to admit that he had not a hint of where the old monk was taking them.

"Where do you think he is taking us, *mon ami?*" Louis voiced Smoke's thoughts in a low whisper.

"I haven't the least idea."

"He could be taking us directly to Murchison," came the source of Louis's worry.

"I doubt that. He could have left us for those railroad thugs."

"Umm. You have a point."

They walked on in silence for a while, ignorant of their

destination, or even of where they had been. Then Louis put voice to his concern again.

"He could be taking us to Xiang Lee," he proposed.

Smoke produced a wide, white grin. "Then all the better for us. We can gun down Xiang Lee and end of problem."

Louis got a startled expression. "You do not really mean that, my friend."

Smoke sobered and left only a hint of smile on his full lips. "Only halfway, old pard. I would never kill an unarmed man. But I could gladly tom-turkey-tromp the crap out of him."

Louis looked relieved and pleased. "Now, that's the Smoke Jensen I have always known. Only, I would feel better if I knew where we were going."

"As I said, we will have to wait and see."

They walked along in silence for several lengthy minutes. Suddenly Smoke received a hint of their destination. The sharp tang of salt air reached his nostrils. He cut his eyes to Louis, who nodded his understanding. They made another turn and it came to Smoke's attention that someone had come along behind them to snuff out the torches. Even if they tried, they could not find their way back through the mystifying maze of tunnels.

Ahead of them, Tai Chiu stopped abruptly before what appeared to be the inner side of the wall of a building. When Smoke and Louis came up to him, he lifted a thick iron ring and gave it a twist. A rusty bolt screeched in its latch. Then a section of the "wall" swung inward. Bright sunlight and the stinging tang of sea air, mingled with the fishy smell of the bay, poured in.

"This way, please," Tai urged.

They followed him out of the building onto a street that paralleled a section of San Francisco Bay. Tai Chiu directed them to a tall, wide wire gate in a high fence at the street end of a long pier. Tai used a key to open the fat padlock and ushered them inside. At the far end of the wharf Smoke saw an odd-shaped ship. Its sails had been furled and the masts were stepped at a steep backward angle. The stern rose in the likeness of a turret from a castle in the Middle Ages, even more so than the caravels of fifteenth-century Spain. On a large plank, mounted below the aft weather rail, picked out in Chinese ideograms and English letters, was the name of the ship, the *Whang Fai*.

The bow also jutted high and square, with murlons to accommodate archers. A likeness of a human eye had been painted a couple of feet above the plimsol line. Louis Longmont soon apprised Smoke of its origin and type.

"It is a Chinese junk. The largest one I have ever seen."

"How astute, Mr. Longmont," Tai Chiu complimented him. "It is an oceangoing junk. You will find it curious to see that it appears even bigger from inside. Our Chinese builders have a talent that way."

Tai led them to a rickety gangway that gave access to the deck of the junk. There, he directed them below decks to an aft cabin decorated in an opulent Oriental style. Statuary in the form of dragons and lions, several of them covered in gold leaf, ranged around the bulkheads, which had been hung with heavy silk brocade tapestries. These depicted various subjects, among them, lovely young ladies of the court, solemn mandarins, fierce warriors astride snorting stallions, bows drawn until the wicked barbs of the arrowheads touched the arms of the bow, and a lordly emperor. Incense burned in tall brass braziers. Cushions abounded, though there was nary a chair. Low tables held porcelain bottles and small, footed cups. It truly did look as if it were too large to fit into the junk's aft quarter.

Smoke took it in and found it a bit too fancy for his liking. Fringe-lined lanterns hung from the overhead in bright colors of red, yellow, and green. They swayed slightly with the movement of the water beyond the bulkheads. The junk creaked and groaned like any wooden sailing ship. From beyond the bulkhead that divided the cabin from the rest of the belowdecks area came the twitter of distinctly feminine voices. Tai Chiu clapped his hands in a signal and the owners of those voices appeared.

One bore a tray with a large, steaming pot, and small, handleless cups. The other had a plate of savory smelling tidbits of foods. "*Dim sum,* little bites," Tai explained. "There are Chinese dumplings, steamed wonton, oysters in peanut sauce—oh, and many more things. Refresh yourselves while I summon our doctor."

Lacking any chairs, Smoke and Louis made themselves comfortable on cushions around the low table on which the young women placed their tea and snacks. Louis made an attempt with chopsticks; Smoke settled for his fingers. He lifted a plump prawn from a scarlet sauce and bit off half of it. At once his tastebuds gave off the alarm. Sweat broke out on his forehead and his eyes began to water as he chose to chew rapidly as the best means of eliminating the fiery morsel. He did not want to spit it out; that, he knew, would be bad manners.

"Szechuan," one of the lovelies provided helpfully.

"I don't know what that is, but it sure is hot," Smoke responded.

They turned their heads away and covered their mouths and broke into a fit of giggles. Smoke noticed in detail how comely they appeared. More than twenty years of fidelity to Sally protected him from their blandishments, a fact for which he gave great gratitude. Louis, however, showed signs of becoming enthralled. He answered Smoke's unasked question in a distant voice.

"She said 'Szechuan.' It's the name of a province in China, and also a style of cooking that uses a lot of garlic and chili peppers."

"More than the Mexicans, I'll grant you," Smoke gasped out.

"Don't use tea to douse the fire," Louis cautioned; "that would only make it hotter. Try some of that rice wine in the ceramic bottle."

Smoke shook his head in wonder. "Is there no place

you have not visited, Louis, no one's food you have not sampled?"

Louis produced a depreciating smile. *"Oui.* There are many places I have never gone. Such as Greece, the principalities of Lesser Asia, the islands of the South Pacific, with their dusky maidens . . ." He would have gone on, except that Smoke raised a hand in a warding-off gesture.

"Enough. I get your point. I hope our gracious host hurries. That bullet I took along my ribs left a world of smarting behind it."

"Let me take a look at it."

When Louis removed Smoke's coat, the China dolls turned away in twittering honor at the sight of the bloody shirt worn by Smoke Jensen. Louis cut away the sodden garment and Smoke swore hotly.

"Damn, that's the only Sunday-go-to-meetin' shirt I brought from home."

Louis studied the wound. "Better it is for you that you had it along. Good, clean linen. Less chance of a suppuration. This should heal nicely. But it will leave another nasty scar."

Another scar, Smoke Jensen thought resignedly. His torso and limbs had accumulated a veritable criss-cross of the patterns of violence. He had received wounds from knife and tomahawk, bullet and buckshot, gouges from the sharp stabs of broken branches, flesh ground off by gravel, and painful burns. His body could serve as a road map of his many close encounters with death. He shook his head to dislodge the grim images from his mind.

Having recovered from their initial shock, the enchanting Chinese women—hardly more than girls—hovered over their guests once more. In halting English they urged each man to eat more of the delicacies, to drink their tea. There would be a sea of rice wine afterward, they promised. Half an hour went by, according to Smoke's big Hambleton turnip watch, before Tai Chiu returned with a black-clad, bowed older man, his lined face reminiscent of a prune in all but color. With only a perfunctory greeting he set right to work.

From a little black bag—just like the kind a *real* doctor carried—he produced an assortment of herbs and lotions and a large roll of bandage gauze. He treated both Smoke and Louis, then leaned back on his small, skinny buttocks to chatter in rapid-fire Chinese at the priest.

Tai Chiu translated for the benefit of the Occidentals. "The doctor says you must take this powder in a little rice wine three times a day."

Smoke eyed the packet suspiciously. "What's in it?"

Tai Chiu smiled deceptively. "It is better that you are not knowing," he said through his spread lips.

"No. I want to know."

The priest sighed and named off the ingredients. "Ground rhinoceros horn, dried fungus from the yew tree, and processed gum of the poppy." He gave a little shrug. "There are, perhaps, other things, secrets of the doctor, you understand. The potion will ease any pain, strengthen you until your body overcomes the blood loss, while the unguents he put on the wound will prevent infection."

Dubious, Smoke responded uneasily. "I'm not so sure about all this."

Enigma coated the lips of Tai Chiu. "Do not your *qua'lo* doctors do the same? They mix roots, bark, and herbs and give them to their patients. The gum of the poppy, in your language, is called laudanum. And does it not ease pain?"

Smoke decided to make the best of it. "You've got me there. And, to top it off, our croakers give everything queer foreign names, so a common feller don't know what it is he's getting."

"Just so. There are no mysteries in Chinese healing. Now, to explain why I brought you here. Your courage and your skill with weapons have been observed and have convinced the high council of our humble order, and the elders of the community, that you have been sent by the ancestors to lead a great battle against the evil dragons of the Triad Society."

What a flowery way to say we're here to break up the alliance between the Tongs and Murchison's thugs, Smoke thought. A quick, silent counsel passed between Smoke and Louis. They acknowledged that they weren't too sure about that. The exchange also conveyed that both agreed to go along for the time being.

"How are we to go about this?" Smoke asked.

"You are to wait here. Men will come, young men who wish to rid Chinatown from the curse of the Tongs for all time. They are strong and good fighters. Students at the temple, for the most part. Now that your wounds have been mended, you will eat and rest and wait for the others to join you."

"When will that be?" Louis inquired.

"Later. In the dark of night. It is our hope to catch Xiang Wai Lee by stealth and deal a death blow to his army of hatchetmen. Now, enjoy. These delightful young ladies have prepared a feast for you. And afterward, you may avail yourselves of the baths in another part of the ship. I will return with the last of our young warriors to make certain none were followed."

After Tai Chiu swept out of the cabin, Smoke Jensen went to one porthole to watch his departure from the wharf. Strangely, the frail old monk seemed to have completely disappeared. He turned to Louis, who pressed on him a plaguing question.

"What was that in service of, *mon ami?*"

Smoke flashed an appreciative smile. "I think we have found the key to dealing with the Tongs, and Xiang Lee in particular. For now, my stomach thinks my throat's been slit. Let's eat."

Steaming bowls and platters of exotic Chinese dishes came one course at a time, in a steady procession. Few, if any, did Smoke Jensen recognize. He enjoyed the pork and noodles, the egg foo yong, and the sweet-and-sour shrimp.

He balked, though, at the baby squid in their own ink—another Szechuan delicacy, which he wisely avoided after his eyes watered from the chili oil and plethora of peppers, when he sniffed the pedestal bowl in which they were served. As was his custom, he tried to eat sparingly, yet when the parade of food at last ceased, he felt stuffed to the point of discomfort.

"That was some feed," he remarked, stifling a belch. "The soup was good, only why did they serve it last?"

"It is their custom," Louis informed him.

Smoke sucked at his teeth a moment. "Tasty, even if it came as dessert. What was in it?"

"It was bird's nest soup," Louis answered simply.

Smoke swallowed hard, as his stomach gave a lurch. "You're funnin' me, Louis. Aren't you?"

"Not at all. Of course, they clean them first. I won't go into how the nests are made."

"No. Please don't." Smoke said no more with the appearance of the sweet young ladies.

"You come bath now?" one of them chirped.

"Sounds good," Smoke agreed, as he came to his boots. All the way to the small, humid chamber that held the bubbling wooden bath, Smoke Jensen tried to puzzle out the slightly amused, esoteric smile on the lips of Louis Longmont.

When they reached the tiny cabin, Smoke quickly learned the reason why. "You undress now," the charming daughter of Han told them. Both girls and Louis began to remove their clothing.

"What! Whoa, now, hold it," Smoke pleaded. Images of the reaction Sally would have boiled in his mind.

Soft light glowed on the nubile bodies of the delightful creatures while Smoke Jensen continued to gobble his protests. With lithe movements, the girls became water nymphs as they climbed the two short steps and waded into the steaming water. Buck naked, Louis Longmont quickly joined them.

"Louis? What are you doing?"

"I have always appreciated a good bath, *mon ami*. You should join us. There are delights that surpass the imagination that follow the laving."

Smoke gulped down his trepidation and pulled a somber face. "Thanks, partner, I think I'll pass."

Puzzled by this exchange, beyond their capacity for English, one of the girls cut her eyes to the other. "What is this? The barbarian will not clean himself?"

Although the language mystified him, Louis Longmont caught the drift of what had been said. It summoned a deep, rich guffaw. "I think the young ladies are disturbed over your aversion to taking a bath."

"I do have that gouge along my ribs. Wouldn't do to get that wet."

Louis sobered. "You have a point. Ah, well, *mon ami*, I suppose I can force myself to uphold the honor of Western man."

Confounded at last, Smoke Jensen stomped from the room, though not without a backward, longing glance at the precious physical endowments of the giggling girls.

Cyrus Murchison and Gaylord Huntley took their post-prandial stroll through the minute park named after St. Francis of Assisi, patron of the city, in the center of the cluster of municipal buildings. Tall marble columns surrounded them, while pigeons and seagulls made merry sport of the imposing bronze figure on horseback that occupied the center of the swatch of green. It was there that Heck Granger found him and spoiled the repose Murchison had generated from this good meal they had consumed.

In fact, it soured Murchison's stomach. "They whupped the hell out of 'em."

"What?"

"Those two, Jensen and Longmont, blasted their way through twenty-seven of my men and flat disappeared."

Murchison's visage grew thunderous. "That is impossible. I will not accept that. No two men can outgun twenty-five plus."

Fearing the outburst that would be sure to follow, Granger answered meekly, "These two did. They ran into a Chinee temple and when my men got in there, they were nowhere to be seen."

"They went out a back door," Cyrus Murchison suggested.

"There weren't none. No side doors, either. There was . . . no place for them to escape."

"Nonsense. I want you to take more men, go there, and tear that place apart until you find how they got out of there."

"That—wouldn't be wise, Mr. Murchison. That temple is in Chinatown. Even the Tongs would turn on us if we did. We only got them behind us a little while ago. It's touchy, I say."

A ruby color suffused the angry expression on the face of Cyrus Murchison. "Damn the Tongs. I never approved of allying ourselves with them in the first place."

"I hate to mention it, sir. But there are more of them than there are of us. I won't risk my men for that. We'll find those two. And we'll do it our way."

It was blatant defiance, and Granger all but quailed at the boldness he had displayed. To his surprise, it worked. Murchison's expression softened. "All right, Heck. I understand your anxiety. Do it the way you see best. Only . . . don't fail this time."

Brian Pullen appeared before Judge Timothy Flannery in the judge's chambers. Aware of Flannery's aversion to wasting time on small talk, he came right to the point.

"Your Honor, I have reliable information that several powerful men in this community have conspired to wrest control of a building owned by a client of mine from him.

In furtherance of this conspiracy, they have made false representations to the police of this city that the property had been sold for back taxes, which it had not. Also regarding acts committed by my client and an associate. These acts were, in fact, self-defense. The result is that the police are looking for my client and his associate as fugitives from justice."

Judge Flannery steepled his fingers. "What is it you wish me to do, Counselor?"

"Inasmuch as these persons are actively engaged in an attempt to seize my client's property and using police pressure to accomplish their goal, I have here a petition for a restraining order, which will relieve my clients from the loss of said property until such time as the matter can be resolved. It also asks that the police be restrained from hunting down my client and his associate, and to prevent agents of the conspirators from doing the same."

"I . . . see." Judge Flannery considered that a moment. "I'll see your brief and make my decision within two hours. By the way, who are these men you allege are co-conspirators?"

Brian Pullen swallowed hard. "Cyrus Murchison and Titus Hobson. Also Gaylord Huntley."

Flannery's eyebrows rose. "Your client picked some big enemies, I must say." Brian asked, "Will that have an effect on your decision, Your Honor?"

A frown creased Flannery's brow. "Certainly not. Come back in two hours."

Shortly after sundown, slim, hard-faced young Chinese men began to drift aboard the *Whang Fai*. Smoke Jensen and Louis Longmont inspected them critically. They exchanged worried glances over the odd assortment of weapons these volunteers possessed. Some carried pikes with odd-shaped blades. Several had swords with blades so broad that they resembled overgrown meat cleavers. A few had knives of varying blade length. More than half bore only stout oak staffs.

Smoke cut his eyes to Louis. "They expect to use those to fight the Tong soldiers and any of Murchison's railroad detectives we come across?"

Louis sighed. "It is a most discouraging prospect, *mon ami.*"

Tai Chiu merely smiled and bowed. "Honorable warriors, it is my humble duty to introduce you to Quo Chung Wu." He indicated a fresh-faced youth who could not be past his twentieth year. "He is the leader of these students that it is my humble privilege to instruct."

"Students? Are they studying to be priests?"

"Yes, that, too. What I teach them is *kung fu,* which are our words for what you would call martial arts. The Way of the Warrior. Since they are destined to follow the religious life, most of what they learn is unarmed combat. Yet I believe that when you see Wu and his young men in action, you will both marvel at what can be done. Now, the time draws near. We must lay a course of action."

10

Tyrone Beal and six thick-muscled railroad detectives sat their horses outside the small, wooden frame building that had been sided with galvanized tin. A pale square of yellow light slanted to the ground from the window in an otherwise blank wall to their left. An angled layer of shingles formed a roof over the narrow stoop that gave to a door, the top third of which was a lattice of glass panes. A hand-lettered sign rested at the junction of porch roof and building front. It read in dripping letters: CENTRAL VALLEY FREIGHT. At a nod from Beal, the thugs dismounted.

"Don't look like much," one hard case grumbled.

"Heck Granger said Mr. Huntley don't want the competition, so we take care of it," Beal told him. "The sooner, the better, I say. This is my last job up here in the nowhere, then it's back to San Francisco for me."

A local tough glanced at Beal quizzically. "You don't like it out here?"

"Nope. It's too wide open for me. I grew up with buildings all around me. This kinda country makes me feel like I'm gonna fall right off the earth." Beal motioned to a pair of the local gang. "You two take the back. Make sure no one gets away."

Beal and the other four climbed the open, rough-hewn plank steps to the stoop. Beal took the lead, his big hand smacking the door hard enough to slam it against the inside wall. From behind the counter a man with the look of a farmer gave them a startled glance.

"Wh-what do you gentlemen need?" he asked shakily.

"You're out of business, Harper," Beal growled.

Gus Harper backed away from the counter that separated him from the hard cases. He raised both hands in protest. "Now, see here . . ."

"No, you listen and do as you are told."

"Who are you?"

Beal gave Harper a nasty smirk. "Names don't mean a lot."

"Then who sent you?"

"I think you know the answer to that. We come to give you a different outlook on what's what in this world. There ain't gonna be any competition in the freighting business."

"I have every right," Harper blustered. Then he weighed the menace in Beal's expression. His next words came in a stammered rush. "N-now, let's not do anything hasty."

Beal pointed at the counter and rolltop desk behind. "We'll not, just so long as you put an end to this crazy notion of yours. You're a farmer, Harper. Go back to clod-hoppin'." He glanced left and right to the thugs with him. "Spread out, boys. This place needs a little rearrangin'."

Harper made a fateful mistake. "Stop right there. There's law in this valley, and it's on my side."

Beal nodded to a pair of thugs. "You two take ahold of him. Now, Mr. Farmer-Turned-Freight Master, for the last time, go back to your plow. There ain't gonna be another freight company in the Central Valley."

Harper made one final, weak effort to make reason prevail. "But the railroad and Huntley's Dray Service have raised rates twice this year already and harvest is three months away."

"Don't matter how many times the prices go up, you and all the rest are going to pay and keep your mouths shut."

Beal moved in then, through the small gate at one end of the counter. He balled his big fists while the two thugs grabbed onto Harper. They spread the former farmer out so his middle was open to the vicious attack Beal leveled on him. Beal worked on Harper's belly first, pounded hard, twisting blows into the muscle of the abdomen, then worked up to the chest. A severe blow right over the heart turned Harper's face ashen.

For a moment he went rigid and his eyes glazed. Slowly he came around in time for Beal to start in on his face. Knuckles protected by leather gloves, Beal put a cut on Harper's left cheekbone, and a weal on his forehead. Beal mashed his victim's lips and broke his nose. Harper went limp in the grasp of the hard cases.

Beal showed no mercy. He went back to the gut. Soft, meaty smacks sounded with each punch. Harper hung from the grip of strong hands. Beal aimed for the ribs. He felt two give on his third left hook. It gave him an idea.

"Let him go," he ordered.

Harper sank to the floor, a soft moan escaped though battered, split lips. Beal toed him onto his back and began to methodically kick Harper in the ribs. The bones broke one by one. When all on the right side had been broken, Beal went around to the other side and began to slam the toe of his boot into the vulnerable ribs. They, too, snapped with sharp pops. When the last gave, Beal went to work on Harper's stomach.

Unprotected, the internal organs suffered great damage. Sometime while Beal worked on Harper's liver, the man died. The first Beal and his henchmen knew of it was when the body, relaxed in death, voided. The outhouse stench rose around them.

"He's gone, Mr. Beal," Spencer said quietly.

"Then drag him outside. Let that be a lesson for the others. The rest of us are going to torch this place."

* * *

It did not seem like much of a plan to Smoke Jensen. Tai Chiu had described to them the dens habituated by the Tong soldiers. One was an opium parlor. There, the wretched individuals in the thrall of the evil poppy idled away their lives, many filth-encrusted and never off their rude pallets, where they smoked the black, tarlike substance that gave them their life-sapping dreams. That is how Tai Chiu described them.

At least they sounded incapable of putting up any resistance, Smoke speculated. That still left some two hundred Tong members. Tai Chiu had been quite certain of the number. The count varied from time to time, though never exceeding a hundred members for each of the three Tongs. Tai Chiu had named them the Iron Fan Tong, the Blue Lotus Tong, and the Celestial Hatchets. Smoke considered the names odd and a bit pretentious. Louis had explained the reasoning behind them.

"These Tong members choose a name based on the power a Tong has. Some of them go back centuries. Anything with 'Celestial' in it is most powerful. It is likely that Xiang Wai Lee is from this Tong."

"Quite right, Mr. Longmont," Tai Chiu confirmed. "You know much about the darker side of our ancient culture."

"There were, for a time, some Tongs in New Orleans."

Tai Chiu's eyes danced with interest. "Might I ask what happened to them?"

"Myself, and some of my friends, ah, persuaded them to depart."

"I presume you did not use gentle persuasion on them?"

"Right you are, Mr. Tai. We used six-guns and some rope."

Tai Chiu's white eyebrows rose. "I think we have the answer to why they so readily came after you. No doubt some of the survivors came here, to San Francisco. You might have been recognized the first time you were seen."

Louis considered that. "Sounds reasonable. Now, as I understand it, each of the three of us will take on one of the Tongs. When one of their meeting places has been pacified, those of us who fought there will go on to another location."

"That is correct," Tai Chiu verified. "The Celestial Hatchets are currently the strongest of the three. You do not feel uncomfortable assuming that task, Mr. Jensen?"

"Not too much. Considering I'm going to have only fifteen of your student-fighters along," Smoke answered dryly.

"Be advised that it is your prowess with firearms that will tip the balance. The Tongs are not loath to use modern weapons."

Smoke looked hard at the old priest. "Thanks very much, Mr. Tai. If I thought I was goin' up against fellers armed only with hatchets, I couldn't live with myself."

Tai Chiu studied Smoke's face a moment. "Your face tells me you are serious, yet your eyes speak of a jest. You are having fun with me, yes?"

"It's that or walk away from this whole thing. Sixteen against a hundred is mighty long odds."

"Bear in mind, not all of them will be there at one time. You must deal with them as they come in answer to the rallying call. That will make your task simpler, I think."

Smoke checked the loads in his right-hand six-gun. He slid a sixth cartridge into the usually empty chamber. Then he did the same for the second revolver. "All together, I have about thirty rounds. After that, it's going to get quite interesting."

"We go now," Tai Chiu answered simply.

To their surprise, Smoke Jensen and Louis Longmont found Chinatown brightly lighted even at the midnight hour. Families streamed in and out of restaurants, many with sleepy-eyed little tykes tugged along by their small hands. Westerners as well as Chinese thronged the shops, clutching their purchases by the strings that bound the gaudy red-and-gold or green-and-silver tissue paper. Musical bursts of conversation in Cantonese and Mandarin filled the air. All of that added an unexpected complication for Smoke Jensen. Their small force had divided before entering Chinatown and Smoke felt uncomfortably exposed.

His target, the Celestial Hatchets, had a building on the far side of the market square, near the Chinese opera house. He and his volunteers would be in the open the longest. Quo Chung Wu took the lead as they rounded the corner. Two youthful Chinese lounged against the wall outside the door to the Tong headquarters. One of them roused himself when he caught sight of Quo in his saffron temple robe. He stepped out to block the walkway and raised a hand to signal that Quo should halt.

"You are in the wrong place, *shunfoo go,*" he snarled insolently.

"'Dog of a priest,' am I?" Quo Chung Wu rasped back.

Then, in only the time it took Smoke Jensen to blink, Quo made his move. His body pivoted and bent backward. A weird birdlike sound came from his throat as he lashed out a foot in a powerful kick that knocked the Tong thug back into his companion, who had only begun to straighten up, sensing at last that trouble had come to their lair. Quo followed up the unconventional kick with a full swing that brought him back face-to-face with the Tong soldiers. Elbows akimbo, he formed his long-fingered hands into the shape of tiger claws and darted one out to rake sharp, thick nails across the face of the slow-awakening Tong man. To Smoke's surprise, the youth did not scream as long, red lines appeared on his cheek. Quo's fist closed and he smashed the injured man in the nose with a back-blow.

His left elbow struck the chest next. Then he sent a side-kick that knocked the insulting one to his knees. A pointed toe rose under the Tong hatchetman's chin and stilled his opposition. His companion had regained his feet and leaped into the air to deliver a flying kick that rocked Quo back, though it did not faze him. He pivoted to the right and drove hard fists, the middle knuckles extended, into the breastbone of his attacker. Staggering back until his shoulders collided with the wall, the thug drew a hatchet.

It gave off a musical whistle as it swung through the air. When the blade passed him, Quo stepped in and drove an open palm to the already damaged nose. Bone and cartilage cracked and popped and sliced through the thin partition into his brain. He fell twitching to the ground. Smiling sardonically, Quo stepped to one side and made a sweeping gesture of welcome to the door.

Smoke entered, his .45 Colt at the ready. Two more Tong henchmen sat on ornate plush chairs. One leaped up with a Smith American .44 in his hand. He didn't get to use it as Smoke upset him into a heap on the floor with a fat .45 slug in his chest. Beside him, his partner shrieked curses in Cantonese and loosed a round from his .38 Colt Lightning. It knocked the hat from the head of Smoke Jensen and smacked into the wall beyond.

Superior weapons skills put Smoke's round right on target. Eyes bulging, the Chinese hoodlum slammed back into his chair, which tipped over to spill him onto the hall carpet. Smoke stepped over his twitching legs and advanced along the hall. A steady drone of conversation in Chinese ended with the roar of the guns. How many would be waiting? Smoke didn't let it worry him. He stepped through the archway at the end of the hall with his Peacemaker ablaze.

A squat, rotund Chinese with a sawed-off shotgun discharged a barrel into the ceiling on his way over backward in his chair. To his left, another hurled a hatchet at the head of Smoke Jensen. Ducking below the deadly device, Smoke popped a hole in the Tong soldier's chest that broke his collarbone and severed the subclavian artery. Another Tong bully came at Smoke, his face twisted in the fury of his scream, at the same moment Quo Chung Wu stepped into the room beside Smoke.

Quo gave the thug a front kick, high in his throat, that cut off the scream like a switch. Then he pivoted and delivered a side-kick to the chest and a second to the descending head. To Smoke's surprise, he had accomplished this in less time than it took Smoke to cock his Colt. The Tong butcher dropped his hatchet and skidded on his nose to the feet of Smoke Jensen. Quo smiled and bowed slightly.

Stacks of coins and paper currency went flying as another Tong hatchetman leaped onto the table and jerked back his arm to unloose a hatchet. He pitched over on the back of his head when Smoke plunked a .45 slug into his belly, an inch above the navel. A scrabbling sound came from the corner of the room.

A youthful Tong henchman tried desperately to fling up the sash of a window. When the muzzle of Smoke Jensen's .45 Colt tracked toward him, his fear overcame him and he threw himself through the pane. Broken glass rang down musically. One of the student volunteers rushed to the gaping frame and drew a fancy carved bow. The arrow sped down the alley and took the fleeing Tong gangster between the shoulder blades. A thin, high wail ended his life. Smoke touched a finger to his bare forehead.

"Obliged," he told the archer.

Others of the young priests had fanned out through the house. The sound of breaking glass came again as a youthful Tong member made his escape. By ones and twos the volunteers began to return to this central room to report the place as empty. Smoke looked around at the havoc they had created.

"That happened too easy," Smoke told them.

Their young, happily smiling faces contradicted him. "We have no objection to that," Quo spoke for them all.

"What I'm getting at is, there are a whole lot more of them out there. They will be coming, you can be sure of that."

"Then we will not be going on to help the others?" Quo asked, uncertain.

"Not right away, Quo. We'll have our hands full any minute now," Smoke responded, as he opened the loading gate of his Peacemaker and began shucking out empty shell casings.

Louis Longmont eased his way along a dark alley in Chinatown. Close at his side came five of his fifteen volunteer priests. For all the danger they faced, these young men held uniform expressions of calm and confidence. An unusually tall, lean Chinese beside him clutched a bo stick with supple fingers. They came to a dark, recessed entrance to a cellar and the youthful martial artist tensed slightly, glided forward a step, and swung his stick.

It made a sharp *klock!* against the head of a sentry and the Tong soldier went down hard. The youth with the bo stick nodded slightly and slid on past. He raised a hand and indicated first one, then a second, ground-level doorway. The other ten young men had offered to take the place from the front. Theirs would be the risky job, Louis considered. He glanced down at the unconscious sentry as he passed the steps to the basement.

That stick, he thought. Something like a quarter-staff. Right out of the Middle Ages. Louis Longmont had been a gunfighter long enough to know that the "right" weapon did not exist. Whatever did the job when it had to be done worked. He caught up to the Chinese youth with the bo stick. Now all they had to do was wait until the rest hit the front door.

It turned out not to be a long wait. Shouts of alarm and cries of pain came from inside the Tong headquarters less than two minutes later. At first, no one showed at the rear entrance, then the door flung open and a skinny man with a waist-long pigtail rushed out. A hatchet in his left hand reflected moonlight as he raised it defensively. One of the temple students closed on him, a halberd with an elongated tip blade held ready. The hatchetman changed his weapon from the defensive to the offensive. Metal clanged as he batted the pike head with the flat of his blade. His opponent lunged, driving the shaft of his device forward in a lightning move.

No sound came when the slender blade drove into the gut of the Tong soldier. His eyes went wide and his mouth formed a pain-twisted "O." His knees went out from under him and he dragged the halberd down as he collapsed on the steps. The youthful volunteer wrenched his blade free. It made a soft sucking sound as it left the dying flesh. Two more of the Iron Fan Tong warriors burst through the open doorway. Louis took quick aim and shot the first. He kept on running for enough steps to pitch headlong off the stoop. Already, the high, rounded front sight of the gun in the hand of Louis Longmont lined up on the second target.

His revolver gave a comfortable, familiar jolt to his hand when the hammer fell on a fresh cartridge. The Tong thug broke stride and looked down at his chest. Surprise registered a moment before he keeled over to one side and fell heavily on his right shoulder. Even then, he tried to throw his hatchet at Louis, who shot him again. The sounds of a scuffle came from inside. Although the back hallway had been darkened, Louis could make out the figures of two men. They flowed rapidly through the postures of several recognizable creatures. Now a crane, now a tiger, now a snake. With each ripple, an arm or foot would lash out and strike at the other. Louis well appreciated the skill they exhibited, yet he had no time to be an interested observer.

Two Tong members came down a wooden fire escape attached to the rear wall. One paused to hurl his hand-ax at Louis. It stuck in the siding six inches from the head of the man from New Orleans. Louis reacted instantly. His shot knocked the man from the ladder, and the scream he uttered lasted until he hit the ground. The other hatchetman flung his weapon at Louis. It struck Louis on the left shoulder with the handle. Sharp pain, quickly stifled, radiated from the point of impact.

Louis put a bullet in the thrower's head, ending his days of ruthlessness. When the sound of the shot reverberated down the alleyway, Louis found it totally silent inside the building. He entered to find the Tong's nest in the hands of his young fighters.

"We could burn this place, but it would take the whole block," Louis informed his troops. "Five of you, stay here, in case any of the rest of the Tong comes back. The others, come with me. We'll go lend a hand to Smoke."

Tai Chiu found most of the Blue Lotus Tong at home. They boiled out of the dilapidated godown they used as a headquarters like a swarm of aroused bees. Passersby looked away and scurried for safety as their hatchets flashed in the red-and-yellow light of lanterns strung from post to post. Without hesitation, Tai's pupils waded in.

One avoided a hatchet blow with a rising forearm block, then kicked the Tong member in the gut. Air whooshed out of a distorted mouth, only to be battered back inside by an open palm smash to the lips. Blood flew black in the colored illumination. Two of the hatchetmen came for Tai Chiu.

Their weapons did no harm as the old man melted away from in front of them. Crouched low, Tai lashed out with a side-kick that knocked the legs from under one of his attackers. Chiu's robe fluttered like wings as he spun on the ball of one foot and delivered another kick to the exposed chest of the second thug. The Tong hatchet swished by just an inch short of Tai Chiu's extended leg.

Without a blink, he took a crane stance and snapped extended fingers at the face of the hatchetman. Blood sprang from four fine lines along his face. He tried another swing with the hatchet, only to have his nose smashed by a backhand blow. Before he could recover, the elderly monk kicked him three times under the chin. The hatchetman dropped to the ground to twitch out his life. Tai Chiu moved on to engage a short, stout thug with a revolver in his hand.

His first attack kicked the gun from the startled gangster's grip. The Chinese thug had not even gotten off a shot. Tai knocked him senseless with a smooth routine of fist and elbow blows and well-aimed kicks. Beyond him, two of the Blue Lotus members sprinted away from the center of the melee. There would be more coming soon, he realized regretfully.

Smoke Jensen considered it better to fight in the open, so he led his volunteers out of the Celestial Hatchets Tong headquarters to take on the reinforcements who had arrived during the past five minutes. Several of them carried swords similar to the ones with which the student priests had armed themselves. One of these darted forward and made an overhand swing at a Tong thug. The sword in the hard case's hand rose swiftly to parry the swing.

The edges met with a ring. Like lightning, the young student's left hand flashed out and slammed into his opponent's face. At once, another Tong member leaped toward the volunteer. He never made it. Breaking the engagement of their blades, the supple youth made a horizontal slash with his sword and all but decapitated the Tong thug. The last hatchetman, with an oversized cutlass, raised his weapon and set himself for a blow to the back of the exposed head of the young student.

Smoke Jensen shot the Tong member between the eyes. A shout came from down the street and Smoke looked that way to see some ten railroad detectives. In their uniforms of brown suits and derby hats, they rushed toward the scene of conflict, pick handles in their hands.

11

They were in for it now, Smoke judged. A moment later, the yard bulls crashed into the line of students. The fighting spread out, two of the enemy on each one of the students. When one of Murchison's gunhawks pulled iron, Smoke Jensen stepped in. The Colt Peacemaker bucked in Smoke's hand and spat a slug that pulverized the gunman's right shoulder.

He howled and staggered off, only to be given a kick to the head by a young Chinese. Down he went, limp and unmoving. More of Heck Grange's henchmen poured into the narrow side street in Chinatown. They went after the allies of Smoke Jensen, only to be knocked down and out time after time. Three closed in on Smoke. The one in the lead, a thick-chested brute with a snarling face, drew a pocket pistol and fired hastily.

His bullet cracked past Smoke's head and the last mountain man pumped a round into the man's chest. He shook himself and came on. He cocked his pistol again and took aim at Smoke. The .45 Colt in Smoke's hand bucked and a second slug ripped into his attacker's chest. Still the man remained on his feet. Smoke shot him once again.

This time, Smoke noticed that not a drop of blood flew from the wound. Smoke raised his aim and put a round in his opponent's forehead. Quickly he swung his Peacemaker to another of the armed thugs. They traded shots. The yard bull missed. Smoke Jensen didn't.

Facing only a single enemy, Smoke leveled his .45 Colt and fired the last round in the cylinder. The thug took it in his belly, an inch above his hipbone. Quickly Smoke changed revolvers. He made it just in time. A lance of flame spurted from the Merwin and Hulbert the hard case carried. His bullet punched a hole through the body of the coat worn by Smoke Jensen and exited out the back. Too close a call.

Smoke ended the man's railroad career with a sizzling .45 slug in the heart. Smoke went forward to inspect the corpse of the man who had absorbed so many bullets. Bending low, he pulled open the shirt. Just as he had suspected: the dead man wore a fitted piece of boiler plate, its backside thickly padded with cotton quilting. Smoke's soft lead bullets had smashed against it and spread out to the diameter of a quarter. If he ran into too many like that one, he would really be in trouble, Smoke reckoned. Another shout rose among the battling figures in the middle of the block. Smoke looked up in time to see more Tong soldiers storming down the street.

Jing Gow had run all the way from the Celestial Hatchets Tong club house to the Wu Fong theater, where most of the members were attending a recital by a famous Chinese lute player. They filled the balcony and two of the larger boxes to the side of the stage. Word went around quickly and nearly half of the audience walked out in the middle of the performance. Now, he trotted along Plum Seed Street with his Tong brothers toward the sounds of a fight.

He did not feel the cuts made by the glass from when he had jumped through the window. In the second floor leap he had also sprained an ankle, and he limped painfully. All he could think of was the huge *qua'lo* who had burst into the room during counting time for their weekly squeeze money. That one had the ferocity of a dragon. Jing had jumped through a curtained doorway and run up-stairs. Now, blood dripped down his chest and belly. When they rounded the corner to face the battle scene, Jing Gow felt light-headed. How long had be been cut and not taken care of it?

A haze seemed to settle over the street. Jing swiped at his eyes to try to ward off the fuzzy vision. He found his hand covered with dried blood. The fog remained. It even grew darker. Jing saw the giant foreign devil and raised his hatchet. A howl of fury ripped from his throat.

Jing Gow threw his hatchet, only the big man dodged to one side. Then a terrible force struck Jing in the chest and he saw smoke and flame gush from the *qua'lo's* gun. Awful pain radiated from the area around his heart and the world turned dark for Jing Gow. He did not feel a thing when he fell face-first onto the cobblestones.

It appeared to Louis Longmont that every person under the age of fifty in Chinatown was a Tong member. They kept coming from buildings and down both ends of the street near the building used by the Iron Fan Tong as a headquarters. He had run dangerously low on ammuni-tion. The thought occurred, Why hadn't the police come?

It didn't matter, he decided, as he jammed a hard fist into the face of another Tong hatchetman to save on car-tridges. He heard the crack of a shot from behind him and whirled to reply. In so doing, he nearly shot Brian Pullen. The young lawyer competently held a .44 Colt Lightning in his hand, a dead Tong member at his feet.

"I heard about this Tong war and thought I'd come lend a hand," Pullen explained.

Louis nodded to the corpse. "You got here just in time. I hope you brought enough ammunition."

"I have two boxes of cartridges. Will that be enough?"

"I doubt it. What we need is a shotgun. Something to clear the street with."

Brian Pullen looked blankly at Louis Longmont and snapped his fingers. "I never thought of that. Hang on, I'll be back." He ran through the back of the house before Louis could reply.

Twenty minutes went by in a frenzy of fighting, the likes of which Louis had never seen. The young Chinese volunteers used a form of personal combat unlike anything he had heard of. Three of them went down, victims of hatchet blows, yet the rest continued to take a bloody, deadly toll on the Tong fighters. When Brian Pullen returned, he brought along two finely made, expensive Parker 10-gauge shotguns and a large net bag filled with brass cartridges.

Louis Longmont hid his surprise. "That should do the job."

He took one, loaded it, and blasted two Tong thugs off the stoop of the building with a single round. Pullen put the other Parker to good use, ending the career of a short, squat extortionist. Quickly the men reloaded and pushed out into the street. Four more loads of buckshot broke the fanatic assault of the Tong hatchetmen. Six of their companions had been killed in a matter of seconds. The two grim-faced *qua'lo* did not hesitate as they advanced. They reloaded on the move, paused, and then downed more Tong members. At first, a trickle of young gangsters faded away. Then the remaining street thugs abandoned the battle and fled out of sight.

"I think we should check the Blue Lotus Tong," Louis calmly suggested.

Wang Toy had successfully hidden from the enraged priests from the Golden Harmony temple. He had watched his Tong brothers being beaten and some of them killed by those led by the old priest, Tai Chiu. The aged one had never had the proper respect for those of the Triad Society.

He should have been disposed of long ago. Although the killing of priests was frowned upon by Xiang Wai Lee, Wang Toy would have been pleased to carry out that assignment.

Now he skulked in the dusty attic of the Blue Lotus club house and worried about his own safety. When the last of his companions had run away, he had been left behind, unable to come out of hiding so long as the practitioners of *kung fu* remained around the building. They had left, after a short while, yet he remained in his undiscovered lair. In all his seventeen years he had never been so frightened. At last he goaded himself into opening the square hatch in the floor and lowered himself to the second-floor hallway.

Embarrassed and shamed by his cowardly behavior, Wang Toy slunk to the stairwell and started down. At the landing, he pulled his hatchet from his belt and held it at the ready. He would find his brothers and rally them. Wang reached the last step at the same time the front door flew open. The first person through it was a *qua'lo* with a double-barreled shotgun. That was the last thing Wang Toy saw because Louis Longmont blew his head off with a load of buckshot.

Smoke Jensen had barely finished counting the number of Tong gangsters when a hoard of more young Chinese men rounded the far corner. It took him a moment to real-ize that several of them wore the saffron robes of the student priests. They fell on the hatchetmen from behind and began to chop and kick them with terrible efficiency. Only the guns of the railroad detectives saved the Tong members from total destruction.

Two burly hard cases shot the same student at one time. One of them did not get to crow about it, for Smoke Jensen blasted the life out of him. His partner whirled and threw a shot in Smoke's direction. The bullet slammed into the doorjamb behind Smoke. His assailant tried for another round, only to be blasted to perdition by a slug from the .45

Colt in Smoke's hand. In the far distance, Smoke heard the shrill of police whistles. Recalling the incident at the bordello, he wondered whose side they would take.

He decided to leave when the first bluecoats arrived on the scene and began to club the students with their nightsticks. "Time to be moving on," he told Quo Chung Wu, who stood steadfastly at his side.

"You will run from these men?" Quo asked in disbelief.

"The last I heard, I was a wanted man. The police have gone over to the yard bulls. What do you think they will do when they reach us?"

Quo nodded and shouted to his companions in Cantonese. "We will go to the temple. Make these men bring the fight to us."

At once the volunteers broke off their fighting and sprinted off down the street. Smoke Jensen and Quo Chung Wu formed the rear guard. It did not take much convincing to delay pursuit. Smoke shot one of the Tong henchmen in the leg and the whole crowd hung back. Smoke saw the last of them, shouting among themselves, as he rounded the corner into a wide boulevard that led to the market square.

A sharp pang of unease nearly doubled Sally Jensen over as she sat on the edge of her bed. Smoke was in dreadful danger; she had no idea from what or whom. She only knew, as clearly as the September harvest moon shone a silver pool on the braided rug which covered the smooth planks of the floor, that her man was close to losing his life. She had awakened only a few moments before, and the fragments of the dream that had disturbed her still clung to her.

She tried to make sense of the strange images which had tumbled through her dozing mind. Odd-looking lanterns bobbed in a breeze. Men in yellow robes wielded strange weapons. A heavy mist or fog hung over black water. There were screams and cries that echoed in her head. And Smoke was somehow mixed up with it all. She hadn't seen him in that kaleidoscope of weird impressions, only sensed his involvement. Hugging herself across her stomach, she rose and headed for the kitchen. A cup of coffee might help.

Sally scratched a lucifer to life and lighted the oil lamp on the table. Still troubled, she added wood to the stove and put water to boil in the pot. While she scooped coffee into the basket of the percolator, she tried again to piece together her premonition. To her annoyance, nothing meaningful came to the surface. She started when a soft knock came on the back door.

"Anything wrong, Miss Sally?" Cole Travis stood, hat in hand, a worried expression on his face.

"No," Sally replied promptly, then added, "yes. No, I don't know. That's what is so bothersome, Cole." She tried to force a smile and swiped at a stray lock of raven hair that hung over one cheek. "I'm not given to womanly vapors," she said lightly. "But I was awakened a while ago by the strongest impression that Smoke was in trouble."

Their winter foreman put on a sympathetic face. "Any idea what or where?"

Sally considered the shards of her dream. "In San Francisco, obviously. Only I can't make sense of what I remember of the dream." She abandoned the subject. "I was fixing coffee, Cole. Would you like a cup?"

Despite his silver hair, Cole Travis took on the expression of an impish boy. "Would you happen to have a piece of that pie left from supper to go with it?"

That brought the sunniness back to Sally's face. "Of course I do. Come on in. Maybe we can figure out what is going on around Smoke."

People scattered before the retreating students. Their movement through the market square set off ripples like a stone dropped in water. In the forefront of those who pursued them came the railroad police. Indifferent to the Chinese citizens of San Francisco, they roughly shoved those who impeded them out of the way. Even so, they made little headway. When the men they sought veered toward the Golden Harmony Temple, they redoubled their efforts.

They looked on from halfway across the square as the last to arrive, Smoke Jensen and Quo Chung Wu, paused long enough to swing closed a spike-topped gate in the Moon arch that fronted the temple grounds. Snarling at this impediment, they pushed through the late-night shoppers. When they reached the closed partition, several of Murchison's henchmen grabbed on and began to yank it furiously.

A police sergeant and several of his subordinates shouldered their way to where the men struggled with the gateway. "Here, now," he bellowed. "We can't go in there. It's sacred ground. A sanctuary."

"Don't mean nothin' to us. Mr. Murchison wants this stopped, and we reckon to do just that," Heck Grange growled.

The sergeant scowled at him, unmoved by the declaration. "Not with our help. We got orders, all the way down from the mayor. Treat these Chinee places with respect."

"What are you going to do?"

"What we can; surround the temple and make sure no one gets out."

Granger's voice turned nasty with contempt. "While you're doing that, we'll just open up this little box and see what's inside."

Stubborn was the sergeant's middle name. "You try it and we'll arrest you. We believe there's a wanted man in there, and he belongs to the police."

For the first time, Heck Grange regretted his idea about reporting the shootings to the police. If he killed Longmont and Jensen outright, it could get sticky. No matter, his thug's brain reasoned, they wouldn't give up without a

fight. And anything could happen then. He turned a disarming smile on the lawman.

"Go on, then. I'll send some of my boys along to take up
the slack."

"I appreciate that," the sergeant said stiffly. "Don't worry.
We'll get them if we have to wait until morning.

"What about these Chinee fellers with the hatchets?"

Looking around him, the sergeant shrugged. "If they
want to go in there, there's nothing I can do about it," he
dismissed.

At once, the young Tong members started for the walls.

Inside the temple, Tai Chiu urged his diminished force
to take the hidden passageway so as to come out behind
their enemies. Smoke Jensen considered it a moment.

"We should hold out here for as long as we can," he advised. "Everyone could use the rest. If we only had some
surprises to slow down anyone coming in after us," he
added wishfully.

Old Tai Chiu smiled enigmatically. "There are . . . certain
defenses built into the temple. They are activated by levers.
We can engage them as we leave."

Smoke began to look around. It took a while, though finally he began to recognize a number of clever obstacles,
or what might be turned into such. A large log hung suspended from two ropes. It appeared to be intended for
ringing a huge brass gong. The position of the line that propelled it had been placed in such a way that it could be used
to draw the thick cleaned and polished tree limb upward to
one side. In front of it, a too-regular line in the flooring indicated to Smoke the presence of a pressure pad. He
smiled.

Other things came to his sight. A large candelabra hung
suspended over the center of the worship area. Directly
under it was another hidden trip device. He did not know
that for centuries, this particular caste of warrior-monks

had been harassed by the warlords in China. He did appreciate that they had become wise in the ways of secret defenses. Slits in the domed roof suggested that arrows could be fired through them, or objects dropped on unsuspecting heads. Well, now, that was fine and dandy with him. His thoughts took another line.

Where was Louis? Had he encountered trouble? One of the volunteers hurried up to interrupt his musings. "The Triads are scaling the walls," the young Chinese informed him.

"All we need," Smoke snapped. He quickly checked and reloaded his six-guns. His fingers told him he had only nine spare rounds. Well, let them come, he thought of the enemy outside. We'll welcome them in style.

None of the Blue Lotus Tong returned to their club house. Louis Longmont rounded up the volunteers who had come with him. "We will go to this Celestial Hatchets building. They are the largest Tong, *non?*"

He thought primarily of his friend Smoke Jensen. Smoke had taken on the greater number because that was the way Smoke Jensen did things. While the students had ransacked the Tong headquarters and scrawled signs on the wall in Chinese warning the gangsters that they were no longer welcome in Chinatown, Louis had stood guard outside. In the distance he had heard the shrill sound of police whistles. Like Smoke, his mind went to the visit by police to Francie's. If the law joined in, it would hamper how they dealt with those who opposed them. It wouldn't do to kill a legitimate policeman.

When the last of the young monks had finished smashing furniture and breaking glass inside, Louis called them together and made his announcement. Eagerness shined in their eyes, though most kept their faces impassive. At once, they left in a body.

Disappointment waited for Louis Longmont when his

contingent of trash collectors reached the converted warehouse occupied by the Celestial Hatchets Tong. The place had been demolished inside. A few bodies lay about, among them some Occidentals Louis figured for railroad bulls. Silence filled both floors. Not a sign of Smoke Jensen.

"If they had finished here, and heard the police come . . ." Quo Chung Wu suggested; then he added, "Yes, I heard their whistles, too."

Louis understood at once. "The only safe place would be back at the temple, or on the junk." He paused only a moment. "I say the temple; it is closer."

They started that way. Along the route, Louis noted more injured, unconscious, or dead Tong thugs and railroad detectives in their brown bowler hats. No question that the night had taken a terrible toll on the Triad Society. It pleased him. At the edge of the market square, Louis halted his followers abruptly. He pointed toward the temple.

"I believe we arrived a bit too late." He noted of the swarm of police, railroad thugs, and Tong members around the walls of the temple courtyard.

"Not necessarily," Brian Pullen offered at the side of Louis Longmont. "I believe that is Sergeant O'Malley over there. In all that's happened, I forgot to tell you of one piece of good news.

"Actually, it's the reason I made such an effort to find you and Mr. Jensen. I received an injunction against the California Central Railroad, enjoining them to cease and desist in any attempt to apprehend you or Mr. Jensen." Pullen patted the breast pocket of his suit coat. "I also have a writ from the court ordering the police to disregard any complaint made against the two of you. All I have to do is serve them and the odds go down dramatically."

"What says either side will obey them?" Louis asked sensibly.

"O'Malley will. Above all other things, he is an honest cop. He'll take the writ back to the stationhouse and give it to his lieutenant. That will effectively end the police man-hunt for the both of you."

"And if Murchison's minions refuse?"

"Not a chance. They will have been served right in front of O'Malley. If they keep at it, O'Malley and the boys in blue will arrest the lot and throw them in jail."

Louis called after Pullen as the young lawyer stepped off on his errand. "I wish I shared your confidence."

"Not a problem," Pullen gave back jauntily.

Matters did not go quite so smoothly as Brian Pullen had predicted. Sergeant O'Malley spluttered and fussed awhile when handed the writ. "Ye should have delivered this to the stationhouse."

"I tried, and was told everyone was out in the field—in Chinatown, to be exact. If your lieutenant is handy, I'll be glad to give it to him."

O'Malley looked one way and the next, then murmured, "He's at that big red an' gold gate at the front of this place, don't ye know?"

"I came in another way. What do you say, O'Malley?" He turned to Heck Grange. "I have a little something for you, Chief." He continued after slapping the paper into Grange's hand. "It is a temporary restraining order stopping your railroad police from any punitive action against Misters Jensen and Longmont. They are to be left alone."

Grange went scarlet in the face. "I take my orders from Cyrus Murchison, not some goddamned judge."

Brian Pullen turned to Paddy O'Malley. "Sergeant, you know your duty. If these—hooligans violate this injunction, now or in the future, I'm sure you'll do it."

O'Malley's broad Irish face beamed. He had always fig-ured this Grange feller a bit too smooth an operator. It would be his pleasure to raise a few lumps on that oversized skull. He also recalled that the big one with the six-gun had been careful not to fire on any of his policemen. Might be there was somethin' to what young Pullen said, not just some fancy lawyer tricks. He came to his decision.

"Ye'll be movin' yer men on now, Mr. Grange, won't ye, now?" His brogue thickened with the assertion of his authority.

Heck Grange found himself up against someone impossible to take odds with. He deflated and pulled a sour face. "Yes. But we'll get those two, you mark my words, O'Malley."

12

By that time, the first of the Tong members had scaled the top of the temple wall. They went over with a shout and others scrambled to follow. Heck Grange made curt gestures to two of his henchmen and sent them off to round up their number among the railroad police detachment. He'd see to an end of this, he thought furiously. Cyrus Murchison owned more than one judge. What one had done, another of them could undo.

He headed off to care for that at once, tossing behind him a curt command to Earl Rankin. "Get 'em out of here, Earl."

"Yes, sir, Chief," Rankin answered, somewhat relieved. Being around all these roused-up Chinamen with hatchets made him nervous. A chilling shout from inside the compound added speed to his feet.

Watching first the railroad police, then the city police, withdraw, Louis Longmont nodded in approval. That feisty lawyer had some sand. He spoke to Quo Chung Wu. "Now, we catch the men of the Tongs between us."

A shot came from inside the temple grounds and the volunteers in the marketplace started forward. Recognizing friends, no one made a move to get in their way. Louis Longmont had his shotgun and that of Brian Pullen. When he reached the young attorney, he handed one of the Parkers to him.

"Maybe we should have asked the police to stay to take charge of the Tong members," Brian asked.

"Sometimes, it is not wise to think like a lawyer. I don't think these students are in much of a mood to take prisoners," Louis told him grimly.

Consternation mingled with doubt on Brian's face. "But . . . these men have broken laws here for years. They deserve to be punished."

"*Dead* is about as punished as one can get, mon ami, don't you think?"

Brian paled. "I—uh—never looked at it that way before."

"Start to, or you may wind up with a hatchet between your eyes."

Unobserved, Xiang Wai Lee joined his underlings outside the cursed temple of those twice-cursed *Chau Chu* monks. His face grew thunderous as he took note of how few of the Society remained among the fighters. This could not be tolerated. His cheeks burned in sympathetic humiliation while he watched that puny lawyer take the face from both the police and their supposed allies from the railroad.

Then his expression hardened into bitter contempt. He had personally opposed the Triad Society joining forces with these foreign devils. What did they know of the honor and tradition of the Society? What, indeed, did they know of ruling by fear? A few, quick words sent new energy through his flagged-out men.

Even while the *qua'lo* argued over the meaningless bits of paper, the Tongs united and rushed the walls. A smile broke his stony expression a while as he recalled that glorious day when his Celestial Hatchets had come down through the hills and stormed that other *Chau Chu* temple. Blood had run in rivers and the riches of the frugal monks had been theirs. It had financed their journey to this strange land of foreign devils and established their power in San Francisco. Truly the Goddess of Fortune had smiled upon him that day. Just as she had done in making it his destiny to be away when these students and the two *qua'lo* had attacked.

Xiang had viewed the destruction and death only minutes before. "This must not happen," he had hissed to his second in command, Tang Hu Li. "We must find our brothers and see that they bring me the heads of these white devils."

Now, he observed that busy hands had been at work on the gate and went that way. A gunshot roared from inside and his followers ducked low. Xiang made a stately figure as he advanced without even a flinch. As he had calculated, it inspired the drove of hatchetmen. They stormed through the open gate and flowed across the lawn. Only one firearm barked in defiance.

What of the other man? Out of ammunition, or injured? Either way, it boded fortuitously for the Triad. Xiang had moved up in the Society since coming to America. Under his bloody direction, the wasteful inter-Tong warfare had been ended. Now he ruled over all three in Chinatown, and had liaison with Tongs in other cities. He had literally murdered his way to the top, with more than fifty killings to his credit. One day a network would extend from every Chinese settlement in every major city in this country. And he would rule it all. The euphoria of his recurring fantasy lifted him even now.

Then reality came crashing back as a segment of the inner face of the compound wall suddenly lost its integrity and crashed downward onto seven Tong warriors. They died, screaming horribly. Dust billowed and obscured the front of the temple. Yellow-orange flame lanced through the murk and another member shrieked and grabbed at his chest. Xiang looked anxiously around him in consternation.

A second later, two shotguns blasted from the gateway

through which Xiang had walked only moments before. To his left a stout Tong hatchetman's head turned into a red pulp. Another groaned softly and sagged to the ground, his white shirt speckled with red. All Xiang could do was hurry forward into the mouth of that deadly six-gun. As he did, he broke with tradition. From his coat pocket he pulled a light-framed .38 Smith and Wesson. He had found it useful in his rise to power for the sort of killing he usually did. Right here, he had doubts of how effective it would be, though better to have it out and ready than not to have it at all.

He might have regretted that line of thought if Smoke Jensen had given him time.

Smoke saw the distinguished man with the long black queue swaying behind his head start up the steps to the temple. He also saw the small revolver in his hand and the deferential way the other Tong gangsters behaved toward him. Rage glittered in the ebony eyes, and the face held a cruel cast. This had to be the bossman of them all!

"Ho, Coolie-Boy!" Smoke taunted him. "It's me you're looking for. Face me like a man, not a dog."

Xiang Wai Lee hissed a command in Cantonese and made a harsh gesture that scattered his minions. "So, white devil, you have some courage, after all. You have a twisty mouth." His accent gave the English words an unpleasant flavor. "Are you brave enough to fight me in my own style?"

Smoke nodded at the Triad leader. "You have a gun in your hand, use it."

Insolently, Xiang thought, Smoke returned his own six-gun to its holster. It proved too much for Xiang's pride. He took another step toward Smoke Jensen and raised his gunarm. Taking careful aim, he squeezed on the trigger. Slowly the hammer started backward. Then the impossible happened.

With lightning speed, Smoke Jensen drew. Before

Xiang's hammer reached its apex, the big Colt roared and blinding pain exploded in the chest of Xiang Wai Lee. He staggered and took a step back. His own weapon discharged. The slug gouged stone from a step above him. An unfamiliar numbness began to spread through him. Was this what his enemies had felt before they'd died?

He banished the thought with a Chinese curse and tried to raise his arm to fire again. A flash of excruciating pain exploded in his head and a balloon of blackness quickly filled it. Xiang Wai Lee went over backward and rolled head over heels to the bottom of the steps. His dreams of a Tong empire went with him.

With the death of Xiang Wai Lee, the fight went out of the Tong members. The three nearest to where their leader had been slain spread the word quickly. Then, shouting their defiance and rage, they spent their lives in an attempt to avenge their leader and recover his face. They made the terrible error of attacking Smoke Jensen all at once. He welcomed the first one with a bullet, his last, which split the Chinese thug's breastbone and riddled his heart with bone chips.

He went rubber-legged and sprawled halfway up on the steps. Then the hatchetmen discovered that their enemy had a hand-ax of his own. With his last round expended, Smoke reholstered his six-gun and pulled his tomahawk free. A well-made, perfectly balanced weapon, the 'hawk had been made by a master Dakota craftsman. The head was steel and it honed down to a keen, long-lasting edge. Genuine stone beads dangled on rawhide strips from the base of the haft.

That 'hawk had saved the life of Smoke Jensen more times than he could recall. Old Spotted Elk Runs, who'd made it, told him; "I fashioned this in the proper time of the moon, said all the proper prayers, even gave of it a bit of my blood to drink. So long as you prove worthy to own it, this warhawk will never fail you."

Knew what he was talking about, too, Smoke reckoned. It had a fine balance and sure, deep bite. A Tong assassin named Quon Khan had learned the hard way when he'd closed in on Smoke and raised his own Tong hatchet. Quon had come up against wooden handles before, but this time his studded iron haft failed to perform its usual magic.

When he swung, Smoke Jensen parried with the Sioux warhawk. The Osage orangewood of the handle was springy and incredibly tough. It bent slightly—the best war bows were made from the same wood—and held. Smoke used the moment of stalemate to punch his enemy in the chest. Air whooshed from Quon's lungs and dark spots danced before his eyes as he tried to reply with a kick.

Then Smoke make a quick disengagement by bending his knees and pivoting to his left. Every knife fighter knows that save for a period of sizing up an opponent, the actual engagement lasts only seconds. So it was for Quon Khan. As the pressure of his attack eased on Smoke's 'hawk, the mountain man struck his own blow. The keen edge of the warhawk sliced through knuckles and laid bare a long portion of forearm.

Quon screamed and dropped his weapon. Instantly, Smoke struck again. White Wolf's Fang—the Dakota craftsman had insisted that Smoke give his tomahawk a name, for strong medicine, he had maintained—struck Quon and split his skull. The blade sank to the haft. It cleaved Quon's brow and split a part of his nose. Immediately, Smoke wrenched it free, with the aid of a kick, and turned to face his third opponent, while Quon sank in a welter of gore.

Bug-eyed, the skinny teen-aged thug with a bad rash of pimples froze in astonishment. No one, especially a *qua'lo*, could move so fast and strike so hard. Only two in the Triad Society had reputations for such prowess. And this foreign devil was not one of them. He felt his knees go weak and a warm wetness spread from his crotch, down both legs, as the huge *qua'lo* turned his attentions toward him. To his consternation, the white fiend smiled, then spoke.

"Do you want to live?" Dumbly the Tong brat nodded affirmatively. "Then drop that thing and get out of here."

At first he hesitated. He raised the hatchet in a menacing manner, and the big *qua'lo* took a step forward. That decided him. His Tong hatchet clanged on the stone step and he turned tail. Black, slipperlike shoes made a soft scrabble on the walkway of crushed white rock. Quon looked neither to left nor right, and certainly not behind, as he took flight. First one, then another of his comrades saw him and joined in.

Spurred on by the steady boom of the shotguns, they cleared the temple grounds in what became the first of a concerted rush.

Apprehension began to fill Agatha Murchison when a messenger arrived from Chief Grange's railroad police. It had been at midnight, and she had awakened to the rumble of her husband's bass voice, clear down in the front hall.

"At last, by God, we've got them cornered. Get back to Grange and tell him to keep pressing. I want those two finished off tonight. Tell him I want regular reports."

Cyrus Murchison had seen the man out, then padded through the house to the two-room suite next to the kitchen that housed the cook and her husband, the butler. He roused cook and put her to preparing coffee. Agatha had managed to remain in bed for another three-quarters of an hour. A voluminous velvet robe over her nightdress, she came to where Cyrus awaited further news in the breakfast room. The coffee service, her good porcelain one, sat on the table, along with three cherry tarts left over from dinner. Cyrus looked up at her entrance.

"You needn't have discomfited yourself, my dear. It is only a matter of business."

"What sort of business, Cyrus?"

"The usual," Murchison evaded, and began to demolish the tarts one after another.

"I'm worried, Cyrus," Agatha announced. "Ever since this alliance you worked up with Gaylord and Titus, you've been a changed man. It seems you never have time to rest . . . or for me."

Murchison's face crumpled and he put aside the fork, with its burden of red cherries and crust. "That's not so, my dear. I think of you always. Lord knows, there are enough reminders around my office. As you know, I have replaced that old tintype with an oil portrait of you, and there are those new-fangled glass plate photographs. And we do have many nights together." He looked miserable.

"'Many,'" Agatha repeated. "But not like it used to be, not *most* nights. What is this about fighting in Chinatown?"

"You overheard?" Murchison asked, his face suddenly drawn and secretive.

"I could not help but hear, with all the noise you two were making. Whatever have those heathen Chinese to do with your railroad?"

That prompted a harsh, albeit evasive, reply. "Outside of the fact that a lot of them helped build it, nothing."

"Then why are your men mixing in their affairs?"

Murchison's brow furrowed and he took a moment to contain himself. "It is not their affairs. Two very dangerous men, who mean harm to the California Central, have been seen there. Grange sent some of his men after them. Somehow it got the Chinese aroused."

"I shouldn't wonder. After all, it is the only place they may live as they are accustomed." A sudden insight came to her. "Was there any shooting?"

"*Of course* there was shooting," Murchison responded testily.

Agatha replied mildly. "Then I don't blame the Chinese for being upset." For her it was the end of the subject.

In his usual manner, Cyrus also saw it that way, this time with relief. They sat in silence a while, until the knocker resounded through the hallway loudly enough to be heard in the breakfast room. Cyrus rose to answer the summons. Agatha clutched at her lace handkerchief. Worry teased her mind. She seriously believed this alliance to be a terrible mistake. It had an aura of something illegal about it. For all his standing among the elite of San Francisco, Agatha knew that there were limits set by the power structure that could not be crossed with impunity. For a moment, a secret smile lifted the corners of her mouth.

For all the frivolous nature of the lives of society women, Agatha Marie Endicott Murchison had a fine, quick, and active mind. She had learned early to mask it under the usual vapid expressions practiced by her chums at school. Agatha Marie Endicott had been a lively, lovely young girl. She wore her long blond hair in the stylish sausage curls of her youth and had a trim figure. She had never gone through that leggy, coltish stage in her early teens. She had been lithe and graceful at her matriculation at her debutante ball at the end of May in 1860. It was there that she had met the dashing, handsome older man who would become her husband.

Cyrus Roland Murchison came from wealth. Old money had resided in his family for three generations. His great-grandfather had made the family fortune in whaling on Nantucket Island. His grandfather had added to the vast resources by pioneering a railroad in New York State that eventually put the Erie Canal out of business. His father had answered the siren call of the California gold fields and moved his fledgling family—his wife, his eldest, Cyrus, and three siblings—to Sacramento.

Quincy Murchison soon found he had no eye or hand for prospecting. When subterranean mining began, he fell back on the family talent. He engineered and supervised the installation of tracks for ore cars. He expanded to trestle bridges and eventually worked for Leland Stanford on his Union Pacific Railroad. Cyrus Murchison had followed in his father's footsteps. He had attended Harvard and an advanced technical institute and had been working as an engineer for the UP for a year when he attended the cotillion where he met Agatha.

For her part, Agatha Endicott maintained a cool demeanor, though her heart pounded at each glance at her ardent suitor. Cyrus had fallen in love at first sight. When the ball ended, he asked permission to call on her. Coquettishly, she had stalled him, said she must consult her social calendar. Two days later, she'd sent her calling card around to the Murchison mansion, now located in San Francisco. On the back, she had penned a brief message.

"Friday? A carriage in the park? Eleven o'clock of the morning."

It had stunned her when he replied with a huge armload of long-stemmed roses and an attached note. *"My world will remain in dreariness until blessed Friday. Eleven will be delightful, my dear Miss Agatha. I shall bring a hamper."* It was signed, *"CM."*

He called for her in a spanking surrey. A dappled gray pranced in glittering harness. With consummate gallantry, Cyrus handed her into the carriage, mounted and took up the reins. They rode off with Agatha in a rosy glow of anticipation.

Now his angry voice brought Agatha out of the pink warmth of reflection.

"What the hell do you mean, they took on the Tongs?" The answer came in a low, indistinguishable murmur. "Did the Triad Society kill Jensen and Longmont?"

This time she heard everything clearly. "No, sir. It was the other way around. By now most of them are either dead, wounded, or runned off."

"What about your men? What did Grange do?"

"We tried. We really did. Only the cops turned on us. Some mealy-mouthed lawyer feller showed up when we had 'em trapped in some Chinee church. He had papers from the court ordering us and the police to lay off this Jensen and Longmont."

Murchison exploded. "What the hell! What judge would have the grit to defy my wishes?"

"I reckon you'd have to take that up with Chief Grange, sir."

A low growl came from Cyrus. "You get back there and tell Grange I want to see him now. Not tomorrow morning, right now."

"Yes, sir. Right away, sir. An-anything else, sir?"

Agatha could hear her husband's teeth grind. "Just don't let Jensen and Longmont get away."

Cyrus Murchison returned to the breakfast room with a thunderstorm in his visage. Agatha Murchison sighed and poured more coffee.

An uneasy silence had fallen over Chinatown. Without a word, old men with wheelbarrows went about collecting the dead and wounded Tong men. The Occidentals of Murchison's railroad police waited to the last. These the elderly carted to the main entrance to Chinatown and deposited on the curb across the street. While they went about it, Smoke Jensen, Louis Longmont, and Tai Chiu discussed their situation.

"Is it to be back to the *Wang Fai?*" Louis asked.

"I'll tell you, pard, this street fighting isn't to my liking. I'm out of my element," Smoke allowed.

Tai Chiu stared at this big warrior in astonishment. Less than thirty-five Tong members, roughly divided among all three Tongs, remained in Chinatown. Yet this fighter with his gun—aha! gunfighter—said he was out of his element. What more could he do there?

Louis Longmont appeared to have read the old monk's mind. Through a low chuckle, he spoke to Smoke Jensen. "You wanted to finish them all, is that it, *mon ami?*

"At least break their backs. Have you ever seen a rattler with a broken back?"

"I do not believe I have," Tai Chiu responded hesitantly.

Louis shook his head in the negative. "There are not so many rattlesnakes in New Orleans. Now, water moccasins I know about. And other such vipers."

Smoke smiled. "Then I'm sure you know what I'm talking about. A rattler with a broken back gets so worked up about his body not doing what his brain tells it to that it begins to bite itself. Of course, rattlers are immune to their own venom."

Louis joined in with a chuckle. "It is the same with other venomous snakes, eh? What they do is use up all their poison striking at themselves. Then they can be safely picked up."

Smoke nodded. "I've been acquainted with those other deadly critters. To me, there's none of them worth picking up. Except for the rattler. His meat is mighty tasty, and a feller can always sell his skin and rattles to tenderfeet. Other than that, what use are they to anyone but themselves?"

Tai Chiu nodded enthusiastically. "Yes. Snake meat is quite a delicacy to my people. But this is not solving our immediate problem. What do you suggest we do now, Mr. Smoke Jensen?"

Smoke considered it a moment. "Going back to the ship—er—junk seems to me to be like giving up. Can your students and the other volunteers keep at it a while?" At Tai's nod in the affirmative, he went on, "Then I suggest you put them to cleaning up the last of the Tongs. It might be wise to send some of them through that tunnel of yours and hit the Tong hatchetmen by surprise. It can only serve to discompose them."

Tai Chiu smiled fleetingly. "And what will you be doing while we accomplish this?"

Smoke nodded to Louis and Brian. "The three of us have to go to the heart of this thing. We're going after Murchison and his co-conspirators."

13

Pearlescent light filtered through the fog of a pale dawn when Smoke Jensen, Louis Longmont, and Brian Pullen left Chinatown. Behind them, the house-to-house and shop-to-shop search for the remaining Tong members had already borne fruit. Kicking and screaming, several youths, still in the black trouser and white shirt uniforms of the Tongs, had been dragged from their homes. Frightened and helpless, parents stood uselessly to the side, looking on with shocked eyes.

Pitiful cries and pleas for mercy rose from frightened throats as these callow youths had their bottoms bared and slatted bamboo rods appeared in the hands of stern, muscular Chinese disciplinarians. Stroke after stroke fell on the exposed backsides of the former Tong terrorists. Smoke made a backward glance to take in all this. He stifled a smile and gave a satisfied nod.

Humiliation alone, from this ignominious form of punishment, would drive the Tong trash from the city, he reasoned. A loud rumble in his belly reminded the last mountain man that he had not eaten since early the previous morning. Not that he had not gone longer without food; many were the times he had been compelled to fast for three or more days. Like that time when wet powder and a horse with a broken leg had compelled him to evade a party of blood-lusting Snake warriors . . .

. . . Smoke Jensen had ridden into what had appeared to be a friendly village of the Snake tribe, along the middle fork of the Salmon River. He had been welcomed, given meat and salt, and a generous portion of roasted cammus bulbs. Years before, he had learned the traditional lore of Indian customs.

"Iffin' they feed ya'. Especially if they share their precious salt with ye," Preacher had solemnly told him. "Then ye can be certain they'll never lift yer hair while ye stay in they's camp."

"Sort of . . . safe passage?" the sixteen-year-old Kirby Jensen had offered.

"Well, naw. Once you leave their lodges an' clear the ground they count as their campsite, you jist might be fair game again."

"Ain't that sort of—ah—treacherous?"

"Nope, Kirb. It's all in how they sees things. Once you've been tooken in, they's honor bound to treat you fair and square. Once you've left the bosom of their hearth, you become jist another white man an' an enemy."

And so it had proved to be for Smoke Jensen when he'd set out alone from the Snake village. Within half an hour he became aware of pursuit. He pulled off the trail, circled back, and watched. Sure enough, here came better than a dozen Snakes, war clubs, lances, and bows clutched in hands; the men's faces were painted for war.

Once they had passed him, Smoke crossed the trail, then returned to wipe out his sign. He led his stout horse, Sunfish, deep into the thick tangle of fir and bracken north of the trail he had ridden out on. He continued northward for a day.

Often he doubled back, wiped out his sign, then moved along on a parallel track. Twice he laid dead-falls. It was late in his second day when the thunderstorm formed over the mountains and sent down torrents of water. Sunfish slipped on a clay bank and went down. A squirrel gun pop sounded when the stallion's cannon bone broke. A shrill whinny told Smoke the disaster was beyond repair. Flash-flooding threatened to take the stream he traveled along out of its banks. Yet in this unending downpour, he could not cap and fire his big Hall .70 pistol.

He considered any other means of ending the suffering of Sunfish to be unacceptable cruelty to an animal that had so unstintingly served him. The suffering of the horse tore at his heart. The tempest thrashed and whipped at the man and horse for long minutes, then swept on to the east, leaving a light drizzle behind. Quickly, Smoke wiped the nipple of his pistol, capped it, and fired a .70 caliber into the brain of his faithful companion. He dared not stay here, and he could not make any time with the saddle over his back.

Regretfully, Smoke stripped the saddlebags, which contained his scant possessions, and his bedroll from the saddle and left his valiant mount behind. Even with the storm, sharp ears would have heard the report of his mercy round. It still rained too hard for Smoke to reload, so he would have to rely on his other two pistols and the Hawken rifle he had yanked from the saddle scabbard.

No matter. He had been alone, and afoot, with less. He trudged off along the edge of the roiling mountain stream, far enough into the torrent to wash out his footprints. The storm had hardly abated three hours later. That's when the Snakes caught up to him.

With triumphant whoops and yips, mud-smeared warriors materialized out of the mist of rain to one side and from behind. Their bowstrings softened to uselessness by the deluge, they relied on lances and warhawks. Smoke dropped one with a .70 Hall, then a second. The Hawken rifle at his shoulder, he aimed for the most elaborately festooned Snake, the man he remembered had been most outgoing in his welcome to the village. One who had been introduced as the greatest fighter of all the Snakes.

He needed to down this war leader to buy even a small

bit of time. The Hawken fired and the ball sped toward its target. A pipebone chest plate exploded into fragments when the .54 caliber projectile slammed into it. It smashed through his chest wall and flattened somewhat before it ripped a jagged hole in his heart. He dropped like a fallen pine. Hoots of victory changed into howls of outrage and superstitious fear.

Grabbing up their dead leader, the Snake warriors flitted off through the trees. Quickly, Smoke sheltered the muzzle of the rifle and reloaded. His three pistols quickly followed. Rather than set off in a panicked run, he held his ground. Nightfall swept over the canyon and the Snakes had not returned. That didn't mean they wouldn't, Smoke reminded himself. The rain had ceased to fall an hour before, yet Smoke could not risk a small fire, even if he could find dry wood.

Back against a tree, the last mountain man settled in for a long, miserable night. From his saddlebags, he withdrew a strip of venison jerky and a ball of fry bread left from the Snake village. His munched thoughtfully while his eyes adjusted to the gathering darkness. He was not even aware of when he slipped into an uneasy slumber.

Morning brought back the Snakes. They slithered through a ground mist so thick that it obscured the cattails along the stream. Smoke saw them at the last moment and wished wistfully for at least one cup of coffee before they hit his camp. He snapped a cap on the Hawkin and downed a bold warrior who leaped at him from a huge granite boulder. Two more burst out of the brush, warhawks raised to strike. Smoke set aside his rifle and filled both hands with the butts of pistols.

First one, then the second Hall bucked and spat flame. Big, whistling .70 caliber balls cut through the air. The first cut a swath through the gut of a howling Snake. He dropped to his knees, a hand over the seeping entry wound, eyes wide. Smoke's other round found meat in the shoulder of a thick-waisted warrior of middle age. He made a grimace and gave testimony to the canine nature of Smoke's ancestry. Smoke Jensen hastily drew his remaining pistol.

He cocked the weapon and triggered it. The hammer fell on the cap, which made its characteristic flat crack. Nothing else happened, except the Snake kept coming. Quickly Smoke drew his 'hawk and hefted it. He ran his hand through the trailing thong, so it could not be wrenched from his grasp. Then he went after the wounded warrior. Four more of them, all that remained, gathered around, anticipating a quick end for this white dog . . .

. . . It had been one hell of a fight, Smoke recalled. The wet powder in his last pistol had put him in terrible danger. The wounded man had been no problem. He quickly dispatched the Snake with a feint and an overhand blow that split the warrior's skull. That still left four more. Awed by his obvious fighting ferocity, they held back. Smoke had not been granted that luxury. With a wolf-howl, he had waded in. The nearest of the four went down with a slashed belly.

His intestines spilled on the ground as Smoke whipped past him and whirled the warhawk in a circular motion that denied his enemy an opening. He spun and lashed out with a foot. His boot sole smacked solidly into the chest of a younger warrior, hardly more than a boy, who flew backward to splash noisily in the stream. He howled in frustration as the current, still high from the recent rains, rapidly whirled him out of sight. That left him with two.

Had Smoke been a seriously religious man, he might have prayed for strength, or for victory. Instead, he offered himself up to the Great Spirit. "It's a good day to die!" he had yelled into the startled face of the Snake facing him.

And, as Smoke now recalled, it had been the Snake who had done the dying. The last one had turned tail and run. That left Smoke Jensen alone to find his way on foot out of the Yellowjacket Mountains. He had made it, or he would not be in San Francisco, on the edge of Chinatown, walking down a street toward the offices of his present enemy. Another rumble of hunger reminded him again.

"What say we take on some grub before we face down Murchison?" he suggested.

"Suits," Brian Pullen readily agreed.

Louis Longmont looked around in trepidation. "Is there anyplace . . . suitable?"

Smoke made a sour face. "Louis, you disappoint me. I'm sure we can find something. Although I doubt they'll have escargots."

Smoke Jensen finished a last cup of coffee and pushed back his chair. The ham had been fresh, juicy, and thick. Three eggs and a mound of fried potatoes, liberally laced with onions, rounded out their repast. The walk to Murchison's office on Market Street took little time.

Early employees strolled toward the Murchison offices when the four grim-faced men rounded the corner and approached the building. Quo Chung Wu had caught up to the other three at the cafe. His sincerity could not be doubted, and he had been welcomed to the party determined to crush Murchison's dark scheme. Smoke Jensen signaled a halt and they stepped back against shop fronts on the opposite side of the street.

To make their presence less conspicuous, Brian Pullen purchased a copy of the morning *Chronicle* from a newsboy with a stack under one arm. He frowned at the dime Brian gave him and turned a button nose up to the well-dressed lawyer. "Don't got any change. That's the first I sold."

"Keep the change," Brian informed him.

Brightening, the kid scuffed the toe of one clodhopper over the other. "Really? Thanks, Mister." A small, newsprint-blackened hand shoved the ten-cent piece into a pocket and he set off to hawk his papers. "Read all about it! Big battle in Chinatown!"

Brian cut his eyes to Smoke Jensen. "Looks like we made the papers."

"Not by name, I hope," Smoke returned.

Quickly, Brian scanned the front-page story. While he read, a fancy carriage arrived and a portly, well-dressed gentleman stepped down and entered the building. "Who is that?" Smoke asked.

Brian looked up. "Cyrus Murchison." He went back to his perusal of the article. A flicker of relieved smile lifted Brian's lips. "Not by name, anyway. It says here that it looks like a band of dockworkers invaded Chinatown for some unknown reason and laid waste to a number of residents and store owners. Promises more details to follow."

Smoke's observation came out dry and sour. "No doubt what those 'details' will be like. Unless we can make an end of this right now."

Brian grew serious "We'll have to catch them red-handed 'fore anyone will believe us."

"Murchison has that much influence?"

"Oh, hell, Smoke, they all three do," Brian advised him.

"Then we'd best be gettin' in there and find proof of what they have in mind," the last mountain man suggested.

The determined quartet crossed the street diagonally and brushed aside several California Central employees. They ignored the startled yelps of complaint, quickly silenced when the offended parties got a look at the grim faces of the four men. Smoke Jensen shoved ahead of a prissy-looking clerk type and the others followed. They entered the lobby of the California Central building and came face-to-face with a trio of burly rock-faced railroad detectives, in their brown suits and matching derbies.

Murchison's minions took in the grim, powder-grimed faces, the belligerent postures, the number of weapons, and the scarred black leather gloves on the hands of Smoke Jensen. Without any need to consult one another, they began to sidle around the edge of the room, never taking their eyes off the four intruders. Their actions did nothing to deter Smoke and his companions. They walked purposefully toward the gate behind a railing that separated the lobby from the business portion of the first floor. Behind them, the three railroad detectives bolted out the door.

A dandified secretary looked up from his desk at their approach. His eyes went wide and he knew in the depth of his heart that these men certainly had no legitimate business here. He raised a soft, well-manicured hand in a halting gesture.

"I say, there, gentlemen—you cannot go in there." He gasped in exasperation when he saw they had no intention of obeying. "Please, fellows, let's not be hasty."

Brian turned to the sissified secretary. "We're here to serve a warrant on Cyrus Murchison."

Already wide eyes rolled in pique. "I will accept service on his behalf."

"Sorry," Brian pressed. "It has to be served in person."

"Mr. Murchison is not in at the present," the defender of the gate lied smoothly.

Smoke Jensen took a menacing step forward, the fingers of his gloved right hand flexing suggestively. "Sonny, we just saw him come in. Are you going to show us the way, or do I squeeze your Adam's apple until it pops outten your mouth like a skun grape?"

Defeated and demoralized, the secretary raised a feeble arm and pointed the way. "Upstairs, third floor, at the back," he bleated.

Quo Chung Wu remained behind to keep the secretary in line, while Smoke and his companions strode quickly down the hall and started up the staircase toward Murchison's office. Behind them, they heard the dulcet voice of the secretary purring.

"Ooh, a Chinese boy. How very nice. I *love* Oriental food."

Brian Pullen made gagging signs; Smoke Jensen twisted his face with a look of disgust; Louis Longmont produced a sardonic expression. Then they stood before the door.

Smoke positioned Brian and Louis to either side, their shot-guns at the ready. Then he raised a foot and kicked in the heavy portal. Wood shattered around the thick latch.

Moving smoothly on oiled hinges, the thick oak panel swung noiselessly until it collided with the inside wall. Beyond, Smoke saw a large expensive desk, ranks of book-shelves, an ornate sideboard with decanters of brandy and sherry, and flag poles with the United States flag and that of the California Central Railroad. He also noted heavy curtains that billowed into the room, driven by the breeze through open windows. Of Cyrus Murchison they found no sign.

"He got away," Smoke spoke plainly.

Brian gasped. "It's three stories down."

Smoke led the way to the window. Outside, an iron fire escape clung to the brick wall. Somehow, Murchison had learned of their presence and eluded them by this handy way out. From the direction of the stairwell, Smoke heard the sounds of a fight in the lobby below. He nodded that way.

"Sounds like those hard cases came back."

In the lobby, the secretary quailed under his desk while Quo Chung Wu tore into half a dozen railroad detectives. The timid soul peeped from the legwell of the rolltop from time to time when a strange warble or animal cry came from the lips of the Chinese student. He could not believe his eyes.

Two men already lay on the floor, writhing in agony. The Chinese boy moved so quickly and unpredictably that the others were unable to get a clear shot. He whirled and pranced, then came up on one toe and lashed out a blurred kick that rocked back the head of one detective. Staggered, the man crashed into the dividing rail and draped himself over it, unconscious and bleeding from the mouth. The handsome boy, the secretary had heard him called Quo, did not hesitate to enjoy his victory.

At once he spun and ducked and blocked a blow from
an ax handle. The owner of that deadly device stared stupidly while Quo kicked him three times: in the chest, the
gut, and the crotch. He went to his knees with a moan. Quo
moved on. At the same time, a dozen more bully boys
rushed into the lobby. Their charge was checked by the
bellow of a 12-gauge Parker shotgun.

Brian Pullen arrived on the scene in time to drop two
gunhands who had taken aim at Quo Chung Wu. The roar
of the scattergun froze everyone in the lobby for a moment.
It gave Brian time to reload. He needed it. Three hard cases
turned his way slowly, as though under water. The Parker
bucked in Brian's hands and a load of buckshot slashed
into one before he had completed his move.

He did not make a sound as he flew backward into another railroad thug. They sprawled on the floor in a heap;
the unwounded one squirmed and kicked to free himself.
Quo had not delayed. The moment he knew where the
shotgun pointed, he went into action.

Instead of avoiding the new threat, he waded into the
middle of it; elbow, back-fist, knee blows, and kicks rained
on the stunned henchmen of Cyrus Murchison. One of the
railroad policemen, accustomed to dealing with brawling
hobos, leaped at Quo, only to end up hurtling through the
air in his original direction bent double, his shoulder dislo-
cated and an arm broken at the elbow. It had the effect of
a bowling ball among ninepins.

Brown suits flew in all directions. Brian butt-stroked a
lantern jaw of one and stepped aside to allow the unconscious man to skid into the railing. Before the railroad
detectives could organize themselves, Smoke Jensen and
Louis Longmont arrived on the scene.

Smoke waded right in. He grabbed the coat of a hard
case by one lapel and yanked him into a hard fist to the jaw.
Saliva flew and his lips twisted into an ugly pucker. Smoke
popped him again and threw him aside. A yard bull

grabbed Smoke by one shoulder and heaved to spin him around.

Jensen did not even budge. Instead, he shrugged the thug off and drove an elbow into the man's gut. Air hissed out and the face of the company policeman turned scarlet. Before he could recover, Smoke gave him a right-left in the face that split one cheek and mashed his lips.

Two more turned on Smoke Jensen. One had a thick chest, with bulges of muscles for arms. He stood on tree-trunk legs, with long, wide boots to hold it all up. His partner weighed in at only a bit less menacing. Growling, they went for Smoke with their bare hands. First to reach him, the smaller giant tried for a bear hug.

Smoke batted one arm away and sent a sizzling left up inside the loop it formed to crash in right under the big man's ribs. He grunted and blinked . . . and kept on coming. A quick sidestep by Smoke evaded his clutching arms. Smoke popped him on the ear with a sharp right.

Again, all he did was blink. This could get tiresome right quick, Smoke reasoned. He disliked the idea of shooting an apparently unarmed man. Yet, from the corner of his eye he saw the other brute moving to find an opening. End it now, Smoke demanded of himself.

His left hand found the haft of his tomahawk and pulled it free. He dodged back a step and swung from his toes. The flat of the blade smacked into the forehead of the colossus with a soft ringing sound. His eyes crossed and he went to his knees. Smoke reached out quickly and pushed him to one side. He fell silently. Smoke looked up in time to see a fist slam into his face.

Starbursts went off in his head and he dropped his 'hawk. Bells rang and he felt himself losing control of his legs. He gulped air, rocked back, and swung in the blind. Due to the eagerness of the huge railroad detective to follow up his advantage, Smoke landed a good one. It gave Smoke time to recover his sight.

It went quickly then. He pumped lefts and rights to the

gut of the gargantuan. Liquor-tainted air boiled out over his lips. Smoke waded in. His opponent lowered his guard to protect his stomach. Smoke went for his face. The hard case recognized the need for a change of tactics and reached under his coat for a holdout gun.

Lightning fast, Smoke snatched his warhawk from the floor and swung in a circular motion. The keen edge whirred through the air and neatly severed the man's wrist. Hand and gun hit the floor. Gaping at the torrent of blood that flowed from the cut artery, the man gave a soft moan and passed out.

"Smoke, behind you," Louis Longmont warned.

Smoke whirled, his right-hand Colt appearing in his hand as he moved. A hard case with a short-barreled H&R .44 Bulldog gritted his teeth as he tightened his finger on the trigger. Fire and smoke leaped from the muzzle of Smoke's Peacemaker. His slug punched into the protruding belly behind the small revolver and its owner dropped the Bulldog to cover the hole in his gut.

"The door," Smoke yelled to his companions.

Understanding, they changed their tactics. Every move Louis, Quo, Brian, and Smoke made took them closer to the tall double doors of the main entrance. By studied effort, they cut a swath through their enemy. Aching, wounded, and dead reeled in their wake. Smoke Jensen broke free first, then turned back to batter an open face and create a pathway for his friends.

He jerked two hard cases together so violently that their heads clunked together loudly and they fell as though hit with sledgehammers. It took some time for the dazed thugs to realize the purpose of their opponents. Deafened by the loud reports of shotgun and six-shooter, they reeled in confusion while the four companions fought their way clear.

Smoke and Louis barreled into the street together, followed shortly by Brian and Quo. With an angry roar, the railroad's hoodlums recognized what had happened and charged the doorway. Smoke and his Western companions laid down a blistering fire that kept the hard cases inside while the quartet backed down the street. At the corner, they rounded a building and sprinted off into the center of the city.

"Where now?" Louis asked.

"We have to find Murchison," Smoke stated the obvious. "My bet he'll be somewhere around his railroad yards. First stop is the livery to get horses. Quo, can you ride?"

A blank expression came over the young Chinese student's face. "I have never done so before. But, if I can master T'ai Chi, I can stay on top of a horse."

Smoke did not know what T'ai Chi might be, but he already had doubts about the student priest's horsemanship. Nothing for it, they had to move fast.

14

Not until the full extent of damage had been assessed did Cyrus Murchison realize the danger in which he found himself. With the pale pink light of dawn spreading over the hills of San Francisco, he sent urgent messages to his co-conspirators. Not a one of the judges whom he had wined and dined so lavishly, always making certain they departed with fat envelopes of large-denomination currency for their "campaign chests," would even receive Cyrus in his time of peril. Nor, he was certain, would they seriously consider overruling a decision by a colleague.

That resulted in the plain and urgent summons to Titus Hobbs and Gaylord Huntley. It urged them to gather what men they had on hand and go directly to the California Central yard office. All were to bring horses. He dispatched Heck Grange on the same errand, with additional instructions to have the yard master assemble a "special"—at least six livestock cars, four chair cars, and his private coach. It was to be stocked with food and liquor and held in readiness at the yard office.

That settled, Cyrus Murchison went about his usual morning routine. He shaved, and he brushed and patted his thick shock of white hair into place. Then removed his dressing gown. His gentlemen's gentleman assisted him in donning his usual starched white shirt, pinstriped blue-gray trousers, vest, and suit coat. He put his feet in glossy black shoes and sat patiently while his manservant adjusted pearl-gray spats. He would select a suitable hat from the rack in the front hall. On his way out the door to his bedroom, he looked back at the servant.

"Oh, Henry, will you see to packing my field clothes? That's a good man. See that they are delivered to the yard office at once."

"Yes, sir. Very good, sir."

"And while you're at it, select a rifle and brace of revolvers, with ample ammunition for a long stay, and send them along also."

Henry's eyes widened, though he reserved comment. Like all of the servants, he had become aware of the turmoil in the latter half of the night. Something boded quite wrong for the master if he made such preparations so early in the morning. Henry would bide his time and see what developed.

Downstairs, Agatha had breakfast waiting for them. A fresh pot of Arabica coffee, date muffins, a favorite of Cyrus's, eggs scrambled with sausage and topped with a lemony Hollandaise sauce, ham, fried potatoes lyonnaise, and a compote of mixed fruit. In spite of his troubled thoughts, Cyrus ate wolfishly. He and Agatha chatted of inconsequences until he had had his fill. Then, pushed back with a final cup of coffee and another muffin, Cyrus invited the remarks he felt certain would come.

"We're going to be in for some sort of change, aren't we, dear?" Agatha asked.

Cyrus considered, for a moment, revealing the full extent of the change he anticipated. "There have been setbacks, yes," he allowed. "Nothing to concern you greatly. Although I will be required to be out of town for a while. At least until certain matters are—ah—attended to."

Agatha frowned. "You mean the killing of those two men who upset your plans," she stated flatly.

"Tut-tut, my dear, that is hardly a concern of yours."

Agatha Endicott Murchison had the proverbial bull by the horns and had no intention of letting go. "Come, Cyrus. I may choose to appear as vapid and vacant as my society sisters, but you know full well I am no fool. If you must leave town, this must be serious indeed. How badly can it affect our fortune?"

A rapid shift came to the expression of mild disdain on the face of Cyrus Murchison. A scowl replaced it. "I could be disgraced, humiliated, ruined," he listed harshly.

"Prison?" Agatha prompted.

"Possibly. It would remain to be seen how much could be traced directly to me."

"How much of what, Cyrus?"

Cyrus Murchison pressed himself up from his chair. "*That* I will not go into in detail with you, my dear. You are better off knowing nothing. I realize that women, even in your favored position, are still considered chattel. Even so, that does not exempt them from going to prison for not reporting prior knowledge of criminal events. I'm going east for a while. I'll not be home tonight, nor for some time to come, I fear. Keep your chin up, and always insist you know nothing of anything I may be accused of having done. Goodbye, my dearest."

They kissed as usual on the porch and Cyrus Murchison took his shiny carriage to the California Central Building on Market Street as he would any other day. There he found himself compelled to beat a hasty retreat far sooner than anticipated. He arrived at the railroad yard office short of breath, his usually impeccable clothes in disarray.

"Get everyone aboard at once," he demanded of the yard master.

"Horses are already loaded, Mr. Murchison," that worthy responded in his defense.

"Excellent. Did you send for my bay?"

"Chief Grange arranged for that. Oh, and Mr. Hobson

and Mr. Huntley are waiting in the drawing room of your car, sir."

"Good. I'll join them. Heck," he raised his voice to summon. "Get this motley collection of ne'er-do-wells aboard. Did you arrange for food?"

"I did. And whiskey, too."

Murchison scowled. "Keep a tight lid on that. All we need is a load of drunken protectors."

Any attempt to trail Cyrus Murchison through the early morning rush of people on the way to work would be useless. Smoke Jensen announced that conclusion to the others as they stood in the alleyway behind the California Central Building. He then offered an alternate approach.

"Odds are, he's headed for the trainyard. We can go directly there, or try to find if his partners in this are still around. I say we do the latter."

That received quick agreement and the four hunters set out. At the offices of Hobson's mining company, they learned that he was not in and had sent word that he would not be in that day. In the dockyard office of Huntley's maritime shipping company, one of those newfangled telephones jangled on the desk of the receptionist. He looked at it aggrievedly and assured them that Mr. Huntley had telephoned early to say he would be out of town for a few days.

"They're all at the railroad," Smoke summed up. "We'd best get over there."

They rode at what speed they could through the throng of milling pedestrians—all to no avail, they soon discovered. Reluctant to make any answer, the yard master had a change of heart when Smoke Jensen used one big hand to bunch the bib of the man's striped railroad overalls and lifted him clear of the ground.

"Y-you just missed them. Mr. Murchison and his associates had a 'special' made up. They and a whole lot of rough-looking characters rolled out of here not fifteen minutes ago."

"Headed which way?" Smoke demanded.

Newfound defiance rang in the voice of the yard master. "I don't reckon I should tell you that."

Smoke gave him a shake and got his face down close to that of the other man. "I reckon you'd better, or I'll have these fellers string you up by the ankles and I'll slit your throat and let you bleed out like a sheep."

Face suddenly gone white, the yard master bleated like one of the woolly critters. "E-E-East! Th-They went east on the Main Line. Clear to Carson City, in Nevada Territory."

"Why, thank you, Mr. Yard Master," Smoke drawled. "We're obliged. When's the next train go that way?"

"N-not until tonight. The local leaves at five o'clock, to pick up freight along the run."

"Won't do. See what you can do about rustlin' us up another train to take out right now," Smoke demanded.

"B-but that's impossible!" the yard boss stammered. "Running one train right behind the other is too dangerous."

"Suppose you let me worry about danger. Are there cars and a locomotive in the yard now?"

"Well, yes, of course. But . . ."

Smoke's gray eyes turned to black ice. "But nothing. Like I said, we'll worry about any danger. Where'd we find a likely train?"

"Out—out there," came the reply from the yard master, his eyes wide with fear.

Smoke thought on it for a minute. "Quo, you an' Louis go scout out a train that'll suit us. Let me know pronto." After they left, he turned back to the hapless captive. "I see you got one of Mr. Bell's squawk boxes." He lowered the thoroughly cowed yard boss to the floor and released him. Smoke's Green River blade appeared in his hand. "I think we'll just take that along with us. That telegraph key, too. That way, if you get the urge to send word down the line and warn Mr. Murchison about us, you'll have a hard time doing it."

"But—but that's railroad property," the man sputtered.

Smoke snorted through his aquiline nose his opinion of the severity of taking railroad property. "So's that train we're taking."

Quo Chung Wu returned, excitement lighting his face. "We found one. A locomotive, tender, baggage car, and stock car. Louis said they were just making it up."

"What's Louis doing?" Smoke asked.

Quo broke into a grin. "He's keeping the engineer and fireman peaceful. Also making them back up to a chair car."

"Now, that's nice. But we can do without the extra weight. It'll only slow us. Run tell Louis to forget it. We'll be with you shortly."

After Quo departed, Brian Pullen offered some advice. "Whatever we do, word will get out fairly soon. Even tied up, when the yard master is found, he'll spill everything."

Smoke made a tight smile. "Well, then, we take him along. If he's not to be found, everyone will assume he's off on some business."

"I ain't goin'," the yard master blurted. Smoke glowered him into silence.

Ten minutes later, they boarded the train. The yard master cowered in one corner of the baggage car. Quo remained in the cab of the locomotive to, as he put it, "keep the engineer and fireman honest." This he did with T'ai Chi kicks and painful pressure holds. With a nervous eye on the young Chinese, the engineer opened the throttle and the train steamed out of the yard.

Five miles down the track, with San Francisco dwindling in the distance, Smoke Jensen signaled for a halt. He dismounted from the baggage car and scaled a telegraph pole. He cut the three lines and descended. He would do the same several times more.

Once under way, Smoke settled down for a strategy session with Louis and Brian. "There's not a hell of a lot we can do except chase after them. At full throttle we can close the distance, given time."

"And then?" Louis prompted.

Smoke frowned, considering it. He was not an expert on trains, even though he had worked for the Denver and Rio Grande as a right-of-way scout. He visualized the exterior of the locomotive that pulled them. "There's a walkway along both sides of the boiler on our locomotive. I reckon we can use that to board the other train. When we do that, what we have to do is take on Murchison and his partners without their hard cases mixing in."

"Easier said," Brian began, to be cut off by Louis.

"Do not despair. Once in that private car we can jam the doors at both ends so no one can enter. That will make our task much easier."

"What if there's a nest of them in there already?" Brian persisted.

Louis Longmont shrugged. "That is for Smoke and myself to deal with, *non?* For that matter, you do quite well with that shotgun. Quo Chung Wu is . . . Quo Chung Wu. He may eschew firearms, but the truth is, he is a weapon himself. We will do all right."

Brian Pullen sighed heavily, resigned. "I hope you are right."

Sally Jensen drove the dasher into her churn for the last time. She pushed back a stray lock of black hair, then removed the lid and beater. With a dainty finger, she wiped the blades clean, then reached into the conical wooden device and removed a large ball of pale white butter. She dropped it into a large crockery bowl and lifted the heavy churn, made up of wooden slats like a barrel.

From it, she poured a stream of buttermilk into a hinged-top jug. Setting it aside, she selected a large pinch of dried dandelion blossoms and powdered them between her palms. She dropped the yellow substance into the bowl with her butter, added salt, and began to knead it, to work out the last of the buttermilk. A pale, amber hue spread through the blob. Without warning, an enormous wave of relief washed through her bosom.

So intense was the dissolving of tension that her head sank to her chest and she uttered a violent sob of release. Smoke no longer faced such immense danger; she knew it. It made her heart sing. She wanted to break into a joyful ditty. In fact, she did begin to hum to herself.

"Oh, Susannah, don't you cry for me." The words rang in her head. She wanted to tell someone. Quickly she looked around. To her surprise and pleasure, she saw Monte Carson cantering up the lane from the far-off main gate to Sugarloaf.

Monte brought more substantial good news. "I've heard from Smoke. He telegraphed to say he was about to wind up his business in San Francisco. Should be home in a week."

"When did it come, Monte?" Sally asked eagerly.

"This mornin'. I come on out right away I seened it."

"Oh, thank you. I just know everything will be all right now."

Cyrus Murchison set down the brandy decanter and offered glasses to Titus Hobson and Gaylord Huntley. They had finished a sumptuous dinner at noon, in the dining room of Murchison's private car. Over coffee and rolls that morning, Murchison had explained the current situation to his partners in crime. Since then, Titus Hobson had complained about the moderate speed of the special train.

"Can't go any faster," Cyrus Murchison explained. "The *Daylight Express* is ahead of us by only half an hour. The slightest delay for them would result in a disaster when we rear-ended the other train."

Hobson frowned. "Can't word of an unexpected halt be sent to us by telegraph?"

"There's no such thing as wireless telegraphy. Won't ever be." Murchison loaded his words with scorn for the uninitiated. "One has to be attached to the wire to get a message. So we run in the blind."

"Did you send along word of our 'special'?" Gaylord Huntley asked.

"Of course I did."

"Then we could get flagged down in case of trouble, right?"

"True. But the faster we're going, the longer it takes to slow down and stop. Relax. Enjoy your brandy. There's no one chasing us. At least, none who can go as fast as we're going now."

"What do we do now?" Hobson bleated.

Murchison frowned. He had never seen this yellow streak in the mining magnate before. What caused it? He carefully chose the words he wanted. "We go as far east as we need to. Lie low, wait and see if anything is done officially. Actually, there's nothing that can be done. Only the three of us know what we have in mind. I assure you, Jensen and Longmont have no idea where we are going. *They* are our only enemy. When we have a chance to regroup, we'll strike back at them. And believe me, the consequences for Jensen and Longmont will be dire indeed."

At the insistence of the engineer, the pirated train that bore Smoke Jensen and his allies made a water stop at a small tank-town located on the eastern downslope of the coastal range. Even though it was the gateway to the Central Valley, all the roads to be seen from the water tank were narrow and rutted. Truly, Smoke Jensen mused, the California Central could be considered the single vital artery to the area. To the south by twenty miles ran the tracks of the Union Pacific, which curved through the San Joaquin Mountains, from the first rail terminus at Sacramento to San Francisco.

No doubt the pressure of competition from the larger, more robust UP had been a factor in the decision for a power grab by Cyrus Murchison. No matter the man's reasons, he had gone far outside the law and had harmed untold innocent people in his determination to amass control over all of Central California and he had to be stopped. Smoke Jensen considered himself the right person to bring an end to Murchison's reign of bloodshed and terror.

His speculations interrupted by a hiss of steam and single hoot of the whistle, Smoke Jensen climbed back aboard the baggage car. A moment later, the train creaked and groaned and began to roll down the track. Louis had taken care of cutting the telegraph line. There would be so many breaks that it would take a week to repair them all, Smoke mused. Too bad. Catching Murchison and his partners came first. A question he had left unspoken so far came to him.

"Louis, what brought you to San Francisco in the first place?"

To Smoke's surprise, Louis flushed a deep pink. "A certain situation had become untenable for me in New Orleans. You know I had invested extensively in certain establishments in the Vieux Carré. Restaurants, a casino. Another casino on a riverboat. In fact, I had overextended. We had a run of heavy losses. Money became tight. One individual in particular, who sought to gain control of my businesses, pressed hard.

"He became obnoxious over it. Silly as it may sound, I found myself forced into an affair of honor with him. Dueling has been outlawed since the Recent Unpleasantness. One of the gifts of Reconstruction. In spite of that, we fought . . . and I killed him." Louis paused, wiped at imaginary perspiration on his forehead. "Fortunately, I was exonerated. I later found out this man worked as an agent for Cyrus Murchison of San Francisco. Digging deeper, I found out about Murchison's grand scheme. It appeared he could not be content with Central California, he wanted to expand. So I came here to find out all I could."

"Why didn't you tell me this from the git-go?" Smoke pressed.

Louis sighed. "Because I am convinced I behaved so foolishly. Like a twenty-year-old who still believes he is immortal. What could I do, alone, against such powerful men?"

"So you contacted me."

Louis eyed Smoke levelly. "Only after I learned much of the scope of their plans. Three days later, Francie was killed. I knew I had to see it out. I loved that woman, *mon ami.* She was truly *une belle femme.* We set her up in that lavish establishment, do you remember? It was after you got her out of that tight spot in Denver."

"Only so well, my friend. And I agree. Francie was indeed the lovely lady. She—deserved much better." Smoke Jensen did not waste his time on if-onlies, yet the thought flitted briefly through his mind: *If only Francie had chosen a different life.* He turned to look out the open door.

Fields ripe for the harvest flashed past as the train gained speed. A short conference with the reluctant engineer provided him the information they would reach the town of Parkerville shortly after noon. Smoke wondered what they would meet there.

When the "special" slowed to a stop at the depot in Parkerville, Heck Grange prevailed upon Cyrus Murchison to give the men in the chair cars an opportunity to stretch their legs. With permission granted, they began to climb from the train. At once, Heck Grange spotted a familiar face.

"Ty!" he shouted above the hiss and chuff of the locomotive. "Tyrone Beal."

Beal turned, then headed his way. Before Beal could speak, Grange pushed on. "You were supposed to be back in San Fran on the *Midnight Flyer.*"

"I know. Only there was some delay. Some hick-town sheriff got on our case about the fire and the dead man at that freight company. By the time he could verify our identity as railroad detectives, I missed the train." Beal nodded to the throng of hard cases. "What's going on here?"

"We could have used you in town. One hell of a fight with Longmont and his friend Jensen. Ol' Cyrus Murchison's got some wind up his tail. Seems he thinks those two are chasin' after him and he wants to fall back and regroup. You and those others might as well throw in with us for now."

"Glad to, though except for Monk Diller, the rest ain't worth a pinch of coon crap."

"Bring who you see as best, then. And after you get them aboard, come back to Mr. Murchison's car."

In five minutes, hat in hand, Tyrone Beal stood on the observation platform of Murchison's private car. He stepped across the threshold of the rear door on invitation. Murchison sat behind a large, highly polished rosewood desk, Hobson and Huntley in wingback chairs to either side.

"Ah, Mr. Beal. I am sure Gaylord here is anxious to hear your report."

"Yes, sir. We got that farmer all right. Burned his freight office to the ground. Pounded on him hard enough to get some sense into him, too. Actually, he got a bit much of a pounding. He died."

A sardonic, cynical smile flickered on Huntley's face. "Too bad. At least that's one gnat out of our faces. You do good work, Mr. Beal."

"Thank you, sir."

"You can do some more for us. I have only this minute learned from the station master that the lines are all dead west of us. The telegrapher received only part of a message that spoke of a runaway train headed this way. It is my belief that Longmont and Jensen, and whatever ragtag band of vigilantes they could round up, are in pursuit of us. I would be obliged if you took some of Heck's men and set up a delaying action. It would mean a considerable bonus for you if you succeeded."

Ty Beal inflated his chest in sudden pride. "You can count on me, Mr. Murchison. We'll hold 'em, never you mind. Hold them long enough, anyway."

"Fine. I'm counting on you. Now I rather think we should be on our way. Pick your men, and good luck."

Forty-five minutes later, the commandeered train commanded by Smoke Jensen rolled into Parkerville. Nothing seemed untoward at first glance. Five boxcars stood coupled together on one of three sidings. On the other side, beyond the double tracks of the main line, a passenger car idled, attached to a standard caboose. Like a suckling pig, the locomotive nosed up to the water tank and took on precious liquid. The fireman hurled wood aboard the tender, aided by Quo Chung Wu and the brakeman.

Relieved to be out of their cramped quarters, if only for a little while, Smoke Jensen, Louis Longmont, and Brian Pullen walked out the kinks, stretched legs at an angle from a wooden slat bench, and breathed deeply of the country air. They had only begun to relax when a fusillade erupted from the boxcars.

15

Hot lead flew swift and thick. Trapped in the open, Smoke Jensen and his companions had no choice than to duck low and return fire. Smoke concentrated on the open door of a boxcar. The hardwood planking of the inner walls deflected his bullets and they ricocheted around the interior with bloody results. Yelps of pain, groans, and ouches came from the occupants.

Louis Longmont quickly duplicated Smoke Jensen's efforts. The results proved spectacular. Curses and howls came from inside the cars. Then, from the opposite sides, away from the supposedly trapped quartet of avengers, came the sound of steel wheels in roller tracks. Light shone through the opening doors. Moments later, the hard cases left by Heck Grange deserted their vantage points, which had suddenly become hot spots.

Quo Chung Wu soon became frustrated with his inability to close with the enemy enough to be effective. He turned to Brian Pullen. "How do you use one of those?" he asked, with a nod toward Brian's six-gun.

Brian gave it a moment's thought. "Best use one of these," he announced, giving a toss to his Parker and the net bag of brass cartridges. "Beginners do better with a shotgun."

Grinning, Quo hefted the weapon, shouldered it, and squeezed the trigger. Nothing happened. Brian shook his head in frustration. "You have to cock the hammer first. Then, when you've fired both barrels, open it with that lever between the barrels, take out the spent shells, and re-place them with fresh."

"Oh, yes. I see. Thank you." Quo's first shot ground the shoulder of one hard case into gory hamburger. "I think I have it now," he called out cheerily.

"I suppose you do," Brian responded dryly, as he watched the wounded thug stumble away.

Gunfire continued unabated from the other cars and from beyond the second siding, where the grade had been built up to keep the track level. It was from there that the charge came. Half a dozen gunmen rose up and rushed the idling train with six-guns blazing. Return fire was spo-radic at best. Louis Longmont downed one hard case, then ducked low behind the steel wheels of the lead truck of one car to reload. The shotgun in the hands of Quo belched smoke and fire and another of Murchison's gang screamed his way to oblivion.

"One can apply the principles of *Chi* to shooting," Quo observed wonderingly.

That left four gunhawks. Smoke Jensen zeroed in on one and cut his legs out from under. With the enemy routed on one side, Smoke took quick stock.

"Get back on board," he commanded. He raised his voice to the engineer. "Get this thing moving!" He re-mained as a rear guard.

Quo seemed unhappy at having to give up on his new-found skill. He went up the ladder to the cab with agile speed, even with the shotgun in one hand.

Louis Longmont reduced the attacking force to half its original size before boarding the baggage car. The remain-ing trio faltered. At that moment, a burly figure stepped out of the depot, a smoking six-gun in one hand. "Which one of you is Smoke Jensen?"

Smoke answered quietly. "I am."

Eyes narrowed, Tyrone Beal took a menacing step toward the mountain man. "I want you, Jensen. I'm gonna take you down hard."

Smoke laughed. "Not likely."

"You've got a gun in your hand, Jensen. Use it."

For a moment, Smoke Jensen stared in disbelief at this cocky gunhawk. Confidence? Or was he completely loco? "If I do, you'll die, whoever you are." Slowly and deliberately, he holstered his Colt.

"M'name's Tyrone Beal. I had a good thing goin' before you showed up. Now, I'm gonna make you pay for upsettin' my apple cart."

The more mouth a man used, the less shoot he had in him, Smoke Jensen had learned long ago from Preacher. He decided to goad this lippy one further. "Road apples, if you ask me."

Beal's face clouded. "C'mon, you loudmouthed bastid, make your play."

"You're too easy, Beal. I'd feel guilty about it. It would be like killing a kid."

Froth formed at the corners of Beal's mouth. The locomotive whistle gave a preliminary hoot and steam hissed into the driver pistons. The big drivers spun with a metallic screech. Tyrone Beal's eyes went wide and white a moment before he swung the muzzle of his six-gun up in line with the chest of Smoke Jensen. His thumb reached for the hammer.

Smoke Jensen whipped out the .45 Peacemaker and shot Tyrone Beal through the chest before the first click of Beal's sear notch sounded. Disbelief warred with agony on the face of Tyrone Beal. He made a small, tottery step toward Smoke Jensen, then abruptly sat on his rump.

"I'm kilt," he gasped. "Goddamn you . . . Smoke . . . Jensen!"

Then he died. Smoke quickly boarded the already moving train and settled down in the baggage car.

* * *

Rolling through the peaceful autumn countryside, Cyrus Murchison was almost able to forget he had been forced to flee an empire he believed to have firmly in his grasp. At least, he did until those meddling sons of mangy dogs interfered. Titus Hobson had told him that Smoke Jensen was a one-man army. Ruefully, he recalled that he had scoffed at that. He knew better now.

Louis Longmont, who was considered to be a dandy, a fop, had proved far tougher than anticipated, also. How did a New Orleans gambler get to be so accomplished a shootist? If he moved in company like Smoke Jensen's, he must be one of the best gunmen in the country.

And that little snit Pullen. Until now, Brian Pullen had been the least-feared lawyer in San Francisco. Where did he learn to fight like that? Where did he learn to shoot?

The way the three of them had gone through the Tong gangs impressed Cyrus Murchison. For all his fine education and refined manners, he actually preferred using raw brute force to accomplish his goals. As a boy, he had dominated his friends, always been the one to decide what games they played. Later, when away from home at school, Cyrus had been fiercely competitive. He would brook not the slightest error in the work of his lab or his student engineering partners.

When at home during the summer, he worked with his father on the Union Pacific and frequently used his superior intellect, fast reactions, and utter fearlessness to knock resentful gandy dancers and other underlings into line. Yet here he sat, in his private car, running away from a fight. The mere thought of it infuriated him. A burning indignation rose within his chest and he decided to change his tactics.

At their last stop, a fragmentary message had caught up to him. It told enough. The men pursuing him had not been stopped at Parkerville. Beal had failed, and was dead in the bargain. Cyrus pounded a fist on the arm of his chair in frustration. From now on, Jensen and Longmont would have to pay for every inch of track they gained.

For the past hour, the commandeered train had been climbing a barely perceptible upgrade. The foothills of the Sierra Madre lay ahead. To keep up to the top speed safety would allow consumed far more fuel. The engineer conveyed that to Quo Chung Wu, who relayed the message via a pulley-and-rope device rigged between the baggage car and cab. Smoke Jensen replied that the train was to stop at the next station and take on all the wood it could hold.

When the train with the four avengers aboard arrived at Grass Valley, all appeared peaceful and serene. Only the engineer recognized a familiar car on the end of a train on the main line, alongside the depot. Suddenly, a switch was thrown and their stolen train rolled onto a siding and all hell broke loose.

From the three parlor cars, a torrent of lead blasted toward the three-car train. After the first stunned moment, Smoke Jensen saw that none of the rounds seemed aimed at the stock car. Relieved for the safety of the horses, he concentrated on returning fire. At once a hard case in the window of a chair car went down behind a shower of shattered glass. Up ahead, Smoke caught a quick look at the switch. A red ball atop the upright told him the switch was set against them. Fully occupied with suppressing the volume of incoming rounds, he hadn't the time to scribble a message and send it to Quo. Fortunately, the thick, heavy desks used for sorting mail successfully absorbed the bullets flying through the doorway. It became a very dangerous waiting game.

When at last the baggage car of the slowing train rolled past the lead passenger car of the other train, Smoke seized the chance to write a brief note. *"Quo, send the switchman to throw the switch and let us through,"* it read. Smoke affixed it to the signal cord on the far side of the train and ran it forward. He did not expect a reply and did not get one. Meanwhile, the thugs in the other train were trashing the coach behind the baggage car. A shout came from two of them when they spotted the switchman heading forward to change the switch.

They fired in unison and their bullets struck the hapless man in the back. He jerked, spun, and fell in the ballast along the track. A sudden lull came in the firing and Smoke steeled himself for what he knew must come next. He alerted his companions.

Feeling quite smug, Cyrus Murchison ordered his henchmen out of the train and to rush the one opposite on the siding. They ran forward eagerly, unaware of how well Smoke Jensen had instructed his three companions. With a shout, three of the hard cases rushed up to the grab-iron and ladder to the locomotive. They didn't know it at the time, but they were about to get a lesson in the etiquette of boarding a train, though unwelcomed.

First to reach the ladder, one thug clambered toward the cab, shouting an order for the engineer and fireman to go down the other side. For his efforts, he received a foot in the face that broke his nose and jaw. He flew off the iron rungs with a strangled cry. He hit in the gravel and cinders of the track ballast, a moaning, bloodied wreck. Those with him hesitated only a second.

Six-guns crashed and bullets spanged off the metal walls and roof of the cab. Their momentary delay had given Quo time to dodge below the protecting wall of metal beside the cringing engineer. Quo looked at the terrified railroad employee with disdain—if one could not conquer fear, one could never fully know oneself. Outside, the situation quickly changed.

Covered by fire from both, one of the remaining hard

cases climbed the ladder. The hand holding his six-gun came above the steel plates of the cab flooring first. Quo saw it and shifted position. When a hatless head slid up next, Quo set himself and aimed a deadly, full-thrust kick. Bushy brows followed and Quo let fly.

His training-hardened sole crashed into the exposed forehead and snapped the skull backward with such force that Quo could clearly hear the snap of vertebra. Not a sound came from the thug as he fell, twitching, to his death, his neck broken. That convinced his companion, who headed in the opposite direction. A shotgun roared from the open doorway of the baggage car and a swath of buckshot swept the fleeing hoodlum off his feet.

A rifle and six-gun took up the defense and a withering fire came from the riddled car that rapidly thinned the ranks. It slowed, then halted the advance. From their exposed position, most of the hard cases saw no advantage in rushing men barricaded behind thick counters. Several made to withdraw. A sudden ragged volley came from both sides of the track that slashed into the armed longshoremen and railroad police caught between the trains.

"What the hell is this?" Cyrus Murchison bellowed at the sight of his henchmen retreating toward the train.

Titus Hobson peered from the window, the red velvet curtain held aside in his rough hand. "It appears to me your local farmers and merchants have failed to be cowed by the thugs you sent out here, Cyrus," he replied sarcastically.

A bullet hole appeared noisily in the window out of which Gaylord Huntley gazed. He yelped and flopped on the floor. Cyrus Murchison cast a worried glance in his direction.

"Are you injured, Gaylord?"

"N-no, but it was a close call. Let's get the hell out of here."

Cyrus Murchison cut his eyes to Heck Grange. "Get those men back on board."

Reluctantly, then, he reached for the signal cord after Grange left for the observation platform. Three mournful hoots came in reply from the distant locomotive and steam hissed from all the relief valves. Slowly the pistons began to shove against the walking beams. The big drivers rolled forward, spun, and regained purchase. A moment later, the creak, groan, and jolt of the cars elongating trembled through the train. Ponderously, it began to move forward.

Only then did an expression of abject relief cross the face of Gaylord Huntley. Some of the color returned to the features of Titus Hobson, who reached for the brandy decanter with trembling fingers. Cyrus Murchison covered his face with an unsteady paw and repeated the dying words of Tyrone Beal.

"Goddamn you . . . Smoke . . . Jensen!"

Agatha Murchison read with horror the bold, black headline of the afternoon *Chronicle*, her heart fluttering in her breast.

RAILROAD POLICE AND TONGS FIGHT IT OUT!

Was this the problem that had taken Cyrus from home and office? If his police minions had clashed with those heathen Chinese, his life must be in danger. Tears stung Agatha's eyes. She did not want to read further, but she knew she must.

Late last night, elements of the California Central Railroad police clashed with members of the secret societies of Chinatown, variously called the Tongs or Triad Society. Much bloodshed resulted. More than twenty men died in the conflict, with a hundred more injured. Listed among the dead was an ominous figure known as Xiang Wai Lee, reputed Triad Society leader. When the smoke cleared, no sign could be found of the railroad police or of the sinister foreign gangsters of the Tongs.

Attempts early this morning by the *Chronicle* to contact Chief Hector Grange of the Central California Police elicited the information that the chief was not available. Likewise, attempts to reach Cyrus Murchison, President of the California Central Railroad, proved fruitless. Sources in the railroad offices stated that Mr. Murchison had left the city on business and was not expected back for several days. Our Chinatown contacts responded with terse replies of "No comment." The *Chronicle*'s Chinatown reporter, Robert Gee, informed us that a sect of Buddhist priests were also attacked by the Tongs. We have often spoken out against vigilantism in our fair city, and this time is no exception. However, until we learn the motivation behind this most recent outbreak of citizen violence, we must reserve judgment.

Yet duty clearly calls for this newspaper to demand an investigation . . .

Agatha laid aside the fiery words of the editorializing journalist and swallowed to banish the tightness in her throat. Something became undeniably clear to her sharp mind: if whatever had compelled Cyrus to order his police into Chinatown had been a legitimate reason, he would have had no reason to go into hiding. Unless, of course, there had been some—some—She could not use the word "criminal." Had there been something unlawful about the association of her husband with those Chinese? Suddenly she went cold and still.

Hadn't that one in the article, that Xiang Wai Lee, been

right in this very house not long ago? Slowly she lowered her head and covered her face with hands that trembled. Hadn't he?

When Murchison's train began slowly to gain momentum, Smoke Jensen climbed from the baggage car and waved his thanks to the local citizens. They cheered him and a few fired parting shots at the fleeing moguls. Smoke took his hat from his head and waved it to quiet the local vigilantes.

"If that fight didn't give you a bellyful, we could use some help. Anyone who wants to come along, put your mount on board and take a seat in that parlor car."

More cheers answered him, and men headed for their horses. Smoke went forward and swung up into the cab. His stern, powder-grimed face struck pure terror in the heart of the engineer, not a man to show yellow before anyone. But with the muzzle of Smoke Jensen's Peacemaker jammed against his head, he decided now would not be the time to show undue bravado.

"I want you to explain to my friend here how to throw that switch when that train clears it. Don't steer him wrong, or you'll answer to me."

"I won't, Mister. I surely won't." At once he began to outline the steps to activate the switch.

Quo Chung Wu listened intently, then dismounted and ran forward. By then, Murchison's "special" had cleared the switch. Looking down, Quo located the lever that swung the hinged tracks to give the siding access to the main line. Only minutes separated the two trains, and every second counted. Quo raised the arm into the position described and heaved on it.

Total resistance. The wrong way. Sweating, Quo reversed his stance and pushed. With a metallic creak, the steel rails swung away from the closed position and rode across the space between tracks. When the thin end of the right-hand rail mated to the inside edge of the main line track. Behind him, he heard the locomotive gather itself to rush forward.

He stood upright and gave a friendly wave. Then, fists on hips, he waited for the stolen train to come to him. More time was lost to allow horses and volunteers to board. Then Quo stepped aside to allow the locomotive to rumble past. When the grab iron came next to him, he reached out and swung aboard with all the ease of one who had had years of practice. He was surprised to see that Smoke Jensen had gone back to the bullet-riddled baggage car. Flame leaped from the open door of the firebox and Quo gave it a satisfied smile. They would catch up soon.

Speed came on the runaway as it rattled through and beyond the switch. Behind it, in the bay window section of the depot, the telegrapher frantically worked his key. The dots and dashes of Morse code sped down the line with the speed of an electric spark. Tersely, he advised stations to the east of two extras, one a stolen runaway, hurtling in their direction. Abruptly, he looked up when his sounder took on that flat buzz that came from talking to no one.

His eyes narrowed as he saw a local merchant shinny down a telegraph pole. The line sagged to the ground in both directions from the cross arm. "Thunderation, Hiram, why in hell did you do that?" he roared in his frustration.

Hiram made an obscene gesture. "We're tired of takin' hind tit to the likes of Cyrus Murchison. I tell you, he's up to somethin' no good, Rupe. I seed the flash of a marshal's badge on one o' them fellers shootin' at his train. A U.S. marshal's badge."

For the first time since he had gone to work for the railroad at the age of twelve, Rupe gave serious thought to ending his career.

16

Gaylord Huntley looked back apprehensively along the track. Greasy sweat popped out on his forehead. "By God, they're gainin' on us."

"We still have them outgunned," Cyrus Murchison responded, with a tone of indifference he certainly did not feel.

"I don't think so anymore," Heck Grange injected. "I saw some of those local bumpkins jump on board back there."

"Well, Zach Bourchard is a trustworthy man. He'll send word along the line. Up ahead there's a siding just beyond a wide curve. When we reach it, we'll pull onto it and throw the switch against them. I don't like wrecking a locomotive, but I'll do it if it stops those damnable gunfighters."

"Sort of costly, isn't it?" Titus Hobson suggested.

Cyrus Murchison revealed his anxiety in a flash. His fist pounded the edge of his desk. "Damn the expense! These men are not dolts. That they are on the verge of ruining us right now should prove it." His eyes narrowed. "We could still lose it all, gentlemen. I have an idea. I own this fine long-range hunting rifle. It has a telescope on it. You are such an excellent shot, Gaylord—what say you stop worrying and make yourself useful? See if you can pick off the engineer of that train."

Huntley pulled a droll expression. "I thought you just finished praising his loyalty?"

Impatience at such dullness flashed on Murchison's face. "I was talking about the stationmaster at Grass Valley. Although you have to admit, I have a point about Terry O'Brian, the engineer. Otherwise, he would not be running that locomotive, would he?"

Doubt in his face, Gaylord Huntley turned away from his vigil and reached for the rifle. He pushed in the loading gate cover and checked that a round was ready to chamber. With care he raised the muzzle to the ceiling and turned back to the platform door. His shoulders, slumped in resignation, more noticeable than his words, he opened the door and walked out on the observation deck. He knelt and brought the rifle to his shoulder.

Carefully he eased the eyepiece closer and established a field. The sway of the train made it difficult to settle the cross-hairs on the head and left shoulder of the engineer. Satisfied, Huntley worked the lever action and chambered a long, fat .45-70-500 Express round. Then he returned to his study of the target.

Steady . . . steady . . . lower now . . . easy . . . Damn it! The train lurched violently and destroyed his aim. Gaylord Huntley eased off the telescope and let the bright spot fade in his right eye. Try again. Lord, that loco must be a thousand yards off. He fined his sight picture, elevated the muzzle, and squeezed off.

The powerful Winchester Express slammed into his shoulder. A second later he saw the flash of a spark as the bullet whanged off the face plate of the cab a foot above the open window. A quick glimpse through the scope revealed that the engineer had not even flinched. Quickly he ejected the spent cartridge and chambered another.

His second shot screamed along the outside of the boiler and burst into a shower of lead fragments when it hit the thick iron plate of the cab face. Quickly he reloaded. The third round went two feet wide of the cab when the private car hurtled sharply to the left as the speeding train swung into a curve. Gaylord did some quick mental arithmetic. Four rounds left. He rose from his cramped pose and eased his numb legs.

When he returned to his position, he quickly expended two more bullets. They did no more good than the other three. Time to reload, he figured. He'd fire one more round first. A wild lurch of the car sent his bullet high; had he been on board the pursuing locomotive, he'd have heard the bell halfway down the boiler clang with a fractured tone.

Back in the plush interior of Murchison's private car, Huntley went to the gun cabinet and located and shoved fresh cartridges into the Winchester. He ran a nervous hand through his oily black hair and worked his foreshortened upper lip over his rodent-like teeth. Huntley knew what he needed and went directly to it.

Three fingers of brandy warmed the cold specter of defeat in his gut and spread calm through his limbs. Thus fortified, he returned to the observation platform and knelt to steady his aim. Huntley failed to notice that in his absence, someone else had entered the cab of the locomotive behind them. He also did not observe that the newcomer held a Winchester Express like his own.

Huntley took aim and took up the slack in the trigger. Then, through the circular rescale of the telescopic sight, he saw a lance of flame and a curl of smoke. A split second later, hot lead spanged against the brass cap of the platform rail and showered shards of metal into the face of Gaylord Huntley. Sharp pains radiated from the wounds and he screamed in horror as he felt a sliver pierce his exposed eye.

Reflexively he dropped the rifle and fell backward onto his butt. Beyond the rail, his tearing eyes took in another flash. Terrible pain erupted in his chest and he was flung backward against the doorjamb. Gaylord Huntley's mouth sagged and darkness swarmed over him. Beyond him in the parlor section, unaware of what had happened, Cyrus

Murchison froze, half out of his chair, hands flat on the desk, eyes bugged, as he stared in confused astonishment at the body of his former associate.

Smoke Jensen lowered the Winchester Express from his shoulder when he saw the body of Gaylord Huntley sprawl backward in his death throes. One less, he thought grimly. The chase continued, though the gap had rapidly closed. Hauling more cars, the lead locomotive could not maintain its distance advantage for long. At the suggestion of the suddenly and surprisingly cooperative engineer, the whistle shrilled constantly, a tactic that Smoke Jensen thought would unnerve those they pursued. Torn snatches of answering screams came from sidetracked westbound trains as the two locomotives ran headlong through the foothills of the Sierra Nevada mountains. Train crews stared after them with eyes wide and mouths agape. Tediously, the distance shortened to half the original 1,000 yards.

From there on, time was suspended as the trailing locomotive rushed toward the private car of Cyrus Murchison. Smoke judged it time to put his rough plan in motion. He left the baggage car to talk to the volunteers in the chair coach behind. The two dozen of farmers and townies who had jumped aboard Smoke's commandeered train gathered around at his summons. He eyed them with concentration.

"Now, this is going to be tricky. None of you are required to do what I'm going to ask. First off, I want to know how many among you consider yourselves surefooted."

Nearly all hands went up. Smoke suppressed a smile and nodded. "Take a look outside and forward." By turns they went to the open windows and did so. Several recoiled from the blast of wind created by their swift passage. "See that catwalk along the boiler? How many of you surefooted ones think you can walk that while the train is moving?"

Not so many hands went up this time. Smoke considered that with himself and Louis, and six of these willing volunteers, they could carry off his plan. It didn't matter to him what happened to the rest of the train. What they needed to do was isolate the rear car containing Murchison and Hobson. Now for the tricky part.

"That's good. We need six men to come with Louis and me. What we are going to try to do is close in and ram that observation car. The idea is to derail it." Startled expressions broke out among the plain country folk facing Smoke Jensen. "Failing that, those of you who come with us are to be ready to advance along the catwalks on both sides of the locomotive and board the other train while we are in motion."

"That sounds a tall order, Mister," a farmer with sun-reddened face observed.

"Yeah," a pimply store clerk picked it up. "Why should we take such a risk for you? Besides, who are you, anyway?"

"Folks call me Smoke Jensen."

Color drained from the lippy clerk's face. "Oh, Jesus. I've heard of you. Read all about you in them Ned Buntline books."

Smoke gave him a hard, straight face. "Buntline lies. I've never shot a man in the back who hadn't turned it after I squeezed the trigger."

Eyes widened, the clerk gulped, "You've read all them dime novels?"

"A fellah needs to know what others are sayin' about him," Smoke said simply. "Now, like I say, do you think you can walk that narrow track and jump, if need be?"

Seven responded in the affirmative. "Better than I expected," Louis Longmont stated dryly.

Smoke let the other shoe drop. "Remember, there are still a lot of hard cases aboard that train. If we don't isolate the rear car, the fighting will be rough."

Only one of the hands went down. "All right," Smoke announced. "I'll lead you. Louis here will give you the word when the time is right."

* * *

Terence O'Brian did not mind shattering the nerves of those they pursued. Besides, he reasoned, it gave them more of a chance by warning approaching trains onto sidings. When he heard the blathering of that crazy man he knew the boy-o had slipped a cog somewhere. Jumping from one train to another? Pure madness. When the tough-faced gilly ordered the throttle opened to full again, he said, as much.

"That's a lunatic idea if I ever heard one. Why, at the speed we're goin', we could ram that train ahead of us." Smoke Jensen's reply left him thunder blasted.

"Exactly what I had in mind."

"Not with my beautiful baby, ye won't," Terry O'Brian blurted in indignation. "Ye'll derail us both!"

Smoke Jensen pulled an amused face. "The thought occurred to me. Only, I want you to just knock them off the track, not us."

Gloved hand on hip, O'Brian snapped his defiance. "Can't be done. We hit them hard enough to derail that heavy car, we go off, too."

Smoke though a moment. "You're the engineer. If you say that's the case, I'll believe you. Can you do this? Get us close enough that men can jump from the front of this locomotive to the rear car of that train?"

"Sure. Easy. If anyone is crazy enough to try makin' the leap. Thing is, I don't want to ram them."

"I understand. Only, give it a try and see what we can do."

"You're stark ravin' crazy, ye are," O'Brian offered his opinion again. Then, in exasperation, he put hand to throttle and shoved it forward.

It took a while for the big drivers to respond. With the rush of steam, they spun free of traction for a moment, then O'Brian added sand and the engine leaped forward. The gap quickly closed. At two hundred yards, four men appeared on the top of the private car. Two took up sitting positions, while one knelt and the other flattened out prone. Smoke took note of it and hefted his Express rifle.

Aiming through the forward window, opposite the engineer, Smoke squeezed off a round. One of the seated hard cases reared backward, fell to one side, and rolled off the car. The others opened fire.

"Get down!" Smoke shouted to O'Brian. "Not you," he barked at the fireman. "Keep stoking that boiler."

Bullets spanged off the metal plates of the locomotive. Smoke hunkered down and took aim again. The Winchester bucked and another thug sprang backward from his kneeling position and sprawled flat on the walkway atop Murchison's car. A slug cracked past Smoke's left ear and he reflexively jerked his head to the side. Damn, they have some good shots over there, Smoke thought. Not the time to ease up.

He fired again. As the hammer fell, the private car swayed to the left and their locomotive jinked right. Smoke's bullet sped through empty air. He cycled a fresh cartridge into the chamber. When the careening rolling stock settled down, he drew a bead on the chubby gunhand lying on his belly.

At the bullet's impact, the fat hard case jerked upward and flopped back down, shot though the top of his head. Not bad, Smoke judged his performance. At the last moment, before Smoke could sight in on him, the fourth of Murchison's gunmen gave it up and ran for the safety of the car ahead. Smoke held his fire as the thug's head disappeared below the lip of the roof overhang. Time to get ready, he decided, and turned away.

When he returned to the cab, the distance had narrowed to less than a hundred feet. Gingerly, O'Brian brought his behemoth up to within twenty feet, his hand playing the throttle like an organist at a mighty pipe organ console. Smoke gave him the nod. Swallowing against the lump of fear in his throat, the engineer opened the throttle again and the big Baldwin 4-6-2 sped into the rear of the Pullman-manufactured private car.

Violent impact knocked many of the volunteers off their

feet. One clung desperately to the grab-rail to keep from falling down among the spinning drivers. Smoke staggered as the two vehicles slammed together. With a terrible screech, the observation platform rail sheered off and went flying to the sides of the track.

Murchison's car jolted forcefully and the rear truck raised, then slammed back. Unasked, O'Brian eased back. The blunt nose of the locomotive withdrew from its menace over the beleaguered carriage and held steady, three yards off the shattered rear platform. Terence O'Brian looked pleadingly at Smoke Jensen. Smoke nodded to him.

"Bring it in as close as possible. We'll jump."

Cyrus Murchison could not believe what he saw through the open door at the rear of his private car. Beyond the gap between it and the chase train, men stood on both sides of the locomotive boiler, slowly advancing to the nose of the steaming monster. He had been knocked out of his chair by the collision. At first he could not figure out what these lunatics had in mind. Then the reality struck him.

They intended to jump from the speeding locomotive to his car! If they made it, it would be all over, he thought in a panic. He waved to a slowly recovering Heck Grange. "Got to get some of the men in here. Those crazy bastards are coming after us."

"How?" Heck demanded.

"They are going to jump over here, you idiot. Now, do as I say. Get a dozen, no, twenty guns in here right now."

Heck started for the front door of the car. He worked the latch handle and passed through at an uneven gait. Wobbling on unsteady legs, Grange pushed into the next car. Concerned faces looked up. He stared them down, swaying with the roll of the car, one hand on the butt of his six-gun.

"We're in for it, boys. Jensen's comin' after us. Gonna jump from train to train. The boss wants twenty of you in his car right now."

"Hell, Chief, we can't get twenty men in there. Maybe eight or ten. Even then, we'd be crammed so close it would be like shootin' fish in a stock tank."

"I know that, Miller. Best thing is to be ready on the vestibule, in case those gunhawks get through. Mr. Murchison will never know if there's twenty or five in there. Now, let's get going."

Smoke Jensen looked down at the dizzying blur of ballast and cross-ties in the space between the cowcatcher of the Baldwin loco and the rocking platform ahead. He swallowed to regain his equilibrium, flexed his knees, and prepared to spring. Behind him he heard a voice raised in sincere prayer.

". . . *Holy Mary, mother of God, pray for us sinners, now and at the hour of our death . . .*"

Well, that might be right now, the last mountain man considered. What he proposed to do, what they were about to do, could easily be considered suicidal. One or all of them could be dead within the next two minutes. The rail-like bars of the cowcatcher inched closer, closer. Another foot. Two feet. Smoke Jensen reached forward with his gloved hands. Smoke took his mind off the rush of death below and sucked in a breath.

Jump! Smoke left his insecure perch and sailed over the gap between the two trains. He seemed to pause in the middle, while the gap widened. A moment later the Baldwin surged forward and Smoke hit the platform on hands and knees. He landed solidly, thankful for the gloves he wore. A burly farmer crashed to the platform beside him. Smoke looked up to see the car interior was empty.

He came to his feet as two more men landed on the observation deck. A moment later, the door at the far end flew open. Five men poured in. Smoke filled his hand with a .45 Colt and set it to barking. Crystal shattered and tinkled down on the expensive Oriental carpets that covered the floor. The hard case in the lead jerked and spilled on his face in the narrow passage that paralleled the bedrooms. The man behind him threw a wild shot and tripped over the supine corpse.

More glass shattered, this time an etched panel between the dining room and the parlor area. Smoke sidestepped and a shotgun behind him roared. Two thugs screamed and slapped at invisible wasps that stung them with buckshot fury. More gunhands pushed through the vestibule door. By now, four of the volunteers had gained the hurtling lead train.

Louis Longmont appeared at Smoke Jensen's side. "The last two are on their way."

"Good. No chance to secure that door now. No reason, really. Murchison and Hobson got away."

"They can't go far," Louis stated the obvious.

With the arrival of the last volunteers, the volume of fire became too much for the armed ruffians. Their ranks devastated, they chose to withdraw from the hail of lead that cut them down mercilessly. Smoke Jensen's last slug slammed into the thick wooden door of the private car. A muffled howl of pain came from the other side.

"Not as sturdy as I thought," Smoke said lightly to Louis. "I say we go ahead."

Louis cocked an eyebrow. "They will be waiting for us."

Smoke grinned. "Yep. I know. That's why I brought these." From the pocket of his vest, Smoke produced half a dozen bright red packets, covered and sealed with tin foil.

"What are those?" Louis asked.

"Railroad torpedoes," Smoke explained. "I picked them up from the utility box in the cab of the other train."

Louis still did not follow. "What do you do with those?"

Smoke showed mischief in his twinkling gray eyes. "We have one of these fine gentlemen toss them through the far door, one at a time, and shoot them like clay pigeons.

"What good will that do, mon ami?"

"They make a hell of a bang. Enough explosive to jar the

lead truck of a locomotive and be heard over the noise of the engine."

"Powerful. What gave you the idea?"

"I learned about these torpedoes when I worked for the D&RG. When a train breaks down on the main line and there is no siding, a trackwalker goes back half a mile and lays out a series of torpedoes. The number of bangs tells the engineer what is wrong and prepares him to slow and stop his train. In the construction camp we used to shoot them for sport, so I know it will work."

A sardonic smile turned down the lips of Louis Longmont. "Then, by all means, let us get to it, my friend."

Smoke turned to the volunteers. "Any of you good at Abner Doubleday's game of baseball?" Three of the Valley men nodded their heads. "One of you consider yourself a good hurler?"

"Ay bin fairly good, Mr. Yensen," a cotton-haired Swede declared with suppressed pride.

"Olie's right," one of his companions offered. "He's hell at the pitch."

Smoke smiled. "Good, then. Here, I want you to take these," he began, explaining his plan to the Swede pitcher.

Two minutes later, Smoke, Louis, and Olie crossed the gap between vestibules and got ready. Louis yanked open the door. Olie gave a slow underhand pitch that sailed one of the red torpedoes down the aisle, flat side toward the door. Smoke brought up his .45 Colt before the startled hard cases could react, and fired.

A bright flash and shattering explosion followed. Glass rang musically as windows blew out all along the car. Men screamed and clutched their ears. At Smoke's nod, Olie pitched another one. One man, blood streaming from his nose, leaped from his seat and stumbled down the passage toward the far end of the coach. A strong odor of kerosene rose from pools under the broken lamps. Smoke signaled for another.

With an expression of awe on his broad face, Olie flung

another torpedo. A weakened portion of the sidewall, complete with blown-out window sash, ripped away from the side of the car. It whipped off along the rushing train. The gunhands who remained conscious could stand it no longer. Pandemonium broke out as they surged toward the next car forward.

Smoke signaled to the waiting volunteers and led the way after the fleeing enemy. He skidded to a stop and jumped to one side when a torrent of bullets ripped through the facing wall and the door. Tinted-edged glass shattered in the upper panel of the door and one clipped the shoulder of a farmer from the Central Valley.

"Ow, damn them," he complained. "Toss in some o' them bombs, Olie."

Smoke gave the nod and Olie complied. The first one went off before Smoke could fire. The startled gunhand who had shot it gaped in disbelief. Olie recovered instantly and hurled another. Smoke blasted it a third of the way down the car. Windowpanes disappeared. Men groaned and cursed. Powder smoke filled the afternoon air. Sunlight filtered through the billows of dust and burnt explosive in sickly orange shafts. Another torpedo put the defenders in panic.

They raced off to find security in the next car. Smoke watched as the last man through the entry paused to throw the lock. He cut his eyes to Louis.

"We're going to have to do this the hard way," Smoke stated flatly, as he paused to reload. The vision haunted him. Someone among his volunteers would die before this was over.

17

Smoke Jensen stationed three men at the vestibule door, to keep the attention of the hard cases beyond. Then he and Louis led the others to the rear of that car and out onto the narrow platform. He pointed to a set of iron rungs which led to the roof. With difficulty they climbed the ladder, fighting against the jerk and sway of the careening train.

On top of the car, Smoke went forward with the volunteers following. Clouds had formed, Smoke noticed, as he worked his way toward the car-full of gunmen. A light misty rain fell, whipped into their faces by the rush of wind. The air smelled of woodsmoke, which gushed from the tall, grinder-fitted stack. It was filled with fine, gritty cinders and inky exhaust, which quickly blackened their faces and clothing. Footing became treacherous on the damp strips of wood that formed the walkway. When they reached the gap between cars, Smoke stopped to consider the alternatives.

Climb down, cross over and climb back up, or jump. He tested his boot soles against the wood to gauge the security of the roof walk. He took a quick, appraising glance at the strained faces behind him, then he moved back toward them, took three, quick, running steps, and jumped. At the last instant, his foot slipped.

Smoke hurtled in an awkward sprawl toward the forward chair car roof. The toe of his boot caught on the trailing lip of the walkway and sent him to his hands and knees. He hung there, painfully aware that he could have cost them the element of surprise. After two, long, worrisome minutes, he inched forward. Still challenging fire to come up through the roof, he paused again. Perhaps the idea did not occur to those below that they could penetrate the thin roof of the car. Smoke pressed himself up onto his boots and motioned for the others to follow.

To his relief, they made it without undue noise. When they had gathered as best they could, Smoke explained what he had in mind. "Spread out. We're going to fire at random through the roof. May not hit anyone, but it will stir them up some. The next coach is the smoking car. My bet is that Murchison and Hobson are in there. If we can rig the doors of the next car, jam them somehow, we can trap his gunmen there and go after the leaders with little risk."

"Sounds good," a thick-shouldered feed store owner judged.

"Then let's get to it," Smoke urged.

Smoke and Louis went forward and climbed down. Two volunteers went down the nearer ladder. Smoke used the coupler release bar to tightly jam the latch to the parlor car. To his disappointment, they could find nothing to do the same to the rear entrance to the smoking coach. Accepting the setback, they returned to the top. Seconds later, bullets punched through the roof to send showers of splinters and shards of the stamped tin ceiling down onto the unsuspecting gunhawks. Already demoralized by the exploding torpedoes, they made as one for the doors at each end. Slugs continued to snap and crack past them. More bullets smashed through the ceiling.

One man cried out in pain, shot through the top of his shoulder. His ragged breath and the pink froth on his lips told his companions the round had gone through his right lung from top to bottom. He wasn't long for this world. Another hard case uttered a groan and fell heavily to the floor. From ahead a shout of rage rang through the car when Murchison's gunsels found the latch somehow secured against them.

Shots sounded from within the car and shards of glass tinkled out onto the vestibule platform. Eager hands reached through to wrestle with the obstructing bar. After ample curses and some furious struggle, it came free. Men sprang instantly across to the smoking car. Smoke Jensen had no choice but to make the best of a failed plan. He prepared to lead the volunteers forward when a sudden jolt nearly knocked them all off their feet and over the side.

"Cut it loose! Cut it loose!" the familiar voice of Cyrus Murchison shouted from the open doorway to the smoking lounge.

Metal grated against metal, and with a lurch, the couplers opened and the front part of the train sped away from the rear portion, which began to lose forward momentum. Smoke cut his eyes behind them and saw the chase locomotive swelling rapidly in size.

"Get down and hold on!" he shouted.

Beyond Smoke, the second train plowed into the rear of the first. The force of the impact telescoped along the line of cars. The momentum drove the open couplers together, momentarily reattaching the last three cars. The men clinging to the catwalk bounced and whipped about like rag dolls in the hands of an angry child. With an explosive roar, steam exploded from the ruptured boiler of the trailing locomotive. The good and bad alike sprawled in the aisles. Men in the baggage car of the rear train slammed forward, tumbled over sorting tables and crashed into the front wall of the car. Worse was yet to come.

First, the private car of Cyrus Murchison left the rails, crumpling in on itself as it drove forward. The coach ahead teetered and began to lean to the left. It fell ponderously. Domino-like, the next chair car began to cant to one side. Only the remaining forward motion of the reconnected cars prevented total disaster. When the car under them began to waver, Smoke Jensen shouted to the men with him, "Get off of here. Jump to the right."

Unmindful of possible broken bones, the eight clinging men threw themselves away from the reeling car. The unsecured coupler twisted at the joint and separated. It let the car pitch over onto one side, to skid a distance before it came to rest at an acute angle. The eight wheels on the trucks spun as it lay in a cloud of dust. Beyond them, the train with Murchison aboard rolled serenely away. A man next to Smoke Jensen groaned.

"I think I broke my leg," he stated, his mind dulled by the sudden crisis.

"Hang on. I'll get you some help." Smoke looked beyond the billows of dirt and steam to see the occupants of the wounded locomotive leap clear to escape the explosion that would surely follow. With banshee screams, the 140 tons of iron and steel ground to a stop.

Smoke came to his boots to take stock of the disaster. He saw that the Baldwin had derailed on only one side, the lead truck of the tender dangling in empty space above the rails. Miraculously, the stock car had not jumped the track. Even more astonishing, the boiler did not explode. It hissed and belched steam, and remained intact. Gloved fists on hips, Smoke watched while Brian Pullen and the rest of the volunteers climbed shakily from the baggage car.

"What the hell happened?" Pullen asked, his tone of voice clearly conveying his disturbed condition.

Smoke's reply cut through the fog in Brian's mind. "Murchison cut the rear of the train loose. You ran into it."

Brian shook his head, as though to clear it of fog. "Well,

hell's-fire, if that just don't beat all." Then he remembered the chase. "What happened to Murchison?"

"They went on. Let's get those horses out and head after them," Smoke urged. "Chances are we've lost them for now, but we can try."

Pullen took stock of the destruction all around them. "I'm not sure that's a good idea."

Cyrus Murchison, acting as conductor, signaled the engineer to slow the train when he observed the marker indicating a curve and a siding. A switchman dropped off the side and ran forward as the big 2-4-4-0 American Locomotive Works mainliner slowed even more. He threw the switch and the bobtailed train rolled smoothly through the switch onto the siding.

"What are you doing?" Titus Hobson demanded.

"We do not know if the other locomotive derailed. In light of that, we cannot take the chance of remaining on this train." He turned to Heck Grange. "Off-load mounts for everyone remaining, with a spare, if possible. We'll go to Carson City by horseback."

Titus Hobson winced as he recalled how long it had been since he had sat astride a horse. The remaining—how many?—miles to Carson City would be sheer torture. His tightly squinched features reflected his thoughts. To his outrage, Cyrus Murchison read his opinion and laughed at him.

"Think of it as a pleasant outing in the bracing mountain air, Titus. Come, we'll sleep in tents, under the stars, feast on venison and bear, clear our lungs of the city's miasma, and commune with nature."

Hobson chose primness for his reply. "I hardly think this is a time for levity, Cyrus."

"Why not?" Murchison's face darkened with suspicion.

"If you cannot laugh at adversity, you're doomed. Don't you know that?"

Hobson reacted from his fear-driven anger. "My God, you're priggish when you get philosophical, Cyrus."

Heck Grange's return took away a need for Cyrus Murchison to make a reply. "The horses are coming off now. We can leave in ten minutes."

"Good," Murchison snapped testily. "We may not have that much time."

"We're ten miles from where we cut loose those cars. With luck, them and their rolling stock are all busted up."

"You're right, Heck. Only we cannot rely on that."

Unaffected by the mindset of his boss, Heck came right back. "So? Even if they got out of that mess, it will take the better part of two hours to get here from there."

Murchison relented. "You're right, of course. See to everything, Heck. Be sure to off-load those chests from the baggage car."

Grange left to see to the task. Murchison set to work poking into the drawers and shelves of the smoking car. He retrieved two boxes of excellent hand-rolled cigars made in Havana, five bottles of brandy, tinned sardines, cheeses, and other delicacies. He stuffed all of it into a hinged-top box. The brandy he wrapped in bar towels. He looked up into the startled expression of Titus Hobson.

"No reason to deprive ourselves, is there, Titus? The amenities of life are what make us appreciate it."

"It will slow us down."

"No more than the tents and other supplies I had the forethought to put aboard. One more pannier on the back of a packhorse will not hinder our progress."

Titus Hobson looked at his partner with new eyes. "You anticipated this happening?"

Murchison made a deprecating gesture. "Nothing quite so drastic, old boy. But I did have grounds to suspect that all would not go smoothly. Come, we can make this small setback into a lark. How long has it been since you've been away from your wife's sharp tongue, and those cloying children?"

A wistful expression came onto Hobson's face. A man who had married late in life, he found his brood of five children, all under the age of thirteen, to be a burden he would prefer not to have to bear. And his wife had become more acid-tongued with the birth of each offspring—as though it was *his* fault she kept cropping a new brat. A tiny light began to glow in his mind. Perhaps this enforced separation would prove to be a boon.

"All right, Cyrus. I'll give you your due. This could turn out to be . . . interesting."

"Yes. But, only if we hurry. Jensen and Longmont are still back there."

Shaken, though essentially unharmed, the volunteers who had joined Smoke Jensen and Louis Longmont went quickly about saddling horses. They prowled through the kitchen of Cyrus Murchison's ruined private car and provisioned themselves with a wide variety of expensive and exotic food. Smoke gathered them when everything had been gotten into readiness.

"This is going to be rough. Those who have been injured or wounded should head back. There's no telling how long we will be on the trail."

"How far do you intend to go, Mr. Jensen?" a grizzled older farmer asked.

"All the way to Carson City, if necessary."

The oldster shrugged. "Then I'd best go back with the rest. My rhumatiz won't let me abide with damp ground and cold nights for that long."

"Go ahead," Smoke prompted. "And no shame be on you. The rest of us will start off along the tracks, see if we can catch up to that train."

* * *

"We'll leave a few men behind, to delay them if they do come," Murchison directed.

Heck Grange disagreed. "It will only waste lives needlessly. Jensen's not dumb. He'll be lookin' for that. I reckon the place to lay an ambush is up around Piney Creek, just ahead of the upgrade into the Sierras."

Murchison considered that. He accepted that Heck Grange, with his war experiences with the Union Army had a better grasp of tactics than himself. Yet he was loath to appear to not be entirely in charge. Now was not the time for vanity, Cyrus reminded himself

"All right, let's do it that way."

They rode for two hours. Bluejays and woodpeckers flitted from tree to tree, scolding the interlopers with shrill squawks. Squirrels took up the protest in wild chatter. A bad moment developed when a fat, old, near-sighted skunk waddled out onto the trail and set the nearest horses into a panic. For men accustomed to walking or riding everywhere in wheeled vehicles, it took some doing to bring the beasts under control. At last, Heck Grange was compelled to shoot the skunk.

That caused more trouble as its scent glands voided. An almost visible miasma fogged over the trail, contaminating the clothing of one and sundry among the collection of thugs, riffraff, and hard cases. Curses turned the air blue and fifteen minutes were lost trying to gain the upper hand over wall-eyed horses and red-faced, tear-streaked men. A halt resulted to allow everyone to wash off the strident effluvium from Mr. Skunk.

Back in the saddle, Murchison's henchmen grumbled among themselves. The majority were city-bred and -raised. The skunk unsettled them. What more, and worse, might be out there? The grade steepened and even this complaining died out. At three o'clock the big party reached the banks of Piney Creek.

Cyrus Murchison had Heck Grange toll off nine men to set up an ambush in the rocks and cluster of willows that lined the stream bed. None of the hard cases liked being left behind, yet the possibility of ending their ongoing problem appealed to most. They dug in, arranging stones and making dirt parapets in front of scooped-out hollows in the creek bank. When all met the approval of Heck Grange, he reported to Murchison.

"We're ready. Might as well head out."

"You've done a fine job, Heck. This should rid us of Jensen and Longmont. I'll sleep better tonight knowing that."

The rumble of departing hoofbeats had barely faded out when the first uncertainties arose over the idea of the ambush. "I hear there are bears around here, Harvey," one slightly built, long-necked thug remarked to a companion who had also been left behind at the ambush site.

"Don't think so, Caleb," the other railroad cop said around a stalk of rye grass. Unlike the skinny one, who worked as a clerk in the California Central police office, he had a barrel chest, thick, corded muscles in arms and legs, and a flat belly ridged with more brawn. "They keep to the high country up in the Snowy Mountains," he added, using a rough English translation of the Spanish, "Sierra Nevada."

When the Spanish first came to California, the mountain peaks to the east had worn a constant mantle of snow, hence the name "Sierra Nevada." In the three centuries since they had first sighted those awesome ramparts, the climate had altered enough that only the highest remained white all year. It had not done the Donner Party much good, because the snows in even the lower passes began early. The big railroad bull's assurance about bears did ease the worries of his friend. Perhaps it should not have.

Smoke Jensen kept pushing the volunteers. At his own insistence, Louis Longmont rode the drag to make certain they hadn't any stragglers. The afternoon seemed to have too few hours in it. Long red shafts of sunlight slanted through the broken overcast to warn of approaching evening. Smoke wanted to get as far along the trail as possible.

He had not had any difficulty finding signs of what direction the fleeing men had taken. Heavy-laden packhorses had left deep gouges in the soft soil of the gentle slopes, and it seemed the inexperienced riders could not keep their mounts in a single file. Within ten minutes of reaching the abandoned train, Smoke had an accurate count of the numbers they faced. It was more than he would have liked, yet far less than had started out. Now he gave consideration to the twenty-five riders and the possibility someone in charge might consider an ambush.

"We'll stop here for a while," Smoke announced, his decision made. "That map I found shows Piney Creek not far from here. The stream runs through the easiest pass leading to the high country." Smoke's eyes twinkled with suspicion. "The creek would also make a good place for an ambush."

"You are going to scout it out, I assume," Louis offered.

"That I am, my friend. You are welcome to come along."

Louis did not hesitate. "Perhaps next time."

Smoke chuckled. "I'll remember that."

"I'll see to making camp. No fires, I assume?"

"No, Louis. They are running from us. I doubt they'll turn back and attack. A cold camp won't make our friends very happy. It'll give them a chance to cook some of those fancy victuals they took from Murchison's private larder."

Five minutes later, he rode out in a circuitous route that would take him up on the blind side of Piney Creek.

Caleb Varner cut his eyes away from the distant glow of campfires to gaze pointedly at Harvey Moran. "They ain't comin', Harvey."

Harvey let his gaze wander away from the face of his companion, to stare at where the burble of water over stones located Piney Creek. "At least, not tonight, I'd wager."

Caleb looked ghastly in the sickly light of the high-altitude twilight. "That means we have to spend the night here?"

"Sure does."

"But there's bears, Harvey."

"Dang it now, Caleb, I've done told you there are no bears anywhere around here."

Caleb considered that and found a new horror. "What about timber rattlers? I hear they like to crawl right inside a feller's bedroll with him to keep warm."

Harvey did not feel like playing this game. "String a rope around your sleepin' place. Snake won't cross a rope. Thinks it's a brother."

"Really? I don't know."

"Shut up, you two," another ambusher called harshly. "Can't a man grab a snooze in peace? What with the two of you flappin' yer jaws, ain't nobody gonna get any rest tonight."

"Don't you have first watch?" Harvey challenged. "Got no business sleepin' if you do." That should hold him, Harvey thought.

Unseen by any of the neophyte woodsmen, Smoke Jensen slipped away from the camp set up by those manning the ambush. He moved soundlessly through the underbrush with a big smirk on his face. He knew what he could do now. When he reached the ancient Sequoia where he had ground anchored his horse, he reached into one saddlebag. He rummaged around for a moment and came out with what he wanted.

Simple in construction, the first item had come from a friendly Cheyenne youngster he had often taken fishing. The boy had made it himself and proudly gave it to Smoke. It consisted of a gourd on a thin oak stick. Inside were polished pebbles. When shaken just right, it sounded like the grandfather of all rattlesnakes. The second object came from Smoke's past.

Preacher had helped him make it, on a lark, one deep, frigid winter night when they had had nothing else to do. It was a boxlike affair, with a hollowed reed for a mouthpiece. Inside Preacher had fastened an assortment of gut and sinew strings of varying length and thickness. By changes of intensity in breath and a hand waved over the open end, it could be made to produce a remarkably realistic sound. With nothing to do for several hours, Smoke waited calmly beside his 'Palouse stallion.

At near on midnight, Smoke Jensen roused himself. He dusted off his trousers and set out for the camp. When he settled on a position upstream from the enemy site, he eased back against a large granite boulder and gave his thoughts to being a giant timber rattler.

"B'zzziiiiit! B'zzzzzziiiiiit! B'zzzziiit!"

Smoke went still while the voices came to him from the darkness. "M'God, Harvey, you hear that?"

"Hush up, Caleb," came a muzzy reply. Then, head clearing, Harvey asked, "Hear what?"

"I heard a rattler. A *big* rattlesnake."

"Horse pucky. Ain't no snakes around here," Harvey grumbled, his patience with this tenderfoot near an end.

"B'zzzzziiiiit!"

"Awh . . . shit," Harvey grunted out.

Blankets rustled in the darkness. "I'm gettin' outta here, Harvey. That thing sounds big enough to eat us whole."

"Where *you* gonna go in the dark, Caleb?"

"I dunno. Somewhere, anywhere there ain't any rattlers."

"Git in a tree. Snakes can't climb, yu'know," Harvey said calmly, trying not to let his own worry show.

A moment later, a heavy snuffling came from downwind. Even Harvey froze at that. He counted heartbeats between it and the next time. Louder now, the snuffle had a low snarl mixed in. Another pause, then the crash of brush sounded near the edge of the campsite. The full-throated roar of an enraged bear split the silence that followed.

"Oh, Jesus! *It's a bear!*" Caleb wailed. A warm wetness spread from his groin.

"Emory, Emory, do somethin' for chrissakes!" a thoroughly shaken Harvey cried.

Emory and Harvey opened fire at the same time. The grizzly roared again and charged.

18

Smoke Jensen shoved on the huge boulder and sent it thundering downhill through the underbrush. Immediately he dived behind a larger slab of granite. He made it with scant seconds to spare. Six-guns roared and a Winchester cracked in the camp below. The mammoth stone careened forward on a zigzag course and splashed turbulently into Piney Creek.

A regular battlefield of gunshots boomed off the hillsides. Muzzle flashes reflected off the undersides of pine boughs. Lead cracked and whined through the air. Shouts of fright and confusion rose in a mad babble. Unable to contain his glee over the success of his toys, Smoke Jensen grinned like a kid in a vacant candy store.

Then Emory Yates spoiled it all. "Stop it! Stop it! Quit shooting at nothing, you idiots. There ain't no bear!" Slowly the discharge of weapons ceased. Emory immediately jumped on the men he led. "Don't you ever use your heads? They could hear you all the way to Parkerville. Do you think those gunfighters we're supposed to ambush can't hear? They all deef?"

He slammed his hat on the ground in disgust. "We ain't gonna surprise nobody after that dumb-ass stunt. Shootin' at shadows and funny noises."

Before he could say more, the hairs on the back of his neck rose as the awesome growl of the bear came again. "Jeeezus! First light, we're gonna pull out of here. Can't do an ambush here anymore. Four of you keep watch through the rest of the night."

"Hell, *all of us* are gonna watch. Ain't nobody gonna sleep with that bear around," Caleb stammered.

Red-faced, Emory bellowed at Caleb, up close in the man's face. "There ain't no goddamned bear."

Chuckling softly to himself, Smoke Jensen eased from behind the chunk of granite and silently stole off into the night.

In the camp established by Cyrus Murchison, the main fire had died down to a low, rose-orange glow of pulsing coals. Murchison sat with his back propped against the bole of an aged ponderosa pine. He had a half-filled bottle of brandy in one hand and an unlighted cigar in the other. He did not want to let go of the liquor in order to light his stogie, though he dearly wanted the consolation of the rich smoke. An uneasy Titus Hobson approached.

"Light me a strip of kindling and bring it, will you, Titus?" Murchison greeted his partner.

Hobson did as bidden, ignited the cigar, then settled down beside Murchison and reached for the bottle. "That thunder sound we heard a little while ago? I have a feeling it wasn't caused by the weather."

"Sorry to say, I agree. Either those people chasing us stumbled into the ambush and it's all over. Or . . ."

"Or they rode right over the men you left back there," Hobson completed the unwelcome thought.

Shortly after dark, the men left behind by Heck Grange to spy on the approaching avengers had ridden into camp to report a force of some twenty hot on the trail. That many could easily overwhelm the seven men at Piney Creek. That news had sent Cyrus Murchison to the bottle. Then, about two hours ago, the sounds of a brief, ferocious battle came to them, muffled by distance. Could it be that late?

Cyrus pulled his fat, gold-cased watch from his vest pocket. Half past two o'clock. There would be no sleep this night. A sudden crash in the brush banished his gloom. Startled from his lethargy, Murchison jerked away from the tree trunk and listened intently.

More crackling of small branches and shrubs came from above the camp. Dulled by years in large cities and aboard the locomotives of two railroads, the ears of Cyrus Murchison only dimly picked out a grunting, snuffling sound. Growls followed, growing louder. Then the full-throated bellow of an enraged grizzly split the night. Cyrus Murchison did not take time to consider that nothing larger than roly-poly brown bears still lived in the Sierra Nevada. He immediately tried to scale the trunk of the overhanging ponderosa. The slick surface of the bark gave him scant help. The smooth leather soles of his boots scrabbled for purchase, propelled by a repeat of the ferocious roar. He jammed the toes of his custom-made boots into cracks and climbed about ten feet. Sweating with effort, he clung there, paralyzed by the sting from broken fingernails. From below came the fearful bleating of Titus Hobson.

"Shoot him! Kill that bear!"

His bear act had played rather well at the ambush, Smoke allowed, so he decided to try it again. In the larger camp, it created even more pandemonium. Groggy figures jumped from blanket rolls, ghostlike in their longjohns. Blindly they fired into the darkness in all directions. Some traded shots with others equally disorganized. The cooler heads among the gang of misfits lay low in an attempt not to attract a bullet. The bear bellowed a third time.

Horses began to whinny and shy at the picket line. Several reared, their squeals of terror bright in the blackness. That brought forth another fusillade. Three horses, struck by bullets, went splay-legged and sagged down loose-limbed. From his panic-driven perch, Cyrus Murchison cried out in alarm, "Stop it! Stop! You're killing the horses."

A fourth snarling whoop from the bear removed any chance of compliance. Bullets flew in a hailstorm of deadly lead. Heck Grange, smarter than any of his men, rushed to dump wood on the firepit. He kept low to avoid the whirlwind of slugs while he added more. The blaze caught slowly, then went up with a *whoosh*.

Over its roar Heck shouted to the frenzied men. "This way. Get around the fire. Bears don't like fire. And stop that damned shooting!"

When the volume of fire reduced, Smoke Jensen crept out of his hiding place and stealthily approached the picketed horses. His Green River knife flickered in the pale starlight for a moment, then slashed upward and severed the rope to which the mounts had been tethered. He loosed half a dozen, then stepped back quickly to cup his hands around his mouth. A guttural snarl ripped up past his lips.

When the panther cough reached the ears of the horses, they lost their minds. Those who had been freed dashed off pell-mell into the night. The rest reared and stomped and jerked at the picket line until they broke it and stormed off in a loose-knit herd. Reality suddenly took root in the brain of Cyrus Murchison. Enlightenment brought with it misery. He knew . . . he *knew* the cause behind it.

"God . . . damn . . . you . . . Smoke Jensen," he groaned into the rough bark of the pine he hugged.

Morning found eyelids heavy and tempers short. Few of the hard cases had managed more than an hour's sleep. Cyrus Murchison chafed while riders went out to recover their horses. His mood did not improve when the men from the ambush straggled in reeking of defeat.

"Why aren't you lying in wait for them?" he bellowed, rising from the fire, a cup of coffee steaming in his hand.

"We got attacked," Emory Yates explained limply.

"I gathered that. We heard the shooting. Did you stop any of them?"

"It weren't men," Caleb butted in. "It was critters. A giant rattlesnake and a bear."

A cold fist closed around the heart of Cyrus Murchison. "I think you will find that your rattler and bear are named Smoke Jensen."

"Huh?" Caleb gulped.

"You have been bamboozled, my parochial friend," Cyrus grated. "So, for that matter, have we. Smoke Jensen got around you, found your camp, and engaged in a little leg-pulling. Disastrous play, if you ask me."

"What now, Mr. Murchison?" Caleb asked.

"What? Well, once we get our horses back . . ." His face flushed crimson. "Once we get our horses back, we keep going. It is a good three days to the pass. Somewhere along the way we'll lay another ambush."

"You reckon they'll follow us?" Emory inquired, hoping to get a negative answer.

"Of course they'll follow. Louis Longmont and Smoke Jensen are determined to ruin me—ruin Titus and me," he hastily amended. "Only we'll have to outsmart them. So long as I have the support of you, my loyal employees, I am confident we will prevail."

Smoke Jensen paused long enough for the volunteers to examine the ambush site. It would help make them aware of what they faced, he reasoned. It had the desired effect. When they set out again, their usual chatter dried up by seeming mutual consent. Silence held the higher they went into the foothills. When they came to the place where Murchison had camped the previous night, the impromptu posse halted again.

Everyone listened intently while Smoke interpreted the sign left behind. Then he described what he had done to cause them to create the disorganized scuffs and gouges in the dirt. That brought full, hearty laughs. Aware now that riches and power, and a lot of hired guns, did not make anyone invincible, they resumed their good-natured ragging when the column set off again.

Three hours later, they came upon the scene of last night's disaster in the main camp. Smoke's modest recounting of what transpired delighted them and bolstered their fortitude. Smoke found the trail their enemy left to be wide and clear. He called that to the attention of Louis.

"They're not making any effort to hide their tracks. Makes a feller wonder."

Louis Longmont chuckled sardonically. "Not for long, though, eh? It seems they want us to know where they are going and follow along at all good speed."

"You've not lost your trailcraft, old friend," Smoke praised. "I think I'll take Quo Wu and scout ahead. You bring the others along, only at a nice, easy pace. Try to keep no more than a mile between us."

Louis nodded knowingly. "*Très bon, mon ami.* Very good indeed. This way, if they are brazen enough to lay another ambush, the cavalry will be close at hand to ride to the rescue."

Smoke shook his head ruefully. "I can't figure what's so funny about that, but it suits what I've got in mind. Take care, now, old friend."

"I always do," Louis replied jauntily.

To his pleased satisfaction, Smoke Jensen had already found Quo Chung Wu to be nearly as skilled at silent movement as himself. It would come in handy on this little jaunt, he felt certain. On the hunch that Murchison would want to have as much space between the main body and any ambush he might set up, Smoke called a halt a quarter mile short of five miles.

"We'll go on foot from here on. Circle wide of the trail they left and keep off the skyline," Smoke instructed.

Quo Wu bowed his head and spoke without the least condescension. "The art of remaining unseen is ancient in our order. It is a shame that talent does not extend to our horses," he added wryly.

Smoke was ready for that one. "Among the Spirit Walkers of the Cheyenne, it is believed that they can extend their cloak of invisibility to their ponies. It might be they have something there, after all. I've had half a dozen of them pop up on me on open prairie sort of out of nowhere."

"You are possessed of this magic?" Quo Wu asked, impressed.

A modest reply seemed called for. "Somewhat. At least, enough that if there is anyone out there waitin' for us, they won't know Thunder and me are anywhere close until it's too late."

"How does it work?"

Smoke smiled at Quo. "Accordin' to the Cheyenne, all we have to do is think of ourselves and our horses as grass. Or in our case here, as trees."

Quo seemed taken aback. "That is all? We are taught to think of ourselves as birds, flying high above the gaze of our enemies."

"Seems a mite complicated, masterin' all those motions a bird has to go through to stay in the air."

Realizing that Smoke was teasing him, Quo flushed a light pink under his pale brown cheeks. "I have . . . flown twice."

Smoke did not know what to make of that. He did have to suppress a laugh. "No foolin'?"

Quo blurted his explanation through the embarrassment of having shown such unworthy pride. "Of course, my body never left the ground. Only my spirit soared."

Considering that, Smoke clapped a big hand on one

muscular thigh. "That fits with what the Cheyenne say. So, you an' your horse will be birds, an' me an' Thunder will be trees. Either way, if there's anyone out there, we'll be in among them, raisin' hell, before they have an inkling."

Orville Dooling, known as "Doolie" to his fellow railroad police, thought he caught a hint of movement from the corner of one eye. He turned his head and peered in that direction. Nothing. He switched his gaze back down the wide, well-marked trail that had been left from the camp beyond Piney Creek. Once more a flicker of motion impinged on his awareness. Orville shook his head as though to rid it of such notions. An instant later he froze at the soft sound of a whispering voice.

"Say goodnight."

A shower of stars, quickly extinguished by a wave of darkness, filled Doolie Dooling's head. The accompanying pain lasted only a second. Smoke Jensen stepped over the supine gunman and removed his weapons. No sense in leaving them for the rest of this rabble. That accounted for the right flank guard, Smoke noted, as he moved back behind the arc of the ambush to pick another target.

Two hard cases lounged close to each other, backs supported by a thick bush. Smoke glided soundlessly up to them and reached his arms wide. With a swift, powerful sweep, he grasped them over their ears and banged their heads together. The rest of those involved in the ambush remained oblivious to his actions, particularly the one being throttled by Quo Chung Wu at that very moment. Faintly, Smoke's superb hearing picked out the drum of hooves on the spongy terrain beyond the rise where the ambush had been laid.

A second later, the lead element of the posse rode into view and a shot banged flatly from one of the hidden gunhands. Four more thugs opened up, one from so close to

Smoke Jensen, he felt the heat of the muzzle blast. Smoke drew and fired.

His shot dissolved his seeming invisibility. It appeared that all five of the remaining hard cases saw him at once. Smoke flexed his legs and dived to one side, while hot lead smacked into trees and screamed off rocks where he had stood a moment before. From the opposite end of the arc of gunhawks, a shotgun boomed and two of Murchison's henchmen screamed in torment.

Immediately, the hidden shooters turned toward this new threat. That gave Smoke a chance to account for another thug. A street brawler born and bred, he reared up from his concealed position to take a shot at Quo Chung Wu. Smoke cocked his Peacemaker and called to him.

"Over here!"

The slow-witted lout began to swing his .44 Smith, eyes widening at the presence of someone right in among them. His surprise did not get to register on his face. A bullet from Smoke Jensen's .45 Colt reached him first. The red knob of his nose turned into a black hole, its edges splashed with scarlet. He went over backward, draped across the fallen pine trunk he had used for shelter.

Disorganized by the sudden appearance of two men in their midst, the railroad police and dockwallopers completely forgot about the eighteen armed vigilantes riding down on them. That proved a fatal error. Feeding on long-accumulated anger over their mistreatment, the farmers and merchants of the Central Valley swarmed in among their would-be assassins and wrought terrible vengeance.

In less than five minutes the battle ended. Only the unconscious among the hard cases remained alive. Those were trussed up like hogs for the slaughter and left behind, to be retrieved later. "When you come back through here, don't forget these men," Smoke advised.

* * *

Nightfall found Cyrus Murchison and his henchmen in a cold, miserable camp. Considering the events of the previous night, Heck Grange had insisted on no fires. The assortment of longshoremen, railroad police, and freelance would-be gunfighters grumbled noisily while they ate cold sardines and other preserved food from tins crudely hacked open by their knives. They had not been close enough to hear the detail of the brief, furious fight at the ambush site. It had sounded like nothing more than a loosened boulder rolling downhill.

Considering the debacle of the previous night, Cyrus Murchison put another meaning on it. Now, guided only by starlight, he made his way across the encampment to find Titus Hobson and share his revelation. He found Heck Grange seated beside Titus and poured each of them a generous dollop of brandy. He opened his mouth to speak when the chilling howl of a gray wolf broke the silence of the night.

Smoke Jensen had spent four tedious hours creeping up on the area in which he had estimated Murchison would make camp. He found them within three hundred yards of his picked spot. They could have done better to have reasoned like Smoke. Yet the chosen place appeared secure enough.

On the top of a small, domed knoll, the tired, uncertain hard cases sprawled in uneasy slumber. Unlike the previous night, someone had shown sense enough not to light fires, and to put out roving sentries, with pickets posted closer in. It would make his task harder, yet Smoke Jensen flowed through them as though truly invisible. He came up behind one less-than-observant hard case with laughable ease.

Smoke's braided rawhide lariat snaked out soundlessly and settled around the rider's shoulders, pinning his arms to his sides. A swift yank whipped him out of the saddle before he could give an alarm. His butt's contact with the solid ground drove the air from his lungs and blackness swam before his eyes, while Smoke Jensen walked the rope to the captive and klonked him solidly behind one ear.

Using pigging strings from his saddlebags, he secured the unconscious man. Then he dragged the musclebound longshoreman to a shallow ravine and unceremoniously rolled him in. Soundlessly whistling a jolly tune, Smoke recoiled his lariat and strode off into the night. Near the base of the hillock, he found a lone tree, which he scaled with ease. Poised on a sturdy limb, he waited for the passage of another guard.

Within five minutes, Smoke's patience was rewarded. Dozing in the saddle, an exhausted railroad policeman approached, his unguided mount in a self-directed amble. Smoke tensed as the animal wandered by under his branch. A moment later, he launched himself. His bootheels struck solidly between the thug's shoulder blades. Smoke did an immediate backroll off the rump of the startled, shying mount and landed on his feet.

His target did not fare so well. He ended up on his head. The bones of his neck made a nasty sound when they broke. Smoke Jensen spared only a split second for regret, then moved on.

He next surprised an adenoidal youth, far too young and green to be in the company of such reprobates as those who surrounded him. His eyes went wide and he wet his drawers when Smoke took him from behind and clamped a big, callused hand over the boy's mouth. Wisely, the youngster did not struggle. He appreciated his good sense a moment later when Smoke laid the flat of the blade of his Green River against the teenager's neck.

Smoke's urgency carried through the whisper. "If you want to live, make up your mind to take this horse I brought for you and ride clear the hell out of here. Don't stop and don't even look back. It's that, or I slit your gullet and send you off to your Maker."

If he could have, the kid would have wet himself again. He certainly wanted to. With effort, he nodded his head up and down. "Mummmf, unnnh—hunnn."

"Does that mean you agree?" Smoke whisper-probed.

"Unnnn—hunnn."

Smoke's voice hissed like Old Man Death himself in the youth's ear. "If I let you go, you won't give the alarm?"

"Nuuh-uuuh."

Smoke eased his grip and reached behind him. "All right. Here's the reins. Walk him about a mile, then hit the saddle and ride like the hounds of hell are after you." He paused for effect, then put an ominous tone in his voice, knowing what he planned next. "You never know . . . they might be."

Panting, the boy showed his gratitude. "Thank you, thankyou-thankyou-thankyou."

Smoke looked after the young man as he led the horse off from the mound. Then the last mountain man turned and started uphill. Half way to the top, he paused. He gave the kid another five minutes, then threw back his head, cupped palms around his mouth and gave the mournful howl of a timber wolf.

19

Hairs rose at the nape of the neck of every man in the hilltop camp. This time, Heck Grange's discipline took hold and no one fired wildly into the darkness. That did not keep them from filling their hands with any close-by weapon. Eyes showing a lot of white, they peered tensely into the stygian night. Most had barely conquered their nerves when the wolf howled again.

This time it seemed to come from closer in. Another wolf answered it from the opposite side of the camp. Fear gripped all of them, especially Cyrus Murchison. His childhood had been filled with thoroughly spuriously stories about wolves carrying off children and devouring them. Now this ingrained myth came back to haunt him.

"That can't be Jensen," he stated shakily to Titus Hobson. "He couldn't move that fast. There are real wolves out there."

His own unease gnawing at his vitals, Titus answered in a subdued voice. "I couldn't agree more. What are we going to do?"

"Do? We'll have to build a fire. No matter those behind us will see it now. We do it or those wolves will be in among us before we know it."

"Who is going to move and draw their attention?" Hobson queried.

"Grange, of course," Murchison courageously suggested. He raised his voice. "Heck, get a fire started."

"Already under way, Mr. Murchison," the boss gunman answered blandly. "Look for the fire glow reflected in their eyes. We'll know how many there are that way."

A tiny point of light bloomed at the top of the knoll. Kindling began to blaze, and men instinctively moved that way. The two wolves howled again.

Smoke Jensen could not believe his good fortune. A live, breathing wolf had answered his call. He raised his head again and uttered another wail, answered almost at once from the other side of the mound. *Scare the be-Jazus outta them,* he thought in the manner of Paddy Flynn, an old mountain man friend of Preacher's.

Another wolf howl, answered promptly, and then he readied the three horses he had collected from the incautious sentries. He loosened their saddles and removed bits, reins, and headstalls. He got them pointed in the general direction of the hilltop camp and stepped away into the night. A fourth ululating lupine howl sent them off in a panicked canter. Smoke listened intently for the results.

Cries of alarm and consternation came from the camp moments later, when the frightened creatures blundered in among the men and raced mindlessly past the fire. Three men opened fire. Sparks rose as one of the horses blundered into the fire pit. A man's voice rose to a shriek.

"My God, they're here, they're after us."

Smoke started to make his way back to Thunder when he caught a hint of movement off to his right. A gray-white-and-black object moved stealthily through the darkness. Smoke waited patiently. Then he saw it clearly. Even the distant firelight put a yellow-green phosphorescent glow in those big, intelligent eyes.

Smoke hunkered down, extended a hand, and uttered the low whine that conveyed friendly submission among wolves. The great, shaggy beast advanced, crouched low, and came forward at a crouch. He sniffed, his educated scent telling a lot about this two-legged being. Slowly, he closed. Another inspection by nose, then the long, wet tongue shot out and licked at the hand of Smoke Jensen.

"Good boy, good boy," Smoke whispered. "You came to help. I could send you up there among them to cap this off nicely, but I'm afraid you'd get shot. Go on, now. Go run down a couple of fit raccoons for your supper." Cautiously, Smoke reached out and patted the wolf. It might be more intelligent than a domesticated dog, Smoke reminded himself but it was still wild.

A soft whine came from the long gray muzzle and the wolf rolled over on its back, exposing its vulnerable belly. Smoke petted it and then made a shooing motion. He turned and walked away, back toward Thunder. A good night's work, he reasoned. When they found the lookouts in the morning, that would spook them even more.

When the roving patrol failed to return at the end of their four-hour stint, alarm spread through the camp again. Cyrus Murchison and Heck Grange barely managed to quell the general decision to search at once. By morning's early light, the gang managed to locate the missing sentries.

Bound and gagged, all were fully conscious and furious. "It was that goddamned Jensen, I tell you," one outraged thug growled.

"There was two wolves out here last night," Monk Diller stated positively.

"They sure as hell don't carry pieces of rope an' tie up a feller," the complaining sentry countered. "It was Smoke Jensen."

"*God . . . damn . . . you . . . Smoke Jensen,*" Cyrus Murchison thought, though he did not give voice to his impotent curse.

Those with even a scant talent toward it cooked up a breakfast of fatback, potatoes, and skillet cornbread. One man with a passing skill as a woodsman found a clump of wild onions to add to the potatoes, and another dug a huge, fat yucca root to bake in the coals. Their bellies filled, the company of hard cases rode out, headed for the distant pass and Carson City beyond. Try as they might, none of them could find evidence of the presence of Smoke Jensen beyond the bits of rope.

Winds born over the far-off Pacific Ocean pushed thick cumulus clouds toward the coast. They grew as they progressed eastward. Many with fat black bellies climbed beyond 35,000 feet, their heads flattening out into the anvil shape of cumulonimbus. Storm clouds, thunderheads. Steadily they climbed as they raced over San Francisco and beyond to the Central Valley.

Their outriders arrived over the Sierra Nevada at ten o'-clock in the morning. For the past half hour, Smoke Jensen had been marking the threatening appearance of the sky to the west. When the first dirty-gray billows whisked across the sun, he nodded in understanding and acceptance. Wise in the ways of mountains, Smoke knew for certain a tremendous thunderstorm would soon sweep over them. He made his companions aware of it.

"Storm's comin'. Better get out your rain slickers."

Tyler Estes, the barber in Grass Valley, gave him a concerned look. "A lot of us don't have anything. These are borrowed horses and such."

Smoke shrugged, indifferent to physical discomfort. "You'll just get wet, then. Or you can wrap up in your ground sheets."

"Our blankets will get wet that way," Estes protested.

A quick smile flickered on Smoke's face. "One way or the other, something is going to get wet."

Half an hour later, the first fat drops of rain fell from the solid sea of gray-black clouds. The wind whipped up and whirled last winter's fallen leaves around the legs and heads of their horses. In a sudden plunge, the temperature fell twenty degrees. "Here it comes," Smoke warned.

Already in his bright yellow India rubber slicker, Smoke had only to button up and turn his collar. The brim of his sturdy 5X Stetson kept most of the water out of his face. With their backs to the storm, the posse continued on its way. A trickle of cold rain ran down the back of Smoke Jensen's collar. The wind gusted higher as he worked to snug it tighter. Then the core of the storm struck.

Thunder bellowed around then and bright streaks lanced to the ground and trees to one side. The air smelled heavily of ozone. Smoke curled from a lightning-shattered ponderosa. A big hickory smouldered on the opposite side. They had been bracketed by near simultaneous shafts of celestial electricity.

"B'God, it hit both sides of us," Estes gulped out the obvious.

With a seething rattle, like the rush of the tide on a pebbly beach, a curtain of white hurtled toward them from the rear. Visibility dropped to zero and a wall of ice pebbles swept across the huddled men.

"Owie! Ouch! Hey, this stuff is tearing me up," a young livery stable hand yelped when the line of hail rushed over the rear of the column.

"Let's get under the trees!" Tyler Estes shouted.

"No!" Smoke turned his mount to stare them down. "You saw what the lightning did to those trees back there, right? Picture bein' under one of them when it hit. You'd be right sure fried."

Estes shivered at the image created by the words of

Smoke Jensen. He looked around for some escape, while the hail battered at them all. "What can we do, then?"

"Dismount and control your horses. Get on the downwind side of them and use them for what shelter it provides. It'll be over 'fore long."

It proved to be damned little protection. Quarter-sized ice balls pelted down to bruise skin protected by no more than a light coat or flannel shirt. Smoke had been right about the duration. Within ten minutes, the hailstorm crashed on to the northeast. It had been with them long enough to turn the ground a glittering white, to a thickness of some three inches.

"Give me snow anytime," Brice Rucker complained. "That stuff ain't hard."

Smoke favored him with a glance. "You've never seen snow on the high plains, have you? I was there one time with Preacher. We had a heavy snow, followed by an ice storm. The wind got up so that it flung the ice-coated snow at us. It was like razors, it was so sharp. Be thankful for small favors. All we come out of this with is a few bruises."

"Few," the always complaining barber repeated. "I'll be black and blue for a month."

"Too tender a hide, Tyler," Rucker teased him.

"Go kiss yer mule, Rucker," Tyler pouted.

"One bright spot," Smoke said through the rain to defuse the testy volunteers. "Think how that storm is going to play hell with those fellers ahead of us."

Wistfulness filled the voice of Tyler Estes. "Yes. They can't fare any better than us. Worse, more likely."

Louis Longmont entered the conversation. "Murchison and Hobson are soft from years of easy living. I would imagine they are completely miserable about now."

Cyrus Murchison and his motley crew lacked Smoke Jensen's knowledge of the outdoors, so the storm caught them by surprise. Instantly soaked to the skin, they had not even covered themselves with slickers before the hail had hit. Two men were driven from their saddles by now fist-sized stones of ice. Their horses ran off screaming in misery.

Turned instantly into a rabble, the men milled about in confusion. The sky turned stark white and a tremendous crash of thunder followed in the blink of an eye. The huge green top of a spectacular lone Sequoia burst into flame and the upper two thirds canted dangerously toward the trail. Then it fell with aching slowness. Fearing for their lives, the hard cases scattered.

Blazing furiously, the tree dropped across the trail to block forward progress. Its resin-rich leaves spat and hissed in the torrent of rain that fell, unable to quell the flames.

"If the wind was down, we could put up tents."

Cyrus Murchison looked blankly at Titus Hobson. Could the man have completely forgotten everything he had learned about such storms during his mining days? "What good would that do?" he demanded. "The hail would only punch holes through the canvas the minute we stretched it tight."

Titus blinked. Why had he not thought of that? He made steeples of his shoulders to hide his embarrassment. "It's a while since I've been out in anything like this."

"So I gather," his partner responded. "We might as well hold fast here until that fire goes out. No sense in taking the risk of men falling into the flames going around it." He decided to relent on his harsh outburst at Titus. "You're right, though. When the hail quits, we should set up the tents. A warm, dry camp is bound to be appreciated."

Despite the storm-induced darkness, Cyrus judged it to be no more than mid-afternoon. They would lose nearly half a day, yet it would be important to let the runoff firm up the trail. No matter how many men pursued them, they would have been caught in the open, too, he reasoned. And, it might dampen the penchant of Smoke Jensen for those childish, although dangerous, pranks. Only time would tell.

Late that night, Smoke Jensen worked quietly and alone. It had taken him a quarter of an hour to select the right tent and the most suitable sapling. He spent another fifteen minutes in attaching the end of a rope to the springy young tree. Half an hour went by while he painstakingly pulled the limber trunk downward over a pivot point made of a smooth, barkless length of ash limb. He secured it there, then took the other end of the rope and tied it off to the peak of the tent roof.

With everything in readiness, Smoke stepped back to inspect his handiwork. It pleased him. All he had to do was cut the pigging string that held the spring trap in place and nature would take care of the rest. Suddenly he stiffened at the rustle of sound from inside the tent next to the one he had rigged.

Groggy with sleep, one of the hard cases stepped through the flap and headed for the low fire in a large stone ring. He had a coffeepot in one hand. The thug must have caught sight of Smoke from the corner of one eye. He turned that way and spoke softly.

"What's up? You drainin' yer lily?"

Smoke muffled his voice, turned three-quarters away from his challenger. "Yep."

"Too much coffee, or too small a bladder, eh?"

"Unh-huh."

"I reckon I'd best be joinin' you," his questioner suggested, as he tucked his speckled blue granite cup behind his belt and reached for his fly.

He stepped closer and Smoke tensed. The bearded thug fumbled with the buttons as he came up to Smoke. He opened his mouth to make another remark and met a fist-full of knuckles. Bright lights exploded in his head and he rocked over backward. Smoke hit him again under the hinge of his jaw and the man sighed his way into unconsciousness.

Smoke Jensen stepped quickly to where he had secured the line between the bent sapling and the tent roof. His Green River knife came out and flashed down toward the pigging string. It severed with a snap and the tree instantly swung back toward its natural position. Smoke cut loose with a panther cough and yowl while the tent tie-downs sang musically as they strained, then let go. Like the conjuring trick of a medicine show magician, the tent whisked away, skyward, exposing the sleeping men inside.

Before anyone could react, Smoke Jensen slipped away into the darkness.

Several of the volunteers gathered around Smoke Jensen the next morning at the breakfast fire. The big granite pot of coffee made its final round. They had eaten well on shaved ham and gravy over biscuits, with the ubiquitous fried potatoes and onions, and tins of peaches and cherries, courtesy of the larder in the private car of Cyrus Murchison. They laughed heartily when he recounted what he had done the night before.

"Them fellers must have filled their drawers," Brice Rucker chortled. "Those that were in them, at least. I bet more'n a few jumped right out of their longjohns."

"I didn't wait to see," Smoke answered dryly. That brought more whoops of lighter. "Saddle up, men, we've got them running scared now."

Smoke led his small force away only scant minutes after the sun broke over the distant ramparts of the Sierra Nevada. He had told them that by the next day they would be high in the mountains. Another day after that they would be able to sweep down on Murchison's gang and bring an end to it. His words received powerful support shortly before midmorning.

Four tired, harried-looking men rode toward them from up the trail. When they sighted the vigilantes, they halted and waited quietly. As Smoke Jensen and Louis Longmont came within fifty yards of them, they raised their empty hands over their heads.

"We're out of it," their self-appointed leader informed the gunfighters. "We done quit the railroad police and left Murchison to his own ends. There was sixty of us when we started. Now there's less than half." His eyes narrowed. "Which one of you is Smoke Jensen?"

"I am," Smoke told him, readying his hand to draw his .45 Colt.

A chuckle, not a challenge, came from the former railroad bull. "You sure got 'em stirred up, Mr. Jensen. Got us all exercised, that's for sure. Those boys up there are quaking in their boots. After what happened to that tent, we quit first thing this morning. An' there's about a dozen more ready to give it up, too."

"Good to hear, gentlemen. You're free to ride on. Only one thing," he added, a hand raised to stop them. "We'd be obliged if you left all but five rounds of ammunition with us. We're a little short as it is, and every round will be appreciated."

Their leader snickered, a gloved hand over his mustache and full lips. "And, it sort of makes certain we can't turn back and hit you in the rear, don't it?"

Smoke nodded and joined his laughter. "That possibility did occur to me. So, what do you say?" His eyes narrowed to glittering slits of gray. "Lighten your load and ride free? Or open the dance right now?"

The jovial one quickly showed both hands, open and empty. "Ain't got time to waltz, Mr. Jensen. We'll just leave some cartridges with you and be on our way."

Smoke's smile held the breezy warmth of a June day.

"That's mighty thoughtful of you. I'll take you up on that and then we can ride on."

In ten minutes it was done and the volunteer posse grew richer by two hundred thirty rounds. Smoke watched the deserters from Murchison's cause from time to time until they rode out of sight. He showed a sunny mood to everyone as he picked up the pace.

Wilber Evers spoke around a hard knot of grief in his throat that night in the vigilante camp. "He was my brother. My brother, and they shot him down like a dog. One of . . . one of them took a rope to his kids and beat them. Raised welts on their backs."

Another sorrow-softened voice responded. "Yeah, I know. You hear about Ruby Benson?"

"The widow Benson?" Evers asked.

"Yep. That's the one. Only she's not so much an old widow. She's rather young. Anyway, some of these riff-raff came along from the railroad and told her to sell out the farm to Murchison. She refused. So they jumped her, had their way with her and left her a ruined woman. She—she's my sister."

"I'm sorry," Smoke Jensen added his feelings to the discussion around the supper fire. "What did you reckon to do about it?"

"She described them to me. If I find them among those with Murchison, I'm gonna hang the lot of them."

Smoke nodded. "Suits. Preacher hanged some rapists more than once. I know, because I was with him a couple of times. There's even a story going around that he one time hanged a man who messed around with children."

"Served him right, I say," the brother of Ruby Benson growled.

"What else has been done that you know of for certain?" Smoke probed.

Several voices clamored for his attention. One bull

bellow overrode the others. "They burnt my barn and shot my cows. Scared my wife so much she delivered early. We lost the baby."

"Do you know them?"

"Sort of. They had flour sacks over their heads, but two of them didn't change clothes from earlier in the day. I'd know those two anywhere. They work at the depot in Parkerville. Name of Dawkins and Lusk. I meant to go shoot them when I ran into these other fellows and joined in on this little affair."

Angry mutters went around the firepit. "I had myself primed to set my sights on one of Huntley's bullies. He tormented me an' my wife until I was forced to sell two freight wagons to Huntley's outfit. I cussed myself as a yellow-belly ever since. When I heard there was trouble in Grass Valley, I hightailed it for there right away." The gray-haired man stopped there and looked around for approval from his companions.

It came quickly. "Ain't nothin' yeller about you, Paul. Why, we was right pleased to see you join us."

Paul drew himself up and came to his boots. "Well, I thank ye, Lester. Boys, I think I've got enough jawin' for one night. I'm for my bedroll. We got a bushel of work to do tomorrow."

Smoke Jensen silently agreed and pushed away from the circle of gabbers. What he had heard angered and disturbed him. All of their atrocities considered, he doubted that Murchison and his gang would be inclined to give up easily.

20

Crouched in a jumble of rocks, Smoke Jensen cracked a satisfied smile. After hearing the accounts of those victimized on Murchison's orders, he decided to try a different approach. He did not wait as long as he had for the previous night visits to the gangster camp. He wanted the men up and moving around. Smoke had selected his spot carefully and settled in to observe.

Tensions had thickened, what with so many fellows forced to rub elbows for so long, he marked first. No longer did they all crowd around a large, central fire. Seven smaller blazes lighted the night, with men grouped in twos and threes, with a solitary loner at one. Smoke settled on him for his first dirty trick of the night. That determined, he slid away into the darkness around the camp.

After he had circled the campsite, he paused to relocate his target. Then, holding a deep breath, he ghosted up on the unsuspecting thug hunkered down by the fire. With panther swiftness, Smoke whipped an arm around the brute's neck and gave a sudden yank. Unseen by the comrades of the hard case, Smoke whisked him out of sight.

Using a trick of the Cheyenne Dog Soldiers, Smoke increased the pressure of his arm until he stifled the thug into unconsciousness. Then he hefted the limp form over one shoulder and carried him away. Far away. When next the man woke up, he would find himself tied to a tree in a strange place, well out of sight of the camp he had last seen. Smoke Jensen made certain it would be on the route to be taken by Murchison and the gang the next morning. Making sure that the rope that his captive could not escape on his own, Smoke returned to wipe out all trace of his presence.

"That went so smooth, there's no reason not to try for another one," Smoke muttered to himself.

He found another one easily enough. A city dude had gone out in the trees to relieve himself. And, naturally, he plain got lost. In his wandering, he blundered into Smoke Jensen. That quick he became the next to disappear without a trace.

Unaware of the doings of Smoke Jensen, and the fact that Smoke now crouched in some rocks not thirty feet away, Cyrus Murchison and his partners discussed his decision to move on to Carson City.

"We could go back to the main line," Murchison said agreeably. "Only those miserable sons of perdition are between us and it. No, Titus, Heck, it will take longer, but to continue on horseback is the wisest choice."

Titus Hobson answered testily. "*I* say the wisest thing would have been to stay in San Francisco. You own the mayor and the city fathers. And, between us, we own nearly all the judges. The chief of police plays poker with us and gets drunk in that gentlemen's club of yours. There's no way Longmont or Jensen can show any proof of our involvement in anything illegal. *They can't bring any charges.*"

For the first time, Cyrus Murchison found it necessary to reveal his real fear. "You said it yourself, Titus. Smoke Jensen is a gunfighter. The best there is. And there's not a hair's breadth between him and Longmont. Listen to me, our life depends on it. Those two are not in the habit of oringing charges . . . *except the ones in their six-guns.*"

Hobson paled. "You mean, they'll just . . . kill us?"

"Precisely. For men like them, justice comes out of the barrel of a gun. No, we'll keep on overland. The Central's racks have been extended into Carson City. We can get reinforcements there. Then we'll return to California and wipe out these interfering scum." Cyrus Murchison came up on his scuffed, dusty, although once highly polished, boots. Buoyed by his self-delusion, he spoke lightly. "It is time to turn in. I'm looking forward to a sound night's sleep."

"I wish you the joy of it," Titus Hobson grumbled, uncomfortable at being reminded he was the one to identify exactly what Smoke Jensen and Louis Longmont were.

A sudden shout stopped them. "Chief! Chief, there's two of us missin'."

Heck Grange came upright. "Did you see any sign of Smoke Jensen?"

"Nope. Nothin'. Just some tracks where the boys was. They've plum disappeared."

Early the next morning, Smoke Jensen changed his tactics. In the faint gray light that preceded sunrise, he led the posse of vigilantes out at a fair pace. "We're through chasing Murchison and his mob of butchers," he informed his companions. "Today we get ahead of them and see how they enjoy an ambush." Expectant smiles answered him. "With a good early start, we can swing wide and bypass their present camp."

Everyone rode with high spirits. As the day grew brighter, Smoke increased the pace. Every hour, they dismounted and walked their horses for ten minutes. Many of those who lacked experience with saddle mounts marveled at the stamina that this provided their animals. Shortly before the noon hour, Smoke called a halt.

He gestured to where the sheer hillsides closed in on the trail. It narrowed and the grade grew much steeper. "Up there a ways is the place we'll start. Some of you see if you can locate any fallen logs. Make sure they're not bigger around than a man's body and not too dried out."

"Why don't we cut what we want?" Tyler Estes asked.

"We don't have a lot of time, Mr. Estes. The less we have to spend on this the better," Smoke informed him. "Those of you with shovels come with me. I'll show you what to do."

They worked quickly and well. Smoke supervised the building of an even dozen nasty surprises for Murchison's hirelings. Two long, narrow pits had been dug parallel to the trail, covered with leaves and brush. At a point farther along, where the mountain's breast overhung the narrow trace, Smoke saw an ideal place for a particularly nasty trap. He set men to work weaving a large net from vines and ropes.

While they did that, Smoke himself climbed to the top of the lip and sprawled out flat. Working by feel, he drove the pointed end of an arm-thick limb into the soil. He draped a double twist of lariat over the beam it formed and lowered it to the ground. Then he returned to the busy weavers.

"When you get that done, fill it with rocks and attach these ropes at the top to keep it closed. Then stick brush in the net, to make it look like a big bush."

"Then what?" Estes asked.

"We attach the trip line." Smoke turned away to check on other progress while he let them figure that one out.

Three and a half hours later, the project neared completion. Smoke Jensen made a final, careful check, then gathered the volunteers. "Everyone pick a position up above the last trap. Make sure you have a clear field of fire. And be careful going up there. You don't want to set off one of those things on yourself."

"You can say that again," Tyler Estes blurted out. When he had taken in the scope of what Smoke had in mind, his eyes bugged and the usually timid barber had thrilled in the blood lust that heated him at the thought of all these awful things going off in the midst of that gang of thugs. He remained impressed as he worked his way up above the deadly ambush site.

"Do you expect them to fall for this?" Louis Longmont asked, a critical eye roving over the concealed traps and trip lines.

Smoke gave it some thought. "For most of it. It depends on how well those boys can shoot up there whether we break them right here." Smoke cast a glance at the sun. "Either way, we'll know soon enough."

Cyrus Murchison and his army of gunslingers set out a leisurely two hours after sunrise. Everything went well for the first three hours. Then the two men in the lead flew from the backs of their horses, driven off by a long, supple sapling that had been bent back behind a pile of rocks along the trail. They landed hard, both breaking ribs. One of them snapped a leg.

"That damn well ties it!" Heck Grange shouted. "We'll be forever getting to the top of the pass now. How many more of these things are out there waiting for us?"

Cyrus Murchison responded with an air of indifference. "Tell the men to go slow and we'll find out. But keep them going."

With the column on the move again, Murchison settled down to a gloomy contemplation of exactly *how many* such traps they would find. And worse, how much harm would be done.

Nervous, and made more cautious, the band of thugs continued on toward the top of the pass. No more hidden dangers had shown up by the time Murchison's henchmen stopped for their nooning. Titus Hobson had managed to convince himself that someone other than Smoke Jensen had rigged that trap. An Indian, perhaps, to catch some form of game. He shared his thought with Cyrus Murchison. Oddly, Murchison found himself agreeing. Until now he had harbored the sneaking suspicion that the two wily gunfighters had gotten ahead of them, yet he said nothing to Hobson. Half an hour further along the trail he quickly learned to regret that decision.

An agonized scream echoed along the high, enclosing walls of the gorge that led to the high pass of the Sierra Nevada. Its eerie wail jerked Cyrus Murchison out of his dark ruminations and sent a chill down his spine. Up ahead, he saw a thigh-thick log swish back and forth, after striking the lead rider. Jagged flakes of quartz protruded from the face, three of them dripped blood.

Unthinkingly, Murchison spoke his thoughts aloud. "Hideous. It's hideous. They—they're nothing but barbarians."

Heck Grange took charge. "Dismount! Walk your horses and look where you are going."

Severely shaken, his face pale, Cyrus Murchison did as the rest. He reached the spot where the man lay dead, his blood a pool around his crumpled form, when a rope twanged musically ahead and four saplings swished out to slap men and horses in the face. The hard cases shouted in alarm and jumped to the side of the trail. Fragile brush crackled and gave way under their weight. Their yells changed to screams of agony as they impaled themselves on sharpened stakes in the bottom of shallow trenches.

A voice came from one thug behind Murchison. "That does it. I'm getting out of here."

Murchison whirled. "No, wait. Stay with us. There can't be much more of this."

"*Any more* is too damn much for me, Mr. Murchison. You can send my pay to my house."

An idea struck Cyrus Murchison. "Anyone who deserts won't get paid!" he shouted.

"Who cares? At least we'll be alive," another truculent voice replied.

Four men took to their horses, turned tail, and fled without a backward look. Cyrus Murchison cursed and stomped his boot on the hard ground. Up ahead a trigger tripped and a loud roar filled the air. Hundreds of large rocks rained down on the men and horses below.

Whinnies of the frightened critters filled the air as the stones bruised and cut their hide. Dust rose in thick clouds. The rumble of bounding boulders drowned out the shrieks of pain from the injured hard cases. Those the farthest along the trail broke free only to be met with a wall of powder smoke. Bullets cracked through the air. Thugs died horribly.

Belatedly, those behind recovered and drew weapons. They surged forward, yelling to their fellow stupefied comrades over the tumult to keep moving forward. The thrust became a rallying point, which grew into a concerted charge. Six-guns and rifles blazing, they mounted and dashed at the ambush, indifferent to any possible traps that remained.

By sheer force of numbers, they stormed through the weak center of the hidden vigilantes. In a matter of seconds the last of Murchison's shattered column thundered over a rise and out of sight. Louis Longmont came out of the rocks where he had forted up. Smoke Jensen appeared on the slope opposite him. He quickly read the question on the face of Louis.

"We go after them, of course," Smoke said duly.

"We can't keep going on," Titus Hobson raged at Cyrus Murchison. "They've been ahead of us at every turn. Look at those poor wretches we found along the trail this morning. This is suicidal."

Murchison fought to remain calm. "No, it's not. We got through them, didn't we? The thing is, we're nearly at the summit. When we get there we'll dig in and make them come to us."

"I think it's a dangerous mistake," Titus objected.

Basically a coward at heart, Titus Hobson had been a schoolyard bully as a child. He used his strength and size to intimidate smaller children. Later, as a prospector, he had developed his brawn to an impressive degree. His bulging muscles, craggy face, and bushy brows made it easier to cow those who sought to oppose him. His confidence grew, and with it, his wealth. Not until this wild flight into the wilderness had he been effectively challenged.

Now it frightened him witless. He had been close enough to the unfortunate lout who took the log in the chest to have blood splatter on his shirt and face. He knew Smoke Jensen was too dangerous for them to provoke. Why had he let Cyrus drag him into this? Yet he knew that Murchison was also dangerous. A man all too quick to use the final solution of death to end any opposition. Titus knew he dare not let his true feelings be seen too clearly. He tried to placate Murchison before this discussion took a hazardous turn.

"All right, Cyrus. We have little choice anyway. I suggest we make an effort to block the trail further on. Anything to slow them. I gather that this gorge narrows, the farther up we go?" At Murchison's nod, he outlined an idea that had worked in the gold fields against a band of outlaws led by the notorious Mexican bandit Gilberto Oliveras. "When we reach the top, we should close off the entire pass. Fell trees and build firing stands of them. Move rocks, boulders, seal off the trail. Then we can hold off that scum until they run out of ammunition."

Murchison considered that a moment. "Good idea, Titus. Where did you come up with this?"

Hobson showed a hint of modesty. "I was at the Battle of Wheeler's Meadow."

"My Lord, I never knew that. Well, old fellow, I propose you take charge of our delaying actions and the fortifications. Is it true that there were only seventeen of you against nearly a hundred Mexican bandits?"

"Yes. But we had all the tools and we built well. They couldn't get to us. We held them until they ran out of powder and shot. Simple after that."

"I like that. I do like that. We'll do it your way, and watch Smoke Jensen dash his brains out against our stout walls."

Smoke Jensen stood with his right fist on his hip, his left hand on the slanted holster high on his left side. Fallen trees blocked the trail ahead. Louis Longmont joined him while the volunteers labored to clear the obstacles. With a shout from Brian Pullen, horses strained on ropes attached to the first trunk and it swung slowly, ponderously.

"What are you thinking, *mon ami?*"

"They are waiting for us up ahead. I'd bet my last cigar that we'll run into more of these roadblocks, and finally reach the place they're forted up."

Louis nodded. "I think you are right. And no doubt you are going out there to find them tonight. This time I'm going with you."

Smoke made a fake shocked expression. "Louis, you astonish me. Whatever brought you to this? How can you think of risking that elegant neck?"

Louis produced a look of such wounded pride, only to be spoiled by the laughter that bubbled up deep inside himself. "I know you prefer to work alone, my friend. But they have grown bold after breaking out of our nice little trap, non? It would be well that for tonight you had someone to watch your back."

Without a show of any reluctance, Smoke agreed. His spirit lightened when the second downed pine had been dragged clear of the narrow spot in the trail. Smoke took the lead, with Louis at his side. Brian Pullen and Quo Chung Wu brought up the rear. Already Smoke's fertile imagination labored to concoct new nastiness to inflict upon Murchison and his henchmen.

Three more blockades had to be torn down by the time Smoke Jensen called a halt for the day. He had ridden ahead and scouted out the fortifications erected by Murchison's mongrels. Murchison, or someone, had chosen well. Located at the restricted point, at the crest of the high pass, it had taken little effort to build a thick, impenetrable wall. They seemed determined to stand and fight, he reasoned. It might be he could change their minds.

Smoke would have liked to use fire. If he did, he knew, he took the risk that the whole of the forest would be wiped out. Sort of like swatting a fly with a scoop shovel, he reckoned it. That left him with the three other elements as the Indians saw their universe: air, earth, and water. By the time he had returned to discuss it with Louis, he had made up his mind which they would use.

The breeze cooperated nicely, having whipped up into a stiff blow. It would mask any sounds they might make. Thankfully, it held even after the sun had set. Clouds had built up over the late afternoon, another gift of nature, and blotted out the blanket of stars and the thin crescent of moon. Smoke and Louis set out when total darkness descended.

They left their horses three hundred yards from the barrier erected by the hard cases. When they stealthily approached, they found that, rather than looming over them, the bulwark had been built only to shoulder height. All the better, Smoke saw it. He held a whispered conference with Louis and they took position near one end.

Less than five minutes went by before a roving sentry appeared on the opposite side of the barricade. Louis Longmont waited until he went past, then rose on tiptoe to stare over the wall.

"Psssst!" Louis hissed.

Galvanized by the unexpected sound, the hard case spun in Louis's direction, his rifle headed for his shoulder. Smoke Jensen came up behind him and clamped one hand over his mouth, the other on his throat, and yanked him over the wall. Louis stepped close and rapped the man on the head with the butt of his revolver. Smoke tied him tightly and they moved along the wall to wait again.

Another lookout paced his bit of the defenses, his attention wandering between the convivial firelight behind and the thick blackness beyond the bastion. Louis popped up and hissed again when the guard looked inward. He turned abruptly and Smoke hauled him off his feet. He wound up as tightly bound as the first one, unconscious on the outside of the partition.

Smoke and Louis repeated their little ruse until every watcher had been removed from the rampart. With that accomplished, they stole off into the night. When the thugs found their friends in the morning, they might not be so sure the wall would protect them.

"Here they come!" one lookout shouted from the barricade.

Cyrus Murchison and his riff-raff had only finished cussing and stomping about the waylaid sentries of the night before and gone back to breakfast. That clever bastard, Cyrus Murchison thought of Smoke Jensen. He would be smart enough to wait for the last shift to pull that. They weren't even missed until daylight. Now, before a man could even enjoy a decent breakfast, the whole lot of that rabble is attacking. With a regretful sigh, Murchison set aside his plate and reached for the rifle resting against a boulder beside him.

"Hold your fire until they get in close," Heck Grange advised. "Pick a few of them out of the saddle and the rest will turn tail. I know these bumpkins."

It turned out he didn't know them as well as he believed.

Twenty-four strong, led by Smoke Jensen and Louis Longmont, the vigilante posse rode up toward the barrier. At a hundred yards, those with rifles opened fire. Anyone shooting from a moving horse had to be blessed with a lot of luck. It turned out two of the avengers were.

One hard case made a strangled cry when a bullet tore through his throat. He went down in a welter of blood. Off to the left, a second thug made a harsh grunt when a slug angled off the top of the receiver of his rifle and popped through his right eye. Already misshapen, the hunk of lead shredded a path through his brain and blew out the back of his skull.

That ended all restraint. Rifles crackled along the wall of earth and logs. One volunteer flew from his saddle, shot through the heart. He bounced twice when he reached the ground. Another took a bullet in the shoulder and slumped forward along the neck of his mount. A third, gut-shot, made a pitiful cry and turned his horse aside.

That caused several others to falter. Singly, at first, then the whole body spun their mounts and streaked off downhill to the shelter of a cluster of trees. For the time being, the fight turned into a contest of long-range sniping. Not for long, though.

After half an hour, Smoke Jensen's Winchester Express flattened a hard case who had bent over to pour a cup of coffee across the fire pit. When several of his comrades ran to his rescue, Smoke exhorted his volunteers.

"Time to hit them again. Mount up and let's ride."

21

Whooping like wild Indians, the vigilantes charged the fortifications. Caught unprepared, clearly half of the gunmen were wolfing down biscuits and gulping fresh coffee. Three of them did not make it back to the barrier.

At one hundred yards, the posse opened up again. The exposed men died in that first fusillade. At fifty yards, the toughs who manned the wall began to return fire. At first, they had little effect. Then their jangled nerves smoothed and their bullets began to find flesh.

Two of Smoke's volunteers took slugs, one in the shoulder, the other through a thigh. His horse didn't fare well, either. The hot lead punched through its hide and into a lung. Pink froth appeared on its muzzle and lips and it faltered abruptly, then its legs folded under it and the wounded rider pitched over its head.

"Get me outta here," he wailed.

A farmer, who fancied himself a good hand at horsemanship, cut to his right and bent at the waist. Arm hooked, he snagged the injured man and yanked him up behind.

"Ow, damn it!" the victim complained ungratefully. "That hurt worse than bein' shot."

"Be glad I looked out for you, you old fool," his rescuer grumped.

Tyler Estes found shooting from horseback to be rather a pain. He had just gotten the hang of it when all the targets disappeared. "Show yourselves and fight like a man," he challenged, as he jumped his horse to within thirty yards of the wall.

A head appeared, followed by shoulders and a rifle. The gunman fired and cut the hat from the head of Estes. His eyes went wide and he let out a little bleat before he clapped the cheek plate of his rifle to his face and took aim. His horse obediently halted for him and Tyler Estes released the reins for a moment to steady the barrel of his long gun. The .44 Winchester cracked sharply and the head of the thug who had shot at him snapped backward in a shower of red spray.

"That'll learn ya," Estes chortled, then wheeled away to find another target.

Another posseman cut across in front of Smoke Jensen, causing the last mountain man to rein in sharply. That saved Smoke's life, although it did not do much for the unfortunate eager one. He died in Smoke's place, drilled through the head. The suddenness of it changed Smoke Jensen's mind. They could never outlast the number of guns they faced.

"Pull back!" he shouted over the crackle of gunfire. "Pull back to the trees."

Smoke Jensen led the way to a campsite well out of sight of the forted-up gunmen. When the last of the wounded limped in, Smoke called the posse together. His face wore a serious, concerned expression. The losses they had taken preyed on his mind. These men deserved the opportunity to clean up their own yards, he reckoned. Yet they deserved to live. This fight belonged to him and Louis alone. From here on they would carry it through that way. He told that to them in a calm, quiet voice.

Brian Pullen spoke up forcefully. "Don't think you are going to get rid of me that easily. I'm in to the end."

"These . . . honored gentlemen have . . . families . . . and property . . . to care for. It is . . . reasonable that they return to them at this time. But," Quo Chung Wu went on with a fleeting smile, "it would be . . . unmanly for a priest . . . with neither wife and child . . . nor even a home . . . of my own . . . to take the path of . . . safety. I . . . too . . . will stay . . . beside you." He bowed to Smoke.

"There's no need," Smoke started his protest. Then he correctly read the expression on Quo's face. "I am honored to have your help," he amended.

Consternation ran among the men from the Central Valley. "What about us? Ain't we got a say in this?" one complained.

Smoke Jensen shook his head. "Five of you are dead and seven wounded. You've done your share. Now is the time for you to leave the rest to those who are trained for the killing game. Believe me, what we are going to have to do you don't want on your consciences."

"You mean you're goin' to lynch them all?" Tyler Estes blurted.

"No," Smoke answered levelly. "Those who give up we'll let the law handle."

"When do you want us to leave?" a disappointed posseman asked.

"You don't have to leave. Come morning, I'm sure Murchison will believe he won a big victory and pull out. We'll be going after them. You can stay here, rest up for a day or two, and give the wounded a chance to knit some before heading to your homes."

Tyler Estes scratched the balding spot on the crown of his head, and summed up for all of them. "Well, it'll be nice to get back to the shop. I reckon little Joey Pitchel will be needin' a trim, before them red locks o' his turns into long sissy curls."

That brought an understanding laugh, yet a gloomy

pall settled over the volunteers, even though they faced the happy prospect of safely returning to their homes and families. Smoke Jensen sat long into the night, thinking about it.

Emboldened by their apparent easy success, particularly when nothing happened during the night, Cyrus Murchson pushed on with his surviving henchmen. He left two men behind to report of the defeated posse. They waited in the shade of a big oak a ways behind the wall, which had been left in place. The drowsy warmth of mid-morning got to them and they soon dozed off.

They heard nothing when the four riders approached. Smoke Jensen saw them at once and halted. Signing the other three to remain silent, he eased over the wall and cautiously closed in on the sleeping men. A fly buzzed around a thick lock of hair that hung down on the forehead of one lout. It had made three more circles by the time Smoke reached the slumbering hard case. Then, as Smoke stepped up to him, it landed on his nose.

With a start and a sodden mutter, the thug took a blind swipe at the offending insect. His last conscious thought must have been that for a darned fly, it sure packed a wallop. Still clutching the cylinder of his .45 Colt, Smoke turned to the other snoozing lout and smacked him on the head also.

"We'll take their horses," he called back to the others. "Without mounts, they won't go forward. If they move fast, they can catch up to the posse before those fellers leave."

"That's cold, Smoke," Brian Pullen objected. "Leaving a man without a horse in this country can get him killed."

"Only if he's stupid. The old mountain men, like Preacher, walked the whole of the High Lonesome more than one time."

"Mr. Smoke . . . is right, Mr. Brian," Quo Chung Wu offered. "This is . . . the first time I know of . . . that one of our Order has . . . ever ridden anywhere. We walked . . . for centuries in China. It is . . . a requirement," he added with his cheeks flushed.

"I am sure that Tai Chiu will forgive you," Louis Longmont told Quo Chung Wu.

Quo blushed again. "He . . . already has . . . before we . . . left. I was . . . thinking . . . of the . . . Lord Buddha."

Smoke pulled a face. "Well, considerin' what we're headed into, now's sure the time to get religion, as Preacher would say."

Louis Longmont looked from the wall to the unconscious thugs. "Too bad you knocked out those scrudy trash. Now we have to clear the trail ourselves."

"Allergic to hard, dirty work, Louis?" Smoke jibed.

Louis wrinkled his nose. "Only when I can't get a bath. We had better proceed."

It took the four companions an hour to open a pathway through the barricade. With that accomplished, they struck out on the wide trail left by Murchison and his mob. Most of the day's travel was downhill with only a single file of peaks between them and the long, deceptive grade through a lush meadow that led to Donner Pass.

Smoke estimated they would catch up to Murchison's gang at that fateful spot where less than forty years ago, men and women stranded by an early blizzard had been forced to commit the most appalling of human failings. Starving in the snow-blocked pass, they had fallen upon the corpses of their fellows to sustain their lives. How ironic it would be if Cyrus Murchison met his end there, Smoke mused.

He would find out, Smoke promised himself, two days from now.

Shouts of disgust and outrage awakened Cyrus Murchison the next morning. He pulled on trousers and boots

and fumbled with sleep-numbed fingers to button his shirt
A quick splash of frigid water removed the gumminess from
his eyes. He had gone to bed feeling rather better about
their enforced exile.

When the two men left behind to spy out the posse had
not returned by nightfall, he preferred to assume that they
had nothing to report so far. Which would indicate, he convinced himself, that Jensen and Longmont and those local
malcontents had turned back. Now, this, whatever it turned
out to be, riling up the men. He reached for his hat as the
flap opened and Heck Grange entered, his face grim, lips
drawn in a hard line.

"What is it out there that has them all stirred up?"

Words clipped and sharp-edged, Heck Grange told him,
"We're not shut of Smoke Jensen yet. He was here some
time last night. He left us three of my men as a warning."
Finally the enormity of what he had seen overcame his
forced restraint. "Goddamnit, they were strung up by the
ankles, throats slit, and bled out like sheep."

For all his cruel nature, that affected Cyrus Murchison
more than anything else. His face went white, his mouth
sagged, and he placed the hat on his head with a shaking
hand. "That's an abomination," he gasped out.

"You haven't actually seen it as yet. Which you'll have to
do soon or we'll lose men like rats off a swamped barge."
Grange went on to instruct his employer. "One thing you
should point out is that it looks like one of the boys got a
piece of Jensen. His knife is bloody."

Murchison pursed his thick lips. "More likely, Jensen
used it to do for them."

Grange studied on that a moment. "I don't think so. The
knife was on the ground, right below his outstretched
hand, which was bloody, too."

Cyrus drew himself up. "Well, then, we'll dwell on that.
Anything to keep the men together."

It proved to be too little, too late. Already, three of Hunt

ey's remaining longshoremen had pulled stakes and left
amp. By nightfall, five more would desert the cause.

Tom, Dick, and Harry Newcomb—their father obviously
had a twisted sense of humor—topped the first rise outside
Murchison's camp and started on the long downgrade to
the valley floor. For defeated men, they showed consider-
ble energy in the way they kept their heads up and studied
heir surroundings in great detail. It did them little good,
hough. They rode right past two men sheltered in a thicket
of brush along the trail.

They swiveled their heads once more, and when they
ooked forward again, two men appeared on the trace in
ront of them, six-guns in hand. Tom, Dick, and Harry
eined their horses furiously in an attempt to turn and flee
ack to the camp, only to find two more people blocking
heir way, weapons at the ready. Desperately they spun their
mounts again.

"Who are you?" Tom demanded, for want of something
better to say.

The hard-faced one with cold eyes answered him. "We're
our worst dream come true."

Somewhat less daunted than his brothers, Dick pushed
he issue. "What's your name, Mister?"

"Smoke Jensen."

Awareness dawned. "Awh, Jesus," Tom groaned.

"We're dead men for sure," Harry concluded for his
brother.

"Not necessarily," the hard-faced messenger of death told
him.

"We saw what you did to those fellers last night."

Fire flashed in the ruddy eyes. "One of them came after
me with a knife."

The brothers saw it then, a thickness of the left shoulder
of Smoke Jensen. Tom also noted a rent in the cloth of the

jacket, with red-brown stains around it. It fed him a dose of false bravado.

"What about the other two?"

"They got in the way." Then Smoke read the expression on their faces. "Don't worry, they were dead when I strung them up."

Dick, worried over the condition of his hide, asked Smoke the fateful question. "You gonna do the same to us?"

"Not unless I have to," Smoke answered calmly. "I gather you have given up on Mr. Murchison's little enterprise?"

"Yessir, yes, we sure have," Harry hastened to say. "Anyway, we worked for Mr. Huntley, an' he's long gone."

"Then you are free to go. All we ask is that you limit yourselves to a single weapon each, and leave all but five rounds with us."

Shocked by this, Tom blurted, "That ain't fair."

"I think you will find that life is not fair. Do it that way or be left for the buzzards and wolves."

"God, you're a hard man, Mr. Jensen," Tom blustered.

"Enough talk," a man with a Frenchy-sounding accent told Tom, Dick, and Harry. "Do it or die."

Quickly, Tom, Dick, and Harry divested themselves of six-guns, hideout pistols, and one spare rifle, and pockets-full of ammunition. Sweating profusely they rode off down the trail.

"That's a good start," Smoke Jensen told his companions. "Though there's a lot more where they came from."

The next dawn brought a cold, sharp wind and thick-bellied clouds Smoke Jensen knew to be laden with snow. All four ate heartily and fortified themselves with plenty of coffee. Smoke gnawed on a final biscuit while Brian Pullen covered the fire pit. The first lacy white flakes danced in the air as they took to saddle and set off.

Two miles down the trail, they encountered five disgruntled former employees of the California Central Railroad.

The exchange went much as the one with the Newcomb brothers. None of the demoralized hard cases liked the idea of travel in this country so lightly armed, yet the alternative held not the least attraction. They did provide one gem of information. Their departure had left Murchison with only twenty-three men.

"Better odds, wouldn't you say?" Smoke Jensen quipped, as the five men rode away.

Louis Longmont answered him drily. "We have them outnumbered, *mon ami.*"

"When do you propose hitting them again?" Brian Pullen asked.

Smoke made an unusual admission. "This arm smarts like the fires of hell. I'd as soon get it over with. But I think we should let them tire themselves out a bit more. It'll be time enough at Donner Pass."

They rode on in silence for an hour, the snow falling heavier by the minute. Every tree and bush wore a mantle of white. Except for the mournful wail of the wind off the sheer rock faces, their surroundings had taken on a cotton-wool quiet. Three inches accumulated almost before they knew it. Their horses' hooves creaked eerily in that underfoot. Smoke called for a halt.

"We had better gather some wood. Otherwise it will be too wet later on."

He set the example by rounding up an armful and wrapping it in his slicker. He tied the bundle behind his saddle. When they pointed the noses of their horses east again, the snow had deepened to six inches.

"I don't like this at all," Brian Pullen lamented. "It never snows in San Francisco."

Smoke spoke through a snort of laughter. "Get used to it. I reckon we'll have a lot more before this storm moves on."

City men all, except for Titus Hobson and his mine police, the snow storm caught the column of Cyrus Murchison's men by surprise. It slowed, then halted their movement. By mid-afternoon, the horses stood knee-deep in cold discomfort. Heck Grange urged his boss to have the men keep going. He reminded Murchison of the fate of the Donner party, and again suggested that they could rig some sort of plow to clear a lane, dragging it by horseback.

"To what purpose? It will exhaust the men and animals. Have the tents set up here and we'll shelter until the storm blows over." An icy gale whipped his words away.

Folding tin stoves came from the back of one packhorse and men installed them as soon as the tents had been erected. Stove pipes poked through specially prepared openings, and before long, ribbons of blue-gray smoke rose into the air to be shattered into ragged wisps by the turning whirl of the wind. Because of their thin walls, the stoves could burn only thin twigs and small branches. Fuel went up at a rapid rate, yet the drawback held one positive side. Heat radiated quickly, warmed the men, and boiled water for coffee.

Before long, savory aromas came from each tent as pots of stew began to simmer. In his large, well-appointed shelter, Cyrus Murchison opened a bottle of sherry and poured a glass for Titus Hobson and himself. He also cracked the lid on a blue, hinge-gate Mason jar that held neat stacks of small, white spheroids.

"Pickled quail eggs," he offered them to Hobson. "Quite tasty. Only so rich, one does not want more than a few at a time." Murchison helped himself and lifted his glass. "To better times."

"Oh, quite well put," a tired, cold, and wet Titus Hobson responded. He swallowed a sip, munched an egg, and peered at the jar. "Say, what's this in the bottom?"

"What is left of the shells. After boiling the eggs, they are put in with the shells on. The vinegar dissolves the calcium and the residue falls to the bottom."

"Clever. I suppose picking the shells off of hundreds of these little things could drive someone quite dotty."

"Tedious work at best," Murchison agreed. Then he spoke the fear that still rode them both. "After the other night, there's no question Jensen and Longmont are still on our trail. I admit I am at my wits end to find a way to stop them."

"Short of losing all of our men, you mean?"

"Exactly, Titus. Has anything occurred to you?"

Hobson took his time answering. "Other than surrendering, I haven't much to say that is encouraging. You do realize we are in one damnable position, don't you? If those left with Jensen and Longmont come at us now, we are about equally matched in numbers. Our men are fighting for money. Those valley yokels are fighting for they see as a cause. They won't give up. If we have to face them we badly need reinforcements."

Cyrus Murchison scowled. "That's why we have to keep going to Carson City. It's only seventy miles, once we reach Donner Pass. There are enough track layers and more yard police there to fill our needs."

Titus canted his head to indicate the tempest outside the tent. "And if we get trapped in the pass by a storm like this? Do we feed on one another like the Donner party?"

Impatience painted lines on Murchison's face. "Spare me the grotesqueries." Then he argued from a basis of reason. "This is the first storm of the year. The snow will not last past the first few hours of sun on it. There probably won't be another until we are well down on the desert."

"You have no way of knowing that. It only seems to me that your way takes a whole lot for granted."

"Titus, Titus, you disappoint me. I always believed prospectors and mine owners were classical gamblers. Given what is at stake, don't you think that risking all is in order?"

Silently, Hobson considered this, his face a morose study. "Yes, I suppose so," he admitted reluctantly. Then he downed his sherry. "I need something stronger than this. How's the brandy supply?"

"Still holding out. Courvoisier VSOP, to be exact. I'll take one, too." With snifters poured, Murchison raised his in a toast. "Confusion to the enemy."

Smoke Jensen did not stay confused for long. Another night wasted. When the day dawned clear and cold, he rolled out of the snow-dusted blankets. The stockpile of wood soon provided a small fire to warm the stiffness from fingers and toes. He let the others sleep while he gnawed on a cold biscuit and set water to boil for coffee. Louis Longmont turned out next.

"Hell of a morning, *mon ami*," he greeted Smoke.

"It'll pass. Sun's already got some heat in it. Way I measure, we have two feet of snow. Soon as it begins to slag down we'll head out. Coffee's ready."

Louis accepted a cup. "Is there any cornmeal?"

"Enough, I'd say," Smoke told him.

"I'll make some Southern-style mush. It will warm us and last a while."

Smoke Jensen knew all about Southern mush. It had shreds of bacon in it, plenty of eggs, when available, and cooked to the consistency of wall plaster. Some old-timers still called it belly plaster. Smoke nodded.

"There's enough ham to fry some, if you want."

"Done. Too bad we have no eggs." Louis shrugged it off. He downed his coffee and went to work.

They left an hour later. Snow-melt trickled down summer-sun-dried water courses. Slowly the birds found new life and cause to celebrate a fresh day. Their music filled the air. As a boy, Smoke often wondered if they were telling each other about the storm that had blown away at last, sharing gossip. A foolish notion he soon abandoned in the cold light of being alone and a kid in the awesome vastness of the High Lonesome.

Now he had a scrap of that youthful fantasy return to him. Somehow it turned out to be comforting. Endless days and nights of fighting and bloodshed needed a counterpoint. For years it had been his lovely, raven-haired Sally. Out here in these strange mountains, he needed to cling to something.

"Cling to yourself, you maudlin old fool!" Preacher's voice roared at him in his head. And so he did. By one hour after noon, they came upon the site of Murchison's encampment. From the condition of the ground, he estimated the hard cases had been gone no more than three hours. There would be a little catch-up tonight.

22

Angry voices rasped around the campfires the next morning to wash away the good feelings of Cyrus Murchison on the previous evening. During the night, six more men deserted the camp. Now only seventeen gunmen remained. Cursing under his breath, Murchison stuffed himself into clothes, donned a heavy sheepskin coat, and stomped out to quell the upheaval.

"Nothing has changed, men. Nothing at all. We still outnumber them even if they all come after us."

"Yeah, and they kicked our butts right good every time before," one wag taunted.

"What's to say that the fighting and the weather haven't had a similar effect on them?" He wanted to avoid direct acknowledgment of the desertions.

No one could come up with an answer for that. Murchison seized on it to regain control. "Break camp and make ready to ride."

Muttering, some of those on the fringe of the angry assembly turned away to begin packing. Gradually, the remainder joined them, stared down by an aroused Cyrus Murchison. When the last had left, Murchison turned to his partner.

"Titus, is it going to be like this every day?"

Hobson sighed and jinked one shoulder. "Don't ask me. If they leave us alone, I don't think so. But another storm like that last one, and I won't hold out much hope."

"Bugger the weather," Murchison grumped. "If we push ourselves, we can be to the next pass before nightfall." He withheld the fateful name "Donner."

"I agree. It is critical that we make it. I'll talk to my men."

Murchison clapped him on the back. "Good. It can only help. Oh, and at noon, we won't stop to cook a meal. Have everyone bring along something they can eat in the saddle. I am going to beat Smoke Jensen at his own game."

By noon, Smoke Jensen had put his small band a good five miles beyond Murchison's overnight camp. Most of the snow had melted; only on the shady northern sides did drifts and patches still remain. In its wake it left a quagmire of slippery mud.

Smoke nodded to this. "It will slow them down more than us. Those heavy-loaded packhorses will make hard goin' of the mud."

"Shall we be visiting them tonight?" Louis asked.

"Oh, yes, I am sure we will. The ground is wet enough to use a little fire this time."

They came an hour after sundown. Smoke Jensen led the way, a flaming torch held at arm's length in his left hand. His right worked a big .45 Colt. The reins hung over the saddle horn and he steered Thunder with his knees. Louis Longmont rode to his left with another torch. Behind them came Brian Pullen and Quo Chung Wu.

Quo fired the Purdy shotgun one-handed and clung to his saddle with the other. Brian emptied one of the four revolvers he carried into one of the smaller tents as he raced past. Thugs cried in alarm and crashed through the low door flaps of other canvas lodges. Smoke reined in sharply and hurled his flambeau onto the roof of the tent that housed Cyrus Murchison. Cries of alarm came from inside as the heavy billet burned its way through. The blazing canvas illuminated the entire campsite.

Louis fired the other large tent, sheets of flame rushing up from the fringed roof overhang. This time the shouts of alarm came from outside.

"The supplies! They're burning the supplies."

"Get away. There's ammunition in there," Heck Grange shouted. "There's dynamite in there, too."

Cyrus Murchison burst clear of his doomed tent, his clothes in hasty disarray. He waved an awkward, long-barreled Smith and Wesson American in one hand and shouted for Heck Grange. Grange reached his side in a moment and the agitated railroad mogul made frantic gestures back toward the tent.

"Titus Hobson is still in there. Get some men to pull him out. A wall support hit him on the head."

"Right away, Mr. Murchison." Heck Grange sent two men into the burning tent to retrieve the unconscious form of Titus Hobson.

When they laid him on the ground, Titus Hobson swam slowly back into the real world. He coughed clear a phlegmy throat and tried to sit upright. Everything swirled around him. He caught himself with one hand before he could fall back. Fuzzily, he made out the face of Cyrus Murchison as it hovered over him.

"Are you all right, Titus?" Murchison queried.

"I think . . ." Titus Hobson began his answer, when the detonator caps in the supply tent let go.

The dynamite quickly followed from sympathetic detonation. A tremendous white flash and crushing blast followed. The ground heaved, heat waves washed over everything, and the concussion knocked Titus Hobson flat, along with nearly everyone else. A huge cloud of dust and powder smoke filled the clearing. The horrendous sound echoed off the surrounding peaks for a long time, while the stunned men tried to regain their feet.

"We should have never brought that along," Titus stated with feeling.

Quo Chung Wu found himself faced by five men made more dangerous by their desperation. He downed one with the last round in his shotgun. With no time to reload, he put the weapon aside and met their charge with fists and feet when the remaining four swarmed over him. His kicks found their targets and two men fell back. The other pair came at Quo from opposite directions.

He dodged the first lout and the other thug connected with a knife in the shoulder of the one facing him. The city trash howled and Quo jumped nimbly from between them. By then the first hard cases had recovered enough to return to the fight. They circled Quo, one with a knife, the other with his clubbed, empty revolver. Quo kept pace with them . . . at least until the knife artist who had stabbed his comrade chose to try again.

Now, Quo faced enemies on three sides. He used every bit of his martial arts skill to keep them at bay. They circled, feinted, snarled, and cursed. Quo made small whistling and warbling sounds, his hands and arms describing figures in the air, weaving his spell, lulling these dull-witted qua'lo. It worked rather well, until the fourth gunhand joined his companions.

Quo realized at once he had to take the offensive. He spun, lashed out a foot, and kicked one thug low in the gut. The injured dolt bent double and vomited up his supper. Quo pivoted gracefully and delivered another jolt to the side of the exposed head. The hard case went down, twitched, and lay still. The other three rushed Quo at once. The young priest's fists and feet moved in blurs. Another went down, then one with a knife got in close and drove the blade into Quo's back, over a kidney.

His mouth opened in a soundless scream and the strength left his legs. Quo stumbled forward and the knife twisted clear of his back. The grinning goon who held it thrust again, the keen edge sliding between two of Quo's ribs and into a lung. A fountain of blood gushed from his pain-twisted lips. Blackness swarmed over Quo Chung Wu as he pitched forward onto his face, never to rise again.

Smoke Jensen saw Quo Chung Wu go down and a moment of sharp regret filled him. The young Chinese priest had known the dangers involved in this battle and had come along at his own wish. Any of them, all of them, could die right here in this mountain pass, where so many had perished before. His lament for Quo ended, Smoke turned to check on Brian.

Exhibiting a skill at gunfighting unusual for a young lawyer, Brian held off three men with a coolness lacking in many a more experienced shootist. Disoriented by the wavering flames and billows of smoke, the trio of rascals threw wild shots in the general direction of Brian.

He obliged them by gunning down one of their number and smoothly replacing his spent revolver with the third of his quartet. The .45 Peacemaker in Brian's hand bucked and snorted and sent another hard case off to explain himself to his Maker. The third experienced a momentary flash of brilliance. He emptied his hands and thrust them high over his head.

Brian stepped in and smacked the man behind one ear. He dropped like a stone. Taking a deep breath, Brian turned to find another enemy. Disappointment flashed on his face as two reprobates fled from the conflict, thoroughly defeated. That left only Heck Grange, Cyrus Murchison, and Titus Hobson, who had once more regained consciousness.

Forced back on their own resources, the three candidates for hell reverted to their basic savagery. Heck Grange put a bullet through the left shoulder of Brian Pullen. A second later, he found himself facing Smoke Jensen. This would be nowhere as easy. Heck cocked his .44 Frontier Colt and the hammer dropped on a spent primer.

Frantically, he let go of the weapon and clawed for another thrust into the waistband of his trousers. Smoke Jensen waited for him. The muzzle came free and Heck Grange saw a momentary glimmer of hope. Then Smoke Jensen filled his hand with a .45 Peacemaker and triggered a round.

Smoke's bullet hit Heck in the meaty portion of his shoulder. Rocked by the slug, the chief lawman of the railroad grimly completed his intended action. Flame leapt from the muzzle of his six-gun. A solid impact rocked Smoke Jensen and he stumbled to the left, a sharp pain in his side. Gradually that numbed as he centered his Colt on the chest of Heck Grange. Smoke eared back the hammer of his Peacemaker a fraction of a second before a chunk of firewood, hurled by Titus Hobson, crashed into the side of his head.

Stars and vivid colors exploded inside the skull of Smoke Jensen. His six-gun blasted harmlessly into the ground at the feet of Heck Grange. That gave Grange a chance to fire again. The hot slug broke skin on the side of Smoke Jensen's neck. A sheet of blood washed warmly downward. Through the throbbing in his head, Smoke tried to steady himself.

Concentrating desperately, he willed his vision to return. Heck Grange swam erratically in the involuntary tears that filled Smoke's eyes when he could at last see. He steadied his hand and eared back the hammer. The Peacemaker roared once more. Heck Grange's knees buckled and he went down hard.

He caught himself with his free hand and cried out at the pain that lanced through his body from his wounded shoulder. Once again he tried to finish off Smoke Jensen. The six-gun in Smoke's hand spoke first.

Hot lead spat from the muzzle and caught Heck Grange in his left nostril. Grange reared backward and kept on going to land on the back of his head, which had been blown off along with his hat.

Smoke spared the hard case no more time. He felt dizzy and light-headed. Dimly he saw Louis Longmont turn toward Titus Hobson as though wading under the ocean. Hobson also moved in slow motion. He pulled a .44 Colt Lightning from his Coggshell Saddlery shoulder holster and fired almost immediately.

His bullet struck Louis Longmont in the upper right thigh. Louis went to one knee, although he continued his swing. His own six-gun bucked in his hand and the slug sped true. The eyes of Titus Hobson went wide and white when pain exploded in his chest. He tried to cycle the double-action revolver again. This time the projectile missed Longmont entirely.

Weakened by rapid blood loss, Louis Longmont fired his last bullet and missed. He sank to his side on the ground. Head still whirling, Smoke Jensen went to the side of his friend. Hobson, light-headed from his wound, came at the two of them, firing recklessly. Smoke returned the favor and his bullet tore a chunk from the heaving side of Hobson. The Colt Lightning struck an expended cartridge and a expression of shock washed Hobson's face white.

Smoke Jensen knew that he had fired his last round. When the wounded Hobson recovered himself, he snatched up another stick of firewood and advanced on Smoke. Determined to save the life of his friend, Smoke Jensen drew his war-hawk and readied himself. Hobson, though unsteady on his feet, gave him little time for that.

Titus Hobson swung the billet like an ax handle. It swished past over the head of Smoke Jensen, who had ducked. Smoke feinted with the tomahawk and the fighters separated. They appeared to be nothing more than two vicious predators quarreling over a choice bit of carrion. Smoke carefully kept himself between Hobson and Louis. Titus Hobson tried a fake on Smoke Jensen.

It failed and the war-hawk sailed by dangerously close to the face of Hobson. They backed off. Smoke risked a glance at Louis and saw the light in those gray eyes begin to dim.

"Louis, if you can hear me, cover that wound and use your belt for a tourniquet. Do it now!"

His concern for Longmont almost cost Smoke that fight that moment. Titus Hobson lunged and swung the wrist-thick stick at the side of Smoke's head. Smoke spun and parried the blow, did a quick reverse, and cleaved the length of wood in half. Hobson let out a startled yelp and jumped back.

"Damn you, Smoke Jensen. Damn you straight to hell."

Smoke laughed at Hobson. His side had become a continuous lightning strike. Quickly he changed hands with his war-hawk. The movement confused Titus Hobson and he stood blinking. That hesitation proved enough for Smoke Jensen. Swiftly he swung the deadly 'hawk and felt the solid impact as the keen edge sank into flesh and bone near the base of the neck of Titus Hobson. Muscles and tendon severed, Hobson's head drooped to the opposite side at an odd angle.

A gurgle came from deep in his throat and his eyes rolled up. The foreshortened piece of wood fell from numb fingers and Titus Hobson spilled onto the ground, taking Smoke Jensen's tomahawk with him. Smoke took time only for two quick, deep gulps of air, then turned to Louis.

Louis Longmont sat upright now, shoulders drooped, chest heaving with the effort to breathe. His leg wore a tightly drawn belt above the wound and a square of impeccably white linen kerchief covered the bullet hole. He raised his head and cut his eyes to Smoke Jensen.

"You know, we're getting too old for this sort of thing, *mon ami.*"

"Speak for yourself, Louis," Smoke panted. Then he remembered Cyrus Murchison.

Quickly as his injured body would obey, Smoke Jensen turned to his left to find Cyrus Murchison on his knees, trembling hands raised in abject surrender. His lips quivered as he spoke.

"I—I've never seen anyone fight so ferociously. D-Don't hurt me. I'm giving myself up. I'll fight the charges in court." A sardonic smile replaced the fear in the man. "And I'll win, too."

Smoke Jensen looked from him to Louis Longmont, then cut his eyes to Brian Pullen. Pullen's expression told Smoke volumes. Smoke sighed. "With his money, he likely will win." Then he returned to the matter at hand. "Let's patch one another up and take in our prisoner. There's been enough blood shed in the Donner Pass."

A day's journey to the east and those who had come out of the Donner Pass alive turned south. At the insistence of Smoke Jensen, they had brought along the bodies of Quo Chung Wu, Titus Hobson, and Heck Grange. The rest they buried as well as they could. Two more long, hard days to the south put them alongside the tracks of the California Central Railroad.

Cyrus Murchison proved entirely cooperative. He instructed Smoke Jensen in how to rig a signal that would stop the first westbound train. Half a day went by before the distant wail of a steam whistle announced the approach of the daily express run. To the relief of them all, the signal worked.

"We could be in a tight spot rather fast," a weakened Louis Longmont advised from the travois on which he rode as he and the others studied the hard faces of the crew.

"We still have a few things going for us, old friend," Smoke Jensen advised him lightly.

"Such as what?"

"We do have their boss as a prisoner," Smoke suggested.

"That is precisely what I see as the source of our problems," Louis stated drily.

Smoke showed no reaction. "Let's see what they say . . . or do first."

The engineer braced them first. "Isn't that Mr. Murchison you have trussed up like a Christmas goose?" Smoke Jensen allowed as how it was indeed. "What the hell is that all about?" the locomotive driver demanded.

This time, Louis Longmont replied. "He is under arrest."

"By whose authority?" the truculent engineer snapped.

Smoke took a step forward. "By mine. We are going to board your train and ride to San Francisco and turn him over to the police."

A defiant curl came to the thick lips of the trainman. "You will, like hell."

Smoke flashed his badge. "I think we will. I'm a deputy U. S. marshal. If I'm forced to, I'll simply commandeer the train, throw your ass in irons and run it myself."

Two burly switchmen grumbled at this, yet they made no move to interfere. That quickly decided the engineer. "All right, all right. You can board. But you'll have to ride in a chair car. Ain't got no fancy coach hooked up."

"I'm sure Mr. Murchison won't mind," Smoke quipped.

They arrived in San Francisco an hour before sundown. The huge red-orange globe rested a finger's width above the flat, glassy sea and sent long shafts of magenta over the rippling water of the bay. The first order of business was to take Cyrus Murchison to the police station. Smoke surrendered him directly to the chief of police and listed the charges.

After a sad journey to the Golden Harmony temple in Chinatown with the body of Quo Chung Wu, Smoke, Louis, and Brian headed for the bordello. Two of their hired protectors met them on the porch. A minute later, Lucy Glover dashed out to join them.

"I was afraid something had happened to you," she blurted, staring directly into the face of Brian Pullen.

It instantly became obvious to Smoke and Louis that the pair shared mutual stars in their eyes. Smoke cleared his throat. That broke the thick web of enthrallment. Reluctantly, Lucy and Brian turned their attention to the big man with a white bandage on his neck.

"Brian and I have been talking about the future of this—er—establishment. I have decided to ask you to continue in charge of the—ah—operation. Louis is going to stay in San Francisco and make arrangements to sell my latest acquisition."

Shock and worry clouded Lucy's face. "You're going to *sell?*"

Smoke chuckled softly. "Yes, and as quickly and quietly as possible."

"Don't you realize that this place can make a fortune for you?"

"Granted," Smoke declared. "And if my dear Sally ever found out about it, she would have a fit."

"But—but, what will I—I and the girls—*do* after it's sold?"

"The girls can pool their resources and make a bid. Anything reasonable will be considered. For your own part, if I'm not mistaken, young woman, you have a career change ahead in the near future."

Lucy Clover cut her eyes from Smoke Jensen to Brian Pullen, who blushed furiously. "You're right, Smoke, if I have anything to say about it," the young lawyer said softly.

The two gunfighters chuckled indulgently. Then Smoke Jensen ended their embarrassment. "I'll just gather my things and be on my way."

Lucy was shaken. "You're leaving so soon?"

"I have to. I've been away from the Sugarloaf too long."

"But your wounds," Lucy and Brian protested together.

Smoke gave Lucy a sunny smile. "They'll heal better in

he High Lonesome. Especially with Sally there to pamper
ne." He turned to Louis Longmont. "Louis, it's been good
working with you again. After you have this out of the way,
come up to the Sugarloaf for a while. The latch-string is
always out."

"I appreciate, that, *mon ami*, and I will give the invitation
serious consideration. For now, then, I will only say *adieu*."

"Farewell, old friend, and ride an easy saddle."

With that, Smoke Jensen was gone.

The groom is beaming. The church is filled.
The music is starting.

The ceremony is about to begin.

There's only one thing missing...

The Bride!

Runaway Brides

YESTERDAY ONCE MORE
by Debbie Macomber

FULL CIRCLE
by Paula Detmer Riggs

THAT'S WHAT FRIENDS ARE FOR
by Annette Broadrick

Because you can't have a wedding
without them...

DEBBIE MACOMBER

has always enjoyed telling stories, first to baby-sitting clients, and then to her own children. An avid reader, she wanted to share her stories with a wider audience. Debbie's first book was published by Silhouette in 1983, and she was off and running. Now, more than fifty books later, she is a two-time winner of the B. Dalton Bestseller Award. In addition to her Silhouette books, Debbie also writes mainstream novels.

PAULA DETMER RIGGS

discovers material for her writing in her varied life experiences. During her first five years of marriage to a naval officer, she lived in nineteen different locations on the West Coast, gaining familiarity with places as diverse as San Diego and Seattle. While working at a historical site in San Diego she wrote, directed and narrated fashion shows and became fascinated with the early history of California.

She writes romance novels because "I think we all need an escape from the high-tech pressures that face us every day, and I believe in happy endings. Isn't that why we keep trying, in spite of all the roadblocks and disappointments along the way?"

ANNETTE BROADRICK

believes in romance and the magic of life. Since 1984, when her first book was published, Annette has shared her view of life and love with readers all over the world. In addition to being nominated by *Romantic Times* as one of the Best New Authors of that year, she also has won the *Romantic Times* Reviewer's Choice Award for Best in its Series for *Heat of the Night, Mystery Lover* and *Irresistible;* the *Romantic Times* WISH Award for her heroes in *Strange Enchantment, Marriage Texas Style!* and *Impromptu Bride;* and the *Romantic Times* Lifetime Achievement awards for Series Romance and Series Romantic Fantasy.

Runaway Brides

DEBBIE MACOMBER
PAULA DETMER RIGGS
ANNETTE BROADRICK

Silhouette Books

Published by Silhouette Books
America's Publisher of Contemporary Romance

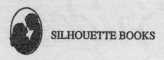

SILHOUETTE BOOKS

ISBN 0-373-20124-9

by Request

Copyright © 1996 by Harlequin Books S.A.

RUNAWAY BRIDES

YESTERDAY ONCE MORE
Copyright © 1986 by Debbie Macomber
FULL CIRCLE
Copyright © 1988 by Paula Detmer Riggs
THAT'S WHAT FRIENDS ARE FOR
Copyright © 1987 by Annette Broadrick

CONTENTS

A Note from Debbie Macomber

Dear Reader,

This year my husband, Wayne, and I will celebrate our twenty-eighth wedding anniversary. In those years we've lived and loved, argued and cried, and laughed. It was the laughter that got us through the tears and the arguments. But even when we disagreed I never doubted my husband's love for me. This is what I believe is so special about marriage. This bonding of two hearts, this blending of two very different personalities into one harmonious relationship, which hasn't always been easy. In this world of quick fixes and miracle cures, we are often guilty of looking for easy answers when it comes to building a solid marriage. Unfortunately, there's no magic formula. It's living one day at a time, helping each other, listening, loving, crying and laughing together. It's respecting and learning from our differences, of leaving our hearts and our lives open to one another.

I'm pleased and excited that Silhouette has decided to reissue *Yesterday Once More*. This is one of my early romance novels and tells the story of Daniel and Julie, two people obviously in love. When matters overwhelmed her, Julie did what most of us have tried at one time or another: the quick fix. Julie, the runaway bride, left Daniel, only to realize later what a terrible mistake she had made.

I invite you to settle back with a tall glass of iced tea and relax as you read about Daniel and Julie. As always, I enjoy hearing from my readers. You can reach me at P.O. Box 1458, Port Orchard, WA 98366.

Debbie Macomber

For my brother, Terry Archer, who was responsible for my "best seller." He made copies of my diary and sold them to the boys in my eighth-grade class. And to his saintly wife, Miki,

With Love

Chapter One

Julie Houser pushed the elevator button and stepped back to wait. An older woman whose office was on the same floor joined her and they exchanged lazy smiles.

Absently Julie glanced at her watch; she'd have plenty of time to finish unpacking tonight. Not wanting to take the trouble to cook a meal, she toyed with the idea of stopping off and picking up something simple from the local drive-in.

The giant metal doors swooshed open and then the two women moved to the rear of the elevator, anticipating the five-thirty rush. By the time the car emptied on the bottom floor it would be filled to capacity.

The next floor down it stopped again. This time three men boarded. Julie's concentration was centered on the lighted numbers above the door when the elevator came to a third halt. Another man entered and absently Julie squeezed herself into the far corner to make room.

The strap of her purse slid off her shoulder and as she eased it back up she felt someone's eyes roam over her. Accustomed to the appreciative gaze of men, Julie ignored the look and the man. The close scrutiny continued and she could all but feel the heated stare that started at the top of her shoulder length chestnut-colored hair and ran over her smooth oval features. Color seeped into her high cheek-bones and the gentle curve of her mouth tightened. Abruptly Julie turned her head, her blue eyes snapping.

But after one look at her admirer, she nearly choked. She felt chilled and burning at the same moment. Her heart rate hammered wildly like that of a captured fledgling. The whole world came to a sudden, jangling halt. Her hand tightened around the purse strap as if the flimsy piece of leather would hold her upright.

"Daniel." The name slipped from her lips as her eyes met and held those of the man standing closest to her. His dark eyes narrowed and an impassive expression masked his strikingly handsome features.

Unable to bear his impassive gaze any longer, Julie lowered her eyes, her long lashes fluttering closed.

The elevator stopped and everyone filed out until she stood alone in the empty shell, her breath coming in deep, uneven gasps as her throat filled with a painful hoarseness. So soon? She'd only been back to Wichita six days. Never had she dreamed she'd see Daniel so quickly. And in her own building. Was his office here? *Oh, please*, she begged, *not yet; I'm not ready.*

"You coming or going?" An irritated voice from the large foyer broke into her thoughts and Julie moved on unsteady legs out of the elevator.

Her heels clicked noisily across the marble floor and the echo was deafening. The downtown sidewalks were filled with people rushing about and Julie weaved her way through the crowds uncertain where she'd parked her car that morning. Pausing at a red light, she realized she was walking in the wrong direction and turned around. Ten minutes later her hand trembled uncontrollably as she placed the key in the car door and turned the lock.

Her heart felt as if she'd been running a marathon as she slipped into the driver's seat and pressed her forehead against the steering wheel. Nothing could have prepared her for this meeting. Three long years had passed since the last time she'd seen Daniel. Years of change. She'd only been nineteen when she'd fled in panic. He had cause to be bitter and she was sorry, so terribly sorry. The regret she felt for hurting the man she loved so intensely was almost more than she could bear.

And she had loved Daniel. The evening he'd slipped the diamond engagement ring on her finger had been the happiest of her young life. No one should ever expect that kind of contentment at nineteen.

Julie let her thoughts drift back to that night as she started her car and headed toward her apartment. Daniel had taken her to an elegant French restaurant. The lights were dim, and flickering candlelight sent shadows dancing over the white linen tablecloth. Julie tried not to reveal how ill-at-ease she was in the fancy place. She had been so worried that she'd pick up the wrong fork, or worse, dump her soup in her lap. She was so much in love with Daniel and she desperately wanted to please him.

"Happy?" he asked.

Julie glanced over the top of the gold-tasseled menu and nodded shyly. Everything on the menu was written in French with an English translation below. Even with that she didn't know half of what was offered, having never sampled frog legs or sweetbreads. "What would you suggest?"

Daniel set his menu aside, his thoughts occupied. Julie noticed that from the moment he picked her up that evening he'd been unnaturally quiet. Nerves tightened the sensitive muscles of her stomach.

"Daniel, is something the matter?" she ventured, fighting off a troubled frown.

He stared at her blankly and shook his head.

"I'm not wearing the right kind of dress, am I?" She'd changed outfits three times before he'd arrived, parading each one in front of her mother until Margaret Houser had demanded that Julie stop being so particular. Any one of the outfits was perfectly fine.

"You're beautiful," Daniel whispered and the look in his eyes confirmed the softly murmured words.

Pleased, Julie lowered her gaze until her thick lashes fluttered against the high arch of her cheek. Her hand smoothed an imaginary crease from her crisp skirt. "I wanted everything to be perfect tonight."

"Why?"

Julie's tongue felt thick and she answered him with a delicate shrug of one shoulder. She wanted everything to be perfect for Daniel every time. "You've been very quiet," she noted. "Have I done something to upset you?"

His deep, resonant chuckle sent her heart rate into double time. "Oh, my sweet, adorable Julie, is it any wonder I love you so?" His hand reached for hers, gripping her fingers with his on top of the table. "I've been trying to find a way to ask you a question."

"But, Daniel, all you need to do is ask."

He sighed expressively. "It's not that simple, my love."

Julie couldn't imagine what was troubling him. Daniel was usually so thoughtful that he did everything possible to make her comfortable. When they met his friends, he kept her at his side because he knew she was a bit reserved. A thousand times over the last six months, he'd been so loving and caring that it hadn't taken Julie long to lose her heart to him. Slowly he'd brought her into his world. He often took her to the Country Club and had taught her how to play golf and tennis. Gradually his friends had become hers until the reticent Julie had flowered under his love.

But a blossom had its season and soon wilted and drooped. Maybe Daniel was trying to think of a way to gently let her down. Maybe he was tired of her. Maybe he didn't want to see her again. Panic filled her mind and she tightly clenched the linen napkin in her lap, praying that she wouldn't make a fool out of herself and burst into tears when he told her.

"I've been accepted into the law practice of McFife, Lawson and Garrison."

Julie jerked her head up happily. "That's wonderful news. Congratulations."

A smile worked its way to his eyes. "It's only a junior partnership."

"But, Daniel, that's the firm you were hoping would accept you."

"Yes, it is, for more reasons than you know."

Her hand tightened around the stem of her waterglass. Now she understood why he'd chosen such an expensive restaurant. "We're here to celebrate then."

"Not quite yet." He leaned forward and clasped her hand with both of his. "Honey, these last months have been the happiest of my life."

"Mine, too," she whispered.

"I know you're only nineteen and I probably should wait a couple of years."

Julie's heart was pounding so loudly she was afraid he could hear it. Briefly, her eyes met his. "Yes, Daniel?"

"What I'm trying to say is...I love you, Julie. I've never made any secret of how I feel about you. Now that I've been accepted into the law firm and can offer you a future, I'm asking you to marry me."

The words came to her like a gentle, calming breeze after a turbulent storm. Julie closed her eyes savoring the warmth of his words.

"For heaven's sake," Daniel growled. "Say something."

Julie bit into her bottom lip, convinced if she said anything, she'd start to cry.

"Julie," he pleaded.

She nodded wildly.

"Does that mean yes?"

The words trembled from her lips. "Yes, Daniel, yes! I love you so much. I can't think of anything that would make me happier than to spend the rest of my life with you."

The loving look in Daniel's eyes was enough to melt her bones. "I didn't think anything could be so heavy," he said pulling the jeweler's box from his coat pocket. He opened the lid and the size of the diamond caused Julie to gasp.

"Oh, Daniel." Unbidden tears blurred her gaze.

"Do you like it? The jeweler assured me that we can exchange it if you want."

"It's the most beautiful ring I've ever seen."

"Here." He took her hand again and slowly slipped the diamond onto her finger, his eyes alight with a heart full of love. . . .

Battling to put an end to the memories that were flooding her thoughts, Julie pulled into the apartment parking lot and sat for several long moments. Absently, her fingers toyed with the gold chain that hung around her slender neck, seeking the diamond. She kept the engagement ring there and would continue to wear it all her life until it was back on her finger where it belonged. But after seeing Daniel today, Julie realized how difficult the task was going to be. Daniel wouldn't forgive her easily. With a determined effort she climbed out of her car and walked to her apartment.

Uninspired and drab best described her quarters. The bright, sunny apartment she'd left in California had been shared with good friends, people who loved and appreciated her.

Resolutely, she'd returned to the unhappiness facing her in Wichita. She had no choice.

The most difficult decision she'd ever made was to flee Wichita three years ago. The second hardest was to come back. But she had no option. Love demanded that she return and set things right—if possible.

Julie hung her purse on the bedroom doorknob and placed her coat in the closet. Several large boxes littered the living room floor, but she felt exhausted, the kind of fatigue that had nothing to do with physical exertion.

Everything had happened just as she'd hoped. The job had been lined up even before the move, then, in a relatively good area, she'd located an apartment within her budget. The transition had been a smooth one. But to have inadvertently run into Daniel after only six days seemed unreal. That she hadn't counted on. She sat on the couch and rested her head against the back cushion.

Straightening, Julie moved onto the floor and crawled along the carpet until she located the box that contained their engagement portrait. With a sense of unreality, she stared at the two smiling faces. They'd been so much in love. Tears filled her eyes and the happy faces swam in and out of her vision.

Lovingly her fingers traced Daniel's face. The smiling good looks had disappeared. The years had added a harshness to him, an arrogant aloofness. Even the sandy-colored hair that had always seemed to be tousled by the wind was urbanely styled. The powerful male features were apparent even then, but more pronounced now. Her finger idly moved over the lean, proud jaw and paused at the tiny cleft in his chin.

A sad smile touched her eyes as the memories rolled back. She had loved to kiss him there. To tease him unmercifully with her lips. And he had been so wonderful. Conscious of her innocence, Daniel had held his desire in tight rein. Julie wondered if he regretted that now. The opportunities to make her completely his had been many but Daniel had been the one to put a stop to their foreplay, never letting things develop beyond his control. She'd respected him and loved him for that until her heart ached. He wouldn't accept the ring when she tried to return it. Julie wore it around her neck. It rested at the hollow between her breasts, near her heart. Daniel would always be close to her no matter how many miles separated them. Or how much pain.

Early the next morning Julie arrived at work intent on checking the occupant listings of the office complex. The Inland Empire Building housed fifteen floors of offices. The directory was against the wall in the foyer.

Daniel Van Deen, Attorney seemed to leap off the register at her. Again Julie experienced that hot, cold, chilled, burning feeling. Only one floor separated her from Daniel. For five of the six days since she'd been in Wichita they'd crossed paths without even knowing it. A multitude of questions and doubts buzzed through her mind like bees around an active, busy hive.

Unexpectedly a tingling sensation swept through her and she didn't need to be told that Daniel had entered the building. Slowly she turned her head to see him walk to the elevator, a newspaper clenched under his arm. He pushed the button and almost immediately the wide doors opened. Stepping inside, he turned around. Their eyes clashed and locked from across the width of the foyer.

Shivering, she watched an angry frustration sweep over his features. His magnetic dark eyes narrowed as he stared back at her. A muscle leaped uncontrollably in his cheek before the huge doors glided shut.

Julie released a quivering breath, unaware that she'd been holding one in. Daniel hadn't forgotten or forgiven her. The look he'd given her just now had sliced into her heart like the jagged edge of a carving knife.

Her legs felt unsteady as she took the next elevator and stepped into the office of Cheney Trust and Mortgage Company. Grateful that she was the first one to arrive that morning, Julie sat at her desk, striving to regain her usual poise. Her hand trembled visibly as she opened the bottom desk drawer and deposited her purse.

Sherry Adams, a pert blonde, strolled in about fifteen minutes late. Their employer, Jack Barrett, had arrived earlier and pointedly stared at the empty desk, noting Sherry's absence. Julie had only been working at the office a few days, and although Sherry had her faults, it was easy to see that the young divorcee was a valuable asset.

"Morning," Julie responded to the warmth in her co-worker's voice. "You look like the cat who got into the cream."

"I am." She gave a brilliant imitation of a fashion model, her skirts flaring as she whirled around for effect.

"I take it you want me to guess?" Julie asked, falling prey to Sherry's playfulness.

"Not really. I just thought you'd be interested in knowing that I was recently asked to dinner by the most eligible man in town."

"Congratulations."

"Thank you. Actually this is the culmination of five weeks of plotting and fine-tuning some basic womanly skills. I must admit that this guy has been one tough fish to catch."

"Well double congratulations then," Julie said with a soft laugh.

Sherry sat and rolled her chair over to Julie's desk. "I don't suppose...you-know-who...has arrived." Sherry quirked her head toward the closed door of their employer's office.

" 'Fraid so, about fifteen minutes ago."

"Did he say anything about me being late?" she asked, but didn't look the least bit concerned.

"Not to me he didn't."

"One of these days, old Barrett is going to fire me, and with good reason."

"I doubt that," Julie commented with confidence. "Now tell me about your hot date."

"It's with Danny Van Deen."

Julie bit back a gasp of shocked disbelief and lowered her gaze, hoping to hide her surprise.

"He's a lawyer in the building," Sherry continued. "Cagey fellow, but I've set my sights on him for a long time now. He's only taken the first nibble, but I swear it won't be long before I reel him in."

"Good luck." Julie forced her voice to maintain the same level of cheerfulness.

"Of course I can't let him know I'm interested. That would be the kiss of death as far as Danny's concerned. Maintaining a cool facade shouldn't be so difficult. By the time we're standing at the altar he'll think it was all his idea."

"I, uh, I thought you were soured on wedded bliss."

"Not me. It didn't work out with Andy. I feel badly about that, but we both just fell out of love with each other. Not much either one of us could do about it, really."

"And . . . this Van Deen . . . has he been disillusioned with marriage?"

"Nope. That's the amazing thing. Danny's never married. I can't understand it either. He's perfect husband material: handsome, intelligent and sensitive under that cool exterior of his. He dates often enough, but nothing ever comes of it. Until now." She laughed softly. "I'll have him to the altar before he knows what hit him."

"Best wishes then." Somehow Julie managed to murmur the words.

"I'm going to need all the luck I can get," Sherry added and made a pretense of straightening her desk. "Are you taking first lunch today?"

"If you like," Julie replied absently as she flipped through the pages of a report she was studying.

"Would you mind cutting it short so I could get out of here by twelve-thirty? I'll make up the time for you later, I promise." Sherry's brilliant blue eyes contained a pleading look. "There's a dress I saw in a boutique window and I want to try it on. That's the reason I was late this morning. Wait until Danny Van Deen sees me in that." She rolled her eyes dramatically.

"Sure," Julie agreed. "I can be back early."

The remainder of the morning was peaceful. The two women took turns answering the phone. Because she wasn't fully accustomed to the office, Julie relied on Sherry for help, which the blonde supplied willingly. Sherry was a generous soul who harbored no ill against anyone. That's what made her divorce so difficult to understand. Julie couldn't imagine her newfound friend giving up on anything as important as a marriage.

A couple of minutes after noon Sherry reminded Julie of the time. Julie stood, ready to leave for her lunch break. As she took her purse out of the desk drawer, her boss, Jack Barrett, strolled into the outer room.

"Are you going out for lunch?" the balding, middle-aged man asked Julie.

"Would you like me to get you something?" she volunteered.

"Not today." He handed her a large manila envelope. "But would you mind dropping this off at Daniel Van Deen's office?"

Chapter Two

Panic filled Julie's eyes as she cast a pleading glance at Sherry.

"Go on. You might catch a glimpse of him and then you'll know what I mean when I say hunk!" Apparently Sherry believed Julie's reluctance was due to the claim she'd staked on Daniel.

"Is there a problem?" Jack Barrett glanced from one girl to the other.

"No problem," Sherry answered on Julie's behalf.

With little way to gracefully bow out of the situation, Julie nodded her agreement.

"His office is one floor down. Number 919, I think." Sherry bit her bottom lip. "Yes, 919, I'm sure of it. Not to worry, his name's on the door."

Julie forced a smile and walked out of the office. By the time she rode the elevator and got off on Daniel's floor the envelope felt as if it weighed fifty pounds.

The palm of her hand felt clammy as she turned the knob and walked into the plush office.

A round-faced secretary glanced up and smiled. "Can I help you?"

The first thing Julie noticed about the woman was her diamond ring. She was married. Why it should matter to her that Daniel's secretary was married was beyond Julie.

"I . . . have a package for Mr. Van Deen from Jack Barrett," she managed at last.

"Agnes, did you find—" Abruptly, Daniel stopped midsentence as soon as he caught sight of Julie. The hard look in his eyes was directed solely at her.

For a crazy second, Julie imagined this was the way Daniel would look before going into battle. Intent and intense, prepared to lay down his life for the sake of righteousness. Then unexpectedly his gaze softened and an emotion Julie couldn't define came over his features.

"Mr. Barrett's sent the papers you asked about this morning," Agnes supplied.

Although Julie heard Daniel's secretary speak, she felt as if she and Daniel were trapped in a hazy fog that swirled around the room.

"You did ask about the Macmillan papers?" The woman's words seemed slurred and distant.

"Yes." Daniel broke the spell, but his dark, unreadable eyes continued to hold Julie captive.

The secretary took the envelope out of her frozen hand. The woman's sharp gaze went first to Julie then to Daniel. "Was that all?"

"Pardon?" Julie tore her attention from Daniel.

"Was there something else?"

"No," she mumbled. "Thank you."

A puzzled look marred the woman's brow. "Thank you for bringing them," she murmured.

Julie turned and managed to walk out of the office with her head held high.

The remainder of the day passed in a blur and by the time she returned home that night, Julie felt physically and mentally drained.

The first thing to greet Julie as she walked into her apartment was her new phone. The installer had apparently come by. The first person she decided to call was her mother.

"Hi, Mom," she greeted with a falsely cheerful note.

"Julie. How are you?"

"Fine. Everything's fine."

"I'm so glad, dear. I've been worried."

Margaret Houser lived in a retirement community in Southern California. None of Julie's family was in Wichita anymore. Her older brother lived in Montana, but both Julie and Joe, her brother, had been born and raised in Kansas.

"Have you looked up any of your old high school friends?"

"Not yet." Actually Julie doubted that she would. The only real friends she'd had in Wichita had married and moved elsewhere. "Mom." She took in a deep breath. "I've seen Daniel."

Instantly, her mother was concerned. "How is he?"

"We...we haven't talked. But he's changed. In some ways I hardly know him. He never understood why I left. He's not likely to understand why I came back."

"Don't be so sure, sweetheart." Margaret's soft voice was reassuring. "He's been hurt, and the years are bound to have changed him."

"Mom, I don't think he will talk to me."

"I've never known you to be a defeatist," her mother said in a confident, supportive tone. "But I worry about Daniel's mother. Be careful of her."

"I will." Idly Julie's fingers flipped through the white pages of the telephone directory as they spoke. Clara Van Deen's phone was unlisted. But Daniel's was there. Her mother continued to speak, and Julie made a few monosyllabic replies as her finger ran back and forth over Daniel's name. The movement had a strange calming effect on her, as if she was reaching out to him.

"Did you hear me, Julie?"

The remark pulled Julie back into the conversation. "I'll be careful of Mrs. Van Deen, I promise."

"The woman can be completely unreasonable. Remember I was the one who had to deal with her after you left."

"I know and I'm sorry about that."

"You did the right thing, honey."

Julie wasn't sure. After three years, she still didn't know. She'd been so stupid, so naive. A hundred times she should have said something. She'd wanted to put a stop to the outrageous wedding plans. But like Daniel, she had been caught in the overwhelming force of his mother's personality. Even when she did tell Mrs. Van Deen how she felt, her wishes were pushed aside.

"Julie, are you there?" Margaret asked.

"Yes, I'm here. Sorry, Mom, it's been a long day. I'll talk to you next week."

"I'll be thinking about you."

"Thanks, Mom, I can use all the happy thoughts I can get." Her mother's love had gotten her through the most difficult times and it was sure to help her now.

"Are you sure you're doing the right thing?"

"I'm sure," Julie returned confidently.

Gently Julie replaced the receiver in its cradle. She slumped forward on the couch and buried her face in her hands. A tightness was building in her throat. It was as if three years had never passed. The anxiety was as keen now as it had been that spring.

From the beginning, Julie was aware that Daniel's mother wanted her son to marry a more socially prominent girl. But to her credit, Clara Van Deen accepted Julie as Daniel's choice. Then she immediately set about to make Julie into something she would never be. First she completely remade Julie's appearance. Clara had her hair cut and styled, then purchased an entire wardrobe of what she claimed were outfits more suitable for Daniel's wife.

Julie swallowed her pride a hundred times and tried to do exactly as Mrs. Van Deen wished. She did so want to make Daniel proud. He was a man coming up in the world and

Julie didn't want to do anything to hamper his success, as his mother claimed the wrong woman would surely do.

The wedding plans were what had finally caused Julie to buckle and run. All Julie had wanted was a simple ceremony with only their immediate families. Before she knew what had happened, Daniel's mother had issued invitations to four hundred close and intimate friends she couldn't possibly insult by not inviting to the wedding.

"But, Daniel," Julie had protested, "I don't know any of these people." At the time, Julie knew that she should have told him the truth. She never knew why she didn't. Maybe it was because she was afraid he wouldn't want her if he knew how shy she actually was.

"Don't worry about it," Daniel had said and kissed the tip of her nose, never fully understanding the depth of Julie's anxieties. "They'll love you as much as I do."

Daniel had negated any further protests with a searing kiss that left Julie too weak to argue.

As the date drew closer, Julie was the focus of attention at a variety of teas and social events. She felt as if the phony smile she'd painted on her mouth would become permanently engraved on her pale features.

After each event, Mrs. Van Deen would run through a list of taboos that Julie had violated. No matter how hard Julie tried, there was always something she'd done wrong or shouldn't have said. Someone she might have offended.

"I can't take it anymore," Julie cried to her mother in a fit of tears after one such event.

"Say something," her mother advised.

"Don't you think I've tried?" Julie shouted and buried her face in her hands. "This isn't a wedding anymore, it's a Hollywood production."

Every day the pressure mounted. The whole wedding grew until what had started out as an uncomplicated ceremony was a monster that loomed ready to devour Julie. The caterers, musicians, soloist, organist. The flower girl, the dresses, the bridesmaids. Mrs. Van Deen even made the arrangements for their honeymoon.

"Daniel, please listen to me," Julie had begged a week before the wedding. "I don't want any of this."

"Honey, I know you're nervous," he'd whispered soothingly. "But everything will be over in one day and we can go on with the rest of our lives as we wish."

But Julie doubted that they could. Every incident with his mother reinforced her belief that this was only the beginning. Soon, Julie believed, Mrs. Van Deen would take over every aspect of their marriage as she had the wedding. Her suspicions were confirmed when Julie learned that Daniel's mother had made a large down payment on a house for them.

"It's her wedding gift to us," Daniel explained to Julie. But the house was only a few minutes from his mother's and the handwriting was bold and clear on the freshly painted walls. His mother insisted she would help Julie with decorating and choosing the furniture. Such things couldn't be left in the hands of an immature nineteen-year-old.

"Doesn't it bother you the way she's taken over our lives?" Julie cried.

In that second, Julie could see that Daniel did care, but would do nothing.

"For the first time since Dad died, my mother's got purpose. She's loving every minute of this. Can't you see the difference our wedding has made in her?"

No, Julie couldn't see. All she could feel was a growing case of claustrophobia. That night she couldn't sleep. By the time the sun rose early the next morning, Julie had packed her bags.

"You can't do this," Margaret Houser argued, aghast when she realized her daughter's plans.

"I've got to," Julie cried, her eyes red and haunted. "I'm not marrying Daniel. I'm marrying his mother."

"But the wedding's in five days."

"There will be no wedding," Julie replied adamantly. "What could have been a simple and beautiful ceremony has been turned into a three-ring circus and I won't be part of it."

"But Julie—"

"I know what you're going to say," she interrupted her mother. "This is far more than pre-wedding jitters. Daniel and I are never alone anymore. His mother has taken over every aspect of our relationship."

"Talk to him, dear. Explain how you feel," Margaret Houser advised. "At least do that much. This is a serious step you're considering."

Julie took her mother's advice and went to Daniel's office. They met as he was on his way out the door.

"Julie." He seemed surprised to see her.

"I need to talk to you." Her hands were clenched tightly in front of her.

Daniel glanced at his watch. "Honey, I don't have the time. Can it wait?"

"No." She shook her head forcefully. "It can't wait."

Daniel apparently had noted her agitated manner. He pressed a hand to the small of her back and led her into his office. "All right, honey, I know things have been hectic lately, but it's bound to get better once we're married. We'll have lots of time together then, I promise."

"That's just it, Daniel," Julie informed him vigorously. "We aren't going to be married."

Daniel inhaled sharply. "What do you mean?" He looked around a moment, shocked at her statement. "What's this all about?"

"I can't marry you, Daniel." Her finger trembling, she slipped the diamond off and held it out to him in the palm of her hand.

"Julie!" He was stunned. Shocked. "Put that ring back where it belongs," he muttered harshly.

"I can't," she repeated.

"I don't understand." He slumped onto the arm of his office chair.

"I don't imagine that you do." Julie bowed her head, preferring not to reveal the pain in her eyes. "Do you remember last week when I suggested we drive across the border and get married? You laughed." Her voice wobbled and threatened to crack. "But I was serious. Dead serious."

"Mother would never forgive us if we did something like that." He defended his actions.

Julie released a short, harsh breath. "I think that's the crux of the situation. You wouldn't dream of crossing your mother, but it doesn't seem to matter what all this is doing to me."

"But she loves you."

"She loves the woman she's created. Haven't you noticed anything? Look at me, Daniel," she cried. "Am I the same woman I was three months ago?"

"I don't know what you're talking about."

"Look at me," she repeated, her voice high-pitched. "My hair is different, my nails are groomed, and my...my clothes..." Tears welled in her blue eyes as her voice broke. "Did you realize I have to phone your mother every morning to ask her what she wants me to wear? I haven't had on a pair of jeans in weeks. It's unbecoming, you know," she cried flippantly, and gestured weakly with her hand. "I'm slowly being molded, shaped, carved into what she thinks would be the picture of the right woman for you. I've had it. I can't take it anymore."

Daniel stood and threaded his fingers through his hair. "Why don't you stand up to her?"

"Do you think I haven't tried? But no one listens to me. Even you, Daniel. What I think or feel doesn't seem to matter anymore. I'm...not even sure how I feel about you anymore."

"Is that so?" He exhaled a sharp breath.

"That's right," Julie insisted huskily, her chin jutting out defensively. "I want out. Here." Again she tried to return the ring.

For an agonizing moment Daniel stared at her and then the ring. With barely suppressed violence he stalked to the far side of the room and looked out the window, his back to her. He rammed his hands into his pockets. "Keep it."

"But Daniel," she pleaded.

"I said keep it," he grated. When he turned around, his mouth had twisted into a rigid line. The piercing dark eyes clouded with hurt and pain. "Now get out of my life and stay out."

Tears ran down her face. Julie turned and left. She drove straight to her mother's. The clothes, the wedding dress, everything Mrs. Van Deen had purchased was left strewn across the bed. Julie had then loaded her suitcases into the back of her car and driven to California and her aunt's.

That had been three years ago and every night since she'd wondered if she'd done the right thing. Slowly Julie straightened from her position on the sofa. The guilt had pressed down on her oppressively, but the love they'd shared had never died. At least not for Julie. She'd hurt Daniel and his mother. Right or wrong there were better ways to have handled the situation.

Now after three years, she'd come back to ask Daniel's and Mrs. Van Deen's forgiveness. She wouldn't return to California without it.

Chapter Three

The next morning Julie stood inside the Inland Empire foyer and waited until Daniel entered the building. She longed to talk to him. She'd dreamed of it for months, praying that her heartfelt apology could wipe out the pain she'd caused him. Then, only then, could they start to rebuild their crippled relationship. She'd found him so much sooner than she'd expected. Surely that was a positive sign.

As had happened previously, her body reacted to his presence even before she saw him. The tingling awareness struck the moment he pushed past the large double glass doors.

Julie straightened and watched him advance toward the elevator. If he realized she was there, he gave no outward indication. Without a sound she moved behind him so that when the metal doors glided open she could enter when he did.

Frustration knotted her stomach as two others stepped inside the tiny cubicle and the four ascended together.

If Daniel was aware of her presence he refused to react. But Julie had never been more aware of anyone or anything in her life. Daniel's tall, handsome figure, looming beside her, seemed to fill the elevator. The years had been good to him. He'd been boyishly good-looking three years ago; now he was devastating. No wonder Sherry had set her sights on him. Daniel could have any woman he wanted. However, from the information Sherry had given her, Daniel didn't seem to notice or care about his effect on the opposite sex.

A tortured minute passed and Julie yearned to reach out and touch him, anything to force him to acknowledge that she was there. He couldn't go on ignoring her forever. Sooner or later they'd need to talk. Surely he recognized that.

His gaze focused straight ahead and Julie's heart throbbed painfully as the creases around his mouth hardened. He resembled a jungle panther trapped in a cage too compact for him to pace.

Her stomach tightened in nervous reaction, but she couldn't tear her gaze from him. His features were so achingly familiar, but upon close inspection the changes in Daniel were even more prominent. Streaks of gray were mingled with the sandy-colored hair at the side of his meticulously groomed head.

Again she had to restrain herself from brushing the hair from his temple. Her legs were shaking so badly she could hardly remain upright, so she leaned against the back wall for support.

The two strangers exited on the fifth floor and a surprised Julie found herself alone with Daniel. This was exactly what she'd planned, yet her tongue suddenly felt uncooperative. There was so much she wanted to say, and she'd practiced exactly how to begin so many times. But now that the opportunity was there, she found herself incapable of uttering a single sound.

"Hello, Daniel," she managed after several awkward moments. Charged currents vibrated in the short space separating them. The high voltage added to Julie's discomfort.

He ignored her, staring straight ahead.

"We need to talk." Her voice was barely above a whisper.

Silence.

"Daniel, please."

She noted the way his mouth twisted into a hard line as he turned and directed his attention away from her.

Gently she laid her hand on his forearm. A deep sigh rumbled from her throat at the look in his eyes. The hopelessness of the situation overwhelmed her. As stinging tears filled her eyes, the tall figure that towered beside her became a watery blur, and Julie dropped her hand. The elevator stopped and she watched him leave. Daniel had refused to look at her.

Again Julie was grateful to be the first one in the office. She collapsed into her chair, fighting off waves of nausea. Pain pounded at her temple. It was too soon. She was expecting too much. Time. Daniel needed time. There was nothing she could do until he was ready to talk. She had to be patient. When he was ready, she'd be waiting.

"Morning." Sherry strolled into the office five minutes early, her eyes twinkling.

Hiding her expression, Julie feigned absorption in a paper she was studying on her desk.

"Aren't you interested in how my hot date went?"

Julie didn't want to hear any of it, but was uncertain how she could effectively disguise her feelings. "Sure." She swallowed tightly and banished the mental image of Daniel holding Sherry passionately in his arms.

"Awful," Sherry admitted with a wry grin. "Talk about disappointment! I could have had two heads for all the notice he gave me and my new dress."

"Maybe he was worried about a case or something." Julie couldn't repress a surge of gladness. If Sherry was to become involved with Daniel, the situation would be unpleasant.

"Or something, is right," Sherry shot back.

"If last night was such a disaster, how come you're so cheerful this morning?"

"Because Danny apologized and asked me out again this weekend." Sherry's voice contained a lilt of excitement. "And when he takes a woman out, believe me when I say he spares no expense. We went to the best restaurant in town. What a waste. Danny barely tasted his dinner."

Danny! Julie's mind rejected the casual use of his name. Daniel used to hate it. No one called him Danny.

"I hope everything works out better the next time," Julie replied, and smiled stiffly.

"It will," Sherry said, her voice high with confidence. "Next time, he won't be able to take his eyes off me." She paused and laughed lightly. "I won't let him." She smiled to herself, apparently over some private joke, hung her bright jacket on a hanger and placed it inside the office closet.

"Are you doing anything special this weekend?" Sherry asked as an afterthought. Her blond head tilted curiously, lighting her expressive face.

"Painting my living room walls." Filling her time was vital at the moment. Anything to keep her mind from Sherry doing her utmost to lure Daniel into falling in love with her. For part of the morning Julie debated if she should say something to her newfound friend. But what? Julie had relinquished him when she'd left Wichita. She had no right to claim Daniel now.

When Julie woke Saturday morning the sun was shining and the early spring day was glorious. Much too beautiful to spend indoors. She recalled how Daniel's mother loved to work in her flower garden. Clara Van Deen had grown the most gorgeous irises.

When Julie climbed into her car, her intention had been to drive to the paint store, but instead she found herself on the street that led to Clara Van Deen's house.

She pulled to a stop across the street and stared at the lovely two-story home with the meticulously landscaped front yard. A fancy sports car was parked in the driveway. Julie doubted that Mrs. Van Deen would ever drive that type of vehicle. Since she was butting her head against a brick wall with Daniel, Julie debated whether she should gather her courage and approach his mother.

The long circular driveway was bordered on both sides by flowering red azaleas. Julie stared at the house for a long time, undecided about what to do. She wondered what had become of Daniel's mother. From past experience Julie realized that Clara Van Deen could be a greater challenge than her son.

Julie rubbed a weary hand over her eyes. No. Now wasn't the time. Not when she was dressed in jeans and a sweatshirt. When she faced Mrs. Van Deen she would need to look and feel her best. The desire to get the confrontation over with as quickly as possible would profit neither of them. Before her resolution wavered, she shifted gears and headed toward the closest shopping center.

The paint she chose for the living room was an antique white that was sure to cheer the drab room. Filled with purpose, her spirits lifted as she returned to the apartment. She actually looked forward to spending a quiet afternoon painting.

First she unhooked the drapes and carefully laid them across the back of the davenport. Intent on spreading out newspapers, she jerked upright as the sound of the doorbell caught her off guard. In her rush to get to the front door, she stumbled over the ottoman.

Stooping to rub her hand over the injured shin, she opened the door. "Yes?"

Daniel's tall figure towered above her and filled the doorway. The look on his face sent a cold shaft of apprehension racing through her blood.

"Leave my mother alone."

Julie stared back at him speechlessly, then slowly straightened.

"Did you hear what I said?" he demanded. Anger smoldered in his hard gaze.

Numbly she nodded.

"I saw you this morning parked in front of her house. Stay away, Julie, I'm warning you."

Inwardly Julie flinched and jutted her chin out in a gesture of defiance. "The time will come when I'll have to talk to her."

"Not if I can help it."

"You can't."

"Don't bet on it." His eyes were as frigid as a glacier snowpack.

"Daniel, I've come a thousand miles to talk to you and your mother."

"Then you wasted your time because neither one of us cares to see you."

Levelly, Julie met his gaze, realizing the task she had set before her would be more difficult than she'd thought possible. "I didn't come back to hurt you or your mother. I've come to make amends."

"Amends?" Viciously, he threw the word back at her as he paced the carpet, his hand buried deep in his pant pockets. "Do you think you could ever undo the humiliation I suffered when you walked out?"

"I'm sure I can't, but I'd like to try. Don't you understand? I was young and stupid. A thousand times I've regretted what I did—"

"Regretted." He paused and turned to face her. "I used to dream you'd say that to me. Now that you have, it means nothing. Nothing," he repeated. "I look at you and I don't feel a thing. You came back to apologize, then fine, you've made your peace. Just don't go to my mother, bringing up the past. She has no desire to see you. Whatever you and I shared is over and done with."

Julie hung her head and closed her eyes at the sting in his voice. She wouldn't be easily swayed from her goal. "Oh, Daniel," she whispered. "You don't mean that."

"Does that bother you?" he asked. "You taught me a lot of things. I've blocked you from my mind, but unfortunately my mother has never been the same. I can't forgive you for what you've done to her."

"But that's the reason I've come back," she said with forced calm. Her stomach churned violently and her eyes pleaded desperately with his. "I want to make it up to you both. Can't you see how sorry I am? I couldn't stop thinking about you. Not for a day. Not for a minute. For three long years you've haunted me."

"Do you want me to pat you on the head and tell you everything's just fine and we can pick up where we left off?" His dark eyes hardened. "It's not that easy."

Julie lowered her gaze and struggled to maintain a grip on her composure. "You've changed so much. Oh, Daniel, have I done this to you?"

His dark eyes raked her from head to toe, and Julie could see that he wouldn't answer her.

Unaware she would even do such a thing, Julie raised her hand to his mouth. Lightly her fingertips caressed his lips. Abruptly, Daniel jerked his head back and retreated a step as if she'd seared him.

"I don't want to hurt or upset you or your mother," she began softly.

"Then leave before you do both."

"Oh, Daniel, I wish I could. But this is too important to me. I've got to make things right."

"You'll never be able to do that. Sometimes it's better when the past remains buried."

"I can't. Believe me, I tried. For a long time I tried."

Daniel looked exhausted. "Leave, Julie. You could do more harm now."

"Didn't you hear what I just said? I won't go," she returned forcefully. "Not until I've talked to your mother. Not until I pay her back every penny."

"Why now?" He sank onto the sofa and leaned forward until his elbows rested on his knees.

"Just as you've changed, Daniel, so have I. I'm not a naive nineteen-year-old anymore. I'm a mature woman willing to admit I made a terrible mistake. I was wrong to have run away instead of confronting the problems we faced. I regret what I did, but more than that I realize that there isn't anyone I could ever feel as strongly about as you. All these years I've dreamed of you. When another man held me, I found myself wanting him to be you. It's you I came back for. You, Daniel."

He stared at her disbelievingly. "You mean to tell me that after all these years your conscience hasn't quit bothering you?"

"Yes, but it's so much more than that. If possible I want to make everything up to you."

"That's fine and dandy. You've come, we've talked and now you've done everything you can. Now you can go. I absolve you from everything. Just stay out of my life. Understand?"

A look of pain flashed across his face, and for a fleeting moment Julie saw a glimmer of the old Daniel. Something was troubling him, something deep and intense.

"Daniel." She moved to his side, fighting back the urge to touch him. Something was bothering him and she yearned to comfort the man she loved. Carefully, she weighed her words. "Something's wrong. Won't you tell me what it is?"

He looked right through her and Julie knew he was lost to another world.

Defiantly he stood, impatiently shaking off his mood. "Leave my mother alone. Do you understand?"

"I'm sorry." Julie hung her head. Her long, brown hair fell forward, wreathing her oval face. Everything she'd tried to explain had meant nothing.

"Julie?" A wealth of emotion weighted her name.

With controlled movements, she stood and faced him. "I promise not to do anything to hurt her. Can you trust me for that at least?"

"I shouldn't." A nerve moved in his jaw and again Julie was aware of the battle struggling inside him. Without another word, he turned and walked out of the apartment.

Numb, Julie stood exactly where she was for what could have been a split second or a half hour. Her hands felt moist with nervous perspiration. Forcing herself into action, she finished spreading the old newspapers across the floor and opened the first gallon of paint.

Julie worked until well past midnight. When she finished, the old room was barely recognizable. The feeling of accomplishment helped lift her heavy heart. Had she thought confronting Daniel and his mother would be easy? No. From the beginning she'd known what to expect.

Absently her hand fingered the ring dangling from around her neck. She was physically exhausted as she cleaned the paint brushes under the kitchen faucet, but her mind continued to work double time.

As she worked, Julie remembered Daniel's words. Maybe he was right. Perhaps contacting Clara Van Deen now could do more harm than good. Hours later, lying in bed, staring at the darkened ceiling, Julie couldn't let the thought go. She'd come this far. The clock dial illuminated the time in the dark bedroom. Two A.M. and although she was physically exhausted, she hadn't been able to sleep. Pounding her pillow, Julie rolled over and faced the wall.

Write her.

The idea flashed through her mind like a laser beam. Instantly, Julie sat up and threw back the covers and searched for a pen and pad.

Sitting on top of the bed, her bedside lamp burning, Julie drafted the letter:

Dear Mrs. Van Deen:
I know this letter will come as a shock to you. My hope is that you will accept it in the light in which it is written.

I wonder if you've ever done anything in your life that you've regretted. Something that has haunted you over the years. Something you would give anything to do over again. I have. For three years I've carried the guilt of what I did to you and Daniel. Mere words could never undo the acute embarrassment or the deep hurt my actions inflicted. I won't even attempt to make retribution with a simple apology. I would beg your for-

giveness, and ask that you allow me to make this up to
you in some way. Anything.

My address reads as above with my telephone number. If you desire to contact me please do so. I will await
word from you.

Julie read the letter again the following morning. The next
move would be Mrs. Van Deen's.

A week passed before she heard from the older woman.
Seven long, anxious days for Julie. Every one of those days
she saw Daniel. Not once did he speak to her, but his eyes
held a warning light that said more than an angry tirade.
Julie wondered if his mother had told him about the letter.
With that thought came another. Would Daniel hate her all
the more for not heeding his request?

The scented envelope with the delicate handwriting captured her attention the minute she picked up her mail early
Saturday afternoon. Julie's heart rate soared.

She was barely inside her apartment door when she ripped
open the envelope. Her fingers shook as she took out the
single sheet of stationery.

It read simply: *Saturday at four.*

"That's today." Julie spoke out loud. Frantically she shot
a look at the kitchen clock. Just after one. She had only
three hours to prepare herself. Mrs. Van Deen had done that
deliberately, hoping to catch her off guard. But Daniel's
mother would be disappointed. Julie was prepared for this
confrontation. She knew what had to be said and she was
willing to deal with the difficult task.

After carefully surveying her wardrobe, Julie finally decided to wear a simple business suit of blue gabardine. It was
the same one she'd worn to the job interview with Mr. Barrett six weeks earlier. She wanted to show Mrs. Van Deen
that she wasn't an awkward teenager any longer, but a mature woman. At precisely four o'clock, Julie pulled into the
curved driveway.

The doorbell was answered by Mrs. Batten, the elderly cook who had been with the family for years. If she recognized Julie, she said nothing.

"Yes?" The woman's low tone was barely civil.

"Good afternoon. I'm here to see Mrs. Van Deen."

Mrs. Batten hesitated.

"I'm expected," Julie added.

Again the woman paused before stepping aside and allowing Julie to enter the foyer.

The interior of the house hadn't changed. Everything was exactly as she remembered. The same mahogany table and vase sat beside the carpeted stairway that led to the second floor. To her left was the salon, as Mrs. Van Deen called it. At one time Julie had thought of it as a torture chamber. To her right was a massive dining room.

"This way," Mrs. Batten instructed, her tone only slightly less frosty.

Like an errant student being brought to the school principal, Julie followed two steps behind the elderly woman. She was led through the house to the back garden Mrs. Van Deen prized so highly.

"You may wait here." Mrs. Batten pointed to a heavy cast-iron chair separated from an identical one by a small table.

Julie did as requested.

"Would you like something to drink while you wait?" The woman's eyes refused to meet Julie's.

"No. Thank you," she mumbled, clasping her hands together in her lap.

Fifteen minutes passed and still Julie sat alone. Every second was another trial. Daniel's mother was doing this deliberately. Testing her. But Julie was determined to sit there until midnight if necessary.

The sound of soft footsteps behind her caused Julie to tense.

"Hello, Julie." The words were low and trembling.

Julie stood and turned around. Daniel's mother was frail and obviously weak. She leaned heavily upon a cane, her back hunched. Yet she was elegant as ever. Her hair was completely white now and she was thin, far thinner than Julie remembered.

"Sit down." Mrs. Van Deen motioned with her hand and Julie sank into the uncomfortable chair, grateful for the chair's support.

Daniel's mother took the seat beside her. Both hands rested on top of the wooden cane. "To say I was surprised to receive your letter would be an understatement."

"I imagine it was." Julie's grip on her purse tightened.

"Does Daniel know you're back?"

She nodded. "We work in the same building."

The frail woman didn't comment, but smiled weakly.

If Daniel was different it was nothing compared to the changes in his mother.

"You have a Wichita address."

"Yes, I moved back." Her voice quavered slightly.

"Why?"

"Because—" Julie swallowed around the thickness building in her throat "—because I wanted to make amends and I didn't think I could do that if I flew in for a weekend."

"That was wise, dear."

"I came because I deeply regret my actions. I—"

"Do you still love my son?" Clara Van Deen interrupted.

Julie focused her attention on her hands, tightly coiled around the small leather purse. The question was one she'd avoided since her return, afraid of the answer. "Yes," she admitted without hesitation. "Yes, I do, but I . . ."

"But you hate me?"

"Oh, no." Julie snapped her head up. "The only person I've hated over the years was myself."

The old woman's smile was wan. "There comes a time in a woman's life when she can look at things more clearly. In my life it comes as I face death. As you've probably guessed, I'm not well."

Unexpected tears filled Julie's eyes. She hadn't expected Daniel's mother to be kind or understanding.

"There's no need to cry. I've lived a full life, but my heart is weak and I can't do much of anything these days. Ill health gives one an opportunity to gain perspective."

"Then you do forgive me?" Julie asked in a mere whisper, her voice dangerously close to cracking.

The veined hand tightened around the cane. "No."

Julie closed her eyes to the disappointment and hurt. An apology would have been too easy; she should have realized that. Mrs. Van Deen would want so much more. "What can I do?" Julie asked softly.

"I want you to forgive me." Daniel's mother spoke gently and reached across the short space separating them and patted Julie's hand. "I was the reason you did what you did. All these years I've buried that guilt deep in my heart. I behaved like an interfering old woman."

Julie noticed a tear that slid down the weathered cheek, followed by several more. Her own face was moist.

"We've both been fools."

"But there's no fool like an old one." Clara Van Deen wiped her cheek with the back of her hand. She looked pale and tired, but a radiance came from her eyes.

As if on cue, Mrs. Batten carried in a silver tray with a coffeepot and two china cups. Mrs. Van Deen waited until the woman had left before asking Julie to do the honors.

A smile lit up her face as Julie poured the coffee, stirred sugar into Daniel's mother's and presented her with the first cup and saucer.

"Very good." Mrs. Van Deen nodded approvingly.

Julie laughed, perhaps her first real laugh in three years. "I had a marvelous teacher." She sat back and crossed her legs, the saucer held in her hand.

"Tell me what you've done with yourself all this time." Mrs. Van Deen looked genuinely interested.

"I went to school for a while in California and lived with my aunt. Later my mother joined me and I got a job with a bank as a teller and worked my way into the loan department. From there I got a job in a trust company. Nothing very exciting."

"What about men?"

"I . . . dated some." The abrupt question flustered her.

"Anyone seriously?"

Julie shook her head. "No one. What . . . what about Daniel?"

The former radiance dimmed. "He never tells me."

"He's changed."

"Yes, he has." Mrs. Van Deen didn't deny the obvious. "And not for the good I fear. He's an intense young man. Some days he reminds me of . . ." She paused and stared straight ahead.

"Mrs. Van Deen, are you feeling all right?"

"I'm fine, child. You're beginning to sound like Daniel. He's always worried about me. And please, I'd prefer it if you called me Clara."

Even when engaged to Daniel, Julie had never been allotted the honor of using Mrs. Van Deen's first name. The privilege to do so now was a confirmation of their new understanding.

"All right, Clara." The name felt awkward on her tongue.

"I do have regrets." The older woman looked as if she were in another world. "I would so have liked to hold a grandchild."

Julie took a sip of her coffee, hoping the liquid would ease the coiled tightness in her throat.

"I know what it's cost you to come to me," Mrs. Van Deen continued. "You have far more character than I gave you credit—" The woman's tired eyes widened and she paused to take in deep breaths. "I'm sorry, Julie, but I'm not feeling well." The older woman's hand covered her heart. "I think you should call Mrs. Batten."

Panic filled Julie. Daniel's mother was a lot more than weak and unwell. Clara Van Deen was on the verge of collapsing. "Mrs. Batten," she cried as she bounded to her feet and ran toward the kitchen. "Call Medic One and tell them to hurry."

Tears were streaming down Julie's face as she struggled to recall the lessons she'd taken in pulmonary resuscitation. She fell to her knees beside Daniel's mother and took the weathered hand in hers.

"Don't worry so, child," Clara assured her. The frail voice was incredibly weak. Julie had to strain to make out the words.

Julie began loosening the older woman's clothes, words of reassurance tumbling from her lips. She couldn't bear to lose Clara now. Slowly, Mrs. Van Deen was losing consciousness. Dear Lord, why was it taking the medics so long? Daniel's mother's life was held on a delicate balance as Julie lowered her to the floor and knelt at her side. The sound of sirens could be heard screaming in the distance and Julie breathed easier.

Heavy footsteps followed and Julie stumbled aside as the two men entered and began working frantically over the unconscious woman. A flurry of questions came from another team of men who brought in a stretcher and loaded Mrs. Van Deen into the waiting vehicle. Tubes and needles were inserted into Clara's arm by the trained medics.

Her own heart pounded so loudly that Julie was unable to hear any of the commotion around her. Mrs. Batten walked to the front lawn with Julie as they carried Daniel's mother to the mobile unit.

"I'm going to the hospital," Julie told the housekeeper. She'd go crazy waiting around here. For a second Julie questioned whether she was in any condition to drive. Her hands were shaking so badly she had trouble inserting the key into the ignition.

The hospital was a whirlwind of activity when Julie arrived. She almost collided with Daniel as she hurried down the wide corridor. He stopped and his look sliced into her with a fine cutting edge, as if he wanted to blame her for his mother's ill health. After a moment he entered the waiting room, leaving her standing alone in the hall.

Julie's fingers were clenched so tightly the blood flow to her fingers were severely hampered. To hide her own fears, she bit into the corner of her bottom lip.

Daniel didn't want her with him, and yet she couldn't leave without knowing what had happened.

The chapel offered her the solitude she desired. Needing the time to think, she buried her face in her hands as she sat in the back pew. Her mind was in such turmoil that clear thought was impossible. An eternity passed before Julie stood.

Daniel was pacing the small waiting area when she returned. He turned toward her as she entered the room.

"Don't ask me to leave," she pleaded.

He rammed his fingers through his hair, and not for the first time if the sandy rumpled mass was any indication. "The ambulance driver was in. He told me you were responsible for calling them in time to save her life."

Julie didn't answer. Her arms cradled her stomach as she paced the enclosure with him. They didn't speak. They didn't touch. But Julie couldn't remember a closer communication with anyone. It was as if they were reaching out mentally to each other, offering encouragement and hope when there seemed little.

The whole universe seemed to come to a stop when the doctor stepped into the room. "She's resting comfortably," he announced without preamble.

"Thank God," Daniel said with a shuddering breath.

"Your mother's a stubborn woman. She insists upon seeing both of you. But only take a minute. Understand?"

Julie glanced at Daniel. "You go."

"Both," the doctor repeated.

Clara Van Deen looked as pale as the sheets she was lying against when Julie and Daniel entered the intensive care unit.

She opened her eyes and attempted to smile when she saw they were there. "My dears," she began, "I'm so sorry to cause you all this worry."

"Rest, mother." Daniel whispered.

"Not yet." She fluttered her eyes open. "Julie, you said you'd do anything to gain my forgiveness?"

"Yes." That strange voice hardly sounded like her own.

"And Daniel, my son, will you do one last thing for me?"

"Anything, you know that." He didn't sound any more controlled.

The tired, old eyes closed and opened again as if she was on the brink of slipping away. "My dears, won't you please marry . . . for my sake."

Chapter Four

Julie woke in the gray light of early morning. She hadn't slept well and imagined Daniel hadn't either. They'd hardly spoken as they left the hospital and scarcely looked at one another. The white line that circled Daniel's mouth revealed his feelings in the matter of any marriage between them. Words weren't necessary.

When she'd arrived home Julie undressed and made herself a cup of strong coffee. She sat in the living room, bracing her feet against the coffee table as she slouched down on the sofa. Her thoughts were troubled and confused. Clara was so different from what she'd expected. Julie had braced herself for a confrontation, confident the older woman would lash out at her. Instead she'd discovered a sick, gentle woman who had suffered many regrets. Deep within her, Julie longed to ease Clara's mind. Daniel's mother lay weak in a hospital bed, facing death. She needed the assurance that her son would be happy.

But, Julie knew, they wouldn't have any kind of marriage when Daniel resented her so much.

Her mind continued to be troubled as she readied for bed. As she lay staring at the wall, a calm came over her. She loved Daniel, had loved him when she ran away all those years ago and, if possible, loved him even more now. Every time she looked at him, his features so lovingly familiar, her heart ached with that love. Closing her eyes, Julie reminded herself over and over again of the reasons she'd returned to Wichita.

Even at midmorning the hospital parking lot was full. Although Julie hadn't reached a decision, she had peace in her heart. She'd talk to Daniel, really talk. Together they would decide what to do.

The faint antiseptic odor greeted her as she pushed through the large double glass doors that led to the hospital foyer. The sound of her shoes clapping against the polished floor seemed to echo a hundredfold as she walked down the wide corridor.

Daniel was in the waiting area outside the intensive care unit. He glanced up as Julie approached, his eyes heavy from lack of sleep.

"Good morning," she said in a soft tone. "How's Clara?"

"My mother," he returned stiffly, "rested comfortably."

Julie took the seat opposite Daniel. "Can we talk?" Sitting on the edge of the cushion, Julie leaned slightly forward and linked her fingers.

Daniel shrugged his muscular shoulders and ran a hand over his face.

"Did you sleep at all?"

A quick shake of his head confirmed her suspicions. "I couldn't. What about you?" he asked without lifting his gaze.

"Some." She noticed that Daniel wouldn't look at her, not directly. Even when she'd entered the room his intense gaze had met hers only briefly before focusing on something behind her.

"The doctor's with her now."

"Daniel." Julie found it difficult to speak. "What are we going to do?"

His laughter was mirthless, chilling. "What do you mean *do*? My mother didn't know what she was saying. They'd given her so many drugs yesterday she wasn't thinking straight. Today she won't remember a word."

Julie didn't believe that any more than Daniel did, but if he wished to avoid the issue there was little she could say.

They didn't speak and while his gaze was directed at the floor, Julie had the opportunity to study him. The lines about his mouth and eyes were more pronounced now, deeply etched with his concern. His brow was creased in thick furrows. Julie knew that his mother was all the family Daniel had.

A coffee machine across the hall caught her attention and Julie took several coins from her purse and stood. She added sugar to each of their cups and cream to Daniel's. His gaze bounced off her as he accepted the Styrofoam container. She watched as surprise flickered over his face and knew that he hadn't expected her to remember he used sugar and cream.

They both set the coffee aside and looked up expectantly when the doctor entered the room.

The white-haired man smiled reassuringly and Julie noticed for the first time the gentleness that seemed to emanate from the man.

"How is she?" Daniel spoke first.

"She's incredibly weak, but better than we expected. For her to have survived the night is nothing short of a miracle." The doctor paused to study them both. "Your mother seems to have decided she wants to live. And since she's come this far the possibilities of her making a complete recovery are good."

Julie bit into her bottom lip to keep from crying out with relief.

"She's resting now and from the look of things, both of you should do the same."

Daniel nodded. "I didn't want to leave until I was sure she was going to be all right."

The doctor shook his head. "I don't know what she said to you last night, but whatever it was has made the world of difference in her attitude. From that moment on, she started to recover."

Julie's eyes clashed with Daniel's. If possible he paled all the more.

"Now go home and get some rest. There's nothing you can do here. I'll phone you the minute there's any change."

"Thank you, Doctor," Daniel said, his voice husky with appreciation.

They remained standing even after the doctor left. Daniel closed his eyes and released a long, exhausted sigh.

"Can I drop you off at your place?" Julie asked quietly. Daniel didn't look as if he was in any condition to drive.

He looked at her and shook his head. "No."

"You'll phone me if you hear anything?"

He answered her with an affirmative shake of his head.

"Everything's going to work out for the best," she whispered and walked away, leaving the hospital and heading back to her apartment.

Julie didn't mean to sleep, but after arriving home and phoning her mother to tell her about Clara Van Deen's attack, she decided to stretch out on the sofa and rest her eyes a few minutes. The next thing she knew someone was knocking on the door.

Abruptly rising to a sitting position, Julie glanced at her wristwatch and was shocked to notice that it was after two.

"Just a minute," she called and hurriedly slipped her feet back into her shoes and ran her fingers through her tangled hair. "Who is it?" she asked before releasing the lock.

"Daniel," came the taut reply.

Immediately, Julie threw open the door. "Is she all right? I mean, she's not worse, is she?"

"No." He shook his head. "She's doing remarkably well."

"Thank God," Julie whispered as she stepped aside to let Daniel into her apartment.

"I do," Daniel murmured under his breath as he walked past her. "Did I wake you?"

With a dry smile, Julie nodded. "It's a good thing you did or I wouldn't be able to sleep tonight."

"They let me see her for a few minutes," he said and stood uneasily in the center of the room.

"And?" Julie prompted.

"And—" he paused and ran a hand through his thick hair, rumpling the urbane effect "—she asked when we were planning to have the wedding."

Julie walked to the sofa and sat down. "I was afraid of that."

Daniel remained standing. "Apparently she's been talking to the nurses about us. The head nurse told me she firmly believed the fact you and I are going to be married was what kept mother alive last night. It was what the doctor called her sudden will to live."

"And," Julie finished for him, "you're afraid telling her otherwise could kill her."

Daniel stalked to the far side of the room and spoke with his back to her. "I talked to the doctor again. He explained that if mother can grow strong enough in the next few months there's a possibility that heart surgery could correct her condition."

"That's wonderful news."

He turned to her then and the hard look in his dark eyes raked over her. "Yes, in some ways it's given me reason to hope. But in others..." He shook his head and let the rest of his words fade into nothingness. "Why did you come back, Julie? Why couldn't you have left well enough alone?"

"I already explained," she answered quietly and squeezed her hands tightly together. "I want— No," she amended, "I need your forgiveness."

"My forgiveness," he repeated and lifted his head so that she could read the exasperation into his eyes. "I wish to God that I had never seen you again."

The pain of his words slammed into Julie and she struggled to disguise her response. "But I am here and I won't leave until I've accomplished that."

"You have a long wait."

"I didn't expect it to be easy."

Forcefully he muttered a curse under his breath. "I don't know what to do. I can't see us getting married. Not the way I feel about you."

"No," she agreed, "I can't see adding that complication to our relationship."

"We have no relationship." His voice grated as he stalked from the apartment.

Julie stopped at the hospital with a flower arrangement on her way home from work Monday afternoon. Since Mrs. Van Deen remained in the intensive care unit, Julie doubted that she would be able to see her. But when she reached the nurses' station she was informed that special permission had been granted for her to visit. The same five-minute limitation applied.

Clara looked pale against the white sheets. She opened her eyes and gave Julie a feeble smile.

"I'm so pleased you came," she whispered, squeezing Julie's hand.

"I can only stay a few minutes," Julie told her in a soft voice.

"I know."

"How are you feeling?"

"Much better now that I know Daniel will be happy."

A strangling sensation gripped Julie's throat. She couldn't think of any way to tell Clara Van Deen that she and Daniel weren't going to be married.

"It was all my fault, I realize that now." The frail voice wavered. "With you and Daniel married I can undo some of the harm I did."

"But..." Julie groaned inwardly. "Marriage isn't something to rush into. I'm still very much in love with Daniel, but he's been badly hurt and needs time to forget the pain I caused him."

The tired eyes fluttered closed. "Daniel loves you. He always has. His pride's been hurt, but he'll come around. I know he will."

So much for that argument, Julie mused unhappily.

"Trust me, child. The reason he's hurting so much is because he loves you."

The nurse stepped up to the bedside. "I'm sorry, but I'm going to have to ask you to leave now."

Julie leaned down and gently kissed the weathered cheek. "Rest now, and I'll stop in tomorrow afternoon."

The old eyes opened again. "Tell Daniel you love him," she whispered, her voice barely audible. "He needs to know that."

Julie didn't answer one way or the other. How could she admit something like that to a man who fought her in every way he could? Julie had more pride than to set herself up for that kind of pain.

Daniel was in the waiting room when she came into the hallway. He stood and glanced at her expectantly when she entered the area.

"She looks much better today."

He nodded, but Julie was sure he hadn't heard anything she'd said.

"Can we go someplace and talk?" he asked tightly.

The hospital cafeteria was almost empty. A few people were sitting at circular tables near the window.

"Go ahead and sit down and I'll bring us something. Iced tea?" he quizzed, arching a questioning brow.

The afternoon was sunny and warm for early spring and Julie smiled her thanks. Iced tea was her favorite summertime drink. She hadn't expected Daniel to remember that.

He carried the two tall glasses on an orange-colored tray and deposited it on a nearby table after removing their drinks.

"I talked to Dr. Berube again this afternoon," he said, staring into the tea.

Julie's hand curled around the icy glass, the cold seeping up her arm.

"The doctor seems to feel that if we...if I...was to disappoint mother about this marriage it could be extremely detrimental to her recovery."

The icy coldness stopped at Julie's heart. "Does this mean you want to go ahead with the wedding?" Her voice sounded incredibly soft.

"No." he breathed out a sigh. "A marriage between us would never work. The possibility of a life together ended when you left. But my mother's health—"

"Daniel," she said, her voice gaining volume, "I know you may find this hard to believe after all these years, but I never stopped loving you."

His eyes hardened. "If you had loved me, you would never have walked out. You don't know what it is to love, Julie. It isn't in the core of stone hanging where your heart should be."

Her mouth trembled with the effort to restrain stinging tears. She had done as Daniel's mother suggested and humbled herself. Daniel had to know how difficult it was for her to bare her soul to him and yet he tossed her declaration of love back in her face. "If you honestly believe that, there's no point in having this discussion." Abruptly, she stood and hurried out of the room. Shimmering tears blurred her vision as she made her way to the parking lot.

Suddenly, a male hand gripped her upper arm and turned her around before she reached her vehicle.

"Running away again?" he rasped. "I won't let you this time. You're marrying me, Julie, as soon as I can make the arrangements."

"I'd be crazy to marry a man like you."

His laughter was harsh. "Do you think you can carry the guilt of my mother's death on your shoulders? If you walk out now, that's what will happen. It'll kill her. Are you ready to face that, Julie? Or don't you care?"

Julie pulled herself free from his grip. "Daniel," she pleaded, "marriage is sacred."

"Not in this instance," he insisted. "It'll be one of convenience."

"Will it remain that way?" Her questioning eyes sought his.

His steady gaze didn't flicker. "I couldn't touch you."

Biting into the soft, spongy flesh in her inner cheek, Julie struggled not to reveal the hurt his honesty had inflicted. It shouldn't matter to her. The way he felt about her, Julie didn't want Daniel to make love to her. "And after your mother..." She couldn't bring herself to mention the possibility of Clara Van Deen's death.

"You will be free to go, no strings attached. An annulment will be fairly simple."

"I don't know." Julie smoothed a hand across her forehead. "I need time to think."

"No," Daniel shot back sharply. "I need to know now. This minute."

In some ways he was right. What choice did she have? Slowly, deliberately, Julie nodded her head. "All right, Daniel, I'll marry you, but only for your mother's sake."

His lip curled up sardonically. "Do you think I'd marry you otherwise?"

"No, I don't suppose you would." Unfastening the chain from around her neck, Julie handed him her original engagement ring.

"You kept it?" Shock rang through his voice.

Julie stared wistfully into his dark eyes and gave him a gentle smile. "I couldn't bear to part with it. I wore it all these years. Close to my heart. Surely that must tell you something."

He laughed shortly. "It must have given you a sense of triumph to have kept that all this time. To be honest, I'm surprised there's only one. In three years I would have expected you to add at least that many more."

Again Julie struggled to hide the pain. "No," she answered, lowering her gaze, "there was never anyone but you."

"You don't honestly expect me to believe that, do you?"

"It doesn't matter what you believe."

"Keep the ring around your neck. It represented a lot of devotion and feeling I don't have now. I'll buy another one later."

"If that's what you want," Julie whispered in defeat.

"I'll make the arrangements and get back to you with the details."

"Fine."

Julie didn't have to wait long to hear. Daniel phoned her the following afternoon with the information. The wedding was set for one week. Daniel picked her up after work Tuesday night so they could have the blood tests done and apply for the wedding license. After the required three-day wait, they would be married. Everything was cut-and-dried. Even as he relayed the details, Daniel had remained emotionless.

Julie's mother was shocked, but pleased, and planned to fly in for the wedding. Unfortunately Margaret Houser had to get back for volunteer work the next day. Julie was relieved that her mother's stay would be cut short. She wasn't sure how effectively she could act out the role of a happy bride.

The night before the wedding, with her mother sleeping in her bed, Julie tossed restlessly on the sofa. Just before dawn, she decided to give up on trying to sleep and moved from the couch. She doubted that she'd slept more than a couple of hours.

Standing at the window she stared into the night. The moon's silver rays fell upon the glistening dew of early morning.

Nervously she tugged at her lip. This was her wedding day and now in these last hours before the ceremony, her freedom was like sand silently slipping through her fingers. Nervous tension produced waves of nausea. Even now, Julie wasn't sure she was doing the right thing. Of one thing she was certain: right or wrong, she wouldn't walk out on Daniel a second time.

Several hours later, long after the last of the brilliant stars had faded with the morning sun, a car came to deliver Julie and her mother to the church. Clara Van Deen had insisted that her minister marry them. Julie had no objections and apparently Daniel didn't either.

Daniel met them at the church door. His eyes roamed over the white street-length dress Julie had chosen and something unreadable flickered across his face. Julie didn't know what he was thinking, and doubted that she really knew this man at all.

His casual "Are you ready?" stirred the gnawed sense she was making a terrible mistake. Swallowing, Julie decided to ignore it.

The ceremony was short. Daniel's steady voice responded to the minister's instructions as if the words held no meaning for him. In contrast, Julie's strained speech wobbled uncontrollably as she repeated her vows.

Daniel glanced at her when she pledged her love and a glint of challenge entered his gaze.

Her fingers trembled slightly as he slipped a plain gold band on her slim finger. The simplicity of the ring suited her, but she was sure Daniel had chosen something so plain as a contrast to the beautiful diamond he had given to her the first time. Julie was confident the contrast didn't stop there.

Julie's mother hugged them both, her eyes shining with happiness. All three rode to the hospital together and were allowed a short visit with Daniel's mother.

Clara Van Deen smiled as a tear of happiness slipped from the corner of her eye and dampened the pillowcase.

"Trust me, Julie," she whispered. "Things will work out."

Julie nodded, smiling feebly as she kissed the wrinkled brow.

From the hospital, Daniel and Julie drove her mother to the airport. Margaret Houser insisted on paying for everyone's lunch. If she noticed the stilted silence between the groom and bride, she said nothing.

Julie would have liked to visit longer with her mother. She yearned to hold onto her old life as long as possible, but Daniel was clearly in a hurry and after a few abrupt words, he ushered Julie back to the car.

Watching him as he drove, Julie's fingers clenched the small bouquet of flowers her mother had given her. The unfamiliar gold band felt strange against her finger and unconsciously she toyed with it, running it back and forth over her knuckle.

Stopped at a red light, Daniel caught her gazing at her hand. "Don't be so anxious to remove that wedding band. It's there for as long as I say. Understand?"

Julie tossed him an angry glare and murmured tightly, "Of course, I understand. You've made your feelings toward me and this marriage perfectly clear."

Neither spoke again until Daniel had parked. He owned a condominium in Wichita's most prestigious downtown area. The doorman smiled his welcome and held open the shiny glass door for Julie.

"Good afternoon, Mr. Van Deen," he said politely, his eyes widening with undisguised curiosity at the sight of Julie and the two suitcases Daniel carried.

Nodding curtly, Daniel placed his hand under Julie's elbow, hurrying her toward the elevator. The huge metal doors parted at the press of his finger and Julie was quickly ushered inside. The strained silence continued until he unlocked the door of the condominium, swinging it wide to allow Julie to enter first.

Reluctant to move inside, Julie hesitated, wondering what lay before her.

"Don't tell me you expect me to carry you over the threshold as well." The taunting arch of his brow brought a rush of embarrassed color to Julie's cheeks.

"No," she replied shortly and, with as much dignity as possible, entered her new life.

The condominium was surprisingly spacious. The tiled entryway led to a sunken living room carpeted in a plush brown pile. Two huge picture windows overlooked the downtown area and Julie paused to admire the fantastic view from fifteen floors up.

Pointedly, Daniel moved around her and briskly delivered her suitcase to what was apparently to be her bedroom. He stopped outside the door in the wide hallway.

"This is your room," he called abruptly, interrupting her search for familiar sights.

Julie lifted her eyes from the Century II Convention, Cultural Center, the Broadview Hotel and Holiday Inn Plaza and followed the sound of Daniel's voice to the hallway.

A glance inside the room confirmed her belief that this had been a guest room. Fitting, Julie realized, since she was little more than an unwelcome guest in Daniel's life.

"The rest of your things will be delivered sometime this afternoon," he informed her. "I have to get back to the office for a couple of hours."

Back to the office! Julie's mind shouted. They'd barely been married three hours. She'd taken the day off work. He could have at least done the same. They were in this marriage together.

"What am I supposed to do?" she asked mockingly in an attempt to hide her disappointment. "Make myself at home in a strange house, alone?"

"Unpack," he replied flippantly.

"That should take all of five minutes. What should I do then?"

"Don't tell me I have to stay home and baby-sit you for the next twenty years."

"No," Julie tossed out recklessly. "Go ahead and leave. There's no need to hurry back on my account."

Daniel's laugh was mirthless as he headed out the front door. "Don't worry."

Her calculation was correct. Five minutes later both suitcases were empty. After a quick inspection of the remainder of the condominium, Julie returned to her room. She yawned, raising her hands above her head and stretching. Her neck hurt from a sleepless night on the sofa. Slowly rotating her head, Julie hoped to ease the tightness from her tired muscles. She'd slept so little that she decided to take a nap. The bed yielded, soft and welcoming under her. Within minutes she fell into a deep, comfortable slumber.

Refreshed, she woke after four. Daniel had been gone a couple of hours. After leafing through a magazine, Julie toyed with the idea of going out for dinner and letting him come home to an empty apartment. It would serve him right. But, no, being antagonistic wouldn't help their situation. She pushed the hair away from her temple and released a slow breath. She would cook their meal and try to make the best of things.

The compact kitchen was beautifully arranged and well stocked. Apparently Daniel enjoyed cooking and ate at home regularly or he had someone come in to cook for him. Julie's hand tightened against the counter. The thought of Daniel bringing another woman into this kitchen produced an unaccustomed feeling of jealousy. She'd managed to squelch those uncomfortable sensations when he'd dated Sherry, but now they washed over her, surprising Julie with their intensity.

Working quickly, she prepared a fresh salad and dessert, and then thawed two large steaks in the microwave until they were ready to grill.

She had the option of setting the dining room table or the small area of the kitchen. After only a moment's deliberation she chose the dining room. This was, after all, their wedding day, although Daniel seemed to be doing his best to forget just that. If they were going to build any kind of meaningful life, then she would have to be the one to take the first step.

Another suitcase and several boxes from her apartment were delivered shortly after five and Julie spent the next hour unpacking and arranging her things with Daniel's. She wasn't surprised to find that they shared similar tastes in literature and artwork. More than once, as she placed her books on the shelf, she discovered that Daniel already had the same book.

Why the fact amazed her, Julie didn't know. They had been surprisingly alike from their first meeting. Fleetingly Julie wondered if Daniel still played tennis. It was on the courts that they'd first met. The attraction had been immediate and intense. They'd been so much in love.

As dusk fell over the city, Julie lit the candles, creating a warm, romantic mood. She regretted the harsh parting words with Daniel that afternoon. Maybe the dinner would show him that she was willing to work things out. She'd made the first step. But the next one had to come from Daniel.

Glancing at the table, she noted that the candle flames dancing against the illumination of city lights was breathtaking and alluringly poetic. Julie doubted that she would ever tire of looking at it.

The tiresome minutes ticked into drawn out hours and at eleven Julie accepted the fact that Daniel wouldn't be coming home for dinner. She didn't know if he'd be home at all. But if he walked in on the homey scene she'd created it would only amuse him.

After blowing out the candles and turning on the lights, she began to clear the table piece by piece, returning the china place settings to the rosewood cabinet.

When only half the dishes were cleared, the front door opened. Julie paused, her hand clenching the expensive plate tightly to her stomach, her heart pounding wildly.

From across the sizable room, Daniel's bold eyes held hers mesmerized.

Lowering her gaze, Julie offered him a nervous smile and resumed her task, praying he wouldn't comment. She should have known better.

"A romantic dinner complete with candlelight and the best dishes. What's this, Julie? An invitation to your bed?"

Chapter Five

"No," she said, forcing her voice to sound light and carefree, "it wasn't that at all."

"Pity," he mumbled under his breath, but loud enough for her to hear.

Julie had to bite her tongue to keep from asking where he'd been. That was exactly what he wanted her to do, but she refused to play his games.

"If you'll excuse me, I think I'll go to bed."

Daniel remained standing in the tiled entryway, staring at her, his serious eyes searching her expression. "I didn't know if you'd eaten or not."

Averting her gaze, Julie shook her head. "No, I thought I'd wait for you."

"I'm surprised you did."

Wordlessly, Julie moved past him and down the hall to her room. Daniel had made it clear they wouldn't make the pretense of a honeymoon and she was scheduled to return to work in the morning. As she undressed, Julie could hear Daniel's movements in the kitchen.

Zipping up her housecoat, Julie moved across the hall to the bathroom to brush her teeth. The appealing aroma of broiling steak reminded her she hadn't eaten since early afternoon. Squaring her shoulders, she attacked her teeth with the brush. Not for anything would she go into that kitchen.

Back in her room, she sat on top of the bed and opened a recent best-seller. The light tap against the door shocked her.

"Your steak is ready." Daniel stuck his head in and smiled. "Medium rare, as I recall."

Julie opened her mouth to tell him exactly what he could do with the dinner, then abruptly stopped herself. It had been a tiring day for both of them and the last thing they needed was an argument to complicate matters.

"I'll be there in a minute." Feeling strangely pleased with the turn of events, Julie put on her slippers and joined him in the kitchen.

The table was set for two. Their steaks were served with grilled tomatoes and melted cheddar cheese on huge platters.

Smiling, Julie opened the refrigerator and brought out the crisp vegetable salad she'd made.

As she set the bowl on the table, Daniel commented nonchalantly, "There were some briefs I needed to review for a court case in the morning."

Julie paused as she sat at the table, her hand clenching the fork. Daniel was telling her why he was late. She hadn't expected it, confident he'd wanted her to fret. And she had.

"Perhaps it would be best if either one of us is going to be late to let the other know," she said evenly as the knife slid smoothly across the thick steak.

"Sounds fair," Daniel commented.

A soft smile touched her eyes as Julie continued eating. The evening had gotten off to an uneasy start, but they were working things out and that pleased her.

"We should probably make some other living arrangements," she suggested, forcing a conversational lightness to her voice.

"Like?"

"Since you did the cooking, I'll do the dishes."

"That sounds reasonable." His warm gaze touched her and Julie felt a weak sensation attack her stomach. Daniel hadn't smiled at her, really smiled, since she'd returned. She'd almost forgotten how potent one of his glances could be.

Julie continued to study him from beneath the thick lashes that veiled her eyes. Laying her knife across the curve of the plate, she looked up. "That was wonderful. I don't remember you being such an excellent cook."

"I've managed to pick up a few skills during the last couple of years," he murmured dryly.

Julie stood and carried their plates to the sink while Daniel poured them each a cup of coffee.

"Why don't we drink this in the living room?" he invited unexpectedly.

"I'll be there in a minute. I want to stick these things in the dishwasher."

When Julie joined him, Daniel was standing at the window looking out at the sparkling lights of the city.

"Mother seemed much improved today, didn't she?"

Julie took the coffee cup from the end table and sat down. "Yes, she did. There was some color in her cheeks for the first time since the attack."

"It's going to be a long uphill haul for her in the coming months."

"I know. I'll do anything possible to help her," Julie said and took a sip from the coffee cup. Daniel remained at the window with his back to her.

"I think we should agree that no matter what happens between us we won't take our squabbles to my mother."

"Of course not." Julie blinked. She was surprised that Daniel would think she'd run to his mother with every complaint. "If we need to talk something over, the person I'll come to is you," she said as matter-of-factly as possible.

"Good." He turned around and sat in the wing-backed chair beside her. "Don't worry about the housework. The cleaning lady comes in twice a week."

"What about the cooking?" Her hands cupped the mug as she avoided eye contact. "I hate to admit it, but I'm not much good in the kitchen. You're probably more adept at this cooking business than me. Do you want to take turns?"

"If you like."

"It might work out best for a while." She shrugged carelessly. How could they sit beside one another—man and wife—and talk of trivialities? Julie didn't want her marriage to begin with all these uncertainties gnawing at her. Twice before the wedding she'd tried to settle their past. Both times Daniel had abruptly cut her off. As much as possible he wanted to leave that time in their relationship behind them. Sadly the thought flashed through Julie's mind that they had no future until they faced the hurts and misunderstandings of the past. But tonight wasn't the time.

"You're looking thoughtful," Daniel commented.

"Sorry." She shook her head to clear her thoughts. "I guess I'm tired."

"I think I'll turn in too."

Together they carried their cups into the kitchen. Julie placed them in the dishwasher with the other dishes and Daniel showed her how to work it. The soft hum of running water followed them into the hallway.

He flipped off the light switch and the condominium went dark.

Julie's eyes adjusted quickly to the moonlit room.

"Can you find your way?"

"Sure," she murmured confidently. Their gazes met in the darkness and suddenly everything went still. Daniel's look held her motionless. She couldn't see his eyes well enough to know what he was thinking. How long they stood there not speaking, Julie didn't know. It seemed an eternity.

When his hand reached out and caressed her cheek, a warming sensation spread down her neck. Releasing a soft sigh, she closed her eyes and placed her hand over his.

"Good night, Julie," he said tenderly and removed his hand. He walked her to her room and hesitated long enough in the open doorway for her heartbeat to quicken.

Their eyes met and for a fleeting moment the hurt that had driven them apart all but faded. Unconsciously, Julie took a wishful step in his direction. This man was her husband. They were meant to be together.

"If you'd like, I'll cook breakfast in the morning," she offered, wanting an excuse to linger with him in the darkness even if it meant asking inane questions.

He didn't answer for so long that Julie wondered if he'd heard her speak. "I thought you said you weren't much of a cook."

"I can manage breakfast."

"Did you dine out so often?"

The question caught her completely off guard. "I don't understand."

He raised his voice with tight impatience. "Is the reason you can't cook because you dated so much?"

"No," she answered simply. "I hardly went out at all." She couldn't when she'd left her heart with him.

Silvery moonlight filled the narrow hallway as Julie intently studied her husband, waiting for a reaction.

"I wish I could believe that," he said with a sigh, "but you're much too beautiful not to have men fawning over you." Abruptly he turned away.

The alarm on the clock radio went off at six, filling the silent room with instant music. Julie lay in bed several minutes, listening to a couple of songs before throwing back the covers and climbing out of bed.

Slipping into her housecoat, she ambled into the kitchen, yawning as she put on a pot of coffee. Already the morning was glorious. The sun was shining and Julie stood at the window looking down on the city as it stirred to life.

When she turned around, she found Daniel standing at the coffeepot waiting for enough liquid to drain through so he could have a cup.

"Good morning," she greeted him with a warm smile.

Daniel mumbled something unintelligible under his breath.

"Did you say something?" she asked as she took the empty cup out of his hand, and poured what little coffee had drained through into his mug.

"No," he grumbled.

"No one told me you were such a grouch in the mornings," she teased.

"Do you have to smile so brightly?"

"No," she said, laughing softly. "I'll go get dressed and stay out of your way until you're civil."

"That's probably a good idea."

Humming, Julie returned to her bedroom and dressed. The outfit she chose was a new one, a two-piece gray-and-blue striped dress with a wide vee neckline. In normal circumstances she probably wouldn't have chosen the dress for work, but she considered her choice a means of wooing her husband. Slipping the pumps on her feet, she completed the final touches to her makeup and hair before entering the kitchen.

The bacon was sizzling in the pan when Daniel came in and poured himself a second cup of coffee.

"How do you want your eggs? Over easy?" She turned and was surprised to see the scowl that twisted his mouth in disapproval.

"Is something wrong?"

"That dress."

"It's new. Don't you like it?" She swallowed tightly. Julie hadn't needed a saleslady to tell her the outfit was becoming on her. The blue tones matched the color of her eyes perfectly.

"It's a little revealing, don't you think?"

"Revealing?" Julie gasped. "Where?"

Daniel picked up the morning paper and sat down. "The neckline."

"The neckline?" Julie's hand flew to the V-shaped front. She'd always dressed modestly and there was nothing about this outfit or anything else she owned that could be considered less than proper. "There's nothing wrong with this dress," she replied in even tones.

"That's a matter of opinion," he returned from behind the open newspaper.

"How do you want your eggs?" Julie repeated her question, fighting back her impatience.

The newspaper didn't move, effectively blocking her out. "I've lost my appetite."

"So have I," she whispered brokenly and turned off the burner.

The drive to the office took only a few minutes. Neither spoke. Julie's hands were clenched in her lap like a schoolchild, her head held rigid with her eyes focused straight ahead. She hadn't changed clothes, nor would she. Daniel was being unreasonable. A wry smile touched her mouth. And she'd anticipated gently courting him with the new dress.

Daniel pulled into a parking garage across the street and into the allotted space.

"I may be late tonight."

Julie answered without looking at him. "I thought I'd go to the hospital after work."

"Then I'll meet you there."

They sounded like robots, their voices clipped and emotionless.

Sherry was at her desk when Julie walked in the office. Julie paused and did a double take.

"Is that really you, Sherry?" she joked as she closed the door. "Or are my eyes playing tricks on me again? Sherry early? That's impossible."

The returning smile was weak and wavering. "Morning." She lowered her head and blew her nose in a tissue. "I guess it's a shock to see me, isn't it?'' The soft voice faltered slightly.

"Sherry, what's wrong?"

"Wrong?" She laughed. "What makes you think something's wrong?"

"Maybe it's the mountain of wet tissues, or the red eyes and weak smile. But then I've always had the reputation of being a good sleuth."

Sherry made a gallant effort at smiling. She gestured weakly, waving the palm of her hand.

Julie had worried something like this would happen when Sherry learned she'd married Daniel.

"I guess I should have said something the first time you mentioned Daniel," Julie murmured apologetically. "I wouldn't want to hurt you, Sherry, not for anything. Daniel and I have known each other for several years."

Sherry glanced up with a blank look. "What are you talking about?"

"Daniel and me. I should have explained that we've known each other for several years."

"I didn't think either of you were crazy enough to get married after a two-week courtship. That sounds like something I'd do. But not you and Daniel."

"Then why the tears and the dismal look?"

"Andy." Sherry's voice wobbled.

"Your ex-husband?"

Sherry tugged another Kleenex from the brightly colored box and nodded. "The divorce isn't final until the end of the month."

"Second thoughts?" Julie only knew a little about Sherry's marriage from the bits of information her friend had let drop a couple of times. They didn't have any real reason to separate. Both had been overly involved in their jobs. They'd grown apart and apparently out of love. The trial separation had led to the decision to file for the divorce. In the short time Julie had known her co-worker it hadn't been difficult to recognize that Sherry had set out to prove how much fun she could have without her husband.

"I . . . I saw Andy last night."

"Did you get a chance to talk?" Julie questioned softly. She didn't want to pry but thought that Sherry might feel better if she confided in someone.

"Talk!" She hiccuped loudly. "There was a voluptuous blonde draped all over him."

"But Sherry, that shouldn't bother you. For heaven's sake, you've gone out a dozen times with as many different men just since I've known you."

"Yes, but that was different."

"How?"

"Andy didn't care if I saw someone else."

"How can you be so sure?" Julie interjected the question. "Maybe he cares very much. Maybe he's decided the time has come for him to start dating again too."

"Not Andy. He's always hated blondes."

"You're blond," Julie chided.

"I know, but the type of woman he was with last night isn't like anyone that would interest him." Sherry wiped the moisture from her cheeks and inhaled slowly. "There's irony in this whole thing. I'd set my sights on Danny, convinced that he was the perfect man for me . . . and he's another Andy. They're so much alike it's ridiculous. How could I have been so blind—" she paused to take in a deep breath "—and stupid?"

"I've done some stupid things in my life," Julie admitted with a wry smile.

Their boss, Mr. Barrett, came into the room and absently nodded his greeting as he hung his coat in the closet. He seemed about to say something when he noticed Sherry's red face. Swiftly he retreated into his office, closing the door. With a grin, Julie said, "Why don't we see if we can take lunch together and talk some more."

"I'd like that."

The phone rang and Julie pushed down the button to take the call.

Ten minutes later, Julie replaced the phone and took the top file from her In basket.

"I meant to tell you earlier how nice you look today. Is that a new outfit?"

"Yes." Julie's head snapped up. "Do you like it?"

"It's perfect for you."

"What about the neckline?" She tilted her head up and arched her shoulders.

"What about it?"

"It's not too revealing?"

"Revealing?" Sherry echoed. "No way."

"That's what I thought," she mumbled and turned back to the file.

Clara Van Deen attempted to smile when Julie entered the intensive care unit that afternoon. She lifted her hand to Julie, who clasped it between hers.

"How's my new daughter?"

"How's my new mother?"

Clara closed her eyes and when she opened them again they were glistening with unshed tears. "Better now that I'm assured I've made up for some of the pain I've caused you and Daniel."

"I love him," Julie admitted gently. "I came back because of my love for him."

"And Daniel loves you. Don't ever doubt that, Julie. Though I know little of his life anymore, I realize he saw lots of women. But, Julie, there was never anyone he truly loved. No one but you."

Gently, Julie squeezed the old woman's hand. "I'll make him a good wife."

"I don't doubt for a minute that you will." The returning smile was weak but infinitely happy.

Daniel arrived thirty minutes later. Julie was in the waiting room leafing through a dog-eared magazine she'd already read through twice. She glanced up expectantly when he entered the area.

Daniel's gaze dwelled on her neckline and the fullness of her breasts. A closed expression masked his features.

"Your mother's looking very good," Julie said softly.

Daniel nodded abruptly. "I'll spend some time with her and then we'll leave."

Of their own volition Julie's eyes were drawn to her husband. His rugged appeal gave the impression that he worked out of doors. His face was tanned for early spring and Julie suspected he had continued to play tennis although he hadn't mentioned it. But then they hadn't talked about a lot of things. The sensuous mouth was compressed into a tight line.

"I talked to the doctor this afternoon," Daniel announced casually and rubbed his hand along the back of his neck as he paced the waiting room.

"And?" Julie set the magazine aside and uncrossed her legs.

"He said mother's improving enough for him to consider doing the open-heart surgery."

"When?" Julie asked and breathed in deeply.

"A month from now, maybe longer."

"That's wonderful news." If the surgery was a success the possibility of Daniel's mother returning to a normal life would be greatly increased.

"Is it?" Daniel returned almost flippantly. "If she gains enough strength to make it to surgery her chances are only fifty-fifty she'll survive the ordeal."

"But what are they without it?"

He stalked to the far side of the room and pivoted sharply. "Far less than that."

"Is there a choice?" She could understand and shared his concern, but the chance of a longer, healthier life for his mother was worth the risk. Daniel, however, didn't look nearly as confident. "Everything's going to be fine."

"How do you know that?"

"I don't," Julie admitted, "but your mother's content, her spirits are good and she has the will to live. Her attitude is positive and that's bound to help." It was on the tip of her tongue to tell Daniel that on the day Clara had taken ill, she'd mentioned to Julie how she longed to hold her grandchildren. Julie knew sheer willpower would see her mother-in-law through this surgery.

Daniel's expression tightened as he studied her.

The nurse arrived and directed him into the intensive care area. Julie stayed behind since the staff preferred that their patients have only one visitor at a time.

As they drove home Julie noticed that a spark of amusement seemed to flicker in and out of Daniel's eyes.

"What's so funny?" she asked him later as she set the table for dinner.

"What makes you think something's amusing?"

Julie pretended an interest in the fresh green salad she was tossing. "Every time I look up it seems you're trying to keep from laughing."

"Something mother said, that's all." He didn't elaborate.

"About me?" she asked stiffly, disliking the fact she could have been the brunt of their joke.

"Indirectly."

They ate in almost total silence. Not an intended silence, at least not on Julie's part. They were married but shared nothing in common as yet. Daniel hadn't allowed her into his life. Julie was confident that the sharing would come with time. The one thing they desperately needed to talk about, Daniel refused to discuss.

"Do you still play tennis?" Julie asked as she cleared the small table, hoping that he'd follow through with her question and suggest that they play again.

"Often enough."

Julie noticed that he didn't ask if she still played. They'd met on the courts and had been a popular doubles team. Julie still enjoyed the game, but didn't know how to volunteer the information without making it look as if she was looking for an invitation, which she was.

"I'll do the dishes later." Daniel broke into her unhappy thoughts. "There are a few papers I want to go over tonight."

"Do you bring work home often?" Julie hadn't meant the question derogatorily, but the look Daniel flashed her showed his disapproval.

"Hardly at all."

"I'll do the dishes," she volunteered.

"No," he said abruptly. "When I say I'm going to do something, I do it."

Julie gripped the edge of the oak table and exhaled. "In other words you don't walk out five days before the wedding. That's what you're saying isn't it, Daniel?"

"That's exactly what I'm saying," he said in steel-sharp tones.

In a haze of pain, Julie stood and scooted her chair to the table. Soundlessly she moved out of the kitchen, reached for a sweater and headed for the front door.

"Where are you going?" Daniel demanded.

"Out," she replied with a saccharine sweet smile and closed the door behind her. Half hoping Daniel would come after her, Julie lingered in the hall outside the condominium. She should have known better.

Without her purse and nowhere to go, Julie was back within an hour, having done nothing more than take a brisk walk.

When she returned to the condo, Daniel was in his den, or at least she assumed he was. The two pans from their meal were washed and stacked on the kitchen counter. Julie dried them and put them away. When she'd finished she glanced up to note that Daniel was standing in the open doorway of the den watching her.

"So you came back."

"What's the matter," she said flippantly, "were you hoping I wouldn't?"

A muscle twitched in his jaw and the pencil in his hands snapped in two. He pivoted and returned to his den.

Julie closed her eyes and took in several calming breaths. This grueling tension between them was fast taking its toll. She hated any kind of discord. At eighteen she'd avoided confrontations and had paid dearly for her mistake. She wasn't the same Julie she had been then. She didn't avoid conflict these days, but she didn't wish to instigate it either.

Daniel remained in his den, the door closed, while Julie sat alone in the living room reading. Although her eyelashes fluttered closed more than once, she shook herself awake, determined to be up when Daniel came out. She wasn't going to run away, not anymore. It was important that he recognize that.

Again and again her eyelids drooped closed until Julie gave up the effort and closed her book. Flipping the light switch to its lowest setting, she leaned her head against the back of the chair to rest her eyes and obediently surrendered to the welcoming tide of slumber.

"Julie." Daniel's whisper woke her. "You'll get a crick in your neck."

Her blue eyes opened slowly and she straightened. The soft glow from the lamp was the only light in the house. Daniel stood above her, his shirt open to reveal the mat of hair on his chest. He studied her and time seemed to come to a halt. Julie felt herself drowning in the tender look in her husband's eyes. She yearned to reach out to him, slip her arms around his neck and gently place her mouth over his. He hadn't kissed her, had avoided touching her, and Julie felt if he turned and walked away from her now she'd die.

"Julie." Her name came on a tormented whisper as he brushed a long strand of hair from her temple.

She knew the look in her eyes must have revealed the hunger she felt for his touch. The desperate need she had to be loved, forgiven and trusted again.

He helped her stand, his touch almost impersonal.

"Daniel," she pleaded softly, wanting to cry with frustration.

Without a word he slipped his arms around her, his dark gaze feasting on her softly parted lips as he slowly, silently, eliminated the distance between them.

Julie released a trembling sigh as she slid her hands over his shoulders and linked her fingers at the base of his neck. "Oh, Daniel," she whispered, "I've waited so long."

He crushed her to his chest, his mouth moving sweetly over hers as he arched her closer.

Mindlessly, Julie obeyed as he kissed her again and again. She thrilled to the urgency of his mouth as if he couldn't receive enough. As if she couldn't give enough. When he buried his face against the curve of her neck, Julie smiled contentedly, while her hands sought his thick hair.

Daniel straightened and looked into her eyes. Smiling, Julie brushed her mouth over his and kissed the tiny cleft in his chin. The very spot she'd loved to tease with her tongue all those years ago. She wanted him to know she hadn't forgotten, not anything.

He stiffened against her and abruptly tugged his arms free. "Good night, Julie," he murmured stiffly before turning and walking away. He was telling her he hadn't forgotten anything, either.

For one unbearable moment, Julie didn't breathe. How many times would he walk away from her to make up for the one time she'd left him? How many hurts must she suffer to compensate for the damage she had inflicted against his male pride? Standing alone in the darkened room, Julie could find no answers. Slowly she turned and went into her room, hoping to find some peace in sleep.

The next day was almost identical to the one before. Silently, they rode to work together. From work they went to the hospital, taking turns visiting his mother. Daniel cooked dinner while she changed clothes.

"I'm going to the library," she announced as she placed their plates in the dishwasher.

"How long will you be?" Daniel asked without looking up from the mail.

"An hour." Anything was better than sitting in a silent house again while Daniel closed himself off from her in his den.

He shrugged as if what she did was of little concern to him.

Julie hesitated. "Would you like to come?"

"I've got things to do around here."

Julie let herself out the front door, her heart aching. The first night she'd accused Daniel of playing games. Now she was the one escaping, hoping that he'd say something to prove that he wanted her to stay. He didn't.

Chapter Six

Saturday morning Daniel left the condominium before Julie climbed out of bed. Lying awake with her bedroom door partially open, Julie listened to his hushed movements as he walked down the hall. She expected him to go into the kitchen and was mildly surprised to hear the front door click a few moments later.

Carelessly tossing back the covers, she slipped out of bed and found a pot of coffee and a note on the kitchen counter top. The message read: *Playing tennis all day.*

All day, Julie mused resentfully. They'd talked about the game earlier in the week. There had been ample opportunity for him to have included her in today's outing had he wished . . . which he obviously hadn't.

After brewing a fresh pot of coffee, Julie sat at the round oak table, her palms cupping the mug. An abundance of pride tilted her chin at a sharp, upward angle. She'd known when she agreed to marry Daniel that there were several factors working against them. Some days Julie was convinced that Daniel would never forgive nor forget the hurt she'd inflicted on him by leaving. Then at other times, odd moments when he didn't think she'd noticed, she could feel his gaze studying her. Daniel had been unable to disguise the tender look fast enough. He hadn't kissed her or touched her since that one night. Julie recognized he regretted that one slip and had taken measures to ensure that it wouldn't happen again.

Restless, she killed time by cooking a light breakfast, then dressed casually in washed-out jeans and a plain sweat-shirt. The last of her things had been moved from the apartment. Almost everything had been unpacked and what remained needed to be placed in storage. Only a few of her everyday items were necessary since Daniel's condominium was fully furnished.

Stacking the cardboard crates in the bottom of her closet, Julie located the box that was filled with mementos of her courtship with Daniel. Now that they were married, she could set them out freely. If she placed their engagement photo in full view it might prompt him to discuss the very things he chose to ignore.

Encouraged at the thought, she set the gold-framed pic-ture on top of the television and stepped back to examine it. As always, her heart constricted at the bright hope and promise that shone from their eyes. Daniel's appearance had altered over the years, but Julie vowed that in time all that would change and the special light of his love for her would again shine.

She placed a few other items here and there and then stood in the middle of the room, hands on her hips, to ad-mire her efforts. The condominium, bit by bit, reflected a part of them as a loving, happy couple. Daniel couldn't help but be affected by it. Undoubtedly he would be surprised that she'd kept those things, but she wanted him to under-stand that although she'd left Wichita, she'd never forgot-ten him nor stopped loving him.

After a hot shower, Julie had lunch and decided to stop in at the hospital and visit her mother-in-law.

The older woman turned her face toward Julie as she en-tered the intensive care unit.

"Good afternoon," Julie said with a warm smile and lightly brushed her lips across Clara's cheek. "How are you feeling today?"

"Much better."

She looked improved and Julie felt encouraged.

"Where's Daniel?" Clara wanted to know.

"He's playing tennis." Silently Julie hoped that her mother-in-law wouldn't ask for any more details because she wouldn't know what to tell the older woman. As much as possible, Julie hoped to paint an optimistic picture of their marriage, but she was unwilling to lie.

"That's right," Mrs. Van Deen murmured and smiled softly, "Daniel mentioned something about playing in a tournament this weekend. I'm surprised you aren't at the Country Club with him. As I recall, you two made an excellent doubles team."

So he'd told his mother and hadn't bothered to mention it to her. Maybe he had another partner and didn't want Julie interfering with his prearranged plans. The thought produced a flicker of jealous anger. Quickly she squashed it before her mother-in-law could read her expression.

"Julie, you still play, don't you?"

"I'm a bit rusty," she claimed with a feeble effort at smiling. The Country Club; Julie could vividly recall how uncomfortable she'd been around those people. Daniel had taken her there several times to dinner or for a set of tennis, but Julie had been unable to overcome her feelings of inferiority.

"I thought you'd want to be with him," Clara continued, studying Julie.

"I came to give you our love before meeting Daniel later." Julie told the white lie uneasily. But she would show up at the Country Club. The time had come for her to face some of the other insecurities of the past.

"There's no need to disrupt your day coming to visit me," Clara said with a tired sigh. "I already know how much you care about me. If I live or die is of no consequence to me. All I want before I go is the assurance that the two of you are happy." The white-haired woman regarded Julie seriously. "I wouldn't, however, be upset to hold a grandchild or two." She paused and attempted a smile. "Daniel seemed quite amused when I mentioned how much I was looking forward to grandchildren."

So that was what he'd been so smug about the other night. "I think he feels we should wait," Julie improvised quickly.

"His words exactly. But try to convince him, Julie. I don't have all the time in the world. And he's at the age when he should be thinking of starting a family."

Gently, Julie brushed the hair from Clara's face. "I'll mention it," she promised. "But remember we've only been married a short while."

The tired eyes fluttered closed. "It seems so much longer. In my muddled mind I find it difficult to remember you were gone all those years."

"My heart was here," Julie said softly.

"Would you read to me, dear?" she asked. "My eyes are so weak."

"I'd be happy to."

Although her thoughts were troubled, Julie read until she was certain Clara was asleep, then she quietly slipped from the room. Her mind was set on facing Daniel at the Country Club, but her determination wavered. Her unexpected arrival could be uncomfortable for everyone involved. No, she reasoned. As his wife she had the right to go and watch her husband. Resolutely, she left the hospital, got into her car and headed for the outskirts of town.

Julie was lucky to find a parking place in the crowded lot. The tennis courts and surrounding areas were jammed with spectators. Julie signed in as Daniel's wife and was grateful no one questioned her.

It only took her a few minutes to find her husband. He was on the courts in what she learned was the semifinal singles match. There was a space for her in the bleachers, and she sat there silently engrossed in the competition. A feeling of pride filled her when Daniel won the match. The championship game was played fifteen minutes later. Julie clenched her fists several times at tense moments. Daniel's composure astonished her. He lost the title, but shook hands with his opponent and came off the court joking and smiling.

The crowd gathered around the winner as the stands emptied. Julie made her way to her husband.

Daniel was wiping his face with a hand towel.

"Nice game," she said from behind him.

He didn't pause or give any indication he was surprised as he turned toward her. "How'd you know where to find me?" His look revealed little.

"Your mother mentioned the tournament, so I thought I'd stop by and cheer you on." She offered him a fabricated smile.

"I saw you take a seat in the stands."

"You were good." She noticed that he didn't indicate one way or another how he felt about her unexpected arrival. "Your game's improved."

"I've played better." He made busywork of packing away his racket.

"Good game, Van Deen," a deep baritone voice intoned from behind them.

Julie sensed Daniel stiffen. "Thanks." Casually he looped the towel around his neck.

Julie didn't recognize the tall, athletic man who had joined them.

"I see you've brought your own cheering section along."

Daniel slipped his hands around Julie's waist, bringing her to his side. "Patterson, meet my wife, Julie. Julie, this is my friend and associate, Jim Patterson."

"Your wife!" he echoed. "When did all this happen?"

"Recently."

Jim chuckled and rubbed the side of his jaw in a bemused action. "It had to have been recent. Real recent. Does Kali know?"

At the mention of the other woman's name, Julie eyed her husband speculatively. She had wondered before their wedding if there was another woman Daniel was seeing seriously and at the time had doubted it. Sherry would have known if he'd been romantically involved with someone else. But it was obvious Jim knew more than her co-worker.

"I haven't talked to Kali yet," Daniel replied stiffly.

"This calls for a celebration," Jim said hurriedly, trying to cover the awkward moment. "Let me buy you two a drink."

"Not today," Daniel answered for them. "Unfortunately, Julie has an appointment and must leave." His arm slid possessively from her waist to the back of her neck. "I'll see you to your car, honey." His hand tightened as he steered her toward the parking area.

"It's a pleasure to have met you... Patterson." Julie twisted her head to look back.

"We'll have that drink another time," Jim promised with a brief salute.

Once they were free of spectators, Julie pushed Daniel's hand loose. "What was that all about? And who is Kali?" She was so frustrated she could hardly speak.

A muscle leaped in his determined jaw. "No one who need concern you."

"And why couldn't we have stayed for a drink?" she sputtered out breathlessly. "It's time I met your friends. I'm your wife."

"Don't remind me."

His words couldn't have hurt more had he reached out and physically slapped her. Tears brimmed from the depths of her eyes, threatening to crash over the thick wall of her lashes. She inhaled sharply and refused to give him the satisfaction of seeing her tears.

Daniel rammed his hands into his pockets and looked as if he was about to say something more, but Julie didn't wait to find out. Pride dictating her actions, she briskly turned and walked away. She couldn't get out of the parking lot fast enough.

Unwilling to return to the empty condominium, she drove around until the hurt and anger had dissipated enough for her to think clearly. So there'd been another woman. All right, she could accept that as long as this Kali remained in the past. She'd need to be told soon, however, that Daniel had married or it could cause awkward moments in the future.

Julie released a ragged breath. She was adult enough to realize that Daniel hadn't buried his head in the sand during the years she was gone. It would be unreasonable to expect anything less, but it hurt more than she thought possible. What worried her more was his determination not to tell her about Kali.

When she arrived home two hours later, Daniel was restlessly pacing the living room carpet.

"Julie." He stopped and walked a couple of steps toward her before pausing and jerking a hand through his hair. "Where were you?"

"I went for a drive. I needed time to think a few things through."

He scowled and nodded.

She glanced at her watch. "I didn't realize it was so late. It's my turn to cook isn't it?" she continued, chattering nervously. "I'll put something on right away. You must be starved."

The sound of his voice followed her as she headed for the kitchen. "I thought I'd take you out tonight."

"Take me out?"

"As you said earlier, it's time you and I were seen together."

Julie inhaled a quivering breath of pleasure. The dinner invitation was his way of telling her he was sorry for what had happened that afternoon. It wasn't an eloquent apology, but one that encouraged her immeasurably.

"Well?" Hands buried deep in his pockets, he studied her.

She replied with a slow, sensual smile. "I'd like that."

"Wear something fancy."

The soft smile faltered. "I'm afraid I may not have anything appropriate. Would you mind if we went someplace less formal?" she asked him stiffly.

"Why? As I recall, you liked the party scene."

"I was nineteen years old and incredibly stupid," she told him in a shaky voice. "I never liked any of it, but I couldn't tell you that. I was afraid if you knew how shy I really was, you wouldn't want me."

A flicker of surprise touched Daniel's rugged features. "Our relationship seems riddled with misunderstandings, doesn't it? Why didn't you tell me how you felt?"

"I was so crazy about you, I was ready to become anything you wanted."

"Everything but my wife," he said, his expression impassive, almost stoic.

"I couldn't," she cried. "Not then." She left the kitchen and moved into her bedroom. Leaning against the door, she closed her eyes. Surely Daniel must realize that if they'd gone through with the wedding three years ago their marriage would have been doomed. Sighing unevenly, Julie recognized that their union wasn't any more secure now. The thought saddened her.

Swallowing down the hurts that crowded in around her, Julie changed into a pale blue dress with a matching white jacket. A glance in the mirror confirmed that even the most critical eye would find no fault with the neckline. White high-heeled sandals graced her feet while a single strand of pearls hung elegantly around her throat. Daniel had given her the pearls, but she doubted that he would remember that. He'd given her so many beautiful things.

She moved into the living room, where her husband was waiting. He wore dark poplin slacks with a color-coordinated shirt under a sports coat.

The atmosphere was congenial as he pulled out of the parking garage. "I made a phone call and was able to get last minute tickets for the dinner theater."

Julie nodded agreeably. "That sounds wonderful. What's playing?"

His mouth twisted wryly. "*Never Too Late*," he said and cast an amused glance at Julie.

"Seems appropriate," she murmured as she returned his smile. Deep within herself she prayed that it wasn't too late for them.

When his hand reached for hers, Julie felt a shimmering warmth skid up her arm from his touch. It had always been like that. Daniel was capable of stirring sensations in her she had only dreamed existed. Never would she be able to respond like this to another man.

The dinner was wonderful and the comedy had both of them amused and laughing. At least for those few hours, they set aside their difficulties and were man and wife without the past intruding.

"Would you like to go someplace for a drink?" Daniel asked on their way out of the Crown Uptown Dinner Theater.

"We could if you like," she agreed, "but I think I'd prefer a hot cup of coffee in our own kitchen so I can prop up my feet. I should have known better than to wear tight shoes."

"If you promise to be sensible the next time I take you to dinner, then I'll rub them for you." Daniel admonished with a lazy smile.

"You're on." It felt so good to joke with him. Tonight it was so easy to pretend that they were exactly as they appeared to be: a loving husband and wife enjoying an evening out together.

While Julie made them a cup of cappuccino, Daniel turned on the stereo. Mellow music filled the condominium, a love ballad so beautiful that for a moment Julie was lost in the meaningful words.

She carried the cups into the living room and sat on the opposite end of the sofa from her husband. "Here." She swung her feet onto his lap. "Do your magic."

While she sipped from the tiny cup of creamy coffee, Daniel gently massaged her feet, rubbing the aches until she sighed with pleasure.

"Why do you wear those silly things? You've got a blister on your heel."

"I know," she muttered, "but they're the only decent pair of dress shoes I have."

"Is that a hint for me to buy you a new wardrobe?"

Julie went completely still. She swung her feet onto the floor. "No," she answered evenly. It was difficult to infer from his tone of voice if he was teasing or sincere. She studied his face, but any telling emotion was hidden behind a noncommittal expression.

"A husband enjoys buying his wife gifts. You certainly had no difficulty accepting things from me in the past. You've kept them too, if the pearls are an indication."

"I kept every part of you I could," she whispered through the uncertainty. Her gaze fell on the television and she stiffened with bewilderment. The framed engagement picture was missing. Her eyes shot to the bookcase, thinking he may have moved it.

"What happened to the picture?" She rolled to her bare feet. "I put it here this morning and now it's gone."

"I put it away."

"Away?" she echoed in disbelief. "What do you mean by away?"

Daniel stood and stalked to the opposite side of the living room. "It's in your bedroom."

"But why?" she cried again, watching his reaction. She felt unbelievably hurt.

"Because I was angry and took it out on the photo."

Julie went pale. "You . . . didn't destroy it, did you?"

"No, but I was tempted. I don't want anything around to remind me of that time in my life."

"I see," she said and breathed heavily, fighting off the pain that came at her in waves. She refused to give in to the tears. For a minute she thought she glimpsed pain in his eyes. But he didn't answer her. Instead he walked into his den and closed the door.

Julie was shaking so badly that the cappuccino sloshed over the rim of the cup and into the saucer as she carried it into the kitchen. After rinsing out the cups she returned to the living room and removed the other mementos she'd placed there. Those items, however small, meant a great deal to her. She couldn't bear to have Daniel reject them as he had the photograph.

Her sleep was troubled. She woke from a fitful slumber at three, her heart heavy. Just when it looked like she was making some progress with Daniel, something would happen and she'd realize how far they had to go.

Slipping from the bed, she wandered into the kitchen and poured herself a glass of milk. She stood at the picture window, looking down on the silent, sleeping city below. She sensed, more than heard Daniel come up behind her. Not moving, Julie remained as she was.

"You couldn't sleep?"

"No." The one word tumbled from her throat as the tears filled and shimmered in her eyes.

Gently, his hand clasped her shoulders and he pressed his face into her hair. "Julie, I'm sorry about the picture. The minute I saw how much it meant to you I regretted taking it down. To be honest, I wasn't sure why you put it out. I thought you wanted to torment me." His fingers smoothed the dark hair from her temple.

"Torment you?" Abruptly, she turned, her eyes seeking his in the moonlight. Dark, dancing shadows flickered against the opposite wall, making it impossible to read his expression.

He took the glass of milk from her hand and set it aside. With an infinite tenderness he brought her into the warm circle of his arms. His chin rested against the top of her head as his hands roamed up and down her back in a massaging, rotating motion.

How long he held her, Julie didn't know. It felt so right to be in his arms again. In some ways it was as if she'd never left.

A finger under her chin lifted her mouth to his. Her response was automatic. Julie stood on tiptoes and fit her body to his, feeling Daniel resist momentarily as she melted against him.

"I'm sorry, Julie," he whispered on a husky note and relaxed, kissing her again.

"I know," she whispered and tantalizingly brushed her lips over his. Daniel moaned and hungrily claimed her mouth, holding her so close it was difficult to breathe.

"I won't make you cry again," he promised as his fingers smoothed the dark hair from her temple. His eyes were shining into hers and Julie sighed longingly and pressed her face to his shoulder. Nestled in the comfort of his embrace, she tried unsuccessfully to stifle a yawn.

"Come on, sleepyhead," he whispered and kissed the top of her head. "I'll tuck you in." With arms around each other's waists, Daniel led her back to the bedroom. Her heart thundered in her breast as he helped her into the bed and stood above her. He wanted her, Julie was sure of it. She was his wife and he longed to take her in his arms and love her as a husband. Yet he stood as he was, his face revealing the battle he waged within himself.

"Good night," he whispered finally, turning away.

"Good night," she repeated, struggling to disguise her own frustration. He lingered in the doorway and Julie's heart was beating like a locomotive. She sat up, using her elbows for leverage. "Daniel?"

"Yes?" He turned back eagerly.

"Thank you for tonight. I enjoyed the show."

"I did too," he said softly. "We'll do it again soon." He hesitated. "Next time I'll take you to Gatsby's."

"Really?"

"If you'd like we could take up tennis again."

"I'd like that," she responded happily, "very much."

"Tomorrow?"

"All right, if you want."

To his credit, Daniel did play a set of tennis with her the following morning. But he repeatedly glanced at his wristwatch, obviously not enjoying their match. He beat her easily, but then it had been a long time since Julie had played anyone who challenged her the way Daniel did. He seemed uncommunicative and out of sorts by the time they finished. It would have been better not to have played at all. She couldn't understand his attitude. And part of the reason she wanted to play was so she could meet his friends. Daniel introduced her to no one.

"Half the morning's gone," he commented on their way off the courts. Again he glanced at his watch impatiently. "I've got several things that need to be done this afternoon."

Julie remained tight-lipped as they returned to the condominium. He'd been the one to suggest the game, not her. Almost immediately Daniel closed himself in his den. When lunch was ready a half hour later, Julie went into his room to find him poring over books and papers. He barely noticed that she was there.

"Would you prefer to eat in here or in the kitchen?"

Daniel glanced up surprised. "Here."

Julie brought in a tray with tomato soup and two grilled cheese sandwiches.

"Thanks," he muttered.

Julie ate a silent meal while leafing through the thick Sunday paper. Later in the afternoon she did the weekly shopping and a few other errands. On her way back to the condominium, Julie stopped off at the hospital. Clara Van Deen was being transferred out of intensive care the next morning and Julie promised to stop in for a visit on her way home from work the following evening.

On the return trip home, Julie picked up hamburgers at a drive-in for their dinner. To her surprise, Daniel remained in his den. "You're still at it?"

He looked up and nodded. "This case is more involved than I thought."

"I brought you some dinner."

"Good, I can use a break. What'd you make?"

Julie glanced at him guiltily. "Well, I didn't exactly cook anything. I brought hamburgers home."

Chapter Seven

"Married life doesn't seem to agree with you," Sherry commented, watching Julie work.

"What do you mean?" Julie knew she wasn't doing a good job of hiding her feelings. Another week had passed and just when she thought the tension was lessening between her and Daniel something would happen to set them back. They hardly spoke in the mornings. Even during the drive downtown he was strangely quiet, preoccupied. In the evenings they visited his mother, came home and ate dinner. Almost immediately afterward, he'd hole himself up in his den. Sometimes Julie wondered if he was aware of her at all. He treated her more like a roommate than a wife. She didn't know when he slept. He seemed to be avoiding her as much as possible.

"Maybe I should keep my mouth shut," Sherry continued, "but you don't have the look of a happy bride."

Julie bit into her trembling bottom lip as she opened a file and looked at the names with unseeing eyes. "I don't feel much like a bride."

"But why?"

A tear traced a wet trail down Julie's pale cheek. "Daniel's busy right now. It seems I hardly see him."

Sherry rolled her chair close to Julie's desk and handed her friend a tissue. "Believe me," Sherry said sympathetically, "I know the feeling of abandonment well. That's how all my problems with Andy started. He worked so many long hours that we didn't have time to be a couple anymore. He was so involved with his job that eventually we drifted apart. It got to be that he was home so little of the time that I'd been gone a week before he even knew I was missing."

Julie tried to laugh but her voice came out sounding like a sick toad. Just then their employer came out of his office. He started to say something before noticing Julie blowing her nose. He paused, glanced from Sherry to Julie and quickly retreated into his office again. The two women looked at each other and broke into helpless giggles.

Ten minutes later, Mr. Barrett returned. "I was wondering..." he said and nervously cleared his throat. "Would you two like to take an extra half hour for lunch today? It's been a hectic week."

Julie and Sherry exchanged surprised glances. "We'd love it. Right, Julie?"

"Right," Julie concurred, doing her best to hide a second giggle. Poor Mr. Barrett, he didn't know what to think.

The long lunch with Sherry proved to be just the tonic Julie needed to raise her sagging spirits.

"You know," Sherry said between bites of her chicken and cashew salad, "if I had it to do all over I'd make it so Andy never wanted to leave the house again."

Julie stirred her clam chowder without much interest. Her appetite had been nonexistent lately and with little wonder. "How do you mean?"

"Think about it." Sherry leaned against the table, her eyes sparkling mischievously. "We're both reasonably attractive women. There are ways for a wife to keep a husband home nights." Demurely she lowered her thick lashes. "Subtle ways, of course."

"Of course," Julie repeated, her thoughts spinning. Sherry didn't know the details of her problems with Daniel, but her co-worker was so amazingly astute that Julie wondered if Sherry had somehow discovered her secret.

As the day progressed, Julie gave more thought to Daniel's actions. In the beginning he'd been bitter, but as the weeks progressed, time had healed that aggressive hostility. He'd told her after taking down their engagement photo that he wouldn't hurt her again. And he hadn't. If anything, he was all the more gentle with her. Only the other night, she'd found him holding their photo and studying their young, happy faces. Julie had held her breath, worrying about his reaction. She feared he would look at their picture and remember the pain and embarrassment she had caused him. Instead his gaze had held an odd tenderness. He hadn't known she'd seen him and she'd been puzzled when he retreated into his den. It made sense that if he'd forgiven her, if he loved her and wanted her, that he'd come to her. Julie was beginning to hate that guest bedroom. She didn't belong there; she was his wife, and she longed to be so in every way.

In the weeks since their wedding, Daniel had only touched and kissed her a few times and yet she'd seen the desire in his eyes. He wanted her. He spent the evenings avoiding her for fear of what would happen otherwise. His male pride and ego were punishing them both.

A secret smile touched Julie's eyes as she recalled the pearly-white satin nightgown she'd recently admired in a department store window. Perhaps she could do as Sherry suggested and lure her husband to her bed without injuring either of their sensitive egos. The more she contemplated such an action, the more confident she became.

After work that evening Julie and Daniel drove silently to the hospital. Mrs. Van Deen was sitting up in bed and smiled warmly, holding out her hand to Julie as they came into the room.

"My dears," she murmured with a happy light glinting from her tired eyes, "it's so good to see you."

"Mother." Daniel kissed her wrinkled cheek and held Julie close to his side with a hand at her neck.

"Julie, you're looking especially pretty. That color agrees with you."

Daniel looked at his wife as if seeing her for the first time that day. His eyes softened measurably as he noted the way the soft pink dress molded gracefully to her. A smile touched his eyes. "She certainly does," he said as his hand slipped around her waist.

"How are you feeling?" Julie centered her attention on Daniel's mother, thinking how good it felt when Daniel played the role of the loving husband. Soon he wouldn't be pretending, she vowed.

"Better," Clara said with a sigh. "The doctor said he'd never seen a woman make a swifter recovery. But I told him I have something to live for now. My son has the wife he's always wanted and I shall soon have the grandchildren I've dreamed about holding."

Daniel's fingers bit unmercifully into Julie's middle and she had to suck in her breath to keep from crying out. Her hand moved over his and it was an effective way of letting him know he was hurting her. Immediately, his grip slackened.

"My grandchild will have the bluest eyes," Mrs. Van Deen continued, oblivious to the tension in the room. "My husband's eyes were blue. So blue I swear they were deeper than any sea. I wish you'd known him, Julie," she continued, lost in a world of happy memories. "He would have loved you just as I do. He was a fine man."

"I'm sure he was," Julie replied thoughtfully.

"A lot like Daniel."

Julie glanced up at her husband; her eyes were captured by the warmth of his look. Daniel's mother continued speaking, reminiscing about her life with August Van Deen.

When Julie and Daniel returned to the condominium that evening Julie released a long sigh.

"What was that about?" Daniel asked gruffly.

"What?"

"That moan. Do you want me to apologize because my mother likes to remember the happy years she spent with my father?"

Julie stared back at him in shocked disbelief. She'd thought they'd made more progress than to have Daniel accuse her of something like that. "Of course not," she murmured, unable to disguise the hurt.

"Then why the sigh?" He remained defensive.

"I . . . I was thinking how much I wanted our lives to be as rich and rewarding."

"I'm sorry, Julie, I didn't mean to snap at you." Daniel's rich dark eyes softened before he turned and delivered his briefcase into his den.

"I understand," she whispered in return. It was nearly seven and they hadn't eaten dinner. They were both hungry and tired.

While the noodles were cooking, Julie changed clothes, donning tight navy-blue cords and a thin sweater that outlined the ripe fullness of her breasts. For good measure she refreshed her makeup and dabbed on Daniel's favorite perfume, then returned to finish preparing dinner.

Daniel looked surprised as he joined her in the kitchen. He studied her for a tense moment as if noting something was different.

"I didn't want to spill anything on my dress," she told him, hiding a smile.

He answered her with a short nod, but he couldn't seem to keep his eyes off her as she deftly moved around the tiny kitchen.

He didn't talk much while they ate, but that wasn't unusual. Perhaps Julie was reading too much into his actions. After so many years of living alone he could simply prefer to keep his thoughts to himself.

With seduction plots brewing in her head, every bite of her dinner seemed to stick in her throat and after a few minutes she stood and scraped half her dinner down the garbage disposal. Absently she placed her plate in the dishwasher.

"I thought I was doing dishes."

"There are only a few things."

"Hey, we made a deal. When you cook, I wash the dishes," he said. "Now scoot."

Having been ousted from the kitchen, Julie sat watching the television, but her mind was not on the situation comedy.

Daniel worked in the kitchen, but several times Julie felt his eyes rest on her. A couple of times she glanced up and smiled sweetly at him.

"A penny for your thoughts," he said, bringing her a cup of fresh coffee.

Julie swallowed a laughing gasp. "You wouldn't want to know," she teased. "You'd run in the opposite direction."

"That sounds interesting."

"I promise you it is."

Daniel surprised her by sitting in the wing-backed chair beside her. "Julie." He took the remote control and muted the television. "Can we talk a minute?"

"Sure." Expectantly, she turned toward him.

"I haven't been the best of company lately." He hesitated.

"There's no need to apologize," she told him. "I understand."

"How do you mean?"

"You must be exhausted. Heaven only knows when you sleep. You've been working yourself half to death this last month." Crossing her legs, Julie leaned back against the velvet cushion. "And then this evening your mother started talking about grandchildren and neither one of us has the courage to tell her we aren't sharing a bed." Nervously she glanced down at the steaming coffee. It was on the tip of her tongue to admit how much she wanted that to change, how much she longed to be his wife in the full sense of the word and give life to his children.

"Julie, listen." His voice was filled with a wealth of emotion.

The phone rang, directing their attention to the kitchen.

"I'll get it," Julie volunteered. Whoever it was, she'd get rid of him in a hurry. For the first time Julie felt like they were making giant strides in their marriage. Their conversation was far more important than someone who wanted to sell them siding for a house or steam clean their carpet. "Hello," she said into the receiver.

A pregnant pause followed.

"Hello," Julie repeated.

"Who's this?" the husky female voice returned.

"Julie Van Deen," she answered.

"So it's true," came the hushed words, coated with shocked pain.

"And you're...?" Julie squared her shoulders, already knowing it had to be the woman Jim Patterson had mentioned on the tennis courts that day. A hundred times since, Julie had bitten back questions about the other woman. But something deep inside had held her back.

"Kali Morgan," the woman answered.

An icy chill raced up Julie's spine. "Would you like to talk to Daniel?"

Kali paused. "No. Just...just give him my best...to you both."

"Thank you," Julie murmured. Hurt and confused, she replaced the phone.

"Who was it?" Daniel was looking at her expectantly.

Twisting around, Julie clasped her hands together behind her back. "An old friend of yours." Her voice was incredibly weak.

"Who?" Daniel repeated.

"Someone who obviously didn't know you had a wife."

"Kali." The word was a statement, not a question.

All this time Julie had assumed that Daniel really wanted her as his wife. Now that she'd heard the shocked pain of the other woman's voice, Julie's confidence crumbled. "You didn't tell her, did you?"

Daniel stood, but the width of the living room remained between them. "Julie." He sounded unsure, worried. "What did Kali say?"

Her eyes searched his face, silently studying him. The man who stared back had become a stranger. Her heart throbbed painfully and she pressed her palm over it, not understanding how any pain could be so intense. Daniel seemed to think that he needn't tell Kali that he had married. Maybe he believed that given time, Julie would leave him and he could go back to his old life. As callous as it sounded, perhaps he was holding on to his options so that if his mother didn't survive this ordeal he could quickly annul their marriage. Maybe he was looking for ways to hurt her as she'd hurt him. If so, he'd succeeded. She'd been so stupid. So naive.

Slowly Daniel took a step toward her. "Julie, don't look at me like that."

Paralysis gripped her throat as she moved down the hall to her room. The bag containing her lovely new nightgown rested on the top of her bed. She stared at it in disbelief. Only minutes before she'd plotted to seduce her husband.

Daniel followed her down the hall. "Julie, be reasonable. Surely you didn't think I've lived the last few years like a priest."

Everything went incredibly still as hot tears filled her eyes, scalding her cheeks as they crashed over the wall of her lashes. "For three years my heart grieved for you until I couldn't take it anymore...and I came back because... because facing your bitterness was easier than trying to forget you."

"Julie." His voice took on a soft, pleading quality. He paused as if desperately searching for the right words.

"Kali and I have been dating for several months," he assured her. "But Kali's in the past. I haven't touched her since the day I saw you in the elevator."

"Touched her," Julie repeated shakily. "Is that supposed to reassure me?" she cried. "You haven't touched me either!" Her stomach heaved convulsively and she rushed into the bathroom.

Daniel followed her. Julie stood in front of the sink and pressed a cool rag over her face, attempting to ignore him.

"What did you expect me to do the rest of my life?" he shouted. "You walked out on me!"

Julie turned and raked her eyes over him with open disdain. "You didn't tell her we were married!" She hiccuped on a sob, convinced Daniel hadn't a hint why she was so upset. "And...and all these years I've loved you until coming back was better than facing life without you."

"Don't tell me that there hasn't been anyone in—"

"Yes," she shouted. "I seldom dated. You were the only man I ever loved. The only man I could ever love." She wept into the wash cloth.

"Julie," he pleaded softly, standing behind her, a gentle hand on each shoulder.

"Don't touch me," she shouted and shrugged her upper torso to break his light hold. "Your tastes have changed, haven't they, Daniel? You must find me incredibly stupid to have cherished the belief you still care." She couldn't finish and abruptly turned from him.

Roughly he pulled her into his arms. "You're going to listen to me, Julie. Perhaps for the first time since we met one another we're going to have an honest discussion."

Julie was in no mood to be reasonable. "No," she cried, rushing back to her room. Grabbing the package from her bed, she shoved it in his arms. "Here. Once I'm gone you might find this useful for one of your other women." With that she slammed the door, and collapsed into tears.

Sherry was at her desk when Julie entered the office the following morning.

"Morning," Julie greeted the other woman, doing her best to disguise her unhappiness. She knew she looked terrible. Cosmetics had been unable to camouflage the effects of the sleepless night. For the first time since their marriage, Daniel left for work without Julie. When she'd stirred with the alarm, the condominium had been as silent as a tomb and just about as welcoming.

"Morning," Sherry replied without looking up.

Although she was tied up with her own problems, it was obvious Sherry had been crying again. It took all her restraint not to join her friend and burst into tears. "What happened now?" Julie pried gently.

Wiping the moisture aside with the back of her hand, Sherry sat up and sniffled. "After our talk yesterday, I got to thinking about how much I miss Andy...so I saw him last night."

"Was he with another woman again?" That would explain Sherry's tears.

"No, this time he was with me. I...I told him I wasn't positive I wanted the divorce and that I thought we should talk things over more thoroughly before we take such a serious step."

"I think that's wise." Julie recognized how difficult it had been for Sherry to contact her husband and suggest that they meet. She and Daniel weren't the only ones with an overabundance of pride.

"We sat and talked for ages and, well, Andy ended up spending the night." She cast her gaze to the desktop. Her fingers nervously toyed with a tissue.

"Well it seems that not all lines of communication are down," Julie murmured, thinking how much she'd wanted to 'communicate' with her own husband.

"I...I thought so too. But this morning when I woke up, Andy was gone. No note. Nothing. He regrets everything; I know he does. Now I feel cheap and used and..." She paused and blew into the tissue.

"Sherry." While battling her own unhappiness, Julie moved behind the other girl and gently patted her back. Only the day before they'd been like teenagers, sharing girlish secrets. So much for the best-laid plans. Like a pair of idealistic fools, they had hoped everything would be perfect because they were in love with their husbands. "I'm sure there's a perfectly logical explanation why Andy left." Julie tried to sound optimistic, but knew she'd failed.

"I feel like a one-night stand."

"You are married." So was she, for that matter, and it didn't seem to help how she felt.

"Yes, but not for very much longer."

"Things have a way of working out for the best." Julie tried to sound confident, but she didn't know whom she was speaking to: Sherry or herself. "If you love Andy then I wouldn't worry."

Sherry shook her head, doing her best to smile. "How did everything go for you?"

"Fine," she lied and, at Sherry's narrowed look, amended, "Terrible." Sniffling, she reached for a tissue.

The office door opened and Julie and Sherry immediately lowered their heads, pretending to be absorbed in their work. Mr. Barrett passed through the room with little more than the usual morning greeting.

"He must think we've gone off the deep end," Sherry whispered once he was safely inside his office.

"Maybe we have."

"Maybe," Sherry agreed.

They worked companionably, taking turns answering the demands of the telephone. When she had a free moment, Sherry lifted her purse to the desk and took out her makeup case. "Count your blessings, Julie. You're much too level-headed to do some of the dumb things I've done with this marriage. Can you imagine anyone walking out and leaving a man as good as Andy?"

Julie had to struggle not to confess that she had done exactly that. "Maybe you should contact Andy yourself," Julie suggested in a low voice that bordered on tremulous.

"I couldn't...not after what happened."

"I'm sure he'd be willing to talk, especially after last night," Julie insisted.

"I wish that was true," Sherry stated miserably. "But somehow, I doubt it."

Daniel was already in his den when Julie returned home that evening. Clara had let it slip that her son had been by earlier to visit. Her astute mother-in-law studied the dark shadows under Julie's eyes, but didn't comment. Julie was grateful. Her composure was paper thin as it was. Answering questions would have been her undoing.

Hanging up her jacket in the hall closet, Julie headed for the kitchen. A package of veal cutlets rested on the countertop and, releasing a sigh, Julie reached for the frying pan.

"I thought it was my turn to cook," Daniel said heavily from behind her.

"All right," she murmured without turning. "But I'm not very hungry. If you don't mind, I think I'll lie down for a while."

He was so long answering her that Julie feared another confrontation.

"Okay," he said at last. "I'll call you when dinner's ready."

"Fine." They were treating each other like polite strangers. Worse. They seemed afraid to even look at each other.

Flipping the light switch, Julie moved into the room and sat dejectedly on the side of the mattress. A month into her marriage and she was little more than an unwelcome guest in Daniel's life. The pillow comforted her head as she leaned back and closed her eyes.

It seemed only minutes later when Daniel knocked softly against the open door. "Dinner's ready."

Momentarily Julie toyed with the idea of telling him she wasn't feeling well. But Daniel would easily see through that excuse. No, it was better to face him. Things couldn't possibly get much worse.

The table was already set when Julie pulled out the chair and sat. Daniel joined her.

"Your mother looked better tonight."

Daniel deposited a spoonful of wild rice on his plate before he answered. "She asked about you. I didn't know if you'd be stopping in to see her or not."

"I did," she told him inanely.

"So I surmised."

Five minutes passed and neither spoke. Julie looked out the window and noted the thick gray clouds rolling in. Daniel's gaze followed hers. "It looks like rain."

Julie nodded. Since they had nothing in common—no shared interests—there was little to discuss beyond his mother and the weather.

Another awkward silence filled the kitchen until Julie stood and started to load the dishwasher.

"I'll do that," Daniel volunteered.

"It's my turn."

"You're beat."

"No more than you," she countered, stubbornly filling the sink with hot tap water.

The dishes took all of ten minutes. The hum of the dishwasher followed her into the hallway. The thought of spending another night in front of the television was intolerable. But going out was equally unsavory. Daniel had disappeared inside his den and Julie doubted that she'd be seeing him again that evening, which was just as well.

Deciding to read, she returned to her room. It wasn't until she turned that a glimmer of satin caught her attention. Setting the book aside, she discovered that the lovely, alluring gown she'd shoved at Daniel was hanging in her closet. Lovingly her fingers touched the silky smoothness. Tears jammed her throat. She'd so wanted things to be different. A soft sob escaped and she bit into the corner of her mouth.

"Julie." Daniel spoke from outside her room. "Are you all right?"

Angrily she turned on him. "I'm just wonderful. Just leave me alone." With a sweep of her arm, she closed her door, effectively cutting him off.

For a stunned moment nothing happened. Then her door was knocked open with such force that it was a wonder it wasn't ripped from the wall.

Julie gasped as Daniel marched into her room and lifted her from the floor and hauled her in his arms.

"Put me down," she cried, kicking her legs uselessly, but her efforts only caused him to tighten his grip.

Chapter Eight

Furiously Julie wiped the tears from her face. "You didn't even tell Kali you were married," she shouted.

"I couldn't," he shouted right back. "She was in England on a business trip."

Julie's anger died a swift and sudden death. She went completely still and stared into her husband's dark, angry eyes. "Gone?"

"I don't know what's going on in that twisted little mind of yours. I'm not even sure why it matters if Kali knows or not. For heaven's sake—we're married. What the hell has Kali got to do with us now?"

She offered him a trembling smile through her tears. "Nothing," she whispered, laughing softly. "Nothing at all."

"What's so amusing now?" he barked, clearly not understanding the swift change in her mood. He sank onto the side of his bed, his hold on her loosening as she rested in his lap.

"You wouldn't understand," she murmured linking her arms around his neck and kissing the corner of his mouth.

"I thought you were planning... Never mind." Gently she covered his mouth with hers.

"Julie," he groaned, his hands folding her in his embrace.

"Are you really tired of playing games?" she asked, spreading a series of sweet kisses over his face. Her eager lips sought his temple and nose, slowly progressing downward toward his mouth, teasing him with short, playful kisses along the way.

"Yes," he moaned, gripping the back of her head and directing her lips to his. "Oh, Lord, yes."

A pervading warmth flowed through her. "Oh, Daniel, Daniel, what took you so long?"

Slowly his hands slid across her breasts as he began unfastening the tiny buttons of her blouse. All the while his mouth moved over hers in eager passion. Frustrated with the small pearl-shaped fastenings, he abandoned the effort and broke the kiss long enough to try to pull the blouse over her head.

Breathless and smiling softly, Julie stopped him. "You've waited a whole month for me. Another thirty seconds shouldn't matter."

As she freed her blouse, Daniel cupped the soft mounds of her breasts and buried his face in the fragile hollow of her throat. "I couldn't live another month like the last one," he told her, his gaze drinking in the velvet smoothness of her ivory skin. "I couldn't sleep knowing you were just down the hall from me. Every time I closed my eyes all I could see was you. The only thing that helped was working until I was ready to drop."

"Oh, love, and I wanted you so much." Sliding her hands up and down his muscled shoulders, she felt the coiled tension ease out of him.

Hungrily he devoured her mouth. "You're my wife, Julie, the way you were always meant to be."

"I know, love, I know." Her heart singing, Julie gave herself to the only man she had ever loved. She had accom-

plished everything she'd set out to do in Wichita and more.
So much more.

"Wake up, sleepyhead," Daniel whispered lovingly in her
ear. "It's morning."

"Already," Julie groaned, running her hand over her
husband's muscular ribs and resting her head in the crook
of his arm. Her eyes refused to open.

"Are you happy?" Daniel asked, kissing the crown of her
head.

"Oh, yes."

"Me, too." In long soothing movements, he stroked her
bare arm. "I never stopped loving you, Julie. I tried, believe me I tried every way I could to forget you. For a time
I convinced myself I hated you. But the day I saw you in the
elevator, I knew I'd been fooling myself. One look and I realized I'd never love another woman the way I love you."

Raising her head, Julie rolled onto her stomach and kissed
him with infinite sweetness, slanting her mouth over his.

The hunger of his response surprised her. Quickly he altered their positions so that Julie was on her back looking
up at him. His eyes burned into hers.

"Daniel," she protested, but not too strenuously, "we'll
be late for work."

"Yes, we will," he agreed, "very late."

An hour later, while Julie dressed, Daniel fried their eggs,
humming as he worked.

"My, you're in a good mood this morning," she teased,
sliding her arms around his middle and pressing her face
against the muscular back.

Daniel chuckled. "And with good reason." He twisted
around and pulled her into his arms, kissing her soundly. "I
love you."

Her eyes drank in the tenderness in his expression as she
slowly nodded. "I know."

"I think it's time we took that diamond ring hanging
around your neck and put it on your finger, where it be-

longs," he told her gently. He helped her remove the chain and slid the solitaire diamond onto her finger with a solemnness that told her how seriously he took his vows. "I wanted you the minute the minister pronounced us man and wife," he admitted sheepishly. "I had to get out of the condominium that day because I knew what would happen if I stayed."

"And I thought—"

"I know what you thought," he said, taking her back into his embrace. "It was exactly what I wanted you to believe. My ego had suffered enough for one day. I couldn't tolerate it if you knew how badly I wanted to make love to you then." His chin brushed the top of her head.

The workdays flew by and after a wonderful weekend together, Julie and Daniel spent a quiet Sunday with his mother at the hospital. Clara Van Deen's heart surgery was scheduled for the next Tuesday and both Julie and Daniel wanted to be with her as much as possible.

"Have you told Julie about her surprise yet?" Clara questioned Daniel as he wheeled his mother into the brilliant sunshine of the hospital courtyard. The day was glorious, birds chirped a contented chorus and the sky was as blue as Julie could ever remember seeing it.

"Surprise?" Julie's attention wandered from the beauty of the day. "What surprise?"

"Oh, dear." Mrs. Van Deen twisted in the chair and glanced over her shoulder at her son. "I didn't let the cat out of the bag, did I?"

Leaning forward, Daniel kissed his mother's pale cheek. "Only a little," he whispered reassuringly. "I was waiting until later."

"Later?" Julie spoke again. "What's happening later? Daniel, you know how much I hate secrets."

"This one you'll enjoy," her husband promised. His eyes held a special light that was meant for her alone. He laughed at her puzzled expression and slid a hand around her waist and kissed her lightly on the cheek. "I won't make you wait any longer than this after-noon,'' he whispered in her ear. The tender look in his eyes was enough to make her feel light-headed.

After an hour in the glorious sunshine, Clara Van Deen announced in a frail voice, ''I think it's time for me to go back inside. I tire so easily.''

Immediately, Daniel stood, gripped the wheelchair and prepared to wheel her inside. ''We shouldn't have kept you out so long.''

''Nonsense,'' Clara protested. ''I've been wanting to feel the sun for days.''

Julie followed them back into the hospital corridor and her mother-in-law's room. Within half an hour Clara was in bed and asleep, her tired features relaxed.

Standing on opposite sides of the hospital bed with the railing raised, Daniel whispered, ''Are you ready for your surprise now?''

Julie nodded eagerly. For days she'd been aware he was planning something. The last two mornings they'd driven to work separately because he had late business appointments. Or so he claimed. Julie wasn't sure. He had a gleam in his eye and several times he looked as if he wanted to tell her something, but swallowed back whatever it was.

During the past few days, Julie had never known such blissful happiness. Daniel was more tender and loving then she'd ever dreamed. It astonished her how much he desired and loved her.

Their hands joined, they strolled out of the hospital to the parking lot. Daniel opened and closed her car door for her and stole a lingering kiss when no one was looking.

''Aren't you going to give me any hints?'' Julie felt his gaze rest on her warmly.

''Not a one. You'll just have to be patient,'' he admonished her gently.

He smiled at her and Julie felt the magnetic pull of sensual excitement only he was able to generate within her. Julie couldn't imagine loving him any more than she did right this moment, this hour, this day.

Daniel took the freeway that led out of town and drove past the densely populated suburbs. Finally, he exited and turned down a long winding road that led into the countryside.

"For heaven's sake, Daniel, where are you taking me? Timbuktu?"

He chuckled. "Wait and see."

Again Julie was pulled into the magnetic aura of this man she loved. Everything was so perfect. So right.

When he pulled the car into a long driveway that led to a newly built two-story house, Julie was awestruck.

"What do you think?" His eyes sought hers; one brow lifted inquisitively.

"What do I think?" she repeated, feeling the waves of shock dissipate. "You mean this...house...is my surprise?"

"We're signing the final papers for it Monday morning. There are several things that are awaiting your decision. The builder needs to know what color you want for the kitchen countertop, the design of the tile for the bathrooms. From what I understand there are several swatches of carpet for you to look at while we're here."

Julie nodded, not knowing what to say. She couldn't understand why Daniel wanted a place so far from the city. It would mean a long drive both ways in heavy traffic every day. Julie loved the city. Daniel knew that.

"Come inside and I'll give you the grand tour." He climbed out of the car, walked around to her side and gave her his hand. "You're going to love this place."

Julie wasn't convinced as his words echoed through her numb brain. Why would he pick out something as important as a house without consulting her? Shock waves trembled through her body as Daniel took out the key and opened the front door, pushing it aside so she could enter before him. At first she was overwhelmed by the magnificence of the home. A sunken living room contained a massive floor-to-ceiling brick fireplace. The crystal chandelier in the formal dining room looked like something out of a

Hollywood movie. No expense had been spared to make this home an opulent showplace. But the kitchen was compact and the only real eating space was in the formal dining room. Nor did the house have a family room.

"What do you think?" Daniel asked eagerly.

"Nice." Julie couldn't think of anything else to say. It was a beautiful home, that she couldn't deny, but it wasn't something she would have chosen. In many ways it was exactly what she wouldn't want.

"The swimming pool is this way." He led her to the sliding glass doors off the kitchen and to a deck. A kidney-shaped pool was just outside. Although the cement structure was empty, Julie could picture aqua-blue water gently lapping against the tiled side.

"Nice," she repeated when he glanced expectantly toward her, seeking her reaction.

"If you think this is impressive, wait until you see the master bedroom." Daniel took her limp hand and pulled her through the hallway.

The room was so huge that Julie blinked twice. Fireplace, walk-in closets, sunken tub in the private bath. Everything anyone could ever want. But not Julie.

"What about the other bedrooms?" By some miracle she was able to force the question from her parched throat.

"Upstairs." His low voice was almost a caress.

Like a robot Julie followed him up the open stairway. Three large rooms led off a wide hallway. Another bedroom and a bath. The second room, without a closet, Julie assumed would become Daniel's den. The third room looked as if it was meant to be an art room with huge glass windows that overlooked the front of the house.

Although she made the appropriate comments, Julie felt as if someone had a strangle hold on her throat. Speaking became nearly impossible and she didn't know how much more of this she could take. Abruptly, she turned and walked down the stairs.

"Julie." Daniel followed her out the front door. "What's the matter?" His troubled gaze pierced her numbed senses.

Shaking her head, Julie tilted her chin to the sky, and fought for control of her raging emotions. That Daniel would look for and buy a house without consulting her struck her like arrows from the past. Memories returned to haunt her. She wasn't a naive teenager anymore. His mother had picked out their first home as a wedding present without consulting Julie. And now Daniel was doing it again. Anger, hurt and a myriad of emotions seemed to swarm around her like troublesome bees, stinging her pride and wounding her ego.

"You don't like it, do you?" A hint of challenge was evident in his voice.

"That's not it," she admitted flatly. She was angry with Daniel, and equally upset with herself. Most women would love a home like this. Unfortunately, she wasn't one of them.

"All right," Daniel breathed, his gaze scrutinizing her. "What don't you like? I'm sure whatever it is can be changed."

"Changed?" she flared back. "Can you change the location? I love Wichita. I want to live in the city. You've lived there all your life so what suddenly made the thought of the country so appealing?"

"Peace, solitude—"

She didn't allow him to finish. "What about the hour's commute in heavy traffic every morning and night?"

"I'll get used to it," he said, attempting to reason.

Her eyes flashed angrily at him. "Sure you will."

Crossing his arms over his muscular chest he seemed to be physically blocking out her words. "Is there anything else?"

Julie swallowed at the lump choking her throat. "Three years ago I didn't say anything when your mother bought a house without me so much as looking at it. I let everything build up inside until it exploded and I fled. I can't do that anymore. This is a beautiful home, but it's not a place for us. Someday I'd like to have children. This house isn't a family home. It's for a retired couple, or for a family with teenagers." She waved her hand accusingly at the two-story structure that seemed to be laughing back at her with all its magnificence.

Daniel frowned and the action drove deep grooves into his forehead.

"I . . . I appreciate what you're trying to do, but—"

"Be honest, Julie. You don't appreciate a thing about this house." A cynical smile twisted his mouth. He held open the car door for her and shut it once she was inside.

She waited until he was in the driver's seat. "Daniel." His name rushed out in a low breath as she exhaled. "I'm sorry I sound so ungrateful. But something as important as a home should be decided upon by both of us." She drew in a shaky breath. "I realize you were saving this as a surprise and I'm sorry if I ruined that."

Either he was caught up in his own disappointment and didn't hear her or he chose to ignore her. The tires squealed as he pulled out of the long driveway and onto the road.

On the drive home Julie sat miserably with her arms crossed. Moving into that house feeling the way she did would have destroyed her hard-won resolve. She'd come too far in three years to allow something like this to happen to her a second time.

The silence in the car was deafening. Daniel had wanted to surprise her. Maybe she hadn't expressed her feelings in the most subtle way, but surely he recalled what had happened with his mother.

Daniel looked pale under his tan, or maybe it was her imagination, Julie didn't know. When they arrived back at the condominium, he went directly into his den and made a series of phone calls while Julie struggled to understand what had motivated him. A dark cloud seemed to hang over their heads. Only that afternoon, Julie had doubted that anything could destroy their utopia. Now she realized how fleeting their happiness was.

Julie was cooking their evening meal when Daniel joined her. With her back to her husband, Julie made busywork at the stove, needlessly turning the few slices of beef every few seconds. "I wish you hadn't closed yourself off in the den," she began nervously. "I thought we were beyond that. I think it's important that we talk this out."

He didn't answer her.

"Daniel," she pleaded and turned to find him sitting at the table, reading the newspaper. "Are you giving me the silent treatment?"

He lowered the paper. "No."

"Then let's talk." Again she spoke to the front page of the paper. "If... if that house means so much to you then I'll adjust." Making a concession like this was the most difficult thing Julie had ever done. But her marriage was worth more than her pride.

Apparently engrossed in his paper, Daniel didn't speak for several long minutes. "You're right, it wasn't a good idea for me to have taken the bull by the horns."

"Then why are you so angry?" she pleaded.

With a slow deliberate motion he set the paper aside and wiped a hand over his face. "I don't know," he admitted honestly. "My mother claimed when you left that you were ungrateful for all we'd done for you. I'm beginning to understand what she meant. I bought that house for you, Julie, and for our lives together."

Julie could hardly believe what she'd heard. "What a horrible thing to drag up now. You're being completely unfair."

"Was it fair of you to walk out on me three years ago? Don't talk to me about fair."

The color washed out of her face as the shock of his words hit her.

Oblivious to her pain, Daniel raised the newspaper and continued reading.

A full minute passed before Julie could move. Numb with emotional turmoil, she turned off the stove and walked out of the kitchen.

Daniel claimed to have forgiven her, but he hadn't. Not in his heart. Tonight he'd wanted to hurt her because of his disappointment.

"Julie." His voice was filled with regret.

She heard his chair scrape against the floor before he followed her into the living room. "I didn't mean that."

"I doubt if that's true. I believe you meant every word." Julie swallowed tightly and by the sheer force of her will restrained the tears.

"Maybe I did at that," he said tightly.

The next thing Julie heard was the front door closing softly.

The following morning Julie left the condominium early, not waiting for Daniel. She was already at her desk when Sherry arrived for work.

"You're punctual as always," Sherry commented as she sat in her rollback chair and stuck her purse in the bottom desk drawer.

"I try to be," Julie said without looking up from her paperwork.

"I'm going to run down and grab a maple bar and coffee. Do you want me to pick up one for you?"

"Sure," Julie agreed rather than make an excuse as to why she wasn't hungry. She was counting out the change to hand Sherry when the office door opened.

Framed in the doorway was Daniel. A muscle worked convulsively in his lean jaw as he glared at her. Julie could see and feel his anger and the effort he made to control it.

Sherry glanced from one to the other and took in a deep breath. "If you'll excuse me, I'll run downstairs."

Silently, Julie's eyes thanked her friend. Understanding, Sherry winked and edged her way past Daniel.

"Don't do that to me again," he commanded in a low growl.

"I needed some time alone," she explained. "I thought you'd understand that.... You felt the same way yesterday."

"That was different," he snapped.

"If you can vanish until the small hours of the morning without an explanation then I have the right to leave for work unannounced.'' Angry now, Julie was astonished at how level her voice remained.

The phone rang and she swiveled around to answer it, presenting Daniel with a clear view of her back. Halfway through the conversation, she sensed he'd left. She couldn't see him, but the prickly sensation at the back of her neck eased and she felt the tense muscles of her shoulders relax.

Sherry returned by the time Julie had finished with the customer on the telephone. Her eyes were filled with questions, but Julie didn't feel up to making explanations.

''You have tomorrow off, don't you?'' she asked instead.

Julie had nearly forgotten. ''Yes. Daniel's mother is going in for heart surgery.''

A lump lodged in Julie's throat. With so many pressures tugging at Daniel he didn't need a cold war between them. Tonight, she'd insist they put an end to this. They were both adults and should be able to put their grievances aside.

The day dragged by and the visit with her mother-in-law that evening went well. Although Julie stopped at the hospital immediately after work, she learned that Daniel had already been and gone and they had only missed each other by a matter of a few minutes. If his mother noticed that anything was different, she said nothing.

Julie stayed later than usual with Clara. They chatted together, and talked about flowers, which Clara loved. Then the nurse arrived and gave the older woman a shot to help her relax. Julie stayed until she was confident Clara was asleep and resting comfortably.

Her heart burdened, Julie walked to the parking lot and her car. This misunderstanding with Daniel about the house couldn't have happened at a worse time. The first test of love in their marriage and they had both failed. Utterly and completely.

Daniel wasn't home when she came through the front door and Julie felt as if she were carrying the weight of the world on her shoulders. Where could he be? Briefly she wondered if he'd gone to Kali. Julie felt her heart constrict with pain. He wouldn't. She couldn't love him as much as she did and believe he could do something like that.

She forced herself to cook dinner, but had no appetite and only picked at the cutlet and salad. After washing her few dishes, she turned on the television. Every five minutes her eyes drifted to the wall clock. Where was Daniel? His mother was having major heart surgery in the morning. This was the time they needed each other more than ever. Julie turned off the television and went to bed.

Shadows flickered like old-time movies against the dark bedroom wall as Julie lay staring at the ceiling. Her tension-filled body produced a curious ache as if every part of her being was affected by the events of the past two days.

The front door clicked softly and Julie sat upright, her ears picking up even the slightest noise. When the sound of the first footsteps could be heard, she released her breath, unaware she'd been holding it. A quick look at the clock confirmed that it was after midnight.

Daniel paused in the open doorway of their room. Their eyes dueled in the dark. His were filled with challenge as if he dared her to comment on how late it was or demand to know where he'd been. She wouldn't, not when there were so many other things to say.

He loosened his tie as his eyes continued to hold hers in the moonlight. Still he didn't speak, his eyes mocking her with every movement as he took off the suit coat and carelessly tossed it over the back of a chair. The air in the room contained the stillness that settles over the earth before an electrical storm. Tension seemed to arc between them.

Frantically her mind searched for the right words. All the hours that she'd lain awake she could have been rehearsing what to say. Now her mind was a blank, empty.

Of its own volition, her hand reached out to him. For one heart-stopping moment Julie thought he was going to reject her. She watched as he stiffened and closed his eyes as though he couldn't bear to look at her. The dark lashes flickered open and with a muted groan he crossed the room and reached for her as a dying man reaches for life.

"I'm sorry," she whispered, the words rushing from her in a breathy murmur. "Oh, Daniel, I'm so sorry. We need each other now more than ever. Let's forget the house." She wrapped her arms around his neck and hugged him as if she could never let him go again. Julie discovered that she wanted to laugh away their hurts and at the same time had trouble restraining the tears of release.

Roughly his hands brushed the hair from her face and lifted it to study the light in her eyes.

Julie was confident every emotion she was experiencing was there for him to read.

"Julie," he groaned in a husky voice. The harshness began to leave his expression as if he couldn't believe the love she was offering him. He buried his face in the slim column of her neck and inhaled deeply. "I need you."

Julie understood what he was saying. "Yes," she breathed and weaved her hands through his hair, holding him against her. "I love you," she murmured, and with a contented sigh she pulled his mouth to hers.

An hour later, her head nestled against the cushion of his chest, Julie lovingly ran her fingers over her husband's ribs. "We can't settle all our arguments this way."

Daniel chuckled, his breath caressing the hairs at the top of her head. Gently his hand ran down the length of her spine and back in a soothing motion. "I think it has its advantages." His voice was both tender and warm.

"I feel terrible about Sunday. Everything I said and did was wrong. You wanted to surprise me and—"

"No." His hold tightened momentarily. "You were right. Anything as important as a house should be a mutual decision. Later when I got over being angry, I realized how unreasonable I'd been."

"I might not have overreacted if that hadn't happened before. It was like living a nightmare all over again." She shrugged one ivory shoulder, unsure of dragging the past into this moment. "Do you really want to live in the country?"

The pause was long enough to cause her to raise her head. "Not if you don't," he answered finally.

"My home is with you." She felt his smile against her hair and nestled closer to his warm body. Something was troubling Daniel, something more than his mother's ill health and pending surgery. Whatever it was had to do with their marriage. Julie didn't know what, but she had the feeling she would soon.

Chapter Nine

Daniel paced the waiting room as Julie sat in the vinyl-cushioned chair and attempted to read. Repeatedly, her concentration wandered from the magazine and she glanced at her wristwatch.

"What time is it?" Daniel inquired with a worried frown.

What he really wanted to know, Julie realized, was how much longer it would be. The doctor had assured them the surgical procedure would take at least five hours, and possibly longer.

"Anytime now," Julie answered and exhaled softly. They'd been in the waiting room most of the day. A nurse came at noon and suggested Julie and Daniel have lunch. But Julie couldn't have forced down anything and apparently Daniel felt the same way.

Her husband took the seat beside her and reached for her hand. "Have I told you how much I love you?" His eyes filled with tenderness.

Before Julie could answer, the doctor, clad in a green surgical gown, walked into the room. His brow was moist and he looked as exhausted as she felt. Automatically, both

Julie and Daniel stood. Daniel held onto her trembling hand with such force that her diamond cut into her fingers.

"Your mother did amazingly well," the doctor began without preamble. "Her chances appear to be excellent."

A pent-up breath escaped Julie's lungs and she smiled brightly at her husband, feeling as if the weight of the world had been lifted from her back.

"Can we see her?" Daniel inquired, his own relief evident in his voice.

Julie knew her husband well enough to know that he needed visual assurance of his mother's condition.

"Yes, but only for a few minutes. You both can go in. She'll be in intensive care for a few days, then if everything goes well she'll be placed on the surgical floor."

"How long will it be before she can come home?"

The doctor shook his head lightly. "It would be hard to say. As soon as two weeks, or as long as a month."

Julie had appreciated from the beginning the quiet support the doctors and staff had given regarding her mother-in-law's condition.

"Thank you, doctor." Julie gave him one of her brightest smiles. "Thank you very much."

With their hands linked, Julie and Daniel were led into the intensive care area. When Julie saw Daniel's mother her heart lurched. The tubes and bottles surrounding her mother-in-law gave the older woman a ghostly look. She was deathly pale. White hair against the white sheets... The figure blurred and for a moment Julie thought she was going to faint.

"Are you okay?" Daniel's voice was filled with concern as he placed a hand around her waist to hold her upright.

"I'm fine," she assured him, but was glad for the supporting arm.

Clara Van Deen's eyes fluttered open and she attempted to speak, but the words were slurred and unintelligible. She tried to lift one hand, but it was taped to a board to hold the IV in place.

Lovingly Daniel laid his hand over his mother's.

"I'm afraid I'm going to have to ask you to leave." The efficient looking woman in the spotless white uniform requested softly a couple of minutes later. "You're welcome to come back tomorrow, but for now Mrs. Van Deen needs to rest."

Julie thanked the nurse with a smile and watched an expression of tenderness move across her husband's face.

"We'll be back, Mother," he whispered softly.

The air outside the hospital felt fresh and clean. Julie paused to inhale several deep breaths. Although they had done nothing to require physical exertion Julie was exhausted. With her head resting against the back of the seat, she closed her eyes as Daniel drove the short distance to the condominium.

"Julie." A warm, caressing voice spoke softly in her ear. "Wake up. We're home."

Her eyes fluttered open and she did her best to suppress a yawn. "My goodness, I don't know why I should be so tired."

"We didn't get much sleep last night," he reminded her with a roguish grin. "And the way I feel right now we may not tonight either." He helped her out of the car and held her close to his side until they reached their door.

Daniel led her directly into the bedroom and pulled back the covers. "I want you to take a nice long nap and when you're rested Mother has ordered us to have a night on the town."

Julie opened and closed her eyes, already feeling the pull of slumber. Maybe today had been harder on her than she realized. "A night on the town?"

"I'm not teasing. Mother and I had a long talk yesterday and she feels that after we spent today at the hospital we deserve to go out."

Julie was about to protest.

"No arguing," Daniel said sternly, "Mother insisted."

The bed felt warm and welcoming. Daniel tucked her in and kissed her lightly across her brow.

"Aren't you going to rest?" Julie wanted to know.

"Honey, if I crawl in that bed with you it won't be to sleep." The sound of his chuckle was caressing and deep. He brushed the hair from her temple. "Actually I've got some papers to go over. That should take an hour or two. Just enough time for you to catch up on some sleep."

Julie relaxed against the fluffy pillow and pulled the blanket over her shoulder. Her mind drifted easily into happy, serene thoughts as she closed her eyes and sleep commanded the deepest recesses of her mind.

The next thing Julie knew, Daniel was beside her, holding her close, his breath fanning her cheek.

"Is it time to get ready for dinner?" she muttered, reveling in the delicious warmth of her bed and keeping her eyes closed.

"I think breakfast is more in order."

"Breakfast?" Her lashes flew up. "I couldn't have slept through the night. Could I?" She looked around, confused.

"I paraded a marching band through here late yesterday afternoon and you wouldn't budge."

Wiping the sleep from her face, Julie sat up and leaned against the oak headboard. "I can't believe I slept like that. I was dead to the world for fifteen hours or more."

"I imagine you're starved."

Strangely she wasn't. Even her usual morning cup of coffee didn't appeal to her. Once she ate breakfast, however, she realized how famished she actually had been.

"I'm sorry I ruined your night."

Daniel looked up from his plate and smiled tenderly. He reached out and traced the delicate line of her jaw. "You didn't ruin anything," he whispered. "Do you know how incredibly beautiful you are in your sleep? I could have watched you for hours. In fact I did."

Somewhat embarrassed, Julie lowered her thick lashes and shook her head. A finger under her chin raised it to meet his eyes.

"I lay awake last night, my heart full of love, and I realized I'm the luckiest man in the world."

"Yesterday was a day to think that. Your mother survived the surgery, and we've been given a second chance to build a solid marriage."

"Yes, we have," Daniel whispered, his mouth seeking hers.

"What did you and Daniel decide on this house business?" Sherry asked over lunch later that week.

Julie shrugged, and set aside her turkey sandwich. "It's on hold. We've more or less decided to wait until we had a reason to move."

Sherry averted her gaze. "Do you want to start a family right away?"

"Yes." And no. Julie hadn't been naive enough to believe that once they were sharing a bed everything would be perfect. It wasn't. The incident with the house had proven that. Daniel loved her, but Julie was convinced he didn't completely trust her. It was almost as if he were waiting for her to pack her bags and walk out on him a second time. Julie realized that only time would persuade him otherwise. And Julie wanted a secure marriage before they had children.

After finishing lunch, the two women returned to work. The phone was ringing when they entered the office.

"I'll get it," Sherry volunteered, reaching for the telephone receiver.

Julie didn't pay much attention to the ensuing conversation until Sherry laughed and handed the phone to her. "It's for you. Personal."

"Daniel?"

"Nope, Jim Patterson."

Instantly Julie remembered Jim as Daniel's associate who had introduced himself the day of the tennis match. "Hello, Jim," she greeted cheerfully, somewhat surprised that he'd be contacting her.

"Julie. Sorry to call you at the office, but I didn't want Daniel to answer the phone and there was always that possibility if I rang your place."

"What can I do for you?"

"The Country Club has voted Daniel as The Man of The Year. We like to keep it a secret until the big night so don't let on that you know."

Julie's heart swelled with pride. "I won't breathe a word. Daniel will be so pleased."

"Each year we do a skit that tells the life story of the recipient of the award. You know, *This Is Your Life* type of thing. Of course we tend to ham it up a bit."

Julie giggled, her mind conjuring up the type of crazy stunts the men would pull.

"I was wondering if there was a time you and I could get together and go over some of the details of Daniel's life. I'd talk to his mother, but apparently she's in the hospital."

"I'd be happy to do that. When would you suggest?"

They agreed on a time and Julie was beaming with pride when she set the telephone receiver in its cradle.

"What was that all about?" Sherry inquired, not bothering to disguise her curiosity.

"Daniel's been named the Country Club's Man of the Year."

"That's wonderful!"

"I think so too," Julie agreed.

Daniel came into her office at quitting time. Usually Julie walked down the one flight of stairs to his suite and waited for him. But she was the last one to leave today, having made arrangements to stay a few minutes later to sign final escrow papers with a young couple. Both husband and wife worked full time and couldn't make it into the office any earlier than five. Julie was with the Daleys when Daniel walked through the door. She hadn't told him she would be later tonight, but not because she'd forgotten. Usually she was left waiting ten or fifteen minutes in his office and didn't think these few minutes would matter.

Julie smiled at her husband and gestured with her hand for him to take a seat. "I'll be done in a minute," she told him.

"I didn't realize it was so late." Mrs. Daley cast Julie an apologetic smile, glancing up from her wristwatch. "We've got to pick up the baby at the day care. You don't need me to sign anything more, do you?"

Quickly, Julie scanned the documents. "No, you're both free to go as soon as I've received the cashier's check."

"I've got that now," Mr. Daley announced.

Completing the transaction took only a few minutes longer. Mr. Daley enthusiastically shook Julie's hand and thanked her again for her help. This was the part of her job that she enjoyed the most. The house the Daleys were buying was their first and a dream they'd saved toward for three years.

The Daleys left the office and Julie quickly sorted through the remaining paperwork.

"Why couldn't Sherry have stayed?" Daniel asked stiffly.

"Because I volunteered," she answered on the tail end of a yawn. Placing her hand over her mouth, she lightly shook her head from side to side. "I don't know what's the matter with me lately. I've been so tired."

Daniel set his briefcase aside and claimed the chair recently vacated by the young husband. "I don't understand why you continue to work. There's no need. I make a decent living."

"I'd be bored if I didn't work." Julie immediately shelved the idea, surprised he'd even suggest it.

"You might have the time to learn how to cook."

"Are you complaining about my meals?" she joked, knowing he had every right to grumble. As long as she stuck to the basics, she was fine. But their menu was limited to only a handful of dishes and Daniel was obviously bored with the lack of variety.

"I'm not actually complaining," he began, treading carefully. "But I want you to give serious consideration to quitting your job. I don't like the idea of you having to work so hard."

"It's not hard," she protested. "And I enjoy it. Sherry and I make a great team."

"Whatever you want," he grumbled, but he wasn't pleased and Julie couldn't understand why.

A week after open-heart surgery and Clara Van Deen was sitting up in bed looking healthier than Julie could remember since returning to Wichita.

"I can't tell you how grateful I'll be to go home," she said, her voice rising slightly with enthusiasm. "Everyone's been wonderful here. I can't complain, but I do so miss my garden."

"And your garden misses you," Julie said with a wink to her husband.

"That's right, Mother." Looking grave, Daniel shook his head. "Weeds all the way up to my knees. I can hardly see the flowers in what was once the showplace of Willowbrook Street."

Clara Van Deen grimaced and shook her head. "I can't bear to think of what months of neglect have done to my precious yard."

Unable to continue the game any longer, Julie patted her mother-in-law's hand reassuringly. "Your garden looks lovely. Now don't you fret."

"Thanks to Julie," Daniel inserted. "She spent a good portion of the weekend on her hands and knees weeding."

"I should have been thinking of ways to torture a husband with a loose tongue," Julie admonished with a sigh. "It was supposed to be a surprise."

"My dear, Julie. You didn't really?"

"She has the blisters to prove it," Daniel inserted.

"Daniel! I didn't know your mouth was so big."

The hand across her back gently squeezed her shoulder. "All the better to kiss you with, my dear."

Julie tried unsuccessfully to hide a smile. "It's times like these that I wonder what kind of family I married into."

"One that loves you," Clara Van Deen replied with a warm smile. "Say, Julie, isn't today the day you were meeting with—"

"No," she interrupted hurriedly, warning her mother-in-law with her eyes not to say anything more. After Jim had contacted her about Daniel's award, Julie had shared the good news with his mother. Apparently the older woman had forgotten that the award was supposed to be a surprise.

Daniel made a show of glancing at his watch. "What's this about Julie meeting someone?"

"Nothing," Julie returned hastily.

"It's a surprise, son." The lined mouth twisted with self-derisive anger. "I nearly let the cat out of the bag the second time. Forgive an old woman, Julie."

"There's nothing to forgive."

"Will you two kindly let me know what is going on?"

"My lips are sealed," Julie taunted.

"Mine, too," Clara chimed and shared a conspiratorial wink with her daughter-in-law. "It's sometime this week, isn't it?"

Julie knew Clara was referring to her meeting with Jim. "Yes, over lunch. I'll let you know how everything goes."

"I will," Julie promised, squeezing Clara's hand.

Daniel's expression altered from amused to concerned on the way to the hospital parking lot. "You're not going to tell me, are you?"

"Nope."

"At least let me know whom you're meeting with."

"Never."

"I could torture it out of you," he whispered seductively.

"I'll look forward to that." She slid an arm around his waist and smiled up at him. He looked so handsome that she couldn't resist stealing a kiss.

"What was that for?"

"Because I love you."

A brief look passed over his features. One so fleeting that Julie was almost sure she'd imagined it. But she hadn't. Daniel doubted her. After everything that had transpired between them, her husband didn't believe she loved him. Julie was so utterly astonished that she didn't know what to say or how to react. Time, she told herself, he only needed time. As the years passed he'd learn.

On the ride home, Julie was introspective. They'd traveled this same route so many times over the past six weeks that sights along the way blended into one another.

"Daniel?" Julie sat upright.

"Humm?"

"Take a right here," she directed, pointing with her hand.

"Whatever for?"

"There's a house on the corner that's for sale." They must have passed the place a thousand times. Julie had noted the realtor's sign on each occasion and hadn't given the place a second thought. Now something about the house reached out to her.

Daniel made a sharp right-hand turn and eased to a stop at the tree-lined curb in front of the older, two-story Colonial home. The paint was peeling from the white exterior and several of the green shutters were hanging by a single hinge. "Julie," he groaned, "it doesn't even look like anyone lives there."

Julie glanced around her and noticed the other homes in the neighborhood. They were family oriented and well maintained. "All this place needs is a bit of tender, loving care."

"It's the neighborhood eyesore," Daniel said with more than a hint of impatience.

"I'd like to see the inside. Can we contact the realtor?" Already she was writing down the phone number.

"Julie, you can't be serious."

"But I am."

That same evening they met the realtor. "I'm afraid this place has been vacant for several months," James Derek, the realtor, told them.

"What did I tell you?" Daniel whispered near her ear. "This isn't what we're looking for—"

"No," Julie interrupted as she climbed out of the car, "but I like it. I like it very much."

"Julie," Daniel moaned as he joined her on the cracked sidewalk that led to the neglected house.

James Derek hesitated and Julie sensed that his sentiments were close to Daniel's. Undoubtedly, because of its run-down condition, this home would mean a much lower sales commission than the newer, more expensive homes they could afford.

"Can we go inside?" She directed her question to the realtor.

"Yes, of course."

The moment Julie walked through the door she knew. "Daniel," she breathed solemnly, her hand reaching for her husband, "this is it. This is the house."

"But, Julie, you haven't even looked around."

"I don't need to, I can feel it."

The entryway was small and led to an open stairway and a long mahogany banister that rounded at the top of the steps. To her right was a huge family living room and to her left a smaller room obviously meant to be a library or den. Dust covered everything and a musty smell permeated the house. The hardwood floors were dented and badly in need of buffeting.

"You'd probably want to have these old floors carpeted," the agent suggested.

Julie tossed him a disbelieving glare. Maybe oriental rugs, but it would be a shame to cover those solid wood floors.

The formal dining room had built-in china cabinets and a window seat. The kitchen was huge with a large eating area. The main level had two bedrooms and the upstairs had three more. The full basement was ideal for storage.

"It doesn't have a family room," Daniel commented after a silent tour. "That's something you've insisted on with the other house." His look wasn't encouraging and Julie realized he was grasping at straws.

"This house doesn't need one," Julie insisted. Desperately she hoped that Daniel could see the potential of the house. "It's perfect. Right down to the fenced backyard, patio and tree house."

"Perhaps you'd care to make a few comparisons with some other homes," the realtor interjected.

Determined, Julie shook her head. "I wouldn't." Her eyes met Daniel's. She realized their tastes were different. She even understood his doubts. This house would require weeks of expensive repairs, but the asking price was reasonable. Far below anything else they'd seen.

"In all fairness I feel you should be aware of several things."

James Derek's voice seemed to fade into the background as Julie sauntered from one room to the next. Her mind was whirling at breakneck speed as she viewed each room the way she would decorate it. Two bedrooms downstairs were ideal. After their family was old enough to move upstairs she could use that room as a sewing area. Next she wandered through the kitchen. The only problem she could foresee was having the washer and dryer in the basement. But the back porch was large enough to move the appliances out there. Of course, that would require some minor remodeling.

"Julie." Daniel found her and placed a hand on her shoulder. "I think we should go home and think this over before we make our final decision."

"What's there to decide?" For an instant she couldn't understand his reluctance. "If we don't put down earnest money now, someone else will."

"That's highly unlikely, Mrs. Van Deen," the realtor interrupted. "This place has been on the market for six months."

On the drive back to the realtor's office it was all Julie could do to keep her mouth shut. Before she and Daniel climbed into their own car, Daniel and James Derek scheduled another time for them to go and look at other houses.

With a numbed sense of disbelief, Julie closed her car door and stared straight ahead.

"Why'd you do that?" she demanded when Daniel climbed into the driver's side of their car a few minutes later.

"Do what?" He looked surprised at the anger in her voice.

"Set up another appointment."

"To look at houses—"

"But I've found the one I want," she declared. "Daniel, I love that house. We can look for another ten years and we wouldn't find anything more perfect. And best of all it's only a few blocks from your mother's. It's got a den for you and..."

"That house would be like living in a nightmare. The repair cost alone would be more than the value of the house. The roof's got to be replaced. There's dry rot in the basement."

"I don't care," Julie stated emphatically.

"I'm not going to fight with you about it. If we're going to buy a house then it's one we both agree on."

Julie had no argument. That house was everything Julie wanted. Hot tears brimmed in her eyes and blurred her vision. Something was definitely the matter with her lately. She couldn't believe she would cry over something as silly as a house.

The day Clara Van Deen came home from the hospital was the happiest Julie could remember. With Mrs. Batten's help Julie had the house spotless.

Although weak, the smile on her mother-in-law's face was reward enough for the long hours Julie had spent weeding and caring for her much-loved garden.

Mrs. Batten arranged huge floral bouquets around the living room and cooked a dinner of roast, potatoes and fresh strawberry shortcake, which had long been a family favorite.

Sitting with Clara on the patio, in the late afternoon sun, Julie lifted her face to the golden rays.

"Is everything all right with you, dear?"

The abrupt question surprised Julie. "Of course. What could possibly be wrong?"

Clara took a sip of tea from the delicate china cup. "I'm not sure, but you haven't been yourself the last couple of weeks. Has this house business got you down?"

"Not really." Julie straightened in the wrought-iron chair. The question struck a raw nerve. "Daniel and I have more or less agreed to wait. There's no rush."

"But there was one house you liked?"

Julie knew the smile of reassurance she gave her mother-in-law spoke more of disappointment than any confidence. "We agreed to disagree." She changed the subject as quickly as possible. "Have you noticed how pink the camellias are this year?"

Clara didn't answer; her look was thoughtful. Daniel's look was almost identical when he unlocked the front door of the condo an hour later.

Julie felt uncomfortable under his gaze. "Is something bothering you?"

Daniel's mouth twisted wryly into a smile. "I thought we agreed not to take our disagreements to my mother."

Julie blanched, understanding immediately what had happened. Clara had spoken to Daniel about the house. "We did," she admitted stiffly.

"Mother had a talk with me before we left tonight."

"I know what it sounds like," Julie cut in, "but please believe me when I tell you that I didn't do anything more than mention it. I tried to change the subject."

A brooding silence followed and Julie watched as her husband's mouth thinned with impatience.

"If anything," she said, pausing to exhale, "I think I should have a talk with your mother. She's going to have to learn that although we love her dearly, she can't become involved in our lives to the point that she takes sides of an issue. Okay?"

"Definitely."

Julie walked across the room, her arms cradling her middle in an instinctively protective action. They were both walking on thin ice. Each desperately wished to maintain the fragile balance of their relationship. In some ways they seemed to be miraculously suited to each another and in other ways they were complete opposites. The house was a prime example. Daniel preferred the ultra-modern home. But Julie wanted something more traditional. She didn't know if they would ever be able to compromise.

Daniel cleared his throat and came to stand behind her. "I can see that this house issue could grow into a major problem."

Julie gave a determined shake of her head. "I won't let it. As far as I'm concerned all I want is to be your wife. It doesn't matter where we live."

His arms went around her and gathered her close within his loving circle. "I've been giving the house you wanted considerable thought," he whispered in a grave voice.

"And?" It was difficult to maintain her paper-thin poise.

"I think that we should be able to come up with a compromise."

"A compromise?"

"Yes." He drew back, his hands linked at the small of her back as he smiled at her upturned face. "I'll buy it if you agree to quit your job."

Chapter Ten

"Quit my job?" Julie repeated incredulously. "You have got to be joking." Her eyes studied the lines of strain about Daniel's mouth.

"That house is going to need extensive remodeling. Someone should be there to supervise the work."

Again her wide, troubled eyes searched his face. "It isn't remodeling the house needs, but repairs, most of which will have to be done before we move in." Breaking from his hold, Julie walked to the far side of the room. "I've seen it in you several times, but didn't bring it up hoping—"

"You're speaking in riddles," Daniel countered.

"The house isn't the real reason you want me to quit."

"I want you to be my wife."

"And I'm not now?" she responded in a stark voice. "I enjoy my job." Her hand made a sweeping gesture, slicing the air in front of her. "I've seen it in your eyes, Daniel. You think I'm going to walk out on you again. It's almost as if you're waiting for it to happen."

"You're being ridiculous."

"Am I?" she asked softly. "First it was the house you bought me that happened to be an hour out of town. It was like you wanted to close me off from the rest of the world."

Daniel stalked across the living room floor, and ran a hand along the back of his neck.

"And most recently you've suggested I quit working."

"I saw you with Jim Patterson last week," Daniel announced harshly.

"And you immediately jumped to conclusions."

"No." He turned around and Julie noted the heavy lines of strain around his eyes. She'd known something was wrong for days, but couldn't put her finger on it. He held her and loved her and gave no outward appearance that anything was troubling him. Only at odd moments when she caught him looking at her and witnessed the doubt and pain in his eyes did she guess.

"Will you tell me why you and Jim found it necessary to have lunch together?"

"I can't," she whispered miserably. "But I'm asking you to trust me. Surely you don't believe Jim and I are involved in any way?"

"I've tried. A hundred times I've told myself that you must love me. You wouldn't have come back or married me if you didn't."

"I do love you," she cried. "What makes you think I would even look at another man?" The hurt she was feeling must have been expressed in her eyes.

Daniel lowered his gaze and ran a hand over his weary eyes. "Sometimes I hate myself." The admission came with a bitter laugh.

"You don't trust me."

His returning look confirmed her worst suspicions. A sob rose to her throat, but she inhaled a deep breath and forced it down. "I love you so much I could never think about another man, nor could I leave you. What will it take to convince you of that?"

Daniel couldn't meet her eyes. "I don't know." He paced the carpet in front of her. "When I first saw you with Jim,

I felt sick inside, then explosive. Even though I'd heard you joke with my mother about this meeting, I couldn't believe I'd see my wife and a good friend together. For two days I expected to wake up and find you gone.''

''You actually believe that I'd run away with Jim Patterson?''

''Why not? You ran away from me before.''

Julie closed her eyes feeling frustrated and furious. ''I haven't even thought about anyone else since I moved to Wichita.''

''But you had lunch with my friend.''

''Yes.'' She couldn't deny it and wouldn't have, even if she could have lied.

''And you won't tell me why you met him?'' He scowled.

''No. I'm asking you to trust me.''

His dark eyes narrowed. ''I'm trying. Lord knows I want to, but I don't know if I can,'' he whispered, his eyes revealing his torment.

''Julie, you don't look as if you slept at all last night,'' Sherry said when Julie walked into the office the following morning.

''I didn't.''

''Why not?''

Julie had felt the weight of the world pressing down on her when they'd gone to bed after their discussion. Daniel stayed on his side of the mattress and although they were separated by only a few inches, he could well have been on the other side of the world for all the warmth and comfort they shared.

''It's a long story,'' Julie answered finally. She made busywork around her desk for a couple of minutes, then asked, ''What would you think if I told you that Daniel wants me to quit my job?''

''Does he?'' Sherry's baby-blue eyes rounded with concern.

''Let's make this a hypothetical question.''

Julie wondered if, without knowing the background of her relationship with Daniel, Sherry would read the same meaning into her husband's strange behavior.

"Well, first off he wanted to move you into that house in the boondocks," Sherry said thoughtfully, rolling her chair the short distance between their two desks. "And now he wants you home all day. My guess is that he's insecure about something. But I can't imagine why. It's obvious to anyone how much you love him."

"I only wish Daniel recognized that."

"You're not going to quit working, are you? I suppose I'm being selfish," Sherry admitted sheepishly. "You've helped me so much through this ordeal with Andy. I can tell you things I wouldn't speak of to anyone else. I'd miss your friendship."

"No, I'm not going to do it." She refused to give in to his insecurities. Doing so could lead to an unhealthy pattern in their marriage that she wanted to avoid. "Enough about my problems. How's everything between you and Andy?"

"I get depressed so easily." Sherry lowered her gaze to her desk. "Who would ever have thought wooing my husband back could be so difficult?"

Julie smiled secretly to herself. She knew exactly what Sherry meant. She was shocked by how far she had to go to mend the hurts of the past three years.

The phone buzzed and Sherry looked up. Suddenly pale, she motioned for Julie to answer it as she rushed into the bathroom. Not for the first time in the past couple of weeks, Julie suspected her friend was pregnant.

Julie was off the phone by the time Sherry returned. "Are you going to tell me or are you going to make me ask?"

"How'd you know?" Sherry protested.

"Sherry, honestly. I can't believe you sometimes. I'd have to have my head buried in a hole not to have guessed. Does Andy know?"

Bright tears sparkled from her eyelashes. "No. If we do get back together, I want it to be because he loves and wants me. Not because of the baby."

"The divorce proceedings were halted, weren't they?"

Sherry nodded. "But only because Andy and I felt we needed time to think things out more thoroughly. We're not living together."

"You're not going to be able to hide it from him much longer," Julie advised softly.

Sherry propped her chin up with the palm of one hand and shrugged her shoulder. "I know. That's why I've given him three weeks to decide what he wants. If I'm going to lose him, then I'd prefer to face that now and be done with it."

"How does Andy feel about having an ultimatum?"

Sherry giggled and the tears glistened in her eyes. The contrast reminded Julie of a rainbow.

"Andy doesn't know."

"Oh, Sherry," Julie groaned.

A tear slid down her friend's cheek. "I realize this whole scheme sounds crazy, but I've thought everything out. I firmly believe I'm doing the right thing. If Andy found out about the baby and we reconciled then I'd never be sure. This way I'll have the confidence I need that Andy really loves me and wants to make this marriage work."

The phone rang again and the two were quickly involved in the business of maintaining an escrow office.

Not until that night when Julie took pains to cook Daniel's favorite dinner did he notice something was different.

"Did I miss something?" he asked teasingly.

"Miss something?"

"It's not my birthday, is it? I've got it! You overdrew the checking account. Right?"

"Just because I cook stroganoff does it mean I'm up to something?" Julie inquired with feigned righteousness.

"In my short experience as a husband, my immediate reaction is...yes!"

"Well, you're wrong. I've taken all your complaints to heart and bought a cookbook. I can't have my husband fainting away from lack of the proper nourishment."

"Would you like me to demonstrate how weak I am?" he asked, slipping his hands over her breasts and pulling her against him.

"Daniel, not now."

"Why not?" he growled against her neck.

"Dinner will burn."

"That has never bothered you before."

"I thought you were hungry."

"I am. Come to bed and I'll show you how hungry I am."

Julie switched off the stove and turned into her husband's arms, meeting the hungry urgency of his kiss with a willingness that surprised even Julie. She did love this man. Someday he'd realize how much.

Dusk had settled over the city before they stirred an hour later. Lovingly, Daniel's hand caressed her bare shoulder. "I'll be happy when you're pregnant," he whispered.

Involuntarily Julie stiffened. "Why?"

She could feel Daniel's frown. "I thought you wanted a family."

"I do." But she wanted the two of them secure in their marriage before they started a family.

"Then why the questions?"

"I want to know why you want a baby." A chill settled over the area of her heart. Her greatest fear was that Daniel would see a child as the means of binding her to him.

"For all the reasons a man usually wants to be a father." He tossed aside the blankets and sat on the edge of the mattress. "As I recall, we agreed that when you were pregnant, you'd quit your job."

Reaching for her robe at the foot of the bed, Julie buried her arms deep within the blue silk. She didn't know how any man and woman could make such beautiful love together and then argue. "I think you should know I've made an appointment with the doctor."

The silence grew and grew.

"So you think you might be pregnant."

"No, I want to make darn sure that doesn't happen."

* * *

As the days passed Julie had never been more miserable. Daniel treated her with icy politeness as if she were little more than a guest in her own home. If she'd thought the first days of their marriage were a test of her love it was nothing compared to the cold war that was being waged between them now.

Daniel threw himself into his work and Julie did her best to give the outward appearance that everything was fine. With Daniel gone so much of the time, Julie spent more and more of her evenings with her mother-in-law.

The two women worked at getting Clara's beloved yard into shape. Julie did her best to disguise her unhappiness, but she was convinced that her mother-in-law knew something wasn't right.

"I was surprised to see that old engagement picture of you and Daniel on the television," Clara remarked casually, working the border of the bed. Clara had recently visited the condominium for the first time since Julie and Daniel's marriage.

"We both look young, don't we?" Julie asked wistfully.

"It's difficult to remember you like that."

Julie had the impression her mother-in-law wasn't referring to looks. "We've all changed."

They continued working, each silently caught up in changes the years had produced.

"Something's bothering Daniel," Clara announced, studying her daughter-in-law closely.

"Oh?"

"I saw him briefly the other day and was shocked by his appearance."

"He's been working a lot of extra hours lately."

"Is it necessary?"

"I . . . I don't know." Avoiding her mother-in-law's gaze, Julie weeded another section of the flower bed.

"You look a bit peaked yourself," Clara Van Deen continued. "What's the matter with you two?"

Settling back on her heels, Julie sighed heavily. "Clara, Daniel and I agreed . . ."

"I know," she murmured. "Daniel said the same thing. But I can't help worrying about you both. You love each other and yet you're obviously miserable."

"I do love Daniel."

"And he loves you. I don't know that he's ever told you, but he knew where you were in California. All these years he's known and loved you. Whatever is bothering you two can't be worth all this torment. Believe me I know how stubborn my son can be. Just be patient with him."

"I'm trying," Julie whispered, struggling not to cry.

Back at the condominium an hour later, Julie soaked in a tub filled with hot water and perfumed bubble bath. She had no idea where Daniel was. Although it was Saturday, he'd left early that morning before she was awake.

Julie had hoped that a bubble bath would raise her spirits. Her head rested against the back of the porcelain bath. Forcing her eyes closed, she mused that without much effort she could easily fall asleep. She'd been so tired lately. It was ridiculous. It seemed she went to bed every night before Daniel and had trouble dragging herself up in the morning. That wasn't like her. Nor was the unbalanced diet she'd been developing lately. She was starving one moment and feeling like she'd overeaten the next. Her appointment with the doctor was in the first part of the week; she'd mention it to him. Her body had been doing funny things lately. It was probably a reaction to all the stress. Heaven knew she'd had enough of that to last a lifetime.

Abruptly, Julie sat up in the tub, causing hot water to slosh over the sides. In a flash she knew. She was pregnant. So much had been happening that she'd completely lost track of time. Biting into her trembling bottom lip, Julie leaned back and placed a hand on her flat stomach. Daniel would be pleased. This was exactly what he was hoping would happen. Despite her misgivings, Julie's heart swelled with joy. Just as quickly, tears flooded her eyes. She cried so easily these days and now she understood the reason why. All in one breath she was ecstatic with joy and unbelievably sad. Desperately she wanted this child, but she wanted the baby to come into a warm, secure marriage and not one torn by tension and mistrust. Sniffling, she wiped the moisture from her face.

Dripping water and bubbles over the bathroom floor, Julie climbed out of the tub and wrapped a towel around her body. An array of mixed emotions flew at her from all directions until she wanted to thrash out her arms to ward them off.

Sitting on top of their bed, she reached for the phone and dialed the number to Daniel's office where she suspected he'd be. The phone rang twice before Julie abruptly cut the connection. What could she possibly say?

Sniffling anew, Julie dialed again and waited several long rings. "Sherry," she said, relieved that her friend was home. "Congratulate me, we're both pregnant." With that she burst into sobs.

Chapter Eleven

"Here," Sherry said, handing Julie another tissue. "You're going to need this."

A dry-eyed Julie glanced at the Kleenex, then back to her friend. "I'm through crying. It was a shock, that's all." Within fifteen minutes after receiving the call, her co-worker and best friend had arrived at the condominium, flushed and excited.

"Discovering I was pregnant was a shock for me, too, if you recall. At first I was ecstatic, then I was flooded with doubts. Three days later I leveled out at 'great.'"

Julie's smile was wan. "A baby is exactly what Daniel wants."

"But for all the wrong reasons," Sherry claimed heatedly. "If Andy knew about me, I suspect he'd be thrilled; again for all the wrong reasons."

Julie nodded, feeling slightly ill. She hadn't eaten since breakfast, but the thought of food was enough to nauseate her.

"What did Daniel say?" Sherry sat across from Julie and laced her fingers.

"He doesn't know yet."

"You haven't told him?"

Julie laughed at the sound of incredulity in her friend's voice. "I learned that trick from you."

"What are you going to do?"

"I don't know yet. He has to be told, but I don't know when. He's... hardly around anymore."

"So he's pulling that trick again," Sherry huffed.

"He's working himself to death."

"Or he could be out having the time of his life as Andy did."

Julie doubted that. "I don't think so."

"Ha! That's what I thought about Andy. You aren't going to sit here and sulk. I won't let you."

"I'm not sulking."

"No, you're crying." She gave Julie another tissue. "Come on, I'm taking you out."

"Sherry, honestly, I appreciate your efforts, but the last thing in the world I want is to be seen in public. I look a mess."

"So, it'll take a bit of inventive application with your makeup."

"And twenty years."

Sherry giggled. "My friend, I'm going to let you in on one of life's important secrets."

"Oh?" Julie was dubious.

"When the going gets tough, then the tough go shopping."

"Sherry," Julie groaned. "I don't feel up to anything like—"

"Trust me, you'll feel a hundred percent better. Afterward I'll treat you to dinner."

"But Daniel..."

"Did he bother to tell you he wouldn't be home for dinner the last three nights?"

"No." She lowered her gaze to disguise the pain.

"Then it's time you quit moping around and do something positive for yourself."

Squaring her shoulders, Julie realized her friend was right. However Julie knew that Daniel probably wouldn't know she was gone. And worse, wouldn't care. If he was to return before she did, he would suspect she'd left him. It was almost as if he were driving her to that. Then her disappearance would only confirm what he believed would eventually happen anyway.

"All right," Julie agreed, "I'll go."

It took the better part of an hour to get ready, but Sherry was right, she felt better for it. Before they left the apartment, Julie penned Daniel a short note, telling him whom she was with. He may not care or want to know, but Julie felt better for having done it.

Sherry seemed intent on having a good time. First they frequented the mall stores, scouting out baby items and trying on maternity dresses until they laughed themselves sick.

Next they took in a movie and had an Italian dinner afterward. On the way home, Sherry insisted that they stop off at her house so Julie could see the baby blanket she was knitting.

"I think I'd better call Daniel," Julie said, sipping her cup of tea. The evening had slipped past so quickly. Already it was after eleven and although she had left the note, he might be worried. All right, she *hoped* he'd be worried.

"Don't," Sherry chastised. "He hasn't phoned you lately, has he?"

"No," Julie admitted reluctantly. She had barely seen him in the last week. They were like strangers who just happened to live together.

"I think I'll put on some music and let it soothe our souls."

"Good idea," Julie chimed.

The next thing Julie knew, she was lying on the sofa, wrapped in a thick comforter. Struggling to sit upright, she rubbed the sleep from her eyes so she could glance at her watch.

"I was wondering what time you'd wake up," Sherry called from the kitchen. "How do you want your eggs?"

"It's morning?" Julie was incredulous.

"Right, and almost ten. You were tired, my friend."

"But..."

"I turned on the radio last night and the next thing I knew you were sound asleep."

"Oh, good grief." Untwining the comforter from around her legs, she stood. "I'd better call Daniel."

"Go ahead. The phone's on the counter." She pointed to it with her spatula.

While Julie dialed, Sherry handed her a small glass of orange juice and two soda crackers. Julie smiled her appreciation. Her stomach was queasy and had been for several mornings. Only Julie had attributed the reason to nerves.

Ten rings later, she hesitantly replaced the receiver.

"No answer?" asked Sherry.

"No." Rubbing the palms of her hands together, Julie gave her co-worker a feeble smile. "Maybe he was in the shower."

"Maybe," Sherry echoed. "Try again in five minutes."

"At least he knows whom I'm with. If he was worried he would have called."

Sherry turned back to the stove. "He didn't know."

"I left a note."

"I stuck it in my pocket before we left your place. Heavens, I didn't know you were going to fall asleep on me and spend the night. I thought if Daniel worried a little it would be good for him."

"Oh, Sherry."

"It was a rotten thing to do. Are you mad?"

Julie shook her head, feeling utterly defeated. Sherry had no way of knowing that she had walked out on Daniel once and he was sure to believe she'd done it again.

"No," Julie mumbled. "He doesn't appear to be overly concerned at any rate. He's not even home." For that matter he could have returned late, as he had every night of the previous week, crawled into bed and not even noticed she was missing.

Fifteen minutes later, Julie used her key to open her front door. The condominium was dark, and absently Julie walked across the living room to open the drapes.

"Julie?"

Abruptly, she swiveled around to find Daniel sitting on the edge of the chair, leaning forward, his elbows braced against his knees. His dark eyes were wide and disbelieving.

"Hello, Daniel." He looked the picture of such utter dejection that she fought back the tears that clogged her throat. Julie didn't know how any two people who loved each other so much could come to this point.

Quickly the proud mask he wore slid into place and he stood, ramming his hands into the side pockets of his slacks. "I suppose you came back for your things."

"No." Somehow she managed to let the lone word escape. His clothes were badly wrinkled and his hair was rumpled as if he'd run his fingers through it several times. The dark stubble on his face was so unlike the neatly groomed man she'd lived with all these months that Julie looked away.

Apparently he didn't hear her. "Well go ahead and get them. Don't let me stop you."

"You want me to leave?" she asked, her voice little more than a breathless whisper.

"I won't stop you."

She dropped her gaze as the pain washed over her. "I see." Not knowing how to explain that she wasn't going, Julie took a step toward the hallway.

Daniel jerked his head up as she moved. His face was deathly pale, the fine lines about his mouth drawn and pinched.

"Julie." He murmured her name forcefully.

She turned back expectantly. Their eyes met and held. Neither seemed willing to break the contact. The tears filled her eyes and she wiped them aside with the back of her hand.

"I don't blame you for walking out on me," he spoke at last. "I drove you to it." He jerked his hand through his hair. "I let you out of my life the first time and blamed you for it. God help me, I can't do it again." He took a tentative step toward her. "Once you're gone, there won't be any more sunshine in my life. I lived for three long years in the dark and I won't go back to that. Julie—" his voice softened perceptibly "—don't leave me," he pleaded. "Let me make up for all the unhappiness I've caused you."

With a cry of joy, Julie reached out to him and they came together with all the desperation of young lovers separated by war. Daniel crushed her into his embrace and buried his face into her hair, taking in deep breaths as he struggled with emotion.

"It doesn't matter why you saw Jim or any other man. I was a fool to think everything would be solved by having you quit your job."

"Daniel, listen—"

"Moving into the country was just as ridiculous," he interrupted. "I love you, Julie, you're the most important person in my life. I can't let you go."

Cupping his ears, Julie lifted his head and spread tiny kisses over his face. "Would you kindly listen to me for one minute? I'm not leaving and never was. That was all a mix-up that we have to thank Sherry for. And as for my job, I plan to work for about another six months and then think about quitting."

"That sounds fair," he said and blinked. "Why six months?"

"Because by then the baby—"

"The baby?" Daniel repeated, stunned. His frown deepened as he searched her face. "Julie, are you telling me you're pregnant?"

Twenty-four hours ago, Julie would have been just as shocked had anyone mentioned her condition, but since then she had acknowledged and accepted the baby so readily that Julie had forgotten that Daniel didn't know.

"How? When?" He looked completely flustered.

Julie laughed and lovingly ran her hand along the side of his proud jaw. "You don't honestly need an answer to that, do you?"

"No," he agreed on a husky murmur. His eyes shone with pride and happiness. "All these weeks I'd hoped that you would be. I wanted a child to bind you to me. Now I realize how wrong that was. You've always been with me. Even while you lived in California, you were here in my heart."

Slipping her arms around her husband's neck, Julie smiled into the loving depth of his tender gaze. "We're already bound."

"By our love," he finished for her. When his mouth sought hers, Julie surrendered to her husband's deep hunger, secure in his love. "You needn't worry, Julie. I learned some valuable lessons about myself last night while I sat here alone. I was convinced my selfishness had driven you away a second time. What I didn't know was if I could bear to let you go." The doorbell chimed and Daniel glanced at it irritably. "I'll get rid of whoever it is," he promised, kissing the edge of her mouth with a fleeting contact that promised more.

"Hello," the man's voice came from the open door. "I'm looking for Julie Van Deen."

Julie cast an inquisitive glance at Daniel and shrugged. "That's me," she said, joining Daniel and loping an arm around his waist.

"Excuse me for intruding on you like this," he began as a pair of golden-brown eyes narrowed on her.

A salesman, Julie mused to herself, and one with the world's worst timing.

"I'm Andy Adams," he began haltingly, "Sherry's husband."

"Of course." Julie brightened immediately. "I've heard a lot about you."

"Yes." He cleared his throat and glanced at Daniel. "I'm sure you have. Sherry has mentioned you on several occasions."

"Come in. Can I get you a cup of coffee or something?"

"No, thanks. If you don't mind I'd like to ask you a few questions." He stepped into the condo, closing the door behind him.

"About Sherry?" Julie didn't want to get caught in the middle of her friend's marital difficulties, but knew that she probably already was.

"Yes. That is if you have no objections."

"I know that she's decided to stop seeing you and—"

"But why?" he demanded and paused to rumple his thick dark brown hair. "I apologize. I didn't mean to shout."

He'd hardly raised his voice. "You didn't," she assured him. Andy and Sherry were as different as two people could be. Her flighty friend was married to this intense young man with the soft-spoken voice. Julie would never have pictured Andy in a three-piece suit.

"This whole thing is driving me crazy. I love my wife. I loved her when we separated the first time. It wasn't me who wanted that stupid divorce. Sherry seemed to need space to find herself and I thought the best thing I could do was give it to her, but I've always loved her."

A soft smile touched Julie's eyes. "But then you decided to taste a little of that freedom yourself."

"It was all a game. I knew Sherry was going to be there that night. By that time I was desperate and thought a taste of her own medicine would help."

"It did," Julie returned, recalling her friend's reaction.

"A little too well," Andy admitted with a self-derisive smile. "Maybe that was the mistake, I don't know. We were to the point of moving back in together when—whamo—Sherry announces it's over and she doesn't want to see me again." He took a few brisk steps before pivoting and pacing back.

"I thought you were the one who—"

"No," he said forcefully. "It's true I thought this new relationship should progress slowly. I wanted Sherry to be sure of her feelings."

"I think she's very sure how she feels."

"But I thought—"

"Andy." Julie took in a deep breath. "I want you to think about something. When you and Sherry separated, she went off her birth control pills. Does that mean anything to you?"

The silence grew more intense with every passing second. "I'm going to be a father?" The words were issued in a disbelieving whisper.

"I'd say you've hit the nail right on the head."

"I'm going to be a father," he repeated as a contented smile lit up his eyes until they sparkled like rare jewels. "Then why in the sam hill did she tell me it was over? This doesn't make any sense."

"I think that's something you're going to have to ask Sherry."

"I will."

"Good." Julie couldn't help smiling.

"Thank you, thank you."

He took her hand and pumped it until Julie's fingers lost feeling, then reached for Daniel's hand, shaking it with the same enthusiasm.

"I've got to talk to Sherry."

"It'd be a solid bet to say she's anxious to see you."

"I can't thank you enough," he called as he opened the door and left, nearly tripping in his rush.

"I know exactly how he feels," Daniel said, taking his wife in his arms. "I feel like a fool who's been given a second chance at happiness. Believe me, this time I'm not going to blow it."

"We're home," Julie said gently as she saw her mother-in-law rocking her three-month-old son a year later. She paused in the living room. Daniel had bought the house she'd loved and made extensive repairs. Most of the work they'd done together during Julie's pregnancy. "You know who you remind me of?" Julie asked, lifting the sleeping baby from Clara's arms.

"Probably Whistler's mother," the older woman answered with a soft chuckle. She had spent the evening with little Ted while Julie and Daniel attended a banquet at the Country Club.

"Was Jim surprised to be named Man of The Year?" Clara asked.

"Not anymore than I was last year," Daniel answered with a chuckle. "But then last year was a very good year."

"It was indeed," Clara murmured wistfully. "I was given a new lease on life."

"So was I." Daniel slipped an arm around his wife's trim waist and lovingly kissed the brow of his sleeping son.

Julie smiled down on her baby. "Was he good?"

"Not a peep. I must admit to being a bit frightened by him yet. He's so small. Theodore August Van Deen seems such a big name for such a tiny baby."

"He'll grow," Daniel said confidently. "And be joined by several more if his mother agrees."

"Oh, I'm in full agreement."

The baby let out a small cry.

"It isn't his feeding time, is it?" Clara looked up to Julie, the weathered brow knit with concern.

"Not yet," Julie assured her. "Don't worry, Grandma, babies sometimes cry for no reason."

"Teddy-boy, Grandma's joy." Clara took the baby from Julie and placed him over her shoulder. Gently, she patted his tiny back.

With infinite tenderness Daniel turned Julie into his arms, burying his face in the warm hollow of her throat. "I love you, Julie Van Deen." He raised his head and looked deeply into her soft blue eyes.

"And I you, my husband."

"The hurts and doubts are gone forever. I've buried my yesterdays."

"And look with happy excitement toward our tomorrows," she whispered softly and smiled.

*   *   *   *   *

A Note from Paula Detmer Riggs

Dear Reader,

Every young woman dreams of her wedding. Well, anyway, I did. I wanted it all—the fit-for-a-princess dress, traditional music, my friends cheering me on, proud parents (okay, so maybe an astute observer might have noticed a large measure of relief in those pleased expressions, but hey, you know parents).

My husband-to-be was an officer in the navy, assigned to a destroyer plying the South China Sea. Not really hazardous duty, thank goodness, but since this was during the Vietnam War, the captain of said ship had this quirky belief that his officers should put their duties before minor distractions like weddings and frantic fiancées. After much delicate negotiating on the part of my clever intended, the skipper finally consented to grant him two weeks' leave after the ship returned to port.

Cleverly—or so I'd thought—I set the date for two weeks after the ship was due back to San Diego. Sorority sisters were flying in from various parts of the country, the cake was ordered, the two pastors' schedules coordinated, the caterer was set. We were styling!

Then came word from my apologetic fiancé. The cruise had been extended. Excuse me? In navy terms, that meant the ship wasn't going to be home until well after the event. In other words, I'd been left at the altar, even before the wedding!

Fortunately, like the love story in *Full Circle,* my story had a happy ending. Six months later my handsome sailor was home, the church was filled with relieved family and friends, and I got to walk down the aisle in my beautiful white dress.

Paula Detmer Riggs

FULL CIRCLE

Paula Detmer Riggs

Chapter 1

The Clayton High School band swung into a rousing rendition of the "Washington Post March" as Jillian Anderson, high heels clattering and long auburn hair flying, bounded up the steps of the bunting-draped platform.

The four other members of the town council had already arrived and were gathered around the podium in the center of the stage, their eyes trained in her direction. Jillian could almost hear their collective sigh of relief as she hurried across the rough boards.

From below the platform, where most of the spectators were bunched, she heard the shouts of the crowd egging her on.

"Yeah, Jillian."

"Go get 'em, Mayor."

With a sunny but slightly breathless smile, she dropped her speech and her purse onto the nearest folding chair and returned the friendly waves of her neighbors.

"Whew, that was much too close," she managed between ragged breaths as she joined the others. Her wide green eyes sparkled as she glanced down at her watch. "Two minutes to spare."

The ceremony was scheduled to begin at ten, and she'd jogged in a narrow skirt and heels most of the distance from the parking lot outside the fence in order to make it on time.

Her cheeks tingled from the brisk September wind, and her sun-streaked auburn bob, unruly even on the best of days, tumbled wildly over the trim collar of her tailored blue blazer, framing her face with exotic color.

The three men on the welcoming committee exchanged pained looks, and Jillian hid a smile. In the 142 years since the town had been founded by two survivors of the Donner Party, Clayton, California, had never had a woman mayor—until now.

Three years ago she'd been elected by a landslide. At the time, she'd promised to bring increased employment to the economically depressed area, and today she was keeping that promise.

Wilderness Horizons, a drug treatment facility based in Seattle, was opening its newest unit on a twenty-five-acre plot outside of town, and nearly forty-five local citizens were starting new jobs there this morning.

The town was celebrating, and Jillian was scheduled to give the first speech.

"Here, have a program," said the only other woman on the stage. "Wouldn't you know, they just arrived from the printer an hour ago? Talk about small-town casual."

Adrian Franklin was the town's only doctor and Jillian's best friend. She was a small pretty woman with short dark brown hair, snapping black eyes and a mischievous sense of humor.

Jillian laughed and used the program as a fan. "I feel as though I've been circling the parking lot for days," she told Adrian with a quick look over her shoulder.

The newly renovated grounds were packed with casually dressed visitors, with more streaming past the uniformed guard at the gate. Family groups on blankets dotted the wide open space under the flagpole, while others clustered along the edges of the swimming pool and spilled over onto the volleyball court.

"I know what you mean," Adrian replied, tossing her long straight bangs away from her face. "My Jeep's crammed into a spot better suited to a bicycle. It's a good thing the people from Horizons are coming by helicopter. Clayton is definitely not set up to handle a crowd this size."

"Don't talk about crowds, Addie. You know how nervous I get when I have to speak in public. Every time I stand in front of a microphone I'm absolutely convinced that I'm going to open my mouth and gibberish will come out."

Adrian laughed. "Not you, Jill. You're never at a loss for words."

"That comes from living with a teenager. You learn to think on your feet."

Jillian leaned against the rough two-by-four railing and lifted her face to the sky. The sun was hidden by the thick overhanging clouds, and the cool breeze carried a hint of winter. To the west the green slopes of the Sierra Nevada slanted sharply upward to disappear into the gray fog. It was a gloomy day for a celebration, but no one seemed to mind.

Adrian looked around. "Where *is* Jason?"

Jillian's face softened into a dimpled smile as she thought about her son. He was a small miniature of her, with his flyaway red hair and pale freckled skin, but in many ways he was different, too. Jason was far too stubborn for his own good, she admitted, and impossibly quick-tempered, just as his father had been.

"He's at home," she told Adrian with a quick smile. "Said he had homework."

"Good kid."

Jillian laughed. "Actually I think he was afraid I'd embarrass him. He's at that awkward age where he hates to admit that he even has a mother. You know, when girls are calling at every hour of the day and night, and a pimple is an occasion for panic."

Adrian groaned. "How well I remember."

"Don't we all! I was known as 'Jill the Giraffe' until my weight caught up with my height."

Adrian clucked her tongue. "I was 'Old Thunder Thighs.'" She glanced down at her trim form. "They're still there, lurking, waiting for that extra bite of chocolate."

As they shared a laugh, Jillian's idle gaze dropped to the chairs placed directly in front of the podium. Seated there were the boys, fifty in number, who were going to be living at Horizons for the next six months, sentenced by the courts to the strict high-security facility as a last resort.

All were hard-core drug addicts, and most had been arrested more than once. At the moment, each boy wore the sullen look of a half-grown kid forced to be where he didn't want to be.

Even the counselors, dressed as casually as the boys, looked uneasy, as though they were equally uncomfortable. Was something wrong? she wondered, frowning. Something she as mayor should know? Her gaze traced the line of faces again, then stopped abruptly at the last boy.

A ragged open area segregated the group from the rest of the spectators, and at each side of the empty space stood an armed deputy sheriff.

"For God's sake, Mel, are you crazy?" she exclaimed, whirling to lock gazes with a giant of a man wearing the olive drab uniform of the Clayton County sheriff. "You're deliberately humiliating those boys, and I won't have it. It's wrong, and it's cruel."

The loose flesh above the sheriff's tight khaki collar reddened, sending streaks of dusky color along his pugnacious jaw. "Full-fledged hoodlums," he exclaimed in an overly loud voice. "That's what they are, rotten little bastards, all of them. And our tax dollars are supporting them."

"Mel, we've been over this a dozen times," Jillian said with barely concealed impatience. "Wilderness Horizons is a private corporation. Your tax money is safe."

Mirrored in the lenses of his sunglasses, her oval face was pink with outrage, and below her swooping auburn brows, her jade-colored eyes seethed with angry gold sparks.

Stay calm, Jill, she told herself firmly, taking a slow breath. The last thing the town needed at this moment was an ugly scene. Today was supposed to be a happy time for all of them—including the boys sitting in front of her.

"If it'll make you feel better, Sheriff," she told him, instinctively slipping into the same quiet but firm tone she'd once used as a Navy nurse to control belligerent patients twice her size, "I'll assume responsibility for their behavior."

"Sure, you say that now, Jillian," Mel Cobb shot back sarcastically after a moment's hesitation, "but what happens when one of these *boys* gets loose and goes on a rampage? Maybe even rips off your precious Sierra Pharmacy for money or drugs? How're you going to feel then?"

Jillian ignored the sarcasm. "Move the deputies, Mel. Right now."

Cobb gave her a long, tight-lipped look, then spun on his heel and stalked toward the steps.

The two deputies were quickly dispatched to take up other posts in the area, and Jillian breathed a sigh of relief. Mel had good credentials, in spite of a reputation for using force where it wasn't always necessary, and he'd accepted the minimal salary that was all Clayton could afford to pay. Otherwise the town would never have hired him.

"You should have gone out with the guy when he asked you. At least once, anyway," Adrian teased in a low voice. "You know what they say about a man scorned."

"Please, Addie," Jillian told her friend in a long-suffering tone. "Not today."

Adrian's answer was forestalled by a sudden blinding light cocooning the platform.

Two yards away a stocky man in a safari jacket and shorts hefted a minicam to his shoulder, then approached slowly, panning the platform from left to right. Behind him came a young black man in jeans and a sweatshirt carrying a light bar and sound equipment.

The PBS series *Focus*, a popular monthly documentary on health and safety in the eighties, was doing a feature on Horizons' innovative program of combining military survival training with conventional methods to treat chemical dependency.

"Here they come," Adrian exclaimed, clutching Jillian's arm and glancing upward.

The noise of rotor blades thundered in Jillian's ears as a sleek red-and-white helicopter cleared the needle-sharp tops of the tallest pines and settled gently onto the ground. A cloud of red dust billowed upward, and the leaves of the hardwood trees rustled overhead.

Orrie Hughes and Rick Garcia, the other two members of the town council, came to stand behind her. The sheriff returned to the platform and stood alone, a dark scowl on his face.

"This is the most exciting thing that's happened in this ol' town since Hans Baumgartner tried to make beer in his basement and blew out all the windows in his house," Orrie muttered close to her ear.

Jillian chuckled and glanced over her shoulder. Orrie, eighty-three and still working every day in his barbershop, was dressed in a suit for the first time in her memory.

"When was that, Orrie?" she asked with a grin.

"Oh, after the war. Nineteen twenty. Twenty-one, someplace in there."

An excited buzz rose from the spectators, punctuated by the shrill shouts of excited children, most of whom had never been this close to a helicopter before.

As she straightened the collar of her white silk blouse and buttoned the dark blue jacket, Jillian struggled against a queasy feeling of déjà vu. During the Vietnam War she'd seen too many Medevac helicopters carrying too many dead or dying men to enjoy the sight of another one.

"Horizons is obviously not lacking for money," Adrian told her with a grin as the rotors began to slow.

"Actually," Jillian said absently, "the parent corporation is one of the most profitable in the health care field. I checked them out before I opened negotiations, just to be safe."

Suddenly the helicopter door slid open. Three passengers, two men dressed in conservative dark suits and a tall blond woman in beige silk, stepped out into the bright light and began walking toward the platform, ducking their heads against the down draft from the slowly spiraling blades.

Jillian recognized the woman as Robin Bessaman, the executive director of Wilderness Horizons with whom she'd been negotiating the terms of the lease. She didn't know the men.

The band swung into another march, and Jillian absently tapped her foot along with the pounding rhythm. Quickly she ran through her speech in her head. This was going to be a great day for Clayton.

"Now that's what I call a *good*-looking man," Adrian muttered at her side.

"You always were a sucker for a guy with a beard, Addie."

"Uh-uh. I mean the other one, the tough-looking type with the dynamite shoulders and the don't-mess-with-me swagger."

"Control yourself, Doctor," Jillian teased, peering through the swirling dust. "He's probably Horizons' accountant."

"No way. I tell you, Jill, if he's carrying anything but muscle under that Brooks Brothers suit, it's more likely to be a gun than a calculator."

Jillian's pulse tripped as her gaze fastened on the shadowed features of the husky, ramrod-straight man in a gray three-piece suit bringing up the rear. He was bigger than most men she knew, with the shoulders of a lumberjack and long, powerful-looking legs, and he walked with a rolling gait that suggested a barely restrained impatience. Or, she admitted reluctantly, danger. This time Adrian wasn't far off the mark.

The dust began to settle, and she got her first good look at his face. His features were strongly carved, with angular lines and shadows adding to the aura of danger surrounding him. His mouth, slanted now into a controlled white grin, looked hard, as though smiling was something he rarely did. His eyes—

Jillian gasped. Oh, my God. No! It couldn't be.

Only one man had eyes like that, intense, passionate copper eyes that looked almost black when he was aroused. Eyes that had once bathed every inch of her naked body with fire.

"Trevor."

His name shuddered from the darkest part of her memory where she'd fought so hard to bury it.

The air around her thinned, making it hard to breathe, and she blindly groped for the back of the nearest chair. This couldn't be happening, she thought. Not when her life was finally in order, and her wounds were healed.

Her hands were shaking as she ripped open the program Adrian had given her and quickly scanned the names of the guests. He was listed under the executive committee.

Trevor Madison Markus, Chairman of the Board and Founder of Wilderness Horizons. The black letters wavered in front of her eyes, mocking her. She crushed the program between her hands and let it fall to the stage as she stared past the empty chairs toward the steps.

The crisp, sandy blond hair was now a solid gunmetal gray, and the years had added muscle and power to his whipcord frame, but his face was even more ruggedly handsome than she remembered—if that were possible.

Than she remembered . . .

It had taken years of hard work, years of missing him and crying for him, years of lying awake, lonely and aching, but she'd pushed him out of her mind and her heart.

Jillian glanced around hastily, filled with a sudden powerful urge to run. Robin Bessaman had never mentioned his name. Not once, even though she'd spoken highly of the Horizons Board on occasion.

Jillian's heart began to pound and her breath shortened, coming in irregular intervals that hurt her chest. She bit the inside of her lip so hard she tasted blood.

"Jill, are you all right?" Adrian's voice had lost its teasing lilt. "Your face is as white as your blouse."

"I . . . yes, I'm fine. I missed breakfast, that's all."

Jillian glanced back toward the steps. The television lights caught her, and her cheeks burned. She was onstage, held in the spotlight of the camera, her every expression monitored. She was trapped.

At the edge of the stage, Robin paused, an anticipatory smile on her face. As soon as she caught sight of Jillian, her smile broadened, and she waved. Before Jillian could react, the woman had turned back to direct a remark to the two men behind her.

Trevor's head came up abruptly, and his grin faded. As his copper gaze locked with Jillian's, he paled, and his shoulders jerked. He looked like a man who'd just been blindsided by a knockout punch.

His lips moved stiffly, forming her name. The years telescoped, and she felt again the pressure of that hard mouth on hers. Trevor's mouth.

His wide, warm lips had tasted hers with bold masculine relish, each kiss more demanding than the last, until he had only to smile in that special half challenging, half beguiling way, and she'd shivered helplessly in anticipation.

She shivered now, and something barbed and cutting twisted inside her. Once she'd loved the way his lips had smiled against hers. Once she'd loved *him*. But he hadn't loved her.

Robin hurried across the platform, her hand extended eagerly. "This is a terrific welcome, Mayor. I couldn't be more grateful."

"Clayton prides itself on its neighborliness," Jillian managed to get out, her voice unnaturally flat. Inside, her stomach was tumbling violently, and her mouth was dry. "I'm sure everyone here is as pleased as I am to welcome Horizons."

The two men approached, with the leaner, bearded man slightly in the rear. Jillian felt the bloodless chill on her cheeks as she turned to greet them. She concentrated on breathing normally.

Her welcoming gaze included both men, but in her mind she saw only Trevor. The strong, square face, the quizzical lines bracketing his quiet, surprisingly sensual mouth, the slight cleft in his stubborn chin. And the bleak, shuttered look in his eyes.

Robin introduced her to Trevor first, adding with pride in her voice, "Trev doesn't usually attend opening ceremonies, but since Clayton Horizons is our twentieth unit, he's made an exception."

"How nice for us," Jillian murmured, watching his thick sandy lashes lift until those deep-set eyes were resting intently on hers. Something powerful and unreadable shifted in the midnight pupils, tugging at her. *Anguish.* The thought came, then was banished from her mind in the instant it took him to blink.

Ignoring the shiver of uneasiness that shot down her backbone, she fixed a cool smile on her face and extended her hand. Because he was a guest of the town, she would be polite.

"Hello, Trevor," she said in a voice that sounded perfectly calm. "It's been a long time."

His shadowed gaze fell to her small hand. "Yes, a long time." His grip was warm and strong. Too strong. He was hurting her, but she refused to show it.

He cleared his throat. "It's . . . good to see you again . . . Jill."

"Is it?"

"Yes. I've thought about you over the years...wondered what happened to you." His voice deepened, grew husky, more intimate.

"Really?" She tugged her hand from his, but the skin still stung where his long fingers had crushed hers. His touch still had the power to shake her.

A muscle worked along his strong jaw. "Yes, really. But I see that you don't believe me." His mouth twisted down at one corner. "Maybe I don't even blame you. I was a bastard."

Shock shuddered through her. Abruptly she wrenched her gaze away from the eyes that had haunted her dreams for too many years. She wouldn't remember, she told herself, balling the hand that he'd held into a fist. It hurt too much.

"Trev?" Robin's pleased smile slipped, and a look of concern replaced the warmth in her eyes.

"You give the speech today, Rob," Trevor said in a clipped, husky tone. "You're better at it than I am, anyway."

Abruptly he unbuttoned his coat and shoved his hands into the pockets of his trousers. Jillian recognized the unconscious gesture of masculine insecurity, and she felt a sharp stab of satisfaction. He might have stunned her into silence, but Trevor Markus wasn't as confident as he appeared.

"Excuse me," he said curtly.

He moved past them to greet the others on the platform, and Jillian suppressed a sigh of relief as she turned her attention to the bearded man waiting patiently for an introduction.

He was tall, almost as tall as Trevor, with a rangy build and intelligent gray eyes. Robin introduced him as Dr. Henry Stoneson, the director of Clayton Horizons.

Jillian summoned a polite smile. "Dr. Stoneson."

"Call me Hank," he said in a lazy West Texas drawl as they shook hands. She estimated his age at forty-five, give or take a few years.

"I'm Jillian."

"That's an ... unusual name."

Suddenly she had a strong but totally inexplicable conviction that this man knew her or, rather, knew exactly what she was feeling. But that was impossible. She was very good at hiding her feelings. She'd had to be.

Involuntarily she glanced toward Trevor, who'd moved to the rail and was talking with one of the counselors who'd been sitting with the boys. He stood rigidly, tension written in every powerful line of his long body, and his hand gripped the railing so tightly that the knuckles poked white against the bronzed skin.

If she didn't know better, she would have sworn that Trevor had been hurt by her indifferent welcome. But that was a fool's perception. A man had to love a woman before she could hurt him. And Trevor had never loved her.

Suppressing a shiver, she turned away and briskly introduced the other members of the council to the two visitors. There was a flurry of handshaking and polite conversation while the band pounded out the last verse of the march.

As soon as the last notes died away, Jillian stepped up to the podium and switched on the microphone. The others on the platform took their seats, and the crowd settled down.

Directly below her, the cameraman from PBS prowled the area, expertly framing his shots as Jillian smiled warmly at her fellow citizens. The knot in her stomach pulled tighter.

She took a deep breath, praying silently for control, then began to speak. "Ladies and gentlemen, honored guests..."

Jillian spoke the words she'd practiced by rote. Her speech was short and optimistic, laying out all the reasons why the town was welcoming its new neighbors.

"...and we all remember what this town was like four years ago, when Pacific Timber declared bankruptcy and closed their doors. Families were uprooted, homes went into foreclosure, people were scared. But this town, all of you, fought back. You didn't give up. And so today we celebrate a new beginning, a second chance for all of us...."

When she finished, the crowd applauded and whistled, and she waved her thanks. When the applause began to slacken, she quickly introduced Robin Bessaman, then sat down next to Adrian.

From the corner of her eye she saw Trevor sitting across the aisle. His spine was pressed against the back of the metal folding chair back, and his long legs were fully extended in front of him.

His eyes were focused on Robin's back, but his expression was stiffly remote, as though his thoughts were far away. As she watched, his hand slowly tightened into a fist against his heavily muscled thigh, and he lowered his head as though in prayer.

Jillian dropped her gaze to the unpainted planks beneath her feet. Slowly she slid her burgundy pumps backward and tucked them under her chair. Letting Robin's perfectly modulated voice flow over her, she studied the tracks her soles had made in the fine layer of dust covering the bare boards.

Footprints in the sand, she thought. No matter how deep, they were only temporary. Sooner or later the tracks would be swept away—like the promises Trevor had once made her.

Jillian drew in a deep breath of air that smelled of pine and threatening rain. Overhead, the large, jagged leaves of a sycamore shuddered in the brisk wind, twisting and turning on their fragile stems.

The trees outside the big military hospital in Tokyo that summer had been a vivid green. Jillian had loved to sit by the window in the nurses' lounge and watch a pair of little brown birds tend their newly hatched nestling.

The baby, undersized and feeble, had fought hard to survive, but one gloomy July dawn she'd found him lying crumpled and lifeless in the tiny nest.

Like so many of the critically wounded men in her ward, he'd lost the fight to live.

But Trevor had won, against all odds.

The sound of Robin's voice faded as Jillian's thoughts spun backward....

"His name's Markus," the burly corpsman tossed over his shoulder as he positioned the bed carefully against the wall in the small cubicle.

The patient was a big man, with long legs that stretched to the end of the hospital bed, and muscular shoulders that were almost as wide as the pillow. He'd been in surgery for nearly seven hours, and his face was pasty white and lined with pain. "Doc says he probably won't make it through the night."

Jillian quickly scanned the chart. His first name was Trevor, and he was twenty-nine. In six days he'd be thirty, she realized. If he lived.

He was a lieutenant commander in the Navy, a pilot assigned to the carrier *Ranger* which was operating in the South China Sea. His crippled jet had run out of fuel only seconds before he was to land, and the plane had hit the deck instead of the sea. The crash landing had shattered his legs and crushed his spine, but because his fuel tanks had been bone-dry, the plane hadn't exploded on impact. Somehow he'd survived, critically injured and near death, one more wounded Naval officer to add to a lengthening list.

The evac hospital had struggled to stabilize his vital signs and, as soon as he'd been out of immediate danger, had immobilized him for the trip to Tokyo, where the surgeons had worked to save his legs and reconstruct his spine. Most of his body was now encased in plaster, and he had months of almost total immobility ahead of him.

"He's not dead yet," Jillian muttered at the weary-looking corpsman. Together they studied the ashen face half buried in the pillow. The man's nose had been broken in the crash, and one eye was purple and swollen shut. His short sandy hair was damp and matted with sweat.

"Guy looks tough," the enlisted man said with an edge to his voice. "Maybe he *will* make it." He gave Jillian a sympathetic nod and left the room.

An hour later the unconscious pilot started thrashing and moaning in pain as he tried to pull the IV needle from his wide, bronzed forearm.

"Easy, Commander," Jillian murmured, preparing a syringe. The doctor had ordered the maximum dosage of morphine every four hours if he needed it, but she had a feeling it wasn't going to be enough.

As she plunged a needle into his arm, he opened his eyes, blinking in the light. His eyes, deep-set and framed in dark blond lashes, were a startling shade of brown that was almost copper. At the corners, deep weather lines were etched into the tanned skin, and his brows were boldly defined and sun-bleached blond.

"Am I home?" His voice was a ragged whisper, a dark sound of agony.

"No, Commander, not yet. You're in Tokyo, in the hospital." Jillian wiped the sweat from his brow with a cool cloth.

He blinked up at her, trying to smile. "You...have a nice face."

Under several days' growth of whiskers, he had the look of a practiced flirt, a hotshot pilot who knew he was irresistible to women. She'd met her fill of Navy flyers just like him in every officers' club from Newport to Subic Bay.

But there was more than conceit in the pain-filled eyes that stared up at her with such intensity, much more. There was intelligence and humor and tough resilience that gave her hope. Maybe the corpsman was right. Maybe he wouldn't die.

"I bet you say that to all the girls," she said with a teasing grin.

His thick crescent lashes drooped, then raised. "No, just you. Who...are...you?"

Each word was an effort, and Jillian moved closer. The man was in for a rough time, rougher than he could even imagine. She made her voice light and cheerful, trying to distract him from the pain. "My name is Jillian. I'm your nurse."

"Pretty name," he whispered through stiff lips. His hand groped for hers, and she slid her fingers over his, holding his strong brown hand while the morphine worked its way through his veins to numb the screaming nerve endings. He tried not to groan, but the pain was too much for him. He twisted his head on the pillow, trying to escape the agony.

"Hang on to me," she told him, squeezing his hand. "Hold on, Trevor."

His hand crushed hers, but she didn't cry out. His breathing was harsh, and his eyes were tortured.

"Don't...leave me," he whispered through parched lips. "Don't let go. I can make it if you don't let go."

A burst of applause shattered Jillian's inner privacy, jerking her back to the present with a heart-pounding start. She heard the rumble of conversation from the others on the platform and the buzz of the crowd. The band was playing again, and children were laughing. Robin had finished, and the ceremony was over.

She stood.

Trevor came up to her before she could escape.

Without thinking, she moistened her parched lips with the tip of her tongue, and a tiny flare of something hot came and went in his black pupils. Once he'd looked at her just that way before he'd pulled her down for a heated kiss.

"I liked your speech," he said quietly.

She had the oddest feeling that Trevor was holding back, restraining himself in some way. But that was patently ridiculous, she told herself. There had never been *anything* restrained about Trevor Markus.

"Thank you," she said primly, glancing around. The others were all gathered near the steps, where the TV director was interviewing Hank Stoneson.

"I especially liked the part about a second chance."

"Did you?"

"Very much." There was a tense pause, one that seemed to throb between them. "I believe in second chances, too." He glanced down the lean length of his body. "As you can see."

Jillian didn't want to see the solid muscles and rangy sinew that were barely gentled by the civilized pinstripes. She didn't want to measure his length against hers. She didn't want to know where his thighs would press her, where her breasts would touch his chest. She didn't want to know... anything.

"I'm glad to see that you've completely recovered," she said with a chilly nod, preparing to excuse herself. She was shaking so hard inside that she felt as though she would shatter.

"You told me that I would." A glimmer of a smile came and went in the warm copper between his thick lashes.

She gave him an impersonal smile, the kind she reserved for visiting politicians. "At least I was right about some things."

He glanced around, impatience written on his face. "Look, Jill, I know we need to talk, but—"

"No."

He seemed not to have heard her. "Any time you say, any place. You set the terms."

Somewhere deep inside, scar tissue tore away, leaving her raw and unprotected. No terms, she thought wildly. Not for this man.

Her heart began to pound furiously, and her stomach lurched. She needed air; she needed to escape.

"There's nothing to talk about, Mr. Markus. You're an honored guest of this town. As mayor, I'm your hostess. Otherwise, I can assure you that I wouldn't have stayed on the same platform with you for more than the second or two it would have taken to find the stairs.'' She lifted her chin and met his copper gaze defiantly. ''I hope I've made myself perfectly clear.''

One side of his sensual, hard mouth lifted in a half mocking, half amused smile. She remembered that smile. The first time she'd seen it, he'd been trying to get her into his bed.

''In other words, get lost.''

''I couldn't have put it better myself.''

His eyes narrowed only a fraction at the corners, but Jillian noticed, just as she noticed the immediate prickles of warning dotting her skin. This man wasn't used to being crossed.

''Suppose, as an *honored* guest, I ask for a personal escort?''

He was at least five inches taller than she was, and she had to tilt her head to look at him. She hated the advantage it gave him.

''I'm sure one of the men on the council would be happy to oblige,'' she murmured politely.

''I want you.''

For an instant Jillian couldn't move. Echoes of the past bore down on her, nearly smothering her.

I want you, Jill. For now. For always. But always had lasted less than seven months.

''Sorry,'' she said in a cool, steady voice that cost her dearly. ''I'm not available.''

She turned and walked away from him.

She felt sick.

She glanced across the wide expanse of sunburned lawn toward the rear of the administration building, where a group of local citizens lined the large concrete patio. In a central area, a California redwood tree almost six feet tall, its roots balled in burlap, stood to one side of a mound of red dirt. From nearly every branch fluttered a bright yellow ribbon.

According to Robin, every unit of Horizon had such a tree. Trevor had planted the first one nearly ten years ago at the first facility in Seattle. It was a symbol of a new life for each boy who walked through the gate.

"Oh, yeah. I forgot about the tree." Adrian frowned briefly, then brightened. "Listen, I was thinking, how about meeting Peter and me for a drink when we're done here? He has a friend who—"

"Stop!" Jillian held up her hand and scowled. "No more blind dates. I'm still trying to get over the last guy. Remember him? The one who was into alfalfa sprouts and past life regression?" She sighed. "I'm having enough trouble with the life I have right now, thank you very much."

She began walking toward the patio, and Adrian was forced to fall in step or be left behind. The crowd was slowly dispersing, some ambling toward the patio, others heading for the far end of the compound, where members of the Ladies Aid Society of the Community Church were setting out a potluck buffet.

"You're too picky for your own good, Jill. Besides, Pete's friend is an attorney and very good-looking."

Jillian made a face. "That's not the point," she said in the placid, reasonable tone that she usually reserved for her son's more difficult moments. "My conscience tells me I should open the pharmacy for a few hours this afternoon in case anyone needs a prescription filled. You may not have noticed, but I *am* the only pharmacist in town."

Adrian's sleek black brows arched. "I've noticed. I've *also* noticed that you've been as nervous as a cat since you shook hands with one Trevor Markus, who just happens to have the kind of body bachelor ladies like me fantasize about while soaking in a bubble bath.'' A sly look brightened her black eyes as she puffed on her cigarette, then blew out a stream of smoke. ''Dare I hope you've finally met a man who's gotten through that thick armor of yours?''

Armor?

Triple-tested and double-thick, Jillian thought as she sidestepped a discarded paper cup. Guaranteed to keep her safe against charming and selfish men who wanted only the pleasure they could strip from her body before moving on.

''For heaven's sake, Addie, you make me sound like some kind of man hater,'' she groused. ''I'm just . . . particular, that's all.''

''Now that's an understatement if I ever heard one.'' Adrian clucked her tongue in mock despair. ''How many men have there been in your life since you moved here ten years ago?''

Jillian's voice sharpened. ''How should I know? I don't make a mark on a scorecard every time I have a date.''

''Just when *was* your last date?''

Jillian sighed. Adrian was beginning to get on her nerves. ''Last New Year's Eve, the Fourth of July, I can't remember. I have other things to think about, Addie.''

''Like what?''

She let her impatience hurry her speech. ''Like making a living, heading the town council, taking care of my son, minor things like that.''

She increased her pace, her long legs taking one step while Adrian, shorter by at least six inches, was forced to take two. ''And for your information, Doctor, I'm not nervous.''

Adrian detoured to a nearby trash receptacle, where she ground the butt of her cigarette against the metal barrel before discarding it.

''The autocratic Mr. Markus was nervous, too,'' she said as she fell in step again. ''It wasn't obvious, I grant you, but the awareness was definitely there, around the jaw and in the set of those drop-dead shoulders, especially when he looked at you—and he looked at you a lot. I tell you, Jill, the man had the look of a patient facing major surgery. I've seen it dozens of times.''

Jillian snorted in disgust. ''That's a great analogy, Addie, comparing me to major surgery. Thanks a lot.''

Adrian rolled her eyes. ''You know what I mean. The man was shocked clear down to his spit-shined loafers.''

''So? Maybe he was expecting the mayor to be a man.''

Without seeming to, Jillian searched the area for Trevor's tall silhouette. He was standing alone near the rear entrance to the administration building, one arm braced against the large concrete post supporting the latticework overhang.

He'd removed his suit coat, and the sleeves of his pale blue shirt were rolled to the middle of his forearms. He had large, square hands and sailor's wrists, supple and thick and heavily veined where they widened into the oak-hard muscles of his arms.

She remembered the play of those corded muscles against the white sheet when he'd gripped her hand. He'd had a big man's wariness about his own strength, and he'd tried not to squeeze too tightly. But sometimes he hadn't been able to help himself, he'd needed her so desperately.

So many times, late at night as she'd sat next to him, watching him toss and turn restlessly in a drug-induced sleep, she'd tried to imagine what it would be like to stand in the shelter of his long, powerful arms, to be cradled against his chest, to hear the strong beat of his heart, to rest her head on his wide shoulder, listening to the quiet resonance of his breathing.

She inhaled slowly, fighting an irrational urge to walk into those arms and pillow her head on his shoulder. Once, he would have welcomed her....

Jillian glanced up to find Adrian looking at her as though she were some puzzling diagnostic case.

''C'mon,'' Jillian told her in a forced breezy tone, ''we've got fifteen minutes. I'll buy you some cider at the VFW stand, and you can tell me your latest escapades with the handsome Professor Peter Morrow.''

Trevor Markus braced his spine against the rough redwood siding of the building behind him and watched the two women sipping cider by the small red, white and blue stand.

He was sweating, even though the sun was hidden behind a fat gray thunderhead and a sharp breeze was blowing from the north. Inhaling the familiar scent of threatening rain, he shifted from one large foot to the other, trying to ease the knotted muscles of his lower back.

He should have worn his brace, but he hated the damn thing. It was hot and stiff and itched like the very devil.

He *should* have stayed home, that was what he should have done. He couldn't remember the last time he'd sat for more than a few minutes on the deck of his Belleview house.

Damn it, he'd bought the place because it had a fantastic view of Lake Washington, a view he rarely saw.

When he was home, he spent most of his time in his den, working on the latest project for Markus Engineering International, and it was usually dark by the time he finished. Most nights he ate his dinner at his desk, soaked for twenty minutes in the Jacuzzi, then fell into bed.

He ran his hand down the rough post. The ache in his back was beginning to get worse. It was always bad when he was tense.

He needed a drink, he thought grimly. A double Scotch. Or even one of Hank's foul-tasting cigars. Anything to keep from jumping out of his skin.

He hadn't been this edgy for years, not since he'd sunk every dime he'd saved into the civil engineering firm he'd founded a few years before he'd started Horizons.

His hand clenched against the post. The last time he'd seen Jillian Anderson, she'd been walking alongside the stretcher, trying to smile through her tears as he was taken to the Medevac plane.

The dope they'd pumped into him so that he could stand the twelve-hour trip back to the States had made him drowsy, but he'd forced himself to stay awake, struggling to burn her face into his memory. The face of his personal angel.

Nurse Jillian Anderson, he thought. His Jillian.

A thousand times over the years he'd told himself that he would never see her again. When he'd walked out on her, he was full of anger, full of self-hatred and resentment. Against the Navy, against the war, against her, for making him want things he couldn't have.

It had taken months, years, before he'd been able to think about that time in his life without wanting to put his fist through the nearest wall.

He'd been a bastard, all right, and she had every right to resent him. He'd treated her as badly as a man can treat a woman. She knew it and, God help him, so did he.

But he'd changed. He wasn't the same man who'd left her. It had taken him years to find the courage to look at himself in the mirror when he shaved, really look. Even now, he wasn't sure he liked what he saw.

But at least now he could sleep most nights without waking up drenched with sweat and guilt.

He still thought of her. He always would. But over the years she'd become more like an unattainable dream than a real woman. And as long as she'd remained only a memory, he'd been able to live with himself. At least most of the time.

But now, suddenly, when he'd least expected it, she was standing only a few feet away, so achingly lovely that it hurt to look at her. He had only to cross a few feet of concrete to be able to touch her, to feel again that soft, pliant body move sensually beneath his palm.

But he didn't move, didn't try to close the distance between them. He'd forfeited that right a long time ago, a right he knew he'd never have again.

His left hand clenched, the hard edges of his closely clipped nails digging into his palm. He welcomed the pain, even sought it. He needed something, anything, to distract him from the memories Jillian's presence aroused, terrible, accusing memories that had tortured him for months, even years, before he'd wrestled them into oblivion.

But this was a different Jillian, he realized as he watched her closely. The pixie cap of bright curls that used to smell of jasmine was now a thick mane of sun-washed waves, shimmering in the light and so soft-looking they begged to be touched. And her body... Trevor inhaled slowly, fighting the rush of raw need that flared in his loins. Once she'd been willowy, her hips scarcely wider than her tiny waist, and her breasts had been small perfect globes that barely filled his palms. But now, even sheathed in some kind of plain blue suit, her body had a ripeness that was sending his male radar into alarm status.

Damn, he thought. Why hadn't she grown fat or wrinkled? Why had she become even more desirable in her thirties than she'd been at twenty-one?

It didn't seem possible that she was thirty-six. And yet he knew that she'd celebrated her birthday in August, just as he knew that she loved chocolate and rum punch ice cream. And that she loved to be kissed behind her ears, and tickled behind her knees.

God, Trevor thought. He had to stop thinking like this. There'd been no spark of interest in her eyes, no nostalgia, nothing but cool rejection. Not that he could blame her, he admitted with a silent sigh.

No matter how hard he'd tried, he'd never been able to forgive himself for hurting her so terribly.

A familiar restlessness tightened the muscles of his thighs, and he shifted his feet. He needed to burn off the scorching tension that was lashing him.

He allowed himself to look at her again. She was explaining something to the woman with her, gesturing gracefully in the air with her left hand. There was no wedding band on her finger, no jewelry at all.

Over and over he'd told himself that she would marry, would have children and be happy, far happier than he could have made her.

"I want babies, Trev," she'd said with a dreamy smile that last night before he'd been evacuated to the States. "Lots and lots of babies, with your eyes. I want a house in the mountains, where we can hear the birds sing in the morning outside our window. And I want to make love in the thick green grass."

He remembered that she'd frowned then, thinking of the terrible suffering she'd seen every day at the huge hospital. "We'll be so happy, so normal," she'd vowed. "No more pain. No more problems."

Oh, Jill, he thought, closing his eyes to blot out her lovely profile. I wanted to give you all those things. I swear I did.

Instead, he'd buried it all: Vietnam, the endless months in the hospital, Jillian. It had been the only way to put his life back together again.

Flexing his shoulders in an attempt to ease the growing tightness, Trevor looked out over the crowd gathering along the edge of the patio. He'd been the one to okay this facility after Robin had done all the preliminary work.

The lease hadn't been signed when he'd seen it. If it had been, if he'd seen Jillian's signature at the bottom, there would have been no way in hell that he would have okayed this site. No damn way at all.

Hank Stoneson looked first at his watch, then at Jillian, who was standing a few feet away, listening to Adrian and Robin talk about the health problems a chronic drug user faced.

"Ready, Ms. Mayor?" he drawled softly, drawing her gaze.

"Ready, Dr. Stoneson."

"Then let's get this sucker planted."

Hank took her arm and led her over to the tree, where a shiny new shovel adorned with a big yellow bow was propped against the root ball.

"I promise to make this as painless as possible," he told her with a crooked smile that didn't alter the somber, watchful look in his cool gray eyes.

With his rangy loose-hipped walk and laconic way of speaking, Hank reminded Jillian of the heroes in the grainy black-and-white Westerns she'd watched on TV as a child.

"Please don't worry about me, Hank," she said equably. "I'm stronger than I look."

She felt a surge of satisfaction as his eyes suddenly warmed. His head dipped slightly as a slow grin slashed white against his beard. "Yes, ma'am, I do believe you are at that."

Jillian had the distinct impression that her words had pleased him. Even stronger was the feeling that she'd met this man before—or that he'd met her. She relaxed slightly and tried to ignore the butterflies in her stomach.

The crew from PBS fanned out to bracket the area surrounding the tree. The cameraman adjusted his lens, then nodded to his assistant, who turned on the lights and sound.

"Okay, y'all, gather round," Hank drawled, his voice raised to carry over the chatter of the crowd. He waited until the noise subsided and most of the faces were turned toward him. "What we have here is a *Sequoia sempervirens*, better known as a coast redwood." He fingered a branch. "Pretty, isn't it? And this is where it comes from." He reached into the pocket of his coat and pulled out a small pinecone. He held it up for everyone to see. It was barely an inch in diameter. "Hard to believe that a tree that grows as tall and strong as this one will can start from something so small, but it does."

Without warning he tossed the cone to one of the Horizon residents in the front row. Sullen and pale, the teenage boy was smaller than the others and painfully awkward, but he managed to keep the cone from falling.

"This pinecone is like a second chance. Plant it, nurture it with hard work and determination, and it grows. One day at a time."

Hank had a droll, relaxed manner that was entertaining as well as informative, and as he told about Horizons' program, the party attitude of the crowd added to the upbeat mood.

Jillian, waiting to toss a shovelful of dirt into the hole, idly studied the faces surrounding them. The crowd was much smaller now, but it was still sizable, and most of the spectators were smiling.

She noticed Trevor immediately. Taller than most, he was standing to one side, with another group of inmates. There was a tense, almost rigid set to his shoulders, and his jaw was tight. Suddenly, as though her gaze had touched him, he turned to look at her.

He was a stranger, and yet, oddly, he was terribly familiar. The rugged masculine features were the same, the strong almost square chin with a hint of a cleft, the large straight nose, the hollowed cheeks that were now seamed with harsh lines, all terribly familiar. It was the eyes that had changed.

Still strangely hypnotic, the bronzed copper no longer held a boyish exuberance for life. There was experience trapped there, and a deep brooding sadness that caught Jillian off guard.

As she watched him, his eyes darkened, then became completely blank, and his thick lashes lowered, shutting her out.

Flushing, she jerked her gaze away. She shouldn't have touched him, she knew now, shouldn't have let him wrap his large warm hand around hers.

She could still feel the warmth of his hand against hers. She'd never forgotten the way his hands had caressed her, seduced her, thrilled her.

He'd made love to her exactly six times, always with his legs sheathed in plaster. She'd never been able to feel his legs entwining with hers, never felt the power and the tension in those heavy thighs, never felt his thighs slide against hers.

Clenching her teeth, she pretended to concentrate on Hank's words. But in her mind she was hearing Trevor's voice, low like Hank's, but more resonant and filled with a raw masculine hesitancy that had stunned her....

"Marry me, Jill, as soon as I can walk down the aisle with you." Trevor lifted her fingers to his lips and kissed the tips. "Say yes, angel. Say you'll marry me."

"Yes, yes, yes!"

He laughed and pulled her down against his chest for a long, bone-tingling kiss that left them both breathless.

It was the night before Trevor was being shipped back to the States to begin a lengthy and difficult course of therapy for his legs, and they'd just made love.

"Oh, Trevor, I love you so much," she whispered, wanting to go home with him so badly that she ached with it. "I couldn't stand it if I lost you."

Her hushed voice broke, and she bit her lip. Her happiness was like a fragile bubble, suspended in midair. Now that she'd found him, she didn't think she could face life without him.

During the months of his difficult convalescence he'd pursued her relentlessly, taking advantage of every moment she'd spent by his bedside to tease seductively, using his husky voice and his expressive eyes to do what his body couldn't.

But it was during the quiet time they spent alone that he'd won her heart. Terrified that he would spend the rest of his days in a wheelchair, he'd been moody and introspective and vulnerable, sharing his fears with her, along with his deeply buried hopes. She'd seen the real Trevor Markus during those hours, the sensitive, sometimes insecure man behind the devilish facade.

Jillian had convinced him that he would recover. Perhaps he would never fly again, or race his twelve-meter yacht on Puget Sound with his father and brother, but he would certainly walk. He'd believed her, finally, and after that had begun to make rapid progress.

In spite of the lack of privacy and the hard, unyielding casts that restricted Trevor's movement, they'd become lovers. It was always in the middle of the night, when the other men were sleeping, and it hadn't been easy. But Jillian's fellow nurses had helped, moving Trevor's bed to a private room as soon as one became available. Whenever the door was closed, no one intruded.

"You won't lose me," Trevor said with the careless note of arrogance that she'd first hated and then come to love, just as she'd come to love him.

He tugged her closer until he could lightly trace the curve of her lower lip with a long, blunt finger. Lying across his chest, she could feel the heat from his body flowing through the starched cotton of her uniform to warm her breasts.

Jillian allowed her body to soften against his. Her hands cupped his hard shoulders, and her skin tingled as she slid her palms along the hard ridge of his collarbone. His skin was warm and slightly damp, and the muscles below were hard and sharply defined.

Trevor inhaled swiftly as her hands threaded into his thick sandy hair. He kissed her hungrily, probing with his tongue, arousing her with the rough tip against hers. He tasted of chocolate, and his lips were hot.

He slid his hand to the back of her neck, and his fingers massaged the sensitive spot under her hairline. His kiss became hot and insistent, and she met his arrogant demand with a demand of her own.

His hand tangled in her short curls, and she could feel the pads of his blunt fingers pushing against her scalp. His breathing quickened and grew slightly more raspy.

She felt her own pulse trip into a faster rhythm. Boldly she slid the tip of her tongue along his lips, and they parted instantly. He'd taught her to be unrestrained, to unleash the wild sensuality inside her that was as vibrant as her hair.

A hot, sweet urgency began building inside her, and she tempted his tongue with hers. He groaned hoarsely and met her thrust with one of his own.

Tiny beads of sweat erupted on his broad forehead, and he began to caress her back with long, fevered strokes.

Under the sheet draped between his plaster-sheathed legs he was becoming aroused, exciting her as no man had ever excited her before. Jillian was ready, more than ready.

This was Trevor, the man she loved more than her life, the man who loved her.

"It's all set, angel," he said in a tortured voice. "Christmas Eve, on the grounds of the Royal Hawaiian, at sunset. You bring the minister and the witnesses, and I'll bring the champagne."

A tiny dimple appeared at the corner of her soft, full mouth. "And the flowers," she teased. "Don't forget the flowers. Red roses, lots and lots of red roses."

The breeze brushed a long, soft tendril of hair across Jillian's face, and she blinked. Trevor's resonant laugh had once shivered down her spine, like that strong north wind she remembered as she pushed the thick curl into place again.

"Red roses for my angel. I promise," he'd said then, and she'd believed him.

She'd believed everything he told her, until it was too late.

Jillian lifted her head, catching the chilled breeze on her cheek. She was no longer that young nurse, and she no longer believed in love, at least not the kind that Trevor had offered.

She shifted her gaze to Hank's intense face. He sounded as though he was almost finished. And then she could leave.

"... and thank God, most of you good people will never have to live with a ticking bomb in your belly, reminding you every minute, every second, that one slip will send you spinning back into a nightmare that ends only in death."

Hank shoved one hand in his pocket and surveyed the crowd. "The guys here aren't asking for your sympathy, and they'll have to earn your respect, but we *are* asking for a chance to show you that we can be good neighbors."

A ripple of sound ran through the crowd, and the spectators began to applaud. Applauding with them, Jillian felt a flow of pride at the spontaneous outpouring of support. These were good people, generous and kind, and she prayed she hadn't done them a disservice by bringing Horizons to their close-knit community.

Hank grinned and held up his hands. "Thank you very much. The boys and I appreciate the welcome. And now, if Mayor Anderson will help me, we'll put this fine tree in the ground."

Jillian's smile felt stiff as she took the shovel from Hank's hands. Two of the residents came forward and lifted the tree into the hole.

"Give it your best shot," Hank said as he took a step backward.

She nodded and looked up at the crowd. Unerringly her gaze found Trevor's.

He looked sad, as though he'd just lost something precious. But that was impossible, she told herself with bitter scorn. He was probably as impatient for this to end as she was.

Mentally giving herself a shake, she shoved the pointed end of the spade into the mound of rust-colored dirt. The impact stung her hand, but in some strange way the pain felt good.

"Good job," Hank said as she tossed the dirt into the hole. The pellets of clay rattled like hail against the sturdy trunk, and the crowd cheered.

Hank took the shovel from her, duplicated her effort, then raised the shovel above his head. "Let's hear it for Horizons number twenty," he shouted, and the boys began applauding. The crowd joined in.

"Thanks again, Jillian," Hank said, suddenly serious as the crowd closed around them. "I hope we're going to be friends."

"Me, too," Jillian said, smiling into his kind eyes.

They were engulfed by well-wishers, and Jillian turned away, politely acknowledging the congratulations of her fellow citizens as she angled across the patio toward the open space. She'd turned the corner of the building and was starting across the open area when she heard a shout behind her.

"Jillian, wait up!"

What now? she thought, recognizing the sheriff's strident call. She turned around, then sighed. It was Mel all right, red-faced and scowling and heading directly toward her.

"I *warned* you, Jillian," he said in a loud, angry voice as he reached her side. "I warned all of you, but none of you bleeding hearts would listen to me."

Jillian's heart began to pound. "That's enough, Mel. You're making a scene."

"Damn right I am! This town needs to wise up, and the sooner the better." The loose skin below his chin shook violently as he bobbed his head accusingly. "Grady Hendricks, you know, Ralph's son, the one who works here in security, just told me. One of those damn hoodlums is missing. Escaped, doing God only knows what right now."

"Calm down, Mel. You're overreacting."

"Overreacting, hell! You're the one who said we could trust these people. You're the one who ramrodded this through the council. Okay, fine, but now we have a problem, and I want you to call an emergency meeting of the council to discuss this."

Conscious of the stares and whispers directed their way, she counted to five, then said in neutral tone, "Tomorrow, Mel. If we find we really have a problem."

"We have a problem, all right, and I'm beginning to think it's you. What did these guys do, pay you to let them take over PacTimber's lease?'' His voice quivered with disgust as he grabbed her arm.

A searing pain shot into her shoulder, and she tried to twist away. She'd never seen Mel out of control like this.

"Sheriff Cobb!"

The deep voice came from behind and carried the steel of command. Jillian inhaled sharply as Cobb's fingers bit into her arm like the jaws of a vice. "Let her go—*now!*"

The sheriff dropped her arm as though it were a glowing poker, and Jillian spun around, her eyes snapping indignantly. Trevor stood a shadow's length away, his copper eyes trained like twin howitzers on the sheriff's face.

"Now look here, Markus—" the sheriff began in strident anger, only to close his mouth with a snap as Trevor took a deliberate step toward him.

"No, you look here, Sheriff," he said in a quiet voice that hissed past Jillian's stony face like the wind of a mortar shell. "As I see it, you've made two mistakes. Number one, you jumped to the wrong conclusion because you're so damn prejudiced against these boys, you didn't wait to hear the whole story."

Jillian stood rooted to the ground. The Trevor she remembered had been a charming flirt, even a bawdy tease on occasion, but he'd never projected this kind of raw male power, never exuded such potent menace. Flustered, she wondered what kind of a life he'd led during the years since then to change him so drastically.

"What the hell do you mean, wrong conclusion?" Cobb demanded. "The kid is gone, escaped. As soon as I can get some men together, we're going out after him."

"The boy was lost," Trevor said in an even voice. "He'd been following some deer tracks and he got confused. One of the counselors just brought him back. They tell me he never left the grounds."

Mel glared at him, his mouth working, but before he could say another word, Trevor moved closer until his flat torso was only inches from Cobb's fat belly.

Jillian held her breath. She should stop this, but suddenly she was powerless to move.

"And number two," Trevor continued softly, "you took out your anger on someone who doesn't deserve it. That's not what I call smart."

Cobb blanched, and his voice shook as he took an awkward step backward, his heel crunching against a discarded candy wrapper. "Don't threaten me, mister. Your money doesn't mean anything here."

"I don't need money to bring you down, Cobb. Take off that badge, and I'll show you I mean what I say."

The two men locked glances, and the air seemed to crackle around them. Jillian stood in frozen disbelief, her heavy bag clutched to her breast like a shield.

Trevor and Mel were about the same height. The sheriff had the advantage in weight, but Trevor had more powerful shoulders and, Jillian noted as though from a great distance, the sinewy look of superb conditioning under the trim vest and pleated trousers.

Nearby the buzz of curiosity swelled. Mel's mouth opened and closed like a catfish scavenging on a lake bottom, and his watery eyes bulged wildly.

"This is only round one, Markus. Sooner or later one of those rotten kids will step over the line, and I'll be waiting."

He tugged the bill of his cap another inch closer to his blond brows and turned on his heel, stomping across the tennis court toward the parking lot, his gun slapping his fat thigh.

The comments of the crowd swirled around Jillian's head, and she struggled to keep her temper in check. Her breath came in short bursts, and her cheeks were burning as she trained her angry gaze on Trevor's bronzed face.

"Don't ever do that to me again!" she said in a harsh whisper.

Her hushed voice was shaking more from reaction than anger, but Trevor couldn't know that. She lifted her chin and glared at him, her back teeth grinding together.

Trevor stared at her. "Do what?" he asked quietly, his face coolly impassive. "Keep that bigoted ape from pawing you?" He jammed his hands into the pockets of his trousers and shifted his weight. His spine was rigid.

Jillian drew a long stream of air into her lungs. The smell of rain had grown stronger, and the clouds above were now swollen and black.

"Mel Cobb's a bully, and he blusters a lot, but he wouldn't deliberately hurt anyone."

Trevor's unruly brows drew together. "Oh, sure, that's why you were trying to get away from him."

"I was trying to get away from him because I don't like anyone touching me without my permission."

"Take a look at your arm tomorrow, and then tell me he didn't hurt you."

Jillian resisted the urge to rub the bruised skin. Trevor was right, but she would never admit it. And the longer she stood talking with him, she realized grimly, the more she was risking.

"Let's just forget it, okay? I'm glad your . . . your inmate is back safely."

His lips tightened. "We call them residents."

Jillian nodded. "Sorry, I'll remember that. And now, if you'll excuse me . . ."

With a scowl she turned away, fighting to keep the memory of this man locked away where it had been for so long. She wouldn't allow herself to remember how he'd touched her so long ago, how his big hand had searched and found all the tender, sensitive spots that had given her so much pleasure. How he'd pleasured her heart and her soul even more deeply.

"I'm sorry, Jill."

Shock shot through every curve and angle of her body. Slowly she turned to look at him. His face was as hard as the granite slope beyond the tree line, and his eyes carried no hint of his feelings.

"Sorry for what? For embarrassing me? For walking out on me fifteen years ago? What are you sorry for, Trevor?"

She swallowed the angry tears that scalded the back of her tongue, tears that were as bitter and poisonous as her thoughts.

"I'm sorry for hurting you, Jill. Fifteen minutes ago *and* fifteen years ago."

Jillian's stomach heaved. "Deftly put, Trevor. You have a real way with words."

One corner of his mouth curled downward. "But you're not impressed."

"I doubt there's anything in this world that you could say or do that would impress me."

Her eyes smoldered as she glared at him, and a tight pressure gripped her chest painfully. No, she wouldn't remember. She wouldn't.

"Goodbye, Trevor."

"Don't go."

Before she could escape, Trevor crossed the distance between them until he was standing between her and the rest of the clearing. Jillian was startled to see that her mouth just reached his strong brown throat. She had only to move forward a few inches and her lips could brush the clean line of his jaw.

Chagrin burned in her blood as she jerked back a step. What was she thinking? This man had once hurt her so terribly that she'd wanted to die. She took another stumbling step backward.

Trevor's eyes darkened to mahogany as he watched her retreat, and a tiny muscle spasmed next to the taut corner of his mouth. "You look great, Jill," he said in a husky voice. "Very elegant. But then, you always were beautiful."

Trevor watched her skin turn so white that he wondered if there could be any blood left in her face. She was angry, and bitter as hell. He'd never seen her eyes so dark, not even when they'd made love.

Suddenly, irrationally, irresistibly, he wanted to kiss that soft, angry mouth. He wanted to hold her, to feel her warmth just one more time against his chest. This time he wanted to feel all of her against him. This time he wanted to be the strong one. This time he wanted to take care of her, this one time.

"Jillian," he began in a husky tone, then faltered. Suddenly he didn't know what to say. He'd been so sure he would never see her again. So damn sure.

He reached for her, his big hand folding gently over her shoulder. With a harsh cry, she wrenched away.

"Don't touch me!" she said desperately, backing toward the side of the building. "I don't want you to touch me."

She hadn't been prepared for the wild spurt of raw desire that had shot through her. This hot urgency was more than she could handle.

"You used to like me to touch you. Remember?" His eyes warmed, and his voice dropped into a rough whisper. "You used to stretch like a cat and beg me to pet you. And then you'd make that sexy growling sound in your throat when I found all the right places."

Jillian's mouth went dry. She couldn't seem to think. She couldn't seem to move. A breathless pleasure filled her lungs, and the same warm tingling that Trevor had always excited in her slowly spread through her body.

"I don't remember," she said woodenly. But she did. Dear God, she did!

She took another step backward, feeling the rough redwood siding of the building snag her skirt. She was trapped.

"This is pointless," she said, tightening her grip on the smooth leather of her bag. She had to get away from him.

"Jill, listen—"

She refused to let him finish. "You don't care a thing about me, and I certainly don't care about you."

His jaw jerked, as though she'd slapped him. "Maybe you don't care about me, Jill, but I...care about you. I always have."

Trevor knew that he should let her go. But even as he told himself to turn around and walk away, he couldn't leave her. Not yet. Not until he'd said the words he should have said fifteen years ago.

Absently he massaged the knotted muscles of his neck. He was stalling, trying to find the courage to look her in the eye without flinching, but it was harder than he'd thought it would be. Just do it, he told himself angrily. He straightened his shoulders, gritting his teeth against the hot flare of pain in his lower back. "Jillian, about Hawaii—"

"No! I don't want to talk about that, ever."

Her anguished cry was like a razor slash across his spine. For the first time he saw the scorching contempt in her eyes, along with the raw pain that had been hidden behind the indifference. A heaviness gripped his chest, and he inhaled deeply, trying to fill the void inside. Payback time, Markus, he thought. With interest. One more debt he had to pay, just as he'd been paying for years.

"I never meant to hurt you, Jill."

Jillian forced herself to ignore the grave lines of suffering around his eyes. "You made your point quite adequately. You didn't want to get married. You didn't want me. Fine. I accept that. Now let's drop it." Her chin jerked upward as she made herself breathe in and out slowly.

Trevor stared down at the sparse grass beneath his feet. What had he expected from her? Absolution? A second chance? Damn, he thought in vicious self-contempt. It hurt. Even after all these years, it still hurt like hell to know he could never have her.

All of a sudden he felt terribly tired, and his back screamed for relief. He nodded curtly, accepting her rejection. "Goodbye, Jill. It was...good to see you again."

He turned away, only to smash into a skinny redheaded kid carrying a skateboard. "Whoa, there...!" Grunting,

the boy bounced off his chest, and the skateboard went flying, tumbling sideways to land upside down on the grass.

Trevor was furious with himself. He couldn't even make
a graceful exit.

The kid was all arms and legs, with a long skinny torso
and restless feet. He looked to be about twelve or thirteen,
the same age as Trevor's brother's son.

He wrapped his hand over the boy's bony shoulder and
looked into his pale, freckled face. "Sorry, son," he said
tersely. "I didn't see you coming. Are you okay?"

The boy shook off his hand and pushed his dark glasses
more firmly against the bridge of his nose.

"Yeah, I'm okay." His voice cracked, and color flooded
his cheeks.

Trevor hid a smile. The kid sounded as though he was
going to have a deep voice someday, but right now it was
changing. He remembered those awkward days very well.
He hoped this kid's father could help him through the agony of puberty as patiently as his father had helped him and
his brothers.

The boy turned his attention to Jillian, ignoring Trevor
completely. "Some of the guys are going over to Truckee to
play video games, and I want to go along, if that's okay with
you, Mom."

Mom?

Trevor froze. He'd always known there would be other
men. Hadn't he told himself over and over that she would
find someone else? That she would marry and have children? She'd wanted four—or was it five? He'd forced himself to forget a long time ago.

He kept his expression carefully neutral as Jillian brushed
a damp red curl away from the boy's freckled forehead. He
didn't want to think about the man who'd fathered her son.
But he knew that he would, often. And that he would envy
him.

"This is Jason, my son," she said calmly, her low voice soft with pride. In her eyes Trevor saw the same loving glow that had once been there for him alone.

He nodded, not trusting himself to speak yet. His stomach burned, and his throat felt as though it had been scalded. So this is regret, he thought numbly as he extended his hand toward Jillian's son. Funny. It had never hurt quite so much before.

"Hello, Jason," he said in a voice that sounded like a stranger's. "I'm Trevor, an old friend of your mom's."

The boy shook his hand halfheartedly, clearly uninterested.

"How 'bout it, Mom?" he asked, ignoring Trevor again.

Jillian took a tighter grip on her purse. "Who's driving?"

"Mike Cobb."

"Jase, he's had two tickets—"

"I know, but he's learned his lesson. Besides, his dad said he'd pull his license if he gets another one."

Jillian hesitated. Mike Cobb had lived with his mother in Los Angeles until six months ago, when she'd sent him to live with Mel. He was sixteen, big for his age, and far too wild for her peace of mind. But Jason liked him, and she'd always trusted her son to pick his own friends.

"It's okay with me, but I want you back before dark. Tell Mike you won't be allowed to go with him again if you're late." Jillian felt Trevor's eyes on her, and she had to force herself to smile at her son.

"Killer! Thanks, Mom." The laces of his high-topped sneakers flapped around his bony ankles as Jason walked over to retrieve his skateboard. As he bent over, the dark glasses slid from his nose and dangled from a cord strung around his neck. He paused, squinting toward the swimming pool, where a group of friends were horsing around, poking one another and laughing.

Suddenly, before Jillian could move, he spun around and looked directly at them. In the light his eyes were a clear, startling copper.

She held her breath as a gray tinge spread under Trevor's dark tan. He looked stunned, his face frozen into a mask of disbelief.

Trevor's mind went blank, and he felt a savage pain twist his gut. It was the same feeling he'd had just before his F-14 had smashed into the deck.

"My God, Jillian," he whispered hoarsely. "How could you?"

Chapter 3

For an instant Jillian couldn't speak. She'd been so sure this moment would never have to happen.

Of course Trevor was shocked, she told herself as she hugged her purse against her stomach. Any man would be when suddenly faced with a part of himself. But the shock would soon pass, just as the shock of his rejection had.

Forcing life into her wooden features, she gave Jason a quick hug. "Be home for dinner, okay?"

"Are you sure you want me to go?" His brow puckered as he stared at Trevor's stony expression. "I can wait."

"No, it's okay. Have fun."

The boy hesitated for an instant, then pushed his dark glasses back onto his nose, spun around and took off at a run, his shirttail flapping. He didn't look back.

Trevor watched the boy until he disappeared into the crowd. A son, he thought, fighting the numbness of shock. Dear sweet God, I have a son. He ran a shaky hand down his jaw and turned to look at Jillian. His heart was thundering in his ears, and his skin felt clammy. He had to clear his voice twice before he could speak.

"I didn't know, Jill," he said harshly. "I swear I didn't know."

Jillian's jaw tightened until her ears hurt. Surely he didn't think that made his desertion forgivable.

"Jason's the surprise I had for you in Hawaii, the one I mentioned in my letters." Her voice thinned. "Or maybe you don't remember."

Remember? Trevor thought in a blazing surge of raw pain. He'd read those letters so often that the paper had worn thin and the writing had faded.

"But why did you...wait to tell me?"

"I'd planned to tell you as soon as I knew for sure," she answered truthfully. "I'd even written the letter, but I tore it up. I wanted you to be able to concentrate on your therapy without worrying about a pregnant fiancée."

Jillian was pleased to hear the lack of emotion in her voice. She'd done her screaming years ago, in private, sitting hunched over on a windswept beach, her tears mingling with the spindrift.

Trevor glanced up at the clouds above as though searching for an answer. Or an escape. "There's nothing I can say that would be enough," he whispered hoarsely as he dropped his gaze to her face. "Except—thank you."

Jillian forced herself to ignore the stark agony that settled in his eyes. She slung her purse over her shoulder. The crowd was clustering around the buffet table, and she and Trevor were alone at the side of the main building.

"I really don't expect you to say anything, Trevor. Not after all these years. Life goes on, and mine has gone on just fine, so you needn't feel any responsibility for me *or* my son." She lifted her chin. "Now, if you'll excuse me, I have things to do." She started to turn away, only to have Trevor stop her with a painful tug on her forearm.

"You can't just walk away, Jill. We have things to talk about." In spite of the pain in his eyes, his voice was edged with granite.

"Why can't I? You did."

Trevor's lips whitened. "What do you want me to say, Jillian? That I was a bastard? I've already said I was, and I meant it." His deep voice roughened. "Some things I can change, and I have, but there isn't one blasted thing I can do to change the past. I can only live in the present. And right now, today, I want to become a part of Jason's life. Whatever it takes, I'll do."

"No!"

The word was torn from her throat before she thought. She pressed shaking fingers against her lips to stop the trembling. She had to stay cool. She had to think.

"Yes, Jillian." His lips thinned. "As Jason's father, I have a right to be a part of his life."

"Rights, Trevor? You have no rights. None at all." Her voice vibrated with anger, and her hands shook uncontrollably.

"Don't push me, Jill. I've already said I was sorry. I screwed up, yes, but now I intend to make things right the best way I can. *Any* way that I can."

Jillian fought to control her temper. How dare he? she thought, her breath hissing past her dry lips.

"We don't need you to make things right, Trevor. Jason and I are doing great without you. He's happy here. I make a good living. We have friends. We don't need you." She glanced toward the front gate. Jason's bright head was a small speck in the jumble of spectators moving toward the exit.

"Look at me, Jill." Trevor's voice was husky. He waited until she reluctantly shifted her gaze to his face. "I'm forty-six years old, and I don't know the first thing about being a father. Hell, I'm still having trouble dealing with the fact that I *am* one. But I can't just walk away and pretend my son doesn't exist. I've walked away from too many problems in my life."

Jillian stared at him. Was that what she'd been to him? A problem? She banished the thought, but not the sick feeling in her stomach.

"What you do or don't do in your life is not my concern, Trevor," she told him. "But Jason is. And he's very happy the way he is. I can't see any advantage in changing things."

Trevor's eyes narrowed. "I won't accept that, Jill. Every boy needs a father."

"There's more to being a father than merely performing a physical act, Trevor. It requires hard work and commitment and a lot of staying power."

His chin jerked. "Did it ever occur to you that I might have changed? That maybe I've paid for what I did to you?"

She stared at him in disbelief. "If you've paid," she said slowly, her voice throbbing with conviction, "it wasn't nearly enough."

His jaw tightened for an instant, then relaxed, as though he were making a conscious effort to restrain himself. "What do you want me to say, Jill? That I've regretted every day I've had to live without you? That I would give everything I own to be able to live that Christmas Eve again? That I've never stopped loving you? Is that what you want to hear?"

Jillian was very close to tears. She didn't want his lies, his excuses, his apologies.

"I don't want to hear anything from you, Trevor. Except goodbye."

He ran his blunt fingers through the pewter hair above his ear. "You're determined to hate me, aren't you?"

"Wrong. I don't feel anything for you."

He exhaled slowly. "Then it shouldn't be difficult for you to let me become a part of our son's life."

The chill in the air had seeped into Jillian's bones, and she repressed a shiver. "He's not *our* son," she told Trevor with that same chill in her voice. "He's mine. He doesn't know about you, and I don't intend to tell him."

Trevor heard the ring of finality in her tone, and he felt sick inside. This wasn't the sweetly adoring woman he'd loved so fiercely in Tokyo. This woman was fiery and passionate and willing to scratch and claw to protect her child from a man she despised. But he knew only one way to fight—no holds barred. And this was a fight he had to win.

"I can take you to court, Jillian. I don't want to do that, but it's up to you." His voice was silky soft and edged with regret. "I have enough money to hire the best family law attorneys in the country."

Jillian felt as though she'd been kicked in the stomach. Even blindsided and off guard, Trevor sounded as though he intended to fight, just as he'd once fought for his life.

"I'm not afraid of you," she lied. "There's no way you can prove Jason's your son. Legally his father is a man named William Paul White."

Trevor's nostrils flared. "The hell he is!"

Jillian lifted her chin. Nausea was climbing from her stomach into her throat. "He was a patient in the hospital the same time you were, a good and decent man. And it's his name I put on Jason's birth certificate. He's dead now, and there's no way you can prove he wasn't my child's father."

Pain ripped along Trevor's backbone, and he inhaled sharply. This wasn't the indifference she claimed to feel toward him. This was hatred, raw, bitter hatred. He knew all about that kind of bitterness. He'd lived with it for a long time.

"I'll find a way," he said with forced calm. "There are things you can't change—the color of his eyes, his blood type."

"I'm not stupid, Trevor. Bill White's blood type is the same as yours. And he had brown eyes, maybe not exactly the same color as Jason's, but close enough."

Trevor's jaw clenched. "Then I'll find something else to use. I'm not giving up. I've always wanted a child, more than you can know. And it hurt a lot when I thought I would never have one. I'm tired of hurting." His voice took on a steely edge. "Hate me if you have to, Jillian, but I won't let you keep me away from my son."

"Never! I'll never give you access to Jason."

She spun on her heel and walked away, moving with mechanical stiffness. Tonight, when she was alone, she would let herself feel. But right now she welcomed the icy numbness spreading through her. It would insulate her against the crippling pain of hating this man.

Trevor watched her until she disappeared into the crowd. Rolling his shoulders back carefully, he looked blindly up at the trees. His eyes stung with remorse, and he closed them convulsively. He had more to pay for than he'd thought. Much, much more.

But no matter what he did, no matter what he gave her, no matter how humbly he begged for forgiveness, it wouldn't be enough.

A son. Jillian had given him a son, a good-looking kid, with her hair and his eyes. Markus eyes.

Suddenly, in his mind's eye, he saw her as she must have been in Hawaii, the tawny skin of her belly swollen with his child, her vibrant green eyes filled with happiness, waiting to surprise him. She would have been so lovely....

"Damn," he whispered, feeling the sting of moisture on his cheeks. The storm was coming closer.

I love you, and I miss you, and I can't wait to feel you next to me. All of you, my dearest Trevor. You are my strength when things get so awful here that I want to run and run and run. You're strong and brave and honorable. And you are my future. My husband. The father of those redheaded little sailors you keep talking about.

He knew the words by heart. She'd written them in the last letter she'd sent him from Tokyo.

Trevor bowed his head and shoved his hands into his pockets. Strong. Brave. Honorable. In the end, he'd been none of those things. And she'd been the one to suffer. No wonder she hated him. But she couldn't hate him any more than he hated himself. Not then, and not now.

Above his head, thunder clapped and the storm broke, pelting his face with cold, hard raindrops. Trevor uttered a harsh oath and glanced toward the helicopter. That damn pilot better be ready to go as soon as the ceiling lifts, he thought, striding stiffly toward the patio. He couldn't wait to get the hell out of this place.

The bell over the door jangled a loud warning, and Jillian looked up to see Adrian ambling into the pharmacy. She was dressed in satin shorts and a loose-fitting tank top, and her pink running shoes were covered with red dust.

Jillian felt a pang of guilt. Tomorrow, she told herself firmly, she'd haul her bicycle out of the shed and put some miles on it before the weather turned cold.

Adrian slid onto a stool in front of the marble soda counter and gave Jillian a curious look. "What are you doing here? I thought Darcy minded the store on Sunday."

"She does, usually. But she's nursing a bad cold. I told her I'd cover today."

Jillian shoved the newspaper she'd been reading aside and reached for a glass. "You want diet soda or water?" she asked as she filled the glass with ice.

"Water, please. And a hot fudge sundae. With everything." Adrian glanced down at her full hips, scowled briefly, then shrugged. Jillian laughed.

"You're something, Addie. You jog for miles every day, and then you pork out on ice cream."

Adrian unwound the sweat-stained bandanna from her forehead and wiped her wet face. Her shiny brown hair was damp and curled around her ears.

"Yeah, I know. I've created the perfect balance."

Jillian filled the glass, and Adrian took it from her hand. She gulped noisily until it was empty, then put it on the counter. "Be sure to give me lots of crumbles," she ordered, reaching into an inside pocket of her running shorts for a crumpled package of cigarettes and a lighter. She started to light up.

"Ahem."

Adrian froze. "What?" she asked guilelessly.

Jillian pointed the ice cream dipper toward a big red sign taped to the large mirror in a carved oak frame behind her. "'Thank you for not smoking,'" she read aloud, slowly. "That means you, Dr. Franklin who, I might add, ought to know better."

Adrian grumbled under her breath, but she put the cigarettes away. "Why do I sometimes feel as though you're my mother?"

"Because someone has to take care of you, Addie, since you do such a bad job of it yourself."

"Hey, I'm a big girl. Thirty-seven on my next birthday."

"If you're around to celebrate." Jillian scowled. "You drive too fast in that rattletrap Jeep of yours, you go hang gliding, for heaven's sake, and you won't eat anything that isn't loaded with preservatives."

She piled whipped cream over the dripping chocolate, plopped a cherry on the top and plunked the concoction down in front of Adrian with a loud thud.

"I'm going for the burn," Adrian said as she picked up her spoon and dug in. "Isn't that what we're supposed to do?"

"We're *supposed* to exercise some good old common sense."

"Hmm. Is that what you were doing when you let Trevor, as in gorgeous, sexy and rich, Markus hit on you yesterday? Being sensible?" She shoved a heaping spoonful into her mouth and watched Jillian with innocent blandness.

"What?" Jillian stared at her friend in consternation. Adrian's black eyes sparkled with impish delight.

"It's all over town. I heard it twice at church this morning, and again when I stopped to chat with Orrie Hughes outside the Mother Lode Inn."

"Oh, for heaven's sake," Jillian muttered, pouring herself another cup of coffee. Absently she reached for her third doughnut. "We were just . . . chatting."

"According to Jason, the aforementioned Mr. Markus was putting the make on you."

Jillian's throat tightened, and she nearly choked on a mouthful of glazed dough. She swallowed convulsively, then stared anxiously at Adrian. "He . . . talked to you about Trevor?"

"Trevor, is it?" Adrian grinned, but her amusement faded when she saw the strained expression on Jillian's face. "Jill, what's wrong? You look green around the edges."

Jillian sighed. "I feel a little green. I didn't get much sleep last night."

She sat down on the step stool she kept behind the bar and rested her elbows on the polished marble. This was home. This was reality, not a man with copper eyes and a short memory.

Jillian glanced around the long, narrow pharmacy. She loved the high ceilings with the ornate, hand-carved moldings and the tall, skinny windows that let in enough light on a sunny day to save her a tidy sum on electricity.

The thick wooden shelves were fully stocked, with the sundry items nicely displayed in neat multicolored rows and stacks of sale items at each end. The air smelled of cough syrup and fresh lemons in the summer, and pine boughs and cider in the winter.

Cheerful scenes of the Sierra, grizzled sourdoughs with their mules, trappers with their long rifles, mothers in their sunbonnets, had been painted on one wall, and Jillian had had the murals cleaned and restored to pristine brightness. The rustic reminders of a less complicated time had never failed to raise her spirits whenever she looked at them—until now.

Jillian stared down at the scarred travertine. She hated Formica. It was so cold and utilitarian. But marble had life and warmth and, most important, permanence.

Her gaze slid involuntarily to the folded newspaper. "Have you seen the paper this morning?" she asked glumly.

"If you mean, did I see the picture of you and Trevor Markus, I did," Adrian said mildly, sneaking a look at Jillian over her spoon. "You look terrific. He looks as though he'd just been struck by lightning."

The *Clayton Clarion* had featured the opening of Wilderness Horizons on the front page. Alongside a photo of Jillian and Trevor shaking hands was a short profile of Horizons' founder, briefly describing his exemplary Naval career as well as his professional credits.

The two corporations that he'd founded, Markus Engineering International and Wilderness Horizons, had been widely acclaimed for the high percentage of handicapped and ex-offenders each employed, and Trevor himself had been cited for his humanitarian efforts in the field of drug abuse and veterans' rights.

But the man behind the public face, Jillian had read, kept a very low profile. He'd conceived the original idea of combining drug treatment with the survival skills taught by the military, and he'd provided the money to open the first unit but, according to the sources cited, he left the running of Horizons to the people he hired.

Other personal details were sketchy. He had never been married, lived in an upscale community near Seattle, where his family was socially prominent, and rarely gave interviews.

I could give you such a scoop, Jillian thought with a silent wince as she pushed her coffee cup to one side. She was down to the dregs, and it tasted like floor sweepings.

Already this morning she had received half a dozen calls congratulating her on her farsightedness in attracting such a quality addition as Wilderness Horizons to Clayton's small business community.

The irony was wonderful, she thought. Clayton gained jobs, while the mayor who'd solicited them might lose her son.

Suddenly she wanted to lay her head on the cool counter and bawl. She hadn't felt so alone in years.

"This was just what I needed, Jill," Adrian said with a sigh of greedy satisfaction. "Now I can skip lunch."

She scraped the spoon around the edge of the glass, then savored the last of the gooey mess. Her expression was one of sublime pleasure, the kind only a true lover of ice cream can produce. She licked the spoon, then dropped it reluctantly into the glass.

"What did you think of the story on, uh, Trevor?" Jillian asked in a neutral tone.

"What's to think? The man is the catch of the century. Of two centuries. If he'd even glanced my way, I'd already be scheming to get him into my net. But alas..." She rolled her eyes, then reached for the paper and unfolded it. "Obviously the gentleman prefers redheads."

Jillian threw Adrian a fond look. Shortly after Jillian had taken over the pharmacy, Adrian had come to her with a prescription. It had been written by a doctor in San Francisco and called for one of the newer antiseizure drugs. Jillian was the only person in Clayton who knew that the bubbly doctor was an epileptic.

It had taken time for their friendship to develop. Both were intensely private people in spite of their congenial public facades. But over the years, at a casual picnic supper on the deck of Jillian's apartment or an occasional brunch at Adrian's redwood-and-glass nest, they'd gradually shared bits and pieces of their personal history.

Jillian had told Adrian of her struggle to combine a nursing career with the demands of raising a toddler, and of her ultimate decision to resign her Navy commission and return to college for a degree in pharmacy in order to have more time for her son.

In turn, Adrian had regaled Jillian with tales of her escapades in medical school, where she'd been known as a terrible practical joker and a dedicated flirt who was really a Puritan underneath the tantalizing bravado.

It had been just two years ago that Jillian had discovered that the kinship she felt with Adrian went deeper than she'd suspected. Adrian had been jilted by a fellow medical student, who'd broken their engagement less than a week after she'd told him about her epilepsy.

"I was so sure it wouldn't make a damn bit of difference," she'd told Jillian with a bitter smile. "He loved me, you see."

Adrian had stopped believing in love after that. She'd had lots of boyfriends, and even the occasional lover, but whenever a man became serious, she broke it off. She would never marry.

Jillian glanced down at the blurred newsprint. The article on Trevor had shaken her more than she wanted to admit. This was not the man whom she'd scorned all those years. This was not the man who, as she'd repeatedly told herself, wasn't fit to be Jason's father.

But maybe the story had been exaggerated. Or slanted for the best effect. She was enough of a realist to understand journalistic license. And public relations. A lot of corporations paid millions every year to generate favorable press releases.

"Addie, what did Jason really say about Trevor?" she asked in a voice that sounded alien to her ears.

Jason hadn't mentioned Trevor to her at all. And during dinner last night, when she'd casually explained that she'd known Mr. Markus during the war, he'd simply stared at her as though he couldn't understand why she was bothering to tell him something so unimportant.

Adrian glanced up from the photograph on the front page. "Just what I told you. We met in the parking lot, and he told me that this big tough-looking dude was putting the make on his mom, and did I think he should stick around? Naturally I told him no." She paused, then glanced quickly down at the paper. "I take it that you weren't terribly receptive?"

"Not very, no." She hesitated, then added softly, "Trevor Markus is Jason's father."

"Dear God!" Adrian looked stunned. "But... but you said... on Jase's medical records his father is listed as deceased."

Jillian bit her lip, then sighed. "Trevor didn't know about Jason. I... was afraid that, if by some remote chance, he ever found out that he had a son, he might try to... to take him."

"You parted badly?" Adrian's tone was sympathetic. She knew all about bad endings.

"You might say that, yes." Jillian's tone was extremely dry.

She stood up quickly and went over to lock the front door and flip the sign dangling in the window to Closed. She returned to the counter, but she was too nervous to sit. Grabbing a clean white cloth and a bottle of glass cleaner, she began to wipe the already spotless marble.

"Trevor wants to be part of Jason's life."

"And you don't want him to be."

"No. I never want to see him again."

Adrian gave Jillian a thoughtful look. "Why do I think there's more to it than that?"

Jillian sighed. "Because there is. He... threatened to take me to court if I refuse to let him see Jase." Her voice wobbled. "I'm scared, Adrian. If he fights me, I could lose."

"Would you like to talk about it?"

Jillian hesitated.

Why not? she thought after a moment's reflection. Adrian was her best friend and, in spite of her eccentricities, very clearheaded. Maybe Addie could help her figure out a way to keep Jason safe.

She returned the spray bottle and cloth to the shelf under the counter and opened the small refrigerator.

She took out a bottle of white wine and carefully eased out the cork, then reached behind her for a single glass. Adrian didn't drink because of the powerful drug she was forced to take daily to control her seizures.

"I need a little Dutch courage," Jillian said with a tight smile. "I've never told anyone what happened after I left Tokyo."

She splashed a generous measure into the glass, and shimmering droplets of Chablis scattered over the counter.

"You told me that you were stationed in Bethesda when Jase was born."

"I was, but before that I was on maternity leave. I flew from Tokyo to Hawaii, where I'd reserved a suite at the Royal Hawaiian. The bridal suite."

Absently Jillian mopped up the spill, then took a sip of Chablis. The wine was cold on her tongue and tasted like half-ripe apricots. "You sure you want to hear this? It's not pretty, and I'd hate to spoil your day off."

Adrian lifted her brows. "Only if you want to tell me about it, Jill. I know all about ghosts."

"Ghosts. I guess that's about it."

Slowly, in a voice so quiet Adrian had to lean forward to hear clearly, Jillian told her everything that had happened, beginning with the moment when Trevor had looked up at her that first morning and ending with a description of her anguish on the day he'd been shipped back to the States.

"He was the bravest man I'd ever met," she said simply in conclusion. "His doctor told me he'd never had a patient fight so hard against such impossible odds."

Adrian looked down at her hands. "Back injuries are the worst, I know. And so are multiple fractures. I've had patients beg for another shot barely an hour after the last one."

Jillian nodded. "It was rough. And parts of his therapy were just as bad. They had to stretch the scar tissue in his legs, and sometimes he passed out from the pain. He didn't tell me that, but his therapist did. I called her once, when I hadn't heard from him for over a week, and she filled me in.''

The other woman nodded. ''You said you were to be married at Christmas after your tour of duty in Tokyo was over. What happened?''

Jillian took another sip, then held the glass tightly and stared into the clear liquid as though it were a window into her past.

''As I said, we'd set the date for Christmas Eve. I'd made all the arrangements....''

The temperature was in the high eighties. Jillian stood at the window overlooking the Pacific and grinned at the thought.

Christmas on the farm in southern Ohio had meant a roaring fire and hot chocolate and warm sweaters. Many times over the years she'd had to wade through knee-deep snow on Christmas morning to reach the barn in order to do her chores.

This Christmas she'd be having both sunshine and snow in the space of a few days.

In two days, after a brief stopover in Seattle to meet his parents, Trevor intended to take her to Canada for their honeymoon, to a small inn he knew up north.

He was tired of sunshine, he'd written in his last letter from San Diego, which had reached her in Tokyo a week ago. He wanted to be snowed in with her, just the two of them in front of a fire.

''I need to see you in the firelight, angel. I need to kiss you and touch you and bury myself so deeply inside you that I won't be able to think of anything but you.''

Soon, my love, she thought, as she shifted her gaze to the flower-bedecked grotto at the far end of the grounds. The florist had done a beautiful job, transforming the small rock garden into a romantic wedding bower.

The chaplain was due in twenty minutes, and the witnesses, the bubbly, deeply tanned night clerk and her fiancé, were having drinks in the bar by the beach.

Jillian hugged her belly, a blissful smile forming slowly on her lips. She'd been in Hawaii for four days, and most of that time she'd spent lying in the sun, working on her tan. She'd also found time to find a black lace nightie cut on the bias to accommodate her swollen stomach.

"It's gorgeous and very sexy, baby. I can't wait for your daddy to see it," she whispered, caressing her belly. The satin of her ivory maternity dress was erotically smooth against her palm, and her heart began to pound.

She wouldn't allow herself to believe that Trevor would find her unattractive. She was carrying his baby, and all pregnant women were beautiful. Hadn't he told her that once during one of their long nocturnal talks?

Trevor had written that he loved surprises, and she fervently prayed he would love this one as much as she did. As though reading her mind, the baby kicked hard. He was so strong and energetic that she'd already decided she was carrying a small replica of his daddy.

"Yes, I know, baby. I probably should have told him, but he sounded so down." Especially in the past few months.

His letters had become shorter, with fewer references to the future. Bachelor jitters, she told herself. She'd had a few prenuptial nerves herself, especially in the past few days, when the baby had become so active. She was beginning to feel like a lumpy blimp.

Jillian glanced at her watch. Trevor's plane had landed nearly an hour ago. She'd wanted to meet him at the airport, but he'd insisted she wait for him in the bridal suite. He didn't want to jinx their future happiness by seeing his bride before the wedding.

A sudden knock at the door startled her. He was here!

Jillian wet her lips and hastily patted her rebellious curls into place. Taking a slow, deep breath, she smiled down at her tummy, then walked quickly to the door and flung it open.

Her joyous smile faded when she saw the bellman. He was carrying a huge bouquet of long-stemmed roses at arm's length. His white beachboy smile was nearly obscured by the crimson blossoms.

"Flowers for Ensign Anderson, ma'am."

"Uh, th-thank you. Put them on the table, please."

He walked by her, and Jillian stuck her head out the door. She looked up and down the corridor, but there was no sign of Trevor.

The bellman refused a tip. "It's been taken care of, ma'am."

"Mahalo," she said self-consciously, thanking him, and he gave her another good-natured grin.

She waited until he'd closed the door behind him, then crossed the room to snatch up the small white card she'd seen buried among the velvet buds.

The writing was in Trevor's familiar slashing backhand, and the ink was black. Several words had been smeared.

It's no good, Jill. I tried, you'll never know how hard. But I don't want to get married, not ever. Find some-one else, someone who wants to settle down, someone who can love you the way you deserve to be loved. Forget about me, just as I intend to forget about you.

For a long time Jillian simply stared at the terse lines. This was a joke. A horrible joke.

But the handwriting was his. She would recognize it any-where. And if it was his handwriting . . .

Hastily she glanced at the florist's name on the envelope, then raced to the phone. Her fingers shook as she dialed in-formation, and her voice was so unsteady that she could barely get the name out when the operator answered.

It took some persuasion, but the florist finally admitted that a tall sandy-haired man on crutches had purchased the flowers less than an hour ago. He'd paid extra to have them delivered on time.

"I hope you enjoy them, ma'am," the woman added cheerily. "The gentleman was most anxious that you receive them by four. Something about a wedding that he was unable to attend?"

Jillian dropped the phone onto the desk. The florist's tinny voice called out sharply several times before it was replaced by the abrupt sound of the dial tone.

"No, please, no," she whispered, an icy numbness beginning to spread through her. "Not Trevor. He wouldn't do this to me. He wouldn't."

Suddenly another knock sounded on the door. "I knew it," she whispered, her breath coming quickly. "It was all a mistake."

She flew across the room, her hands pressed against her belly protectively. Her heart was racing so fast that she felt light-headed as she threw open the door. "Darling—"

The young chaplain's cheerful smile faltered as Jillian grabbed the edge of the door and stared at him. "Is something wrong?" he asked anxiously.

Jillian didn't answer. The man's tanned features began to waver, then blur at the edges. And then they faded to black.

For the first time in her life Jillian had fainted.

Jillian drained her wineglass and set it carefully on the counter.

"I woke up on the bed. The chaplain had called a doctor and then the manager. None of them seemed to know what to do."

"It's a wonder you didn't go into premature labor," Adrian said in a quiet voice. For the first time since Jillian had met her, there was no animation in Adrian's face.

"I know. The doctor gave me a mild sedative, nothing that would hurt the baby, and I slept until the next morning. When I looked out the window, the flowers and the white carpet were gone. Everything was gone."

"And Trevor? What happened to him?"

Jillian felt a chill. Chewing on her lip, she slowly rolled the sleeves of her plaid cotton shirt down to her wrists and carefully buttoned the cuffs.

"It took me a day or two to sort it out, but I finally decided I had to tell him about the baby. He had a right to know."

Adrian nodded but said nothing.

Jillian hesitated, then went on with her story. She might as well tell it all.

"Trevor had been staying in an apartment near Balboa Hospital for several weeks after he'd been reassigned there as an outpatient. He was still undergoing therapy on his legs, and there was one more minor operation still to be done on his spine. So I went to his place, but he'd moved without leaving a forwarding address."

Her throat burned with unwanted tears, and she tried to swallow them away.

"I was desperate, so I went to the hospital. Trevor's therapist was on vacation, and the orthopedic ward charge nurse was noncommittal, until I showed her my Navy ID. As soon as she saw my name, she broke into a big smile. Commander Markus had left something for me, she told me. A package."

Jillian's brief laugh carried no humor. "I couldn't wait. I ripped it open in the car right there in the parking lot." Her voice faltered, and she stopped. She couldn't go on.

Adrian rubbed a spot from the marble with a corner of her bandanna. "If you'd rather not tell me, I understand, Jill. I can see this is hard for you."

Jillian's lips slanted into a bitter smile. "Actually, it feels good to let it out."

Adrian hesitated, then asked softly, "What was in the package?"

"Letters. Stacks of them. Every one I'd ever written him. And the pictures I'd sent him before my pregnancy had begun to show. He was telling me that he no longer wanted them—because he no longer wanted me."

"The bastard," Adrian whispered softly, wiping tears from her lashes with the back of her small hand. "I can't believe he's the same man I just read about, or the man I met on the podium. He has a nice face. And kind eyes, maybe even a little sad, like a man who's suffered a great loss."

Jillian refused to acknowledge her similar thoughts. Trevor was a great actor. Once he'd even convinced her that he loved her.

"Believe it," she said tersely.

Adrian looked concerned. "What reason did you give Jason for your not being married?"

Jillian sighed. "He thinks his father is a man named William White who died a hero before our wedding, and that's what he's always going to think."

Adrian gave her a thoughtful look. "Are you sure that's wise, Jill? Trevor's bound to come back here occasionally, maybe even spend a few days now and then. He could find Jason anytime he wanted. One wrong word and Jason would find out that you've been lying to him. He…he might never get over it, Jill. Kids are very vulnerable when it comes to things like that."

The icy hand of raw fear tightened around Jillian's lungs until she thought she would suffocate. Adrian was right. Clayton was only a matter of hours from Seattle by plane. And nearly everyone knew her—and Jason.

"Trevor won't be back," she said, praying she was right. "At least not to see me—or Jason. Once he's back in Seattle and over the shock, he'll realize that a half-grown son who thinks he's dead and a woman who hates him aren't worth his trouble."

"I thought you said he promised to fight for Jason."

Jillian snorted. "Trevor's good at making promises, but he's rotten at keeping them. I tell you, Addie, he won't be back."

"Well, I won't argue with you," Adrian said as she slipped off the stool and picked up her bandanna. "But, from what I saw of Trevor Markus, if he does come back, you'd better be prepared for the fight of your life."

Chapter 4

Jillian was restless after Adrian left. She kept thinking of Trevor, and the way he'd looked when she'd told him his name wasn't on Jason's birth certificate.

He'd appeared to be angry, certainly, and hurt, but she'd also seen disappointment cross his face, as though he'd expected more of her.

"He has no right to judge me," she muttered fiercely as she paced up and down the aisles.

Jillian stopped in front of a display of baby products, a smile playing over her face as she fingered a soft flannel sleeper adorned with laughing pink and blue teddy bears.

She'd bought Jason his first teddy bear at the airport in Cincinnati when she'd flown back to Ohio to tell her parents about the baby on the way.

The visit had been a nightmare.

Her stepfather had been quietly furious, pacing the shadowed parlor in the old-fashioned farmhouse with angry, lumbering strides.

Her mother had cried quietly, sending Jillian reproachful looks from sad, faded eyes.

"I won't have it, Jillian," Reuben Anderson had said in his nasal Ohio twang. "I raised you right, since you were three. I gave you my name, and it's a proud one. I won't have some playboy pilot throwing dirt on it. I'll get me a lawyer, or a shotgun, I don't care which, and make him do the right thing by you and the child."

Jillian had been appalled and very frightened. Reuben was an obstinate man with very strict ideas of right and wrong. He'd meant to do what he'd threatened, no matter how much he might embarrass her or risk the welfare of her baby.

So when he'd demanded the man's name, in desperation she'd given him the name of a patient who'd died.

As her due date grew closer, she'd been terrified that her stepfather would somehow discover her deception and carry out his threat. For days she worried that Trevor would suddenly appear, demanding her baby.

Now, from the perspective of years, she realized she'd been slightly irrational in those final months of her pregnancy.

She'd been very sick toward the end, and the last weeks had been passed in a daze of weariness and worry. She'd been terrified when her obstetrician had ordered her into the hospital almost six weeks before her due date.

Jason had nearly died during the difficult delivery, and Jillian, struggling to bring Trevor's child into the world, had called his name over and over until her voice had sunk to an inaudible whisper. Afterward, she'd sobbed helplessly when they'd taken Jason from her arms, even though it was to put him into an incubator in order to save him.

Jillian crushed the soft flannel sleeper in her hand and blinked at the hot tears pressing her lids. Her shoulders slumped as she stared down at the smooth, worn boards that bore the scars of countless heels.

From the instant her tiny redheaded son had wrapped his stubby fingers around hers, she'd been filled with so much love that she'd been shaking with it.

He'd been helpless and trusting and precious, a wonderful little person who needed her. As she'd kissed his soft, sweet head, she'd vowed that nothing would ever hurt this child. All the love that Trevor had rejected, all the caring that he'd scorned, she would give to his son.

Her son.

"Why did he have to come here now?" she muttered, stalking up the aisle to the glass-lined cage where she kept the prescription drugs. Opening the safe, she took out her Class Two ledger and sat down at her cluttered desk.

She'd forgotten him, she told herself as she opened the log. She'd gotten on with her life. She didn't want to think about things that might have been. She didn't want to open old wounds. It hurt too much.

Jillian's hands shook as she reached for her pen. She was thirty-six now, not twenty-one. She was no longer at the mercy of her emotions. *She* was in charge of her life, not her hormones, or some half-remembered love that had died long ago.

Right? she asked her reflection in the glass door of an old drug cabinet where she kept her reference books.

The tall, unsmiling, auburn-haired woman who stared back at her didn't look very convinced.

"See you later, Mom. I'm going to Mike's house to study." Jason thundered through the living room, his books under one arm. Dinner was over, and Jillian was tidying the kitchen.

"Be home by nine," Jillian called after him. "Remember, you have a test tomorrow. You need your rest."

The slamming of the screen door was her only answer.

Sighing, Jillian poured a glass of iced tea and sat down at the table under the open window. Jason had been oddly silent during dinner. He'd played with his food and stared down at his plate, answering her cheerful attempts at conversation with monosyllables.

He'd behaved so strangely that she'd felt his forehead to make sure he wasn't feverish. His skin felt normal to the touch, but his freckles had stood out in stark relief, as though he were paler than usual. And he'd drunk three full glasses of water with his meal.

If he was still behaving strangely tomorrow, she decided, she'd call Adrian and take him in for a checkup. Having made her decision, she felt better, and she let her mind wander. It had been a long and difficult week, and she was bone tired.

Idly she stared down at the town square. Main Street was quiet. Not much was happening. Nothing much ever happened on a Sunday in Clayton, unless it was ski season. Then the snow bunnies would descend on the town in parka-clad waves, stopping for hot chocolate or brandy on their way back to their nine-to-five weekdays in the cities down the mountain.

Trevor had been a skier. They'd talked about it once, about the way he and his brothers would race down the steepest slopes, shouting insults at one another. As the eldest, he'd invariably won, until his youngest brother, Tim, cadged lessons from a family friend who was also a former alpine champion. After that, Tim had whipped his big brother on every run. Trevor had been nineteen that season, and it had been the first time he'd ever lost at anything.

"I sulked for days," he'd told her with a self-conscious smile. "And then I decided that I'd better take a few lessons myself. Then, if Timmy beat me, I could live with it, knowing I'd done everything I could to win."

Everything he could to win.

Jillian ran her finger through the condensation on her glass. Trevor had fought hard for his life, too, fought to win against terrible odds. The compound fractures in his legs had become infected. For days he'd been delirious, racked by fever. During her off duty hours she'd stayed with him, sponging his hot face with cool water, holding his hand, talking to him, and she'd heard his disjointed remorse over the unavoidable pain his bombs and missiles had caused. Under the playboy facade Trevor had gradually shown himself to be a very caring man.

Jillian shut her eyes convulsively. She didn't want to re-live that time. She'd locked those four months they'd had together in some deep dark place at the back of her brain and refused to let the memories escape.

But what she'd told Addie was right. Maybe it was better to face the ghosts. Maybe, after all these years, the memories had lost the power to hurt. In any event, she'd better find out. Otherwise, she would be helpless to control her feelings if Trevor surprised her and showed up again.

And she had to be in control. If she showed the slightest sign of weakness, Trevor would start calling the shots. That was the kind of man he was.

Quickly, before she could change her mind, she left the table and went into her bedroom. From the top shelf of her closet she took a small wooden box. Shaking, she placed the box in the middle of her bed and piled pillows against the headboard. She kicked off her sandals and settled back.

Her hands were shaking and her palms were damp as she opened the dusty lid. Inside were two packets of letters. The ones tied with red satin ribbon were the ones Trevor had written to her. The other packet was thicker in spite of the air mail stationery. These were the letters he'd left behind. Her letters to him.

Her heart began to pound as she slipped the rubber band from the packet and sorted through the flimsy envelopes. They were all there but the last one, the long, loving letter she'd written just before she'd left Tokyo. She'd timed it so that Trevor would receive it just before he left San Diego.

She'd poured all of her love and loneliness into those two pages. She'd told him all the things she loved about him. And she'd told him of her dreams for their future together.

Rapidly she checked one more time. The last postmark was December twelfth. But she'd mailed her last letter on the fifteenth, nine days before her wedding day. She remembered distinctly.

He must have torn it up, she thought as she neatly rebundled the letters and slipped the rubber band over the thick pile. Or tossed it out. Either way, it didn't matter.

Besides, she'd simply been stalling, looking for a letter whose contents she knew by heart. It was Trevor's letters that she needed to read. Trevor's words.

Her fingers were clumsy as she untied the knot in the ribbon and lifted the first letter from the packet. Her name was written in large, bold script, with imperious capitals that commanded attention.

The paper rattled as she unfolded the single page. The first time she'd read these words she'd cried. She took a deep breath and began to read.

My Angel:

I did it, by God! I finally made it all the way to the end of the blasted corridor without falling on my can. I used the canes, of course, but I walked, Jill. I really walked!

Denise—my therapist, remember?—was so excited she cried. Okay, so maybe you were right after all. Maybe she wasn't really a Gestapo agent in a former life. Anyway sweetheart, I'm feeling pretty good tonight. Tired as hell, but missing you so much.

I wish you were here right now to crawl in beside me. I want to make love to you so badly I'm hard just thinking about you. Remember the first time, angel? Remember—

Jillian couldn't go on. The poignant words were too blurred by tears for her to see. Fighting back the sobs, she dropped the letter onto the quilt and folded her arms over her stomach. She remembered. Oh, God, how she remembered!

"I look like a damn lizard," Trevor grumbled, straining his neck to look down at his chest. It was late, nearly midnight, and they were alone behind the closed door of Trevor's room.

That afternoon the doctor had removed the cast from his torso. After thirteen weeks in plaster his skin was covered with a crusty layer of dried skin.

Jillian laughed. "You are pretty scaly, at that." She tipped the bottle of lotion into her hand and poured out a generous measure. "Now, lie still and let me work this in."

"Not until I get my kiss." His eyes glowed as he gazed up at her.

The dim light over the bed turned his thick hair to gold, and his lashes cast dark spiky shadows on his cheeks. Jillian felt her heart swell with love as she leaned forward to brush her lips over his.

Instantly his mouth firmed under hers and became hungry. One large hand cupped the back of her head, while the other framed her jaw. "Angel. I want you so much," he whispered before taking her lips again. This time he wasn't gentle. This time he demanded.

Pleasure shot through her as his tongue slipped past her lips. The raspy surface was exciting as it abraded the inside of her mouth, and he tasted sweet.

She could feel the tension in him, and the heat. A faint musky smell mingled with the cherry scent of the lotion, exciting her. He wanted her just as much as she wanted him. She wrapped her hands around his shoulders, feeling the lotion go from her palms to his skin. It felt good, like a sweet, sensual lubrication.

He growled deep in his throat, then let her go. "You're better than any pill," he said with a crooked smile. His gaunt cheeks were flushed, and a vein throbbed violently in his temple. A faint sheen of moisture glistened on his forehead, and he was breathing hard.

Jillian felt the muscles of her face soften into a smile. "A kiss every four hours, you mean?"

"At least." He wiped his brow with his hand and let his forearm rest there, as though he were in pain.

"It's worth thinking about, anyway."

"That's about all I can do," he grumbled as she began massaging his shoulders. "The doctors tell me to be patient, but I feel like a damn eunuch."

"Don't worry. Your body just needs time to heal, that's all," she whispered soothingly. His arousal came swiftly whenever he touched her, but it never lasted.

He sighed and rested his forearm over his eyes to block out the light.

His skin was warm and tough against her palms, and his chest was covered with a fine layer of golden hair. Her fingertips burrowed tiny tracks in the silky thatch, and the lotion turned the gold to brown.

His nipples were tiny flat pebbles, darker than the rest of his skin, and when she touched them they hardened instantly and turned white. Her palms began to tingle, and heat shot up her arm. It felt so good to touch him, to feel his muscles, still hard despite being unused for so long, contract under her fingertips.

She loved the massive lines of his chest and the powerful slant of his shoulders. Beneath the stubborn jaw, he had a strong neck, the kind a woman liked to nuzzle. His tan had faded, but his skin had regained much of the healthy color it had lost.

He was a male animal in his prime, vibrant and virile, in spite of his temporary incapacity.

She poured more lotion, warming it for several seconds in her palms. Then, slowly massaging in gentle circles, she moved down his ribbed torso, feeling the hard slab of muscle that tightened into granite as she pressed.

A thin curling line of golden hair led her lower, and she began to warm inside. Beneath the sheet Trevor was naked. The sheet had been pulled to his waist, and she slowly slid it toward his hips.

Her fingers tangled in the triangle of coarse, tightly curled blond hair below his hard abdomen.

Trevor groaned, and his breath became shallow. Jillian froze, her palms flat against him. His hands covered hers, and he exerted a gentle pressure.

"Don't stop, angel," he whispered, his eyes closed. "I feel alive. For the first time since I hit that damn deck, I feel like a man again."

He was aroused, but this time his arousal didn't disappear as quickly as it had come.

Jillian fought back tears. His face was taut, his brows drawn, his lips compressed. Deep lines bracketed his mouth, lines she knew would never completely disappear, even when he'd recovered. They'd been too harshly imprinted by the fever and pain—and fear.

She felt the tears glisten in her eyes, and she tried to blink them away.

"Hey, don't cry, angel," Trevor said huskily, capturing her hands and rubbing his thumbs over her wrists. "I don't ever want you to cry. If I could, I'd take all the bad things out of your life forever."

The gentle friction was nearly unbearable, and she inhaled sharply. "I'm crying because I'm happy. You make me so happy, Trevor. Just being with you makes all the bad things disappear."

She saw the flush of embarrassment touch his cheeks. He had trouble talking about this feelings. Or hers. But she would be patient. The tenderness was there inside him. She'd felt it in his touch and seen it in his smile.

Trevor's gaze fell to the bulge between his legs. "I'm afraid to move. I think I might explode." His grin was lopsided and tinged with humor, but his eyes were turbulent and intense—and filled with harsh male frustration. "God,

I want you," he whispered with a groan, but he made no move to pull her toward him. "But that door doesn't lock."

Jillian's heart swelled with love. In spite of his need to prove he could still perform as a man, he was leaving the decision up to her. If she were caught making love to a patient, she would be court-martialed.

"Maybe I can do something about that," she whispered, leaning forward to kiss the slanted edge of his mouth. "I'll ask Bev to see we're not disturbed. That is, if you think you can stand the strain."

Her breasts brushed his chest, and he inhaled swiftly. "I want you so damn much I can stand anything to have you."

Jillian kissed him, then hurried into the corridor. Beverly Sons was flipping through a patient's chart when Jillian beckoned to her. "Trevor and I need some privacy, okay?"

Bev's blue eyes twinkled with understanding. "No problem. It's quiet tonight." She grinned. "Give the big hunk a kiss for me."

Jillian blushed and nodded happily before she returned quietly to the room she'd just left. "All taken care of, sir," she said with a snappy salute.

"Come here, Ensign," he said with a growl, and she hurried eagerly across the room.

His arms closed around her, and he hugged her against his chest. She could feel his heart pounding beneath her, and there was desperation in the cadence of his breathing.

"I was afraid you wouldn't come back," he said thickly. "I thought sure you'd have second thoughts."

"Never. I know a good thing when it's offered."

His laugh was a throaty rumble that sent chills down her spine. She smiled against his neck and trailed her hands down the hard muscles of his upper arms. Slowly she pushed upward until he was holding her loosely.

His eyes held hers as she reached up to turn off the light. A silvery glow from the outside lights turned the room to velvet gray, making it seem warmer somehow, and more intimate, as though they were the only two people in the huge, sterile building.

"Let me go a minute, darling," she whispered.

A tiny frown appeared between his dusty blond brows, but he obeyed, and she slid off the bed. With eyes that seemed to glow, he watched her intently.

Jillian felt a deep shiver of love as she slowly untied the waistband of her loose-fitting surgical scrubs. She started to pull the smock free, but he stopped her with a growl.

"Let me."

Trevor's hand shook as he tugged the top from the pants. She hesitated, then straightened quickly and pulled the smock over her head.

She gasped as his hand slid up her rib cage to cup her breast. Her bra was mostly lace and fell away easily as his fingers found the front opening.

Trevor's breath was raspy and urgent, and his eyes were on fire as he watched her step out of the baggy trousers. She stood before him, a trembling smile on her lips as he bathed her in a reverent gaze.

"My fantasies were never this good," he said in a harsh whisper as she slowly removed her silky panties. He reached out and took them from her hand, then tucked them under his pillow. "I've imagined you doing this a hundred times in my mind, but you're even more perfect than I thought."

Slowly she leaned closer. His face tightened with strain as he moved slowly, twisting at the waist until he was on his side at the edge of the mattress. He bracketed her rib cage with his hands, then slid his palms down the curve of her hip.

"You're perfect, angel," he whispered. "Your skin is like cognac on the tongue, so smooth and hot."

Jillian held her breath as his fingers dipped lower. She threaded one hand in his thick hair while the other stroked his hard back. She was afraid to move, afraid to breathe. She wanted him desperately, but she didn't want to cause him any more pain.

His eyes were narrow golden-brown slits as he stroked her with slow absorption, his hard fingers trailing along her inner thighs.

It took some ingenuity, and caused him to inhale sharply against the pain, but Trevor finally maneuvered himself so that he could bury his face against her belly. His breath was hot on her skin as he wrapped his arms around the curve of her hips and pulled her closer.

His tongue trailed long, lazy circles around her navel, dipping into the tiny folds of her belly button to lap her skin. His lips were soft and insistent as he moved lower, licking her into glistening wetness.

"Such a sweet taste," he murmured against her. "I've been so hungry."

Instantly on fire, she buried her fingers in the ragged thickness of his hair and held on. She'd never felt such glorious urgency, such intense longing. Under his tongue, her nerve endings began to flutter in involuntary reaction. He was taking control of her body, exciting sensations in the sensitive receptors that made her shiver.

Suddenly he groaned. "I can't wait," he said in a tortured voice. "Baby, now, please, before I disappoint us both."

Slowly he eased onto his back again. His eyes never left hers as she carefully knelt beside him. His teeth bared, he began breathing in short, raspy bursts as she slid the sheet away from his body.

Both his legs were encased in plaster from his hips to his toes and elevated slightly on pillows. Careful not to jostle him, she straddled his imprisoned hips, bracing her weight on her shins. The plaster casts were hard and rough under her buttocks as her skin brushed against them, and the sheet was slick and cool beneath her knees.

He was ready, his arousal standing between them, hot and hard and swollen. She saw the violent hunger in his eyes and heard the desperate urgency in his breathing.

"Now, angel. Don't wait. Let me feel you."

Heat flooded her face, and her heart thundered as she gently guided him into her. He filled her with throbbing heat.

He groaned and tossed his head from side to side on the pillow, gritting his teeth. He was trying to hold back.

Moaning, she eased forward until she was resting against his wide chest. She slid her arms under his and pressed her face into the moist hollow of his shoulder. Tremors shook him as she began to move, slowly at first, and then, as the fiery heat built inside her, faster and faster, until he was heaving under her.

And then, just when she knew she had to stop or explode, his muscles went rigid beneath her, and his fingers tightened convulsively in her hair. His clenched jaw muffled his groan of release, but she could feel the explosive shower inside bathing her with delicious heat. Her surrender came immediately as wave after wave of pleasure rolled through her.

Trevor wrapped his arms tightly around her and gasped for air. "My angel," he whispered in a hoarse soft voice. "Don't ever leave me. I couldn't stand it if you left me."

Jillian stared blindly at the letter in her hand and started to sob. Hot tears splashed on the thin paper, turning the ink to black pools. "But you left *me*," she whispered, crushing the letter to her heart. "And I still don't know why."

Jillian raised her head to the ceiling, and the tears dripped down her cheeks. She hadn't cried for Trevor in years. Not since the night she'd taken his Academy ring from the chain around her neck, wrapped it in tissue and put it away.

Slowly she let her gaze drop. The ring was still there, a pink wad in the corner of the small box, but she didn't touch it. Instead, sitting cross-legged on the quilt, her tears wetting the flimsy pages, she read his letters one by one. The words weren't eloquent. Sometimes they were funny, but more often they were angry and filled with terrible frustration and loneliness. Still, they were Trevor's words, and she could almost hear him speaking them to her. Her tear-filled gaze dropped to the last lines of the final letter.

I know I'm not the greatest when it comes to words, angel. I've never been in love before, and I'm not sure I tell you the things you want to hear. But that doesn't mean I don't feel them.

Sometimes I wake up in the middle of the night, and I'm so scared of the hard things ahead of me, I'm sick, but then I see your face and hear your voice, and I'm okay again.

You're my lifeline, Jill, and my hope. You're the best thing that ever happened to me. And even if I sometimes let you down, or if I hurt you or disappoint you, always remember that I'm not perfect, but I do love you.

Jillian was filled with such a sense of loss that it nearly strangled her. She pressed the thin paper against her breast and squeezed her eyes tightly shut.

She rocked back and forth on the mattress, Trevor's letters piled around her. "Why, Trevor?" she pleaded through trembling lips. "Why did you do this to us?"

Her only answer was silence.

Sometime after midnight Jillian awakened suddenly, her heart pounding. Something was wrong. She sat up and listened. Adrenaline pumped violently through her system, making it difficult to breathe.

The door to her bedroom was open, and light streamed along the hall. But she'd turned out the light when she'd gone to bed, just as she'd always done.

The sound was coming from the bathroom at the end of the hall. It was a gasping, retching sound that sent shivers up her backbone.

"Jason," she cried in a strangled voice as she tossed off the sheet and reached for her robe. Without bothering with slippers, she ran down the hall, her robe billowing behind her.

Jason was bent over the toilet, his skinny shoulders heaving violently. It took Jillian a moment to realize he was fully dressed.

"Baby, what is it? Are you sick?" She bent over him, her hand against the sweat-dampened curls at the nape of his neck.

He moaned and shook his head. The worst appeared to be over, and he sat back on his haunches. His face was white, and he was sweating.

Jillian flushed the toilet, then wetted a cloth and gently wiped his face. The freckles stood out starkly against his pale skin, and his lips were gray.

"I'm calling Addie," she said, anxiously feeling his forehead. He still wasn't feverish, but he must have picked up some kind of intestinal bug.

"No, Mom," he protested in a slurred voice. "Don't call Dr. Franklin."

A sour odor wrinkled her nostrils, and she pressed her fingers against her nose and mouth as though to block out the smell. "Why not?" she asked quietly, already knowing the answer. Jason was drunk.

His shoulders slumped, and he hung his head. "Don't need a doctor," he muttered, his eyes blinking rapidly. His shoulders swayed back and forth in a jerky, disjointed rhythm, and he was breathing loudly through his nose.

Jillian pressed a hand to her stomach. Now she was feeling sick, as sick as her son had been. "You've been drinking."

Jason shook his head, then groaned. He hung on to the bowl to steady himself.

Jillian bit her lip. The first thing she had to do was get him back into his room. Maybe by then she would have figured out what to do. "Here, sweetie, let me help you up."

He was heavier than he looked, and his legs were rubbery. His arm was heavy on her shoulder, and he staggered as he moved, but she managed to get him into the bedroom. He collapsed on his rumpled bed, and Jillian sat on the edge of the mattress, trying to catch her breath. Jason was already snoring.

She shivered uncontrollably as she looked down at her disheveled son. He'd been a handful as a toddler and a rambunctious little boy. But he'd never been a bad kid. He'd never lied or taken something that didn't belong to him, and his grades, until recently, had always been good.

"So what do I do now?" she muttered under her breath as she hugged herself in a futile effort to stop the violent trembling. Nothing came to her.

Sighing, she shook Jason awake again. "Talk to me, Jase. What's this all about?" His eyes blinked rapidly, and he groaned. Jillian refused to let him sink back into sleep. "I want an answer, Jason."

"It's a club, Mom." He licked his lips. "Mike Cobb and a bunch of other guys and me. We had some champagne to celebrate our first meeting."

Jillian scowled. "A club? You mean, like a fraternity."

Jason's smile beamed crookedly. "Yeah, that's it. A fra-fraternity."

"But isn't that against school policy?"

"Who cares about the dumb school?" he said in slurred derision. "Besides, we meet after school in Mike's garage. Sheriff Cobb says it's okay as long as we don't play the music too loud."

Jillian refused to be blackmailed. Mel Cobb wasn't her idea of a model parent. "Who else is in this club?"

Her tone was sharp, and Jason's brow puckered. Slowly, his voice wavering, he listed the names. The other boys were from good families, and Jillian had known most of them for as long as she'd lived in Clayton.

She bit her lip. The idea of a club seemed harmless enough. In fact, it might even be a positive thing, especially now, when Jason seemed to be having so much trouble making the transition to high school. And all kids Jason's age experimented with alcohol, sooner or later. All the books and magazines said so. She just wouldn't let it go any further.

"There can't be any more drinking, Jason," she said sternly. "You hear me?"

Solemnly he nodded. Some of the color was beginning to come back into his cheeks, and his eyes had lost their wild sheen. "I promise, Mom. It was a stupid thing to do, anyway. I didn't even like the taste." His bloodless lips curved into a tentative smile, and Jillian melted.

This was her son, her baby. Of course he knew better. Jason had always had good sense. She hugged him tightly. He was caught in limbo, this half man, half boy. But he would be fine. She had no doubt at all.

Jillian helped him strip to his shorts, and he slid beneath the covers. He gave her a sweet smile, then snuggled his cheek against the pillow. His red hair was a bright halo around his long, narrow face, and his features were slack with tiredness. He was asleep in seconds.

His body was long, his bones large, with the promise of sturdy strength. He had big wrists and enormous feet. Like his father. And like Trevor, Jason had a smile that seemed to reflect the sun whenever it flashed.

The first time she'd seen that endearing, lopsided grin on Jason's small face she'd cried. It had hurt so much, knowing that Trevor would never stand hand in hand with her next to his son's crib and listen to the sweet, soft breathing. That he would never nuzzle his face against a chubby little neck that smelled of baby powder. That he would never hear his little boy laugh or say his first imperious words or mutter to himself in cheerful toddler nonsense.

Jillian's lips began to tremble, and her throat closed up. It had been Trevor's fault that he'd missed those rare and wonderful moments.

And she'd made it up to Jason for not having a father. She was sure of it.

"I love you, sweetie," she said, smoothing the frown from his brow. "And I won't ever let him take you away from me, I promise."

Chapter 5

Jason perched on the side of Jillian's desk and fiddled with the 1850s ore sample she used as a paperweight. His foot tapped restlessly against the worn floor, and he looked bored.

It was Saturday, the day Jillian spent in the mayor's office in the town hall. It was also the day Jason received his allowance.

"Could I have a little extra this week, Mom?" he asked as she pulled out her wallet. "Darcy and I did a good job washing the windows."

Darcy Hammond was a young mother of four and one of the workers laid off when PacTimber had gone into receivership. Jillian had hired her to clerk in the store on weekends and Wednesdays.

Every Saturday morning Jason helped Darcy clean the store before it opened, and Jillian paid him the same hourly wage as she paid her helper.

"Why do you need extra?" she asked, pulling out some bills. For the past two weeks, since the night she'd found him drunk in the bathroom, Jason had been moody and withdrawn. Guilt, Jillian had told herself. She'd decided to let him work through his feelings in his own way.

Jason's gaze slid sideways to meet hers. "It's my turn to bring the drinks to the club meeting this afternoon."

At her abrupt frown, he added quickly, "Cokes, Mom. Just Cokes. And some chips and things."

Jillian relaxed. She and the other mothers of the club members had agreed to monitor the boys' activities. If the boys drank again or got into trouble of any kind, the mothers would insist the club be disbanded. She hadn't spoken with Mel Cobb. It would have been a waste of time.

Slowly she counted out his wages, then added three dollars more and laid the money on the cluttered desk. Absently she riffled through the remaining bills. "One of these days I'm going to have to get some reading glasses," she muttered in disgust. "Or learn to count."

"Something wrong?"

"No, I just thought I had more money in this sorry old wallet than I have."

For days, since the dedication ceremony, in fact, she'd been horrendously absentminded. Twice she'd misplaced her truck keys, and just last week she'd found a carbon copy of a prescription for codeine she couldn't remember filling. The name of the patient was unfamiliar, but she'd initialed the bottom, just as the state required, and tucked the copy into the ledger, just as she always did.

Jason crumpled the bills in his freckled fist and reached down for his skateboard, which was propped against her desk. "Thanks, Mom. I'm outta here," he said in a rush.

"Sweetie, wait. I need to talk with you about something."

A wary look crowded into Jason's eyes, and his brow furrowed. He held the board in front of him, wheels out. "What about?"

Jillian masked her irritation. She was determined to keep the fragile peace between them. She couldn't stand it when Jason withdrew from her.

"Nothing serious. It's just that Mr. Sizemore called this morning while you were downstairs with Darcy. He really could use you on the team again this year."

The wariness left his eyes, and he grinned. "Ah, Mom, I told you, I'm tired of soccer. I just don't want to play anymore."

"But you've always loved to play. I don't understand why you say you're tired of it."

He lifted one shoulder in a familiar gesture of impatience. "I got better things to do with my Saturdays, that's all. And I might go out for basketball this winter, if I grow a little more. Mike's dad says I'm real good."

Jillian started to brush the matted hair from his forehead, but he jerked away and stood up. A quick hurt shot through her. He didn't want her to touch him anymore.

"Jase, I think you're spending too much time with Mike and not enough time with your other friends. I haven't seen Scott Sizemore around the house since the beginning of summer."

"Scott's a dork." His eyes carried a sneer, and he began to prowl the room, too restless to sit still.

"Jason! Scotty's a very nice boy. And you always said he was your best friend."

"Well, he's not anymore. He's not any fun. Nobody at school likes him."

Jillian leaned back in her chair and tried to keep her rising frustration out of her voice. "By nobody, I suppose you mean Mike?" When Jason didn't answer, she sat forward and gave him a pleading look. "Jase, what's wrong? You've been in a terrible mood since . . . since the opening of Horizons."

She tried to see what he was thinking behind the thick brushes of his lashes, but in the bright morning light his wide pupils conveyed only sullen impatience.

"I'm fine, Mom. I just have a lot on my mind, you know?" he declared emphatically, his lips twisting into a boyish smile that looked forced.

"No, I don't know. That's why I'm asking. You've always told me what's on your mind, but lately every time I try to talk with you, you clam up or find something you have to do."

Jason's brows pulled together in a rebellious frown. "I'm almost fifteen, Mom," he said in a petulant tone that she'd never heard before. "I can handle my own life."

"I know that, Jase. But I'm worried about you."

"I'm too old for that." The petulance had been replaced by anger. "You keep thinking I'm still a kid. It's time you started trusting me more."

Jillian sighed. She wasn't going to win this round. "We'll talk about this later," she said, beckoning him closer. "Give me a kiss, and you can go."

Jason hesitated, then came forward to give her an awkward kiss on the cheek. Then, as though he were terribly embarrassed, he spun around and hurried toward the door.

"Be home by six," she shouted after him.

"Six-thirty," he shouted back as he propelled his board down the deserted corridor. The wheels clattered loudly on the linoleum, and Jillian winced.

Thank God all the offices are closed on the weekend, she thought as she slumped back in the worn leather chair and stared at the ceiling. She closed her eyes and tried to relax, but she was as jumpy as her son.

Since the night she read Trevor's letters she'd been waging an inner battle. Part of her wanted to let go of the past, to forgive Trevor and let him become a part of Jason's life if that was what he wanted, but another part, the vulnerable young woman who'd been so badly scarred, refused to trust him.

What if he decided that an occasional visit wasn't enough? What if he wanted Jason to live with him part-time in Seattle? What if he wanted custody?

No, she thought quickly. She couldn't risk it. She couldn't bear the thought of someone else rearing her son, not even his father. She would fight if she had to. She would—

Suddenly the phone buzzed. Sighing, Jillian reached for the receiver. She was used to these Saturday calls. It was the only time when her constituents could be sure of her undivided attention.

"Jillian Anderson. May I help you?"

Absently she ran a hand through her curly hair. She'd spent an extra half hour in front of the mirror earlier, trying to tame the rebellious thickness into a more sophisticated style, but as soon as she'd stepped outside, the brisk morning breeze had ruined all her hard work.

"Jill, it's Addie. He's here!"

Jillian sat bolt upright and gripped the receiver more tightly. Inside the prickly denim of her tight new jeans, her thighs clenched painfully against the leather seat as she pushed the soles of her sneakers against the floor.

"You mean—Trevor?"

"Yes. I'm at Ray's Service. I saw him go by when I was gassing up the Jeep. He's driving a maroon Jaguar convertible with Washington plates. I know it's him."

Adrenaline poured into Jillian's veins, jolting her heart into a furious pace and spreading a sick feeling in her stomach. "I'm not ready," she said, more to herself than Adrian. Her free hand worried the open collar of her blouse, crushing the emerald silk against her nervous palm.

"I think it's a good sign that he's come back, Jill."

"Are you crazy, Addie? I told you that was the last thing I wanted."

There was a brief pause. "At least give him a chance to make amends to you and Jase. You might regret it if you don't."

Jillian swiveled around to gaze out the window. The town square bustled with Saturday shoppers, and traffic was heavy on the surrounding streets. But there was no sign of a maroon Jaguar, and no sign of Trevor.

She blew a slow stream of air toward her bangs, and some of the tightness eased from her muscles. "Maybe he's not even coming into town." Jillian searched the area below. There was still no sign of a man with Trevor's distinctive swagger. He could have taken the left fork at the crossroads toward Horizons.

"True. I imagine you'll find out soon enough." Jillian heard the sound of a sigh before Adrian added in a sympathetic tone, "For what it's worth, good luck, I'll be at the clinic until seven if you need a friendly ear."

"Thanks. And thanks for the warning."

"De nada."

Adrian hung up, and Jillian slowly replaced the receiver, her gaze still searching the streets. A strange feeling of excitement leaped to life inside her, and her cheeks grew uncomfortably warm.

Trevor *had* come back.

"I'm impressed, Madam Mayor. You have a very efficient early warning system." The voice was raspy and deep and terribly familiar.

Jillian swiveled around so fast that she nearly overbalanced. Trevor was standing in the doorway, one hand braced against the doorjamb, the other holding a manila folder. There was the barest suggestion of masculine amusement in the crooked slant of his hard lips.

"You're not welcome here, Trevor," she said flatly.

"So you said. I was hoping you'd changed your mind."

She'd heard that husky note of resignation in his voice before. It was the tone he'd used when he was bracing to accept the pain of some necessary procedure during his recovery.

She shoved aside the illogical feeling of guilt that rose inside her. "I'll never change my mind about you, Trevor. Never."

He said nothing, only watched her with those fathomless eyes that changed color along with his mood. This morning they were a deep russet and unreadable. But the knuckles of his hand whitened as though he'd suddenly pushed hard against the wooden jamb.

She remembered the strength in that hand. And the gentleness.

But Trevor didn't look gentle. He looked tough and rangy and, in the faded blue work shirt and tight, wear-softened jeans, slightly uncivilized, like the burly, hard-living men from the lumber company who used to take over the town on Saturday night.

He had to be at least six-three, she realized as she measured his lean length against the door, and all muscle, but there was more than rugged masculine strength in his rawboned frame. There was an air of restless magnetism about him that frightened her.

Heat surged into her cheeks, and her palms began to sweat. The mountain air seemed suddenly thinner somehow, as though Trevor's big powerful body had pushed most of the oxygen from the room.

"What do you want, Trevor? This is my day to catch up on my paperwork, and I'm behind."

"What are you offering?" he asked in a neutral tone.

"A polite goodbye." She shifted her gaze toward the empty corridor behind the massive triangle of his torso. "Have a nice day."

"I'm trying, but you're making it very difficult." A wry, lopsided grin creased his cheeks and crinkled his eyes, but Jillian ignored his devilish charm.

She had a fleeting impression that nothing would be too difficult for this man if he really set his mind on it. Or if it was something he really wanted.

Like being a part of his son's life.

She pressed her thighs together tightly and sat up straighter. "You didn't answer my question," she persisted. "Why are you here?"

"To claim my rights as Jason's father."

The teasing light left Trevor's eyes. He dropped his arm and walked toward her. In the close confines of her office she saw that his swaggering gait was the result of a slight but recognizable limp, as though one of his legs was slightly shorter than the other.

With a flip of his powerful wrist he tossed the folder onto the blotter in front of her. There was a deadly stillness about him that she'd never noticed before.

"What's that?" she demanded, glaring at him.

"Open it and see."

Jillian's hand began to shake as she did as he ordered.

"Oh, no," she whispered in horror as she saw the cold, impersonal lines of the deposition on top. Hastily she spread the other pages out in front of her. There were four in all, properly witnessed and notarized, sworn statements testifying that Ensign Jillian Louise Anderson and Lieutenant Commander Trevor Madison Markus had once been lovers.

There were also copies of Jason's birth certificate and a death certificate showing that Lieutenant William Paul White had died ten months and fifteen days before her son was born.

The name of the law firm was unfamiliar, but the stationery was a thick vellum, and the letterhead had been engraved instead of printed. He'd obviously carried out his threat to hire the best.

"The private investigator I hired hasn't found all of the nurses who were assigned to the surgical wing at the same time you were there, but the four who've been interviewed by my attorney so far were all quite cooperative—and talkative. They remembered you very well, Jill. And me." His voice roughened. "And our love affair. It's all there, how you pulled strings to get me assigned to a private room, how you asked them to insure our privacy after lights out." One side of his mouth slanted into a bitter smile. "It doesn't take much imagination to fill in the blanks. Any judge would be able to do it easily."

She raised stricken eyes to his. "You make it seem so tawdry." Her voice choked. "It wasn't like that. It wasn't. You're not being fair."

A harsh tension tightened the planes of his face into a stark mask, and under the soft material of his shirt, his muscles clenched until they seemed forged from steel. "You put another man's name where mine should be. How fair was that?"

"You know why I had to do that," she cried. "You didn't want to be a husband. I had no reason to think you'd want to be a father."

Trevor ran a hand through his hair. Except for the color, the coarse thickness was very much like Jason's, hard to tame and inclined to curl at the ends if it got too long.

"You're right," he said in a rough voice. "I walked away from you, and I've never looked back. Is that what you want me to say?"

"Yes, because it's true. You didn't even leave a forwarding address."

His hands balled into fists at his sides, then slowly uncurled, as though he were consciously controlling himself. "Jill, listen to me. I wasn't in any shape to take care of a wife. I was having trouble taking care of myself in those days." A tiny muscle jerked in his rugged jaw. "But if I'd known about Jason, I swear I would have tried. I wouldn't have let you face that alone."

"It's too late." Her fingers trembled as they pressed against her throat. For some strange reason it had hurt to say those words.

"For you and me, maybe, but Jason is still my son, and I intend to be there for him as I should have been from the first." A flicker of pain darkened his eyes for an instant before his thick lashes lowered. "Hate me if you have to, Jill, but I love my son, and I want him to know that. And as quickly as possible. We've already lost too much time."

Jillian turned to ice. Inside, she began to shiver violently, and her palms felt frozen. "And if I refuse?"

Something raw and powerfully potent simmered in his eyes. "Then I'll show these sworn statements to a judge."

"You . . . you wouldn't!" Jillian pressed her hand to her stomach. A sick dread was rapidly replacing the empty chill.

His skin paled, but his eyes remained hard. "I will if I have to, Jill. I don't like playing dirty, but you made the rules. Jason's the only son I'll ever have, and I'm not going to give him up."

The blood drained from her face in a rush, and she felt light-headed. Tiny pinpricks of light wavered in front of her eyes before she managed to clear her head. "If you do this, I'll never forgive you."

He absorbed the venom in her words with a stiff shrug. "I've never expected your forgiveness, Jill." His voice was flat, without any emotion at all.

She bit her lip. "What if Jason decides he doesn't want you in his life? Then what?"

He flexed his shoulders as though his back had suddenly given him pain. "I never think past today, Jill. If he makes that decision, I'll deal with it then."

Jillian's gaze dropped to the papers in front of her. She could hire an attorney and fight to deny Trevor access. Maybe she would win, maybe she wouldn't. But Jason would be the one to suffer if these affidavits were read in open court.

Her gaze absently noted the signatures, signatures she'd seen hundreds of times on hundreds of patient charts. Sally and Bev. Pat and Barbara.

They'd been young, just out of nursing school, like her. Every day they'd dealt with terrible suffering, just as she had. They'd been allies as well as friends, fighting desperately to keep their horribly wounded patients alive. Too many times they'd lost, but sometimes they'd won. And after every victory, they'd cried together in joy and relief.

Romance had been as rare as a laugh in the wards where they'd worked. So when she and Trevor had fallen in love, the other nurses had been willing conspirators. Helping the lovers escape the stark reality of the war for a time had been their own private expression of hope in that bleak world of suffering and death.

In spite of the terrible things around her, when she'd been with Trevor, she'd been so happy... and so foolish.

Her hand shook as she collected the papers he'd brought and shoved them into the folder. "Here's your evidence," she said stiffly, shoving the folder toward him. "You've made your point."

"It doesn't have to be this way, Jill," Trevor said as he moved forward and took the papers from her trembling hand. He sounded bone weary and very bitter, like a man who'd just run a gruelling race the best way he knew how and lost.

"Oh, yes, it does. You made certain of that when you came here with your tidy little file."

Trevor glanced up at the ceiling, his expression thunderous. "What the hell was I supposed to do?" he said with explosive anger. "If I walked away and let you keep me out of Jason's life, you'd think I didn't care, just the way you think I didn't care about you fifteen years ago. A man can't win with you, lady." He ran a hand through his hair again, this time in a savage gesture of restraint, and glared at her.

"That's right," she shot back. "So give up. Let me alone."

"Like hell I will! I have a lot to prove to you, and I'll be damned if I'll give up until I do." He looked furious, but there was a hint of something that looked like pleading in his eyes.

"Please leave now," she said in a stiff voice that contained the last of her strength. "I think we've said just about all there is to be said."

He exhaled slowly. "Not quite. You haven't given me your answer."

His stormy gaze shifted to the framed picture of Jason on her desk, and Jillian lifted a weary hand in surrender. She would never publicly expose Jason to the damning words in that folder, and Trevor knew it. It was one more reason to hate him.

"I'll talk to Jason tonight. If he wants to meet you, I won't stand in his way. That's the best I can do."

Emotions raced swiftly through his narrowed eyes, emotions she could neither read nor understand. He lifted his shoulders in a shrug that conveyed barely contained impatience.

"You can reach me at Horizons. I've . . . rearranged my schedule so that I can manage some vacation time. I intend to spend it with Jason." His deceptively low tone carried a strange combination of deep sadness and warning.

She folded her hands over her stomach as though to protect the tiny life that was no longer there. "I'll call you."

The harsh lines of his face, first put there by his months in the hospital, seemed deeper as he gave her a brief smile. "Good. I'll be waiting."

"Don't hold your breath."

He stared at her in stony silence for a moment longer, then tucked the folder under his arm and walked away from her.

The streetlight outside her kitchen window began to glow with an eerie orange brightness. Seated across from Jason at the table, Jillian rested her chin in her palm and watched a flock of birds flying eastward in ragged formation.

It was dusk, and the sun had fallen below the horizon, leaving bloody streaks in the dark sky. The air was oppressively hot, and there was going to be a full moon. A lovers' moon.

Ignoring the sudden tremor that shook her, Jillian shifted her gaze to the peaks in the distance. Somewhere between her and those jagged mountains, Trevor was waiting for her call.

She'd tried all afternoon to find the right words to tell Jason the truth about his father, but all the words she'd chosen had sounded stilted and defensive.

No, that wasn't the reason she was stalling. Admit it, Jill, she said silently. You're scared. No, more like terrified.

Trevor was rich. He traveled by helicopter and wore suits that cost more than she made in a month. His life was exciting and glamorous, just the kind of life a young boy would find irresistible.

What if Jason suddenly decided he'd had enough of his mother's quiet ways? What if he decided he wanted to live with his father in Seattle? She'd survived the loss of one person she'd loved desperately. How could she possibly survive the loss of another?

"Mom? Didn't you hear me?"

"What?" She blinked across the table. Jason had finished his dinner and was folding his napkin in the careful way she'd taught him.

"I asked if I could be excused?"

Jason pushed back his chair and started to rise. He looked as though he'd gained back a few of the pounds he'd lost over the past few months of summer vacation.

Jillian put her hand on his arm to stop him. "Not yet. There's . . . something I need to discuss with you."

Jason's thin chest heaved in a sigh. "Mom, I already told you I don't want to play soccer." His face was a curious mixture of teenage rebelliousness and adult exasperation.

Poor baby, she thought, aching for him. He wants to act grown up, but he's not sure how.

"Well?" He sounded impatient.

Jillian bit her lip, then glanced at the folded newspaper that was tucked into the basket under the window where she kept her magazines. "First, I want you to read something, then we'll . . . talk." She cleared the table, making a space.

Jason's pale brow furrowed, and apprehension crept into his eyes. "What's with you tonight, Mom? You're acting funny."

She forced a smile as she unfolded the two-week-old *Clarion* in front of him, pointing to the article beside the pictures of Trevor and herself. "Read this."

Grumbling under his breath, Jason bent his head and began to read.

Jillian ran her wet palms along the sides of her jeans. The hard seams hurt her skin, but she welcomed the pain. She could handle that kind of pain.

"Okay, I've read it. So what?" Jason sat back and looked at her. It was almost as though he were daring her to tell him something he didn't want to hear.

"What... what do you think? About Trevor Markus, I mean."

Jason shrugged disinterestedly. "Says here he's some kind of all-American hero. So what?"

He was edgy, she could see it.

Jillian ached to go to him, to wrap her arms around his thin body and hold him close. She would do anything to keep him from being hurt. *Anything.* But right now she had to get through this.

"I met Trevor when he was a patient in the hospital in Tokyo. You remember, when I was a Navy nurse?"

He nodded, his expression becoming more wary with every second that passed.

"He was a Navy pilot. He, uh, was very badly hurt, and it was four months before they could evacuate him to the Navy hospital in San Diego." She wet her dry lips. "We fell in love."

Her voice choked, and she had to stop. Her heart was pounding so hard that she felt faint, and her hands were clammy with nervous sweat.

The words had to be said, and she had to say them. But now, suddenly, she knew she'd been wrong, terribly, selfishly wrong, in denying her son his true heritage. She had only to look into his bewildered copper eyes to realize the dreadful wrong she'd done him. And Trevor. Whatever his failings, Trevor was Jason's father. Jason was their son, a part of each of them.

Oh, baby, I'm so sorry, she cried silently. Shaking, she took a deep breath, then said softly, "Trevor Markus is your father."

Jason's jaw dropped, then snapped shut. He went white and then red beneath the golden freckles. "You...you said my father was dead. Every time I'd ask you about him, you said he was dead." His voice rose to a shrill protest as he jumped to his feet. He moved a few jerky paces away from her, then stood frozen, staring at her, his eyes wild. "You said my father's name was William White. You said he was killed before you could get married."

"I had my reasons—"

"Yeah, sure." Jason flung out his arm in an awkward, jerky arc. "You're always preaching at me to tell the truth, but you've been lying to me all this time. *Lying!*" He gulped, then moved backward, his feet tangling in the laces of his sneakers. He grabbed the chair and righted himself awkwardly, like a clumsy puppy.

"I don't care who that guy is," he shouted, his voice breaking into a cracking falsetto. "I don't care if he's some kind of damn war hero, or how much money he has. Just keep him away from me. I don't need another parent nagging at me all the time."

Jillian held out a hand beseechingly. "Sweetie, listen, it's not like you think. Trevor and I had a . . . a misunderstanding before I could tell him about you. He didn't know I was going to have a baby. I—"

"So why didn't you just tell me that, huh, Mom? Why the big story that he died in the war?"

"Because I . . . thought it would be easier if you thought he was dead."

Jason looked as though he wanted to cry, but he whirled around and headed for his room. "So let him stay dead. I don't need him."

Jillian stood motionless, one hand clutching the back of the chair where her son had sat. The remnants of their dinner were still on the table, and a mournful country-and-western ballad was playing softly from the radio at the far end of the narrow kitchen. Suddenly Jason's door slammed, and she winced. Half a second later his stereo screeched a metallic guitar riff at top volume.

She hurried into the living room to close the front windows. She could stand the noise just this once. In fact, the discord was a welcome distraction. Maybe if she could summon enough irritation at the dreadful sounds, she might not feel the guilt quite so much.

Moving mechanically, she went into the kitchen and began to run water into the sink. Washing dishes was usually Jason's job, but tonight she would manage without him. She'd always known her son had inherited his father's temper as well as his eyes, but Jason had never exploded as violently as this before. And never at her.

Her shoulders sagged with the weight of her own guilt. She'd deserved his anger. She'd let her own pain override her responsibility to her child. She'd been weak when she should have been strong. She'd let him down.

Oh, Trevor, she thought in deep anguish, how could we have made such a terrible mess of things?

The dish she was holding slipped from her hand and fell to the floor. Shards of thick china hit her bare ankles, leaving a bloody smear of tiny cuts. Her fingers were clumsy as she picked up the pieces one by one. She managed to get even the smallest bits.

It's too late, she thought numbly, staring at the pile of shattered crockery in her palm. Too late to pick up the pieces.

Suddenly she wished with all her heart that it wasn't.

Chapter 6

The night was too quiet. Sometime after midnight the crickets had stopped chirping, and now the leaves hung limp and quiet above his head.

Trevor leaned against the rough bark of a towering white oak and listened to the sound of his own breathing. He felt acutely uncomfortable, as though his skin were stretched too tautly over his bones, and, in his veins, his blood burned like hot lead.

"Damn," he muttered into the moonlit glade. "I haven't felt this wired in years."

A heavy tightness tugged at his belly as he stared at the sky. The stars looked close enough to touch, but no matter how high he climbed, they would always be beyond his reach.

Like Jillian.

He rubbed his jaw with a tired hand. No matter what he did for her now, it would never be enough. Never! She'd given him the greatest gift a woman can give a man, his child, and she wanted nothing from him in return. No, he thought with a silent, bitter chuckle, that wasn't quite true. She wanted him to disappear from her life. Again.

And that was the one thing he couldn't do.

If she'd asked him for anything else, *anything*, he would have worked like a son of a gun to give it to her, but he couldn't walk away again. Not from his son.

His son.

He was still having trouble dealing with the idea of being a father. He'd always wanted children, but over the years, he'd gradually come to terms with not having them.

Sometimes, as he'd watched his brother, Brian, and his sister-in-law, Mary Rose, struggle to raise their two sons, he'd told himself it was just as well that he had none. It had been exhausting work from what he'd seen, and sometimes Mary Rose had been at the end of her emotional strength.

But she'd had the luxury of a husband to help her, a man who loved her and provided a nice home, so that she'd been able to stay home with her boys. And when they'd occasionally become discipline problems, Brian had been there to take charge.

Jillian had had to do it all. For fourteen long years she'd handled more than any woman should have to handle, and from what he'd been able to discover, she'd managed damn well.

He was proud of her, for what it was worth. And he respected her more than any woman he'd ever known. She had guts and determination and a hell of a lot of strength. He had a feeling he was just beginning to find out how much.

Trevor shoved his hands in the pockets of his khaki shorts and stared at the lonely shadows crossing the large open area between him and the main building. Once she'd been a part of him. The best part. She had made him believe in himself in those terrible days when he didn't know if he would ever be a whole man again.

It had been her voice that he'd loved first. Soft and slightly husky, as though she'd just emerged from a deep sleep, her voice had soothed and cajoled and rebuked him.

Listening to her, fighting with her, flirting with her, had kept him alive.

When he'd discovered he'd fallen in love with her, it had terrified him. He'd fought it, telling himself he was horny. That she was available. That he would forget her when he left Tokyo, just as he'd always forgotten the current lady in his bed when he left a duty station.

But somehow Jillian had gotten inside him. When she was with him, he felt . . . complete. Whole. Ready to take on the world, or at least six grinding months of therapy. She'd given him her strength when he'd needed it, and her love when he'd needed that even more.

When she'd been holding his hand, the pain had been bearable. When she kissed him, he forgot the long, hard road ahead. And when, in the last few weeks before he'd been shipped home, she'd given him her love and her body, he'd felt like the luckiest man in the universe. ·

After he'd left her, he'd told himself over and over that he'd saved her from a terrible life with a man who would have eventually destroyed her spirit and taken the joy from her eyes. He'd made his decision, and he'd learned to live with it, but strangely, it hurt to come face-to-face with the woman she'd become without him.

Damn, he thought. He had to stop thinking that way. Jillian had her life, and he had his. That was the way it had to be.

But they both loved Jason. Their son.

With an unfamiliar sense of apprehension, Trevor allowed his thoughts to turn to the boy who was a large question mark in his head. Would he be like him, or more like Jillian? Would he feel resentment toward a man who'd never even known he was alive? Would Jason hate him the way his mother did?

Slowly he rubbed his tired cheeks. His whisker stubble felt as rough as the bark against his bare shoulders.

Fifteen years ago Jillian's skin had felt like fine porcelain under his fingers and had been burnished lightly with golden freckles. Once he'd teased her about the tiny specks that dotted the swell of her breasts. Once his tongue had moistened every one until her skin had glowed.

Trevor glanced down at his bare chest. She'd felt so tiny, so delicate, lying in his arms, so very precious. And yet he'd wanted her with a ravenous hunger that he hadn't been able to drive out of his system.

His body hardened instantly as he thought about the creamy silkiness of those long, graceful legs. He wanted to feel those legs between his. He wanted to stroke and pet her until she was wet and ready for him.

Ten minutes ago he'd left his bed drenched in sweat, the vividly erotic dream he'd been having still throbbing in his head. A few more minutes and he would have disgraced himself as badly as a teenager.

And he still wanted her. Every time he saw her, he wanted her more. But he'd learned a long time ago that wanting and having were often different things.

He muttered a vicious obscenity into the heavy silence, but it didn't help.

The familiar pressure inside him would build and build until it was a terrible ache. He had to move, to work off the tightness. He had to get Jillian out of his head.

He pushed himself away from the tree and headed for the pool. He would swim laps until his legs burned and he couldn't lift his arms. Maybe then the tension would let go, and he could sleep again.

And maybe, if his body was exhausted, he wouldn't dream of a redheaded temptress with sultry green eyes who hated him. Maybe, if his mind was numbed by fatigue, he wouldn't be tortured by memories of all the years he'd thrown away.

Maybe then he could find a way to make peace with a woman he wanted and could never have.

Jillian paced. Back and forth she walked, her bare feet leaving a rut in the plush area rug covering the middle of her living room. Her hands were crossed over her belly, and her face was drawn and pale.

It was nearly dawn, and she'd awakened with the birds. Her body was exhausted, but her mind wouldn't let her rest.

She couldn't stop thinking of Trevor. Over the years, when she'd thought of him at all, it had been with bitterness and hatred, and he'd deserved it.

But now she found she couldn't seem to sustain that anger. Yesterday she'd been furious at the way he'd forced her hand, but today she had to admit she would have done the same thing in his place. She would have used any weapon, resorted to any tactic, to get her son if he'd been denied to her.

The haunting sound of church bells slowly penetrated the deep gray fog that surrounded her. Six-thirty, she realized, time for the early service at the Community Church.

Framed in the open window, the tip of the white steeple was barely visible through the treetops, but it was there, solid and enduring. Slowly, feeling the leaden weight of indecision, she crossed to the window and looked south. Adrian's new clinic was nestled in the tall pines, and beyond the long, low building Miracle Lake glistened in the dawn light.

The early settlers had believed that the icy water pouring out of the mountains during the spring thaw had restorative powers. As soon as the snow had left the ground, they'd jammed the sandy beaches, shivering and hopeful, to wade into the clear water. A display in the *Clarion* office chronicled the claims of miraculous cures of ills ranging from anemia to yaws.

Jillian pushed her toes into the rough nap of the rug. That was what she needed now, she thought, a miracle, a way to erase her mistake and let her start over with her son. Except that miracles happened only in legends and fairy tales.

A gust of pine-scented breeze ruffled the lacy curtain and brushed her bare skin. The air was already warm and heavy, suggesting another muggy Indian summer day. She hugged herself and slumped back against the wall by the window.

She loved Jason so much that it frightened her. She wanted to wrap him in so much love that he would never feel pain.

But now, face-to-face with her son's anger and Trevor's persistence, she found herself doubting her motives. Had she, by denying his parentage, actually been seeking a subtle revenge on the man who'd hurt her so badly, a revenge so complete it would instead hurt the child he'd given her?

She felt the tears clog her throat, and she lifted her gaze to the ceiling. Whatever she and Trevor had once had together was past. But from that love had come a precious and perfect child. He was a part of both of them, maybe the best part. And nothing she could do would ever change that.

Quickly, before she could change her mind, she hurried into the kitchen and picked up the phone. When the night receptionist at Horizons answered, she nearly hung up. Her heart was pounding furiously, and her fingers were stiff on the receiver. "Trevor Markus, please."

"Mr. Markus is in the guest bungalow. I'll ring."

"Thank you."

The phone rang and rang, but there was no answer. A bitter disappointment shot through her. He'd left without waiting for her call.

"Markus."

His voice was rusty from sleep, and she shivered helplessly at the sensual promise of that deep masculine gruffness.

"This is Jillian. I told you I'd call."

There was a brief silence. "Uh, what time is it?"

She could almost see the sensual sweep of his thick lashes as he blinked himself awake. "Almost seven. I'm sorry if I woke you. I can call back, if you prefer."

"No, that's... okay. Just give me a minute to wake up."

She inhaled very slowly, willing her body to relax, but the sleep-slurred voice stirred her imagination irresistibly. Involuntarily she glanced down at the thin cotton gown that barely covered her thighs. It had been a hot night. No doubt Trevor had worn very little to bed.

In the hospital he'd slept in the nude. Even with air-conditioning, the east wing had been unbearably hot in the summertime. Most nights, even when she hadn't been on duty, she'd gone to his room in the early hours to exchange his sweat-soaked pillowcase for a crisp new one.

Sometimes he'd awakened then, his eyes heavy with drug-induced sleep, and he'd pull her down for a hard, demanding kiss. His voice had been husky then, too, and thick with desire.

Jillian gripped the receiver even tighter against her ear. She discovered she was holding her breath, and exhaled the trapped air in a nervous stream.

"How...are you?" he asked in a still-husky voice. She heard the rustle of bedclothes and the sound of his whiskers scraping against the phone.

"Fine," she lied. "And you?"

His chuckle was throaty and oddly infectious. "I think I'm suffering from culture shock. It's too quiet in this place."

"We like it," she said stiffly.

Her teeth ground together as she glanced around her cozy, pine-paneled kitchen. The copper pans hanging above the stove glinted in the light streaming over her shoulder, and the bright green leaves of the creeping Charlie on the baker's rack had a healthy sheen. It was homey and comfortable and no doubt completely alien to the fast-lane life he must lead.

His heavy sigh whispered into her ear. "I'm not criticizing, Jill. I was just trying to make a joke. Sorry."

"I...morning is not my best time," she said with a reluctant trace of apology. "Especially since I've been up most of the night." While he'd been dead asleep, she thought with a sudden pang of bitterness.

"Is something wrong?" he asked quickly. "You're not sick?"

At heart, yes, she thought. "No, just hot. Our apartment isn't air-conditioned."

"Well, maybe this heat wave will break soon."

"Maybe."

Jillian stifled a sigh. They were like two boxers in a ring, circling cautiously, each waiting for the other to throw the first punch. She stood up straighter and glanced toward the shimmering mirror that was Miracle Lake. "I, uh, called to invite you to a picnic. I've done some thinking, and I think that would be the best way for you and Jason to get to know each other."

There was a faint sound, as though Trevor had inhaled suddenly. "A picnic? You mean with paper plates and fried chicken—and ants?" His voice carried a murmur of caution, as though he didn't quite trust his hearing—or her.

"I'm not sure about the ants," she said, a strange and definitely unwanted excitement curling through her.

"Hmm, no ants. Sounds challenging." His velvet voice was low with amusement, and Jillian felt an answering smile shiver the corners of her mouth.

Instantly she twisted the smile into a frown. "I'll expect you at eleven-thirty," she said curtly. "My apartment is above the pharmacy. When you get to the center of town, you can't miss it. I'm right on the square." She heard a faint sound that could have been a sigh whisper into her ear.

"I know where the pharmacy is. Yesterday, when I drove into town, I went there first. The woman behind the counter gave me directions to the town hall."

She ignored the mention of their last meeting. The memory of her anger and frustration was too raw. "Use the outside steps in the back. They lead directly to our apartment."

"No problem. I'll be there at eleven-thirty."

Jillian glanced toward the hall. There was no sound from Jason's room. "There's something you should know before you come," she said quietly.

"What's that?" Suddenly there was a wary edge to his voice that hadn't been there before.

"Jason is pretty upset."

"About me?"

She hesitated. It was tempting to put the blame on Trevor, but she couldn't make herself do it. She'd been the one to tell the lies that now entwined the three of them.

"No, about me. He's angry because I lied to him."

Jason's door opened suddenly, and then the door to the bathroom clicked shut. Jason was up.

"Trevor, I can't talk now," she added hastily before he could say anything more. "I'll see you later, okay?"

"Okay." There was a pause. "Jill, about Jason, we'll handle it."

He hung up before she could answer.

Five hours later Jillian was pacing again, but this time she was angry. Trevor was nearly half an hour late.

Jason was in his room, where he'd gone after eating his breakfast in sullen silence. His eyes had been shadowed and his skin sallow, as though he'd gotten little sleep. He'd flatly refused to go on the picnic.

Her mother's instinct had told her to go slowly, so she'd simply excused him from the table and suggested he go back to bed for a few hours. Obediently he'd gone to his room, but his stereo had been blasting since he'd left her, one loud, raucous song after another.

Let's see how Trevor handles this, she thought grimly, pausing to look out the window for the fifth time in the past twenty minutes. Her breath whistled through her parted lips as she froze. Trevor was standing at the edge of the square, putting money in the parking meter.

As she watched, he ran a large, sun-browned hand through his hair, releasing the rebellious cowlicks and ruining the neat part. The sun caught the sandy blond mixed with the gray, making him look more like the man she remembered. From above, his shoulders looked enormous in the tight blue polo shirt, and his bare arms were deeply tanned and bulged with the kind of firm muscle that can only be built up with years of hard work.

Her skin prickled at the back of her neck, and her breath shortened. All too well, she knew his shoulders would be solid, with a thin layer of fat to round the hard masculine edges. And the lean torso that tapered into the band of his jeans would be ridged and corded and furred with soft blond hair in all the right places where a man should be rough to the touch.

An arrow of swift, primitive desire darted down her spine to bury its point deep inside her, and a warm, fluid feeling of tension spread outward, taunting her.

Phantom feelings, she told herself with a bitter silent laugh, like a man who's lost a leg but swears he feels his toes. Her body was simply remembering the feel of that hard masculinity long after it had been taken away from her forever.

She pressed her fingertips against the window frame, but the painted wood was too hot to touch. Snatching her hand away, she watched him, like a bullfighter sizing up the deadly animal across the arena.

The furious pounding of her heart was loud in her ears, and her mouth was dry. She was experiencing all of the physical manifestations of alarm, she noted, licking her lips. If asked, she could describe them in stark, clinical detail, but that didn't help. She was frightened, and excited, and nervous. And she hated the feeling.

She edged closer to the window. His head was bent, and he was staring down at the concrete beneath his dark blue running shoes. There was a stark, even lonely look to him that puzzled her.

What's he waiting for? she thought, tapping her foot impatiently. Why doesn't he just come up? Surely he wasn't trying to work up his courage, and yet, that was exactly what it seemed like.

But it was inconceivable to her that he could be nervous. Trevor had hurtled off the deck of a carrier at bone-jarring speed, flown into enemy fire and returned to that tiny gray speck in the ocean countless times.

As she watched, he lifted his head and stared directly at her. She stumbled backward quickly, but not before his shoulders had jerked in surprise.

"Great going, Jill," she muttered in irritation.

Jillian licked her dry lips as she heard him slowly climb the outside steps leading to the second-story balcony. Her front door was open, with only the screen door between her and Trevor. She saw him before he saw her.

His expression was somber, but there was a tightness along his jaw and a faint narrowing around his eyes. It was a look of gritty determination, and it was definitely unsettling.

"Hi," he said as she answered his knock. "Sorry I'm late. I had an overseas call from my crew chief in Thailand. I tried to call to let you know, but the phone was busy."

He tried to comb some order into his tousled hair with his hand. He didn't succeed.

"Uh, I guess Jason is using the extension in his room," she said, making a mental note to speak with her son. He was supposed to confine his conversations to the evening hours.

Silently, fighting a sudden moment of doubt, Jillian opened the door and stepped back. She resisted the urge to wipe her palms on her white cotton playsuit. It's the heat, she told herself absently as Trevor walked into her living room like a man with a mission.

He took a few steps, then turned and looked around. "Nice place," he said with a brief smile. "Homey."

Her house was like her, Trevor thought. Comfortable and warm and uncluttered, with nice, big furniture that looked as if it could take his weight. And he liked the colors, beige and brown, with some green here and there. They were restful and soothing, like the hills around the town.

The muffled sound of screaming guitars filled the sudden silence, and Jillian jerked her gaze toward the door leading to the hall.

"Sounds like Jason likes metal," Trevor said with a pained grin.

"Unfortunately." She felt an answering grin curve her lips. "It all sounds like noise to me."

"It did to me, too, until one of my nephews made me listen to his entire collection. I nearly went deaf, but I can now recognize a few of the groups, if I'm pushed." He glanced toward the sound of the screeching tones. "Most of the guys in treatment like that stuff, too."

Jillian frowned. "Great," she muttered, wincing as the throbbing sound smashed against her spine like a punishing fist.

"It helps, sometimes, especially in the first few weeks, when they're still half strung out. Takes their minds off their screaming nerves."

She nodded. He was so close that she could smell his after-shave, a dark musky scent that excited her senses. It was like Trevor himself, arrogant, and slightly dangerous.

He looked around, his gaze coming to rest on the bright orange cooler by the door. "Uh, are you ready? I only had one dime, and the meter said twelve minutes, even on Sunday."

Jillian had to raise her voice to be heard over the music. "Jason has refused to go." There was a husky note in her voice that startled her, and she cleared her throat. "I tried to talk to him, but he just turned up his music and ignored me. He can be very stubborn sometimes."

Trevor's grin was fleeting. "Like his dad."

"Yes."

More than once she'd countered his stubborn resistance with melting kisses. It had become a game, one that they'd both relished. Suddenly the solid oak floor felt unsteady under her feet, and she groped for the back of the wing chair beside her.

Her toes curled tightly in her thin-soled sandals, and her leg muscles strained against her skin as she slid her hand over the quilted chintz.

Trevor ran his tongue along his bottom lip. "Uh, you said he was upset?"

"I shouldn't have lied to him," she admitted in a thin voice. "But I just wanted to protect him. I thought I was doing the right thing."

She stared at the rug beneath her sandals. A shadow fell across her toes as Trevor moved closer. His shoes were scuffed and well-worn on the sides, and the laces were knotted and frayed. Like Jason's.

"Jill, don't do this to yourself. Take it from a guy who knows, regret is a heavy burden to carry, and it doesn't change anything."

Slowly she raised her head to look at him. A stiff sadness strained the edges of his smile, and his eyes were shadowed. She sensed he was telling the truth, and a part of her, the woman who'd once loved him, grieved for what might have been. But the cynical part, the abandoned mother who'd never felt his hands caress her belly or whisper words of encouragement when she'd felt ugly and scared, refused to care.

"I tried to tell him I was sorry, but he just stared at me." She stifled a sigh. "He's never acted this way before."

"We've given him a lot to handle. Give him some time to work it through."

"I'm trying, but he's making it difficult." Absently she wiped the beads of perspiration from her forehead. "He's not very . . . receptive."

Trevor ran a hand across his belly. There was still a trace of moisture over her upper lip. It would taste salty, he knew, and tantalize his palate like the finest wine. He swallowed hard, willing himself to stand still. "In other words, I'm not about to be welcomed with open arms."

"No." She sighed. "He claims he doesn't want a father, but I think he's just scared. Some of his friends, like Mike Cobb, don't have such great ones."

"Are you saying that I would be a good one?" Trevor was afraid to breathe.

"I don't know, Trevor," she said in a low, weary voice. "But I know that a battle between us could only hurt Jason."

He wasn't much for subtlety, so it took him a moment to figure out that she wasn't glaring at him anymore. Instead, she seemed...rigidly controlled. He wasn't sure he liked that any better. He exhaled slowly. "This time I won't let you down, Jill. I promise."

Jillian saw the memories come into his eyes, memories of her, of them together. She saw his lips curve upward at the corners, then part slowly. He stopped breathing, then started again, but this time slowly, as though each breath brought pain.

His gaze slowly warmed, then kindled into a strange light. Jillian couldn't look away. His eyes were filled with a hypnotic mixture of pleading and hunger that held hers. His lashes were still sandy blond and as thick on the bottom as they were on the top, and his brows were an intriguing mix of gray and blond.

"I was such a jerk." He said the words so softly that they sounded more like a tortured breath.

So slowly that it seemed to take forever, his hand came up to touch her cheek. His fingers were slightly raspy and very gentle as they traced the line of her cheekbone as though he were a blind man trying to see her face through his fingertips. His hand slid along her cheekbone and into her hair, and his thumb gently stroked the curve of her cheek.

Jillian couldn't make herself move away. She held her breath as his head tipped slowly to one side. Her lips tingled as his gaze lingered there, caressing her as potently as any touch. She tried not to react, but deep inside, in the part of her that had been cold and empty since his betrayal, a sweet warmth began to spread. Slowly his gaze lifted to her eyes, and she saw the question written in the shadowed pupils. He wanted to kiss her.

"Jill?"

"No, Trevor," she whispered.

Before he could release her, she heard a sound behind her. A split second later she heard Jason's voice.

"Mom? Are you all right? He's not going to hurt you, is he?"

Trevor's gaze jerked past her head, and his hand fell, then clenched into a fist. She twisted around, her cheeks on fire.

Jason was standing at the door to the kitchen, his face contorted and pale. His eyes were two copper circles full of some stormy, unrecognizable emotion, starkly outlined between wide open lashes.

Jillian twisted her hands together in front of her. "Of course he's not going to hurt me. This...this is Trevor. Your father."

Jason's face started to crumple, and for an instant Jillian saw the ravished features of the little boy he'd once been.

"I told you I didn't want him here," he mumbled, scuffling his feet.

"I knew you didn't really mean it, sweetie. Every boy wants to know his father. You've been hurt, I know, but I want you to try to put that aside, at least for today. Please. For...for my sake."

Jillian moved quickly to his side and touched his shoulder, but he jerked away from her and stumbled backward until he crashed into the kitchen table. The vase of giant mums in the center fell over with a loud explosion of breaking glass. Water spread over the table and onto the floor, but Jillian ignored the dripping mess.

"You never listen to me!" Jason shouted, his rubber soles crunching on the glass. "You pretend to listen, but you never do. I always have to do what you want. I never get to do what I want."

"Jase! That's not true. I always listen to you. And I try to do what pleases you, but sometimes I can't. Sometimes I have to do what's best, even if it's not what you want."

"Bull—"

"That's enough, Jason." Trevor's voice startled her, and she uttered a yelp of surprise.

Trevor moved silently to her side. "Your mother's right," he said quietly, but with a steely firmness that tightened Jillian's spine. "I'm here because we both love you. And because it's time for you to know your father."

"Yeah, sure," Jason sneered, his head snapping up defiantly. "That's why you're putting the make on my mother."

Trevor's violent intake of breath startled her. "That's enough talk like that," he said in flat, commanding voice. "Your mother doesn't deserve it, and I won't stand for it."

Surprise surfaced in Jason's glittering eyes. "You can't tell me what to do." His voice cracked, and his pale face flooded with color. He suddenly looked more frightened than angry.

"I can, and I will."

"Trevor, wait," Jillian said urgently, aching for her child. "Jason doesn't understand what you mean."

Trevor's face looked gaunt in the bright midday light, and the stillness was back in his eyes. "I'll handle this, Jillian," he said in an unyielding tone. "Jason and I need to come to an understanding."

Jillian braced herself. If Trevor said one wrong word, if he hurt her child, she would risk the embarrassment and go to court. There were other attorneys with fancy stationery and high-priced skills. She would mortgage everything she owned if she had to in order to protect her child.

"Be very careful," she told Trevor in cold warning.

Trevor heard the threat in her voice. He knew she would fight him with everything she had if he threatened her baby, and a deeply buried feeling of tenderness welled inside him. It was his child she was protecting so fiercely.

"Let's talk about this," he said to his son firmly. "Man to man."

Jason's brow furrowed. "Nothing to talk about," he muttered.

Jillian saw her son's hurt and indecision, and her heart lurched. Jason had been sheltered and protected all his life, and now, when he was the most vulnerable, all the years of stability and security had been ripped away, leaving him confused and angry and upset.

Guilt shuddered through her. If only she could take those lying words back. If only she'd had the foresight to know she'd been making a terrible mistake.

Jason's Adam's apple moved convulsively, and his hands balled into fists. "You'n'me got nothing to talk about," he told his father in a trembling voice.

"Then I'll talk, and you listen." Trevor moved away from her and toward their son. Jillian hugged herself, her eyes fixed on Jason's twisted face.

Trevor halted a foot away from Jason and shoved his hands into his pockets. "I'm the one who blew it, Jason," he said in a steady, slow voice. "Not your mother. I was the one who walked out on her, and on you. I didn't know about you, but that's no excuse. I should have known, but I wasn't around long enough for your mother to tell me." He inhaled deeply, then let the air out in a slow stream. "I wasn't much of a man in those days. I was mad at the world and bitter as hell. I didn't know if I'd ever walk without crutches again."

He glanced down at his feet, then back at Jason, who hadn't moved. "I'd just spent ten months in two godawful military hospitals, and the first civilian I saw when I got out called me a baby killer and told me I deserved to be a cripple for the rest of my life."

Jillian uttered a choked sound of protest. The long, sinewy muscles of Trevor's back rippled as though his body had clenched, but he didn't turn around.

His voice roughened. "I don't blame you for being mad, but take it out on me, not your mother. She was simply protecting you from a guy who would have made a lousy father."

Jason's shoulders jerked. "She could have told me the truth."

Trevor shook his head. "I don't think so, Jason. You needed a father to be proud of, not a spoiled, bitter excuse for a man who ran away from his problems." His shoulders were frozen, and his head didn't move as he added softly, "I'm sorry for hurting your mother, and I'm sorry for hurting you."

Jillian heard the rumble of sincerity in his voice, and the regret. She believed him, and maybe she even understood a little, but she would never forgive him for letting her stand there in her wedding dress, alone, waiting. He could have written, called, anything.

Jason's troubled gaze shifted to Jillian, and she forced the past from her mind. "I know this is hard to take in all at once, but give it time, okay?" she said softly.

The boy bit his lip, his eyes blinking rapidly, his posture drooping. He looked so sad, so vulnerable. Jillian started to go to him, but Trevor stopped her with a hard hand on her shoulder.

"Here's my bottom line, Jason," he said with a grave masculine gentleness that brought a lump to her throat. "You're my son, and I want to be a part of your life. I'm not demanding that you love me, or even like me. That's something that has to be earned, and I intend to do my damnedest to earn it. But I won't let you take this out on your mother. Do you understand what I'm saying, son?"

Jason's lips drooped into a sulky pout, but much of the anger was gone from his eyes. One shoulder lifted in a brief shrug.

Trevor's lips slanted in a wry smile. "Does that mean yes?"

Jason nodded.

"Then please apologize to your mother for upsetting her. She's given you a lot, more than you know, and she doesn't deserve to be hurt."

Jason hesitated, then dropped his gaze to the floor in front of him. "I'm sorry, Mom," he said in a barely audible voice.

"It's okay, sweetie," she said, fighting the urge to cry. "I know this is hard for you. It's . . . hard for all of us."

Trevor flexed his shoulders as though relieving a sudden cramp. "One more thing you need to know, son. I'm not walking out on you again. No matter what happens."

Jillian's face felt as though it were going to shatter. Why hadn't Trevor said that to *her*? Because it wasn't true, that was why, she realized instantly. He was here because of Jason, not her. And that was the way it would always be. Once Jason was grown and on his own, she doubted that she would ever see Trevor again, except at some function or other having to do with their son.

Ignoring the strange feeling of hurt spreading inside, she forced a smile for Jason. Right now she had to get through this day. They all had to get through it.

"Why don't you put on the new bathing suit I got you last week?" she told her son in a persuasive tone. "It's already scorching today, and the lake will be nice and cool."

"Okay," Jason said in a jerky voice, but the flush had receded from his cheeks, and the pain was gone from his eyes. He looked at his father one more time, then turned and headed toward his room.

Jillian waited until she heard his door close before allowing her shoulders to sag. With a muttered curse, Trevor pulled out a chair and pushed her down into it. She felt shaky, and her head was beginning to throb.

Trevor hesitated, then pulled out another chair and gingerly lowered himself into it. "Is he always like that?" he asked with raw intensity.

"What do you mean, like that?" she shot back, her nerves still on edge. "He was upset. He had a right to be."

"Sure, he had a right to be upset, but he was acting like a spoiled brat who wasn't getting his way. He had no right talking to you the way he did. If he'd been a few years younger, I would have turned him over my knee."

Jillian felt her control snap. No one criticized her son. No one. "Don't you ever touch him! I've never spanked Jason, and I never will." She looked around angrily. "This was a mistake. I can see that now. I should have let you take me to court. There were things I could have told the judge, too. Like how you asked me to marry you and then didn't have the guts to tell me in person that you'd changed your mind. What kind of an example is that for a boy?"

Beneath his skin, the thick muscles of his forearm slowly tightened into a hard potent bulge as he clenched his fist. "We're going to get past this, Jillian." Trevor raised his voice slightly. "Right now."

At his harsh command her gaze flew to his face, and alarm raced down her spine. His expression was hard, and his eyes were filled with some intense emotion she didn't dare analyze.

"Say what you have to say," he continued in a harsh voice. "All of it. Hit me if it will make you feel better, but get that damn poison out of your system." His fist slammed the table, and she jumped.

"Don't you dare tell me what to do. Don't you *dare*!" Her lips trembled and her stomach heaved. She felt scalded from head to toe, and it was his fault.

"Then back off, Jill! Damn it, give me a chance to show you that I'm sorry for what I did to you—and to our son." His eyes sparked with barely contained fury and something that looked like frustration.

"I am."

"The hell you are! Every chance you get, you aim one of your acid little remarks at my head."

"You deserve it."

"No, I do not," he said in an emphatic voice. "I've paid for what I did, Jill. More than you can ever imagine. And

I'll be damned if I'll let you put me through any more hell for a mistake that neither of us can change. The past is finished. History. And that's the way it's going to stay."

Jillian gripped the edge of the table. "Get out of my house."

"No." His hand trapped her. "Look, Jill," he said, making a visible effort to control his temper. "We've both made mistakes. I hurt you badly. I know that. But how do you think I feel, knowing you deliberately denied me my son?"

His voice vibrated with anger, but his eyes were hollow. He'd been hurt, too.

"Even if I'd put your name on his birth certificate, it wouldn't have mattered. You made it very plain you didn't want to hear from me again—ever. I couldn't even have sent you a birth announcement, remember?"

His hand tightened, and she winced. "I told you why I did that. I wasn't in any shape to deal with...problems."

Jillian inhaled swiftly. "You're absolutely right, Trevor. An illegitimate baby would certainly have been a problem."

His jaw colored. "That's not what I meant, and you know it."

"Do I?"

Trevor sighed. "This isn't getting us anywhere."

"I couldn't agree more. Let's drop the whole thing," Jillian said stiffly. "If you'll let go of my arm, I'll get the food."

She started to get up, but his big hand moved to her wrist and tugged her back into her seat. The chair was hard against her bare thighs, and her hand felt numb.

"Can we try to put all that behind us, Jill? Can we try to be friends, for our son's sake?"

Sharp, tingling shivers shot up her arm, and she tried to jerk away, but Trevor's fingers tightened around her wrist. He exerted just enough pressure to keep her from escaping.

Jillian stared in stony silence at the convoluted oak grain beneath the spot where he held her. Fifteen years of pride and anger and hurt tumbled in her brain, colliding with some new and as yet unnamed feeling.

"Please, Jill," he said in a gruff voice when she remained silent. His fingers slid past her wrist to capture her hand. His grip was warm and possessive.

"I don't know, Trevor," she answered as honestly as she could. "I just don't know what I'm thinking or feeling right now. So much has happened in a short time."

"Will you at least think about it?" His fingers tightened just enough to convey his urgency.

"Yes," she said, because she couldn't seem to help herself. "I'll think about it.

His jaw tightened, and he released her hand. They sat in strained silence for heartbeats before Trevor pushed himself to his feet and began picking up the jagged pieces of the shattered vase.

Chapter 7

The air was steaming hot. Jason had asked Trevor to lower the top of the convertible, and the sun beat directly down on their heads.

By the time Trevor had driven the twelve miles to the turnoff, Jillian's forehead was beaded with sweat beneath her visor, and the front of her playsuit was sticking to her skin.

"There's Big Pine Road. You turn to the right," she said as the Jaguar rounded another hairpin curve on the twisting mountain road.

Behind the aviator sunglasses, Trevor frowned. "It says Clayton Clinic on the sign."

"Miracle Lake is just past the clinic on the edge of that stand of Douglas fir. Addie—Dr. Franklin—built the clinic here because the water of the lake is supposed to have healing qualities."

Trevor glanced across the console, his brows lifting above the gold rims of his dark glasses. "Hence the name, Miracle Lake. Sounds like Dr. Franklin has a sense of humor."

Jillian nodded. "She claims it was only whimsy—and a good deal on the land. But Addie has a strong mystical streak in her, and I have a hunch she believes in the power of suggestion, if not in the waters themselves."

"She could be right. I've seen guys in the unit make remarkable progress once they finally believed it was possible."

Jillian stared at him. Once he'd told her that the only things he believed in were himself, the U.S. Navy and a strong left hook.

"Are you saying you believe in miracles?"

He flicked her a brief smile. "Yes, I do, but only as a result of a lot of damn hard work."

Silence fell between them. The tires hummed on the cracked pavement, and the scenery whipped by in a gray-green blur. She inhaled slowly, savoring the pungent smell of the mountain sage and pine.

The summer was nearly finished, and soon the tall trees lining the road would be bare. By Thanksgiving there would be snow halfway down the slopes, and by Christmas the streets of Clayton would be lined with dirty piles of plowed drifts.

Where would Trevor be at Christmas? she wondered, twisting restlessly in the low bucket seat. Where had he been for the past fifteen Christmases?

He wouldn't be here, that was one thing she knew for certain. She wouldn't be able to bear it. Even now, she could never listen to the familiar carols without feeling as though she were being torn apart inside. It was only because of Jason that she celebrated at all.

"Hey, look. There's Mike's dad in front of the clinic," Jason called suddenly from the back seat. He released the seat belt that Trevor had insisted he wear and leaned forward.

"Stop for a minute," Jillian said with a frown. "I think something's wrong."

Trevor gave her a quick glance, then flipped on the signal and pulled into the circular driveway leading to the clinic. The sheriff's black-and-white Blazer was parked in front of the wide glass doors. Mel stood behind it, one booted foot resting on the reinforced bumper, a small notebook balanced on his knee.

As Trevor pulled the convertible to a stop next to him, the sheriff looked up and scowled. His expression turned speculative when he caught sight of Jillian.

"What's wrong, Mel?" she asked quickly, absently clutching the edge of the door. The metal was blistering hot, and she snatched her hand away.

His lip curled into an ugly and strangely triumphant smile. "I'll tell you what's wrong," he muttered as the heel of his boot hit the pavement with a hard thump. "At approximately 4:00 a.m. this morning, two men wearing ski masks overpowered Mrs. Montoya, the night charge nurse, and took her keys to the drug cabinet. Cleaned it out. She's in shock, and Adrian says she might have a concussion."

Jillian gasped. "They hit her?"

"Hell, yes, they hit her! With a flashlight, she says." Mel closed his notebook and shoved it into his back pocket.

"How is she?"

Carmen Montoya was a friend, as well as a fellow officer in the Clayton High School PTA. Her son, Ramon, was in Jason's class.

"She has a hell of a headache, and she's sick to her stomach." The sheriff frowned. "I've been back three times to see her, but this was the first time she could remember anything. She's still pretty upset, so I didn't push her too hard."

"Does Mrs. Montoya know who they were?" Jason asked from the back seat. "I mean, do you have any, uh, suspects?"

He sounded boyishly eager, as though this were better than any TV show. Mel's expression softened marginally as he leaned over to cuff Jason's chin lightly with a meaty fist.

"Hey, sport, sounds like you and Mike are just alike," he said with a grin. "Always interested in hearing about the bad guys." His expression sobered. "Carmen says one was big and husky, and the other was taller and skinny. She thought they might be young, although it was hard to tell, because the one who talked disguised his voice." Mel grunted in disgust. "It don't take much detecting to figure out where they came from." He jerked his thumb in the direction of Wilderness Horizons.

"If you're implying the thieves came from Horizons, Sheriff, you're wrong." Trevor's voice was silky and far too calm, and it made the skin of Jillian's bare legs shiver. From the corner of her eye she could see Jason's head swivel toward his father.

"The odds say I'm not, Mr. Markus. There hasn't been a drug theft in Clayton since it was founded by old Josiah Clayton himself. Not one that's on the books, anyway. And then, all of a sudden, this so-called treatment center of yours comes to town and two weeks later the clinic's hit."

Cobb's angry blue gaze shifted from Trevor to Jillian. "We got us a problem here. I can feel it."

He tugged on the bill of his cap and hiked up his sagging trousers. He turned to go, but stopped when Trevor called his name in an icy voice.

"If you intend to charge anyone at Horizons, you'd better be damn sure you can back up any and all allegations you make, or I'll personally see to it that you're finished in this town or anyplace else."

Jillian could almost smell Mel's anger.

"Oh, yeah? Well, maybe I'd better do some checking up on you, hotshot. Maybe you got a few skeletons in your closet you don't want anybody to find."

Mel swung his attention to Jason, and his mouth twisted into a humorless smile. "Mike said you called this morning, sport. Something about your dead daddy showin' up alive?"

Jason looked sick. "I told him not to say nothing," he mumbled, twisting his seat belt over and over in his pale, bony fingers.

Jillian reached between the seats and covered his hand with hers. Jason flinched and jerked his hand away. "Leave me alone," he said in a strangled voice.

Trevor knew he was very close to smashing a quick left into Cobb's beefy face. He could almost hear the distinctive crack as the man's nose shattered, could almost smell the blood as it spurted.

He glanced down at the flattened knuckles of his left hand. From that first summer when he'd gone to work in the shipyard at sixteen, he'd had to fight. As the son of the owner and big for his age, he'd been a target for the rough, hard-bitten steelworkers who'd delighted in goading him into a brawl.

He'd taken their insults and their abuse for as long as he could, and then he'd learned to use his fists to shut them up. But he'd never learned to handle the rage behind his fists. It had taken a lot of hard living to teach him that, and it had been a long time since he'd used his fists to solve his problems.

But it was tempting.

"If that's your way of asking if Jason's my son, Cobb, he is, and I'm damn proud of it. And I'm . . . honored that Jillian is his mother."

Trevor sharpened his voice to a slicing edge. "Now, if you have a problem with me personally, we can go to the wall any time you want. But leave Jillian and Jason out of it, or I swear, you'll be working security in the city dump before I'm through with you." He never took an oath lightly, and he let the man see the truth in his eyes.

Mel took a step backward. "I'm not done with you yet, Markus. Not by a long shot." He set his jaw, then turned and climbed into his Blazer. The tires left black smears of rubber on the pavement as he roared off.

Shaken, Jillian stared down at her fingers. The crimson enamel on her nails shimmered like drops of blood in the sun. "You wanted to hit him, didn't you?" she asked in a hollow voice.

Trevor exhaled heavily. "Do you blame me?" He was visibly trying to calm down.

"No," she said emphatically. "Mel Cobb is a pig, in every sense of the word."

She glanced over her shoulder. Jason was staring at his father, his jaw slack, his eyes wide. She'd never seen him look so lost.

"Jason, Mike's dad was way out of line," she said in an urgent voice. "He's just...upset because he didn't want Horizons to come here, and the council overruled him. He's trying to take it out on all of us."

Jason's face closed up. "I don't wanna talk about it," he mumbled in a barely audible voice.

Jillian bit her lip, then nodded. "We'll drop it for now, Jase, but we have to talk about it sooner or later."

Jason slumped back against the seat and crossed his arms. He didn't look at her.

She and Trevor exchanged looks. Only the faint deepening of the lines fanning into his temple showed he was still angry.

"Don't let a redneck like Cobb bother you, Jason," he said, starting the car. "He's just a bully. He likes to hurt people because it makes him feel like more of a man, but inside he's weak and scared."

Trevor glanced in the mirror. Jason was staring straight ahead.

"He'll tell the whole town that...that I'm a bastard," the boy said in empty voice.

Jillian gasped and looked at Trevor.

"Legally, that's the truth," Trevor said matter-of-factly. "You can let it bother you, or you can shrug it off. Your choice." Jillian wasn't sure whether he was speaking to Jason or her, or to both of them.

Jason's mouth twisted. "I wish you'd hit him!"

Trevor sighed. "That wouldn't have changed the facts. And it would have landed me in jail for assault." A grim look that Jillian hadn't seen before flashed across his face, and the powerful car shot forward with a low-pitched growl. "Somehow I don't think that's the kind of example a father's supposed to set for his son. Do you?"

Jason slumped back against the seat. "How should I know?" he muttered. "I never had one before."

They ate in the shade of a lightning-scarred Douglas fir growing at the edge of the wide beach. Tiny flakes of mica sparkled in the sun, turning the sand black in spots.

The heat was oppressive, even in the shade, and the air was heavy with the kind of dense humidity Jillian had rarely experienced in the high country. She was acutely uncomfortable, but the weather was only part of the reason. She was still shaken by Jason's reaction to Mel's ugly attack.

Reuben Anderson had used that word once in her presence, and at that moment whatever love she'd felt for her stepfather had died. She'd kept his name as a courtesy to her mother, but she'd never again thought of Reuben as her father. She realized now that she'd even blamed Trevor for that. She'd blamed him for a lot of things.

Munching on a cookie, she rested her back against the cooler. She'd been too nervous to eat, and Jason had only picked at his fried chicken and potato salad. Trevor had been the only one whose appetite hadn't been affected by their run-in with Mel. In fact, he'd eaten his share and most of hers.

"*Beat the Rap* is a dud, a real downer album," Jason muttered, slashing the sand by the blanket with a plastic knife. "I don't like any of the songs. I don't know how you can say they're any good."

Jillian sensed he was being deliberately unpleasant, but she didn't have the heart to reprimand him, especially since Trevor seemed to be handling him just fine without her help.

He sat with one leg raised, his wide forearm balanced easily on his knee, his hand relaxed and open. But there was a restless aura surrounding him, as though he was having trouble sitting still, like a mountain cat she'd once seen in a game warden's cage.

"I don't suppose you liked *Dirty Dealings*, either." Trevor finished his Coke and crumpled the can in his fist before tossing it into the trash sack.

"It was bogus."

"You have to admire Glen Trapp's guitar work, though."

Trevor leaned forward and tugged off his shirt, exposing his muscular brown chest. An intricate silver medallion hung from a heavy chain around his neck, and his chest hair was the same mix of gray and blond as his eyebrows.

That soft masculine fur had been sun-bleached to blond when she'd given him his daily rubdown after the cast had come off. His muscles, then as now, had been as hard as seasoned oak, his skin slightly rough from his years of exposure to the sun and the sea. She looked away, concentrating on the jagged outline of the trees against the sky.

"Yeah, Glen's hot. I wish I could play like that." Jason stabbed the knife into the sand and broke it in two. He frowned in disgust and dug the point from the sand.

"I could teach you if you like."

"You can play the guitar?" Jason looked grudgingly impressed.

"Some. Part of my misspent youth was spent at the piano teacher's doing penance for my sins, so I can read music. I taught myself to play the guitar when I was in the hospital."

"You didn't mention that in your letters," Jillian blurted out.

Dusky color flooded his face, and she immediately regretted her words. She'd sounded as though she didn't believe him, when she'd only meant to convey surprise.

Trevor shrugged casually, but his jaw was tight. "I guess I didn't think it was important enough to mention."

She gave him a conciliatory smile. "It's just that I'm surprised, that's all."

Trevor nodded, but he didn't return her smile. "It kept my mind off a lot of things I didn't want to think about."

Like marrying me? she wondered.

Suddenly Jason looked around. "Mom, I need to go to the bathroom, okay?"

"Sure, okay." The public rest rooms were at the far end of the lake, half hidden by a cluster of young pines.

"I'll be back in a minute." Jason avoided looking at his father as he slid his sunglasses over his nose and picked up the black backpack that went with him wherever he went.

Jillian watched him go in silence. He was getting taller. In a few more months she'd be looking up at him.

Trevor folded both arms over his knees and watched Jason walk along the edge of the lake. The boy's head was down, and his shoulders were slumped. "Round one," he muttered with a sigh. "I think I lost."

"More like a draw," she said grudgingly. "The next time will be easier."

"I have a feeling I have a long way to go."

"What did you expect?" she asked out of curiosity, noticing the way he rubbed his thumb over his upper lip. He had done that in the hospital whenever he was having trouble expressing his feelings.

"Just about what I got, actually. I'm not exactly the prodigal dad, although—" he lifted his empty plate "—this has to have been as good as any fatted calf." His tone was so ironic that she had to laugh.

"Have another cookie. Chocolate chips are good for a bruised ego."

Trevor grunted, but he took her advice, devouring the crumbly cookie in two bites. "You're a good cook, Jill. Better than good."

"Actually, these came from the bakery next door."

Trevor's eyes cooled. "My mistake."

He leaned back against the rough trunk and closed his eyes. Sweat glistened on his forehead, and his hairline was damp. His face was wiped clean of expression, but there was a tiny pulse throbbing in his temple.

Jillian drew her legs to her chest and linked her arms around her shins. Above her head the leaves rustled gently. It was a lonely sound. "I'm ... sorry, Trevor," she said stiffly. "The Santa Ana makes everyone uptight."

His thick, sandy lashes rose slowly. His eyes were still cool, but his lower lip relaxed into a wry curve. "Apology accepted."

He picked up an apple, looked at it and put it down again. He extended his leg and rested his palm against his thigh. The restlessness she'd seen in him earlier seemed more pronounced.

"Was Jason a good kid? Growing up, I mean," he asked suddenly, rubbing his knee with his palm.

"Not exactly. One day, when I was still in the Navy, I came home early to take him to his pediatrician for his checkup. I gave him his bath and dressed him in his best pair of shorts. I'd gotten him a new pair of shoes the day before, and they were still nice and white."

She glanced at Trevor to see if he was following her. He was listening intently, a half smile tugging at his mouth. "What happened then?"

She sighed. "While I was changing out of my uniform, Jason decided to go wading—in the john."

Trevor's jaw dropped. "The john? You mean the toilet?" He looked as though he couldn't believe what he'd just heard.

"Yes, that's exactly what I mean. He was having a wonderful time, splashing water all over the bathroom and himself. Of course, his brand-new, terribly expensive shoes were ruined."

Trevor laughed. "He sounds like he was a little terror." She could hear regret in his voice, and pain. He'd missed so much.

"He was, actually. By the time he was eighteen months he could climb anything in the house." Her expression softened. "But he was also very loving, and he loved to cuddle."

Trevor's brows wagged. "Good man."

Memory arched between them, and the sounds of the lake faded. Trevor had loved to cuddle, too, as often as he could talk her into climbing in next to him. His gaze flicked to her chest, and she knew he was remembering the nights when he'd fallen asleep with his cheek pillowed on her breast.

Damn you! she thought, feeling the welcome anger rise in her again. Damn you for saying you loved me when you didn't. Damn you for leaving me.

She took a shallow breath. Easy, Jill, she told herself. They were here because of Jason, and that was the only reason.

"What about you?" she asked coolly, deliberately changing the subject. "How come you're not the president of Markus Shipbuilding, the way you'd planned when you found out you couldn't fly again?"

"How do you know I'm not?"

Jillian removed her visor and wiped her brow with a paper napkin. "There was an article on you in the *Clayton Clarion*. It said you were an engineer."

Trevor shifted restlessly against the tree trunk. "After I resigned my commission, I found I had a problem staying in one place for more than a few months at a time. Since I had a degree in engineering from the Academy, I decided to find something that would let me do most of my work outdoors. My brother Brian runs the yard for Pop now."

"And Horizons?"

Silence stretched between them until she began to suspect he wasn't going to answer. Finally he sighed. "I, uh, told you about my brother Tim? That he was killed when his speedboat hit a log in the Sound and flipped?"

Jillian nodded. His resonant baritone had a hollow tone she'd never heard before.

"He was only nineteen, you said."

"Yeah. He had his whole life ahead of him, but Timmy never wanted to wait for anything. He lived for excitement, for the next high. He loved fast boats, faster cars, and even faster women. We were a lot alike."

His brief smile was bleak. "Then someone turned him on to uppers. Speed, they called it then. Timmy loved the irony of it. He wanted to go fast, he told me once, and he used speed to get him there. He thought that was funny as hell."

Jillian leaned forward, a sick feeling of surprise filling her. "Your brother used drugs?"

"As many as he could get."

"How terrible," she said sadly.

"Yeah, it was terrible, all right. He was high when he lost control of his boat and crashed. The coroner said the concussion killed him instantly."

Jillian thought of the methamphetamine on her shelves. These days the drug was rarely prescribed, and only in cases of extreme obesity.

"When I was in college, I lived on diet pills during finals," she said quietly. "Everyone did. In those days no one knew they were addictive, not even the doctors."

Trevor picked up a pinecone from the sand and, with one violent movement of his powerful arm, threw it toward the lake. It splashed into the water and sank.

"During training the doctor on the carrier passed them out like candy." He hesitated, then added flatly, "I never used them. They made me sick."

Jillian's mind flew back in time. Trevor had gotten violently ill the first time the doctor had prescribed a synthetic painkiller. Morphine, because it was derived from the poppy, had been the only drug that hadn't caused an allergic reaction in his system.

"So you started a drug treatment center because of your brother?"

Trevor shifted again. His face was tight, and the tiny pulse had started again in his temple. "Yes, because of Tim," he said. "And...because of the guys who came back from Nam hooked on one drug or another. Horizons can't help everyone, but we do what we can."

His voice carried a harsh note of finality that Jillian couldn't ignore. A moment ago his large hand had been open and relaxed on his heavy thigh. Now, however, it was clenched into a fist, and the tendons of his thick wrist bulged. She suspected that talking about his brother was something he didn't do very often or, for that matter, very easily.

"I'm sorry about your brother," she said softly. And she was. But she was also very worried. Involuntarily her gaze drifted toward the far side of the lake.

Jason, the red rims of his sunglasses a bright splotch of color against his pale face, was wading along the shore, kicking water high into the air the way he used to do as a small boy.

"Trevor, don't tell Jason about your brother until he gets a chance to know you better. Okay?"

"Why not?"

Jillian heard the deceptive note of calm in his voice, but she took a deep breath and plunged ahead. Protecting Jason was more important than sparing Trevor's feelings.

"He's going to have enough to handle, just getting used to the fact that his father wants to be a part of his life."

"And you think knowing his uncle was an addict would upset him?"

"Yes. It's only natural that he would want to be, well, proud of his new family."

Trevor stared at her impassively for several seconds. Then his big shoulders lifted in a shrug. "Whatever you say, Jill. I guess no one wants to admit he has a junkie in the family."

The raw note in his voice caused her exposed skin to prickle, but she knew she was right to insist. Jason was her only concern.

Silence fell between them. Because he was so big, he took up more than his share of the blanket. Consequently his thigh was only inches from hers, and his shoulder was less than a sigh away from touching hers.

Jillian could feel the tension rising in his body, and a sudden fear shot through her. He'd allowed her to set the rules for his visit this time. And maybe he'd let her call the shots the next time. But after that, she had a feeling Trevor Markus would begin to make his own rules.

We'll just see about that, she thought, frowning. She felt her chest rise and fall under the thin cotton of her outfit. She hadn't been so aware of her body in years.

She felt a sudden shiver, and she looked up to find him watching her with smoldering eyes. He wanted her. She couldn't have been more certain if he'd shouted the words in her face.

"How about a swim?" he asked brusquely. "It's damn hot." Without waiting for an answer, he stripped off his shoes and socks and stood up stiffly, arching his back slowly, one vertebra at a time, like the mountain cat he resembled.

He held out a hand. "Well?"

Jillian ignored his hand as she got to her feet. "Miracle Lake is always cold. You probably won't like it."

"I'll swim fast," he said with a trace of sarcasm.

Trevor stripped off the medallion and tucked it into a fold in his shirt, then reached for the top button of his fly.

"What do you think you're doing?" she asked quickly.

"Undressing," he drawled. He was angry at her, and she didn't know why. "It's customary when a guy goes swimming to shed his jeans first."

Jillian glanced up and down the beach nervously. There was a family of six about twenty yards further along the perimeter, and another group of children and adults across the lake. No one was paying attention to the two people by the scarred tree.

At her worried look, he relented. In spite of the heat, cold beads of sweat dotted his forehead, and his muscles were painfully tight. He couldn't sit still a minute longer. If she wouldn't swim with him, he'd swim alone. He was used to it.

"I wore my suit, if that's what you're worried about."

Her cheeks warmed. "So did I," she muttered, unzipping the front of her playsuit to expose her one-piece suit.

"So you did," he said in a dry voice, watching her intently.

Her swimsuit was white, with a slashing diagonal of emerald across one hip, and a strapless top. She'd bought it on a dare from Adrian one day when they'd been shopping in Sacramento, and today was the first time that she'd worn it.

Suddenly, as his eyes warmed into violet golden flames beneath his angry brows, she wished she'd stuck with her ratty old tank suit. At least it covered slightly more of her generous curves.

She didn't look at Trevor as she stepped out of the jumpsuit and slipped out of her sandals, but she could feel his gaze on her. Carefully she folded the crinkled cotton, lining up the seams with slow precision, listening for the sound of his zipper.

It didn't take long.

"Ready?" he said in a voice that sounded oddly rigid. She put her bundle next to his shirt and looked up. He was wearing black boxer trunks, and they were very tight, hiding little of his potent physique.

Something primitive and hot uncurled inside her. And then she saw his face. He was flushed with embarrassment.

"Pretty bad, huh?" he said grimly, glancing down at his legs. He rubbed his hand against his hip, as though it suddenly hurt. Both legs were brutally scarred from his hips to his shins, the puckered scar tissue very white against his tan.

Jillian forced her features into a nonchalant smile, but inside she was sick. Not because of the way he looked, but because of the grindingly hard hours she knew he'd put in just to make those battered legs work again.

"If you mean, are your legs pretty, no, they're not. But I was there when they choppered you in, remember, and I know that you almost lost those nice long legs."

He went very still. "I remember. You told me I'd walk again, even when the doctors said I wouldn't."

"Doctors only work with muscles and bone. Nurses work with people. I . . . I knew you'd make it."

"For a long time you were the only one."

If he touched her, Trevor thought, he'd touch her there, where the top of her suit met the soft swell of her creamy breasts. But if he touched her now, he'd never be able to stop.

A hot pain traveled through his gut to settle between his thighs. I hope to hell that water's as cold as she says it is, he thought with a hard, silent wince.

"Ready?" he asked.

"Ready."

Jillian's legs felt stiff, and the sand burned the soles of her feet, making her walk faster and faster until she was nearly running. She dropped her towel above the waterline and walked into the lake, which wasn't just cold; it was frigid. Jillian felt her teeth begin to chatter the moment the water closed over the top of her suit.

Trevor was walking beside her, a good three feet away. He was looking toward the far end of the lake, where Jason was lying in the shade of a stunted willow, staring at the sky.

"Doesn't he swim?" he asked, glancing over at her.

"Not much. As a little boy, he used to be afraid of the water. I tried, but I could never get him to put his face under."

Trevor nodded. "I was like that, until one day my dad pitched me off the deck of our house into the Sound. I hit bottom like a rock and had to fight my way to the surface."

Jillian stopped walking and stared at him. "That's a terrible thing for a father to do!"

Trevor glanced at Jason again. Fleetingly he wondered what his son was thinking. The boy was too quiet, too self-contained, almost morose at times. He needed to laugh more, but maybe that would come when he was used to having a father around periodically.

"Pop had tried everything else he could think of to get me to learn, but I'd refused to try. He was afraid I'd walk out on the deck and fall in, so he did what he had to do to keep me from drowning someday."

"So he was being cruel to be kind?"

"Exactly."

She shook her head. "That's not my way. Today is the first time I've ever forced Jason to do something against his will, and you saw how much he resented it. I'm still not sure it was for the best."

"I guess I look at the bottom line. I might be dead now if my dad hadn't thrown me off that pier." He gestured toward the diving raft in the middle of the lake. "Wanna race?" he said, lifting one brow in challenge.

Jillian felt a wicked stab of pleasure. Swimming was one of the few sports she did well, and she was going to enjoy beating him. "Loser cleans up?"

Trevor gave her a measuring look. "You're on."

Before he could seal the bet with a handshake, she lunged forward and began swimming away from him with long, graceful strokes.

"Hey," he shouted, then grinned. He'd been taken. The lady was a fighter, all right, and it looked as though she intended to beat the bejabbers out of him.

He dived forward and began to swim. It took half a dozen strokes before the muscles of his back began to loosen. And another half dozen to find a smooth stroke that didn't twist his spine. By then Jillian was far ahead.

He put his head down and pulled as hard as he could, but she touched the side of the raft a full stroke ahead of him. When he surfaced, she was holding on to the raft and gasping for air, water dripping from her tangled auburn curls.

"You lose," she said, laughing triumphantly.

Trevor watched the sun tip her lashes with pure gold as she gazed directly at him. In the bright light her eyes were a flawless apple-green, and filled with the sunny, innocently sensual glow he remembered so vividly.

"Uh-uh. You jumped the gun." He wiped the lake water from his face and enjoyed the look of mock indignation that wrinkled her freckled nose.

She crossed her arms and glared at him. "I did not!"

Her shoulders were tawny gold above the white suit and dappled with drops of water. The exertion had pulled the suit down a half inch or so, and the white skin below the tan line drew his gaze. His body stirred to life in spite of the cold.

Trevor managed to raise his gaze to her lips. They were slightly blue, and her teeth were beginning to chatter. "You'd better get out of the water," he said. "Here, I'll give you a boost."

Jillian didn't argue. The water was making the skin below the water numb, while above the surface, his heated gaze was making her steam.

His hands bracketed her waist, his fingers exerting just enough pressure to make her aware of his strength. Ignoring the flare of pleasure shooting along her skin under the wet suit, she put both hands on top of the raft and started to heave herself aboard. Unexpectedly the heavy structure lurched violently as she put her weight on it. Off balance, she toppled backward and fell hard against Trevor's chest. His hands splayed against her breasts as he grabbed for her again, and they both went under.

Wrapped together in a tangle of arms and legs they sank into the dark green void. Jillian opened her eyes and blinked against the stinging chill. The water was very clear, with black shadows below and sparkling diamonds of light above.

There was no sound.

The moment her gaze found his, Trevor's arms tightened convulsively, and his lips came down on hers. In spite of the cold, his mouth was hot and insistent, his tongue thrusting arrogantly between her lips.

Pleasure shot through her, filling her, and for an instant she wrapped her legs around his thighs and returned his kiss. His chest was hard, his arousal startling. She rubbed against him, feeling the rough warmth of his chest and legs. She was hot and cold and nearly breathless.

No, she thought. She didn't want this.

His hand tangled in her hair, and she felt a sharp tingle of pain. Her ears began to ring, and she pushed hard against his chest. He released her immediately, and she kicked toward the surface.

Trevor followed, furious with himself. He'd known better than to touch her. But when her soft body had slid against his, his resolve had weakened. And when she'd opened her eyes and looked at him underwater, he'd been lost.

"Don't ever do that again," she sputtered, gazing around angrily. Two bright spots of color dotted her cheekbones, and she was breathing hard. She'd wanted him, and she was furiously angry at herself for being a victim of her hormones. She knew better.

"The winner deserved a victory kiss." Trevor winced inwardly, but it was the best he could do. He was still feeling the impact of her breasts sliding down his bare chest and her thighs pressing against his.

Jillian's teeth were chattering so hard that she couldn't get out another word. Once he'd used that same teasing tone to order her to touch him, to run her fingers through the wiry thatch covering his wide chest, to play with his flat nipples, teasing them into hard little rocks under her fingertips. She'd loved the way she could make him groan before surrendering to the desire shaking her. And then his eyes would turn this same gold and he would wrap his strong arms around her so tightly that she couldn't breathe, just as he'd done a moment ago underwater.

She glared at him for a few seconds more, then began swimming furiously for the shore.

Damn, Trevor thought, watching her swim away from him. Over the years he'd learned to exercise rigorous control over his emotions. His only passion had been building bridges and skyscrapers and roads, each one carefully planned in meticulous detail, just like his days and nights.

But since Jill had come back into his life, he was having trouble handling anything but the most uncomplicated tasks. During the past two weeks it had taken a great deal of concentration on his part to keep from screwing up some very important projects.

Scowling, he muttered a harsh curse, followed by a little prayer for patience. It was going to be a long afternoon.

Jillian rested her head against the seat and closed her eyes. She was exhausted, and her head throbbed in rhythm with the tires droning monotonously on the rutted pavement. Even the thunder of Prokofiev playing on the Jaguar's tape deck sounded discordant filtered through the pain in her temples.

It was nearly five-thirty, but the sun was still warm, and the wind flowing through the open car stung her cheeks. She'd been a nervous wreck from the moment that Trevor had kissed her.

He hadn't been her first lover, but he'd been the first one to show her the difference between sex and making love. With him, she'd felt replenished. With him, she'd learned what it was like to give totally and completely and to receive that same devotion in return. She'd never felt that with any other man. And now she suspected she never would. The sense of loss that had started the night she'd reread his letters grew stronger.

"Is it okay to park here? It says loading zone."

Trevor's husky voice jerked her from her inner reverie. He swung the convertible to the curb behind her bright red minitruck parked near the back door of the pharmacy.

She sat up, rubbing her eyes. "No problem. Mel's pretty lenient on weekends."

His lips tightened. "Don't kid yourself. He'd like nothing better than to slap a parking ticket on me. I'm the enemy, remember?"

Jillian sighed. "Clayton doesn't have enough deputies to enforce the parking laws, even though we lose money that way. That's why we don't offer a free day on the meters. We figure it balances out."

"Sounds like some of the countries where I've had to negotiate contracts."

She glanced at the steps leading to her apartment. Trevor had carried the cooler down for her. He would expect to carry it back up. And then what?

"Mom, can I go to Mike's now?" Jason asked from the back seat.

"Not now, Jason. And carry the cooler upstairs, okay?" Jillian saw the frown form between Trevor's shaggy brows as he rested his arm on the wheel and watched her.

Jason unfastened his seat belt. "Can't Trevor do it? Me and Mike made plans to go to Truckee to play vids as soon as I got back."

Jillian gathered her purse and her tote bag, avoiding Trevor's gaze. The tension between them had grown nearly unbearable. "Video games can wait. You have homework to do," she said firmly.

"It's done. I did it this morning."

Jillian refrained from commenting on the kind of work he must have produced while that terrible music had blared. Instead she gave him a measuring look. His eyes were hidden behind his dark lenses, but he was smiling slightly. And he was bouncing back and forth on the seat like a little boy who'd been confined for too long.

"Okay, you can go, but carry that thing upstairs for me first," she said, relenting. The day had been difficult for all three of them, and Jason had tried to be congenial, at least for a while. When he'd returned from the far side of the lake, he'd been sullen and withdrawn, spending the rest of the afternoon dozing on the blanket.

"Great! I'm outta here." Jason opened the door and started to get out, but Trevor leaned through the opening between the seats and stopped him.

"The guys at Horizons are starting a soccer tournament tomorrow, and one of the teams is shorthanded," he said, keeping his hand on Jason's shoulder. "Your mom tells me you're a great goalie, and we could really use you to fill in." He grinned. "You can be on the team I'm coaching."

Jason glanced away. "I have school."

"The recreation period is from four to six, plenty of time for you to make it. I'll come and pick you up if you'd like."

Jason's blank gaze shifted to Jillian, and she smiled encouragingly. "I think it's a good idea, sweetie. Since you've quit the team, you're not getting nearly as much exercise as you should."

He shrugged. "I got better things to do with my time than hang around a bunch of dumb losers."

Jillian opened her mouth to reprimand him, but Trevor beat her to it.

"Pay attention, Jason, because I'm only going to say this once. I don't *ever* again want to hear you refer to the residents of Horizons as losers." He didn't raise his voice, but the flinty hardness was more frightening to Jillian than the loudest shout.

"They're boys like you who've made some bad mistakes and are trying the best way they can to put their lives back together again. And that's damn hard work, son, because every day they wake up with a craving in their belly that can't even be described. Every night they go to bed clean is a major victory."

He sighed, and Jillian could tell he was trying to contain his anger. "They don't deserve your contempt, or mine, or Sheriff Cobb's, and until you've been in the places where they've been and fought the same fight they're fighting, you don't have a right to judge."

Jason went completely white beneath his sunburn. He stared at Trevor in frozen silence. Suddenly, before Jillian could utter a word, he scrambled out of the car and took off running.

"Damn it to hell!" Trevor exclaimed into the stunned silence. "I guess I blew that royally."

He pounded his fist on the gearshift, and Jillian felt some of her anger dissipate.

"I can build a road that will last for a hundred years, but I can't seem to handle one fourteen-year-old kid." He narrowed his eyes and looked at her. "Go ahead. Say what you're thinking. This time I deserve it."

Jillian opened her mouth, then closed it again. How did he know what she was thinking?

"He's picked up that attitude about Horizons from Mel Cobb," she admitted grudgingly. "Mel's son, Mike, has become his best friend."

"Terrific."

Her temper flared again, and she glared at him. "If I forbid him to spend time with Mike, he'll just dig in harder."

Trevor ran his hand through his hair. The silver thickness had dried in a tousled cap that gleamed in the sun. "You're right. That's exactly what he'd do."

Jillian was having trouble staying mad. He seemed so discouraged, and he'd tried so hard.

"Sometimes, when I hear a statement like Jason's," he told her cynically, "I think we should just round up all the addicts in this country and shoot them. It would be kinder in the long run."

"He's just young. He doesn't understand about prejudice."

"Do you?" he shot back.

"Yes, Trevor, I do," she said angrily. "I'm an unwed mother, remember?"

Trevor took off his glasses and rubbed his stinging eyes. "Sorry, that question was out of line," he muttered, tossing the glasses onto the dashboard. "This hasn't been the easiest day I've ever had."

In the space of five minutes he'd managed to alienate his son and put the anger back in Jillian's eyes. Great going, Markus, he thought grimly. Keep this up, and neither one of them will ever speak to you again.

"C'mon," he told her brusquely, pushing open his door. "I'll help you with the picnic stuff."

Chapter 8

The living room was stifling and smelled musty. While Jillian hurried to open the windows, Trevor carried the cooler to the kitchen. After setting it on the floor by the sink, he rolled his shoulders to release the knots, then ran some water and splashed his hot face.

When he returned to the living room, Jillian was standing by the window overlooking the street. She was staring at the horizon, where the sun was dipping below the tree line like a brilliant orange balloon.

His body stirred, pushing insistently against the tight denim. He'd been without a woman for a long time. Too long.

And she was beautiful, standing there in the golden light. He wanted her. Now.

Violently. Possessively. Totally.

Trevor wiped the drops of water from his jaw, then jammed his hands into his pockets. His jeans tightened over his loins, and he stiffened at the surge of blood that shot through him.

He'd thought that he had this leftover ache handled. But he'd been wrong. He wanted to possess her, to manacle her to him until she let him into her bed again.

But he wanted more than her body. He wanted some of that inner fire, that special one-of-a-kind spirit that had stayed with him even when she'd drifted into a painful memory.

These days he kept his feelings on a short rein, just the way he ran his companies, and he never thought about love. It wasn't a word he used anymore. Not for fifteen years. Most likely he'd never use it again.

But this power that Jillian had over him was different. Special. He didn't quite understand it. He wasn't sure he wanted to understand. Mostly he just knew he *wanted*. With her, he was out of control, and he knew how dangerous that could be. It had nearly killed him once. But there didn't seem to be anything he could do about this gut-deep need she excited in him—except wait it out.

"You took a big chance, talking to Jason like that," Jillian said, turning to look at him. "He may refuse to see you again."

He ambled toward her. "How would you feel about that?"

"I haven't decided." She crossed her arms over her chest and watched his rangy body fill up her cozy living room. He seemed too restless and too powerful to be contained by four walls.

He glanced toward the sofa, but he didn't sit down. Jillian saw the pinched look around his eyes and realized his back must be bothering him. But she couldn't afford to care.

"Robin said you were a tough negotiator," he said with a lazy half smile.

"Is that a criticism?"

He moved closer, pushing into her private space. "No."

Jillian held her ground. "Then why did it sound like one?"

"Damned if I know."

He reached out and took her hand, and she stiffened.

"Are you afraid of me, Jill?" His voice was sheathed in warm steel.

"No." She resisted the powerful urge to pull her fingers from his. She couldn't show fear, not to this man.

Thoughtfully he rubbed her empty ring finger with his thumb. "You could have married. Given Jason a stepfather to be proud of."

"Yes." Tiny shivers of sweet pleasure began shooting up her arm, making it hard to concentrate. It had been a long time since she'd been so aroused by a man's touch.

"Does that mean you never . . . found anyone special?"

"No . . . no one special."

His head was bent, his attention focused on her hand, but she could see the slight lessening of the tension along his jaw. His fingers folded over hers, and his thumb moved to her wrist. "Your pulse is racing so fast your skin feels hot," he said in a husky voice. His thumb moved in a slow circle. "Tell me what you're thinking to make your heart pound like that."

Thinking? Jill blinked. Didn't he know? Couldn't he see the way he upset her every time he came near her? Couldn't he feel the heat in her body?

Inside the small, hot room, the atmosphere changed as the silence lengthened. Every breath she took seemed to heighten the tension building inside her. "I'm . . . not thinking anything," she said.

His hand tightened around hers. "Shame on you, Jill. You should know better than to tell a lie when a man has his hand on your wrist." He slid his hand up her arm to her shoulder. "I've thought about you every day since I saw you on that dais. I thought about . . . kissing you again." Maybe if he gave in, he thought, just once, he could purge the ache from his body—and his soul.

"Don't. I'm warning you."

In the square across the street the birds were beginning to gather in the trees, and the sound of their chirping reminded her of the tiny nest in Tokyo. Trevor had been the one to wipe the tears from her eyes when the frail little bird had lost his fight. And Trevor had been the one who'd turned the cool reserve inside her to fire, making her a woman.

She swallowed the thickness in her throat and stared at him helplessly. What did he want from her? What kind of game was he playing?

"Angel."

His lips were whisper-soft as they took hers. His kiss was tender, without passion. His strong hands slid along her cheekbones and into her hair, cherishing her with their gentleness, and yet she could feel his restraint as his thumbs gently stroked the curve of her cheek.

His lips moved, tasting, nibbling. His breath mingled with hers, warm and moist against her mouth. He tasted good, like the chocolate chip cookies he'd finished off before they left.

"Relax, Jill," he whispered against her lips. "Relax and let it happen."

Jillian stiffened, but her knees felt weak. Gradually, without wanting to, she allowed her body to mold against his. Her arms encircled his hard torso, and her skin tingled as she slid her palms along the hard ridge of his spine.

His body was warm, his shirt damp where it rested against his skin, his muscles hard. He was lean and angular and rugged, all the things a man should be.

Trevor groaned as her hands explored his back, his spine, his hips. The moment her fingers slid under the waistband of his jeans, his kiss grew hard and insistent, as though he'd been waiting for her response.

The pleasure of that realization was sweet, like a stroll through a sunlit meadow in the early morning. She felt her soul unfolding like a tightly furled bud, eager for the heat of the sun.

His kisses became hot, insistent, and she met his arrogant demand with an equal intensity. She could feel the ripple of his muscular back under her palms as he pulled her hard against him. His wide chest crushed her breasts, and the pressure excited a delicious ache in her nipples.

She moaned and opened her mouth to him. His tongue slid inside, tentative at first, and then, when she welcomed him with the tip of her own, his kiss became possessive. She was hot, eager.

A harsh groan shuddered through him. His breath was wonderfully moist against her skin as he trailed hot, urgent kisses along the curve of her cheekbone.

"So damn long," he whispered almost incoherently.

Too long, she echoed mindlessly. She wanted to forget the long, empty years. She wanted reality to fade until there was only Trevor. Only his hard body and demanding lips.

She wanted him, blindly, senselessly. Only him. She didn't want to remember. She wouldn't remember, not while his hands were cupping her buttocks and pulling her against him intimately.

His legs moved, his thigh pushing between hers. The rough pressure of the hard muscle beneath the two layers of cloth sent ripples of moist warmth deep into her center. She began to move, answering his primitive male call.

Glorious, she thought, running her hands over the magnificent width of his shoulders, loving the power there, and the strength. Her warrior knight, her lover. He was that and more.

Giddy with sensual memory, eager to feel all of him again, she clung to him, pressing her body hard against his. She could feel his instant hard response, his raw male need. He hadn't forgotten. He still wanted her.

Warmth spread along the tawny surface of her skin, softening the last of her resistance. His fingers combed her hair, tugging on her scalp, and the sensation was exquisite.

Under her hands she felt his muscles harden, and he jerked against her. Jillian let her hands relax, her palms stroking his biceps until they bulged like burled redwood.

"Take me to bed, angel," Trevor whispered hoarsely against her throat. "I can't take much more of this."

To bed?

To make love? Or to have sex?

Fleetingly Jillian remembered the way it had been between them. But this time it would be different. This was only physical. And it would ruin the special memory of their times together, the only memory he hadn't tarnished.

She couldn't bear it. He'd taken everything else. He couldn't have that, too.

"Let me go, Trevor," she said in a strangled voice. "I don't want this."

She struggled, breaking his hold, and withdrew her arms from around him. Her head was swimming, and her body felt leaden and hot.

"The hell you don't!" Trevor's face was flushed, and he was breathing hard. "What is this, Jill? Some kind of revenge?"

Jillian took a step backward and folded her arms over her quivering belly. Inside, shame was spreading through her like a virus, churning her stomach and chilling her to the bone. Hadn't she learned her lesson yet? Did she really have to be hurt all over again before she could get this man out of her system?

"I think you'd better go," she said stiffly.

A thunderous frown tightened his face, and his eyes seethed, his need raw and plain to see. Both hands were balled into fists at his sides, and his jeans bulged with his unslaked desire.

"I will—this time." His frown twisted into a hard smile. "But the next time I kiss you I won't leave. Remember that when you issue an invitation with those sexy green eyes of yours."

Jillian gasped. "Get out."

Trevor snapped her an exaggerated salute. "Yes, ma'am!" He spun on his heel and walked out, letting the door slam violently behind him.

"I hate you," she shouted after him. But even as she said the words, she knew that she lied. She didn't hate him.

Jillian crumpled onto the sofa behind her and buried her burning face in her hands. She loved him. God help her, she was still in love with Trevor Markus.

It was past midnight. Trevor and Hank sat alone in the cavernous kitchen tucked into the far end of Horizons' main building.

"Cobb's an imbecile," Trevor muttered in controlled fury. "Anyone with any sense at all could tell that damn mask and the bottle of Percodan were planted. The guys we get here are too streetwise to stash anything where it could be found so easily." He raised his foot and sent an empty chair skidding across the newly waxed linoleum to crash into the stainless-steel refrigerator.

"You know that, and I know that, but he's got a pretty good start on an indictment," Hank said with a grim half smile. "All he needs is a fingerprint match on that blasted bottle."

Trevor rubbed his upper lip with his thumb, feeling the whisker stubble scrape his skin. "Could he have planted the pills himself before he went to your office?"

Hank stood up and began pacing. "Not unless he climbed up the ravine and vaulted the fence. Hendricks was at the gate, and he logged him in and called me immediately. I was waiting for him when he got out of the car."

Cobb had arrived shortly after Trevor had returned. The sheriff had brought his two deputies and a search warrant signed by a local judge. In an empty gym locker one of the deputies had found a black ski mask wrapped around a bottle of high-potency painkillers. The clinic's label had been pasted on the small plastic vial.

As soon as the sheriff had left, taking the evidence with him, Trevor had called an emergency meeting of the staff, asking question after question and poring over files until both he and Hank were convinced none of the boys had been involved in the theft and assault. The other members of the staff had long since gone to bed. Only Trevor and Hank remained.

Trevor shifted his feet on the slick floor and tried to find a comfortable position, but the chair was too small and the molded plastic back too hard. As he'd had to do for years, he tried to ignore the clawing pain in his back, but even the shallowest breath hurt. He needed a long soak in a hot tub to relieve his tortured muscles.

"If all our guys were accounted for, someone else put that stuff in the gym, probably one of the guys who boosted the junk," he told Hank in a tired voice. "There's no other explanation."

Hank frowned, then perched on the end of the table, his booted foot swinging restlessly. "I agree. But how?"

Trevor shook his head. "Beats me. But I think you'd better have security check the perimeter again. We've got a lot of fence. Someone who knows the area could find a way to sneak in without being seen."

He stared at the dark residue in the bottom of the white mug. The cold coffee was like acid on his stomach. Or was it frustration that was eating at him?

Forget it, Markus, he told himself one more time. Jillian wasn't the only desirable woman in the world. She wasn't even the prettiest or, damn it, the sexiest. So why did she have him tied in knots?

. For a long moment he allowed himself to think of her swimming to shore ahead of him, her long hair streaming in a vibrant cloud behind her, her luscious body neatly contained in that shimmering white suit that had been more provocative than the briefest bikini.

His body stirred again, and he cursed himself a dozen ways for being a fool. Jill didn't want him. She didn't even like him.

"I need a drink," he muttered, glowering at the foul-tasting coffee.

Hank's chuckle was without humor. "You know the rules. No booze, no drugs on the grounds—except in the infirmary."

Trevor glanced across the table. A bank of fluorescent lights illuminated the stark white area, giving the room a cold look.

"How long's it been since you had your last drink, Hank? Fifteen, sixteen years?" Trevor's long, blunt fingers wrapped around the heavy mug so tightly that the knuckles whitened.

"Fifteen years, six months and thirteen days," Hank said with a challenging look.

"You still want it, don't you?"

"Every day."

Hank had come back from two tours of duty as a field surgeon in Vietnam with a vicious hatred of war and an equally vicious drinking problem. Trevor had met the taciturn Texan at Balboa Naval Hospital, where Hank had been assigned to temporary duty after he'd gotten himself sober by camping out alone for six weeks in the mountains east of San Diego. After Trevor's release, they'd kept in touch, and when Trevor had started Horizons, Hank had been the first one he'd called. The two men shared a mutual regard and affection and had few secrets from each other.

Trevor shoved his cup away and rubbed his eyes. He was exhausted. "I'm calling it a night. Maybe things'll look better in the morning."

"We'll beat that bastard yet," Hank muttered, resting a booted foot on a chair and shoving his hand in his pockets.

Bastard . . .

Suddenly Trevor saw Jason's white face. And Jillian's stricken eyes. He flexed his battered left hand. He should have flattened the jerk when he had the chance. Hell, he had a good lawyer, and Cobb more than deserved it. Any judge would agree.

"Trev, what's with you? I haven't seen that look in years."

"What look?" Trevor asked impatiently, clenching his fist.

"Like you're fixing to take me apart. You got some kind of problem with me I don't know about, partner?" Hank dropped his foot and pulled his hands from his pockets.

He and Trevor had been through a lot, and Hank knew better than most how violent Trevor could be when he lost his temper. Once, in the hospital, he'd seen his friend so angry that he'd smashed his fist through the glass front of a drug cabinet and hadn't even flinched from the pain.

"Hell, it's not you, Hank. It's me." Trevor muttered a harsh obscenity, followed by a terse apology and a brief recounting of the sheriff's veiled insult and Jason's reaction.

Hank's braced body relaxed. "Cobb's the real bastard, not Jason," Hank drawled, kicking the leg of the table. "Don't let it get to you."

"Easy for you to say. You don't have to face the kid. Or his mother." His voice tightened. "Or the damn guilt."

He looked up to find Hank watching him speculatively, a frown on his angular face.

"You did the right thing fifteen years ago, Trev. You had no choice. None at all."

Trevor flexed his tired shoulders. "We always have choices, Hank. I made the wrong one, and that's pretty hard to live with right now."

Hank stood and slid his hands into his pockets. "Start over. Win her back."

"You know what the odds are against that? Too long to even count."

"The odds never bothered you before."

"It's more than that, and you know it. There's a lot she'd have to know, a lot I'd have to tell her. I'm not proud of the man I was in those days, Hank."

Trevor's gut tightened. He'd flown twenty-three missions over North Vietnam before the crash without feeling more than the usual preflight jitters, but now he broke into a cold sweat whenever he thought about that part of his life.

"And you think, if she knew, she'd hate you as much as you hated yourself for too many years?"

Trevor dropped his head, then slowly raised it. His expression was grim. "Right now I don't know what the hell I think. And at the moment I'm too tired to care."

He'd flown back from Thailand on Friday and driven all night to get to Clayton early on Saturday. He desperately needed a few hours of oblivion.

Hank's curt nod signaled his understanding. "I hear you." He ran a long brown hand down the thick neatness of his beard, then glanced at the clock on the wall. It was nearly one.

"I'd better get back to the infirmary. We've got a new admission who's going through detox."

"How's he doing?"

"Not good. It's never easy."

Trevor braced both palms on the slick surface of the table and pushed himself slowly to his feet. The frayed nerves in his back screamed in protest, and he held his breath, waiting for the pain to let up enough so that he could make it across the compound to the guest house.

"No," he said softly, thinking about Jillian's angry eyes and fragile smile, "it's never easy."

"Ouch!"

Jillian sucked her finger and glared at the chef's knife that had just sliced the tip. A splotch of blood glistened on the cutting board next to the celery she'd been dicing, and she grabbed a paper towel to mop it up.

She wrapped her finger in the towel and picked up her knife. She attacked the celery again, venting a tiny piece of her growing frustration with every slice.

It was Wednesday, her day off, and she was fixing an elaborate Chinese dinner for Jason and herself. Cooking had always soothed her nerves and helped her to think.

For the past three days, since the picnic, she'd been at the mercy of her flip-flopping emotions. For the first time since the wedding that never happened she found herself thinking of Trevor in a new way. For the first time she wondered what it had been like for him over the past fifteen years.

In many ways he was the same sexy, provocative man she'd loved, and yet he was different, too. In those long-ago months he'd been boyishly selfish and unabashedly conceited.

What he'd wanted, he'd gone after. At twenty-one and desperately smitten, she'd adored the single-mindedness with which he'd charmed her into his bed, and she'd reveled in the masterful way he'd convinced her to give up nursing and marry him.

"Hey, I've got plenty of money," he'd told her with his wicked grin. "We'll have a good time before we settle down and raise the next brood of Markuses."

Now, however, she sensed a depth in him that hadn't been there before, and a reserve that was somehow more appealing than the brash openness she remembered. And buried deeply in his sexy eyes was a quiet sorrow that was always there, even when he laughed.

Much to her surprise, he'd called early on Monday to tell her about Cobb's visit. But she'd already received a call from the sheriff himself, demanding that she convene a special meeting of the council to discuss the revocation of the lease.

Because she had no choice in the face of the evidence he'd found, she'd agreed. But she'd insisted upon waiting until Orrie Hughes returned from a two-week visit to his daughter in San Francisco to schedule the time and place. Mel had grumbled, but he hadn't challenged her decision.

"What do you think, Jill?" Trevor had asked in a tense tone after she'd told him what had transpired. "Could he have planted those pills himself to discredit us?"

Jillian had taken her time answering. Because she disliked Mel Cobb so intensely, she'd had to sort through her feelings before she could find an objective answer.

"I don't think so, Trevor," she'd answered slowly, but definitely. "I admit Mel is irrational about Horizons, but he's also afraid of losing his job. He's got a son to support, and, according to the things Mike has told Jason, a lot of debts to pay off. The man is a pig, but he's not stupid."

There had been a brief silence.

"So you have no idea who might have planted the so-called evidence on us?"

"Unfortunately, no."

He'd sighed and switched the conversation to Jason. Their son had been subdued and withdrawn when he'd returned at nine Sunday night, she'd admitted, and Trevor hadn't pushed her to explain further.

"Tell him I said hello," he'd said before they hung up.

He hadn't asked about her.

The sharp sound of the screen door banging shut drove the disquieting thoughts of Trevor from her mind, and she looked up quickly to see Jason stalking into the kitchen. His face was flushed, and his hair was disheveled and wild-looking.

"I hate this stinking place," he shouted, his eyes hidden behind the dark glasses he wore almost constantly now. "And I hate that stinking school. I'm not going back."

He threw his books at the wall and stalked out.

Jillian stood in frozen silence, the heavy knife gripped tightly in her hand. She stared at the textbooks piled in a heap against the baseboard. One of the books had gouged a deep chunk from the plasterboard, and white dust powdered the linoleum.

"My God," she whispered in a choked voice before her wits returned.

Throwing down the knife, she hurried after her son. His door was shut. She knocked, but the music blaring full blast from his stereo drowned out the sound. She took a deep breath, pushed open the door and walked in. Jason was lying facedown on his rumpled bed, his hands clenched around his pillow.

"Sweetie, what happened? What's wrong?"

He didn't answer.

Jillian winced as a metallic scream filled the room. Keeping her gaze fixed on Jason's tense form, she crossed the room and lowered the volume to a tinny whisper.

Sitting next to him, she stroked his hair. Her jerked away and sat up, his back pressed firmly against the wall. The springs squeaked as she moved closer to him.

"Jason, tell me what's wrong," she said again, this time more firmly.

"I've been suspended for a week. Mr. Grable's gonna call you."

Jillian blinked. "Why, Jase? Why is the principal going to call me?"

"Because he says I stole twenty bucks from a guy's locker during fifth period gym class." He crossed this arms over his chest and seemed to stare at her from behind the blank dark lenses.

Instinctively she reached out to grip his arm. "Did you take the money, Jason?" she asked in stern voice.

"No," he muttered, then dropped his chin so that he was no longer looking at her. "Not exactly."

Jillian's heart speeded up painfully. "What do you mean, not exactly?"

"Mike and the other guys said it was a test. To see if...if I was man enough to stay in the club."

She inhaled slowly, fighting the surge of anger that shook her. That damn Mike Cobb again! she thought, releasing her grip. Her instincts had been right. Mike was trouble.

"Did you explain all of this to Mr. Grable?" she asked, striving to keep her voice calm.

"Naw, he was too mad to listen."

"I see," she said, stalling for time. What should she do now? she wondered urgently. Call Mel Cobb and tell him what his son was up to? Or call Ed and see if she could get Jason reinstated in school so that he wouldn't fall behind?

Feeling as frightened and helpless as she'd felt when she'd given birth to him, Jillian slowly raised her hand and removed Jason's dark glasses. For her own peace of mind, she needed to see the truth in his eyes.

Tears shimmered in the copper depths, and his pupils were wide with fright, but he met her searching gaze squarely. Jillian exhaled in relief. There was no deceit mirrored there. None.

"What you did was wrong," she said sternly. "But I'm proud of you for telling me the truth."

His shoulders sagged forlornly against the garish poster of a grinning skull behind his back. "I was going to give it back, Mom. Honest."

"Oh, baby," she whispered, pulling him into her arms for an awkward hug. "It's okay. We'll get through this."

"I know it was a dumb thing to do," Jason said, his voice wobbling. "I'm not going to listen to Mike ever again. I promise."

"Good," she said, patting his arm. It was going to be all right. He'd learned his lesson. She was sure of it. "I think that's a wise idea."

Jason wiped his eyes with the back of his hand and dropped his gaze. "Are you mad?" he asked in a low voice, his hands fumbling with the comforter.

"No, I'm not mad, but I am disappointed. I thought you knew better."

He rubbed his back against the wall. "Are you gonna tell *him*?"

Jillian heard the quavering note in his voice and frowned. "Who?"

"You know. Trevor. My... father." He sounded nervous.

She wetted her lips, and glanced through the window toward the mountains. "He has to know."

"He'll just yell at me again," Jason mumbled, flopping down on his back and staring at the ceiling. "He doesn't like me." His voice lowered. "And I don't like him. He's always lookin' at me funny, like he keeps waiting for me to do something stupid.''

''Jase, that's not true!''

''Yes, it is. You wait. He's out to get me. He'll be mad.''

''Not if you explain—''

''You're not the same since he came here,'' he interrupted angrily. ''Nothing I do anymore is right. You're on his side!''

''Jason, there aren't any *sides* here.''

Jillian saw the stubborn set of his jaw and realized further discussion would be useless. He was feeling hurt and threatened, and she had to give him time to work through all the things that had happened to him in the past few days.

''I'll explain your side to your father,'' she said softly. ''He'll understand.'' She hesitated, then added in a sterner voice, ''You're forbidden to see Mike Cobb, except at school, and you're no longer in that club.''

His gaze jerked around the room. ''Aw, Mom—''

''No arguments, Jason. I mean it.'' She forced a smile. ''In the meantime, you rest. Dinner will be ready in half an hour. I'll call you.''

She left the room and closed the door behind her. She went directly to her bedroom and sank down onto her bed, her legs shaking and her stomach churning. Inside her head a strident buzz echoed the music that once more blared from Jason's room.

I have to do something, she thought, wiping her clammy hands on the bedspread. But what? Dear God, how can I fix this? How can I make sure this never happens again?

She clenched her hands in frustration, and the nubby chenille bunched between her fingers.

''Trevor.''

Suddenly she realized she'd called his name aloud, and her heart lurched. She had to tell him before he heard about it from someone else. She'd promised Jason she would.

Her hand shook as she reached for the phone by the bed. Breathing slowly through her mouth in an effort to calm her galloping heart, she punched out the number. But the line to the guest bungalow was busy.

"Damn," she muttered.

She hung up, her hand still resting on the receiver. Then, tightening her lips, she made another call. The principal answered on the second ring.

"I was going to call you, Jillian," Ed Grable said as soon as he heard her voice. "I knew you'd be upset."

"What happened, Ed? I couldn't get much out of Jason."

The principal's heavy sigh throbbed against her ear. "One of the other boys in Jason's gym class saw him taking money from a locker. It wasn't Jason's locker, and it wasn't his money."

Jillian cleared her throat. "He claimed he was going to give it back, that it was a prank, something to do with an initiation requirement for this . . . club he belongs to."

"I've heard rumors about that club, Jillian. Personally I don't like the idea of any group that wants to feel exclusive, and this one certainly seems to have gotten off to a bad start, at least where Jason is concerned."

Jillian heaved a sigh. "I agree. I've forbidden him to be a member."

"Good. In the meantime, a week away from his classes might shake him up enough to get him back on track."

Jillian bit her lip. "I, er, was wondering about that, Ed. You don't have to keep him out so long, do you? He's sure to fall behind."

There was a brief silence. "I have to make an example of him, Jillian. Too many other students saw what was going on. And he can keep up with his work at home. If you stop by tomorrow, I'll have a list of his assignments for the next five days."

"If that's the best you can do . . ."

"It is."

"I'll be by in the morning," she said, accepting defeat grudgingly.

Jillian sat stiffly on the edge of the hard mattress, the receiver pressed tightly to her ear. She was trying to make up her mind.

Finally she decided Jason's welfare as too important for her to let her pride stand in the way. "Ed, Jason's father has just come into his life for...for the first time. Do you think that might be affecting him badly?"

There was a lengthy silence, and then Ed cleared his throat. "It's very possible. Family upheaval can be very upsetting to a sensitive boy like Jason." He paused, then added, "Perhaps it would be a good idea if the boy's father came in for a conference. It might give Jason more confidence, knowing both his parents are concerned with his progress."

Jillian stared down at the oak floor beneath her sneakers. Her bedroom was under the eaves, and she could hear the wind rushing through the boughs of the tall aspen outside her window.

"I'll...mention it to...to Trevor." But she knew such a meeting would only solidify Jason's belief that she and Trevor were somehow conspiring against him.

Teenagers, she thought dejectedly. Who could understand them?

The principal cleared his throat. "If there's anything I can do, Jillian, please ask."

Jillian heard the sincerity in Ed's voice, and she felt slightly better. "Thanks for the offer, Ed. I'll make sure Jason doesn't give you any more trouble."

"Enough said," he told her, and they exchanged goodbyes.

Jillian hung up and stared at the phone. Jason's music was still pounding, and her head was still throbbing. Sighing, she dialed Trevor's number again.

His line was still busy.

Chapter 9

"Evening, ma'am. Welcome to Wilderness Horizons."

The burly guard leaned out of the small square box, a polite smile on his face. Middle-aged, with a deeply tanned face and graying sideburns, Ralph Hendricks was built like a tank, with wide shoulders and a thick torso that strained the seams of his dark blue uniform.

"Hello Mr. Hendricks. I'm here to see . . . Mr. Markus."

The guard did a double take. "Mayor Anderson! I didn't recognize you." His respectful smile bloomed into a friendly grin that lit his blue eyes and split his ruddy cheeks. "If you'll wait, Mayor, I'll call ahead and tell reception you're coming." His voice carried an unspoken apology. "It's routine."

"Of course."

Jillian fidgeted in the seat. She'd tried to reach Trevor again before dinner and twice after Jason had returned to his room. But the line had been busy each time. Finally, after nearly exhausting herself pacing, she'd decided to drive the nine miles to Horizons and speak with him there.

When she'd gone to tell Jason where she was going, she'd found him sprawled across his bed, asleep. After leaving him a note in case he woke up to find her gone, she'd taken a quick shower, reapplied her makeup and dressed in a new pair of white cotton slacks and a lavender shirt.

At least she felt somewhat rejuvenated, although the adrenaline was still prodding her heartbeat into an uncomfortable rhythm, and her stomach felt queasy.

"All set, ma'am," Hendricks said in a hearty voice that made her smile. "Mr. Markus's line is busy, but Dr. Stoneson said it was okay for you to go directly to the guest bungalow."

He handed her a laminated visitor's pass, which she clipped to her collar, and asked her to sign the log. He added the time and initialed the entry.

"Do you know the way?"

Jillian shook her head. She was beginning to have second thoughts. Trevor was a bachelor, after all. He might have simply unplugged his phone for privacy.

"When you get to the split in the driveway, take the right fork and drive all the way to the end. You can't miss it."

"Thanks a lot, Mr. Hendricks."

"My pleasure." He shoved his uniform cap to the back of his head. "If it hadn't been for you, I'd probably still be collecting unemployment instead of picking up a nice paycheck every Friday. This town owes you a lot."

Jillian felt a glow of pleasure that quickly faded as the memory of her conversation with Mel Cobb intruded. "I hope the town remembers that when we have the meeting on Horizons' future in two weeks."

Hendricks scowled. "I tried to tell Mel Cobb he was way off base, but he's like an old bulldog I once had. Once that mutt got his teeth into something, it took a hard rap on the head to make him let go."

Jillian laughed. "What happened to that dog?"

The guard scowled. "He turned plumb mean and chewed up my littlest girl pretty bad." His scowl deepened. "I shot him."

Jillian shuddered, then glanced at the brown gun belt encircling his thick belly. "Best keep your revolver at home if you attend the meeting."

"Yes, ma'am. I intend to. I'd hate to be tempted." His eyes twinkled for an instant before he saluted and stepped back inside the box.

The newly applied gravel crunched beneath the tires as she followed Ralph's directions. The road followed the fence line, and the metal links gleamed like chrome lace in the setting sun.

The guest house stood well away from the main compound and was built of the same redwood and glass as the other buildings. It had a sloped roof and large picture windows on the two sides she could see from the road. She couldn't see a door.

Trevor's convertible was parked about ten yards from the house under a towering sycamore, the top up and the windows closed. Jillian pulled in next to it and shut off the engine.

The silence was so complete that she could hear river frogs croaking at the bottom of the ravine. Above her a shaft of pale sunlight filtered through the trees to pattern the gravel like an expensive Persian carpet. Sighing, she grabbed her purse, left the truck and walked around the building.

The front of the bungalow had a redwood deck surrounded by a low railing. Trevor was sitting at a picnic table, dressed only in his black trunks, a cordless phone clamped between his ear and his bare shoulder. He was peering intently through a pair of tortoiseshell glasses at a set of blueprints spread out in front of him and writing on a legal tablet with his left hand.

Jillian faltered, then stopped, feeling like an intruder but unwilling to retreat now that she'd come so far. He was sure to finish soon, and then they could talk. It wouldn't take long to tell him about the theft and Jason's suspension, and then she would leave him to his work.

In the thick silence every word seemed amplified, and she couldn't help hearing. Trevor was asking questions in a brisk, no-nonsense tone that sent shivers up her spine, and it was obvious from the scowl on his face that he wasn't pleased with the answers.

"That's unacceptable, Nick. Five days ago you assured me you had this job under control. Now you tell me you have a problem with unexplained equipment breakdown. Either it's under control or it isn't. Which is it?"

He tossed his pen down in disgust and looked up at the trees, listening with half-closed eyes. He looked tired, and yet, Jillian decided with an odd little flurry in the pit of her stomach, powerfully sexy and very masculine.

"No, I have more important things to do here in Clayton, and I don't know when I can get away. You messed it up. Now you fix it." He riffled through a stack of papers in an open briefcase on the bench beside him. Raising a sheet of paper to the light, he quickly scanned it. "The penalty is two thousand a day American. I pay you top dollar to accept the responsibility for a mistake like this. If I'm forced to pay, it's coming out of your bonus." He listened for a moment longer. "You do that. Right. Goodbye."

He let the phone fall into his hand, then began punching out another number. He was lifting the phone to his ear when he suddenly looked up. "Jill."

He was clearly surprised to see her, but his face remained carefully impassive as he put the phone down and slowly stood. He leaned forward slightly, resting his hands on the papers in front of him, and regarded her with steady eyes.

Jillian felt the impact of his copper gaze immediately. The hard edge of surprise gave way to a guarded amber, and his lashes dipped quickly, then rose slowly, as though he were trying to take in all of her. The lazy once-over was definitely intimate and very unsettling.

"I tried to phone," she said as she skirted the deck and climbed the steps. His potent gaze followed every move. "It was busy."

Trevor looked oddly sheepish. "Now you know one of my darkest secrets. I'm a workaholic."

"At least that's a positive addiction." Her heels clattered against the rough planks as she walked toward him.

"Somehow I think that's a contradiction in terms, but I'm not about to argue with you. We've done enough of that." He rested his hands on his hips and tilted his head to one side, waiting.

Suddenly she didn't know where to begin. Three days of thinking about him in new and disturbing ways had left her oddly vulnerable. She didn't like the feeling.

"I thought engineers did most of their work in front of a computer terminal nowadays," she said, glancing toward the blueprints.

He shrugged. "That's only half of it," he said matter-of-factly. "The other half is making sure the construction supervisor brings the project in on time and within the budget. A week ago I was in Thailand."

The silver medal on his wide brown chest caught her gaze. "Is that where you got the medallion?" He was wearing the same medal he'd worn on Sunday. It gleamed with dull light against the sandy gray hair on which it rested.

The medallion was interesting in its uniqueness, but it was his body that intrigued her more. She wanted to touch him, to trace the tapering line of curly hair down the corded line of his belly. She curled her fingers into her palm and tried to concentrate on the silver chain.

Trevor glanced down at the heavy oval resting above his heart. It was thicker than most medals and was embossed in a bold masculine pattern that she liked.

"Actually, this was made by a guy in San Diego. There was a street fair in Balboa Park while I was in the hospital there, and I got to talking to this hippy who had antiwar slogans plastered all over his booth."

"Talking?" Jillian asked softly, noting the angry flash of his eyes.

His mouth slanted into a grim line. "I was still wearing braces on my legs, and he could tell right away I was a patient on furlough from the Navy hospital. Patients used to wander through the park a lot in those days."

He paused as though he were remembering, and Jillian could see the memory wasn't pleasant.

"Anyway, we got into this shouting match about the war—after I'd paid for this—" he slipped his hand under the medallion and lifted it toward her "—and a crowd gathered. Pretty soon everyone was shouting." His hand closed over the gleaming silver for an instant, as though to protect it.

"Who won?"

"No one ever wins an argument like that, but before I hobbled off he gave me the chain to go with the medal." He let the medallion fall back against his chest.

"Why did he do that?"

Trevor shrugged. "I suppose he felt sorry for me, or maybe he wanted me to know he didn't think I was personally responsible for the war he hated."

"Is that why you wear it?" she asked. "To remind you it wasn't your fault?"

"More to remind myself that I survived, and that I'd damn well better make the most of it."

"I . . . see."

The dense silence settled around them. Jillian began to feel foolish. She wasn't an impulsive person, but with Trevor she didn't seem capable of making rational decisions.

"I . . . am I interrupting anything important? I can come back—"

"My business can wait. What's wrong?"

The thread of subtle command in his voice jolted her from her train of thought. Didn't he ever relax? Did he always have to be in control?

She rubbed her arm with a nervous hand and darted a quick look behind him. The sliding door to the interior was partially open, and a classical guitar played softly somewhere inside. She hadn't noticed it before.

"I . . . are you alone?"

Trevor's brows arched. "Yes, I'm alone."

He'd been more or less alone for fifteen years, he thought with a cynical, imaginary shrug. None of the lovely and willing ladies he'd bedded over the years had touched him inside. Not the way Jillian had touched him. He'd just never let himself admit it—until now.

He glanced around, but he couldn't see her little red truck. "Is Jason with you?" he asked, trying to read the look in her eyes.

She shook her head. "Jason's the reason I drove out to see you, though."

Trevor hesitated, then removed his glasses and tossed them on top of the blueprints. "C'mon, let's go inside. I'll fix you some tea."

He slipped into a pair of Topsiders that had seen better days and grabbed a pale blue shirt that had been draped over the railing. He shrugged into the shirt and opened the door, stepping aside to let her precede him.

The interior was furnished simply with large, comfortable-looking furniture in restful shades of blue and rose. A thick cranberry rug covered the tiled floor. At one end of the living room was a freestanding metal fireplace, at the other a large picture window facing west, looking out over the deep ravine.

There was a small adjoining kitchen and breakfast area, and a hallway leading to what she took to be the bedroom and bath. In the corner by the dining area stood an acoustic guitar.

The music was coming from a large tape player on the coffee table. Trevor walked over and ejected the tape.

"Very nice," she said, smiling at him nervously.

He watched her wander around the cozy room, his curiosity increasing with every step she took. She was jittery, like a sleek red vixen scenting danger. Her small hands touched the furniture absently, as though her mind were on something else. But he'd learned patience over the years. He would give her all the time she needed.

"All the guest quarters look alike," he told her when she'd finished her inspection. "Once, visiting one of the units in the South, I forgot where I was, and I had to look at my pocket calendar to find out."

Jillian laughed. "Poor Trevor."

"Yeah, well, I manage." He crossed to the kitchen and opened one of the cupboards. "Looks like we have herbal and regular," he said, taking down two boxes of tea bags. "Your choice." He waited.

Jillian sat down on the sofa and tried to relax. "Actually, I'd . . . I'd rather have wine, if you have it."

Trevor tossed the boxes onto the counter. "Sorry, we don't allow any kind of alcohol on the grounds. How about hot chocolate instead? I can have someone bring it over from the cafeteria."

"No, nothing, thanks." She stared across the ravine to the horizon, where the first streaks of pink and orange were striping the low-lying clouds.

Trevor watched her in silence for several seconds. The light coming through the big window touched her skin with gold and set her hair aflame. God, how he wanted her, he thought. Right here, right now. On the table, on the floor. Anyplace.

He tried to ignore the sudden flare of heat in his groin, but it only grew hotter and more insistent. He fastened the two bottom buttons of his shirt, then walked over to one of the chairs placed at right angles to the sofa and sat down.

"So why don't you tell me what's wrong?"

His voice was surprisingly gentle, and for an instant Jillian was disoriented. The last time she'd been with Trevor he'd left in a towering rage. But here he was now, sitting calmly a few feet away, his hands open on his knees instead of clenched at his sides, the lines of his face relaxed instead of rigid with fury.

For the life of her she'd never be able to figure out what he was going to do next. Maybe that was why he made her so uneasy. She liked things organized and predictable.

She took a deep breath, feeling the oxygen expand her lungs. There was a slight breeze blowing through the open door, and the air felt cool against her face.

Say it, she told herself. Get it over with.

"Jason was caught taking twenty dollars from a gym locker this afternoon. There was a . . . witness." Her voice wavered, but her eyes were dry.

Trevor went completely still. "What does Jason say?" he asked carefully.

"He claims it was some kind of initiation ritual for this stupid club he belongs to." She felt her anger begin to build again. Swiftly, in short staccato sentences, she told him about the group of boys that met in Mike Cobb's garage. "I know it's Mike's fault," she concluded angrily. "Jason hasn't been himself since that kid came to town."

Trevor flattened his palms against his thighs and watched the indignation march into her green eyes. Her claws were sheathed now, but she was ready to fight.

"Jill, if Jason took the money," he said slowly, feeling his way carefully, "he's the one who's got to take the heat, not this Cobb kid or anyone else."

Jillian sighed impatiently. "But he's not really guilty! Not in any serious way, I mean."

Trevor raised one brow. "I don't understand. Did he take it or not?"

"Well, yes, but he was going to give it back." Stumbling over her words, she repeated what Jason had told her. "I can tell he's really sorry. I think he even cried himself to sleep."

Trevor ran a hand through hair that was already tousled. He knew exactly how guilty Jason felt, and it hurt to know that the boy he was beginning to care about was in torment. But that didn't change the fact that Jason had to accept the consequences of what he'd done. Trevor slid back against the cushions, bracing his back. He knew all about consequences.

"In the long run this may be a good thing for him, Jill. Getting suspended has to be humiliating, and it'll make him take school and a lot of other things in his life more seriously. There's nothing like being denied something to make you want it more."

Jillian heard the rough emotion in his voice, but she ignored it. He was wrong about Jason. Being humiliated this way was the worst possible thing for his fragile ego.

"I don't agree. All it will do is make Jason more rebellious. He's already talking about hating Clayton, and he's always loved living here."

She traced a random pattern on the rug with her toe. She felt awkward, sitting here fully dressed, while he wore only trunks and a half-buttoned shirt.

Trevor took a deep breath and leaned forward slightly, folding his hands between his knees. "Jill, Jason did wrong. Stealing is stealing, no matter what it's for, and he deserves to be punished for it." He hesitated, then added very gently, "Or he might do it again. Or try something worse."

Jillian's jaw dropped, and her blood pressure soared. "How *dare* you imply my son is some kind of...of criminal!" She stood up and began pacing the room, her arms flailing. "It's not as if he's anything like the boys here."

"But he could be."

"What! Are you calling my son a drug addict?" Jillian whirled around and faced him, her hands curled into fists, her cheeks hot.

Careful, Markus, he warned himself silently. Don't make her mad, or she'll never listen to you. Not that he'd ever been much good with words, but he had to try to make her understand.

"Of course not, Jill. I meant that major crimes can grow from little ones that go unpunished, or sometimes are even excused. It's easy to overlook a single incident, but I don't think that's wise."

"Wise?" she asked in a deceptively calm voice. There were all kinds of memories shooting around in her head. Things, *incidents*, in the past that she'd handled alone. She hadn't needed him then. She didn't need him now.

"Jill, don't look so upset, okay? I'm simply saying that you may be too close to Jason to see him clearly."

"Too close? Too *close*?"

The stress of the past few weeks was finally beginning to get to her, and something snapped inside. "Let me tell you about close, Trevor," she said in a chilled voice that vibrated with anger. "I was there night after night for four months when he had colic and screamed for hours on end in my arms. I was there through an endless series of ear infections when his fever spiked to a 103, and I had to sponge him constantly to keep him from going into convulsions. I was there when he cried all the way to kindergarten on the first day, and when Tiffany George broke his heart in the sixth grade, and I'm still there." She took a breath. "Where were you, Trevor?"

He made himself wait out the sharp swell of anger. He could tell her about the nights when *he'd* walked the floor, wanting her so much he'd had to keep his hands in his pockets to keep from reaching for the phone to beg for another chance. He could tell her about the Christmases he'd spent with a bottle of brandy and a lot of hurting memories. He could tell her a lot of things, but he wouldn't.

"You're right, Jillian. I wasn't there. But I'm trying my damnedest to be here for you now. And for Jason." His brows drew together in an accusing frown. "You're the one who keeps pushing me away."

"Then stop telling me I'm a rotten parent because Jason was caught stealing!" Her voice rose in a shrill crescendo, and her control crumpled. To her intense dismay, tears filled her eyes and cascaded down her cheeks.

"Damn," she muttered, looking around frantically for a tissue. She had to get out of here. Coming to see Trevor had been a mistake.

"Hold still." Trevor was suddenly beside her, his hand steady as he wiped away her tears with his fingers. "You're not a bad parent," he said in a rusty voice. "You're caring and dedicated and the best damn mother I've ever seen. When I found out about Jason, I wanted to get down on my knees to thank you for giving me such a great son."

Jillian blinked up at him, the tears still clinging to her long golden lashes in a sparkling row. Her lips trembled, and she gulped, trying to contain the sobs shaking her. "I just want him to be happy and safe," she whispered. "That's all I've ever wanted."

"I know." Trevor had trouble with his breathing. For too many years he'd told himself he would never have the right to touch her again, or comfort her or to love her. But at least now he could hold her and keep her safe for a few moments, if not a lifetime.

Very gently he pulled her into his arms. She stiffened, and he held his breath, desperately afraid she was going to pull away. If she did, he wasn't sure he could let her go. Not when his body was urging him to pull her even closer.

The moment passed, and she relaxed against him. His hand shook as he pressed her temple against his shoulder and rested his cheek on her silky head.

Suddenly Jillian was enfolded in warmth. His chest was solid, like the granite slopes surrounding the town, but wonderfully warm, as though the sun had heated the hard planes just for her.

She was confused and exhausted, but he held her against him, supporting her, comforting her. He was so strong. Nothing would happen to her while he held her.

"It's going to be okay, angel," he whispered. "We'll get through this together."

Jillian felt his chest rise and fall in a steady cadence. His bronzed skin smelled of soap, and radiated a masculine heat, sending tiny shivers of feminine awareness through her body.

A ray from the sinking sun caught the silver medallion, drawing her gaze. His wide chest was darker than it had been on Sunday, and gleamed like polished teak in the light. Involuntarily she licked her lips, and the muscles of his chest rippled.

"I can't seem to stop wanting you, Jill," he muttered against her hair. "Even when I knew I'd never see you again, I wanted you. The feel of you, the smell of you, you're inside me, and no matter what I do I can't get you out."

She held her breath as his fingers slid under her chin and raised her face to his. Her lips tingled as his gaze brushed them with molten heat. His eyes locked onto hers, pulling her deeply into those glowing depths. She'd never been able to resist, never been able to deny him anything when he looked at her so intently, as though he were trying to touch her soul.

"Kiss me, Jill," he whispered in ragged need, dropping his gaze to her lips. "Kiss me like you used to."

Jillian tried to resist, tried to tell herself she was a fool for even being here, but her body ignored the signal to stop. Trevor had taken control, and she was powerless to resist.

His lips were gentle as they took hers. A sweet warmth spread through her, and she allowed her body to mold against his. Tentatively, her fingers shaking, she ran her hands over the width of his shoulders, loving the power there, the strength.

Trevor shuddered as her hands touched the exposed skin at the back of his neck. His hands moved down her back, stroking, teasing, pressing her closer. The tips of his fingers slid over the rounded contours of her buttocks, and a wild, frantic yearning shook him to the marrow.

He hadn't expected to feel her against him again, not like this. He hadn't marshaled the defenses he needed to protect himself against the hold this woman had over him. He was helpless to restrain himself, powerless to hold himself away from her when she was responding to him with such fire.

This was Jillian, his woman, a part of him. Without her he felt truncated, a man alone. But with her he felt complete and . . . strong.

Trevor groaned, and Jillian smiled against his lips. Instantly his tongue traced the curving line, trailing warm moisture over her mouth. Parting her lips, she invited him closer, inhaling sharply as his tongue entered and began stroking hers. He tasted like good, strong coffee.

Her pleasure shifted, deepened, began to shake her. He caressed her lower lip with his tongue until she shivered, then began trailing moist, hot kisses along her jaw. When he reached the sensitive spot under her ear, she moaned and leaned against him.

Wrapping her arms around his broad torso, she explored the strong contours of his back, her fingers hesitating when they touched the faint indentation of his incision. Her fingertips stroked the hair-roughened hollow of his spine, then pushed past the low waistband of his trunks. Trevor inhaled swiftly, his chest scraping her breasts, and she could feel his hard arousal prodding her abdomen.

His kisses changed, becoming gentler, more persuasive, as though his fiery passion was too threatening, too abandoned, to maintain. He began to stroke her arms, slowly, yet with an arrogant intimacy, as though touching her were his right.

She pressed closer, loving the hard masculine feel of him against her breasts and belly and hips. Nothing had ever been better than this. Nothing.

A hot rush of raw need overpowered her, and she rose to her toes, taking him between her thighs. His arousal surged and throbbed, and Jillian squeezed hard, loving the feel of him. At this moment he was hers, this hard, strong, intensely masculine man with the stillness in his eyes.

She moaned softly, and she could feel him shudder. She felt his muscles bunch under her fingertips as though he were controlling himself. Tension flowed between them, static-charged and dangerous, heightening the savage need that drove her.

She hadn't been with a man in a long time, and never like this. Never with this feverish, primitive abandon. Her hands slid up his neck to tangle in his thick hair. It was silky but resilient and curled around her fingers as though drawn to her by some magnetic force.

"My God," he whispered against her lips as passion surged between them. "Stop me, Jill. Stop me now or I'll never stop." His voice was an agonized groan of sound, raspy and out of control.

"I can't. I want you, too."

He groaned and looked deep into her eyes. It was there again, that look of sweet, helpless need that used to fill him with such happiness. She wanted him.

Trevor led her into the bedroom slowly, not quite believing that the beautiful woman looking up at him with passion-softened eyes was real. Too many times, in his dreams, she'd drifted away before he could reach her.

Inside the small suite, the fiery glow from the setting sun turned the white walls to deepest gold and bathed the bed in warm light. The room was sun-warmed, and a faint breeze scented with pine and mountain sage came through the large open window and brushed his cheek as he slowly raised his hands to her shoulders and turned her toward him.

"Jill, I . . . don't want to make you pregnant again." His face was drawn, his gaze tortured.

Jillian felt a sweet warmth spread inside her. He was taking care of her. "It's okay. I . . . it's the wrong time."

"I want you so much," he whispered, his hand shaking as he reached for the top button of her blouse.

In the soft light her eyes held a beautiful glow that warmed all the lonely dark places inside him, and her tremulous smile filled him with the kind of tenderness he'd thought he would never feel again.

Jillian shivered as his hard fingers brushed against her breasts. She slid her hands up to his shoulders and pushed her way under his shirt. His skin was firm and smooth and so hot in places that it burned her fingertips.

Finished with the buttons, Trevor slid the silky shirt from her shoulders, and Jillian dropped her arms, letting the shirt fall to the floor.

Trevor's breathing grew louder and more labored as he stared at her. Beneath the lacy cup of her bra, her nipples were rosy and erect, and her breasts cast crescent shadows on the pale cream skin. He touched her gently, reverently, feeling tiny shivers spread under his fingers as he removed her bra.

"Beautiful," he whispered in a strangled voice as he dropped the scrap of lace and satin next to the shimmering shirt. "I thought I remembered..."

He dropped his head and kissed each breast in turn, his ragged breath moistening her skin with delicious warmth. She tangled her fingers in his thick hair, playing with the ends.

Her heart was pounding beneath the skin he was kissing, and her knees felt watery. He was so big, so masculine, so demanding. She felt small and delicate and loved.

She bent her head and planted a kiss in the clean-smelling silk of his hair, then pulled his head against her breast.

Groaning, he raised his head to give her a heated kiss, then wrapped his arms around her waist. Holding her tightly against him, he moved toward the bed. The edge of the mattress pressed against the backs of her knees, and she felt suddenly weak.

"Trevor," she whispered, "I—"

"Shh. Don't talk. Just feel."

His lips closed over hers, and Jillian shivered, feeling the powerful need in his kiss and in his body. She was overwhelmed, enveloped in raw emotion that shook her to her toes.

His lips were demanding, his tongue aggressive as it plundered the inside of her mouth. Helplessly, eagerly, her lips softened against his, inviting the arrogant intrusion. It was wonderful, it was terrifying, it was dangerous, but suddenly she craved the wild feeling of freedom he was exciting in her.

The years fell away, and she was once more twenty-one, in love for the first time in her life, and eager to taste all the exotic flavors of Trevor's passion.

She held on to his shoulders, her fingers digging into the tempered steel hardness. She was shivering, but inside she was hot, like a parched desert traveler desperate for water. "Yes," she whispered thickly. "Yes, yes, yes."

Trevor stiffened, and his arms were like thick, unyielding cables encircling her. "Oh, angel, I need you so much. I'll try to be gentle, but I don't know if I can."

Jillian pushed against his chest, and he released her. Her eyes never left his as she slid his shirt off his shoulders, smiling seductively as it joined the pile on the floor.

Trevor groaned and reached for the waistband of her slacks. Together they slid them down her legs to bunch around her feet. She kicked off her sandals and stepped clear.

In turn she helped him remove his trunks, her breathing shortened and labored, and in seconds they were both naked and lying together in the center of the bed.

Trevor's eyes rivaled the fiery sun outside the window as she leaned forward to kiss the hair-roughened skin surrounding one flat nipple. His hands clenched, and the muscles of his chest bulged as he let her work her way downward, using her tongue and her lips to excite him. When she got to the sensitive area around his navel, he stiffened and reached for her, rolling them over so that he was half lying, half leaning over her.

His hands tangled in her hair as he kissed her eyes, her nose, her lips. He moved lower, his hands caressing her breasts, her rib cage, her belly.

Jillian was inundated in a sea of sensation, feeling the need building with each kiss, each touch. Trevor was wrapping her in pleasure, his rough hands gentle and yet controlling, seeking the sensitive spots that made her moan, his eyes half closed against his own need, his hard face strained in the dying light.

Jillian writhed, helpless, her head tossing from side to side on the pillow. Trevor moved upward, his breathing raspy and nearly out of control. With a shaking hand he parted her thighs, caressing her, exploring her.

He shuddered as he slid inside her. She was warm and wet and ready for him. He was ready to explode, but he made himself rest quietly against her, letting the blood that throbbed hotly through him ebb slightly.

This was Jill, his special lady, the only woman he'd ever wanted for his wife. He wanted her like sweet hell, but he didn't want this to end. Too many of his dreams had ended with a sweat-drenched awakening that had left him feeling more empty than ever.

Jillian moaned softly and moved against him. She made a low, sultry sound deep in her throat, and his body responded instantly.

What little control he had disappeared instantly, and he drove into her, thrusting harder and harder, feeling the need build until it was exquisite torture, and still he held off. She wasn't with him. Not yet.

"I need you, angel," he urged hoarsely. "Stay with me."

Jillian whimpered as the scalding pleasure built inside her. She thrashed against his heavy thighs, trying to get closer, trying to release the tingling, searing pressure.

"Jill, baby, hurry." Trevor's voice was a tortured plea, and she arched upward, feeling the explosion burst inside her, lifting her higher and higher in wave after wave.

She clung to him, loving the power and the tenderness in him as he trapped his lower lip between his teeth and groaned out his release.

He rested his head next to hers on the pillow, his hand pressed over hers as it lay on the coverlet. She loved the heavy weight of his body and the musky scent of his sweat-dampened skin.

His breathing slowed gradually, and she smiled, stroking his thick, soft hair. Always before she'd had to make love to him. this time he'd made love to her.

His arms slid under her, and he rolled over to let her rest on top of him, their bodies still joined. She raised her head and looked into his eyes. His hard face was soft, relaxed, and there was a gentleness in his beautiful eyes that she'd never seen before.

"My sweet Lord, that was good," he said in a thick voice.

"Yes," she whispered, and smiled.

He traced the curve of her lips with his finger. "The next time it'll be better. I'm a little out of practice. It's been a long time for me."

His voice slurred, and his eyes closed. He tucked her head against his shoulder, and Jillian snuggled against him.

In a few minutes she would have to leave. In a few minutes she would have to return to the real world, where her problems with Jason and her own internal turmoil were waiting.

Her eyes drifted closed. Her body felt sated and buoyant, and her veins hummed with contentment.

Trevor's big chest rose and fell rhythmically, soothing her, and before she could find the strength for another rational thought, she was asleep.

Trevor came awake suddenly and knew he was in trouble. His back was one excruciating spasm. The muscles were locked in a rigid tension that wouldn't let go for hours, and it hurt so much that he felt an involuntary groan start in his throat.

He bit it back, but not before Jillian stirred against him. His arms tightened around her, and he buried his face in the fragrant tangle of her thick hair.

He couldn't let her leave him. Not yet. It was too soon. He needed to feel her against him, her head pillowed trustingly on his shoulder. He needed to pretend it would always be this way, for just a while longer.

It was dark outside, and the only illumination was the eerie blue glow from the security light outside the window. The room was still warm.

Jillian's leg slid against his, and she stretched. "What time is it?" Her question was muffled by his shoulder and ended in a yawn.

Trevor tried to look over her shoulder to see the clock radio, but the pain was relentless, leaving him nearly breathless. And the familiar sickness was spreading in his stomach. He was trapped, a prisoner of the mangled vertebrae that were punishing him for ignoring the warning twinges.

"I can't see the clock," he said in a taut voice. "You'll have to look."

Jillian raised her head, her eyes still cloudy with sleep. She looked at him questioningly, a half smile playing over her lips.

Trevor tried to return the smile, but it was a failure.

"What's wrong?" she asked instantly, sitting up.

The movement of the mattress sent a hot spur into his already straining muscles, and he gasped. He could feel the clammy sweat popping out on his forehead, and he grabbed the coverlet and held on.

"Spasm," he muttered between clenched teeth.

He hated to have her see him like this, helpless and impotent. He should be making love to her again, branding her with his body until she couldn't remember any man but him.

Instead, he couldn't even move enough to kiss her the way he suddenly wanted to.

"Does this happen often?" she asked softly, recognizing the look of dark frustration in his eyes.

"No."

He was lying.

Jillian bit her lip and glanced down at their naked bodies. Her skin was rosy where it had rested against Trevor's skin.

A flare of desire ignited deep inside her as she remembered the way he'd loved her, but she quickly quelled it. "I . . . we shouldn't have."

"Oh, yes, we should have," he shot back in a low, frustrated growl. "And damn it, we should again." He tried to touch her, but the pain defeated him, and he let his hand fall back against the mattress.

Jillian saw the ashen tinge spread along his jaw, saw the way he was breathing, short bursts that barely moved his chest, and she knew he was in agony. Becoming once more the efficient nurse, she shoved her tumbling feelings aside and began to dress. She fumbled slightly with the buttons in her haste, glancing over her shoulder to find Trevor watching her with turbulent eyes.

"It was more fun taking that off," he muttered, his voice thick with pain. He looked furious and rumpled and very sexy.

She smiled. "Behave yourself."

"Believe me, Jill," he said wryly, "at the moment I don't have a choice."

She chuckled. It sounded like old times, with her ordering him around and him making jokes to forget the pain.

As soon as she finished dressing she went into the bathroom, snapped on the light and opened the medicine cabinet. She found an assortment of male toiletries and a bottle of extra-strength aspirin, but no prescription pain pills.

"Trevor, where are your painkillers?" she asked from the doorway.

"Don't have any," he muttered, his eyes closed, his clenched fist pressed over his forehead.

"For heaven's sake," she retorted, knowing the kind of pain he was experiencing. "Why didn't you bring them with you?"

Trevor opened his eyes and glared at her. "They're only allowed in the infirmary."

"I'll call Hank—"

"Stop fussing and give me a kiss." He sounded angry and embarrassed.

"Lord save me from the male ego," she muttered as she returned to the bathroom. A minute later she returned with a bottle of hand lotion and a glass of water. In the pocket of her slacks she carried the aspirin.

She put the glass on the night table, and only then did she notice the folded heating pad. No doubt Trevor spent most nights with his back on that warm square.

A pang of guilt shot through her, but she forced herself to ignore it. It was almost ten. She had to get home soon in case Jason was awake and wondering what was keeping her.

But first she had to do what she could for Trevor.

"What's that?" he muttered, shifting his gaze to the bottle of lotion in her hand.

"It's hand lotion," she said with exaggerated patience. "I'm going to see if I can loosen some of those knots in your back."

"The hell you are!" he said loudly, trying to sit up.

His face drained of the little color that remained, and he fell back against the pillow. He muttered a rank obscenity and glared at her.

She shook out three aspirin and held them out to him. "Here, take these."

"What are they?" he asked again.

Jillian hung on to her temper with difficulty. Trevor was an impossible patient, but then he'd always been difficult. They'd had some royal battles when she'd been his nurse.

"These are aspirin, acetylsalicylic acid, commonly used to relieve pain," she said in a singsong that brought a bright spot of color to each of his pale cheeks.

"Very funny," he said with a growl, but he let her pop them into his mouth. She held his head while he drank, and he managed to get the aspirins down without gagging. "Thanks," he muttered, lying back.

"You're welcome. And now I'm going to help you turn over onto your stomach.

He exhaled very slowly. "Jillian, leave me alone, please. I feel like a jerk, lying here buck naked and totally helpless with a beautiful, sexy-as-hell woman in my bedroom. At least let me suffer the indignity in private."

His protest was choked off by a groan as she helped him ease to his side and then to his stomach. He lay shaking and gasping, his head buried in the snowy pillow, his hands clenched.

She uncapped the lotion and poured the creamy liquid into her palm, where she let it warm against her skin. Trevor gasped as she touched him, and she stopped. "Does that hurt?"

"Yes," he mumbled against the pillow, "but not the way you think."

She smiled and began massaging his shoulders. She worked slowly and methodically, using her thumbs and the heels of her palms to release the tension bunching his muscles.

He had a wide back, with clearly defined muscles and smooth, tanned skin. She could feel the power in those muscles as she worked, moving lower and lower until she reached the small of his back, where most of the damage had been done. Two long surgical scars, one on each side of his spinal column, reminded her of the precarious balance of those crushed and splintered disks.

He was lucky he could move at all.

Trevor groaned as he felt the pain slowly ease. Her hands were warm and magical. She was touching him skillfully, with the deftness of a professional.

In his dreams she'd touched him with love, with passion, and he wanted that now. He set his jaw, trying not to imagine what it would be like to have those long, slender fingers stroking him, petting him, caressing his body in the same way he'd caressed hers.

Raw hunger shuddered through him in spite of the spiking pain, and he wanted to pull her down beside him and bury himself so deeply inside her that she would never get away from him.

Lousy rotten back, he thought, rubbing his cheek against the pillow. It carried the same flowery scent as Jillian's hair, and he inhaled slowly, loving the sensual memory that shivered through him. Between his thighs his body stirred, but it was hopeless. He couldn't even move without feeling as though he were going to pass out.

Trevor was drowsy and mumbling into his pillow by the time Jillian felt the last of the spasms give way. She'd given him temporary relief, but as soon as he exerted himself at all, the spasms would return.

She turned on the heating pad and laid it next to him. "Help me, Trevor," she whispered, and he obediently let her roll him over onto the warm pad.

He looked exhausted, and his face was still very pale. He lay motionless, his eyes closed, his hands flung out to the sides. Jillian bit her lip as she gazed down at him.

He looked so much like the young flyer she'd loved so desperately. And yet he wasn't. And she was no longer that young nurse.

They'd just made glorious love, but that was transitory. What happens now? was the question she didn't want to ask.

Sighing, she looked around for the closet. On the top shelf, she found a folded wool blanket.

Trevor didn't stir as she unfolded it and spread it over his lean, very masculine body. He was still partially aroused, and an answering moistness warmed the spot between her legs. She would remember this night for a long time.

His breathing settled into a harsh rhythm, and his brow furrowed, but at least he was sleeping. For now, anyway. She hesitated, then decided to leave the light in the bathroom burning.

She moved closer to the bed, tears suddenly welling in her eyes. Carefully, so she wouldn't jar the mattress, she leaned over and kissed him gently on the lips.

His lashes fluttered, and a drowsy smile passed over his hard mouth. He turned his head toward her, as though seeking her warmth, but he didn't open his eyes. "Angel," he mumbled, his voice soft.

Clamping her lip between her teeth, she hurried from the room and closed the door firmly behind her.

Dawn was slipping down the steep slope of the mountain outside her window when Jillian woke up on Thursday morning. Her cheeks were wet, and her heart was pounding. Her body was tangled in the sheets, and her skin was so sensitive that it hurt to move.

The dream had been so vivid, so real. Trevor's eyes had glowed as he'd slid his body over hers.

She moaned and buried her face in the pillow, but the heat flooding her skin only increased. Her body was alive and yearning, eager for the release the dream had promised.

She writhed helplessly, trying to ease the heat stirring inside her. But the friction of the sheet against her breasts only increased the ache, and she turned onto her back.

In her dream she'd felt him, hot and hard against her, and his arms had been so strong. "I love you, angel," he'd whispered. "I love you."

As she fought the memory, her nipples hardened and pushed against the thin cotton of her short gown. "Oh, no," she whispered into the silence, crossing her arms over her chest as the remnants of the dream disappeared in the early-morning light.

She'd made a bad mistake.

Caught in the throes of a passion that had overwhelmed them both, she'd forgotten something very important. In the terse words of apology and regret he'd spoke to her, Trevor had never mentioned love.

The dream she'd just had was a mirror, showing her the way it should have been. He should have said the words. The instant before his body had thrust into hers had been the perfect opportunity, the moment when a man in love wants his woman to know what's in his heart as he makes them one.

But Trevor had said nothing.

Jillian ran her finger over her slightly swollen lower lip. Her body was sore, muscles that she hadn't used in a long time aching in a very special way. But the ache in her heart was worse. She loved him, and she couldn't have him, not in the way she needed him. She needed to come first in his heart, and that would never be.

He'd come back because of Jason, not her. She was simply Jason's mother, a woman who'd once loved him. He still wanted her. Maybe he even loved her a little, in a nostalgic, grateful way, but the powerful mystical feeling that made a man and a woman one heart was missing.

No, Trevor didn't love her, and she couldn't risk loving him.

She would offer him the friendship he'd asked her for, but that was all. For her own sanity she had to rebuild the barriers that had protected her so well for so long.

Jillian stared through the window at the new day. *One day at a time,* she thought. That was the motto she'd seen in Horizons' literature and on a small ceramic plaque in Trevor's bathroom, and that was the way she would manage to live without him.

She sighed and threw off the sheet. She still had Jason. At least he needed her.

* * *

Trevor slowly turned his head and looked at the clock. He'd slept until nearly midnight, then spent the rest of the night alternately cursing his back and missing Jillian.

He still couldn't believe she'd let him make love to her. And yet the bottle of lotion was still on the night table, and his clothes were still in a pile on the floor.

Hank, when he'd come by at six for a cup of coffee, had raised a speculative brow but said very little. He'd been more concerned with helping Trevor to the bathroom and making sure he didn't pass out while he was brushing his teeth.

Trevor ran a hand down his stubbled jaw. He needed a shave and a shower, but just raising his hand sent a searing pain down his spine and into his hips.

Muttering a few choice words he'd learned from a master chief on the *Ranger*, he struggled to reach the phone which Hank had retrieved from the deck and placed on the night table. Lying flat, he started to punch out Jillian's number, then cursed again as he realized she would be at work. He got the number of the pharmacy from information.

She answered on the fourth ring, and his heart began to pound. Just hearing her low, vibrant voice made him ache to feel her against him again.

"How could you just walk out like that on a man in pain?" he asked accusingly, feeling himself smile. They'd made a start on a new relationship, and in spite of the pain in his back, he felt terrific.

He heard her breath catch in her throat, and his smile grew. He hoped she was remembering the way their love-making had begun, not the way it had ended.

"You told me to go," she said, her voice sounding slightly breathless.

"I didn't mean it."

"Yes, you did. You're a rotten patient."

Trevor chuckled and glanced down at his nude body. Just talking with her on the phone was arousing him. "If I promise to be good, will you come and see me?" He closed his eyes and thought about her touching him again. Her fingers were supple and strong and very soothing. He wanted to feel them against his skin.

"No way." She was laughing, but there was an odd note in her voice that he didn't like.

"Jill, is something wrong?"

There was a brief silence. "I was going to call you in a few minutes. There's been another drug theft."

Trevor muttered a harsh expletive before he could stop himself. "At your place?" he asked curtly.

"No, at Addie's office. She called me about half an hour ago, and I've been on the phone with Mel for the past twenty minutes. Her receptionist walked into a mess when she opened up at nine."

"Anyone hurt?" Trevor asked quickly.

"No, it happened sometime in the night. Addie keeps her narcotics in a small safe, so all the thieves got were some syringes and a small amount of petty cash. But from what she told me, they pretty much wrecked the office."

Trevor closed his eyes. "And Cobb? I suppose he's claiming one of our guys did this, too?"

"Of course. I'm surprised he hasn't been out there by now."

"He might have been. I'm still in bed."

He sighed and rubbed his forehead. There was no way he could stay in bed now, but he wasn't sure how he was going to manage.

"Trevor, I'm sorry, but all of this has to come out in the council meeting. I hope you and Hank can make a good case for Horizons, because I've already had some calls. A lot of people are worried."

"Yeah, well, I'm pretty worried myself. I don't want to close this unit, Jill. If I do, these boys will have to go back into custody, and that would be a damn shame."

He ground his teeth at the thought. In the short time he'd been here, he'd come to know a lot of the residents fairly well. They were a tough bunch of guys, and most of them were trying hard to change.

"I...never thought of that," she said.

Trevor could almost see the compassion flood her eyes. She was the warmest, most caring woman he'd ever met. And she'd let him make love to her. He started to smile again. Damn, he felt good.

"Uh, Trevor, there's something else I want to talk with you about."

"What's that, angel?"

There was a sudden silence.

"Jill?"

"Uh, about last night—"

"Last night was hell on wheels," he said quickly. "I'm still high."

"That's just it. It never should have happened."

"The hell it shouldn't have! It should have happened sooner, on Sunday. It was what we both wanted. What we both still want."

"No. It can't happen again, Trevor. Ever. We made a mistake—"

"Not me, Jill. That was no mistake." Trevor's hand gripped the phone so tightly the plastic creaked.

"Then I made a mistake. Either way, it's not going to be repeated. You wanted friendship, you said, not an affair. And I think we'd better leave it at that."

Her voice sounded strained, but firm, and Trevor closed his eyes. The nausea had returned, and he was sweating again.

"It sounds as though you've made up your mind." His voice carried a bitter edge. "Thanks for the good time, and here's your hat. Is that about it?"

Jillian ushered a harsh denial. "Stop thinking about yourself and think about Jason for a change! The gossip about us has already started. How do you think he's going to feel if he finds out we've been . . . been—''

"Making love?" He held his breath. What was she trying to tell him?

"No, that's not what it was, and you know it. That's why it has to stop." He heard the sound of a ragged breath. "This won't affect your relationship with Jason," she added with formal courtesy. "You can see him any time you want."

She hung up.

Trevor stared at the phone in his hand for a heartbeat and then, with a vicious curse, threw it against the wall.

Chapter 10

"This can't be right," Jillian muttered, staring at the three columns of figures on the ledger in front of her.

One represented the quantity of Class Two narcotics on her shelves, while the second showed the amount purchased since the last inventory. The third was a compilation of the prescriptions she'd filled for those stringently regulated drugs. According to the numbers, she had a big discrepancy, much more than the five percent variance allowed by the state. But that had to be wrong. In ten years she'd never been off more than a percentage point or two.

"I'll just have to do it over," she said in a disgusted voice, throwing down her pencil and rubbing her eyes.

It was Saturday, and she'd left her office in the town hall early in order to work on the inventory that had to be filed with the State Board of Pharmacy in two months. But for some reason she was having trouble concentrating.

She pushed aside the pile of prescription carbons and rested her chin in her hand, trying to summon the energy to start over. She was uncommonly tired, and she'd been on edge for days, since the night when she and Trevor had made love, she admitted grimly. The heat Trevor had kindled inside her was still there, and nothing she'd done had been able to douse it.

Yesterday, after she'd closed the store, she'd ridden her bicycle for miles along the twisting back roads, but the ache had only grown worse.

And the cold shower she'd taken when she'd returned home from her ride had cooled her skin but not her desire. Or her love.

An abrupt knock on the door to her tiny office interrupted her thoughts, and she glanced up to see Darcy Hammond peering around the doorframe, a look of anticipation on her round pixie face.

"Jillian, there's someone here to see you."

"Tell me it's not another salesman," Jillian said in a weary voice. "I'm not in the mood."

Darcy's eyes twinkled, and she lowered her voice into a sultry imitation of Mae West. "I think you'll be in the mood for this guy, honey. I certainly am, and I'm a happily married woman."

Jillian laughed, and some of the lines in her brow smoothed. "Did this paragon give a name?"

"Yup. In a very sexy baritone, I might add. Said his name was Trevor Markus."

Jillian stood up so fast that her chair rolled backward and hit the wall with a loud crack. "Uh, thanks, Darcy. I'll be right there."

"Don't take too long." Darcy's ruddy complexion grew even rosier. "That's one gorgeous man. And he has a sweet smile, too."

Sweet? Trevor? Darcy must need glasses. The man was arrogant and demanding and totally selfish, but he wasn't the least bit sweet.

Jillian watched Darcy leave, then exhaled slowly as she counted to ten, but she could still feel her heart pounding a painful tattoo in her chest. Trevor was probably here to see

Jason, she decided after a moment's thought, but Jason had gone to the athletic field behind the high school to cheer for his old soccer team against a local rival.

No problem, she told herself with forced confidence as she tucked her short-sleeved turquoise shirt into the tight waistband of her gray slacks. She would give Trevor directions, and he could talk with Jason there. Her sneakers made little sound on the worn floor as she left the cubicle and headed down the center aisle. Trevor didn't hear her approach.

He was standing in front of the magazine rack by the front window, paging through the latest issue of a business weekly. He was wearing faded jeans and a red polo shirt, through which she could see the rigid contours of a back brace. His glasses were firmly settled on his straight, autocratic nose, and his hair had been carefully brushed, though it still curled slightly at the muscular nape of his neck. He needed a haircut.

"Jason isn't here," she said as she reached his side. His musky after-shave tantalized her nostrils, making her recall instantly the time they'd spent in his bed.

Trevor looked up from the page. "I know. I called earlier, and he said he was going to a soccer game. I came to see you."

He closed the magazine and carefully replaced it in the rack. Light from the front window tangled in his hair and splashed over his shoulders, making them look broader than ever.

"Me?"

Jillian tried not to notice the way his slow, lopsided grin erased years from his face, or the way her pulse was suddenly racing out of control, but she failed.

"Since it was Saturday, I looked for you in the town hall, Madam Mayor, but the place was locked up tight, so I came here."

"Very clever." She let a trace of sarcasm filter through her words.

Trevor's grin widened, creasing his cheeks with devilish amusement. "Hey, I'm not just a pretty face, you know. I occasionally have an intelligent thought."

"Humph." Jillian frowned. He was teasing her, and she wasn't sure she liked the warm glow of pleasure that was slowly spreading inside her.

She'd expected him to be angry with her. Or at least distant. After all, she'd told the man to get lost less than twenty-four hours after giving him her body, and a normal man would be nursing a very bruised ego.

But Trevor wasn't a normal man.

The trouble was, she had no idea what kind of man he was. She just knew he didn't love her.

"I'm busy, Trevor," she said, striving to maintain a cool distance. "What do you want?"

There was an instant connection, and Jillian knew he was remembering their lovemaking, just as she was. But his gaze never wavered. The man was more controlled than anyone she'd ever known.

But then his heart wasn't involved, she realized suddenly. He'd made love to her because he'd wanted her body, not her love. She'd been the one who wanted more. The emptiness inside her yawned wider.

"I came to ask your permission to take Jason on a river rafting trip," he said.

"With you?" she asked more sharply than she intended.

Stay calm, she told herself. He wasn't suggesting a lengthy trip to Seattle, or anything remotely like that. Or was he?

"With me and a group of boys from Horizons. Every three weeks the counselors take ten guys on some kind of outing. This time it's a trip down the Donner River by raft. Since Jason's out of school anyway, I thought it might be a good idea for him to have something to do besides brood." He hooked his thumbs through the loops of his jeans and regarded her gravely.

"Are you crazy, Trevor? You can't raft down the river with your back the way it is!" Her words brought an immediate flush to his stubborn jaw.

"It's a nice, easy trip, very little white water, or so they tell me," he said curtly.

"I'll bet."

Frustration flared in his eyes, and he frowned. "You're not my nurse now, Jill, so back off. I don't want your pity."

No, she thought dejectedly, and he didn't want her love, either. Only her body.

"Okay, okay. Be stubborn and suffer," she said, using sarcasm to cover the hurt that coursed through her.

His lips tightened, but he seemed determined to avoid an argument. "What about it, Jill? When we were at the lake the other day, Jason told me he likes camping, and this sounded like the perfect opportunity."

Jillian considered it. On the surface it sounded like a good plan—if she could get Jason to go.

His moods had been volatile since his suspension, swinging from insolence to indifference, and she'd given up trying to figure out what he was really thinking. Or feeling. She only knew he was hurting, and for the first time since he'd been born, she hadn't been able to help.

"When are you leaving?" she asked cautiously.

"Six a.m. tomorrow. The trip starts upstream, near Truckee, I think Hank said, and ends twenty miles below Clayton. It should take about two and half days to get to Clayton, and I thought we'd end our part of the trip at that point. That should be sometime Tuesday."

The thin, dark rims of his glasses gave him a studious look, but she knew that was deceptive. Trevor was a man of action. And determination.

"He might not want to go with you," she warned. "He's still very uptight about the suspension."

Trevor's face tightened. "Maybe you don't want him to go with me," he said in a low, taut voice. "Is that it, Jill? Are you afraid to trust me?"

"No, of course I'm not afraid." But I am, she thought suddenly. But not of Trevor. Of herself, and the feelings he was exciting in her.

He didn't look convinced. "So you'll come?"

Jillian blinked. "Me? You said Jason."

"He'll never go with me unless you're along. You heard how he feels about the guys at Horizons. A bunch of losers, I think he called us."

His voice deepened slightly, as though it hurt to say the words, and the subtle change touched something deep and caring inside her.

"He wasn't talking about you, Trevor," she said softly, impulsively laying a hand on his arm. At her touch, his brows jerked together as though he'd felt a sudden spasm of pain, and his arm stiffened.

Instantly she removed her hand, regretting the spontaneous gesture. Now that she'd told him she didn't intend to make love to him again, he didn't even want her to touch him.

"About the trip," she said with a smile that felt stiff on her lips. "If you can convince Jason to go with you, I think it would be a good idea."

At least it would keep him away from Mike Cobb for a few more days, she thought, and more importantly, it would give Trevor another chance to bond with his son.

"Once he knows you're going, he won't have a choice."

"But I'm not going," she said flatly, trying to remain calm in spite of the adrenaline flooding her system. "I'm not on vacation like you are."

She couldn't spend three days with Trevor in a small rubber raft. Just being in the same town with him was difficult enough.

Trevor glanced around the store until he spotted Darcy behind the soda fountain washing glasses. "Your assistant minds the store on Sunday, right?" There was the barest suggestion of masculine amusement in the crooked slant of his mouth.

Reluctantly Jillian nodded her head. "Yes, but—"

"Surely she could take your place for two more days."

Trevor wanted to kiss her long and hard until she had no breath left to say no, but he didn't dare touch her. He'd vowed to back off until she invited him closer again. But it was hard, especially when she looked so cute, with a smudge of ink on the small, rounded chin she was lifting so defiantly. Now that she'd given him her body, he wasn't going to give up until he had all of her.

"No, you need time alone with Jason," she said after a moment's hesitation. "I'd only be in the way."

Trevor prayed for patience and the right words. For two days he'd tried to figure out a way to start over with her, and this was the best thing he'd come up with. He took a deep breath that turned into a half gasp as pain knifed through his back. The brace helped, but his muscles were still stiff and tender, and would be for a few days more.

He saw sympathy soften her eyes, and he ground his teeth. "Jill, I need you to come. Being a dad feels... awkward to me right now, and I'm liable to make a real mess of things if you're not there to keep me on track. I... accept the fact that you don't want me for a lover, but I really do need your help as... as a friend. And as Jason's mom."

She was silent for so long that he was sure he'd lost. Her eyes were focused on some inner vision, and her lips were pursed into a frown that heated his blood almost as much as it worried him.

He glanced up at the ceiling where an old-fashioned fan was slowly stirring the air, and Jillian watched him from the corner of her eye. Deep down she knew he was right. He'd made a start on a relationship with Jason, but it was very tenuous. And Jason was particularly vulnerable at the moment.

Even if she managed to convince him to go, the trip would more than likely turn into a disaster. Jason was still convinced his father disliked him, in spite of all the talking she'd done to the contrary, and Trevor was more used to handling adolescents with serious problems than a normal boy like Jase.

"I'll come," she said, meeting his hooded gaze. "If Darcy can take over for me." Jason needed her, and so did Trevor, and at the moment she couldn't deny either of them.

Trevor had to clear his throat twice before he trusted himself to speak. "That's great. It'll be fun. There's a great bunch of guys going, and Hank will be there. You like Hank, don't you?" He wanted her to like his friend, but not too much.

"Yes, I like him." A sudden thought occurred to her, and she frowned. "Will I be the only woman?"

Trevor looked startled. "Uh, I don't know." His brows slid together. "This facility has several women counselors, but I don't know who's planning to make the trip. Is it important?"

Jillian didn't want to sound like some neurotic teenager, but the thought of being the only woman with all those men was strangely intimidating. Or maybe it was just the thought of being so close to Trevor for so long that was making her stomach flutter.

"I was just thinking about . . . about sleeping arrangements." She gave him a frank look. "I assume we're sleeping in tents."

Trevor didn't smile, but the hollows in his cheeks deepened slightly as though he wanted to. "Yes. If there aren't any other women going, you can have a tent all to yourself. I'll see to it personally."

"Fine." She rubbed her palms against her hips, but her skin was still unusually damp.

"If you don't have sleeping bags, we have extras." His voice was suddenly rusty and deep.

"Uh, we have bags."

"Good." Trevor's jaw clenched, and his lashes lowered until they rested for an instant on his cheeks. Slowly he opened his eyes and smiled briefly. "I, uh, better let you get back to work." His voice roughened slightly. "I'll pick you and Jason up at five-thirty tomorrow morning."

"Okay."

He didn't touch her, but suddenly Jillian felt as though he'd pulled her close and kissed her. Under the crisp twill of her slacks, her thighs tingled as though his hand slid against them, and beneath the lace of her bra and the soft knit of her shirt her nipples swelled into hard little buds, as though waiting for his lips to ease the hot ache.

Neither of them spoke as he took another step backward, then turned and walked away from her, his steps unnaturally shortened. At the door he turned and waved. His grin was so full of sensual promise that she began to shake inside.

"Dear God," she whispered into the store that suddenly felt much too hot after he'd walked out. "What have I done?"

The sunset was beautiful. Jillian had never seen such fiery streaks in the sky, and the air was like a warm hand against her skin.

Beyond the gently sloping bank where she sat on a large granite boulder, the river was a smooth golden ribbon, edged by lacy ripples that lapped in a soothing rhythm against the smooth pebbles bordering the wheat-colored grass.

She leaned back and raised her knees, linking her arms around her shins. Arching her neck, she let the slight breeze brush her thick hair away from her face. She'd just polished off a huge helping of steak and beans, and since the cleanup crew had refused her offer of help, she was trying to stay out of the way.

It had been a long day, and she was tired and tense. The current in the Donner had been strong enough to propel the six yellow rafts at a steady pace, but not fast enough to be dangerous. After the first hour she'd stopped worrying about Trevor's back and started worrying about her peace of mind.

The raft was large enough to accommodate three in relative comfort, but far too small for Trevor to fully stretch his long legs. Seated next to him, she'd been acutely aware of the hard brown thigh that now and then brushed hers whenever he moved. Under her life preserver her skin had tingled whenever his shoulder had bumped hers. By the time they'd stopped for the night she was wrung out, and so aware of Trevor that she found it hard to think of anything else.

"Having fun?" a deep voice close by drawled.

Jillian gasped in surprise, then grinned as Hank sank down on the rock next to her and extended his long, jean-clad legs in front of him. "You scared me half to death," she said, waiting for her heartbeat to return to normal.

"Sorry, I thought you heard me coming." He clicked the hard soles of his boots together, and Jillian giggled.

"Do you wear those to bed?" she asked with a shake of her head.

He gave her a sideways look. "Naw, not anymore. I've been around you Northerners so long I've gotten soft."

Jillian sneaked a look at his rangy, muscular body and decided there wasn't anything soft about him, unless it was his heart. "After this trip, I think I'll know just how soft I am," she said with frown.

"Problems?" he asked.

She glanced toward the shadowed spot where Jason sat alone, his back against a rock, earphones clamped over his head. He'd flatly refused to go on the trip, and she'd been forced to threaten him with the loss of his beloved stereo for a month in order to get him to change his mind.

"I was hoping this trip would bring Jason and Trevor closer together, but Jason just sits there, listening to his music. He barely spoke all day. I'm about ready to toss him overboard."

She dropped her gaze to her hands, which were pressed together tightly in her lap. Slowly she flexed her fingers, relieving the tension.

"Trev will handle him," Hank said in a surprisingly serious tone, watching her. "He knows how to be patient."

"He wasn't very patient with that boy who kept insisting he wasn't an addict."

Jillian thought about the group meeting that had been held before dinner. The boys had talked about their day and the things they were grateful for. Most were grateful because they weren't in prison, or because they were learning to handle the cravings inside them. But one short Hispanic boy refused to admit he was grateful for anything or anybody. Trevor ordered him to go off by himself and chop enough wood to last the night. "And while you're chopping, Carlos," Trevor had told him, "think about the things you've done that landed you here with us."

"Trev doesn't compromise, that's for sure," Hank said in a neutral tone. "The guys know he's hard-nosed, but they also know he's on their side. He's on Jason's side, too."

She drew her brows together. "Sometimes I wonder. He's been pretty tough on him."

Hank's wide shoulders hunched slightly. "That's the only way Trev knows how to be." He inhaled slowly. "He's one of the good guys, Jillian, one of the best I've ever known," he said quietly, but with a depth of feeling she couldn't question.

She bent down to pick up a twig and began to peel back the bark, strip by strip. "Hank, that first day when we met, I had the strangest feeling that you...knew me." She looked up quickly, catching surprise in his gray eyes. "You know about Trevor and me, don't you?"

Admiration darkened his eyes. "I met Trevor about three months after he'd...returned from Hawaii. It nearly killed him to leave you, Jillian. I think you should know that."

Jillian looked down at the crooked stick in her hand. "How much did he tell you?"

Hank's hand closed over hers, and he squeezed gently. She could feel the strength in his long fingers.

"He told me everything, and he wasn't very kind to himself in the telling. It wasn't a pretty story, and I have a good idea how badly he hurt you." He hesitated. "He was raw for a long time."

"I hated him," she said evenly, feeling the hard knot of anger form again inside her. But this time it melted away as quickly as it had come.

"He's come a long way since then, Jillian, a very long way. Maybe, someday, you'll know just how far." There was kindness in his eyes and a hard kernel of intelligence. But most of all there was a challenge.

She looked down at their joined hands. She wanted to ask him about Trevor's personal life, about the lovers he must have had over the years, but she didn't know how.

"Hey, you two. What's going on here?"

Jillian looked up to find Trevor standing a few feet away, holding two plastic cups of cider. He was wearing faded khaki shorts and a white T-shirt bearing the logo of the Seattle Seahawks. He was still wearing the brace that restricted his movements.

She returned his smile and took one of the drinks. Taking a sip she licked her lips. The cider was pleasantly warm and very tart.

Hank looked up and grinned. "Go away, Markus. The lady likes me."

"The hell she does." Trevor's voice was teasing, but there was a hard warning in the look he sent Hank.

Hank turned to her and winked. "Sorry, darlin'. The man pays my salary." He leaned over to kiss her cheek, then stood up.

"You're not overdoing it, are you, buddy?" he asked Trevor, his eyes narrowing. "I'd hate to have to carry you out of here if your back seizes up again."

Trevor scowled. "If you don't keep your hands off the mother of my son, you'll be the one who gets carried out of here."

The two men grinned at each other like bickering little boys, and Jillian couldn't help laughing. It was obvious there was a deep affection between the two. Hank punched Trevor lightly on the shoulder, then ambled off.

"What was that all about?" she asked Trevor, looking up at him.

"That?" He walked over and sat down. Unlike Hank, he sat stiffly, his knees flexed to take the strain off his back.

"That look you gave Hank. What were you asking him?"

Trevor shot her a quick glance. "You're dangerous, lady. I'm going to have to watch myself around you, or I won't have any secrets left."

His tone was light, even flirtatious, but there was something in the set of his jaw and the look in his eyes that was suddenly very unsettling. A pang of fear shot through her, and her heart began to pound. "Do you have secrets, Trevor?" she asked bluntly, her gaze fastened on his rugged profile.

He didn't move, but Trevor could feel him withdraw from her. Silently, unable to stop himself, she searched the hard planes of his face for a clue. But the stillness was in his eyes again, and his tanned face was wiped clean of all expression.

There was a part of Trevor that was closed off from her. It was as though, whenever she came too close, he withdrew to a place inside where she wasn't welcome to follow.

"Yes, I have secrets, just like everyone else. Only mine aren't very interesting." He took a sip of cider. "What about you? What were you and Hank talking about?"

"Not much. Mostly the day."

Jillian glanced toward the clearing beyond the tents where the boys who weren't cleaning up were playing a very rough game of touch football. "They're nice boys once you get to know them," she said, sighing. "I wish Jason would let himself like them."

Trevor glanced toward their son. Jason's eyes were shut, closing out the rest of the group. "I wish he'd let himself like *me*," Trevor said in a taut voice. "I must be losing my touch. My nephews like me a lot."

His grin flashed and then faded, but not before Jillian had a glimpse of the sensitive man she'd known in Tokyo. He was hurt because his son was pushing him away, and there was nothing she could do to help.

"He's never handled change very well. He just needs time."

"Has he always been so moody?" His thigh was only inches from hers, and she edged sideways, giving him more room.

"He's always been quiet," she said slowly, "but the intense highs and lows started just about the time he turned fourteen."

She frowned as she thought back over the past eight months. She'd had more trouble with him in that short span of time than in any other period of his life.

Trevor chuckled. "Mary Rose, my sister-in-law, says that adolescence is like an endless electrical storm, with lots of thunder and wind."

Jillian laughed. "That's perfect. She sounds like the mother of boys." She took another quick sip and tried not to notice the way his thigh muscles bulged as he leaned forward slightly.

"She's anxious to meet you and Jason," he said quietly. "Everyone is. My dad actually passed out cigars at the yacht club when he found out about his newest grandson, and my mom is already planning the first meal she's going to serve him."

Jillian felt a sadness deep inside. Trevor's parents sounded like nice people. Jason would like them.

"Maybe someday," she said noncommittally, studying the last inch of cider in the plastic cup. She would never meet

Trevor's family. It would be too hard to be the outsider, the one who would always be a guest, invited because of her son.

Trevor watched the distant look return to her eyes, and he felt like smashing his fist into the rock beneath him. Whatever he'd said to her had been wrong. Maybe it would always be wrong.

"Mr. Markus?" called a voice from across the campsite. "The fire's all made."

Trevor looked up quickly to see one of the older boys standing by the flickering fire, holding his guitar. A ragged chorus of encouragement rose from the group, and Trevor groaned in silent frustration. How could he spend time with Jillian when he was surrounded by ten raucous teenagers?

"Your public calls," Jillian murmured, a look of frank curiosity displacing the wary look he hated.

"Yeah, but it's what they're gonna call me after I play that has me worried."

Jillian laughed at the look of mock terror on his face. These boys treated Trevor with obvious respect, bordering on affection, suggesting that in many ways he was acting as a surrogate father to them.

"You'll do fine," she said with a catch in her voice.

Trevor squeezed her hand. "Save my place," he said in a husky voice as he pushed himself to his feet.

As he walked over to the circle, Trevor felt his face grow warm and his stomach tighten. He liked to play, but as he took the guitar from the boy and sat down on an upended storage box, he was suddenly nervous, knowing that Jillian would be listening.

"Okay, guys. What do you want to hear first?" He strummed a chord, adjusting one of the pegs until the guitar was in tune.

Listening to the shouts and the good-natured banter as Trevor and the boys settled on a song, Jillian found herself watching him. In the glow of the fire the lines and shadows of his face were softened, and he looked like the sexy lighthearted youth he must once have been. Like Jason would someday be.

Slipping off the rock, she went over to sit next to her son. She touched his arm, and he jerked upright, his eyes wide with shock. Smiling, she removed his earphones and pointed toward Trevor.

Jason scowled, but he turned off the tape player clipped to his belt and watched his father with sullen eyes. Jillian wanted to shake him, but she restrained herself. She had to give him time to adjust.

Trevor was good. He took every request and did his best with it. Even when he didn't know a song all the way through, he improvised well enough to please his highly vocal audience.

Gradually, as he played and the light faded from the sky, the requests became more mellow. Jillian was lulled into a peaceful mood as Trevor played more and more ballads, and the boys' banter died to an occasional murmur.

Finally, when the sky was a deep cinnamon overhead, Trevor called a halt. "That's it, guys. I've had it."

"Just one more," the boys called in rough chorus. He shook his head firmly and started to prop the guitar against a large rock.

"One more," Jillian called impulsively, drawing his startled gaze.

"Okay," he said, holding up his hand to stop the shouted requests. "This one's for the lady. What's your pleasure, ma'am?" There was a strained edge to his voice that she'd never heard before.

Instantly curious faces turned her way, and she felt herself blushing. "Uh, let me see...."

Frantically, wishing she hadn't given in to impulse, Jillian searched her mind for a song he hadn't already played. Suddenly she remembered one that had been popular during her college days, one she'd hummed often on the ward in Tokyo to distract herself from the daily horror. She called out the name, which was followed by an immediate buzz of comment. Not one of the boys had heard of the bittersweet ballad.

But Trevor knew it. He'd played it countless times in the privacy of his hospital room in San Diego. Sometimes he'd played it over and over until the desperate anger and loneliness torturing him had lessened, and he'd been able to sleep. He closed his eyes and summoned the image of Jillian's beautiful laughing face that had always been with him whenever he'd played this song.

Jillian sat motionless, listening to the power and beauty of the music. Without words, the melody was hauntingly lovely, and Trevor played it with a depth of feeling that stunned her. It was as though he was trying to tell her something so powerful and sublime that he had no words. Her defenses crumbled, and in the deepening twilight she let the music sweep her into a fantasy world where there was only Trevor, where he loved her and she loved him until the end of time.

It was ethereal. It was passionate. It was a lie.

Trevor came to the end of the song and let the notes fade into the silence. He was breathing hard, and sweat dotted his forehead. Slowly, ignoring the applause and shouts from the boys, he opened his eyes and looked at Jillian.

She was gone.

Trevor glanced around apprehensively, looking for her bright yellow shirt. He spotted her far downstream, walking along the bank, her head down, her shoulders hunched. As he watched, she disappeared behind a pile of large granite boulders that bordered the river.

"Damn," he muttered under his breath as he handed his guitar to one of the boys and stood up. He had to find out what she was thinking.

The sharp pebbles on the bank crunched under his soles as he took off after her, walking as fast as the pain in his back would allow. The sounds of the boy's voices faded as he gradually drew closer to her.

She was walking rapidly, etching narrow footprints into the wet clay, and her arms were crossed tightly over her chest. It was obvious from her jerky stride that she was upset.

"Jill, wait," he called, frustration and uncertainty making his voice harsher than he'd intended.

Her shoulders jerked, and her head came up as she whirled around to face him. Her eyes were dark with pain, and her cheeks were wet. She was crying.

A sharp pain bit deeply into his gut. "Don't cry, Jill," he whispered hoarsely, balling his hands into fists at his sides. "I know you're worried, but Jason's a good kid at heart, and you've done all the right things." He didn't know what else to say.

She swallowed a sob and tried to turn away, but Trevor reached for her, pulling her roughly into his arms. Jillian pushed her face into the hollow of his throat and gulped back the tears.

"I'm getting your shirt all wet," she mumbled, her hands bunching the soft cotton knit where she clung.

"That's okay. I've got plenty of shirts."

She felt him rub his cheek against the top of her head, and she bit her lips to keep from sobbing. Her tears made her vulnerable, and that was something she couldn't risk.

"I'm fine," she muttered, pushing against his chest. He linked his arms around her back to keep her from escaping.

"Sure?" He didn't look convinced.

She nodded, sniffling.

His hard features eased into an indulgent smile as he reached into his back pocket and pulled out a snowy handkerchief. His hand shook slightly as he wiped the tears from her cheeks.

"I know I'm a better engineer than I am a musician, but I've never had my audience in tears before."

"You play beautifully," she said in a voice she knew sounded thin. "I'm just . . . tired."

"Are you sure you're not dredging up old hurts? I wouldn't blame you if you were." He returned the handkerchief to his pocket, then rested both hands on his hips.

"Maybe I am," she admitted, knowing intuitively that the past and the present were all mixed up in her love for him. "I had the past slotted away neat and tidy in my mind, and suddenly, just when I thought my life was in perfect balance, you showed up. And then..." She gestured helplessly and fell silent.

"And then?" His voice carried a cutting edge.

Damn that song, anyway, she thought as she stared into his shadowed eyes. The stillness was there, hiding his thoughts from her.

"And then my carefully constructed present blew up in my face, and now I feel as though I'm...wading through rubble." She gave him an angry look. "I hate it."

Trevor turned away and glanced toward the sharp peaks that were starkly outlined against the orange sky. "No, you hate me. Isn't that what you really mean?"

He turned back to accept the truth he knew he'd see in her eyes. Maybe once she'd said the words it would be easier to convince her to let go of the bitter feelings.

"No," she said in a sad voice. "I don't hate you. I'm not sure I ever did. I think I was just so...hurt that I told myself I despised you."

She didn't look at him. Instead she watched the river surge past a half-buried log. The pressure of the water had wiped the large branch clean of bark, leaving the wood satiny smooth.

"I'm tired of thinking," she said softly.

He moved closer, feeling the subtle warmth of her body touch his skin. "I think about you," he said, telling her the truth. "All the time. I have for years."

He saw the disbelief in her eyes, and it hurt. "Sometimes it was only a fleeting thought when I caught a glimpse of a woman who reminded me of you. And sometimes your presence was so strong I had to swim laps for hours to get you out of my head.''

''Trevor, please—''

He silenced her by putting two fingers against her lips. ''Shh, just listen, okay?''

Her eyes widened until they were almost golden and glowed with uncertainty.

He dropped a quick kiss on her forehead and wrapped his hands over her shoulders. ''I'm asking you to forgive me, Jill. I don't deserve it, I know, but I'm asking anyway. I want a chance to win you back.''

Jillian's heart began to pound, but he didn't say the words she longed to hear. But maybe it was too soon.

''Because of Jason?'' She searched his face for the truth. She had to know.

Trevor heard the tremor in her voice and cursed his clumsiness. ''No, because of me.''

Give him a blueprint and he could build anything, but trying to open himself up to her, to anyone, was damn near impossible.

''I've lived with my mistake for so long.'' His voice grew harsh with feeling. ''I'd rather die than hurt you again.''

Jillian couldn't breathe. ''For a long time I thought you would come back,'' she said in a shaky voice. ''Late at night I'd read your letters aloud so that your child would know his father. I told him his daddy would be so pleased . . .''

Her voice broke, and she clamped her trembling lip between her teeth as tears welled in her eyes again. She started to turn away, but Trevor wouldn't let her go.

''I'm sorry, Jill. So sorry.'' His voice was thick.

Without saying a word, he pulled her closer, as though he were trying to pull himself inside her. His arms were strong, and his body was powerful, but inside he was the same sensitive man she'd fallen in love with so long ago. He'd suffered then because his bombs had fallen on innocent victims, and he was suffering now because she'd forced him to share her pain.

They stood that way for a long time. The night grew purple above them, then black. The stars were bright, twinkling with steady light, and a yellow harvest moon began its slow climb across the jagged peaks in front of them.

Finally Trevor raised his head and looked at her. He kissed her so gently that at first she thought it was the wind brushing her lips. She sighed, and he caught the slight sound with his mouth. His hands bracketed her head as he deepened the kiss. His lips were cool, but his breath was moist and inviting and just as delicious as the cider he'd brought her.

Jillian let the pleasure flow over her, just as the water rippled over the rocks a few feet away. He nibbled at her lips. pushing the tip of his tongue into the corner of her mouth, then withdrawing it, teasing her, tantalizing her, giving her time to resist.

But she couldn't pull away. Not while it felt so good to be held like this. Not while he was stroking her with such absorbing care, letting his fingers trail along her jawline, the inside of her arms, the thin skin covering her wrists.

She liked the feel of his big, hard body rubbing slowly against hers, caressing her, provoking her, and she loved the feel of his hands on her bare arms, gentling her, petting her, inviting her to put those arms around his neck.

He groaned as her hands slid over his shoulders and linked behind his head. He nuzzled her neck with his face, then kissed the tender area below her earlobe before tracing the delicate whorls of her ear with the tip of his tongue.

Heat rocketed through her, and she rubbed against him, letting the friction of his hard chest abrade her nipples until the tiny peaks pushed hard against her shirt.

"My angel," he murmured against her lips as his arms slid around her waist. With masculine insistence, he pulled her closer, letting her feel his need. She knew he wanted her. She had power over this strong, enigmatic man who had tried so hard to hide the caring person inside.

That knowledge put an edge on her desire, making her want him more. As though he could sense her feelings, Trevor slid a hair-roughened thigh between hers and rubbed, sending an electric current deep inside her that made her gasp aloud.

Her body began to hum, and then to vibrate with a primitive force, and she ran her hands over his shoulders and down his arms, pulling him closer, closer.

He took her lips, plunging his tongue between them until she was sucking on him, loving the taste and feel and wetness of him inside her mouth. She moaned helplessly.

Trevor stiffened, then broke off the kiss and slid his hands down to her buttocks. He lifted her to her toes, then began rotating her against him. She could feel the instant response of his large, hard body, and an answering wetness erupted inside her.

"Angel, let me love you," he whispered in a husky, choked voice.

Jillian was lost in a haze of need. She should tell him no, but she couldn't. "Yes," she answered in a low, throbbing voice. At this moment she belonged to him, no matter what happened in the future.

He groaned hoarsely and buried his face in the curve of her neck. A ragged breath shuddered through him, and his arms tightened convulsively.

"Here. Now," he whispered, more a demand than a question.

Jillian knew he would stop if she insisted, but he would suffer for it. And so would she.

"Now," she answered, and he exhaled slowly, as though he'd been holding his breath.

Silently Trevor took her hand and led her into the shelter of the massive rocks. In the private niche the coarse grass was thick and green and smelled of the summer sun. Moonlight cast shadows on the steep walls surrounding them, and chips of mica and quartz sparkled in the light as Trevor drew her down onto the soft natural blanket.

She lay on her back, her legs flexed, her eyes on his face. He looked slightly dangerous in the moonlight, and an involuntary thrill skipped along her veins. He would never take her against her will, but he could, easily.

Slowly Trevor unbuttoned her blouse and opened her bra, letting her breasts spill into his palms. The air was cool on her skin, but his lips were warm as he kissed first one hard nipple, then the other. She reached for him, and her fingers brushed against the hard edge of his brace. She stiffened and started to protest, but he stopped her with a hard, thorough kiss that left her lips tingling and full.

She gasped as his fingers slid along her sides, warm and intimate. She loved the rough feel of his skin and the hard demand of his hands as he pushed the elastic waistband of her shorts down over her thighs.

He was directing her, controlling her, using his hands and his lips to send her soaring. Using only the strength in his arms, he lifted her off the ground and against his chest. He kissed her over and over, finding her lips, her eyelids, her earlobe, trailing fire behind him.

She'd never been so consumed, so masterfully excited. He was totally dedicated to her pleasure, stroking, squeezing, kneading, bringing her to the brink of release over and over until she was moaning his name in helpless urgent need.

"Now," she pleaded in a pleasure-drugged whisper, her fingers digging into the hard expanse of his shoulders. "Inside me, now."

She'd never been so demanding, and yet Trevor was a man who wasn't afraid of her demands, a man who could meet the strongest command with equal strength.

She could unleash the wildest passion, and he would follow. She could soar, and he would climb the heights with her.

She was shaking with need, and her breath was strained to a whimper as he unzipped his shorts and slid them down his strong, hard legs, kicking them aside impatiently, as though he was as eager as she was to join them together.

He kissed her with potent need, then straddled her, his shins pressed against her thighs. She arched against him, feeling him hard and hot and ready for her. He filled her completely, with exquisite tenderness, as he moved slowly, letting her set the rhythm. She clutched his forearms, desperate to feel all of him, and he thrust harder, his face intense in the silver light, his dark gaze focused on her face.

She twisted under him, moaning with throbbing need deep in her throat. He leaned forward, filling her, stroking, thrusting, until she was dizzy, knowing only Trevor and his loving.

Their rasping breaths mingled with the love call of the river frogs, filling the intimate space within the confines of the rocks with the song of loving.

Jillian gasped as he plunged deeply within her, melding them together, promising, fulfilling, sending her over the edge into a mindless state of sublime ecstasy. She clung to him, sobbing in release and love.

Trevor was dripping with sweat and breathing harshly as he slowly extended his legs alongside hers and lay next to her, his body still joined with hers. He buried his face against her shoulder and kissed the hollow of her neck. Jillian was replete and sated, and her body was drugged and heavy, and yet she felt as though she were floating far above the fragrant grass.

Inside, she was smiling, but her lips were trembling and vulnerable as she pressed them against Trevor's tousled hair. He smelled clean, and the tangled pewter mass was slightly damp.

He stroked her arm, bringing her back into her body slowly, and she reveled in the sensation. She stretched languidly, then froze as she realized he was still hot and hard inside her. He hadn't followed her into the heights.

"Trevor?" she whispered, her voice a sultry, sated wave of sound.

He moved, firing her with instant heat, and she gasped. He rocked gently inside her, sending little rockets of instant pleasure shooting into the velvet sheath that contained him.

This time he brought her to the peak slowly, thoroughly, his own need building along with hers. He loved the little sounds she made with each thrust, and the feel of her thighs against his drove him steadily toward the limit of his control. He'd wanted to make it perfect for her, to wrap her in so much passion that she would never escape, but once he'd entered her he'd had to fight his own powerful need.

She was perfection, this lovely woman who had once loved him. And he would never deny her anything again.

Trevor felt the heat building, driving him, consuming him. She cradled him perfectly, enticingly, her skin like warm satin, her hair a silken tangle around his fingers, her breasts ready for kissing.

He called her name over and over in his head as he felt the intimate contractions throbbing against him. He let himself rush over the edge, feeling the hot, violent eruption spill into her. She moaned, her hand grasping the neckline of his shirt, and the material gave way with a soft, ripping sound, exposing the heavy silver chain.

He smiled as he collapsed against her. This woman would always demand his best, and he would give it for as long as she let him.

Jillian tried to smile as Trevor rested his head on her shoulder and sighed. But she was too drowsy with pleasure.

Trevor let her heartbeat settle into a normal rhythm. They had to get back soon, or they would be missed. And he didn't want Jason to worry about his mother.

He nuzzled Jillian's soft curls and inhaled the seductive scent of her. He wanted to keep her here forever, just the two of them alone, with no past behind them and no future to face. But that wasn't possible.

He closed his eyes and thought about the night when he'd asked her to marry him. He'd thought then that he had it all together. Hell, he was rich. His father was ready to hand him a plush job once he was on his feet again. A beautiful, sexy, intelligent woman wanted to be his wife.

Damn straight, Trevor Markus had it all. He could handle anything. But he'd been dead wrong. He hadn't handled anything. His life had come crashing down around him, and he'd run away.

He pulled her tighter, letting the feel of her gentle the harsh, dark thoughts he knew were coming. He'd done terrible things, things that even now made him cringe inside, things he didn't want to admit to anyone, ever.

A dozen times since he'd seen Jillian again he'd told himself he was a different man now. That he'd changed, grown up, learned his lesson.

But before he could believe that, she had to know the truth about the man he'd been. And he had to tell her. But not yet. Not until she'd come to know the man he was now. Not until she'd come to trust him.

Jillian sighed and nestled closer, her breathing becoming more regular. She fit perfectly against him, her lush body tantalizing his even as he tried to gather the strength to sit up.

The familiar restlessness pushed through his exhaustion to torment him. He needed to move, to work through the terrible tension building inside him, but he didn't want to leave her. Sighing, he dropped a kiss on her nose. "Wake up, Jill," he whispered. "It's getting late."

Jillian stirred, a satisfied smile blooming on her lips. "I don't want to move," she murmured.

Trevor groaned and answered the seductive invitation with a kiss before he rolled away. The air was cold on his damp skin, and he reached for his shorts. He pulled them on, then looked around for Jillian's. They were in a crumpled heap by her feet.

"Sweetheart," he murmured, tracing her lips with his finger, "you need to get dressed."

Jillian kissed the tip of his finger and opened her eyes. She would remember this night forever. On the nights when she missed him the most, she would let the memory of his loving soothe her empty soul, and when her heart ached for him in the quiet time before dawn, she would cling to this night.

"I suppose you're going to say you're still out of practice," she said in a throaty voice as she let him pull her to a sitting position.

He laughed, and she felt the infectious, boyish sound bounce off the rocks. He sounded . . . nervous. "I could use a few more sessions like this," he said, helping her with her bra. His fingers were warm against the tender skin around her nipples, and she sighed in pleasure.

She wiggled into her panties and shorts, then looked around for her shirt. She'd been lying on it.

"Jill, before we go, you need to know that I meant what I said." He smoothed her hair away from her cheek and kissed her lightly, then set her away from him firmly. "I want us to start over, to try to make it work between us again. I'll do anything you say, take it slow, court you, anything you want."

Jillian's heart began to pound, and her mouth went suddenly dry. "Court me?"

"Yes, if that's what you want. We could date. You could come visit me in Seattle, go sailing with me." His grin flashed. "I'm pretty rusty in the romance department, but I'll give it my best shot."

Jillian glanced around their private cubbyhole. It was shadowy and dark, but Trevor's lovemaking had made it seem as though it were filled with light. But could he do that with her life?

Jillian tried to summon a smile but failed. She was too shaken. If only he'd said that he loved her . . .

"I don't know what to say."

He stroked her thigh. "Think about it. Okay?"

"Okay," she said in a hushed voice. She had to fight hard to keep the tears from forming in her eyes again.

Dressing in silence, she felt Trevor's eyes on her. But he said nothing as she finished. He simply took her in his arms and kissed her with tenderness, but without passion. It was the kind of kiss a husband gives his wife at the end of a long day.

Chapter 11

"Wake up, Jill."

Jillian fought through the soft gray fog surrounding her. The voice calling her name was husky and deep and wonderfully warm.

Firm lips brushed hers, leaving the taste of minty toothpaste behind, and she smiled. This time the dream of Trevor was so real that she could smell the clean scent of shaving soap on his skin.

"C'mon, sleepyhead. Open your pretty green eyes and look at me."

"Mmm." Jillian rubbed her cheek against the flannel lining of her sleeping bag and kept her eyes firmly closed. She didn't want the dream to end.

"Jill, sweetheart, don't tempt me like this. I'm trying to be a good guy here."

Hard fingers brushed her jaw, and she nuzzled a large, warm palm. Her cheek rubbed a damp cotton sleeve that smelled of woodsmoke, and she wrinkled her nose in surprise.

This is not a dream, she thought, opening her eyes slowly to the hazy light of false dawn. In the shadowed gloom Trevor was watching her. His cheeks were red from the cold, and the collar of his foul-weather jacket was pulled up against his strong throat.

"Morning," she murmured, stretching. Her body was stiff, and there was a tingling soreness deep inside her. Last night he'd made love to her so thoroughly that she was still delightfully aware.

Heat spread upward from the space between her breasts to gather in her cheeks as she remembered the tumultuous way he'd taken her. "Uh, what time is it?" Her voice was thick with sleep, and her head felt fuzzy.

He brushed the tumbled hair away from her cheek before he bent closer. "It's a few minutes before six." His voice was almost as husky as hers.

He knelt beside her, his head bent to avoid the top of the nylon tent. The black jeans that stretched over his powerful thighs had faded to a soft pearly gray, and the neck of his plain gray sweatshirt was torn. His hair was rumpled, and his shoes were covered with mud.

"You look very... earthy this morning. Sexy."

She saw the heat come into his eyes as he slid his hand into the down bag to cup her breast. Her nipple pearled, and he caught it between his thumb and forefinger.

"I feel... sexy when I'm around you. And a lot of other things, too." He cupped her breast intimately, then withdrew his hand and drew the thick covering close to her neck. "You want some coffee?" His voice was a frustrated growl.

She ran her hand down is forearm, wrinkling the thick material covering his wide wrist. "Not necessarily," she teased, her voice low and sultry. She eased herself to a sitting position, and Trevor's gaze fell to the soft swell of her body under her purple sweatshirt. A jagged star of frustration flashed in his copper eyes.

"You're enjoying this!" His voice was low and threatening.

"That's true. It isn't often I have you in my power."

His expression became deadly serious. "Do you want me in your power, Jill?"

"I'm not sure that's possible," she answered, equally serious.

"It's possible. I'm must not sure I want you to know how possible." Before Jillian could answer, he leaned forward to give her a swift, possessive kiss. Her hands encircled his neck trapping him. "Don't tempt me," he said with a harsh groan.

"Why not?"

"Because there's a hell of a storm coming, and we have to get an early start." Gently he removed her arms from his neck and held her hands in his.

"A storm? You mean with lightning and thunder?"

"Looks like. The wind's from the right direction, and it's picked up at least ten knots in the past hour." He released her hands and reached for her tote bag. "If the rain does come, Hank's decided to end the trip as soon as we can find a place to go ashore. Do you have any suggestions?"

Her eyes focused on his drawn face, finding the worry lines furrowing his brows. She unzipped the side of her sleeping bag, and cool air hit her with a shivering rush. She inhaled sharply and reached for the tote bag he held out to her.

"Let me think a minute," she told him through chattering teeth. "There's some pretty wild country between here and town." As she rummaged through the jumble of spare clothing, she traced the river's course in her mind. "The best spot would probably be an old ferry landing about five miles above town. There's still a pier of sorts there, and a road leading to the main highway. It would serve in an emergency."

She pulled out her jacket and started to shrug into the sleeves, but Trevor took it from her cold hands and helped her into the fleece-lined canvas. His fingers were possessive and warm as he lifted her thick hair from the back of her neck and planted a quick kiss on her skin before adjusting the collar for her.

"Okay, I'll tell Hank," he told her with a lazy grin. He started to back out of the tent, then stopped suddenly, his jaw clenching.

"You should be wearing your brace," she admonished instinctively, watching the color drain from his tanned skin.

"Damn thing itches. I'm fine without it."

Trevor met her defiant gaze squarely. "And you wouldn't tell me if you weren't," she said in a good imitation of his brusque tone.

He scowled, then started to laugh. "No, I wouldn't, Miss Smarty." Before she could blink, he rocked forward on his hands and kissed her hard and thoroughly. "By the way, you look sexy as hell in that purple thing," he said with a pleased grin as he left her.

Jillian glanced down at the top of her running suit. Just for that she would keep it on all day.

The storm came in at noon. The sky turned from gray to black, and the wind skimmed the river in furious gusts, bringing the scent of rain long before the first big drop hit.

"Wind's got to be thirty knots, at least," Trevor said with a scowl as he pulled Jillian closer to his side and glared up at the sky. On Puget Sound he'd raced a twelve-meter in stronger winds than this, but that had been a far more sea-worthy craft than the flimsy raft.

"I don't know about knots," Jillian muttered, rubbing her hands together, "but I know it's a lot colder than it was when we started." She huddled under the hood of her jacket and watched the rafts ahead of them rocket from side to side in the churning rapids.

They were in the most dangerous part of the river. The water was well over a man's head, and the current was swift. Both banks were lined with large, jagged boulders that dotted the riverbed in a ragged line, creating a turbulence that could flip a raft in rough weather.

"Some fun, huh, Mom?" Jason called sarcastically from the front of the raft. His expression was petulant, and his eyes were sullen and angry.

Jillian inhaled sharply and sent her son a warning look. "I've had it with your complaints, Jason Gregory. No one can predict the weather."

Overhead, lightning sliced a white line through the towering clouds, and thunder clapped loudly in counterpoint.

Jason looked up with an exaggerated expression of disbelief. "Oh, yeah? I thought you knew everything, like how great this family togetherness stuff was going to be. Just you and me and *him*."

"That's enough, Jason," Trevor told him with quiet firmness. "This was my idea, not your mother's."

Something was wrong with the kid, he thought, watching his son closely. His eyes were dull, and his face was very pale. All morning he'd been jumpy as hell. Trevor was surprised that Jillian hadn't noticed, but maybe that was just as well. She had enough to worry about at the moment.

"Right, *Daddy*," the boy muttered under his breath.

Trevor froze, and he felt Jillian stiffen against his side.

"Cut it out, Jase," she warned, avoiding Trevor's eye. "One more smart-aleck remark like that and you'll be grounded for a month."

Jason shrugged and huddled farther into the pointed bow. The bill of his baseball cap dripped water and beneath the orange life preserver his down-filled parka stuck to his body like scarlet skin. "I hate camping," he muttered into his collar. Suddenly he looked up and glared across the raft at his father.

And I hate you.

Trevor heard the words as clearly as if if Jason had shouted them into the howling wind. He felt the muscles of his throat tighten as he swallowed the sharp, angry words that came immediately to mind. His son needed a good spanking, but he would never touch him, not that way. He didn't trust himself to be gentle enough.

"There's the pier," Jillian said, her voice heavy with relief. "See, near that oak hanging out over the water?"

"I see it." Trevor shifted his gaze to the lead raft, where one of the boys was pointing toward the sagging structure. All but one of the rafts ahead were clear of the rapids and in calmer water.

"Looks like Hank sees it, too. It won't be long now." Ten minutes, he calculated.

Suddenly, without warning, the raft lurched crazily to the left, throwing Jillian on top of him. "What the—"

Jason was leaning halfway over the side, vomiting violently into the turbulent water.

"Jason!" Jillian cried, scrambling toward her son.

Trevor reached for her, catching her by the tail of her jacket, but it was too late. The point of the overbalanced craft hit a partially submerged rock, and Jason tumbled over the side. His forehead hit the rock, and blood spurted over his red curls and into the water as he floated faceup, his life preserver supporting him.

"*Jason!*" Jillian's scream was turned into a sob by the wind, and the spray from the boiling river stung her face. Her eyes were wild as she fought Trevor's hold. "He can't swim. He—"

"Stay here! I'll get him," Trevor shouted, pushing her back against the opposite side of the pitching raft.

He went over the side feetfirst and held on long enough to push the raft away from the rocks, then put his head down and kicked as hard as he could. Jason was already a good five yards ahead of him, carried along by the current.

"Watch out! That rock."

Jillian's cry was splintered by the driving wind, and she scrambled frantically toward the front of the raft. Her feet tangled in the oars, and she sprawled in the sloshing water.

Trevor saw the boulder ahead, a wet gray wall barely inches from Jason's bobbing head. Lunging forward, he grabbed the boy's collar and pulled him backward, away from the rock face.

The raft rocketed by, lurching wildly, and Trevor had a glimpse of Jillian's white face before she sped by him. She was screaming, trying to draw the attention of the others as she paddled awkwardly, slowly wrestling the pitching raft toward shore.

Tightening his grip on the back of Jason's life preserver, Trevor kicked for the center of the river. Without warning, a foaming wave caught him full in the face, and he went under. As he came up coughing, his lungs stinging, his back crashed against the sharp point of a partially submerged rock, sending jagged shards of agony down his spine and into his thighs.

He felt sick, and a familiar light-headedness threatened to overwhelm him, but he fought it off and swam a clumsy sidestroke at an angle toward the shore, pulling Jason behind him. By the time his feet touched the rocky bottom and he was able to drag Jason between the rocks to shore, he was breathing hard, and his legs were numb.

He lay facedown, his arm around Jason's waist, trying to find the strength to move. The pain came in waves, one after the other, punishing him for every gasping breath he took.

Hank reached him first, followed by Jillian and several of the boys. Hank's harsh drawl and Jillian's worried cry blended into a rumble of sound. Trevor felt his hand being lifted from Jason, and he muttered a protest.

"Jason?" He tried not to groan, but it hurt to move.

"Let go, Trev. He's okay. Jason's okay. You got to him in time."

Hank's rough Texas twang cut through the noise. Hank would handle everything. Trevor allowed himself to sink into the clawing gray haze. Jason was okay. His son hadn't drowned.

"Trevor, can you hear me?" Jillian's voice was calm and soothing, just as he remembered. "One of the boys has gone for help. We're taking you and Jason to the clinic."

"No clinic," Trevor whispered hoarsely, opening his eyes and searching for Hank.

Hank knelt down and gripped his arm. "Don't worry, Trev," he said in rough voice. "I'll take you back to Horizons. I'll take care of you."

Trevor nodded and tried to relax. He felt soft fingertips stroking his face, gentle and warm. Jillian was with him, just as she'd always been.

Biting back a groan, he fought for consciousness, but the welcoming grayness beckoned seductively. "Don't let go," he whispered as he reached for her hand and held on tight.

"I won't, darling. I'm here."

Then his eyes closed and the gray turned to black.

"I'm not going! You can't make me." Jason's angry voice grated on Jillian's nerves, but she forced herself to remain calm.

Adrian had wanted him to stay one more day in the clinic, but Jason had adamantly refused. He'd been restless and irritable in the three-bed ward, the only space that had been available, and Jillian had finally relented.

Taking the day off, she'd made him stay in bed most of the morning so that she could watch over him. Every hour she'd checked his vital signs, looking for signs of a concussion, but he seemed fine.

His stomach was still upset, and he was pale, but after a short nap his disposition had greatly improved. For the past two hours, since lunchtime, he'd been pushing her to let him visit his friends. When she'd suggested a visit to Trevor, who was still in the Horizons' infirmary, instead, he'd exploded.

"Jason, your father saved your life. The least you can do is spend a few minutes with him while he's still confined to bed."

Jason flopped on the rumpled blanket and glared at her. "Why? He didn't come to see me."

Jillian inhaled slowly and counted the beats she could hear pounding in her head. When she reached twenty, she felt calm enough to answer. "I've told you this once, but in case you've forgotten, your father didn't come to see you because he twisted a disk in his back pulling you out of the river. Dr. Stoneson put him in traction."

Jason's face turned red, and he dropped his gaze, but she could see the stubborn resistance in the rigid line of his thin shoulders. "You didn't go to see him, either," he mumbled.

"That's because Dr. Stoneson wanted him to rest. Besides, he was probably so doped on painkillers he wouldn't have known whether I was there or not."

"So what's the big deal about today?"

"Today he asked Dr. Stoneson to call and tell me that he was lonely and wanted to see us. Both of us."

"Yeah, I bet."

Jillian bit her lip and reached for the battered black knapsack half hidden under the unmade bed. She needed something to occupy her hands and her mind. The past few days had stretched her patience to the limit.

"What are you doing?" Jason's voice rose sharply, and Jillian looked up in surprise.

"I'm going to do a load of laundry before I drive out to Horizons." She unzipped the top and started pulling out dirty clothes still left from their trip. She would give Jason time to reconsider.

"I'll do it."

"What?"

Jason slid off the bed and stood up. "I'll do it, Mom. It's time I learned." He rocked from side to side, and his eyes darted from her face to the bag in her hands.

Jillian stared at him. "You're offering to do the laundry?" she asked incredulously, and he nodded. A nervous smile spread over his pale face, and Jillian felt a sharp prickle of suspicion. "What do you have in here that you don't want me to see?'' She held the nylon bag in her hand, searching his face for a sign of guilt.

His eyes flickered for an instant, then held steady on hers.

''Do you have something you want to tell me, Jason?'' she asked, letting her tone become stern. He was hiding something.

''You don't trust me,'' he said in a harsh voice, his face mirroring a deep hurt. ''Mike said you'd be bummed because of the club stuff. He said you'd be like his dad, always snooping in his room.'' He glared at her, and his lips stretched into an angry line.

What would make him so defensive all of a sudden? Jillian wondered, casting her mind back over the past few weeks. ''Did you take more money, Jason?'' she asked with forced calm. ''From one of the boys on the trip? Or from your father?''

He dropped his gaze to the open flap of the satchel. ''I told you I wouldn't do that again. Don't you believe me?''

Jillian went cold inside. His expression, the tone of his voice, even the tense lines of his thin body, suggested guilt.

''I want to, Jase, but I have to know for sure. Otherwise I wouldn't be much of a parent, would I?''

With a sense of growing dread she upended the bag and shook it hard. Rumpled shirts and underwear fell at her feet, landing with a soft plop on the toes of her sneakers. On top of the jumble, twisted into a cellophane wad, lay a sandwich bag.

Nausea pushed at her throat as she bent over and slowly picked up the small parcel. Her hand shook as she opened the bag. Inside were six yellow pills.

''This is Percodan,'' she said, raising her gaze to Jason's face. ''Isn't it?'' Her throat was so tight that she could barely get the words out.

The skin around his mouth pinched into a frown, and his gaze slid away from hers. ''I don't know what it is,'' he mumbled, turning his back on her.

Jillian was afraid to move. *Narcotics,* she thought, her mind screaming in resistance. Drugs, used illegally. Potential poison.

Not Jason, she told herself in staunch denial. Not her little boy. It wasn't possible.

She glanced down at the small round pills. She'd filled countless prescriptions for this very potent analgesic. She'd even taken it herself when she'd fallen on the ice one winter and sprained her ankle.

But she didn't keep it in the house. And Jason wasn't allowed to go into the glass cubicle where this and other drugs were stored.

She thought about the numbers that didn't match, and her stomach lurched in sick panic.

Her fingers bit into the bony flesh of his shoulders, and he jerked beneath her hand as she spun him around to face her. Putting her shaking hand under his chin, she forced him to look at her. "Jason, I want the truth. Did you take these from downstairs?"

Jason tried to wrench his head away, but she tightened her grip. He winced in pain, but she refused to let him go.

"Tell me, Jason. Where did you get these pills?"

"Some guy on the trip gave 'em to me," he mumbled. He bit his lip, and his shoulders drooped. Suddenly he looked like a scared little boy bracing for a scolding.

"Which guy?" she asked him urgently. She was shaking uncontrollably, and her voice sounded hollow.

"The black dude with the scar. Raymond." Jason's face was scarlet from his chin to his hairline, and his tongue kept running over his bottom lip as though his mouth were dry. "He . . . he said he got 'em from the clinic. He said he'd be busted back to jail if they found the . . . the pills on him." His eyes flashed wildly. "He made me take 'em, Mom. I was afraid he'd hurt me if I didn't."

Jillian looked for the subtle signs that had always betrayed him when he was lying—the averted glance, the pinched nostrils, the nervous hands.

She saw none of them. He simply looked frightened.

"Stay here," she said sternly, pushing Jason down onto the bed. "Don't move until I get back."

Naked panic flared in his copper eyes. "What're you gonna do?" His voice was high-pitched and wavering.

"I'm going to make a phone call, and then you and I are going to have a very serious talk." She started to leave his room, but his anguished cry stopped her.

"You're not going to tell T-Trevor, are you?" His jaw hung open, and he was breathing hard.

"Yes," she said slowly and distinctly, "but first I'm going to call Sheriff Cobb."

Trevor found Hank in his office. The bearded director was leaning back in his chair, his eyes closed, his feet encased in scuffed boots propped on an open desk drawer. He was smoking a cigar, and the smoke hung like a blue wreath around his head.

As soon as Trevor crossed the threshold, Hank opened one eye and squinted at him. "You should be in bed, partner," he said accusingly. "You ripped that disk pretty good. If you put too much strain on it before it's completely healed, you could end up in a wheelchair again—this time permanently." The heels of his boots thudded loudly against the polished linoleum as he stood up.

"I'll be okay," Trevor muttered, glancing down the length of his own body. His gray sweats were loose-fitting and comfortable but even the slightest brush of fabric against his spine hurt. "I'm going crazy tied to that blasted bed, not knowing what the hell's going on in here."

Impatiently he shoved the sleeves of his sweatshirt past his elbows and perched on the edge of the desk. He'd managed to shower after Jillian called, but shaving had been beyond him. It had hurt too much to raise his arm.

Hank puffed on his cigar, then stubbed it out in the ashtray on his desk. "The guard at the gate called about two minutes ago. Jillian and the sheriff are on their way." He began rolling up the sleeves of his red plaid shirt. "Jason's with them."

"Poor kid. I bet he's scared to death." Trevor ran his hand over his thigh as he watched Hank pour coffee from an oversize thermos into two large mugs.

"Raymond's down in the lab being tested." Hank handed him one of the mugs, then returned to his chair and sat down. "This smells wrong, Trev. If it had been anyone but Raymond—" Hank broke off to mutter a blunt obscenity. "I hate to think I've been wrong about him."

Trevor took a greedy sip of the hot coffee. It was strong enough to strip the whiskers from his jaw. "We'll find out soon enough. Sounds like they're here." He put the mug on the desk and waited.

Hank's chair squeaked as he leaned back against the wall and fixed his hard gray gaze on the open doorway. "That man stomps the ground like a mangy old bull we used to have," he muttered, his brows lowered, his eyes narrowed to slits.

Trevor heard only Jillian's light feminine tread. He hadn't seen her in three days, and he was hungry for the sight of her.

Mel Cobb was the first one to enter. He was dressed in full uniform, with his hat pulled low over his forehead, his thick belt sagging under the weight of his gun and cartridge pouch. He slapped his thigh with a heavy black nightstick as he walked.

Jillian followed a half step behind. She was dressed in the same purple sweat suit she'd worn that last day on the river, only this time it was dry and unrumpled and, Trevor noticed, still sexy as hell.

She walked with her head up, her chin out, and she had her arm around Jason's shoulders in a protective embrace. Her hair was piled on top of her head, exposing the deceptively fragile line of her throat.

As soon as she saw Trevor, her face drained of the little color it possessed. "I didn't expect to see you out of bed," she told him softly. "Are you okay?"

Trevor heard the low tremor in her voice, and wondered what she was feeling. "I'm fine, just a little sore." He needed to hold her, but this wasn't the time.

Tamping down his frustration, he shifted his attention to his son. Jason stood shoulder to shoulder with his mother, dressed in worn jeans and a plain green sweater. The left side of his forehead was purple, and three neat stitches closed an inch-long gash that touched his hairline.

"Hello, Jason," Trevor said, forcing the boy to look at him. "How are you feeling?"

"Okay," Jason mumbled, not quite meeting Trevor's eyes.

"Good. I was worried about you."

Jillian watched Trevor's taut expression grow more strained, and she felt sick. She wanted to tell him that this meeting was Mel's idea, but that wasn't quite the truth. After Jason's confession, she was as concerned about Horizons as the sheriff. But before she could find the right words to express her worry, Mel interrupted.

"That's enough chitchat," he said in a coarse growl. "I came to get me a thief, and that's what I intend to do." His smug gaze swept the room, then locked with Trevor's. "This time I got you, hotshot." His voice was an oily stream of triumph that brought a scowl to Hank's face and a look of sharp anguish to Jason's.

Trevor's hands balled into fists, and he struggled to hold down the instant fury. If he moved, he knew he might not be able to stop himself from beating the man's face to a bloody pulp.

"Dr. Stoneson? I have the test results you wanted." The voice that interrupted was tentative, as though the woman at the door could feel the volatile tension in the big office. She was small and blond and nearly hidden by the large black youth standing next to her.

Raymond Williams was dressed in faded black cords and a black sweatshirt, hacked off at the shoulders to reveal massive upper arms. One side of his smooth black face sported a jagged scar that pulled his mouth up into a sardonic half smile.

Ralph Hendricks stood to one side, his hand on the boy's shoulder, his eyes alert. At Hank's nod the security chief removed his hand and stepped back to take up a post in the corridor.

Jillian resisted the urge to shiver as the youth ambled into the room. His narrowed brown eyes raked Jason with contempt as he passed, and Jillian pulled her son closer. His shoulders jerked under her arm, but he didn't pull away.

Hank took the one-page printout from the woman, thanked her warmly before dismissing her, then briefly recounted the testing procedure as the sound of her footsteps slowly faded. "In order to prevent cheating, Mr. Hendricks was with Raymond at all times during the test. Isn't that right, Ralph?"

Hendricks took a firm step forward and nodded. "Yes, sir, Dr. Stoneson. I can swear to that." His gaze hardened as he directed it toward the sheriff.

Cobb scowled, then held out a beefy hand. Hank scanned the report, then let the sheriff take it. Jillian held her breath as the sheriff quickly read off the results.

"Negative, my butt," he said, the words exploding from him in an angry burst. "I don't believe it. The kid's as dirty as they come."

He gestured with a meaty hand toward Jillian and Jason. "Tell these folks what you told your mom and me, Jase," he ordered. "Tell 'em how this sleaze said he stole the Percs from the clinic, then threatened to hurt you if you told on him."

Jason's head jerked, and his gaze flew to his mother's face. Jillian saw the fright in his eyes, and the helplessness. She glanced toward Raymond who looked ready to explode.

"Go ahead," she said, wishing she could spare him this. But he had to face up to the truth. He'd made a bad mistake, accepting the drugs and not telling anyone, but Raymond Williams had made a worse one. Even Trevor would have to admit that.

Jason wetted his lips and slid his frightened gaze toward his father. Trevor had an immediate sense of déjà vu. Timmy, he thought. Jason looked just like his brother, Tim, when he'd been fourteen. And Tim had died at nineteen.

"Tell the sheriff the truth, Jason," Trevor said as calmly as he could. "All of it."

Jason's face crumpled, and he dropped his gaze. "He said he needed to hide them from...from Trevor and Dr. Stoneson. He said no one could know."

"*Liar!*" Raymond's voice was a strangled roar, filling the room with waves of violent sound.

Jillian saw the muscles in Raymond's arms bunch a split second before he moved. Her heart leaped, and the acid taste of nausea stung her throat as she jumped in front of Jason's shaking body.

"Raymond, stop!" Trevor shouted.

Hank tackled the boy in midstride, and the two of them went down. Raymond fought to free himself, twisting and bucking like a wild bronco, but Hank held on, his back muscles straining with maximum effort as he kept the larger, heavier youth from escaping.

Hendricks rushed into the room and tried to grab Raymond's kicking feet, but the burly young man caught him on the side of the jaw with the toe of his shoe, and the guard sprawled backward.

"Freeze, sucker, or you're dead," Cobb shouted, reaching for his gun. His face was fiery red, and his hand was shaking so violently that he had trouble unsnapping the flap of the holster.

"Mel, *no!*" Jillian shoved Jason toward the open door, feeling his terror as Raymond Williams cursed his name.

Her legs started to shake as she rushed toward Mel. She had to stop this insanity before someone got hurt.

Trevor reached the sheriff before she did. With one hand he grabbed Mel's plain black tie, twisting the sturdy cotton hard against the constricting collar to compress the man's windpipe while the other clamped around the sheriff's thick wrist, keeping him from drawing the .44 Magnum.

With a feral cry Raymond escaped Hank's hold and surged to his feet, his body braced. Cobb's eyes bulged, and he struggled against the choke hold, but Trevor held on. *"Think, man!"* he shouted. "This is no place to start shooting."

Mel froze, his face a distorted mask of hatred, but the fight had gone out of him. Trevor released his hold and took a step backward. His back was knotted and throbbing, and he felt sick to his stomach.

"Let's all calm down here and start making sense," Trevor ordered as quietly as he could manage. He could still feel the fury pounding in his head.

Breathing hard, he glanced at Raymond, who was standing with his legs apart and his fists knotted. "Sit down, Ray. You're in enough trouble," he ordered brusquely, raking his hand through his hair. "And keep your temper buttoned up tight."

The black youth scowled, but he backed up warily until the backs of his knees collided with one of the chairs lined up against the wall. He sat down and braced his big, scarred hands on his knees. His eyes were filled with turbulent fire and a desperate fear.

Turning back, Trevor saw the confusion and fright in Jillian's eyes. Her life was safe and comfortable and predictable. In her world people were solid and responsible. They worked hard and took care of their families. He couldn't expect her to understand the dark side of human nature, where a boy like Raymond had to fight for every scrap of self-respect he possessed. Where he lived with a gut-twisting craving every hour of every day and always would. Where one slip could kill him.

"You want sense?" Cobb asked with a sneer. "I'll give you sense, Markus. I'm arresting this boy here for the theft at the Clayton Clinic and the assault on Mrs. Montoya." He pulled out a card and began reading Raymond his rights.

"It's a damn lie," Raymond shouted, his dark, wild eyes clinging to Trevor's. "I didn't take no pills. I swear." His voice choked, and his face twisted. "You gotta believe me, Mr. Markus. Your son there, he's lying."

Trevor stared into Raymond's pleading eyes. He saw terror there and a terrible helplessness. He'd seen that look before—in his own eyes. He knew what it was like to feel alone and scared and desperate for someone to believe in him.

He had to choose, the son he'd just found or this desperate boy. Either way he was going to lose. He took a deep breath and allowed himself a brief look at Jillian's white face. Damn, they needed more time.

Shoving his hands into his pockets to keep from reaching for her, he straightened his shoulders and looked Raymond straight in the eye. "I believe you, Raymond," he told the anguished boy in a strong voice. "Jason is the one who's lying."

Chapter 12

Trevor saw the shock shudder into Jillian's eyes, and he ground his teeth so hard that he felt something shift in his jaw. He'd never felt so helpless in his life, not even when he'd known his plane was going down and that he wouldn't be able to eject in time.

"What . . . what did you say?" Jillian stared at him, her body frozen.

"He said your son's a liar, Mayor," Mel Cobb told her with a snort. "Talk about a liar. He's the biggest one in the whole damn room. He'd do anything to save this sleazy place."

Jillian's face went white, and her eyes grew huge in her head. "Trevor," she asked in a pleading voice, "are you saying Jason's lying?"

Trevor swore silently and thoroughly as all the eyes in the room swung toward him. His back was one hard spasm of hot pain, and his legs were growing numb again. But he couldn't pass out now. Not when Jillian was looking at him with such horror in her eyes. He needed a few more minutes. Just a few more minutes.

"Jill," he said softly, moving toward her, each step agony. "We need to talk—"

"Answer me. Are you accusing your son of lying?" Her voice was flat, lifeless.

He was losing her; he could feel it happening as plainly as if she'd slammed a door in his face. He wanted to hold her, to beg her to understand, to love her, but he couldn't do any of those things.

His throat closed up. Angel, he begged silently, give me a chance.

"Yes, Jill," he said, hating every word he knew he had to say. "I think he brought those pills with him on the trip, and I think he's hooked on them."

Jillian heard someone gasp, then realized the harsh sound had come from her own throat.

The room was deadly still for the space of a shattered breath, and then it exploded into sound. Both Mel and Hank began shouting at once, angry, ugly words. But none were as ugly as the ones Trevor had just uttered with such harsh certainty.

"I told you he hated me," Jason muttered from somewhere behind her.

In slow motion Jillian turned to link her arm with Jason's. "Tell him you didn't mean it," she told Trevor, her voice stiff. "Tell him, Trevor. Now."

"I meant it, Jill. I wish I didn't." Trevor forced himself to wait. To let her decide.

She would never know what it cost him to accuse his own son, especially in front of a man like Mel Cobb. But he'd had no damn choice.

He'd watched Jason change on the river trip. He'd seen the mood swings, the growing agitation, the signs of narcotics withdrawal, and he'd tried his best to ignore them. But now he knew with cold certainty he'd been right. His son was an addict.

If he compromised here, if he didn't force Jason to face the consequences of his actions, his whole life for the past fifteen years would be a lie.

''You . . . you can't believe that Jason is . . . is an addict.'' Jillian's low voice was a wounded whisper.

Trevor watched the pained disbelief twist her face, and he felt as though he'd been laid open by that same pain. He was used to hurting, and he would gladly have taken her pain from her if he could. But he didn't know how.

''There's one way to find out,'' he said quietly, glancing toward the printout lying on the desk. ''Have him tested. If he's using, it'll show up.''

Jason flinched. With a choked cry he jerked away from his mother and bolted from the office, his sneakers pounding the linoleum as he ran for the front door.

Jillian felt the eyes of the others on her, but she saw only Trevor. His eyes were as shadowed and bleak as the gaping hole opening inside her. He'd known exactly how much his words would hurt her. How could he not have known?

''What kind of a man are you?'' she whispered, raking him with her eyes.

Trevor met her fierce gaze steadily. ''The only kind I know how to be,'' he said quietly.

She couldn't trust herself to stay in the same room with him. She wanted to scream at him. She wanted to rake his face with her nails for making her feel this unbearable pain all over again.

''Excuse me,'' she said with careful courtesy. ''My son needs me.''

Walking mechanically, feeling as though her body were made of thin, brittle glass, she left the office. By the time she reached the front door she was trembling so hard that she was afraid she would stumble and fall.

Clutching the door handle, she hunched over, drawing in great gulps of air. She closed her eyes and waited for her legs to stop trembling.

''Jill, please don't do this to yourself.''

Trevor was standing a foot away, watching her closely, every muscle of his body radiating tension held in rigid check, like a man preparing for a bare-knuckles fight. She hadn't heard him following her.

"Do what? Hate myself because I was beginning to trust you? Because I was beginning to love you again?"

Trevor took a slow, careful breath. He didn't like the dead look in her eyes. "And how do you feel now?" he asked softly.

"Now I know that I was a fool." Her voice wobbled. "You asked me to forgive you, but how can I when you're deliberately hurting your own son?"

Frustration ripped at him, and he dropped his gaze to the floor, struggling for control. She's said that she loved him. And she was leaving him.

He'd longed to hear those words again, fought to earn the right to hear them. He felt as though he were bleeding to death. "What do you want from me, Jill? I've tried to show you that I care about you and Jason. I've tried to be a good father. I've tried to make it up to you for . . . walking out on you when you needed me. What else can I do?"

"You can tell me that you believe your son. And you can walk outside with me right now and tell Jason the same thing."

Trevor broke out in a cold sweat. From the first he'd known it was a long shot. But he'd fought for her as hard as he knew how. If he backed off, if he told her he trusted Jason, he might still have a chance.

And, dear God, more than his life, he wanted that chance.

"I can't, Jill. In my gut I know Jason is in bad trouble."

Trevor watched the denial pinch her brow beneath the soft bangs. She'd made up her mind, and he wasn't going to change it. Not without a lot more proof, anyway, which at the moment he didn't have.

"No, Trevor. Raymond's the one in trouble, and Horizons, but not Jason. He told the truth."

A sick, desolate feeling settled inside him. He'd walked away from Jillian once when he should have faced the truth, and they'd both paid a terrible price. He couldn't live with himself if he walked away from his son when Jason needed him the most.

Trevor cleared his throat. He wouldn't let himself feel. Not anything.

"Let me tell you what it's going to be like for him." His voice was flat. "I think he's maintaining now, just barely. Soon, though, he'll need more and more just to keep from getting the shakes. If he can't get it from your shelves or from the clinic, he'll steal the money, from you if he has to, and buy it from his friendly neighborhood pusher."

Jillian uttered a soft, hurt cry, but Trevor wouldn't let himself quit. If what he suspected was true, she was in for a very rough time. He'd do anything, *anything*, to save her from that kind of pain.

"He won't care where he gets the money or how he gets it. He won't care about you or his friends or anything except that filth he has to put into his body to keep from hurting. And he won't stop until he's in prison or dead."

"No!" Jillian backed away from him instinctively, her arms wrapped over her womb.

"Yes, Jill, *yes*. If he's hooked, he's living a nightmare. And someday he'll hate himself for the things he's doing now. He might even wish he were dead. Is that what you really want?"

"How can you even ask me that?" she gasped in a shredded voice, her face haunted. "I'd do anything for Jason. Fight for him. Die for him."

"I'm fighting for him," Trevor shot back, balling his fists impotently. "As hard as I know how. The only way I know how."

"Are you sure, Trevor? Or are you trying to save Horizons by putting the blame on Jason? We both know this will lead to the revocation of the lease."

Blotchy red stained his cheeks, and sweat darkened the ribbed neck of his sweatshirt as he stared down at her, his copper eyes glinting dangerously. "Horizons is important to me, Jill," he said in a voice so controlled that it was steely smooth. "But I'd *never* do what you're suggesting."

"Then what *are* you doing?" she cried, her voice rising as the anguish built inside her.

Trevor fought desperately for control. The violence that was always inside him was very close to erupting, and he couldn't let that happen. Not with Jill.

"I'm trying to save my son's life."

"By branding him a liar and a . . . a junkie?"

"I didn't have a choice."

"Of course you had a choice," Jillian said impatiently. "We both had choices, and I chose to believe my son instead of a . . . a thief. Because I love him."

"Love shouldn't blind you to the truth, Jill."

"Maybe you really believe Jason is capable of lying and letting an innocent person go to prison. But you're wrong, terribly, terribly wrong. And I don't think Jason will ever get over this . . . this betrayal."

But she'd been wrong, too. She'd believed Trevor when he'd said he wanted to start over. Like the fool she'd sworn never to be again, she'd let him seduce her with his hands and his lips and the promises in his eyes.

"Jill, please try to understand. This isn't easy for me. I hate like hell to think he's hooked on pills. Or anything else."

"He's not."

"Have him tested. Prove me wrong."

Jillian inhaled swiftly, and she stared at him in disbelief. "Are you crazy? He'd think I didn't trust him."

"I'll do it, then," he said in a hard voice. "I'll take the flak, and you can stay out of it completely. But I'll need your written permission."

Jillian felt her temper rise, and her cheeks began to burn. "I told you that Jason was just like all the other teenagers in town, for heaven's sake. Maybe he's a bit moodier sometimes, and we've had our moments, I admit, but that doesn't make him an addict. I mean—" Her words began to tumble angrily, and she stopped short. She was breathing hard.

Surely it wasn't possible, she thought. Surely not.

Jillian's throat worked convulsively. "No," she whispered. "A test like that would only humiliate him more. I can't do that to Jase. Not after today. He needs to know I believe him. He needs me, Trevor."

He saw the rejection come into her eyes again, and he knew it was over. But he couldn't give up. He couldn't lose her. Not when he was so damn close to having everything he'd thought he'd given up forever.

"I need you, too," he said quietly. He'd never said those words to anyone before in his life, not even her. "More than you can imagine."

"No, Trevor," she said sadly, shaking her head. "You want to make love to me."

Trevor gritted his teeth against the hot slash of pain in his spine. "I want to make love to you, and live with you, and grow old with you." Trevor felt his face grow hot, and he knew he was close to the end of his endurance. He would try one more time. "I love you, Jill. I never really stopped."

Jillian stared at him, a blinding joy blurring her vision. *He loved her!* Her heart pounded, but even as she began to smile, the joy faded.

He couldn't love her and do what he'd just done to their son. The man she needed wouldn't sacrifice someone he loved to save a...a thing, even something as valuable as Horizons. Because she knew that was exactly what he was doing, whether he believed it or not.

An icy cold settled over her, and she wrapped her arms around herself, trying to stay warm. She felt vulnerable, exposed, alone. So terribly alone.

"I think it would be best if you never saw Jason again. If you never saw either of us again," she said evenly.

"Don't do this, Jill."

He sounded almost as though he were begging her. But that was nonsense, Jillian assured herself. Trevor would never beg. He hadn't once begged in the hospital. He wouldn't beg for her now, a woman he didn't love.

"Goodbye, Trevor."

Trevor didn't move. In his hard face his eyes went completely blank. Only the subtle tightening of his lips into a thin white line showed he was feeling anything at all.

"I love you," he said quietly. "No matter what you think."

"Maybe you do, in your own way. But I don't want your kind of love."

Feeling as cold as death, she pushed open the door and walked out into the sunshine. It felt like the coldest day in winter.

She was a dream, a vision in white satin, floating gracefully toward him past the vivid clusters of exotic flowers. Her long hair was a silk flame in the bright sunlight, cascading in gold-tipped curls over her creamy throat. Her lips were slightly parted in enticing promise, and her green eyes were filled with vibrant joy. In her dainty white hands she held roses, bright red velvet buds with long green stems.

He stood transfixed, watching her smile curve sweetly just for him. Her lovely, beguiling face was softened by the love she felt for him, and her skin glowed with a rare sensual beauty that brought tears to his eyes. She was his light, his life, his bride.

From this day forward they would be one for all eternity.

"My love," she whispered as she placed her dainty hand in his. "You make me so happy. I will always love you."

She gazed up at him shyly, her shimmering green eyes shining with trust and love. And expectation. She was waiting for him to say the words. Those hard, terrible words.

He struggled, feeling the clawing need inside him. "No," he shouted. *"No!"*

The love in her eyes shattered, turning to glittering emerald hatred. Her smile hardened, shuddered, turned to contempt. Her slender hand flew out, sending his head whipping back, jolting his spine.

"No...no... *No!*"

Trevor jerked awake, the sound of his pounding heart filling the dark room. He balled his fists under the corners of his pillow and waited, his eyes closed, for the dream to leave him. It had been months, years, since he'd awakened in this same cold sweat, his heart racing, his body rigid.

It was cool in the bedroom, but Trevor was drenched. The sheet beneath his body was clammy, and the one covering his thighs was twisted and wet.

Outside the wind hissed through the trees and pushed at the curtain covering the open window. Somewhere nearby a screech owl hooted, and from the shallow ravine below came the sound of churning rapids.

The dream was always so real. He could almost feel Jill in his arms, her soft womanly curves gentling the hard, rough angles of his scarred body, filling him with peace.

She would be fragile and delicate, like a lacy pink flower he'd once seen growing in the thin air on the highest slopes of Mount Rainier. But, like that flower, under the gentleness she was tenacious and strong and determined to survive.

Trevor slowly flexed his legs, feeling some of the tension ease. He opened his eyes and stared at the swooping gray shadows above him on the ceiling.

None of the other women in his life had been like her. None of them ever listened, really listened, with her eyes and her mind and her heart, when he'd talked.

He knew he was good-looking. Hell, women had told him that all his life. But no one had really wanted to know the man behind the face—until Jillian.

For some reason he'd never been able to think of her as just another attractive, willing lady the way he'd thought of the other women he'd bedded.

She'd always been special.

And she'd made him feel special. Because she'd thought he was brave, he'd been able to stand the pain a little better. Because she'd thought he was kindhearted, he'd fought to contain his quick temper. And because she'd believed in him, he'd managed to believe in himself.

He'd tried his damnedest to be the kind of man she'd needed in that terrible hospital. And he wanted with all of his heart to be the kind of man she needed now.

But he didn't know how. Damn it, he didn't even know how to begin.

Holding his breath against the spasm in his back, he slowly pushed himself to a sitting position. Sweat ran down his face and dripped onto his bare chest, and his head swam.

After Cobb had left with Raymond, in handcuffs and under arrest, Hank had slapped him back into traction. He'd stuck it out for three days. Three days of thinking of her and wanting her and worrying about her. Three days of hell. Then he hadn't been able to take it any longer, and he'd made Hank let him get up.

Slowly, carefully, he turned on the light and reached for his wallet. From an inner pocket he took out a folded sheet of thin blue paper. His hands shook as he carefully unfolded the letter. He didn't need his glasses to read these words. He knew them by heart.

Someday, my darling Trevor, I'll tell our children how bravely you fought to live. How you laughed instead of cried. And how you gave me some of your strength when I needed it the most. Maybe they'll need some of that strength, too, someday. And you'll be there. That's why I'll always love you.

His fingers were stiff as he refolded the letter and tucked it away again. But she didn't love him. Not anymore.

He felt the familiar ache of loneliness settle inside his hurting body. He would give all he owned or hoped to own if he could live that Christmas over.

He should have fought for her then, the way he'd tried to fight for her now. But life wasn't like that. He'd made a mistake, and he'd paid for it. He was still paying.

He'd tried as hard as he knew how to become the man she'd thought him to be.

He'd tried to be there for Jason. He'd tried to love his son. He'd tried to love her.

He didn't know what the hell else to do.

* * *

Jillian groaned and turned over onto her back. Her bare legs found a cool spot on the sheet, and she shivered. She couldn't sleep.

She kept thinking of Trevor and the look on his face when she'd walked away from him. He'd looked stunned, like a man who'd just received a mortal wound.

But she'd been right to say the things she'd said. Hadn't she?

She stared at the ceiling, longing for the feel of Trevor's strong, sheltering arms. He'd been in pain; she'd seen it in the lines of his face. He shouldn't have been out of bed. But had he been there for her, or for Horizons?

I love you.

His words haunted her. Paradoxically, in spite of the anger she still felt, she wanted to believe him. But if she believed those words, she had to believe the other, terrible, words, too.

And she couldn't.

Jason wasn't a liar, and he wasn't an addict. For three days and nights she'd watched him. She'd looked for signs, for clues, anything that would show her Trevor had cause for alarm.

Jason had been withdrawn and nervous when they'd come home. He'd spent most of the weekend listening to music in his room. None of his friends had called, but she'd heard him on the phone often, talking with someone.

His appetite had been poor, and he was pale and complained of stomach cramps. This evening, after dinner, he'd thrown up. She'd put him to bed with two aspirins and a hot water bottle. When she'd checked at ten, he'd been sleeping soundly.

But Trevor's words wouldn't leave her head. "Living a nightmare," he'd said, and he'd sounded so...haunted when he'd said it.

Groaning, Jillian threw off the covers. The cool air hit her bare skin, and she shivered. Shrugging into her robe, she hurried down the hall to Jason's room. She needed to make sure he was all right, for her own peace of mind.

Jason's door was closed. Without bothering to knock, she pushed it open and snapped on the light by the bed. She reached out to touch his forehead, but he wasn't there. The sheets were rumpled, and his pillow was bunched against the headboard, but the bed was empty.

Whirling, she raced to the bathroom at the end of the hall. He wasn't there. Calling his name, she ran through the rooms, becoming more and more worried. He wasn't anywhere in the apartment. Wrenching open the front door, she ran out onto the balcony, but he wasn't there. Nor was he anywhere in sight.

Her heart pounding painfully, she returned to his room and searched his closet. As far as she could tell, none of his clothes were missing. Feeling more and more frantic, she searched through his drawers. Where was he? Was he running away? Or only hiding until he could face his friends at school again?

But where would he go? she thought frantically, pulling open the last drawer. She tugged too hard, and the heavy drawer slid free of the runners and fell onto the floor.

"Oh, my God," Jillian whispered in horror. "No, please, no."

Taped to the back was a long white envelope that bulged open. It was filled with pills and capsules, a rainbow array of deadly Class Two drugs. Slowly she pulled it free and shook some of the contents into her palm.

Percodan. Thorazine. Codeine. Narcotics, all of them. Controlled substances.

The pills spilled from her hand into the thick rug, scattering without a sound around her bare feet. Jillian slowly sank to the floor, fighting for control. As though everything were magnified, she could see the lint on the rug and the smudges on the wall. The shadows seemed to take on life, mocking her.

Her son was an addict.

Trevor had been right. Jason, her dear little boy, was just like those hard-faced criminals she'd seen that first day in front of the platform.

In a white haze of pain Jillian ran her hand over the scattered tablets, feeling the different shapes against her palm. Unlike most parents, she knew exactly what effect each of these chemicals had on the human body. She could recite the properties and reactions by rote. She knew why each was used and in what dosage. And she knew exactly and in terrible detail the kind of damage each could do if abused.

Brain trauma, coma, death, all were possible. No, she thought, crushing a handful of pills in her fist. Probable.

And Trevor had known all of those things, too.

"What have I done?" Her voice seemed to come from far away, like a long, tortured groan.

She hadn't been talking about Jason at all that day at Horizons. She'd been talking about herself. Sure, she'd told herself she was defending her son, but in reality she'd been thinking only of herself and her needs.

It was her pain, her needs, her wants, that had driven her to lash out at Trevor. And she'd been oh-so-self-righteous, brutally condemning him for not loving her enough. Or for not loving her the way she thought she should be loved.

But what about her? Her kind of love? Since he'd been back in her life, she'd made him fight for every scrap of affection she'd given him. She'd offered him her body, but withheld her love, even when she'd felt it inside her. She'd demanded he prove himself over and over, that he atone, that he beg....

Suddenly it was all so clear.

She'd wanted to humiliate him, just as she'd been humiliated. She'd wanted him to pay and pay and pay. She'd wanted him to earn her love.

But love couldn't be earned, she realized now. It could only be freely given, or it wasn't really love. Given freely and without strings, just as Trevor had given his love to Jason, with no real hope of having it returned. Just as he'd continued to give it to him by trying to make Jason face the truth about himself, knowing his son would hate him for it. That she would hate him.

Trevor hadn't been trying to humiliate Jason. He'd been trying to save him. And he'd gone on trying, even after she'd ripped into him.

I don't want your kind of love.

But she did. Desperately.

She wanted the kind of love that gave her hope when she needed it. That told her the truth when it had to be told. That wrapped her in a protective embrace when she was lonely or sad or scared.

Jillian's hand began to shake, and she pulled it back against her stomach. She'd told him it wasn't enough. She'd rejected him.

Jillian stared blindly at the shadowy room. The familiar furniture wavered in front of her eyes, coming closer, moving away. An icy gray mist began to blanket the room and seep into her bones. She was so cold, so empty.

Her tongue was thick and sluggish. Her eyes refused to focus, and there was a strange heaviness spreading through her. From a great distance she heard a voice calling her name, saying something, but she couldn't make out the words.

"Put your head down and take deep breaths. In. Out. That's good, Jill. Keep breathing."

The hand rubbing her neck was warm and comforting, and the deep velvet voice was soothing. She was so scared.

"I'm here, Jill. We'll beat this, I promise."

In. Out. Breathe.

Slowly the giddiness passed, and she opened her eyes. "I'm okay now." She raised her head and tried to smile, but her lips were numb.

"Sure?"

Trevor was kneeling stiffly beside her, still rubbing her back. His face was drawn, and his eyes were filled with pity. He knew.

"Why didn't I see?" she asked in a tortured voice, turning to look at him.

"It's called denial," he said quietly. "I haven't met a parent yet who didn't have it to one degree or another."

"You knew."

"Not at first. But when Jason threw up on the river, I started to worry. If things hadn't gotten out of hand so fast, you might have gotten suspicious, too."

Jillian's eyes stung as she shook her head slowly from side to side. He was being kind. Her face burned as she lifted her chin. She didn't want his pity.

"Jill, this isn't your fault," he said in a low, strong voice. "If you never believe another thing I tell you, I want you to believe that."

His face was stiff, and his eyes were wary, as though he expected her to lash out at him.

"Yes, it is," she whispered through stiff, cold lips. "I should have protected him from this. I'm his m-mother."

She'd been so sure she'd given her son everything he'd needed. She'd read the books and done all the right things. She was a good mother. She just hadn't been good enough.

"You're also human, Jill. And you love Jason. Sometimes love makes us look the other way without our even knowing it."

She nodded slowly. He was trying to make her feel better, but they both knew how badly she'd failed Jason. And a small, sad part of her wondered if Trevor would ever forgive her.

"I'm sorry," she said in a faint, weary voice. "I should have believed you."

She raised her head and looked at him, trying to see his thoughts in his eyes. But tears blurred her vision. She blinked, and teardrops spilled from her lashes.

Without a word Trevor reached for her hand, and together they stood up. Gently he gathered her into his strong arms. He held her securely, without passion, making no demands.

"You've had a bad shock," he murmured against her temple, "but you'll get over it. You're too strong to let this throw you."

Jillian let his words flow over her. Words that were meant to comfort. Words uttered in the husky, deep voice she loved.

Her body shook from the cold and from shock, but he held her against him, supporting her, comforting her. He was so strong. Nothing would happen to her while he held her.

She pressed her face against his wide shoulder, feeling the smooth coolness of his leather jacket. She inhaled slowly, letting his masculine scent fill her nostrils. Clean-smelling soap, musky after-shave, good leather, and maybe a hint of cigar smoke. Trevor.

Wrapping her arms around him, she tried to draw on his comforting strength.

"Better now?"

Jillian nodded silently, then raised her head and looked at his face. With a sinking heart she saw there was no fire in his eyes, no passion in his expression, no tautness in his body. No love.

He no longer wanted her. And she couldn't blame him.

"We need to find Jason," he told her gently. "Has he ever run away before?"

Pressed so closely to his chest, she could feel his words as well as hear them. "No," she mumbled. "It's never happened before. Not ever."

His brow furrowed. "Okay. We'll start with his friends. You'd better call, since you know their parents."

Jillian had heard that tone before. Trevor was talking to her in the same commanding way he'd used with the man named Nick. Taking charge. Issuing orders. Relegating her to the same importance in his life. She swallowed the rest of her tears and moved out of his arms. She had a feeling he would never hold her again.

"I'll use the phone in the bedroom," she told him evenly. "My book is in there."

Twenty minutes later Jillian had worked her way through the names of Jason's friends, even the ones she hadn't seen in months. But no one knew where he was.

It had been awkward, deflecting the anxious questions of the sleepy mothers and fathers who'd answered. But she'd simply told them she and Jason had quarreled, and that he'd run out in a fit of temper.

Most of the voices on the other end of the wire had immediately warmed with sympathy. These parents had teenagers, too.

With a heavy sigh she dialed Mike Cobb's number. He was her last hope, but Mike's phone was busy. Anxiously she glanced at the clock. It was a quarter to two.

"No answer?" Trevor asked tersely.

He leaned forward in the small padded chair in front of her grandmother's dressing table, his expression remote. The curved mirror reflected the tired lines of his back and the weary slump of his shoulders. The lamplight silvered his hair and deepened the lines of his face.

Jillian felt a pang of guilt. He looked exhausted. And it was her fault. If she'd believed him, Jason would be safe in bed.

"It's busy." She hung up and dialed again. It was still busy. She put down the phone.

Trevor pressed his palms against his knees. "Looks like we'll have to go look for him." He caught her gaze, and he smiled wearily. "I'll drive, if you tell me where to go. This isn't a very big place. He might be . . . walking."

"Or he might be sick. Or hurt. Or—"

His smile became a bleak, warning frown. "Jill, stop it! You'll just make yourself crazy, and it won't help Jason."

Her guilt intensified. He was right. She was behaving badly. A wry smile curved her lips. How many times, as a critical care nurse, had she counseled frantic waiting relatives in that same calm way?

Too many times to be acting so irrationally, was the answer.

She pushed herself to her feet. She'd decorated this room herself. She'd wanted soothing colors, ivory and beige and cream, around her. And soft, sensuous fabrics to touch. This was her haven, her corner of serenity and peace away from her hectic, stressful life. But now this room was contaminated by the dark fear that filled her.

"Jill, it'll be okay." Trevor stood and came over to her. He took her hand and pressed it between his, warming her cold fingers.

He looked controlled and distant, the way he'd looked that first morning on the platform. Only his eyes had changed. The stillness that shadowed them seemed deeper, more a part of him than ever.

She summoned a smile. "Why did you come here tonight, Trevor? You never said."

His answering smile was surprisingly gentle. "Let's just say I came and let it go at that."

"You must have had a reason," she persisted. Deep down she was hoping he'd come to try again. That he hadn't been able to stay away. That, maybe, he still loved her.

"I came to try to convince you to have Jason tested. I had to try one more time before I left." There was a finality in his voice, and her hopes collapsed. She tugged her hand from his grasp.

"I'll go change. I won't be a minute."

Trevor shoved his hands into the pockets of his jeans. In the lamplight his eyes were the color of molten copper, but without the heat.

"I'll wait on the porch."

Chapter 13

The Jaguar was parked in the loading zone, just beyond the rectangle of grainy light spilling from the back window of the pharmacy.

Jillian huddled into the warmth of her fur-lined suede jacket and waited for Trevor to unlock the passenger door. The moon was sliding toward the west like a cold silver ball, and the air carried the harsh bite of frost. It was a lonely night.

"Do you have someone come in at night to clean up the store?" Trevor asked in a low voice next to her ear.

"No. I clean up before I open. Why?"

"Because there's someone in there."

Jillian's heart began to race as she stared into the dimly lit interior of the pharmacy. As a rule, she kept one light burning over the cash register, another in the rear where the prescription drugs were kept. Both lights were still lit.

"I don't see anyone," she murmured, her eyes straining. Everything looked perfectly normal.

"Someone's there, in the back behind that glass partition." His hand closed over her arm, holding her close.

"Do you think it's Jason?"

Her throat went dry, and her hands were shaking. The streets surrounding the square were empty and dark. They were alone.

"Does he have a key?" Trevor moved slightly, putting his body between her and the window.

"No. Only Darcy and I have keys. And Mel. As sheriff, he has keys to all the businesses in town."

"What about an alarm? You have one, don't you?"

"Of course. I set it myself before I locked up. Darcy and Mel have keys for that, too."

Trevor cast a quick glance around the area. "Okay. You go upstairs and call Cobb. Take off your shoes so you don't make any noise on the stairs. Tell him the guy is big, over six feet, and bulky. And he's wearing dark clothes. I don't know if he's armed."

Jillian strained to see the expression in his eyes, but the light was too dim. "What are you going to do?" Fear pounded in her temples, and her skin was clammy beneath the warm clothes.

"Nothing, unless the guy inside tries to leave. Then I'll stop him."

Jillian clung to his arm, feeling the power in the thick muscles beneath the leather. Trevor was brave, and he was strong, but his injured back made him vulnerable.

"What if he has a gun?"

"Then I'll duck." His voice was thin with impatience. "Enough questions. Go make your call." He gave her a little shove.

Heart pounding, Jillian quickly bent down to remove her sneakers, then hurried to the stairs and began to climb. She didn't want to leave him, but he was right. Mel should handle this.

Five minutes later she returned to find Trevor leaning against the front fender, his arms folded over his chest.

"Mel's on his way. He said not to do anything until he got here." She sat down and put on her shoes, tying the laces haphazardly before she got to her feet again.

"He would."

Jillian brushed the dirt from her jeans, then shoved her hands into the pockets of her jacket and stared at the window. Inside, she could see the tidy shelves and the spotless soda fountain. The long mirror behind the counter seemed to shimmer in the gloom.

"There he is," she whispered excitedly, her hand going to her throat. "I saw him in the mirror. He's as big as you are, and he's wearing dark clothes and carrying something—"

Mel appeared from the shadows, interrupting her. He was bareheaded and looked extra-bulky in his dark wool jacket. "Is the guy still in there?" he whispered when he came abreast of them.

"Yes," Trevor answered. "Jill just saw him. He might be armed."

Cobb drew his gun and clicked a round into the chamber. "Okay, I'm going in. You two stay here. When Howie and Arnold get here, tell them to be careful coming in. I don't want to get shot by my own men."

"Jill can tell them," Trevor said immediately. "I'm going with you."

Cobb whirled on him, his pale blue eyes glinting in the dim light. "No way, hotshot!"

Trevor's voice was flinty. "Don't argue, Cobb. According to your theory, the person inside there is from Horizons. If he is, I want to make sure he doesn't suddenly show up dead."

Jillian felt the sheriff's fury. He wasn't going to back down, and neither was Trevor.

She caught Mel's arm. "Stop arguing, you two. That's my stuff the guy's stealing. While you two fight it out, he could get away with my entire inventory."

The two men looked at her for a long second. Then Mel muttered a crude obscenity and jerked away. "Suit yourself, Markus," he said in furious growl. "But stay the hell out of my way."

Trevor grunted, then turned to Jillian. "Go back upstairs and wait," he ordered, grasping her by the shoulders.

"When you see the deputies arrive, you can come back down."

"No. You might need me."

"Damn it, Jill, I—"

"You comin' or not?" Cobb interrupted impatiently. "'Cause I'm goin' in. Now."

Trevor's hands tightened on her arms, then suddenly dropped away. "Get behind the car, then, and stay down," he ordered as he followed the sheriff to the door.

Jillian hesitated. As long as she kept in the shadows, she would be safe. Walking as silently as she could, she followed the two men, taking care to stay in the dark patch by the steps. She heard the faint metallic click as Cobb tried the door, then saw the tiny triangle of light pattern the sidewalk as he eased it open.

The sheriff entered soundlessly, his gun pointed toward the ceiling, with Trevor right behind him. "Hold it right there!" Mel shouted. He and Trevor crouched side by side behind a display table a few feet away from the prescription counter.

Jillian ran closer, hesitating on the threshold. Inside, two men in dark clothes and ski masks stood frozen in the rear. One of the men clutched a black plastic garbage bag in his hand, while the other, tall and muscular, held a lethal-looking hunting knife.

"Run!" shouted the man with the knife as he sprang toward the front. His hip crashed into a large basket of Halloween candy, sending it flying, and his feet slipped on the slick wrappers littering the floor.

"Freeze, sucker, or you're dead!" Mel lowered his gun and took aim.

"Wait!" Trevor yelled, but it was too late.

The sound of the pistol blasted Jillian's eardrums and reverberated like thunder off the high ceiling. She cried out, and Trevor spun around.

"Get the hell out of here, now!" he shouted, but she shook her head. If the thief was wounded, she had to help.

The second man stood frozen, his hand extended toward a bottle of pills on the shelf. Jillian glanced quickly in his direction, then followed Mel toward the front. Trevor's large, powerful body was between the robber and the back door. He wouldn't get away.

The thief lay in a crumpled heap near the front, blood pooling on the floor beneath his leg. He was moaning harshly and trying to move as Mel handcuffed his hands in front of him. It looked as though the bullet had gone through the fleshly part of his thigh.

"Lie still," Jillian ordered, bending over him. "I'm a nurse."

The man's pale blue eyes watched her through the slits in the mask. The dilated pupils were filled with panic and pain.

"You're going to be okay," she said, gently pulling the mask from his head. He began to sob.

Mel's brutal cry of disbelief echoed her own. The thief was Mike Cobb.

"No, oh, no," Jillian whispered, dropping the mask and stumbling to her feet. Shaking uncontrollably, she turned and stared toward the cubicle in the rear.

Her gaze collided with Trevor's. He was standing next to the second thief, a large black flashlight in his hand. Carmen Montoya had been hit with a flashlight.

Please, no, she thought. But she knew. Dear God, she knew. It had to be Jason under the mask. If she'd been close enough to see his eyes, she would have known immediately.

Jillian forced herself to move forward. Her legs felt disconnected from her body, and she was icy cold.

Trevor waited until she was only a few feet away. Then, with a deep sigh, he reached out and pulled the mask from Jason's head. Their son stood under the light, his face so pale it seemed transparent. His bright curls seemed to flame around his head, and his freckles stood out like dark teardrops against his skin. He stood transfixed, a look of fear on his face as he stared into his father's eyes.

"Where'd you get the key, Jason?" Trevor asked in a harsh voice. "From your mother?"

"Mike got it from his old man," Jason mumbled, glancing toward his sobbing friend.

"What about the clinic and Dr. Franklin's office?"

Jason shrugged. "Mike got us in."

Jillian didn't know what to say, what to feel. This was worse than anything she could possibly have imagined. She felt helpless, adrift, unable to believe her eyes.

"Why, Jase?" she asked in a strangled voice. "Why would you do this terrible thing to yourself?"

His faced changed, and suddenly he was a stranger, a grim, defiant half-grown boy with the eyes of a pain-crazed animal caught in a trap. "Everyone does it," he mumbled, his voice sullen. "Just like you drink wine. It's no big deal."

Trevor glanced at the bottles of Percodan that littered the floor by their feet. He could smell the cloying scent of medicine, and he wanted to gag. He hated the thought of his son putting that stuff into his young, strong body.

Slowly he raised his gaze to Jillian's face. She looked frozen, like a beautiful ice statue, but her eyes were filled with glittering green lights of pain. He'd tried like hell to spare her this, but he'd failed.

"No...no big deal?" she whispered, her voice rising. "No big deal? You stole, and you lied. You...you hit Mrs. Montoya, and you call it no big deal?"

Her voice shook uncontrollably, and in her mind she had an image of Jason lying there on the floor, bleeding, dying. "You could be dead now, do you hear me? Dead!"

"You wouldn't care if I was. You've got him now." Jason's lips twisted as he glared at his father.

Jillian inhaled swiftly, fighting for calm. She'd get through this somehow. She had no choice. "I care. But I hate the thought of the things you've done because of this...this madness. It's not like you didn't know what this stuff could do to you. I've told you over and over."

"Yeah, yeah, I know." His voice cracked, and his lips clamped together.

Jillian felt as though he'd just plunged a knife into her stomach and was twisting the blade. "Jason, I'll help you," she said in hoarse voice. "Together we'll—"

"I don't want your help!" he snarled, his face splotched with crimson. "You're always *helping*, always smothering me, always nagging. There's nothing wrong with me, nothing. So get the hell outta my face and leave me alone."

He spun away, his body braced to run, but Trevor grabbed his arm and jerked him around to face them. "No more running, Jason." Trevor's voice was hard and unyielding as iron. "It ends here. Now. All of it."

"You can't make me quit," Jason shouted. "No one can."

"You didn't hear me, son," Trevor said calmly. "It's over. No more lies. No more stealing. No more hiding."

Some of the bravado left Jason's face. "I...I tried to quit, but...but you don't know what it's like. No one knows what it's like. It's *awful*."

Trevor exhaled slowly. "You're right. It's hell, but I'll help you, Jason. We'll do it together."

Jason dropped his head to his chest. His silky red curls were only inches from Trevor's strong, square chin. "I can't do it."

"You can do anything if you want to badly enough." Trevor forced Jason's chin up and waited until his son met his gaze. "You'll do it, Jason, or you'll die."

Jason stared at him for a long moment. Then, with a deep, wrenching sigh, he buried his face against his father's shoulder.

Cold, stinging rain blew in vicious torrents against the window, rattling the panes. Jillian stood alone in a small waiting room tucked into a corner of the Horizons infirmary. It was like every waiting room in every hospital she'd ever been in. It was nearly twelve-thirty in the morning, almost two full days since she and Trevor had brought Jason here. He was in withdrawal.

Shivering, she huddled in the warm cotton blanket the nurse had given her and watched her breath fog the chilled pane. Inside, she felt as cold and lonely as the black void outside.

During the long endless hours she'd watched Jason slip farther and farther into a nervous, agitated state, his eyes growing more and more desperate as the craving inside him built. She wanted to scream in protest and denial and fury, but she forced herself to simply wait.

Trevor was with him. And Hank.

"Mayor?"

Jillian turned and say Raymond Williams standing just inside the door. He was dressed in wrinkled flannel pajamas and a robe, with black high-topped sneakers on his feet instead of slippers. Mel had released him from custody as soon as the ambulance had taken Mike to the clinic.

Jillian had heard from Adrian that Mel was a shattered man. Faced with his own words and actions, he'd refused to let Adrian transfer Mike to Horizons. Instead, he'd taken him down to Sacramento to a treatment center where his son was undergoing the same hell as Jason. Technically both boys were under arrest, charged with breaking and entering and assault.

"What are you doing up so late, Raymond?" Jillian asked with a weary smile.

"I wanted to see how the kid was doing," Raymond told her in a gruff voice. "He's hangin' in there real good."

Jillian leaned against the wall, her leg muscles rigid, holding her erect. "It's very generous of you to care. After what Jason tried to do to you, I mean. I . . . appreciate it."

"Got ya covered, Mayor," he said with a shrug. He hunched his shoulders and looked around the spare room. "Us junkies got to stick together. As Doc Stoneson says, it's hard enough stayin' clean, even with the help of your friends. Without it, it's a crapshoot."

Jillian tugged the blanket tighter. "I . . . did you go through what Jason's going through now?"

Raymond's face twisted, and his scar looked very white against his dark skin. "Yeah, ain't no other way. Course, it's not as bad as it used to be. Now they got drugs, clonidine, stuff like that, that helps some, but used to be, a junkie had to go cold turkey." He shuddered. "Guys would bang their heads on the floor, trying to knock themselves out."

Jillian shivered. She could only nod.

"Well, I best be gettin' myself back to the dorm. Counselor only gave me leave to be gone twenty minutes." He gave her an almost shy smile. "You hang in there, hear?"

Jillian pushed herself away from the wall and walked over to him. "Thank you, Raymond. You hang in there, too." She opened her arms and hugged him.

Raymond returned the hug like a clumsy grizzly, then turned and jogged away as though he were embarrassed.

Jillian returned to her spot by the window. The storm had intensified. Lightning zigzagged a wicked pattern across the sky, and the thunder rumbled almost continuously.

"How're you doing?"

Jillian looked up to see Hank standing where Raymond had been, a starched white coat looking strangely out of place on his lanky body. His face was shadowed, and he looked tired.

"I'm doing lousy," she told him bluntly. "I need to see him again, Hank. I'm going crazy waiting here like this."

"It's almost over, Jill. Then you can see him."

"Take me to him now. He's my baby. I should be with him."

Hank hesitated, then sighed. "Okay, but just for a minute."

Jillian unwrapped the blanket and dropped it onto the drab brown sofa. In silence she walked with Hank to the closed door at the end of the corridor.

Before she could go in, he stopped her. "This isn't going to be pretty, Jillian," he said soberly. "He's in the acute stage now, when he can't keep anything down, and his muscles are screaming. Even with the medication we can give him to help, his body is fighting him."

Jillian nodded woodenly. "I've seen patients in withdrawal," she said. But only in the early stages, before they'd been transferred to the detox ward. And none of those patients had been her fourteen-year-old son.

Hank's arm circled her shoulder for a brief hug. "Ready?"

"Ready."

They stepped into the room together and stood near the bed. The air reeked of sweat and vomit, and the sheets on the bed were rumpled and damp.

A plump nurse with blunt Oriental features and somber black eyes sat in the only chair. She gave Jillian a sympathetic smile as she entered, and Jillian tried to smile back. Her lips trembled, and she bit down hard.

Trevor and Jason were on the bed, both wearing wrinkled green hospital scrubs and white socks. The back of the bed had been raised, and Jason huddled against Trevor's chest, groaning in an exhausted voice, his face contorted with pain.

Trevor's cheek rested on Jason's sweat-soaked head. His eyes were closed, his face as wet as Jason's. He was rocking his son back and forth as though he were a child.

"Make it stop," Jason pleaded, his voice a mere thread. "*Please*, Trevor. I can't stand it."

Trevor stroked his back, his big hand dark against the gown. "Yes, you can, son," he told him with firm conviction. "You're doing great. Just a little longer and it'll be all over."

Jillian wanted to go to her son, to hold him and rock him and tell him she would make it better, just as she'd done when he'd stubbed his toe or skinned his knee. But she couldn't heal this hurt with a Band-Aid and a kiss.

Oblivious to her presence, Jason burrowed his face against Trevor's wide chest, like a baby seeking comfort. He thrashed violently, his feet pushing at the blanket.

"Please, please make it stop. It hurts," he repeated over and over, sounding more and more frantic.

Trevor glanced up then and saw her. He wasn't wearing his glasses, and his face had a surprisingly naked look. His gaze held hers, but she saw nothing there but exhaustion.

"Are you okay?" he asked in a raspy voice.

"I'm managing. How... how are you?"

His face relaxed for an instant. "I've had better days."

She wanted to tell him how sorry she was, and how much she loved him. She wanted to beg him not to go away and leave her alone again. But the words stuck in her throat.

Her smile was shaky, and his answering one was brief.

Thunder crashed overhead, and Jason moaned again, his hand twisting the sweat-stained neck of Trevor's smock. The boy's clutching fingers tangled in the hair covering Trevor's chest, and he winced.

"Here, hang on to this," he told Jason. Trevor slipped the medallion from his neck and placed it in his son's hand. "Squeeze hard."

Jason's knuckles whitened as his hand clutched the silver medal. His breathing was raspy, and his head bobbed back and forth endlessly. Suddenly his eyes opened, and he saw Jillian.

"I didn't mean it, Mama," he cried. "I'll tell the truth about the pills, I promise. Just get me out of here." His voice was high-pitched and scared, his expression wild and pleading. "I didn't mean to lie. I... was scared you'd hate me."

"I could never do that," she whispered, seeing the guilt and anger and desperation all mixed up together in his wonderful copper eyes. Her beautiful baby boy, an addict and a liar. And a thief.

"Then you'll take me home?" His face twisted. "Right now, huh, Mom? I won't use anything ever again. I promise."

She swallowed hard, forcing herself to maintain a calm expression. "You need professional help, sweetie. I know that now."

Hatred flashed into Jason's eyes, and she pressed her hands tightly together in front of her.

"You don't know nothin'!" Jason shouted, his voice suddenly strident. "You hate me, just like they do!"

"No, Jase. No. I love you. We all love you."

He gagged, then moaned. "I'm going to be sick again."

His thin chest heaved, and he leaned over, vomiting water, the only thing he'd been given since he'd arrived, into the shiny bowl tucked against the bed railing. Trevor waited until the boy had finished, then reached for the damp cloth hanging from the bed rail and gently wiped Jason's white face. "You're doing fine, Jason. Just fine."

Jason began to whisper. Trevor gave her a brief glance, then ducked his head and began soothing the boy with the same endless litany.

Jillian pressed her trembling fingers to her lips and clutched Hank's arm. A clammy cold spread through her, and her head felt as though it were filled with soggy cotton. "How... how much longer?"

"Hard to say. At least a few hours more," he said in a low voice. "C'mon, I'll buy you a cup of coffee."

Jillian shook her head. "I'm not leaving him." A shudder ripped through her, and she hugged herself for warmth.

Trevor lifted his head and blinked at her. There was a smear of blood on the side of his neck where Jason's nail had raked his skin. "Jill, please," he said in an exhausted voice. "Don't argue. Hank knows best."

She started to refuse again, but Hank's rough drawl stopped her. "You'll be doing more for the boy by giving him privacy," he said in a terse professional tone. "Besides, he's going to need you in good shape and not as exhausted as he is when this is over."

Jillian nodded woodenly. Hank was right. She would only be in the way.

Six hours later Trevor stood by the bed and looked down at the face of his sleeping son. The boy's skin was pasty white beneath the freckles, and his features were contorted into an exhausted frown.

Sleep, son, he thought. Sleep while you can. He bent over stiffly and kissed Jason's damp forehead.

"He'll be out for a while now," Hank murmured, taking the boy's pulse. "I'll stay with him. You and Jillian have things to talk about."

"Where is she?"

Trevor's eyes stung with tiredness, and his back throbbed with the kind of deep ache that would invariably end in a spasm if he didn't rest his strained muscles soon.

"In the waiting room. I made her drink some soup at about four, and she promised to lie down for a while."

With a sigh Trevor removed the medallion from Jason's hand and slipped it over his neck. "Take good care of my son, okay? I've done about all I can do for now."

"Don't worry. He's tough, like his dad."

"Yeah, I'm tough, all right."

Hank gave him a thoughtful look. "Trev, she's class all the way. She can take the truth."

"Yeah, but can I handle telling it to her?"

He held his breath against the pain and pulled the sweat-soaked smock over his head. He threw it onto the end of the bed, took the fresh one Mrs. Sung held out to him and pulled it over his tired body.

He needed a shower and a shave and at least eighteen hours of uninterrupted sleep, but first he had to face Jillian. These three days and nights with Jason had taken everything he had, but he'd rather go through them all over again then live through the next few minutes.

Trevor found her in the waiting room where Hank had said she'd be. She was stretched out on the sofa, asleep.

It was dawn, and the storm was over. The rising sun filtered through the window, caressing her face with pale color. She was wearing some kind of fuzzy white sweater that looked soft against her skin, and her bare toes peeped out from beneath the edge of the blanket.

Trevor stood motionless, staring down at her. He longed to rest his head on her breast and pull her warmth and sweetness over him like that same soft blanket she was clutching so tightly. He needed her strength and her fire. And more than anything he needed her to smile for him one more time before he left.

But he hated to wake her. She looked so fragile, with her thick, long hair tousled into dark red ringlets against her pale cheeks, and her slender wrist draped over her eyes.

But his lady was no shrinking violet, for all her daintiness. She was strong and feisty and every damn thing a man could want in a woman.

His lady, he thought with a silent sigh. But only in his dreams. She didn't want his kind of love, and it was the only kind he had to give.

Gritting his teeth against the hot ache in his lower back, Trevor lowered himself onto the sturdy oak coffee table in front of her. His hand shook as he brushed a thick curl away from her forehead. Her skin felt like warm satin, and he let his hand rest against her cheek for a heartbeat, knowing it might be the last time he'd be allowed to touch her.

He squeezed his eyes closed, then sighed and dropped his hand. "Jill, wake up. It's morning." His voice was hoarse, and his throat hurt.

"Mmm."

Her lashes fluttered, and she opened her eyes. Trevor saw the pinched strain around her mouth and the bruised shadows under her eyes as she stared at him in drowsy confusion.

"Is it over?" she asked in the sleep-husky voice he loved.

"For now, yes. He's sleeping."

Jillian blinked, trying to force some life into her leaden limbs.

Trevor looked terrible. Under the gray stubble darkening his jaw, his skin was ashen, and his gaunt cheeks were drawn and shadowed. Beneath his furrowed brow, his eyes were bloodshot and rimmed in red. This was the man she'd accused of not caring enough, she thought, feeling the guilt and the anguish fill her.

She'd been such a fool.

"He's okay," Trevor said in a worn-out voice that hurt her to hear. "He's got guts."

Like his father, she thought.

Aloud, she asked softly, "But when he wakes up, he's still going to be an addict, isn't he?"

Moving carefully, she sat up and swung her legs over the edge of the couch. Ever since she'd left Jason's bedside she'd tried to push the horror from her mind, but she hadn't succeeded.

"Yes," Trevor said in a weary voice. "He'll always be an addict. It doesn't go away. Ever."

He rubbed his hands over his knees. He knew what she was going through, but he couldn't help her. She had to fight this out on her own.

"I could have stopped it," she said. "If I'd seen what was happening, I could have gotten him help."

"Maybe. But that hardly matters now."

"Of course it matters! I failed him."

The helpless tremor in her voice shook him badly. They were in the same room, sharing the same pain, yet they were miles apart. He knew now they always would be.

"Jill," he said wearily, forcing himself to concentrate, "Jason needs you now more than ever. It's not going to do any good to think about what you did or didn't do. He just needs you to love him and forgive him."

"I do. Of course I do," she said, fighting the tears. Last night she'd thought she would never cry again, but she couldn't seem to help herself. "But I can't make this go...go away. All...all his life he'll have to fight this...this awful battle, and the books say that sooner or later most addicts lose the fight and use again."

"Some don't."

She raised tortured eyes to his. "My baby's only fourteen, and his life is ruined."

Trevor's patience gave out. "If he wants to make it, he will. If he doesn't, he won't." He didn't bother to search for gentle words. He was too whipped for tact. "That's the bottom line, no matter what the damn books say. And you're not helping him by feeling sorry for yourself, or for him, either.''

Jillian gaped at him. "How can you say that? You don't know what it's going to be like for him."

"Don't I?" His voice roughened. "When he's tired, or depressed, or sometimes for no damn reason at all, he'll remember the sweet euphoria and the blessed numbness. His veins will burn, and his muscles will tighten until he can't sit still. If he doesn't find something to distract himself, he'll go looking for a fix. But the choice is still his."

"Stop it! I don't want to hear that!"

"But you need to hear it. He'll want it, Jill. For the rest of his life. Every morning when he wakes up, it'll be waiting for him, this monster in his gut. So he'll fight, one day at a time. And he'll win that same way." Trevor ran his hands down his thighs, trying to release the tension building inside him. "He can do it."

"What if he can't?"

"Then he'll die."

She inhaled swiftly, and the air hurt her throat. "No, no, Trevor. Don't say that. I don't want him to die. I . . . I don't want him to be an addict."

Trevor took a deep breath, wanting more than anything to have these next few minutes behind him. "I know, angel. I don't want this kind of a future for my son. I don't want him to be an addict, either. But he is. And...so am I."

Jillian stared at him, her pupils slowly dilating in horror. "No...no," she whispered. "I don't believe you."

Now that he'd started, he would tell her all of it, just as he should have told her weeks ago. It didn't matter now. He'd offered her all the love he had, and she'd rejected him.

A deep sadness settled inside him. He had a lot of empty days and nights ahead of him before he would stop missing her.

"It's true. I'm a junkie, Jill. For a long time, years, I woke up every morning with my gut screaming for a fix." He forced himself to accept the horror in her eyes. "I was hooked, Jill. On that same morphine you used to give me.

That the doctors prescribed to keep me alive. By the time they decided I'd had too much for too long, it was too late. I needed it, I craved it, I'd do anything for it. I tried a dozen times to quit, but I couldn't.''

Jillian saw the naked truth in the eyes she adored and knew that if she moved, she would start screaming and screaming and never stop.

''Your letters, you... you said everything was fine. You said you were getting better.'' Her lips were dry and moved woodenly, as though framing each word in slow motion.

''I lied.'' His attempt at a smile was a failure. ''That's one of the things addicts do, Jill. They lie. They do other things, too. Stupid, senseless, shameful things, like... like betraying the ones they love the most.''

Jillian shivered. Now it all made sense. Terrible, shocking sense. He'd lied when he said he'd be there at the wedding.

When he saw she wasn't going to say anything, Trevor forced himself to tell her the rest. ''You asked me how I knew what Jason was doing. I knew because I'd been there, Jill. I spent all of my money buying black-market morphine. And when it was gone, I lied to my father and got more. When that was gone, I got it from my mother. I told her you needed it for your family. Something about your mother being terminally ill.''

Jillian uttered a small cry, and his face twisted. The scalding guilt came back to him, making him relive the nightmare he'd tried so hard to put behind him, and he shuddered. ''The night before I flew to Honolulu, I went to the hospital to buy the stuff from an orderly there. When he tried to hold out on me, I hit him and took it. I'm not proud of what I did, Jill, but I can't change it, either.''

Jillian groped for the hard cushion behind her. ''You... you never said...''

Trevor saw the pictures in his head, the blurred, shameful images of the things he'd done in those terrible, black months. He'd fought back, one day at a time, slowly regaining the trust of his family, gradually paying off his debts and regaining his self-respect by building the best damn roads and bridges he could. He'd driven himself relentlessly to change his life, to change himself, but it had been years before he'd been able to forgive himself.

"I was there, Jill. At the Royal Hawaiian. I stood there in front of that pretty outdoor chapel you'd made for us, and I started to cry. Everything was so clean and white, so... so decent. I wanted to be with you so much. More than I can make you know. It nearly killed me to walk away without you."

"Why... why didn't you tell me? Why didn't you let me help you?" Jillian felt as though she were choking. She struggled to swallow the lump in her throat, but it wouldn't budge.

Trevor saw the terrible anguish in her, and he wanted to cry. But he hadn't cried in years, not since that first Christmas without her.

"Because I was dirty, Jill. Inside and out. I hated the things I did to get the drugs I craved, and I hated myself because I didn't have the guts to quit. I would have done anything to get it, Jill, even... even lie to you so that you'd get it for me. I loved you too much to put you through that."

Trevor was intensely aware of every breath Jillian took. She looked stricken, as though he'd slapped her hard across the face. But he was afraid to move. Afraid to touch her.

He looked up at the ceiling. "I hit bottom after that. I was broke, my family was disgusted with me, I'd lost all of my self-respect." His voice was thick and tortured. "I'd lost you."

Slowly he dropped his gaze until it rested gently on her face. "One day I woke up in a strange bed with a strange woman, and I knew I would either have to get help or walk off the end of a pier."

Jillian wanted to touch him. To smooth the exhaustion from his face and gentle the bleak look of self-contempt in his eyes. But she was afraid. "What... what did you do?"

"I thought about you, about the things you'd said to me when I was half out of my mind in Tokyo. You told me to fight back, to dig down deep inside and find the guts to live."

He took a slow, deep breath. "Somehow I made it to the VA hospital and checked myself into the special program they'd set up for guys like me. That's where I met Hank. He was in charge of the program. He got me through withdrawal somehow. I still can't remember those first few weeks." He sighed heavily and ran his hand through his sweat-damp hair. "Hank tells me I should be glad I can't."

"Cold turkey," she whispered, her hand at her throat.

"Yeah, some name, huh? I still hate the sound of it."

He dropped his gaze. He couldn't look at her. He wasn't ready to see the revulsion in her eyes. He wanted to remember the way she'd looked at him on the river for just a little longer.

Jillian twisted the blanket in her lap. "I don't know what to say," she whispered, staring into his tired face. "All these years I thought you'd left me because you hadn't loved me. But you did, didn't you? Just like you love Jason."

Trevor braced his shoulders and slowly raised his gaze. She knew it all now, except for one last thing.

Her eyes were shadowed and dark, darker than he'd ever seen them. But she was watching him with wariness, not contempt. His heart began to pound, but he wouldn't let himself hope.

His hand shook as he pulled the silver medallion from its place against his skin. It dangled from his fingers, swinging gently in the dim light.

"I was ashamed to tell you the truth when I saw you again, Jill. I wanted you to get to know me the way I am now before . . . before I had to tell you about the loser I was before."

Jillian stared at him as he pressed a tiny latch on the side, and the top sprung open, spilling a wide golden band studded with diamonds into his hand.

"The first thing I did when I got on my feet was buy this for you," he said in a rough whisper, taking her hand and putting the ring carefully into her palm. "Before I quit using, I sold everything else, but I could never give this up, even when I knew you'd never wear it."

Jillian stared at the wedding band she'd never worn. All those years he'd kept it next to his heart, this man who'd said he loved her. Tears spilled from her eyes and trickled down her cheeks.

"Oh, Trevor, I wish...I wish you'd come to me. We could have fought this...this battle together." Her voice was sad.

"My life was so ugly. I didn't want it to soil you."

He touched her face. One last, sweet touch. He'd had years and years of wanting and not having, only to come so close. So damn close. His eyes burned with tiredness.

How? he thought wearily. How the hell was he ever going to make it without her? Somehow he would have to try, but it was going to be so hard.

She tilted her hand so that the diamonds caught the light. "It's a beautiful ring."

"When I was shipped stateside I felt as though we were already married," he said, touching the gold band with the blunt tip of his finger. "I felt that the ceremony would only be a formality. I—I never really stopped feeling that way."

He closed her fingers over the wedding band, then bent to kiss her hand. Jillian felt the brush of his lips, and she shivered. His firm lips were as cold as her skin.

"Keep the ring, Jill. It's always been yours." His hand tightened over hers. "I'll always love you, angel."

Jillian heard the sigh of goodbye in his voice, and she started to shake.

"Then why...why didn't you come looking for me, after...after you quit?"

Trevor felt the thickness clogging his throat. "It took me a long time to fight my way out of the pit I'd put myself into, Jill. I...I was sure you would have found someone else by then."

He wanted to wipe the tears from her face, but he knew he couldn't touch her. He had to get used to being alone again.

"There was never anyone but you. Not in my heart. There never will be. It's you I want. I love you."

Trevor stared at her helplessly. He'd never learned to pray. He wasn't sure prayers were even heard. But he knew there was a part of him that wanted to believe. Silently he breathed a plea that her love was strong enough to accept the flawed man he would always be.

"I can't make you any promises, Jill," he told her, needing to tell it all. "I can only handle one day at a time."

Jillian felt the lump in her throat dissolve, and a strange peace came over her, as though her life had gone full circle and returned to the place where she and Trevor had started.

"All I want is for you to keep the promise you already made me."

He frowned, and his eyes grew wary. "What promise?"

"A wedding. With champagne and roses."

Her face softened into a beautiful smile as she gazed down at the ring in her palm. "I can put it on now, but I'd rather you gave it to me in front of the chaplain, with Jason and Hank and Addie watching." She held her breath, letting her eyes and her smile tell him how much she loved him.

Trevor stared at her, his face tight. Slowly his eyes warmed until they were the beautiful molten copper she loved. "You'll marry me?"

He sounded shocked, and just a little scared. Jillian touched the tiny dimple that appeared at the corner of his mouth whenever he frowned. "Any time, any place." Her fingers brushed the rumpled locks away from his damp forehead, and a coarse tremor shook him.

Trevor wanted to crush her to him, but he was afraid to move. "I'm still a junkie. And I still want it, Jillian, especially when my back is giving me fits and all I can have is aspirin." He took a slow breath. "Sometimes I . . . I can be hard to live with. Sometimes I just have to . . . go off by myself and fight it through. I never know when that's going to happen, or how long it'll take. Sometimes it's months before I can handle a normal life . . . the kind you deserve."

She caressed his face with warm, loving hands. "Are you trying to warn me off? Because I have to tell you that it won't work. I can be just as tough as you, Trevor Markus."

Trevor felt something hard and mean give way inside him. She meant it. She wasn't afraid. Not of him, or his addiction, or the future.

Sweet, hot joy rushed through his body, more potent than any drug he'd ever craved, and he started to shake. He didn't need anything but her.

Trevor groaned and pulled her onto his lap. Through the double layer of soft cotton he could feel her heart pounding against his chest. His own heart was galloping so fast that he couldn't tell when one beat ended and the other began.

With a grateful sigh he buried his face in her thick hair and gave in to the one craving he would never have to fight. "Christmas Eve," he whispered hoarsely. "On the grounds of the Royal Hawaiian. I'll bring the champagne."

"And the roses. Lots of red roses."

Trevor closed his tired eyes and crushed her to him. He couldn't seem to stop shaking.

Jillian snuggled against his hard, tired body and knew nothing would defeat them ever again. Each had been through hell and survived. Together they could face anything.

"Don't let go, my darling," she begged, her eyes filling with tears. "Don't ever let go."

And Trevor knew he never would.

Epilogue

She was a slender goddess in ivory, floating gracefully toward him past the pink and orange clusters of exotic flowers. Her long hair was a silk flame in the bright sunlight, cascading in gold-tipped curls over her lovely throat. Her lips were slightly parted in enticing promise, and her green eyes were filled with vibrant joy. In her dainty white hands she held roses, bright red velvet buds with long green stems.

He reached for her, his hand folding over hers. Her smile curved, bloomed, warmed, just for him, and her lovely, ethereal face turned up toward his.

Love radiated from her eyes as she said the words, sweet wonderful promises that bonded them together forever. His heart swelled, and tears pressed his eyes, as her wide emerald eyes drew him closer, asking, promising, waiting for him to say the words. Those hard, terrible words.

He struggled, feeling the clawing need inside him. "No," he cried in agony. "No more."

Hurting, he reached for her, feeling the warmth of her light fill him, and the ache began to ease. "My angel," he whispered. "I love you."

The love in her eyes shimmered, grew brighter, soothed him. He bent his head to kiss her, but she floated away, lost to him. He'd waited too long....

"No, no, *no!*"

"Darling, wake up. Trevor, it's just a dream."

Trevor woke up in a cold sweat, his heart pounding, his body rigid. He was breathing hard, and harsh sound filled the bridal suite. Not again, he thought in a haze of pain. He couldn't make it without her.

"Darling, I'm here. It's all right." Her voice was soothing, sweet, and it took him a minute to realize she was really here, the woman he'd longed for for so long. His angel. Jillian.

"Jill," he whispered, feeling his heart throb in his throat. He reached for her, pulling her close so that he could feel her against him, soft and clean-smelling and sweet.

"I'm here, Trevor. Right next to you."

He closed his eyes, feeling the silk of her hair caress his neck. Her skin was warm and smooth, and she smelled of roses and sunshine.

"I was dreaming of the wedding," he whispered, feeling the catch in his throat. "I thought I'd lost you again."

He buried his face in her hair, suddenly ashamed of the need for her love that filled him more and more every day. She was his whole life, but he couldn't tell her. He was still afraid to accept the happiness she was offering with such sweet generosity.

And sometimes he was afraid he wouldn't be able to fight hard enough against the demons that sometimes haunted him, afraid that he would let her down again.

"You'll never lose me," she murmured, pressing her lips against his throat. She could feel the terrible tension in him, straining his powerful muscles against his skin.

A few hours ago they'd made glorious love for the first time as husband and wife. He'd whispered sweet, loving words of longing and need in her ear, and for the first time she'd known how very much he loved her.

Silently she lay against him, stroking his muscular chest with a gentle hand, soothing him, letting him feel her love. Gradually he relaxed, and his breathing gentled.

Over the past weeks she'd discovered that Trevor was a terribly complex man, warm and giving, but also moody and introspective. He drove himself hard, and he rarely allowed himself to relax.

From Hank she'd heard of those wretched hours when the morphine was slowly leaching from his body, the hours when Trevor had screamed her name in agony and pleading. And she'd cried when Hank had told her about the medallion containing her ring. Trevor had held it in his hand, too, just as Jason had. Only they'd had to pry it from Trevor's clenched fist after he'd finally passed out.

At the altar in the same familiar corner of the Royal Hawaiian grounds, watching the painful memories flicker in his eyes as he'd said his vows to her, she'd made a silent vow of her own. Somehow she would take the shadows from his eyes and replace the stillness with the kind of happiness she could feel in her own eyes. That would be her special wedding gift to the husband she loved with all her heart.

Trevor sighed and pulled her closer. "How do you like your wedding day so far?" he whispered, stroking her arm. Most of the tension was gone, and a pleased smile curved his lips.

"So far it's perfect." She inhaled slowly, filling her lungs with the seductive perfume filling the room. "Where did you get all the red roses? There must be a hundred."

"I went to the same florist. I think I had to put all the ghosts behind me, Jill. I loved our wedding, but in a lot of ways it's been hard for me. I had to face a lot of bad memories all over again."

His hand shook as he stroked her hair.

"Me, too, but having Addie and Hank here helped." She laughed, deliberately banishing the past to some far corner of her mind.

There was a soft, comfortable silence. Jillian listened to the quiet beating of Trevor's heart and thought about the weeks following Jason's arrest. He'd been at Horizons the entire time, learning how to deal with the things he'd done to himself.

Trevor had been forced to spend time in Seattle and abroad, but he'd called often and returned for brief visits as often as he could.

Every time he'd returned there had been a silent question in his eyes for the first few moments. He still couldn't believe she'd accepted him, but he would.

Jillian smiled. This was the first full night they'd ever spent together, and she wanted to savor every second.

The soft hair on his chest tickled her nose as she turned her head to peek at the clock. It was a few minutes past midnight. Christmas.

She stretched slowly, feeling the sleek sheets under her bare legs. The bridal suite of the elegant old hotel was huge, big enough for three couples, but she needed only this bed and the man beside her.

"Merry Christmas," she murmured.

Trevor groaned and lifted her face for a warm, loving kiss. "This is the first time in years I haven't been blind drunk by this time," he told her with a rueful chuckle. "I like this better."

"Me, too."

Jillian sighed in slumberous pleasure and traced the strong curve of his shoulder with her fingers. "Jason looked especially handsome today, don't you think?"

Trevor's chuckle was a sexy rumble in the darkened room. "I don't know about handsome, but when he called me Dad, I nearly lost it right there in front of the minister and everyone."

Jillian felt his chest rise and fall with a deep sigh, and tears pushed at her throat. "He's come a long way in two months. I'm so grateful."

Trevor stroked her back. "Me, too. For a lot of things, but especially for you. I still can't believe you're mine."

"You'll believe it when we move into that terrific house you're building for us. I intend to go crazy decorating."

Trevor laughed, and she felt shivers run up her spine. He laughed a lot now, but each time was a special gift.

"You can do anything you want, angel. I've never really had a home before, just a house on the lake. I don't care what you do to it, as long as we spend every night in the same bed."

"I know it was silly, making you stay out at Horizons, but—"

"Not silly. Frustrating, maybe. But you, my dearest wife, are a role model in my adopted hometown. I hated leaving you every night, but I'm proud of you, too." His hand combed her thick hair, spreading the silken strands over her shoulders in a warm fan.

"Do you believe Mel actually asked to have Mike sentenced to Horizons?" she asked incredulously. She still couldn't believe the change in the man.

The sheriff was still obnoxious at times, but his attitude toward Trevor and the others at Horizons had completely changed. He'd even wished the two of them well on their marriage.

"The judge was very generous to both boys," Trevor answered, his voice suddenly serious. "It'll be an incentive for them to stay clean, knowing he'll expunge their records when they're eighteen if there are no more incidents."

"Mmm. We've been so lucky."

He groaned and slid his big hands down to her shoulders. His thumbs stroked the fragile hollow of her neck, exciting her, pleasuring her. His leg slid against hers, and she felt the heat shoot upward, spreading into every part of her. She wanted him—again. And he wanted her.

"No, I've been the lucky one," he murmured. "I don't deserve your love, but I'll take it, because I can't live without you. Not anymore."

She traced the curve of his lips with her finger. "So what do you want for Christmas?"

He swallowed. "I have everything I've ever wanted, Jill. You, here in my bed, wearing my ring, and a son who's finally accepted me as his father. I have it all." His voice was thick with feeling.

Jillian's eyes softened, and a tremulous smile curved her lips. Her hand shook as she took his hand from her face and placed it on her warm belly.

"How about an autumn baby?" she whispered adoringly. "Maybe a little girl this time? With her daddy's beautiful eyes?"

Trevor stiffened. Slowly, gently, his hand pressed against her belly. "A baby? You want another baby?"

He sounded awestruck, as though the thought had never occurred to him.

"I want your baby," she whispered.

A hard tremor passed through his big, strong body. His eyes closed for an instant, then slowly opened, and he looked at her, happiness flaring in those beautiful copper depths.

"I love you, angel," he whispered in a tortured voice. "So much. So damn much."

She moved upward to kiss him. But first, very gently, very lovingly, she wiped the tears from his face.

* * * * *

A Note from Annette Broadrick

Dear Reader,

Getting married seems to be a topic little girls fantasize about. What kind of dress, how many bridesmaids and, most especially, who will be the groom?

In this story, Penny had her daydreams as a child, but as an adult she packed them away. It was time to be practical and mature.

Isn't it nice, though, when those childhood dreams come true, despite all the practical considerations? Sometimes that's exactly what a friend is for.

Annette Broadrick

THAT'S WHAT FRIENDS ARE FOR

Annette Broadrick

Chapter One

A soft summer breeze gently caressed Penny's bikini-clad body. The muted sound of water lapping against the dock where she lay provided a rhythmic accompaniment to the periodic melodies of the birds who made their homes near the shores of Tawakoni Lake.

Penny Blackwell had always enjoyed summer and the opportunity to do nothing more strenuous than work on her tan. Being indolent made a pleasant contrast to the hectic schedule she followed the rest of the year.

She smiled to herself. In another week her usual summer routine would be changing permanently. The tempo of her life would doubtless be increased to the point where days like today would be very rare.

"That's a very secretive smile you're wearing these days, Runt," a deep male voice said from somewhere close by. "I find it quite provocative."

Penny's eyes flew open in shock, not only because she'd thought she was alone but also because that voice from her past should have been two thousand miles away.

"Brad!"

She was suddenly conscious of what a small portion of her body her bathing suit covered. Penny grabbed her matching cover-up robe, and with strangely uncoordinated movements for someone normally graceful, she pulled it on jerkily.

"What are you doing here?" After her first glimpse at the man towering above her, she refused to look up again.

Penny knew very well what Brad Crawford looked like. In that quick glance she'd seen that the only item of clothing he wore was a pair of faded cutoffs that should have been discarded years ago. They hung perilously low on his hips.

"Is that any greeting for a friend and neighbor whom you haven't seen in three years?" he asked. Without making an obvious effort, Brad leaned over and picked her up, placing her on her feet in front of him. Even with Penny standing, Brad continued to tower over her, the top of her head coming only to his collarbone. No one else had the ability to make her as aware of her lack of inches as Brad Crawford.

He slid his hand under her chin and lifted her face until he looked directly into her eyes. "You're looking even more beautiful than I remembered," he said, the warmth in his gaze adding heat to her already sun-kissed body, "and I didn't think I had forgotten anything about you." He paused, as though relearning every feature on her face. "I've really looked forward to seeing you again."

Penny's mind seemed to lose all discipline as thoughts she'd assumed were buried years ago flew around in her head like fragments of a jigsaw puzzle—the scraps indecipherable, creating a confusing mélange. She searched desperately through the hodgepodge of disconnected thoughts for something casual to say in response.

She could hardly parrot his last comment. She certainly had not looked forward to ever seeing Brad Crawford again.

"You surprised me," she replied in a feeble attempt to sound natural. "When did you get home?"

He glanced back to the shoreline where the two homes that had sat side by side for three generations overlooked the lake. "Not too long ago. I've been here long enough to find something to wear that is more in keeping with this Missouri weather," he said with a grin that was as familiar to Penny as her own. "I visited with Mom for a few minutes, but she knew I was eager to come find you, so she sent me off."

Penny fought to ignore the implication in that remark. Pretending that she no longer wished to sunbathe, she gathered up her towel and tanning lotion and started toward her home. Brad kept pace with her.

"Why are you here?" she asked, dreading his answer.

He confirmed her fear by answering, "I received an invitation to your wedding. I decided to come home to meet the knight who stole my princess while I was busy slaying dragons."

Penny fully intended to discuss Brad's invitation with her mother at the very first opportunity. Brad Crawford had definitely not been on the guest list Penny had prepared.

Keeping her eyes on the path in front of her, she grumbled, "I don't know why you always make everything sound so dramatic."

"Don't you, Penny? That surprises me. Seems to me drama comes easily for both of us."

That was true, but she resented being reminded. Why now, of all times? One week, that was all she'd needed. Then her life would be safe and secure, just as she planned. Not that Brad could possibly make any difference to those plans, but he did have an annoying habit of creating confusion and uncertainty in her life.

When she didn't answer him, Brad continued talking, sounding relaxed and companionable. "So tell me about him. The name was unfamiliar. Obviously he's not from Payton."

Penny felt a measure of safety as they drew closer to her home. She had no desire to carry on an intimate conversation with Brad. Once they reached the house she could depend on her mother to bridge any uncomfortable silences.

"Actually, Gregory moved to Payton from St. Louis a couple of years ago."

"What does he do?"

"He's an attorney."

"Ah," Brad responded as though some mystery had been solved for him. "An attorney," he repeated with satisfaction, "a nice, safe, unexciting profession."

She glanced at him with annoyance. "Not all of us crave excitement, you know."

"There was a time when you enjoyed it, as I recall."

"I was only a child. 'When I was a child, I used to speak as a child, think as a child, reason as a child; when I became a woman, I did away with childish things.'"

"My! Reverend Wilder would certainly be proud of you, remembering your Bible verses that way. Let's see, that's from the thirteenth chapter of First Corinthians."

"Your early training still shows, too, you know, otherwise you wouldn't have recognized it," Penny replied in an even tone. She pushed open the screen door to the enclosed porch with relief. "Mom? You'll never guess who's here," she called in a bright voice.

"Oh, yes I would," Helen Blackwell said. Her face beamed a welcome as she stepped out of the kitchen carrying a tray filled with cookies and a frosted pitcher of lemonade. "Brad checked with me to find out where you were." She set the tray down and hugged him. "Oh, it's just so good to see you again after all this time. What a marvelous surprise to everyone, having you show up so unexpectedly."

Brad returned the hug with interest, his buoyant smile lighting up his face. "I'm glad to see that someone is happy to see me," he complained good-naturedly, glancing at Penny out of the corner of his eye. "For a moment there I thought Penny was going to shove me off the dock when she first saw me.''

"Don't be silly. You just startled me, that's all.'' Forcing herself to sound casual, she said, "If you'll excuse me, I'm going to run upstairs and change.''

"Not on my account, I hope,'' Brad offered with an innocent grin. "I'm thoroughly enjoying the view.''

Helen laughed. She would, Penny thought crossly. Her mother had always found Brad amusing. As far as her parents were concerned, Brad could do no wrong. He was the son they had never had.

A small voice inside her told her that, to be fair, she needed to remember that she had been the daughter Brad's parents had never had as well. Penny wasn't in the mood for fairness at the moment. "If you'll excuse me,'' she said politely and left.

Helen poured lemonade in two of the glasses and said, "Sit down, Brad. She probably won't be long. Why don't you tell me how things are going for you. I'm so eager to hear about New York and your life there. Everyone in Payton is so proud of you—the small-town boy who made good.''

Brad continued to stare at the door where Penny had disappeared.

"She's changed,'' he said in a flat voice.

Helen sighed. "Yes, she has,'' she admitted, "and in my opinion the change hasn't been an improvement.''

Brad glanced at her in surprise.

Helen hastened to explain. "She seems to have lost some inner spark of enthusiasm, that enjoyment of life that always used to make her sparkle.''

"I remember,'' Brad said with a smile.

"It could have been getting that teaching job as soon as she finished college. She wasn't all that much older than her high school students, which probably explains why she began to dress and act so much older than she really is.''

"Does she like teaching?''

"Seems to. Of course, what she really enjoys is working with the drama club, directing their plays—she loves anything that has to do with acting."

"That isn't too surprising, since that's what she majored in at the university. She was one of the most talented students in our class. It's a shame she isn't using that talent now."

"I know. I suppose that's what bothers me about her. She seems to be settling for so much less than she's capable of."

"Such as Gregory Duncan?"

"Oh, heavens, no! Gregory is a brilliant man. Absolutely brilliant. He made quite a name for himself in the St. Louis area, I understand. Payton was extremely fortunate that a man like Gregory chose to move here and open a practice." Helen offered Brad the plate of cookies, pleased when he took a couple. "Of course, he's extremely busy. He still has a considerable caseload in St. Louis, so he's been dividing his time between here and there. Penny's hoping his schedule will let up some once they're married."

Brad took a bite of one of the cookies and moaned his pleasure. "Sitting here eating your homemade oatmeal-raisin cookies certainly takes me back, Helen." After swallowing some lemonade, Brad returned to the subject of their conversation. "If Duncan's so well-known and established, he must be considerably older than Penny."

Helen nodded. "Yes, he is. He's thirty-nine, fourteen years older than she is."

"And she doesn't mind?"

"Doesn't seem to bother her in the least. Like I said, she acts so much older—seems so settled and all. You'd think they were much closer in age than they are." Helen reached over and took a cookie. "She seems to have her life all planned out now. Penny intends to continue teaching for a couple of years, then start a family. Gregory does a lot of entertaining. Just playing hostess for him will probably be a full-time job. She seems to be content with everything."

Brad gazed out through the screen that enclosed the large porch and murmured, "I wonder."

As soon as Penny returned downstairs, she could hear the animation in her mother's voice. Brad had that effect on people. He seemed to generate excitement wherever he went.

"Everyone in town watches *Hope for Tomorrow*," she heard Helen say, "wanting to see what outrageous things Drew Derek is going to do next. He's a real corker, isn't he?"

Brad laughed. "That he is."

"Of course I know you're nothing like him, but you sure make him out to be a real ladies' man."

Penny could hear the amusement in Brad's voice at her mother's careful phrasing when he replied, "Yes, he's certainly a real threat to the virtue of every woman he meets, isn't he?"

They laughed companionably. Penny decided it was time to join them and change the subject when she heard her mother say, "Well, I think you're just fantastic in the role and very believable. Why, if I didn't know the real you, I wouldn't let you anywhere near my daughter, that's for sure. Speaking of Penny, I taped your program on the video recorder every day during the school term so Penny could watch it when she got home. She—"

"Is there any lemonade left?" Penny asked, stepping out on the porch as though unaware she'd interrupted her mother. She could tell by the expression on his face that Brad had not been fooled.

"Of course there is," Helen answered. "You know I always keep plenty on hand in the summertime. It's our staple drink around here during these warm months."

"So you watch *Hope for Tomorrow* every day, do you?" Brad asked Penny, a half smile on his face.

Brad looked very much at home. His head rested on the back of the well-padded patio chair, his legs stretched out in front of him, crossed at the ankle. He held his glass balanced on his lean, muscled stomach.

Penny stepped over his legs and sank down in the chair on his other side.

"When I have the time," she responded casually. "Which reminds me. How did you manage to get time off to come home? If you really are here for the wedding, that must mean you plan to stay at least a week."

"What do you mean, if I'm really here for the wedding? Don't you believe me?"

She shrugged. "I don't disbelieve you. I just find it unusual that you'd bother."

"Oh, I don't, Penny," Helen said. "Why, Brad is the closest thing to a brother you've ever had. It's only natural he'd want to be here."

"That's very true. So I asked the powers that be in our production for the time and eventually they decided that Drew really did need some R and R from all of his bedroom activities." He watched Penny's profile while he talked because she refused to look his way. Instead, she stared out at the lake. Of course, it was a very relaxing view, but she was studying it as if she'd never seen it before. Glancing at Helen, seated on his other side, he continued, "So they've put poor old Drew in a coma for a few days."

"Oh, really?" Helen said. "What caused it?"

Brad shrugged his shoulders. "Who knows? Too much sex, probably."

"Brad," Helen said, laughing. "That's awful."

"Sorry," he said in a teasing tone that said he wasn't sorry at all.

How many times over the years had Penny heard that exact inflection in his voice? Somehow it had always managed to get him off the hook. Perhaps because when he was in that mood he was practically irresistible.

"Besides," he went on, "I felt I had to meet the man who stole Penny away from me."

Penny stiffened at his words, but before she could come up with a caustic reply she heard her mother say, "Well, then you should plan to come back over for dinner tonight

Gregory is going to be here. It will give the two of you a chance to visit together, sort of get acquainted and all before the wedding.''

Oh, Mother, how could you? Penny silently pleaded. No two men could be more unalike than Gregory and Brad. The evening would be a total disaster. What in the world would they find to talk about?

"Why, Helen, thank you," Penny heard Brad say, and a definite sinking sensation developed in her stomach. "That would be great." He glanced at his watch. "In that case, I'd better get home so I can visit with Dad when he arrives. I'm sure they'll understand why I'm over here my first night at home."

Damn him. Why did he keep making those little remarks, implying a great deal more than he had reason to? When Helen accepted his comment with an understanding smile, Penny could have thrown something.

Which was exactly why she didn't want Brad Crawford anywhere around her.

Penny considered herself to be a calm, even-tempered person. Everyone at school commented on how well she handled her adolescent students. She did not get upset. She did not lose her temper. She was in control at all times. Brad was the only person who had ever caused her to lose that control, and Penny hated his ability to upset her. Absolutely detested it.

The past three years had been wonderfully serene, and she was looking forward to a lifetime of similar peace and serenity. In other words, she intended to spend her life anywhere that Brad Crawford wasn't.

Penny waited while Brad and Helen made arrangements for his return that evening, smiled politely when Brad said goodbye and watched as he left her home and sauntered across the immense lawn that separated their two places. Then she turned to Helen.

"Do you know anything about how Brad received a wedding invitation, Mother?"

Helen had just picked up the tray to return to the kitchen. She looked puzzled by the question. "I sent him one. Why do you ask?"

"Because his name wasn't on the list."

Helen went into the kitchen; Penny followed. "I knew it was just an oversight. After all, you sent one to his folks. So I just stuck one in the mail to him as well."

"It was no oversight."

Helen set the tray on the kitchen counter and turned around. "Penny! Are you saying that—you mean that you didn't intend for Brad to come to your wedding?" Her shocked surprise could have been no less than if Helen had just heard that Penny was pregnant with triplets.

"That's exactly what I mean."

An expression of pain crossed Helen's face. "Oh, Penny. That's awful."

"What's awful about it, Mother? It's my wedding. I should be able to invite or not invite anyone I please."

"But to leave Brad out, after all you've meant to each other during these years."

"Mother, don't exaggerate. Brad and I grew up together because we lived next door to each other. Since we're almost five miles out of town, we didn't have too many choices as to whom we played with. And if you remember anything, you can certainly recall that we spent most of our time together fighting!"

Helen leaned against the counter, staring at her daughter as though she no longer knew her. "Why, Penny, that isn't true! Of course you squabbled at times—any kids who spent much time together would be likely to bicker. Besides, you're both extremely strong-willed and determined to get your own way. No one would expect that you'd always agree on everything."

Penny absently opened the pantry door and peered inside with absolutely no idea what she was looking for.

"But, Penny, the two of you were friends. Close friends. I don't understand your attitude toward him now."

Penny closed the door and turned around. "Well, I don't suppose it matters now, does it? He's here and he'll be here for dinner. I think I'll go on up and take a bath. I want to look calm and relaxed when Gregory gets here."

Helen stood and watched Penny as she went into the hallway and started up the stairs. There were times she didn't feel she understood her daughter at all.

Penny stared at her reflected image in the mirror. The pale peach of her dress showed off her darkening tan and brought out the red highlights in her russet-colored hair. She had pulled her hair smoothly away from her face into a cluster of curls at the nape of her neck. She looked poised, sophisticated and calm.

If only she felt that way! Her insides had been churning all afternoon, which was absolutely ridiculous. What possible difference could it make that Brad Crawford would be there for dinner? she asked herself.

Unfortunately she could come up with a half-dozen reasons before she had to draw breath. She knew him too well. Depending on his mood, he could be everything a hostess could want in a polite dinner guest. Or he could be perfectly outrageous. Funny, but outrageous. And he knew entirely too many things about her that he could bring up if he felt the urge. It wouldn't be the first time he'd embarrassed her in front of someone important.

"Oh, Mother," she lamented aloud, "If you'd only asked me, I would have told you that Brad's favorite pastime is ignoring the script and improvising in a situation." A reluctant smile played on her face when she thought of some of the things he'd done in the past. He really did have a wicked sense of humor.

She realized that she was being a coward, hovering upstairs when she'd heard him arrive at least fifteen minutes earlier. Penny had justified her delay to herself, knowing that her father would monopolize Brad for a while. Sooner or later she would have to face him. Glancing at her watch, she decided now was as good a time as any. Gregory should be arriving before much longer.

Sure enough, she found Brad and her father in animated conversation. They'd always gotten along well. Her dad had gone to all of Brad's Little League games and stood on the sidelines cheering during his high school football games.

The little voice inside her said, And don't forget, you were right there, cheering with the best of them.

Of course she was. She'd been proud of Brad. He was a natural athlete and she'd enjoyed seeing him play. But that was years ago, after all—just part of her childhood.

Brad stood up as soon as she walked into the room. "Wow!" he said in a reverent voice.

Penny couldn't help it. She began to laugh. "That's one of the things I've always liked about you, Brad," she said, grinning. "You were always so articulate, with such an artful turn of phrase."

He walked over to her and took both her hands, staring down at her. "And that laugh is one of the things I've always liked about you. I had almost given up hope that it was still around."

She could not ignore how well Brad looked in the navy blue blazer and gray slacks. The ensemble set off his blond good looks. Let's face it, she thought, he looked like every woman's dream of the man she hoped would appear in her life and take her away from daily drudgery. No doubt that was one of the reasons *Hope for Tomorrow* had become one of the most successful daily serials.

The doorbell served as a reprieve from Penny's runaway thoughts. "Oh, there's Gregory now," she said, unconsciously betraying her relief.

Brad frowned slightly as he watched her return to the hall. For just a moment he'd seen a glimpse of the Penny he'd known forever, but then she'd disappeared behind the polite, sedate facade of the woman he'd seen this afternoon.

He heard murmured voices in the hallway, and an intimate male chuckle that caused the hair on his neck to rise in protest. Brad determinedly ignored the fact that Penny's lipstick was definitely smudged when she returned to the room, leading a man who must have been Gregory Duncan.

Brad wasn't prepared for the shock he received when he saw Penny's fiancé. There was no denying that he was in his late thirties. The mark of time had added character to his face. What hit Brad like a doubled-up fist in his stomach was that Gregory Duncan looked enough like him to be a close relative.

They were both approximately the same height and build, and their hair was the same shade of blond. Brad felt as though he were looking into the future, at what he would look like in another thirteen years.

And this was the man Penny had chosen to marry.

After the introductions were made, Brad said, "I've looked forward to meeting you, Gregory. I've heard some very good things about you." He didn't miss the exchange of glances between Gregory and Penny.

"It's good to meet a friend of Penny's, Brad," Gregory replied in a deep, mellow voice that Brad was sure could be used to great effect in a courtroom. "Unfortunately, I'm at a disadvantage. She's never mentioned you to me."

Brad glanced at Penny in surprise, and acknowledged to himself the pain Gregory's remark caused him. She had truly dismissed him from her life.

Penny couldn't meet Brad's eyes. She smiled at Gregory and said, "Oh, I'm sure I told you about Brad, Gregory. You've probably just forgotten. He lived next door for years."

"I'm sure you have, love," Gregory said, holding her possessively to his side. "It must have slipped my mind."

Brad was unprepared for the almost despairing rage that swept over him at the sight of Gregory holding Penny so intimately.

What had he expected, for God's sake? She was marrying the man, wasn't she? He found himself clenching his teeth in an effort to control his emotions. Helen earned his undying gratitude when she came into the room and announced that dinner was ready.

Dinner was almost as bad. Brad sat across the table from the engaged couple, a silent witness to their smiles and murmurs. Ralph and Helen kept the conversation going, and Brad determinedly joined them, knowing he would have to deal with his pain later.

Penny began to relax about midway through dinner. As usual, her mother had outdone herself with the meal, and the men were obviously enjoying it. She had just felt the tension in the muscles along her spine ease when Brad said, "Too bad you never learned to cook like your mom, Runt. Maybe she'll take pity on Gregory and have you two for dinner often."

Gregory glanced up from his meal and looked at Brad in surprise. "What did you call her? Runt?"

Brad looked a little abashed. "Sorry. I guess that just slipped out. It was a nickname I gave her years ago."

Gregory's gaze fell on Penny. "I can think of many nicknames I might choose for her, but nothing so revolting as that."

"She was always small for her age, you know," Brad said lightly. "I think she always hoped she'd catch up with me, but by the time we were teenagers she knew she'd well and truly lost the race." He studied Penny for a moment, then smiled. "She's always looked younger than her years, anyway, don't you think so?"

Gregory smiled at her. "Oh, I don't know. I'd hardly confuse her with one of her students, despite her height. She's a very nicely endowed woman."

"Thank you kindly, sir," she said.

"As for her cooking," Gregory went on, "Penny doesn't have to do anything she doesn't want to. I'm not marrying her to gain a housekeeper."

"Of course not," Brad agreed. With a perfectly deadpan expression he went on, "I just hope you don't mind the fact that she snores."

The reaction of those around the table was a study of mixed emotions. Ralph looked as though he were trying not to laugh while Helen looked shocked. From the expression on her face, Penny looked as if she could have easily committed murder. Only Gregory showed little reaction—just a slight narrowing of his eyes.

"I had no idea you knew Penny quite that well."

"He's being obnoxious," Penny said heatedly. "Our families used to go camping together when we were children. Brad always used to accuse me of snoring, just to make me angry."

"And it usually worked," he replied with a grin.

She struggled with her anger now, unwilling to let him know that he had succeeded in riling her once again. She tried to laugh, but wasn't sure that anyone was fooled. "But not now. Your childish tricks no longer have any effect on me."

Brad leaned back in his chair. "That's good to know, Runt. That uncontrollable temper of yours used to get you into lots of trouble."

"Temper?" Gregory repeated, lifting a brow. "You must have Penny confused with someone else. A more even-tempered person I've yet to meet."

Brad began to laugh. "Oh, dear. Are you ever in for a surprise, Counselor." He leaned forward and rested his arms on the table in front of him. "How long have you and Penny known each other?"

"About a year, wouldn't you say?" Gregory answered, turning to Penny.

"Something like that," she muttered.

"And she's never lost her temper?"

"Not that I'm aware of."

"How very interesting," Brad mused.

"Only to you, Brad, dear," Penny said sarcastically. Then she stood and said with a smile, "I'll clear for you, Mother. Who would like some cherry-chocolate cake?" She refused to look at Brad.

No one could pass up such a temptation, so Penny carried the dishes into the kitchen and began to slice the cake and place it on plates. She glanced up when she heard the swinging door open, then frowned.

"You don't need to help, Brad. I can manage."

"I know. I just came in here to apologize."

"It's too late."

"Too late for what? Do you think he's going to beg off or something just because he's found out you have a temper, for God's sake?"

"I mean it's too late for you to think I'm going to always say, 'Oh, that's all right, Brad, it doesn't matter.' You think you can say anything you want, behave in the most outrageous manner, and all you have to do is smile that devastating, knee-weakening smile and I'll forgive you."

"Knee-weakening?"

Trust Brad to pick up on her unfortunate choice of words.

"A figure of speech, Brad, nothing more."

"Does my smile really affect you that way?"

"Would you get out of here?" She picked up two plates filled with cake and shoved them into his hands. "Make yourself useful."

Penny watched as Brad laughingly returned to the other room, looking for all the world as if the two of them had been out in the kitchen laughing over old times.

Something told her that the next week might have a certain lack of peace and serenity. She would count the days until the wedding.

Surely after she and Gregory were married, Brad Crawford would no longer have the ability to disrupt her life.

Penny refused to ask herself why this would be so.

Chapter Two

"Good morning, Mr. Akin," Penny said the next morning. She placed the large package her mother wanted mailed in the window of the Payton post office and waited to have it weighed.

"Well, hello there, Penny," he replied. "Guess you're pretty busy these days, what with getting ready for your wedding and all."

She smiled at the elderly man who had worked at the post office as long as she could remember. "Yes, I have been."

"Did you know young Brad Crawford is back in town?" he asked, his intent gaze letting her know it was no idle question.

"Yes, I did. He had dinner with us last night, as a matter of fact."

"Did he now? That's right interesting, considering you're marrying somebody else."

"What difference does that make?"

"Well, folks around here kinda figured that sooner or

later you and the Crawford boy would end up married to each other.''

"I have no idea why they would think that, Mr. Akin, just because we were next-door neighbors for years.''

"It's probably because the two of you were thicker than fleas on a hound's back, missy,'' he said in a no-nonsense voice. ''Never saw one of you that the other one wasn't right there as well.''

"That was a long time ago, Mr. Akin. We were just kids then.''

"You weren't just kids when you went off to college together. Why, everybody knew that Brad spent his first year out of high school here in Payton, just waiting for you to graduate so you could go to school together.''

"Mr. Akin, Brad worked at the textile mill for his dad the year after he graduated from high school. He was tired of school and wasn't sure what he wanted to do.''

"Hmph. Figured that out quick enough when you decided to go up north to that big university to study acting, though, didn't he?''

Why was she debating the issue with a postal employee? People were going to think whatever they wanted to think, no matter how much she tried to explain. Penny managed a noncommittal response that seemed to appease him and watched as he weighed the package.

After paying him, Penny waved goodbye and went to the grocery store to pick up a few items her mother wanted. When she was ready to check out, she noticed Sonia Henderson had the shortest line of people waiting. She and Sonia had gone through school together, but instead of going to college, Sonia had married her high school sweetheart.

As soon as Penny began to unload her basket onto the moving belt, Sonia saw her.

"Penny! Did you hear that Brad Crawford is in town?''

Why did everyone want to tell her about Brad's visit, for Pete's sake? "As a matter of fact, I did, Sonia.'' Trying to forestall another interrogation, she asked, "So how are Timmy and Sarah?"

"Oh, they're fine. Timmy's glad to be out of school for the summer. Sarah's teething and she's been a little cranky, but Mom says that's only natural." Almost in the same breath she asked, "Have you seen him yet?"

"Seen who?"

"Brad! Have you seen him since he came back?"

"Uh, yes. I saw him yesterday."

"Does he look as good as he does on television?"

Better, Penny thought, but decided there was enough conjecture flitting around town without her adding to it. "About the same, I guess."

"Did he talk to you about what it's like, living in New York and being famous and everything?"

"Actually, no, he didn't."

"I think it's so exciting he's here. I hope I get to see him. Do you suppose his life is anything like Drew Derek's?"

"I have no idea."

Sonia giggled. "He probably wouldn't tell you if it was."

"Probably not," she agreed.

"Can't you just imagine what it's like, being famous and all, knowing all the women are dreaming about wanting to make love to you?"

Penny was saved from having to think up a reply when Sonia rang up the total for the groceries. Penny conscientiously concentrated on writing out her check. By the time she managed to get out of the grocery store, she was thankful her mother hadn't thought of any other errands for her to run. If one more person brought up Brad Crawford's name today...

"Good morning, Penny. I always thought that shade of yellow looked great on you."

Thank God she had a good grip on the two sacks of groceries. "Brad! Where did you come from?"

"Why, Penny, you never cease to amaze me. We had a discussion about the birds and the bees years ago. My, how quickly we forget."

"You're not funny, Brad. How long have you been lurking outside the grocery store?"

"I wasn't lurking. I happened to see your car parked out here when I drove by earlier and decided to see if you'd like to go get something cold and refreshing to drink with me."

"I need to get these groceries home," she explained with a certain amount of relief. Brad was looking every inch the virile male in his prime this morning, in faded jeans that fit him like a second skin and gave no doubt to his gender. The tan sport shirt he wore accented his well-developed shoulders and chest. His blond hair, worn much longer than most of the local men's, gleamed brightly in the morning sunlight.

"That's all right. I'll follow you home and we can go in my car."

She closed the trunk and came around to where he was casually leaning against her car. "Not today. I have too much to do."

"Such as?"

Penny quickly racked her brain, trying to think of something. What did she usually do on Saturdays? In the summertime? Not much. How about the Saturday before her wedding? Surely she had something urgent, something really vital, that could not be postponed another hour.

She couldn't think of a thing.

"Don't you want to have a drink with me?" he asked quietly.

Penny hadn't heard that note in his voice in a long time. It caught her totally off guard. She had heard pain, despite his attempt at lightness.

"It's not that, Brad," she began uncertainly.

"We haven't had a chance to talk since I got home, Penny," he reminded her, reaching out and touching a russet curl at her ear.

"Of course we have," she said, trying to defend herself. "We talked yesterday afternoon, then again last night."

"No, we didn't. You didn't say a half-dozen words around me yesterday, except for telling me off in the kitchen." He studied her in silence for a moment. "Are you still angry at me because of last night?"

Trying to ignore how close he was, she opened the car door and slid behind the steering wheel. After pulling the door shut, she looked up at him. That particular look in his eyes had always been able to sway her, even against her better judgment. And she was aware that she had overreacted to his teasing the night before. "All right," she said, giving up the struggle. "I'll see you at home, then."

His smile lit up his face, and for a moment she could only stare at him. He seemed to glow with it. No wonder he had been an instant hit on television. With that much charisma, he was lethal to a person's peace of mind. Or at least, to her's.

Brad followed her home and pulled into her parents' driveway directly behind her. He helped her carry the groceries into the house. "I'll be right back," he said as soon as he set one of the sacks down. "I'll meet you out front in a few minutes."

Penny hurriedly put the groceries away, found her mother working in the flower garden and told her that she was going out to have a drink with Brad.

"If Gregory should call, tell him I'll be home within the hour."

Helen glanced up at her absently. "I will, dear. Have a good time."

Have a good time. How often had her mother said that to her over the years? Probably every time she had taken off with Brad. Her mother had never seemed to worry about her as long as she and Brad were together.

Penny thought about her instructions to her mother for a moment. She didn't really expect Gregory to call. He'd been out of town all week and had told her last night he would probably have to work at the office all weekend. But they were going to have dinner together that night.

Penny smiled to herself as she walked through the house and out the front door, thinking about next week. They were going to take a week off for their honeymoon, although she had no idea where they were going. Gregory told her it was going to be a surprise. She really didn't care as long as she didn't have to compete for his attention with his law practice. For a few days, anyway, she would have him all to herself.

"There's that wicked smile again, Runt," Brad said, and she realized he'd already returned to his car and was waiting for her. "If I didn't know you better, I'd think the innocent Ms. Blackwell was thinking impure thoughts about something—or somebody."

She could feel the color mounting in her cheeks and cursed her fair complexion that let her reaction to his remark show. She knew from his grin that he hadn't missed her blush. "What makes you so sure I'm all that innocent, Brad?" she drawled. "After all, I'm twenty-five years old."

"Age has nothing to do with your innocence," he said with emphasis, holding the passenger door open for her.

He backed out of the driveway, and because she was so caught up in the conversation, Penny didn't notice that he had turned the opposite way from town when he got to the road.

"You don't know everything about me," she said emphatically. "After all, you haven't seen me in three years."

"So what? That doesn't mean I haven't kept up with what's been happening to you."

Penny turned so that she unconsciously fell into the familiar pose she'd always used whenever they went anywhere in the car together—she leaned against the door and pulled one knee up on the seat so that she was facing him.

He darted a lightning glance at her and immediately returned his gaze to the country road, a slight smile on his face.

"Your mother doesn't know everything I do," she said, irritated that she felt the need to defend herself.

"No, but yours does."

"Hah! Not likely." She was quiet for a moment, then asked, "Are you telling me that Mother has been writing to you?"

"Sometimes. Sometimes she just tells my mom, who passes along any relevant information."

"Which I'm sure you found very boring."

"You might be surprised."

They were quiet for a few minutes. Penny watched the passing countryside without registering that they were leaving Payton farther and farther behind. She was too busy trying to analyze what Brad was telling her.

"Then you knew all along when I started dating Gregory?"

"I knew," he agreed with a smile.

"If that's the case, then why did you ask last night?"

"Just being polite."

"That's a laugh," Penny said, although she didn't sound particularly amused. "You don't know the meaning of the word."

"Aah, Penny. I'm crushed. After I tried so hard."

"I know how hard you tried—to be irritating and aggravating."

"Did it work?"

"What do you mean?" she asked, straightening her back. "Do you think you bothered Gregory with your childish remarks? He's much too mature for that," she added, her tone sounding remarkably pleased.

"I'll say. He's almost old enough to be your father."

"He is not! He's only fourteen years older than I am," Penny responded heatedly, unaware that she and Brad had fallen once again into their age-old conversational pattern of baiting and fencing.

"Does he have any children?" Brad asked with polite interest.

"Since he's never been married, I rather doubt it," she replied with more than a little sarcasm.

"Or if he does, he probably doesn't talk about it," Brad added agreeably.

"Brad!"

"Sorry," he said with a grin, neither looking nor sounding particularly sorry. "So why is he getting married now?"

Penny could feel her temper getting the best of her, which only added to her irritation. How was it that Brad could set her off so quickly with his idiotic remarks? "You are really being insulting, you know that, don't you?" she said, her eyes frosty with disdain.

"Well, of course he loves you, Penny," Brad hastily assured her. "Who wouldn't? I just wonder what other reasons such a logical and analytical person might find to choose you for his mate, particularly since he's waited this long to marry."

Who wouldn't? Penny's mind repeated in surprise, losing much of what he had said after that. Was it possible that Brad had actually intended to pay her a compliment? If so, it was the first she could ever recall receiving from him.

"What other reasons could he have?" she asked, curious about his line of thinking.

"Oh, there are all kinds of reasons to get married. Maybe he's tired of living alone. Maybe he wants a family, a hostess. Maybe he's marrying you for your money...."

"That's a pretty vivid imagination you've got there, Brad. Do you write those stories on television as well as act in them?"

"There's nothing imaginative in any of that. It happens all the time."

"Not with me, it doesn't. I doubt that my teacher's salary attracts him. After all, he's a very successful lawyer."

"Then why did he move to Payton?"

Penny relaxed a little more against the door, watching Brad's profile. "Why not? It's a nice place to live, even though you found it dull."

"I never found it dull," he pointed out mildly. "I just wanted to become a professional actor, and Payton doesn't have that many job openings in that particular field." He glanced over at her and grinned when he saw that she was absently twisting a curl around one of her fingers. She only did that when she was agitated. Good. At least he had her thinking. "Besides," he went on blandly, "I wasn't talking about what you make. You're an only child and your family is very well off."

"So what? I'm certainly not apt to be inheriting anything for years to come, and you know it. Good grief. Mom and Dad are still in their forties."

"I know. They got married very young and they made it work but it was tough, which is why they're against teenage marriages."

Penny looked at him in surprise. "How do you know that?" she asked. "I've never heard them say anything about their early years."

"Never mind," he replied, deciding it was time to change the subject. "So if he isn't interested in your money, Gregory must want you to play hostess for him and preside over his home."

"What's wrong with that?" she asked, puzzled by his tone.

"Oh, Penny, that isn't you, and you know it. You've got too much vitality and sparkle for that kind of life. If you would just be honest with yourself, you'd admit that you're already bored with teaching school. How do you think you're going to feel playing helpful Harriet for a man who could pass as your father?"

"Would you stop with the stupid remarks about Gregory's age? In the first place, Gregory doesn't even look that old. As a matter of fact, you may have noticed that he looks a little like you—same hair coloring, similar build."

He grinned. "Is that why you fell for him? Because he reminded you of me?"

She stared at him in horror. "Of course not! He's absolutely nothing like you, thank God."

"You don't have to sound so thankful. I didn't turn out all that bad, did I?"

She heard the hint of pain in his voice again, and wondered about it. Brad Crawford was too self-confident to be easily offended. And yet twice today she had heard a slight hesitancy in his voice as though he were unsure of himself.

"You're living your life the way you want to, Brad. I can't fault you for that," she said quietly.

"But are you living your life the way you want to? That's my concern at the moment."

She glanced at him, puzzled. "That's the second time you've made a remark like that. I am not bored with teaching. I am very content with my life." She studied him for a moment in silence, then asked, "And why should you care what I do or how I feel, anyway?"

"Come on, Penny, you know me better than that. I have always looked out for you and cared for you, ever since we were kids." He gave her a quick glance from the corner of his eye and smiled. "Why should I stop now?"

She wasn't going to let that statement go unchallenged. "Yet you could hardly wait to leave here once you finished college."

He was quiet for a moment. He heard the hurt in her voice and realized once again what a fine actress she truly was. Until now he had never really known that she had cared when he'd decided to go to New York. An interesting discovery, considering how he'd felt when she had blithely greeted his news three years ago by wishing him well.

"You could have gone with me," he said finally.

The interior of the car seemed to reverberate with sudden emotion. The silence that fell between them seemed to grow like a living thing, until Brad felt that he could almost reach out and touch it. Whatever she was feeling, it wasn't indifference. That he knew. He wished he'd had this conversation with her then, instead of now. He'd paid for his cowardice every day since.

When she did speak, her anger surprised him. "Of course I could have gone. We could have starved together! Why would I have wanted to go to New York, Brad? I was twenty-two years old. It was time for us to grow up, accept responsibility, make something of ourselves. Playtime was over... at least it was for me."

"Is that all that acting was to you, Penny? Playtime?"

She laughed, but she didn't sound in the least amused. "Well, it certainly isn't a way to make a living."

"I haven't done so badly at it."

Penny felt a sudden urge to hit something, she felt so frustrated. Who was she kidding, anyway? Why didn't she just admit the truth?

"Actually," she said, wishing her voice didn't sound quite so uneven, "the biggest reason I didn't go with you to New York was simple. You never asked me."

There. She'd finally said it, spoken the words out loud. In doing so, she finally faced them for the first time.

"Would you have gone?" he asked in a neutral tone.

Who knew the answer to that at this late date? The whole point was he *hadn't* asked. He hadn't even acted as though he'd given such an idea a thought. And Penny had been faced with the harsh reality of their shared life. At one time Brad Crawford had been everything in the world to her while he had considered her a friend—his buddy, a pal.

"It hardly matters at this point, does it?" she asked, staring unseeingly out the window.

"Have you ever thought about trying to make it as an actress?" he asked.

"Not for years, Brad. I'm content with my life."

"You keep saying that, but I'm not sure which one of us you're trying to convince. You were always such a natural on stage, you know. You seemed to come alive. It was a beautiful thing to see." He glanced at her, but she had her head down and he couldn't see her expression. "Don't you ever miss it?"

"Not really. I'm active with the local group... and I directed the high school play this year."

"When you could be starring on Broadway? Penny, that's a shameful waste of your talent and you know it!"

Once again she made no response.

Forcing a lighter tone, Brad asked, "What does Gregory think of your acting abilities?"

"He's never seen them," she muttered.

"But he knows about them, surely."

Penny rested her head against the window. "He knows I've had training in that area and assumes I minored in drama while I was getting my degree in education."

"Why haven't you told him? Showed him your clippings and reviews?"

She shrugged. "There's no reason to. That's just part of my past."

Brad wondered if he was too late. Was it even his place to attempt to save her? Obviously she didn't see herself as needing saving. She had chosen not only the man, but an entire way of life, and she was within days of cementing that relationship.

How could he let her do such a thing? Yet how could he, in good conscience, interfere if that was what she wanted?

He loved her. He had always loved her. He would always love her. And he wanted her to be happy. For years he had hoped that her happiness would lie with him. He'd listened to both sets of parents as they had urged him not to rush into a permanent relationship too early in their lives. They had insisted that each of them needed some space, a chance to mature separately, in order to recognize their own feelings.

So he had taken their advice. Because of it, he had lost Penny. He had wanted to be fair, and to do what was best for both of them. Instead, he had lost the only woman who had ever meant a damn to him.

But even in his worst nightmare it never occurred to him that Penny would turn into this subdued, quiet woman who was willing to accept so little in her life.

Now that Brad had brought up his move to New York, the past began to tumble into Penny's consciousness like a child's building blocks. They fell in colorful disarray around her. Mr. Akin at the post office had been right. She and Brad had been inseparable as far back as she could remember. Had anyone asked her back then, Penny would probably have explained that she and Brad would marry someday.

Strange how things had worked out.

She and Brad had never talked about their feelings for each other. There had been no reason to. They were so much a part of each other's life—until Brad announced his intention to go to New York.

Penny could still remember the day he told her. They had been home from college a week and had taken his family's boat out on the lake. The day had been warm and they had found a quiet spot to anchor and laze in the sun.

Penny had been almost asleep when Brad spoke.

"Have you decided what you want to do now that we're out of school, Runt?"

"I'm doing it," she replied in a sleepy voice.

"I mean, to earn a living?"

"I filled out an application to teach. I suppose I'll wait to hear from the school board. Why do you ask?"

He was silent so long that Penny eventually opened her eyes. He had turned so that he was facing her, and she found herself staring into his eyes. "I've decided to go to New York."

She smiled because they had talked about New York for the past year. "To become rich and famous?" she asked with a grin.

"I won't know until I try," he answered in a quiet tone.

Penny's smile slowly disappeared. "You're serious, aren't you?" she asked, and even now she could recall the sudden jolt to her system as the fear of losing him swept over her.

"Yes."

Penny never knew how she managed to get through that day. She'd fought hard to hide her reaction. Somehow it had been important for her not to let him know how devastated she felt. If he could so calmly plan his life apart from her, then she must not mean as much to him as he meant to her.

She determinedly hung on to her pride.

Penny had kept up the act of well-wishing friend until Brad left home. Only then did the true enormity of what had happened sweep over her.

Brad Crawford had blithely and without a care walked out of Penny's life. He didn't need her to make his life complete. Penny had never known such rejection, nor did she know how to deal with it.

As the months went by Penny mentally packed away all of their shared memories methodically and with grim determination. Obtaining the teaching position had been her salvation. She threw herself into the new experiences of teaching and interacting with students and co-workers. Penny learned to hide her thoughts and feelings from others, relieved to discover after a while that her highly charged emotions seemed to disappear.

When Gregory came into her life she was content. He filled a place in her daily routine. He offered companionship and conversation, all she really wanted anymore in a relationship.

Penny had overcome the pain and desolation she had felt when Brad had left. She'd forgotten, until now, what a hole he'd left in her life. Penny knew she could never allow anyone to become so important to her again.

As they continued following the country road, Penny slowly became aware of their surroundings. They had been steadily winding through the rolling hills for miles, she realized with dismay. Brad turned into the entrance of a state park and followed the road toward the bluffs where they had spent countless hours as children.

"What are we doing out here?" she demanded. "I thought we were going to get a drink?"

Brad began to laugh. "I wondered when you were going to notice."

"Brad, I don't have time to be out here. I've got to get home. I told Mother I'd be back by—" she glanced at her watch "—by now, darn you!"

"Okay, so you're late. Big deal. She knows you're with me. I thought it might be fun to come out here again. I haven't been to the park in years. I threw some snacks in a sack and brought some cold drinks. Why don't we wander around for a while, relax and enjoy the scenery? I'll take you back home whenever you say."

"Why is it I've never trusted you when you've used that tone of voice?"

"I have no idea. Everyone else always has."

"I know. But no one else knows you the way I do."

"Good point, Penny. You might want to think about just what that means to both of us. It could surprise you."

Chapter Three

Brad and Penny spent the next hour hiking along the bluffs, skipping rocks across the water and wading in the shallows—all activities they had shared during their years together.

Penny realized that, like Sonia, she really was interested in hearing how Brad had adjusted to suddenly being thrust into the limelight of the entertainment world. She plied him with countless questions—some serious, others teasing, and he patiently answered them, one by one.

When he grew tired of sitting quietly, Brad started a game of tag, and Penny seemed to forget her dignified years and chased him, convinced that he would be too out of shape to give her much trouble. She was wrong. Whatever he did in New York to keep in condition, it certainly worked.

Eventually they threw themselves on the grassy bank of the slow-moving river where they had left their food. Brad reached into the water and pulled out two soda cans dripping with water and handed her one. Penny was convinced that nothing had ever tasted so good.

"See? I told you I'd buy you a drink," he pointed out with a grin. He couldn't help but appreciate the fact that she no longer looked like the prim and proper Ms. Blackwell who was marrying the regal Mr. Duncan in a week. She'd lost the combs that had held her hair away from her face, so that the curls tumbled riotously around her cheeks and across her forehead.

Her face was flushed from running, and she was still breathing hard. The thin tank top did nothing to disguise the sauciness of her heaving breasts. Perspiration dotted her upper lip, and Brad had an almost uncontrollable urge to reach over and wipe it away with his thumb.

How could he possibly give up this woman? He had thought he would go out of his mind for the first several months he'd spent in New York. Only the remembered conversations with first her parents, then his, enabled him to recognize that before he asked her to marry him, Brad owed Penny a chance to have a life apart from him.

Their parents had known how to get him to give her time. They had pointed out that she would probably marry him out of habit, because she was used to following his lead. Did he really want a bride who accepted him for that reason? They had already known the only answer he could live with.

"What's the matter? Do I have dirt on my face?" Penny asked with a grin, looking totally relaxed and unconcerned with her appearance. She was stretched out on the grass on her side, propped up enough so that she could drink from the can without spilling it. In her shorts and skimpy top she reminded him of the young girl he'd known, free and uninhibited.

"Don't you always?" he teased. "I think you must bury your nose in the dirt every so often."

She broke off some blades of grass and tossed them at him, then laughed as they decorated his shirt. "You aren't much better, you know. Just look at your shoe."

They both gazed at his foot. His shoe and sock still dripped muddy water where he'd slipped off one of the rocks when they'd crossed the shallows. "What would your fans think of you now, Mr. Crawford?"

"I hope they would realize that I haven't enjoyed myself so much in years," he said with a smile. He gave up trying to resist temptation and reached over, running his thumb lightly across her upper lip.

Penny jerked her head, startled by his touch. His eyes were filled with golden sunshine, their toffee color warm and inviting.

"I'm not going to hurt you," he said softly.

"I didn't think you were," she admitted. "You just startled me, that's all."

Brad chose not to pursue her reactions to him. At the moment it was enough for him to see her looking so relaxed and at ease.

He rolled over onto his back and stared up at the trees above them. Sunlight dappled the ground around them, the leaves forming a canopy above. "We had some good times together, didn't we, Runt?" he asked.

She nodded.

"Do you remember the time you lost your glasses and accused me of hiding them from you?"

She laughed. "Yes."

"I almost got a beating for that. My folks believed you."

"I wonder why? You were always hiding something of mine—my baseball glove, my volleyball."

"Maybe so," he admitted, "but never your glasses. You couldn't see a thing without them."

"How well I remember."

"Contacts made a big difference for you, I know."

"You're right. A whole new world opened up. Particularly when I got the extended wear. Do you have any idea how wonderful it is to wake up at night and be able to see the clock without putting on my glasses?"

"Weren't you ashamed of accusing me of taking them and getting me in trouble?"

"Wel-l-l, maybe. But I'm sure you did a lot of things and never got caught, so it probably all evened out."

He reached over and touched her hand. "I've really missed you, Runt."

Penny looked at him a long time without speaking. "I missed you, too," she said, finally. "For the longest time I didn't think I'd ever be happy without you in my life." She began to smile. "Isn't that crazy? Now I have a whole new life separate from yours, and everything in my life is just perfect."

She looked over at him and idly noted that he had closed his eyes. His thick lashes rested on his high cheekbones. "Do you remember how we always used to argue? It drove our mothers nuts."

"Yeah, but all they had to do was find something to get our minds off whatever we were arguing about."

"Are you saying we argued out of boredom? Surely not."

Without opening his eyes he said. "You were always such a tomboy, no bigger than a minute, convinced you could do anything anyone else could do, and you usually managed to prove it no matter how hard I argued against you."

"I can remember a few times when you managed to help me in such a way that nobody else knew I hadn't done it all myself."

He smiled to himself. "That's what friends are for."

"Yes," she said with a hint of surprise. "I guess it is."

The quietness of the park settled over them, and Penny laid her head on her folded arms. She was probably going to be sore tomorrow with all of her unaccustomed exercise today. Her eyes drifted closed. The park was so peaceful. She'd just rest her eyes for a few moments and . . .

"Penny? You'd better wake up. I'm afraid we both fell asleep."

Penny sat up with a start. The sun had almost set, and she glanced at her watch in dismay. "Oh, no! Gregory was supposed to pick me up almost half an hour ago." She came to her feet and stared up at Brad and his rueful expression.

"I'm sorry, Runt. I didn't mean this to happen," he said softly.

The sincerity in his voice couldn't be mistaken. Quickly slipping her sandals on, Penny said, "It was just as much my fault as yours." She hoped Gregory would understand. She'd never been late for a date before. He was such a stickler for promptness.

Her life seemed to be falling into a shambles since Brad had appeared, although she couldn't really hold him responsible. He just seemed to have that effect on her. Life never seemed to be as serious when he was around. And it was a lot more fun.

They were quiet in the car going back. Penny tried to prepare herself for her coming meeting with Gregory. Surely he would understand. The time had seemed to slip away. Besides, she had needed that day. It was a day apart from her life, apart from time, separate and complete. She and Brad had returned to their childhood, the innocence of youth where time was meaningless because there was so much of it.

Surely Gregory would understand. If only she could think of a more logical explanation.

But she wasn't sorry for going to the park with Brad. At least she could be honest about that. She had enjoyed every minute, even the argument in the car with Brad earlier.

There was no reason to expect Brad to approve of the man she married. She was certain that Brad would never find a woman that was good enough for him in her estimation. The thought gave her quite a pang in the region of her heart.

Penny had been careful not to ask Brad about the women he had dated, many of whom he'd been photographed with. She hadn't wanted to know about them. She knew she was being silly, but she couldn't help it. Brad was very special to her and it was time she acknowledged that to herself.

He always would be.

As soon as they pulled up in the driveway, Gregory stepped out on the front porch of the Blackwell home.

Penny took a quick inventory of what she and Brad looked like and almost groaned aloud. They both had grass stains on their clothes, and his shoe looked much the worse for a dip in the river. Her hair, from the glimpse she had gotten in the side mirror, looked as if she had styled it with an egg-beater.

She felt as though they had been caught skipping school as they walked up the sidewalk toward the well-dressed man who waited for them.

"I'm glad to see you two are all right. We'd begun to worry about you," he said calmly.

Penny smiled in relief. He didn't seem at all angry but showed a perfectly natural concern. Before she could say anything, Brad said, "I really am sorry about today, Gregory. But you see, after all that physical exertion we fell asleep and weren't aware of the hours passing." His tone and smile were friendly and nonchalant.

Penny saw Gregory's body stiffen and his expression freeze. Quickly reviewing what Brad had just said, her eyes widened with horror. Of course he'd told the truth, it was just that...

"How interesting," Gregory said. "Perhaps you'd like to go into a little more detail. Helen said you'd gone for a drink. I never considered that to be physically taxing, my-self."

"Oh, Gregory, he didn't mean that the way—" Penny began, only to have Brad interrupt her.

"Why don't you run upstairs and get cleaned up, Runt? I'll be glad to make our explanations to your fiancé. After all, he has every right to want to know how you spend your time with me."

Penny glanced uncertainly at Brad, then at Gregory. Brad still sounded casually friendly, but there was a tautness in his stance as he stood facing Gregory that contradicted his tone.

"Good idea, Penny," Gregory agreed quietly. "We're running quite late as it is."

She glanced over her shoulder at the two men as she opened the screen door. Neither one of them had moved. They seemed to be waiting for her to leave before continuing the conversation.

Penny could have cheerfully wrung Brad's neck. There was absolutely no reason for the innuendos. What was he trying to do, give Gregory the wrong idea about their relationship?

The warm spray from the shower soothed her and Penny tried to relax. Brad had always had the ability to turn her world upside down. Why did she think anything had changed? However, she had complete faith in Gregory's ability to see through Brad's teasing and desire to cause mischief.

It would do no good for her to ask Brad to lay off. He would see that only as a challenge. So the next best thing would be to make sure she kept the two men apart. After all, it would be for only a few days, then Brad would be out of their lives once again.

When she returned downstairs Gregory was waiting alone in the living room.

She looked at him in surprise. "Where is everybody?"

"I convinced your parents to go to their dinner engagement earlier. If something had happened, I told them I'd get in touch."

Once again Penny felt guilty at her unusual and irresponsible behavior. How could she explain what she didn't understand herself?

"I really am sorry for making you wait," she said.

Gregory took her arm and escorted her outside. "Let's forget it, shall we?" he said, helping her into the car. "I managed to get our reservations changed, so there's no harm done."

Gregory was quiet on the way to the restaurant and Penny searched for something to say. Finally she asked, "Did Brad tell you we went to the park?"

He glanced at her with an enigmatic expression. "He did mention that, yes."

"It was so beautiful there. I'd forgotten how much I enjoyed being out of doors." She wondered when she had lost touch with nature. Her schedule didn't seem to include outdoor activities. Impulsively she turned to Gregory and said, "I wish you'd been with us."

Penny tried to picture Gregory hiking and wading but it was difficult. She couldn't see him laughing about his shoes getting wet or muddy. Gregory would have been out of place. She and Brad had been reliving their childhood, falling back into a familiar pattern, one in which Gregory did not fit.

"From the description that Crawford gave, I don't think I would have enjoyed the afternoon very much," Gregory said.

Even though Penny had just reached the same conclusion she was surprised to hear Gregory echo her thoughts. "Why not?"

"I generally get my exercise playing racquetball or tennis."

"Oh." Funny, they'd never discussed hobbies that much. Gregory had been so busy with his law practice since she had met him that she assumed he didn't have time for many activities. Everytime she felt that she knew him, Gregory revealed another facet of his personality. She wondered if he felt the same way about her.

Was it ever possible to find out everything about a person before you married? It wasn't that anyone deliberately omitted telling the other some things. There was just so much to learn about another person. Gregory had spent thirty-nine years doing things she knew nothing about. She'd spent twenty-five. How could you possibly catch up on everything? And how did you decide what was important to know before the wedding, rather than learning about it in the years after?

They had a quiet dinner at one of the nicer restaurants located near the interstate highway. Penny asked intelligent questions about some of Gregory's cases, drawing him out so that she could feel closer to him somehow.

One of the things that she admired most about him was his dignity in all situations. He always handled himself well. Tonight he could have justifiably shown anger and spoiled their time together. Instead, he seemed to have forgotten the less than auspicious beginning of their evening, relegating it to its rightful place of unimportance in their life.

Their life together would be one of consideration and understanding, of communication. There would be no arguments, such as she had with Brad. She and Gregory would calmly discuss then decide what needed to be faced in their shared existence. There would be no sudden bursts of emotion. Instead, they would share a sense of calmness and serenity.

After dinner Gregory suggested they move into the lounge for after-dinner drinks. A small combo played quiet music and Gregory asked her to dance. Penny willingly agreed. Gregory was an excellent dancer. Penny felt relaxed and totally at ease when they returned to their table after dancing a medley of slow numbers.

Gregory took her hand in his. He seemed to study it for some time before he looked up at her, his gray eyes serious.

"Why have you never mentioned Brad to me, Penny?"

She had been lulled into a relaxed state and his question dumped her out of the soft, fluffy cloud she'd been enjoying for the past hour or so. Penny stared at him with dismay. She had never seen quite that look on his face before. She wondered if that was the look he gave a witness just prior to cross-examination?

Not that it mattered, really. She had nothing to hide. "I don't really know, Gregory," she answered with a slight shrug. "I suppose it's because I never thought him important enough to mention."

His expression gave no indication of what he was thinking. "Not important enough, or too important to discuss?" he asked quietly.

How should she answer that? Penny had only begun to realize earlier that day that her feelings toward Brad were not as clear-cut as she had thought. "We're just friends," she offered tentatively, wondering what had prompted Gregory's line of questioning.

"I realize that. Since I've known you, I've met many of your friends, and you've talked of several others—some you knew here in Payton who later moved away, others you met at college with whom you continue to keep in touch. But you never mentioned Brad's name."

How could she not have been aware of the omission? she wondered. She shook her head. "I really can't explain it, Gregory. Is it important?"

"Not particularly. I find it a puzzle, that's all. And I've got the sort of mind that can't leave a puzzle alone until it's solved."

"I don't see much of a puzzle about it," she offered. "Brad's been gone for three years. He's no longer a part of my life."

"But he was."

"Yes. Do you have a problem with that?"

"Not necessarily. How does he feel about our getting married?"

Penny remembered Brad's earlier comments and knew she couldn't share what Brad had said with Gregory. "He wants me to be happy," she finally responded, realizing the truth of that statement.

"I'm surprised he doesn't think you'd be happier with him."

She grinned. "Brad? You mean you think Brad wants to marry me?" She laughed. "No way. He enjoys his freedom too much."

Gregory didn't respond. Instead, he took a sip of his drink and said, "I received a call today that means I have to go back to St. Louis. I'll be there all of next week."

Penny gave him a stricken look. "But I thought you had arranged to be here the week before the wedding."

"I had. I've had to rearrange my entire schedule. Unfortunately, it can't be helped. I doubt that I'll make it back much before the wedding rehearsal Friday night."

Penny felt the weight of her disappointment settle on her. Of course his law practice came first. She had always known that. At least he wasn't suggesting they postpone the wedding. After all the planning and hundreds of details, Penny shuddered to think of what it would take to change their plans now.

"I understand," she said quietly, accepting what she knew she couldn't change.

Gregory smiled. "Thank you for being so understanding. I appreciate your willingness to accommodate yourself to my schedule." He picked up his drink. "I'm glad we decided not to have the rehearsal dinner. I would have been pressed for time to have to arrange one."

"It's okay. My friends understand."

"I feel so fortunate to have found you. Nothing seems to upset you. You handle everything with such calmness."

Penny smiled. "It's taken a while for me to reach this point, let me tell you. I used to have a fiery temper."

"Well, I'm pleased that you are no longer bothered by it. The last thing I want to face at the end of one of my work days is a display of emotional fireworks." He reached over and patted her hand. "Your serenity is one of the first things that drew me to you. That, and your calm ability to handle people. Nothing ever seems to catch you off balance."

Penny thought of Brad's unexpected return and her reaction. Gregory had accurately described the person she thought she was, except when Brad was around. He seemed to trigger emotional depths in her that almost frightened her. She didn't like the emotional, out-of-control-person Brad seemed to bring forth in her with no apparent effort.

What a lucky escape she'd had, discovering what an adverse effect Brad had on her.

Later Gregory drove her home, walked her to the door and refused to come inside with her.

"It's late, love, and I have a full day's work on my desk tomorrow before I can even leave for St. Louis."

"Will I see you before you go?"

"I really don't think so, although there's nothing I'd like more than to spend tomorrow with you. However, I don't see how I can possibly get away, not when I'm going to be gone for a week on our honeymoon."

He leaned down and kissed her. Stepping back, he smiled and said, "If I don't stop that, I'll never get away from you tonight. Sleep well, my love." Gregory waited until she went inside and locked the door, then walked to his car. He glanced at the house next door.

Penny had brushed his questions aside regarding Brad Crawford. But there was something there and Gregory knew it. He'd sensed Brad's carefully concealed emotions the night before and earlier this evening. His light, casual air had been very well done.

Gregory hadn't been misled. He'd made a career studying human behavior. The man was in love with Penny.

The question was, how did Penny feel about Brad? And how would her feelings for Brad affect her marriage to Gregory?

Gregory drove back to town in deep thought.

Chapter Four

Penny slept restlessly that night. Her dreams were all mixed up. There seemed to be two men wandering through them—one calm and filled with authority, the other laughing and teasing her.

Scraps of conversation danced in her head. She heard Brad asking, "Come to New York with me...come with me...with me...me..."

Gregory appeared. He paced before her as she sat at the witness stand. He kept demanding, over and over, "What is your relationship to this man?" He would point to a cage in the corner of the room. When Penny looked inside the cage Brad sat there—a ten-year-old Brad with his baseball cap and ragged sneakers on.

No matter what she tried to say, Gregory continued to ask, "What is your relationship to this man?"

"Penny, you're going to be late for church if you don't get up soon, dear," Helen called through her closed door.

Penny groaned and pulled her pillow over her head, trying to drown out her mother's voice and the bright sunlight that streamed through her window.

What had happened to the night's rest she'd come to take for granted over the years? Penny felt as though she'd been up all night in some philosophical debate. Bits of her dreams came back to her, but they didn't make sense. Why would she have dreamed of a young Brad in a cage?

She forced herself up, trying to get her eyelids to stay open. Having Brad home was having a definite effect on her. She wished she could understand it. For the past three years she had built a life for herself, on her own, without Brad's influence.

Within a day of his return, she'd reverted to allowing him to influence her. Take yesterday, for example. They'd played in the park like a couple of kids. *You enjoyed it, though, didn't you,* the little voice inside of her said.

Of course I enjoyed it.

Then what are you complaining about?

She really wasn't sure. There seemed something rather childish about enjoying herself, but she couldn't quite decide what it was.

Penny wandered into her bathroom and turned on the shower. Her mother had been right. If she didn't hurry, she'd be late for church.

By the time she was dressed and grabbed some toast and coffee, Penny was late for the church service. She waited outside the sanctuary doors until after the opening prayer, then slipped into the pew where her family generally sat.

While she hastily thumbed through the hymnal for the first selection she glanced around her. Gregory had become a member of the church and, unless he was out of town, he usually attended Sunday services, but she didn't see him this morning.

The congregation was well into the second verse of the hymn when someone paused by the pew. Penny became aware that someone else was later than she was. She looked up, half expecting Gregory. Instead, Brad edged into the pew beside her and took one side of her hymnbook in a silent request to share.

He looked rested and well-groomed and when she met his eyes he gave her a smile that would have warmed the heart of the coldest critic.

Penny felt her own heart sink. She didn't want to see Brad Crawford. Not today. Not until she was able to get her life back into some sort of order. Whether she liked it or not, Brad was a definite distraction to her.

What would Gregory think if he saw them standing there together, after his questions last night? Why hadn't she ever mentioned Brad to Gregory before?

Could it be she was ashamed of their relationship? How absurd. That would be the same as saying she was ashamed of herself. Brad was so much a part of her he seemed to be an extension of herself. Funny she'd never really thought about that before this weekend.

She'd been so hurt when he went to New York. But it had been good for her. She'd gotten in touch with herself and her own views and goals. If Brad hadn't gone away she probably would have drifted into marriage with him, just because he was so familiar.

What would be wrong with that? that tiny voice asked.

I'm marrying Gregory! He's more my type, she responded sternly. *I don't want to hear any more of your irresponsible remarks.*

The pew where they stood was full. When the hymn was concluded and everyone sat down, Brad was pressed against her side, from shoulder to thigh. She tried to shift but it didn't seem to help. Finally, he placed his arm on the back of the pew, giving them a little extra space, but creating a visual intimacy between them that Penny could have easily done without.

Whenever she glanced at him, Brad responded with a look of smiling inquiry.

He certainly seemed pleased with himself this morning, she thought waspishly. Obviously nothing had disturbed *his* sleep last night.

Penny realized later that she hadn't heard a word the pastor had said during his sermon. It was only when he mentioned the announcements in the bulletin and she heard her name that Penny became aware that she'd missed most of the service.

"You will note that this coming Saturday Gregory Duncan and Penny Blackwell will be joined in Holy Matrimony before this altar," Reverend Wilder said with a smile. "The Blackwells have extended an invitation to each and every one of you to join them in celebrating their daughter's wedding and hope to see you there."

Penny felt as though a spotlight had fallen on her and Brad as they sat there so closely. She forced herself to keep her eyes trained on Reverend Wilder, whose friendly smile served as a beacon of sanity in her sea of confusion. *This, too, shall pass.* The thought seemed to flow around her and she gained some comfort from it.

As soon as the final song was sung she was ready to bolt from the church and search for solitude.

Instead, it seemed as though everyone who attended church that morning wanted to stop and speak to her...and to Brad, who continued to stand beside her in the crowd.

"My, if it doesn't look natural to see the two of you together again," one woman said with a smile after she had greeted them.

"It's good to see you, Mrs. Fielding," Brad replied easily. Her husband owned the local hardware store and had been Brad's coach during his years of Little League.

"I don't suppose you came back in time to stop the wedding now, did you, young man?" she said archly and Penny suddenly prayed for a trap door that would allow her to drop out of sight.

Brad just laughed.

Mrs. Cantrell joined them. "Where is your young man this morning, Penny? When I first saw you standing there this morning, I thought Brad was your Mr. Duncan."

"I'm not sure where Gregory is, Mrs. Cantrell. How's Mr. Cantrell's leg?"

"Oh, it's healing right nicely. He was just lucky he didn't lose it, being so careless around the farm machinery." Not to be led astray from her subject, she went on. "Guess Mr. Duncan can find better things to do with his time than to go to church on Sunday. Those big city people don't seem to consider it as important as some of us," she said with a sniff.

"Oh, I'm sure it's nothing like that, Mrs. Cantrell. But since we're going to be away for a week, Gregory's been putting in long hours trying to clear his calendar."

"Well, it's sure good to see you here, Brad," Mrs. Cantrell said without commenting on Penny's explanation. "Wish you were going to be back home all the time."

Brad grinned. "Well, if there's some way I could convince the production crew to film *Hope for Tomorrow* here in Payton, I'd move back in a flash."

Everyone laughed, except Penny, who had a sudden vision of what life would be like if Brad lived there full time. Her beautifully planned future would probably become a shambles! She edged her way around the group that had gathered just outside the church doors. She'd almost made it to her car when Brad caught up with her.

"Mind if I get a ride home with you?"

"What's wrong with your car?"

"As you know, I've been using Mom's car. It wouldn't start this morning, so I got a ride in with Mom and Dad. They were on their way to visit friends for the day."

"I'm surprised you didn't go with them," Penny said, giving in to the inevitable and motioning for him to get in.

"I thought about it, but decided I'd rather spend the day with you."

"Why?" she asked baldly.

He looked at her in surprise, noticing for the first time the dark shadows under her eyes. "Why?" he repeated. "Do I have to have a reason to want to spend the day with you?"

She shrugged. "What if I've already made plans?"

"Have you?"

Good question. Gregory hadn't called before she left, but he'd made it clear today would be extremely busy for him. She'd be lucky to receive a phone call before he left for St. Louis.

She glanced over at Brad. "Not really," she admitted.

"Why don't we take the boat out on the lake?" he suggested. "It looks like a perfect day for it."

Penny thought about his suggestion for a moment. She enjoyed nothing more than being out on the water. The lake had been formed by a dam built over the river. When they were younger she and Brad had spent many a day following the river and exploring some of the coves that had formed when the water backed up.

The thought of a peaceful cove somewhere seemed to be an excellent idea. "All right," she agreed.

"Do you suppose you could find your way around your mom's kitchen enough to make us something to take along to eat?" Brad asked with a grin.

She refused to rise to the bait. "I'm sure I can. It would probably astound you how well I manage on my own these days."

He watched her in silence as they turned down the road that led to their homes. "Is something wrong, Penny?"

Funny he should ask. "What could possibly be wrong, Brad? I'm getting married in six days. Everything is perfect." She refused to look at him.

"You look tired."

"I've been keeping a busy schedule. School was just out and I've had a lot to do, getting ready for the wedding."

Brad said nothing more and Penny found some comfort in the ensuing silence.

* * *

Hours later, Penny knew she'd been right to accept Brad's invitation. This was just what she needed. Her sleek, one-piece suit was great to swim in. They had found a cove where they could swim without being afraid of being run over by a boat hauling water-skiers.

Brad and Penny had spent as much time in the water as they could all the years they'd lived at the lake. Consequently they were very much at home in it. They were like a pair of porpoises playing and they quickly returned to the pattern of their childhood. Once again, Penny forgot about Gregory and his promise to call her.

By the time they decided to eat, both of them were laughing and winded.

Penny had cheated. She had raided the refrigerator, knowing her mother wouldn't care. There had been left-over chicken, some ham, potato salad and fresh vegetables, all peeled and sliced. And for dessert, she had cut giant slices of her mother's cherry-chocolate cake.

By the time they finished eating, they felt too lazy to move.

"When do you have to get back?" Brad asked, squinting up at the sun as though trying to decide the time.

"No particular time, I suppose."

"Is Gregory coming over?"

Gregory. She hadn't given him a thought for several hours. A surge of guilt flooded through her. No doubt he'd spent the day working while she was out playing like some carefree teenager.

Brad seemed to have that effect on her. She didn't understand it. When she was with Gregory, she behaved as a mature adult would. Somehow Brad brought out the child in her.

"He didn't say," she finally said, in response to Brad's question.

"I suppose he's really busy."

"Yes."

"He appears to be very successful."

"Yes."

"Must put in some long hours."

"He has, ever since I've known him."

"Doesn't have much time to relax and enjoy himself, then," Brad offered.

Penny glanced over at him thoughtfully. "I think he enjoys himself. His practice is something he enjoys. Not only is it his vocation, it's his avocation as well."

"Do you think you're going to be happy with that sort of life, Penny?" Brad asked. His serious expression let her know he was really concerned.

She leaned back on the cushioned seat. "I won't mind it. I'm busy, too, not only with teaching but with the theater group. We each have our own lives, but we enjoy each other's company as well."

"It seems such a tepid existence for you, of all people."

She sat up and looked at him with a hint of indignation. "What do you mean me, 'of all people'?"

"Oh, you know, Runt. You're so full of life and vitality, your energy never seems to run down. I can't see all of that passion bottled into such a tame existence."

She laughed. "You're crazy. I'm not some wild, passionate creature who craves excitement."

"Maybe not. But you could be. The only time you let it loose is on stage. You've never allowed it to show, except when you lose your temper."

"Which I never do, except when you're around."

"Why do you suppose that is?"

"Besides the fact that you can be extremely aggravating at times and more than a little irritating at other times?" She widened her eyes in an innocent stare. "Why, I have no idea, Mr. Crawford. None at all."

He leaned back so that he was stretched full length across the rear of the boat. "I came home to break up your engagement," he said in a matter-of-fact tone.

His quiet statement caused her to come out of her seat. "You did what?"

"You heard me."

"How dare you even consider it!"

"I know. I finally came to the same conclusion."

She stared at him in disbelief. "But why would you even want to?"

He shrugged. "It doesn't really matter now. Since I've met him, and talked with you, I realize that if he's what you want I have no right to cause problems for you."

The idea that he had even thought of doing such a thing infuriated her. "Just who in the hell do you think you are—God?"

"No. But I am your friend. I care what happens to you. I didn't want you to make a mistake."

"And you think you know better than I do what's best for me?" she demanded to know.

"Obviously not, or I would have gone through with it."

"Fat chance, you egotistical, arrogant boob. I believe your new status and identity have gone to your head!"

"Aw, come on, Runt, you know better than that."

"And stop calling me that revolting name."

"You never used to mind it."

"Well, I certainly do now. It was all right when I was a child. It sounds perfectly ridiculous now."

Penny couldn't remember the last time she had felt such anger. Whenever it was, she was certain that it had been directed toward Brad then, as well. He was the most impossible, infuriating—she couldn't find enough names to call him.

"I want to go home," she said in carefully level tones. *Before I attempt bodily harm on you,* she added silently. To think that she had considered him a friend. But no friend would even consider doing to her what he had admitted planning.

Brad sat up. "Fine with me."

She turned the blower switch on, giving time for the fumes to clear before starting the boat. Without another word, they began to pack up the remains of their lunch. Then Penny, being the closest, started the boat and began to leave the cove.

As soon as they cleared the cove she moved the throttle to pick up speed. Out of the corner of her eye she caught a movement and glanced around in time to see another boat shooting around the point, coming directly at her. Pure reflex saved them from a nasty collision.

Penny yelled and jerked the steering wheel hard, cutting their speed at the same time. The combination of suddenly turning and losing speed caused quite a reaction on board and Penny heard a commotion of bumps and Brad's yell behind her.

The other boat went by. It was filled with a bunch of teenagers who were laughing and waving at her.

"Stupid jerks!" she yelled. "Don't you have any better sense? If you don't know water safety you should stay off the lake!" She doubted that they heard her words, but she felt better. Turning around she began to say, "I'm sorry, Brad, I hope you didn't—"

He was crumpled on the deck, the ice chest lying on top of him.

"Brad!" Penny scrambled over a loose oar, life jackets and other paraphernalia that had spilled out during the near-collision. She knelt by his side. Shoving the cooler aside she reached for him. His color seemed to be gone and he wasn't moving. "Brad?" There was a gash at his temple, and blood seemed to be everywhere. "Oh, God! Brad!"

He didn't respond.

Frantic, Penny looked around. They had come a few miles from home. There was nothing on shore that indicated people might be close by. Even in her panic she knew she had to get help. The closest she could think of was home.

Penny grabbed a towel and began to clean the blood from his face. She held pressure there until the flow eased up.

Then she gently checked to see if she could find any other injuries.

He was out cold and she didn't know how badly he'd been hit. There was nothing more she could do now. She had to get him to the hospital as quickly as possible.

Penny didn't even realize she was crying until she had to keep blinking to see where she was going on the way home.

Brad was hurt and it was her fault. She'd been so mad at him. She'd even thought about doing him bodily harm! And look what had happened. "I didn't mean it, God! You know I didn't mean it. Don't let it be serious. Please. Please let him be all right."

She set new speed records getting home. As soon as she could tie up the boat at her dock she ran up the path. "Mom! Dad! Call the ambulance, Brad's been hurt!"

Penny burst into the house, gasping for breath. Gregory met her by the time she reached the kitchen, her parents right behind him. She absently noticed his casual dress but she had no time to question him.

"What's the matter!" he demanded.

"It's Brad! He fell. Hit his head. He's bleeding and I don't know how badly he's hurt."

He grabbed her by the shoulders. "All right, now. Calm down. You call an ambulance and we'll go check on him."

Quickly she nodded, reaching for the wall phone and glancing at the emergency number posted nearby.

Later, Penny couldn't seem to remember all of the events. She knew Gregory and her dad had gone down to the landing and had brought Brad up to the house. He was still unconscious.

She'd called his parents and they were all there when the ambulance arrived. Without thinking about it, Penny crawled into the ambulance with him, holding his hand and whispering to him. "I'm sorry, Brad. I never meant to hurt you. You know that. It was just a crazy accident. Please get better, Brad. Please don't be hurt bad."

The attendant handed her a tissue and she realized that tears still streamed down her face.

The doctor was waiting for them when they arrived and it was only when they'd taken him into the examining room that Penny realized she was standing barefoot in her bathing suit.

Both sets of parents and Gregory arrived within minutes. Her mother, bless her heart, had grabbed some clean, dry clothes for her and Penny excused herself and went into the ladies' restroom to change.

As soon as she came out she asked, "Have you heard anything?"

They all shook their heads. Gregory led her to a couch that looked as though it had been brought off the ark and sat down beside her. "Can you tell us what happened?"

As coherently as possible, she explained the sequence of events. When she was finished, Gregory asked, "Could you identify the other boat or any of the people in it?"

"I doubt it. It all happened so fast. They were just a bunch of kids out having a good time and not paying attention."

"Without your quick responses, it could have been much worse, you know. They need to be found and reprimanded."

Her eyes filled once again. "It was so awful, Gregory," she said in a choked voice. "We'd been fighting and I was so blasted mad at him, but I didn't want him to get hurt." She lay her head on his shoulder and cried, her sobs shaking her body.

"I know. He's very special to you. I'm beginning to understand that."

He held her until eventually the emotional shock began to abate and she had managed to gain some measure of control.

The doctor on call appeared in the doorway of the waiting room. He was new to the area and none of them knew him.

He smiled at the three couples waiting and said, "This young man was very lucky. He did receive a concussion, but it could have been much worse. Blows to the temple are very tricky things."

Brad's mother asked, "But he's going to be all right. You're sure?"

"Oh, yes. He came to for a few minutes. He's still groggy and we gave him something to ease the pain." He paused and glanced at the three women. "Which one of you is Penny?"

Penny came to her feet. The doctor's smile widened. "You might want to go in and see him for a few minutes. He's disoriented and seems to think something happened to you. He's been calling your name and fighting me, saying he had to find you."

Without a thought Penny joined the doctor in the doorway. "Where is he?"

He turned and started down the hallway. "We put him in this room," he said, opening the door and holding it for her.

Penny tiptoed into the room. The shades were drawn and it was dim. The doctor snapped on a night-light and she could see Brad lying there, his head swathed in white bandages. His eyes were closed and he looked so pale. Penny bit her lip to keep from crying out.

She glanced around and discovered the doctor had left the room. Hesitantly she approached the bed. Brad was in a hospital gown and the sheet was folded neatly over his chest. His hands rested on either side of him. She took his hand and slowly lifted it to her mouth, brushing her lips across his knuckles.

Brad's lashes fluttered, then he slowly opened his eyes. "Penny?" His lips moved but there was very little sound.

"I'm here, Brad."

"You okay?" he managed to say. He was having trouble moving his mouth.

"I'm fine. It's you we've been worried about."

"Wha' happened?"

"A boat almost rammed us. I dodged to miss them and threw you halfway across our boat." Tears began to stream down her face once more. "Oh, Brad. I'm so sorry."

"Wasn't your fault," he said drowsily.

"I'm sorry I got so mad at you. I was afraid you'd been killed and I would never be able to tell you how sorry I am."

"I'm...too hard-headed...to be hurt...by a blow...to my head," he said haltingly, trying to smile. She could see the pain in his eyes and she ached with shared pain. "Besides, you had a right...to get angry at me. Trying to break...engagement...was...childish thing to do."

She smiled. "I'm afraid I have to agree with you there, my friend."

"I'm sorry...forgive me?"

She stroked his cheek with her free hand. "You know me, Brad, I can never stay mad at you for long. I never could."

"Good thing," he replied, his voice slurred. "Or you'd... be angry...all...time."

"I'm sure the doctor wants you to rest," she said. "Your folks are waiting outside. I know they want to see you."

He smiled, a slow, sleepy smile that seemed to increase the ache in her heart.

She leaned over and kissed him. "I'll see you tomorrow, Brad." She laid his hand on his chest, but she didn't let go immediately.

He squeezed her hand but didn't say anything. She patted the hand she still held and slowly released him, suddenly feeling awkward.

Then Penny turned around and left the room.

Chapter Five

Gregory was quiet on the way home and Penny felt too drained to try to make conversation. He followed her into the house and she went to the kitchen to make coffee, motioning him into the living room.

Her parents had stayed at the hospital with the Crawfords. No one had expressed an opinion as to when they'd return.

When she brought the coffee into the living room Penny suddenly realized she had never asked Gregory why he'd been there that afternoon.

"I'm so glad you came today," she said, handing him his cup and settling beside him on the couch. "I'm just sorry I wasn't here. I thought you said you were going to spend the day working."

He looked at her and smiled, a wry smile that she found endearing. "Actually, I had no intention of leaving the office until I had made a dent in the pile of files and papers on my desk." Gregory settled back on the sofa with a sigh. "After a few hours I noticed there was no appreciable difference in the amount of work in front of me." He took a sip of coffee. "I kept thinking of you and how much I wanted to be with you."

Gregory peered into his cup as though looking for an answer to a thorny question. "As a matter of fact, I decided to forget about the work for a while and come get you. I thought we could spend some time together out on the lake."

His eyes met hers. "When I got here your parents mentioned that you and Brad had gone out a few hours earlier."

Penny touched his cheek lightly with her hand. "I wish I'd known. I could have waited."

"Spending the day with you and Brad wasn't what I had in mind."

"What I meant was that if I'd known, I would have waited and gone out with you. Brad would have found someone else to spend the day with."

Gregory studied her face, enjoying the candid expression in her blue eyes, the way her flyaway curls clustered on her forehead. Most of all he enjoyed the unconscious innocence she projected, not so much a sexual innocence, although he was willing to bet that was the case. But Penny had a wholesomeness, such a trusting nature that he sometimes felt he was hundreds of years older than she. The ugliness of the world seemed to have passed her by, as though, like a princess in a fairy tale, she had been locked away and protected from some of the harsher realities of life.

"You mentioned earlier that you and Brad had been arguing," he said with a slight smile.

Penny felt her face flush. "Yes."

"About what?"

She stared at him in dismay. She had no idea what Gregory thought of Brad. He was an expert at keeping his thoughts and opinions to himself. For some reason she didn't want him to know about Brad's intention to break them up. The point was, he hadn't and he was sorry. There was no need to share the details with Gregory.

"I can't even remember," she said, not meeting his eyes. "Brad and I seem to argue every time we're around each other."

"I still find that surprising in you."

"I know. Some people have that effect on others."

He nodded thoughtfully. "Yes, that's true. Sparks fly."

She laughed. "They definitely fly whenever Brad and I get together." She hugged Gregory. "I'm so glad you and I don't react that way to each other. I much prefer our comfortable relationship." When he didn't reply she went on to say, "I never got around to thanking you for your help today. I don't know what I would have done without you."

He held her hard against his chest, unable to resist her lips so close to his. Gregory kissed her, feeling her warmth pressed against him.

When he finally released her he smiled at the picture she made—her cheeks flushed, her eyes sparkling, her mouth slightly swollen. "I was glad to help, but you would have done just fine without me. You handled yourself extremely well in the emergency, never losing your head."

"Oh, no. I almost drowned you in my tears at the hospital."

"Yes, after the crisis was over. But when you needed to be strong you managed to give Brad first aid, then got him home. I was very proud of you today. I want you to know that."

"Oh, Gregory. Your ability to understand me is one of the things I love about you," she said, her arms still around him.

He was quiet for a few moments, then said, "It's interesting, isn't it, the many different ways we can love. Some people seem to have a larger capacity for love than others. You seem to have grown up giving your love to people—your parents, Brad, his parents; later the people who live in Payton. Now me."

She smiled at him.

"I always had trouble understanding that emotion they called love. I've seen some of the tragedies that have occurred in the name of love, witnessed selfishness and possessiveness that have been given the label of love, but until I met you, I never truly experienced what it all meant—the generosity of love for its own sake, and what a difference it could make in life." He looked down at her, trying to memorize the beauty that was in her. "Thank you for showing me how unselfish love can be, how generous."

"It was my pleasure," she said with a mischievous grin. "You've shown me a great deal, too, you know."

"Have I? In what way?"

"You didn't treat me like some fragile doll sitting on a shelf. You've always treated me as an equal, with respect and admiration."

"Hasn't everyone?"

"It's hard to explain. But living in the same small town all my life has meant that everyone has preconceived ideas about me. Until you came along, nobody would even ask me out for a date!"

"Why do you suppose they didn't?"

She grinned. "Because all the eligible men already knew me too well, I guess."

"It couldn't have anything to do with Brad, could it?"

She frowned. "What does Brad have to do with my not being asked on a date?"

"Perhaps everyone thought you two were a pair," he suggested.

Penny rolled her eyes. "That's quite possible. I know everybody acted surprised when you and I announced our engagement. I just assumed they thought you'd been tricked into proposing to me."

Gregory threw his head back and laughed and she began to laugh with him. "Oh, Penny, what an innocent you are!" He studied her for a moment, the light of laughter gradually disappearing out of his eyes. "Then you admit that people saw you and Brad as a couple."

She shrugged. "I can't very well deny it. Since he's been home everyone I've seen has made some comment. But that's their problem. It doesn't really concern you and me. Once we're married, they'll get those silly ideas out of their heads."

"So you don't really wish that it were Brad you were marrying instead of me?"

"Brad and I don't have that sort of a relationship. We never did. You are the man I'm going to marry." She sounded very final.

Gregory smiled. "I'm glad to hear it." He carefully unwrapped her arms from around his neck. "However, at the moment I think I'd better let you get some rest. I've still got to pack and get ready to return to St. Louis."

Penny hated to see him leave. She enjoyed his companionship so much. She felt safe and secure whenever he was around. In particular, she needed his presence this final week before she married him, especially now that Brad was here. She couldn't explain it. She just knew it was true. But she knew she mustn't be selfish, so she walked him to the door in silence.

He paused at the door and looked down at her. "I'm going to be extremely busy, so don't worry if you don't hear from me. I'll be back in time for the rehearsal Friday night. You can count on it."

She nodded. "I'll just think about this time next week when we'll be on our honeymoon," she said with a grin. "That should help fill the next few days."

"I'm sure you'll want to spend some time with Brad while he's recuperating." Gregory waited for a denial, for some sign that, despite everything he had seen and heard, Penny wasn't as attached to Brad as Gregory was finally coming to accept.

"Yes, that's true," she said, unaware of what he was thinking. "You know his television character is supposed to be in a coma. He almost had a chance to find out what that was like firsthand.'' She shook her head. ''I bet he's already regretting having come home for the wedding.''

''Then again, it might have been a very crucial decision for his future. Who knows?'' Gregory said, leaning over and kissing her softly on the mouth. ''I suppose only time will tell.''

I wonder what he meant by that? Penny asked herself when she went upstairs and began to prepare for bed. Gregory could certainly be enigmatic at times. No doubt that trait was one of the reasons he was such a brilliant attorney.

''Oh, how sweet,'' Brad cooed in a cloying falsetto voice, clasping his hands under his chin and giving her an idiotic smile. ''You brought me some candy,'' he said as she walked into his hospital room the next morning carrying a gaily wrapped package.

Penny was relieved to see him looking so much better. His color had improved considerably since the day before. Today he looked almost rakish with his head bandaged, but there were still deep bruises under his eyes.

''What I have is much better for you than candy,'' she informed him, walking over to the bed and handing him the package. ''I've brought you a coloring book and some crayons.'' It was worth the search she'd gone to that morning to see the expression on his face.

Without missing a beat he said, ''Fantastic, what kind?''

''Only the best for you, my friend—a book immortalizing the characters from *Star Wars*.''

Brad started to chuckle, then gently touched his head. ''Please don't make me laugh. My head feels like it's going to topple off my shoulders when I so much as move it. Laughter would destroy me.''

She leaned over and kissed him on the cheek. ''Poor baby. And here I thought you'd be so pleased.''

"I am. I am. You're the only one who knows about my secret passion for the *Star Wars* trilogy."

"Oh, I don't think you managed to keep your deep, dark secret from your mom. Remember, she was the one who attempted to keep order in your room for years."

He smiled. "Yes, but I've learned that I can trust the two women in my life to keep my deeply-guarded secret."

"So how are you feeling?"

"Like I've spent a week wrapped around several bottles of booze and just surfaced."

"That bad, huh?"

"I knew there was a reason I never drank much. Can you imagine someone paying to feel this bad?"

"Who are you kidding? You never wanted to lose your wholesome kid image and you know it."

"Wholesome? Me? Don't let my producer hear you say that. He's convinced I look like the sort who'd start seducing maidens before breakfast and continue throughout the day without pause."

She grinned. "Are you sure that's the appeal? I always thought you looked like the sort women dreamed of being seduced by."

He eyed her speculatively. "Oh, yeah? Tell me more."

"Nothing doing. You're too vain as it is."

Brad patted the side of his bed and she perched on it. "I don't think I remembered to thank you for your help yesterday," he said.

"My help! That blow to the head must have really befuddled you, my friend. I'm afraid I was the one who caused it."

"That's not the way Dad explained it. You probably saved us both from a serious, perhaps even fatal, collision."

Penny couldn't think of anything to say. She glanced around the room, then back at him. "Has the doctor said when you're going to be able to get out of here?"

"Hopefully tomorrow. He said I would have to take it easy for a few days, but since that was the way I'd intended to spend the week anyway, I'm not going to have much trouble following the doctor's orders.''

"Are you sorry you came back?'' she asked quietly.

He waited until her eyes met his. They stared at each other for an indeterminable length of time. "No, I'm not sorry. My only regret is that I didn't come back sooner.''

"Why do you say that?''

"It doesn't matter. Now you're deliriously in love with your handsome lawyer and soon you'll be a blushing bride and will live happily ever after.'' He took her hand and held it between both of his. "You know, Penny, that's all I ever wanted, for you to be happy. I've enjoyed our time together this week—the visit to the park, the fun we had yesterday.''

"Some fun.''

"It was, most of it. Sharing those things with you, one last time, helped me to say goodbye to our shared past. I needed the transition time, a chance to be with you before you become the oh, so proper wife of the esteemed and honorable Gregory Duncan.''

"Now you're making fun of us.''

"Not at all. I'm trying like hell not to envy what the two of you have.''

"You'll find it for yourself, someday.''

He nodded. "Of course I will.''

She made a face. "And I'll hate her on sight,'' she admitted with a slight smile.

His eyebrows arched slightly. "Without even knowing her?''

"Without a doubt. You always had such lousy taste in women, you know.''

"Oh, really?'' he said in a dangerous tone.

"Yes, really! Have you forgotten dating Diana during our second year at college?''

"How could I ever forget the lovely Diana? She was a knockout."

"True. And she was also sleeping with every guy on the campus."

"Yeah, well, no man's education is quite complete without a Diana in his life," he said with a grin.

"What about Beth?"

"What was wrong with Beth?" he asked with surprise. "I thought you liked her."

"Liked her? I felt sorry for her. How she ever managed to get out of grade school, much less find her way into college, always remained a mystery to me."

"So she wasn't the brightest person we've ever known. She was very sweet."

"Yes. And she adored you."

"Can't fault her taste."

"Only her intelligence."

They paused and grinned at each other.

Brad squeezed the hand he still held. "God, I've missed you. Nobody has ever given me such a bad time, or led me in such intricate circles as you."

"*Moi?*" she asked in mock surprise. "Surely not."

"Why didn't you ever come to New York to see me, like I wrote and asked you to?"

Penny gazed out the window, thinking back over the years. "Because I was still too angry with you."

"Angry! What had I done?"

"You left me here and went off to continue playing at life."

"Is that what it seemed to you?"

She nodded. "I guess I had always assumed you'd come back to Payton and go to work with your dad. It never occurred to me that your talk of New York was anything but the usual chatter we all had. About the time when we'd be discovered and cast in a starring role. Or being understudy one night, stopping the show as the lead the next."

"You could still do that, you know."

"Not me. I can't see Gregory content to have a wife living half a continent away."

"There is that."

Penny slipped from the bed and brushed the wrinkles from her skirt. "I don't want to keep you from your coloring, my dear. Maybe the nurse will help you if you get too tired to finish by yourself."

Brad didn't smile but continued to look at her. His hand still grasped hers and he slowly loosened his hold. "I love you, Penny," he said, his voice so low she almost didn't hear him. "Thank you for being a part of my life."

In all the years she had known him, he had never said those words to her before. Hearing them now did something strange to her. She wanted to laugh. She wanted to cry. She wanted to throw her arms around his neck. She wanted to go running down the hall.

"I love you, too, Brad," she finally replied.

"Now's a hell of a time to let me in on that little secret," he pointed out rather grimly.

"You haven't exactly been forthcoming yourself, you know."

"I know. Words of love are too special to use lightly. But then, you're a very special person in my life. You always will be."

Penny couldn't control the tears that suddenly flooded her eyes. "You are, too."

"Remember, if you ever need me, for anything, I'll always be there for you. That's what friends are for."

She couldn't say a word. Not one. For if she did, she would end up making a complete fool of herself. So she squeezed his hand, then turned away and walked out of the room.

When Gregory called her that night she was able to report that Brad was rapidly improving and due to come home the next day.

"That's good news, I'm sure."

"Yes," she said, a little abstracted. Penny had wandered around the house all day, like a lost soul trying to find its home. "How are things going for you?" she asked, determined to concentrate on Gregory.

He filled her in on some of the complications he'd run into and she found her thoughts wandering once again. She loved Gregory; there was no way to deny what she felt for him. But it was so different from the way she felt for Brad.

Would she ever be able to forget how she felt for those few moments when she thought Brad was dead? Penny never wanted to suffer through anything so traumatic again. She couldn't begin to picture what life would be like for her if she didn't know that Brad Crawford was somewhere in the world.

"Penny?"

"Oh, I'm sorry, Gregory, I was distracted for a moment."

There was a silence for a moment before Gregory responded. "I'm not surprised," he finally said. "You've had so much on your mind, lately."

"No more than you, I'm sure."

"Yes, well, different things affect us different ways. I've got to let you go for now. I'll see you Friday night."

"Fine. Take care now."

"You, too."

Penny hung up the phone, feeling oddly restless and discontent.

For a moment she wished she could lie down and go to sleep and wake up Saturday morning in time for her wedding. The prewedding jitters were getting completely out of hand.

Brad had been home for three days when his mother called him to the phone. He assumed it was Penny checking to see how he was feeling, although she generally came over. In fact, she had promised him a game of chess sometime that day before she had to go to the church for the wedding rehearsal.

"Hello?"

"Good morning, Brad. This is Gregory Duncan. How are you feeling these days?"

To say Brad was surprised to hear from Penny's fiancé would be a definite understatement. He had assumed that Penny was reporting his progress to Gregory whenever they spoke to each other. For some reason Brad didn't feel as though he had made Gregory's best friends' list.

"I'm feeling much better, thank you."

"I was wondering if you'd feel up to meeting me somewhere. There's something I would like to discuss with you."

"Today?"

"Yes, if at all possible. Penny may have told you I've been in St. Louis all week. I just got in."

"I see," Brad said, automatically. Actually, he didn't see at all. Why was Gregory calling him? More important, why would he want to meet with him?

"Brad? Are you there?"

"Oh, sorry. I was thinking. Yes, I suppose I could meet you at your office, if that would be convenient."

"Fine. I'll see you whenever you can get here."

Brad hung up the phone, still puzzled. Maybe Penny had told Gregory about their conversation at the hospital. Was Gregory going to tell him to keep away from his wife? That was a little dramatic, but then trial attorneys had been known to use a little drama to get a point across.

Brad absently touched his head, where a small bandage covered the blow he'd received.

Perhaps the blow to his head had caused him to feel all of this confusion. Maybe he was Drew Derek, recovering from his stay at the hospital. This visit home certainly had all the elements that could be found in a soap opera.

He could almost hear the strains of music in the background while the announcer intoned—"Tune in tomorrow to find out... What does Gregory want to say to Brad? Does

Gregory know that Brad is in love with his fiancé and had hoped to break up their engagement? Will Gregory denounce Brad to Penny? Will Brad be barred from the church for fear he might try to stop the proceedings? Stay tuned...''

Brad shook his head. Obviously his vacation had been long overdue. He must be cracking up.

Brad had never seen the building where Gregory Duncan had his law practice. He was impressed. The office itself was even more impressive. A middle-aged woman sat at a secretarial desk in the reception area.

"May I help you?" she asked pleasantly.

"My name is Brad Crawford. I—"

"Oh, yes, Mr. Crawford. Mr. Duncan asked that you be shown in immediately." She came around her desk and led him down a hallway lined with law books. Tapping on the door at the end, she announced, "Mr. Crawford is here," and stepped back, allowing Brad to enter.

The office was a corner one, so two walls were almost entirely made up of glass. Since the building was located on the edge of town, the view from the windows was of meadows, rolling hills and a distant glimpse of the river.

"I'm impressed," Brad said quietly, standing in the doorway.

Gregory had stood when he walked in. Now he walked around his massive desk toward Brad. The room seemed large enough to hold a basketball court. All the furniture, furnishings and the well-dressed man coming toward him spoke of dignity and wealth. How could Brad have been so stupid as to suggest Gregory might be marrying Penny for her future prospects? He could probably buy and sell the Blackwells from his petty cash.

Gregory stuck out his hand. "I appreciate your coming in on such short notice, Brad." He motioned to the chairs that were arranged in front of his desk. "Won't you have a seat?"

"I don't mind. I haven't been all that booked up this week," Brad said casually.

"I'm sure that Penny has kept you company during your convalescence."

Brad tried to read something into that statement—sarcasm, anger, jealousy. He heard none of those things. It had been a simple statement. Brad looked at the older man who had seated himself behind the desk once more. "Yes, she has." He raised one brow slightly. "Does that bother you?"

"To the contrary," Gregory said with a brief smile. "I fully expected to hear it, which is why I called you. There's something I need to say to you."

Feeling as though he were in the middle of a play and had forgotten his lines, Brad waited for Gregory to continue.

Gregory leaned his arms on the desk blotter lying in front of him, clasped his hands and met Brad's gaze with his own. "You're in love with Penny, aren't you?"

He'd been right. Gregory was going to see that he was removed from Penny's life. Brad wished he found the situation a little more amusing. How could he convince the man that his love for Penny was the very thing that would prevent him from doing anything to hurt her marriage to Gregory? Searching for the right words, Brad finally shrugged and admitted, "Yes, I am, but you're the man she's marrying."

"No, I'm not," Gregory replied quietly.

Brad was convinced something was wrong with his hearing. Perhaps the blow to his head had... "I beg your pardon?"

"You heard me."

"Of course you're marrying Penny. The rehearsal is tonight and tomorrow—"

"Tomorrow I will be in California. I discovered earlier today where a key witness is located. I'm flying out tonight to take his deposition."

"But the wedding?"

Gregory leaned back. "Ah, yes, the wedding." He placed his hands behind his head. "An interesting situation, isn't it? Two men who love Penny, discussing a wedding that isn't going to come off."

"Couldn't you postpone your deposition or whatever? Surely Penny is more important than—"

"I understand your concern. Now you need to understand mine. I've had a great deal of time to think this week and I've come to the conclusion that Penny seriously misled me."

"What are you talking about? Penny doesn't lie!"

"Please don't put words in my mouth," Gregory responded.

Brad was now facing the courtroom lawyer and recognized he could be a formidable foe.

"When I met Penny I thought she was everything I wanted in a wife. Since then I've come to know her better, and I've had reason to revise that opinion."

"What's that supposed to mean?"

"I've decided that marrying Penny would be a mistake on my part."

"Why?" Brad demanded to know.

"For over a year I've spent time with the quiet, organized, unflappable woman I knew as Penny Blackwell. Yet in three days a volatile, passionate woman I never knew existed emerged as a result of your presence. I'm not comfortable with that person. I have no room for her in my life." He nodded to the younger man. "I believe I have you to thank for the transformation. As far as I'm concerned, I've had a very narrow escape."

Brad came to his feet. "That's a hell of a thing to say! You wait until the day before your wedding to decide you don't know the woman you intend to marry so you're backing out? How can you do this to Penny? When do you intend to tell her how you feel?"

"I don't."

Brad had never felt such a murderous rage in all of his life. Gregory was calmly explaining that he intended to destroy Penny's life without even bothering to warn her?

"You really are a no-good, son-of-a—"

"Yes, I probably am. However, I did not reach my age or gain the experience I presently possess by being quixotic and foolish. I don't believe Penny understands what it is she feels for me. Whatever she feels, I don't think it's what I want from my wife. It's better to make a clean break now."

Gregory watched the younger man as though evaluating his reaction to what he'd just been told.

He got an immediate response. "You really are cold-blooded, aren't you? You don't care what you do to Penny, how you hurt her. She didn't measure up to some ridiculous standards you seem to have, so you're going to abandon her at the church."

"I don't intend to be that dramatic. I'll leave that sort of thing to you. You seem well-trained for it."

"If you don't intend telling her you've changed your mind, how the hell is she going to know?"

Gregory met his gaze and deliberately smiled. "Why, you'll tell her, of course. Why do you suppose I asked you to come in today?"

"Me? Are you out of your mind? It isn't my place to—"

"You're her friend, aren't you?"

"You're damn right I'm her friend, but—"

"I'm sure she'd rather receive such news from you."

"You're wrong! She'd rather hear it from you!"

"Somehow, I doubt that very much," Gregory said in a dry voice.

"Well, of course, you're right. Nobody wants to be told on the eve of their wedding that the other party has backed out."

"I have to agree."

"But it's none of my business. This is between you and Penny," Brad protested.

Chapter Six

By the time Brad reached home his head felt as though it were going to explode. He didn't even remember leaving Gregory Duncan's office or driving home. Only the intense pain in his head held his attention until he realized he was sitting in his room, staring at the wall.

He had to find Penny and tell her. But how was he going to break the news? Damn the man, anyway. How could anyone be so unfeeling as to walk out on someone the day before the wedding?

It would break Penny's heart.

Forcing himself to go in search of her, Brad started through the kitchen of his home.

"Your head must be really bothering you," his mother said when she saw his expression. "Why don't you lie down and rest awhile?"

He turned, wincing at the sudden movement. "I've got to talk to Penny."

"She should be over here before much longer. Why don't you rest until she gets here?"

Perhaps that was good advice. He would take some of the pain medication the doctor had given him when he left the hospital. He hadn't used it before, but at the moment he was willing to do whatever he could for some relief.

After swallowing the tablets he stretched out on the bed and waited for Penny to come.

Oh, God, Penny. If only you didn't have to go through all of this.

By the time Penny peeked in to see if he still wanted to play chess, she found him sound asleep. His mother had told her that he had gone out for a while and was concerned that he had tried to do too much, too soon. She mentioned that he wanted to see Penny, but they both agreed it would be better to leave him alone and let him rest.

Penny had enough on her mind. She hadn't talked with Gregory since Monday evening, which wasn't like him at all. And he hadn't called to let her know he was back today. What if he was late for the rehearsal, or even worse, unable to make it?

She wouldn't let herself think of that. If he was delayed too much, she was certain he would call. Gregory was an honorable man and dependable. If she hadn't been in such a turmoil all week she wouldn't have worked herself up to such a state now.

Everything was under control. She would see Gregory this evening and they could laugh at her silliness.

Her mother decided not to go to the rehearsal so Penny drove to the church alone. Her dad was coming directly from his office.

When everyone was there but Gregory, Reverend Wilder suggested they begin. "After all, the groom has very little to do. I think that's for a reason," he kidded. "Usually the groom is too nervous to think of much of anything."

They all laughed politely, then followed his instructions.

"Have you talked with Gregory today?" Penny's father asked while they waited their turn to go down the aisle.

"No, I haven't."

"I hope nothing is wrong."

"So do I. Perhaps he just got held up. He's probably on his way now."

"Well, he could have called to let you know."

She gave her father a sidelong glance. "You know, Dad, that thought *had* crossed my mind."

He chuckled and patted her arm. "I'm sorry. I suppose I'm more nervous about the groom's absence than you are."

"Not necessarily. But I don't want anyone to think I'm nervous. What you are presently witnessing is my superb acting ability."

At that moment Reverend Wilder motioned for them to start down the aisle. Penny and her father didn't have a chance to speak in private again.

When Brad woke up he noted with relief that his head felt considerably better. Then he noticed it was dark. "Oh, no!" His sudden effort to sit up on the bed reminded him that he was far from being cured, despite the rest.

By the time he got over to the Blackwells', he knew he'd missed Penny. Helen confirmed his guess. "If you want to see her, you're welcome to wait. I'm sure they'll be home soon."

Brad was too restless at the moment to sit and try to make conversation. What he had to tell Penny had to be said in private. What she chose to do after that was anybody's guess. But it wasn't up to him to inform her mother or anyone else.

Brad spent the next few hours rehearsing what he needed to say to Penny.

"You could always marry her yourself," Gregory had said. The refrain kept running over and over through Brad's head.

There was just one thing wrong with that idea. Penny had no desire to marry him. She was in love with Gregory Duncan. The louse. The no-good, rotten arrogant fool who didn't care that he was leaving her to face the embarrassment and humiliation of a church full of people and no bridegroom.

What was she going to do at this late date? How could she possibly call everyone and explain? What could she say? How could Gregory Duncan have done such a thing to her? If he had any feelings for her at all, he would have talked to her, either in person or even by telephone. At the very least, he could have written her.

Why the hell had he chosen Brad to break the news to her?

That's what friends are for. Was that it? Gregory knew that Brad would do his best to shield Penny as much as possible. He'd even marry her if it would help.

Brad thought about that for a long while. Would it help? It couldn't make things any worse. At least she could have the wedding as planned, the reception. He seriously doubted she'd be interested in a honeymoon. Not with him, anyway. Brad tried not to allow himself to think about a honeymoon where he and Penny would be together, alone, and legally married. That way of thinking led to insanity.

Perhaps he and Penny could work out something so that she wouldn't feel abandoned and forgotten. She would never have a need to feel that way as long as Brad was around.

Ralph and Penny got home at about the same time. Her mother said that Brad had been looking for her. There had been no message from Gregory.

She glanced at the time. It was almost eleven—too late to see what Brad wanted. Her parents went up to bed, knowing they would need their rest for the next day.

Penny almost called Brad anyway. She needed to talk to someone. Not just someone, she needed Brad, she realized. He was the only person she knew with whom she could share her fears and be sure he wouldn't laugh.

But his mother said he was still suffering from considerable pain. No doubt he was already asleep now, and he really needed his rest.

Oh, well. She'd see him at the reception tomorrow, and they could chat before she and Gregory left to go wherever it was that Gregory planned to take her. Once Brad returned to New York, Penny knew her life would resume its normal pace.

She knew that he wasn't to blame for all her restlessness this week, but he seemed to symbolize a certain freedom that she was willingly giving up by marrying Gregory. She knew she'd feel more at peace once Brad wasn't around to remind her.

Quietly climbing the stairs, Penny went into her room and without turning on the light grabbed her nightshirt and went into her bathroom. She went through her nightly ritual, showering and drying her hair. Tonight she needed to remember to soak her contacts. She wouldn't want to be bothered next week while they were traveling. Thank God she knew the way to bed blindfolded, she thought with a grin. It was amazing how dependent she'd become on her extended-wear lenses.

Flipping off the light she felt her way to the bed and had almost reached it when a hand touched her arm and a voice said, "Don't let me scare—"

She was already beginning to scream when a hand clamped over her mouth in a firm grip.

"Oh, for God's sake, Penny. I'm not a rapist! What's the matter with you?"

As soon as she heard his voice, she recognized Brad but she hadn't been able to control her involuntary scream. She went limp in his arms and he released her mouth.

"Are you okay? I didn't hurt you, did I?" he asked in a low voice. Brad reached over to the bedside lamp and turned it on. They both blinked in the sudden light.

"How did you get in here?" she hissed.

"The same way I always got into your room—through the window, remember?" He motioned to the opened window and the oak tree that stood outside.

"What is so important that you have to scare me half out of my mind to tell me? Couldn't it have waited until tomorrow?" She wished she could focus on his face better. Penny couldn't see his expression at all. She sat down on the edge of the bed and glared at him.

"You're wearing my old football jersey," Brad said in a wondering tone.

"You mean you risked your neck climbing that old tree to crawl into my window to tell me that?" she asked incredulously.

"Of course not. I just didn't know you had kept it, that's all."

She sighed. "I kept every one you gave me. I find them very comfortable to sleep in. I've used them for years."

He couldn't help grinning but she didn't seem to notice. Now that he looked more closely, she didn't seem to be looking at him. At least, she was staring at him, but she didn't see him. She had that same vague, unfocused look she used to get when . . . "You don't have your contacts in, do you?" he asked, suddenly comprehending why she seemed somehow different.

Penny began to feel bewildered. Brad didn't seem to be his normal self at all, tonight. Then she remembered, But, of course; he was still recovering from his accident. That blow to the head might have caused more serious damage than anyone had realized.

Oh, how horrible! Maybe there had been some brain damage that was only now beginning to be apparent. Penny got up from the bed and walked over to him. Touching his arm she said in a calm, soothing voice. "That's right, Brad. I have to soak them once a week to keep them clean of protein buildup."

Leading him over to the bed, she coaxed him to sit down. She sat beside him and patted his hand.

"I'm really pleased that you came to see me tonight, Brad. I'm sorry I didn't get a chance to visit with you these past couple of days." She glanced up at him with concern. "I suppose your head still really bothers you."

Brad looked at her and had an almost uncontrollable urge to reach out and haul her into his arms. There she was, looking so concerned about him and his problems, unaware of what was happening in her life.

He loved her so much. She deserved better treatment, she really did. If he hadn't been so shocked when Gregory had informed him of his intentions, Brad would have loved to have laid him out. Let Mr. Duncan appear in California to take depositions with a lovely shiner! He deserved more than that.

Penny stroked his brow, subtly checking to see if he was feverish. "Why don't you go home now and get some rest. We're both tired." She smiled. "It wouldn't do for the bride to be drawn and wan tomorrow, you know."

He flinched at her words, grateful she couldn't see him any better. Otherwise she would read the distress that was obvious on his face.

"Yes, well, that's what I wanted to talk to you about, Penny," Brad finally managed to mumble.

His voice sounded so soft and hesitant, which only increased Penny's alarm. He didn't sound at all like himself. Oh, if only she'd taken the time to check on him during the past couple of days. But he'd seemed to be improving. His mother hadn't reported anything out of the ordinary. What could have happened to have brought on these dismaying symptoms?

"You want to talk about tomorrow, Brad?" she questioned as casually as possible.

"Yes."

She waited a moment, but he didn't say anything more. Finally, she said, "Okay."

Brad sat there, staring at her, remembering all of their shared time together. He'd lost track of how often he'd climbed the tree outside her window and sneaked into her room. She had been just as bad about using the tree as an escape to meet him somewhere.

The innocence of youth. It had not occurred to either of them that there was anything wrong with them shinnying in and out of each other's bedroom windows. It had been a game. Some of their greatest adventures had been planned while sitting on one of their beds cross-legged, letting their imaginations fly before them like kites in the sky.

Brad admitted to himself that he felt different now. He was well aware that they were no longer children. Even with her face freshly scrubbed and her hair brushed into submission, Penny could scarcely pass as a child. His old football jersey did not disguise her womanly form or hide her well-shaped legs. Brad felt such a strong surge of love for her that it set him trembling.

How dare Gregory Duncan hurt her—his wonderful, lovable, gentle Penny. She never harmed anyone; she only saw the good in everyone. Even now, Penny had complete trust and faith in the man who was too cowardly to tell her he wasn't going to marry her tomorrow.

"What about tomorrow?" Penny prodded gently, wondering if she should slip out and try to get one or the other sets of parents. Maybe they should take him to the emergency room tonight. Perhaps something suddenly had come loose inside his head, causing his rather strange and unusual behavior.

"The wedding," he managed to say, desperately seeking the right words to tell her.

"That's right, Brad," she said in the same soothing tone she'd been using for several minutes, "Tomorrow is the wedding. And I'm getting married."

"No, you're not," he said baldly.

Oh, dear. He was getting more and more irrational.

"I'm not?"

"No."

"I see. Why am I not getting married?"

She sounded so calm, as though she were humoring him. Of course she'd been under a great deal of strain this week, herself. "Because Gregory isn't going to marry you." There. He'd told her. He waited for her reaction. He knew the rest of the night was going to be hell. At first she'd try to deny it. That was only to be expected. Then she'd probably cry, and get angry—the anger would help, he decided. He would stay with her through all of it, and whatever she decided to do in the morning, he'd agree. If she wanted him to marry her, he would. That's what friends are for, after all, to help in a time of crisis.

What he hadn't expected was her calm acceptance. "Why isn't Gregory going to marry me?" she asked casually.

"Why?" he repeated, not knowing what to say.

"Um-hmm."

"Oh. Well. It has something to do with me, I think. I'm not sure."

"Brad, are you still feeling guilty because you intended to break up our engagement?" she asked with sudden inspiration and understanding. She put her arms around his waist and lovingly laid her head on his chest. "Oh, you poor darling. That's what we were discussing just before the accident. It must have been haunting you all week." She glanced up, unable to see the glazed look in his eyes. "Brad, love, I have forgiven you for that. Please try to understand. No one is going to hold your intentions against you. After all, you changed your mind. And you were even concerned enough to tell me, which I appreciated, very much." Placing her head back on his chest she continued, "Now I want you to go home and get some rest, okay? I appreciate your coming over tonight, I really do. But I don't want you worrying about anything, you hear me?"

She could feel his heart pounding in his chest, like a bird beating its wings against a cage. Penny felt like crying. There was no telling what was going through his poor, confused mind at the moment. Whatever it was, he was concerned about her. No matter what he was suffering, he was still thinking of her.

"Penny!" he said in a strangled voice, "You don't understand!"

She raised her head and kissed him lightly on the lips. Surely Gregory would understand why she would be kissing another man the night before her wedding. The kiss was meant only to comfort. She had to do whatever it took to calm Brad down until they could get some help for him.

His arms came around her convulsively and he hung on to her like a drowning man. During all the hours he had agonized over how to tell her, how much to tell her, never had Brad envisioned that she wouldn't believe him.

He couldn't understand why not. Was her faith in Gregory Duncan so strong that the only proof she would accept would be entering the church in the morning and finding no groom waiting?

She felt so small against him, and she was so vulnerable. Penny had no idea what she had to face tomorrow, unless he took Gregory's advice and became the substitute bridegroom.

Is that why Gregory had told him, instead of her? Was he giving Brad the option of marrying her, himself?

How could he explain to her? "Penny?"

"Hmm?"

"I love you."

She smiled, her head resting on his shoulder. "I'm so glad."

"No. I really mean it. I want to marry you."

Her head jerked up and she stared at him, truly concerned. "Oh, Brad, please don't talk that way."

"I mean it. Gregory won't marry you, but I will."

"Oh, Brad. Please don't do this to either one of us. Please. It's too late for us. Don't you understand that? Maybe if we'd had this discussion before you left for New York everything would have worked out differently." She pulled back slightly and placed her hands on his neck, cupping his jawline. "You can never go back, Brad, no matter what. Perhaps if I hadn't met Gregory, and I'd known how you feel about me . . ." She paused, wanting him to understand, not wanting to cause him any more grief. "It's too late for us," she finished softly.

"No, it isn't. Believe me, it isn't."

She just shook her head. "Oh, Brad. If only life weren't so complicated." She slipped off the bed and stood in front of him. "Go home, now, Brad. We'll meet tomorrow and pretend this conversation never took place. It's just between you and me, like so many other things that we've shared together."

Brad sat there staring at her. He'd tried to tell her. In fact, he had told her, but for whatever reason, she hadn't believed him. His options at this point were severely limited.

The question was, what would she do tomorrow when she discovered that Gregory wasn't there? Would she allow him to substitute for the missing groom?

Knowing Penny the way he did, he sincerely doubted it. In the first place, she would assume he was doing it out of pity for her because of the humiliation she would suffer. Pity had nothing to do with the feelings he had for this woman.

But he needed time to explain, time to make her understand. And from the looks of things tonight, she wasn't going to listen to what he had to say. She'd been under considerable strain all week. He knew that. Stress could have a strange effect on people.

Feeling a wealth of love for the woman who stood in front of him, Brad made up his mind. He would do whatever he had to do to protect her from a situation not of her own making.

Brad stood and smiled down at her. "Everything's going to be all right, love. I'll take care of it."

She nodded, glad to see that he appeared to be calming down.

He turned and pulled back the covers, helping her as though she were an invalid. Docilely she went along with him. There was no reason to upset him. He certainly wasn't dangerous to anyone—just a little irrational. Hopefully that would pass in a few hours. Surely it wouldn't take more than a few days to help him recover. Penny prayed his condition wouldn't be permanent.

"I'll get you a glass of water," he announced as though coming up with a brilliant idea. "That should help you sleep." He turned away and disappeared into her bathroom. She heard the water running, and he eventually reappeared.

"It will?" she asked, wondering if he had water confused with warm milk.

He carefully handed her a glass filled with water. Penny smiled and took it, dutifully taking a sip.

"Now don't worry about a thing, do you hear me?" Brad asked in an urgent tone. "Everything's going to work out just fine. You know I'll always take care of you."

"Yes," she agreed, nodding.

Brad leaned over and touched her lips softly with his. "I think I'll let myself out the back door rather than go down the tree, if that's all right," he suggested.

"Oh, yes! I wouldn't want you to slip and fall, for heaven's sake. You've had enough bumps to your head for one week!"

They smiled at each other, pleased that they had reached some sort of harmonious understanding.

Penny listened until she heard the faint sound of the back door closing, then sighed and turned out the light.

Now not only did she have to worry about whether or not the groom would show up for his wedding in the morning, she also had to live with the fear that her best friend might have received some sort of brain damage that had gone undetected until now.

Chapter Seven

"Good morning, darling," Helen said to her sleeping daughter. "I thought I'd bring you coffee in bed this morning, since it will be the last time you'll be here with us."

Penny rolled over onto her back and groggily looked up at her mother. She could see that her mother was trying not to cry at the thought that her daughter was leaving home at long last. Too bad she couldn't appreciate that very few women continued to live at home until they were twenty-five, Penny thought with amusement.

She pushed herself up, propping her pillow against the headboard. "Thanks, Mom," she said, sipping the coffee, then holding the cup between her hands.

Her mother sank onto the end of the bed. "I'm being so ridiculous, acting like this, when I've known for months you were leaving."

Penny grinned. "That's true, but I understand. I suppose I feel a little weepy myself."

"However, I'm extremely happy for you, Penny. You know I was always a little concerned before. I'm so glad you decided to go ahead and follow your heart after all, no matter what," Helen said, her face radiant. "I want you to know how proud I am of you."

Penny stared at her mother in confusion. What in the world was she talking about? Follow her heart? She shook her head. It was too early in the morning to try to work out word games.

Helen stood, leaned over and kissed her. "Breakfast will be ready in a few minutes, dear. I know you're excited, but you'll need to eat something before we leave for the church."

"I know, Mom."

Her mother smiled at her from the doorway. "It's hard to believe it. My fondest wish is finally coming true."

Penny stared blankly at the door. Her fondest wish? Had her mother secretly coveted her room for some reason? Why else would she suddenly be so pleased while at the same time lamenting that Penny was leaving home today?

She shrugged. Maybe the excitement of the wedding was getting to her mother. She usually seemed very sane and sensible.

Penny discovered that her father wasn't making much sense, either. He came bounding into the kitchen while she was struggling to eat the breakfast her mother had prepared and gave her a big hug. "My God, Penny! You are simply wonderful. I still can't believe it. I'm so proud of you. I'm not losing a daughter, I'm finally gaining the son I've always wanted."

She watched as he poured himself a cup of coffee and joined her at the table.

"I still find it hard to believe," Ralph said with a wide grin. "The two of you are actually getting married this morning. Unbelievable!"

Perhaps her dad had been in some sort of time warp during the past few months. Otherwise he wouldn't find the idea of her wedding day quite so unbelievable. Although he had always been polite and cordial to Gregory, Penny had never heard her father express such a strong sentiment toward him before. She was pleased to see him warming to the idea.

Penny and her bridesmaids planned to change into their dresses at the church, so all she had to do before leaving home was her makeup and hair. After dutifully eating her breakfast, Penny took her time returning upstairs. She had plenty of time before they had to leave.

After a few moments in the bathroom, she hurried to her bedroom door, trying not to panic. "Mom!"

"Yes, dear," Helen responded from downstairs, a lilt to her voice.

"I hate to bother you, but I can't seem to find my contacts," she said, walking out into the hallway. Her mother came up the stairs and Penny went on, consciously working to stay calm. "I know they were here last night. I soaked them overnight but they aren't where I thought I left them." She turned back into her room.

Her mother followed her and walked over to the bathroom. "I'm not surprised. You were probably so caught up in all the excitement you didn't pay any attention to where you set them down."

"I wish I weren't so blind," Penny muttered. How many times had she said that, or thought it, over the years? She followed her mother into the smaller room, feeling frustrated and helpless. Her mother began to move items around on the countertop, then peeked into the cabinets above the sink.

"Find them?" Penny asked, hopefully.

Helen looked around, puzzled. "Are you sure you took them out? Because I don't see them anywhere."

"Of course I'm sure, Mom. I left them in their soaking solution. Believe me, I know when I've got them in or not."

Helen shook her head. "Well, they aren't here, Penny."

Penny could feel the surge of panic she'd been holding at bay sweep over her. "What do you mean they aren't there?" she cried. "They have to be! Maybe they got knocked off onto the floor.'' She immediately fell to her knees and began to feel around on the smooth surface. Helen joined her until they had covered every square inch of the bathroom floor.

"They aren't here, Penny," Helen said finally, stating the obvious. She and Penny stared at each other, nose to nose on the bathroom floor. The enormity of the missing contacts settled over them slowly.

"What am I going to do?" Penny asked in a pleading voice, begging for reassurance.

"I don't know." Helen pushed herself up and looked around the room, as if hoping the contacts would suddenly appear before her. "Perhaps you could wear your glasses?"

"Oh, Mother," Penny wailed, almost in tears, "I haven't had the prescription changed in years." She walked into her bedroom and glanced around wildly. "I don't even know where they are!" She sank down on the side of the bed, her face in her hands. "Oh, dear God. What am I going to do?"

Helen sat down beside her daughter. "Well, you're not going to panic, for starters. So what if you can't see very well?" she said briskly, making it sound as though Penny was worrying over a hangnail. "We'll call for another set to be made up for you and have them mailed to you. You'll probably only have to do without them for a few days."

"But what about today?"

Helen could see that her daughter was about to fall apart. Poor dear. So many things had been happening to her and she'd handled them all so well. Now here she was going to pieces over such a little thing. But not if Helen could help it.

"I'll do your face and hair and help you dress." She laughed and went on, "And your dad is going to walk you down the aisle. After that you can use your brand-new husband as a Seeing Eye dog for a day or two. I have a feeling he won't mind in the least!"

What a way to start a marriage. And why hadn't she ever ordered an extra set of contacts? Of all days to lose hers.

And what in the world had she done with them? She couldn't imagine, but then, she'd been so distracted last night. For all she knew she might have put them in her cold cream or skin freshener!

Penny tried not to let the missing contacts cast a pall over her preparations. At least she could see shapes and wouldn't walk into any walls or doors. Her mother and dad seemed to be in high enough spirits to make up for any lack on her part. If she didn't know better, she would think they'd already gotten into the champagne.

Time seemed to speed up once they arrived at the church. There was a great deal of laughing and teasing among all of her friends while they dressed, and later, one or more would dash back in to report the swelling crowd. The church seemed to be filled to capacity.

Before she left home, Penny had slipped away long enough to call Gregory's house. There had been no answer. Of course he might have left early, even gone to the office for a final check. There was even the possibility that he had been held up in St. Louis and was even now driving back to be there on time.

But why hadn't he called her?

Penny knew that she could have her fears allayed by simply asking someone if Gregory had arrived, but after the teasing about the missing groom she'd received the night before, she wouldn't give them the satisfaction of knowing that she was worried.

Anyway, she would know soon enough. They certainly wouldn't be able to start without him.

So she waited, trying to be calm. This was her wedding day. The day she had looked forward to for months. The reason that Brad had—

Brad! She had forgotten to tell her parents about his strange behavior the night before! Oh, how could she have forgotten? She'd been so wrapped up in herself that his problems had completely slipped her mind. If his parents hadn't noticed, perhaps she was the only one who could sound a warning...

The door to the room where she waited swung open and Penny could hear the organ music. She heard a voice speaking to the congregation, then a burst of laughter and applause. What in the world?

Her father hurried through the door, a wide grin on his face. "You look beautiful, my darling daughter. Just beautiful. Are you ready to go?"

"Uh, yes. Is everything ... I mean, are we all ... ?"

"Yes, everything's moving on schedule." He took her arm and gave it a squeeze as he escorted her into the foyer to wait their turn. "You have made me a very happy man, you know that, don't you?"

At least her father was making no effort to hide his elation at finally getting rid of his daughter, she decided with wry amusement. "I'm glad," she said softly.

"I just couldn't see you with— No. This isn't the place. I'm just happy that you made the right choice."

The right choice? More cryptic comments. Had it only now occurred to her father that she could have moved in with Gregory first, before the wedding? He needn't have worried. Her upbringing would have prevented her from even entertaining the idea and Gregory had seemed content to wait for all the legalities before he claimed her.

She had no more time to think about her father's remark. Suddenly the music stopped and everyone in the church stood. The slow, stately march began, signaling that it was time for her entrance.

For the first time Penny was grateful she couldn't see more clearly. She was having an awful attack of stage fright, which was absolutely ridiculous. Crowds had never bothered her before. She'd found excitement on the stage. However, always before this she was playing someone else. Today she was Penelope Anne Blackwell and she wasn't at all sure she could make it down the aisle without tripping or in some way making a fool of herself.

She forced herself to take a calming breath, then began to take the slow, gliding steps they had rehearsed the night before.

The light from the stained glass window fell on Gregory's blond hair and Penny suddenly let go of the breath she unconsciously had been holding. He had come. He was here.

She began to smile. Everything was all right. All the last minute details had worked out. And the groom had managed to show up when he was needed. Penny began to plan some of the things she was going to say to him once they were alone. What a scare he'd given her!

When she got close enough Penny saw Reverend Wilder standing before her, smiling. At least she assumed it was he. The man appeared to be the right height and size for it. When she and her father paused she noticed that Gregory stepped beside her and faced the altar with her.

Reverend Wilder's melodious voice filled the sanctuary with the age-old ceremonial words of the wedding vows. Tears began to collect in her eyes at the beauty of the vows they were sharing.

Then the dream seemed to dissolve into a nightmare.

She heard Reverend Wilder say, "Do you, Bradley Aaron Crawford, take this woman—"

Bradley Aaron Crawford? *Bradley Aaron Crawford!* Penny turned her head and stared at the man standing beside her, the man she was in the process of marrying. There was a small white patch gleaming on his left temple.

Brad.

She never clearly remembered anything that happened during the rest of the ceremony. She must have made the right responses since no one seemed to find anything out of the ordinary in the situation. Perhaps it was only her; obviously she was suffering from some sort of delusion, she decided, dazed. Although she'd been convinced she was engaged to Gregory Duncan, she was marrying Brad Crawford.

"I now pronounce you man and wife," Reverend Wilder intoned. "You may kiss the bride."

Slowly Penny turned to the man she had just married. He carefully and tenderly lifted the veil from her face and folded it neatly back, then leaned down to kiss her.

"What are you doing here!" she whispered through barely moving lips.

He smiled and lightly kissed her on the mouth. "Marrying you," he replied as he straightened to his full height.

The triumphant music from the organ filled the large room and the entire audience stood and clapped their welcome to the new couple.

Penny wished she were the fainting type. What a wonderful way that would be to get out of an intolerable situation.

Brad swept her down the aisle, out into the foyer and into a private room. Closing the door, he reached into his pocket and pulled out something. "Here."

She blinked and peered into his hand. "What is it?"

"Your contact lenses."

"My contact lenses?" she repeated stupidly, wondering how he had known she hadn't been able to find them. And then the truth seemed to drop on her like a sudden resounding crash of boulders. "You?" she said, desperately trying to make some sense out of her whirling thoughts and emotions. A rage such as she had not felt in years took control of her. "You—Bradley Aaron Crawford—*you* took my contacts? You hid them from me, knowing I would be blind without them?"

He nodded. "I needed every advantage I could think of. You made it clear last night that if I gave you any warning, you'd refuse to allow me to help you, to save you from the embarrassment of having to call off the wedding."

"What are you talking about? Have you lost your mind?" she demanded. Then hearing her own words, things began to make a twisted sort of sense.

"Of course," she said, pacing, her long train trailing behind her, "That's it! You had that terrible blow to the head and now you've—"

She stopped suddenly and spun around, almost losing her balance in all the satin and lace material that wrapped around her when she turned. She gazed at him, her eyes widening with growing horror. "Gregory! You've done something to him. What did you do, Brad?" She fought the entangling folds of her dress and rushed over to him. Grabbing his arms and trying to shake him she yelled, "What have you done with Gregory, Brad? Answer me!"

"Penny, calm down! I haven't done anything to Gregory Duncan. Don't be so damned dramatic."

"Dramatic! Me? Why, I couldn't begin to compare with you, you no-good, rotten, egotistical louse. Just how much more dramatic did you intend to get? You managed to spirit away my fiancé in some way so you could take his place!"

Once again she began to pace, gathering her dress in both hands and bundling the folds in front of her, as though acting out a scene of a primitive washerwoman striding around the room with her load of clothes.

"Well, I won't stand for it, do you hear me?" Her voice continued to grow in volume. "I have had it with you, do you understand? I have taken all I intend to take from you and your stupid, idiotic pranks! You did your best to ruin my childhood by scaring me with snakes, putting frogs in my bed, hiding my glasses—"

"Damn it! I've told you and told you—I never did a thing to your stupid glasses. Even your mother believed me when I told her I had nothing to do with your losing them!"

She ignored the interruption. "You'd invite me to play with you, then run off and hide so nobody knew where you were, and then you would laugh because I cried when I couldn't find you!"

"Come on, Penny," he said, "be reasonable! That was twenty years ago, for God's sake!"

By now she was caught up in remembering all the many grievances she had against him. Ignoring his comment Penny continued going down her list. "And what about that time when we were in high school, how mortified I was by your absolutely awful teasing in front of Frank Tyler when you knew I had a crush on him!"

"Hey, Runt, you held your own in that department and you know it! How many girls did you tell your ridiculous stories about me so they'd never take me seriously!"

"Take you seriously? You? The original good-time man-about-town? You've never taken anything seriously in your whole life! It's all been fun and games for you, all the times we were growing up, and even when we went away to college."

She stopped pacing and stared at him from across the room, her face flushed and angry. "I was never so glad when you moved to New York and out of my life, do you hear me? Every time you're around crazy things happen. Nothing ever works out the way I plan. It was only after you were gone that I finally managed to get some order in my life and find the man I loved and intended to marry and then you—" The enormity of what had just taken place swept over her like a tidal wave and she began to cry, harsh sobs that shook her body. "No-w-w... yo-you've... com-completely... ruined... m-my life!"

Brad could only stand there and watch her. He had honestly thought he was helping her out. He certainly had no intention of ruining her life. He loved her. He had only wanted to help her... or so he had managed to convince himself when he decided to substitute himself for Gregory at the altar.

Who are you kidding, Crawford? he asked himself. *You've been eating your heart out every day since you learned she was marrying someone else.* When he'd seen his opportunity, he'd grabbed it, using Gregory's desertion to finally get what he wanted.

And Penny hated him for it.

Brad could feel the guilt churn in his stomach. He'd managed to make her his wife, but at what price? What could he possibly do or say that would ever help her forgive him?

Slowly he walked over to her and reached out his hand. She jerked away as if she found the mere thought of his touching her repulsive. He dropped his hand and just looked at her.

Penny fought for control, trying to get her breath. Through sobbing breaths she managed to grate out, "Where...is...Gregory?"

Brad sighed. He slid his hands into his pants pockets and turned away, gazing out the window.

"California."

"California? What's he doing out there?"

"Taking depositions."

She stared at him in disbelief. "You're making this up, aren't you? All of it? Gregory wouldn't have gone off like that, leaving me without some word."

Scrubbing at her face, Penny took a couple of breaths and forced herself into a semblance of calmness. "You warned me last Sunday," she said in a low voice that shook with the intensity of her hurt and rage. "You told me you had come back to break up the engagement! Too bad I didn't realize you were lying when you said you had changed your mind!"

"I wasn't lying, damn it!" he said, spinning on his heel to face her. "I've been telling you the truth!" Brad had finally been goaded beyond control.

"Well, if it wasn't a lie, what was it? You said you'd break us up. I'd say that substituting yourself for the groom certainly managed to do that! You don't care that Gregory and I already had our future planned together. You couldn't stand seeing me happy, could you? Well, Mr. Crawford, this time you managed to get caught in your own trap. Because you are just as married to me as I'm married to you. And I don't want to be married to you. I want Gregory!"

"You've made that good and clear. Believe me, there's nothing I'd rather see than you married to Gregory, damn it. Can't you understand that?"

She crossed her arms, her mutinous expression making it clear that she did not find his remarks appeasing.

"No, I can't understand it. Because you are here and he isn't."

"That isn't my fault."

"Isn't it?" she asked sarcastically.

"Listen to me, you hardheaded, obstinate shrew. If I hadn't married you, you would have been left here this morning having to explain to everybody who showed up why your groom begged off!"

His words were a verbal slap in the face and Penny flinched. "You mean that Gregory changed his mind?"

"That's exactly what I mean!"

"Why?"

"How the hell should I know?"

"He must have told you. Otherwise you wouldn't have known."

He nodded his head curtly. "He told me he had changed his mind. That he wasn't going to marry you. He said something about not really knowing you as well as he thought."

The look she gave him was filled with contempt. "And you really expect me to believe that? There's absolutely no way of knowing what horrible lies you must have told him to cause him to change his mind about marrying me!"

"Stop calling me a liar!"

"Stop behaving like one!"

They had made no attempt to keep their voices down. In truth, the volume of the argument was the last thing they had considered. The sudden silence as they stood glaring at each other seemed to bounce off the walls of the room.

A soft tapping on the door made them look in that direction. "Come in," Brad commanded.

Helen stuck her head around the door and looked from one to the other in shocked dismay. She stepped inside and firmly closed the door behind her, leaning on it.

"I absolutely can't believe the two of you! You haven't been married five minutes and you already sound the way you used to as small children when your mother and I had to drag you apart and make you spend the day at home by yourselves until you could play together without fighting! Do you realize that you can be heard for a city block? Are you aware that the recreation hall is full of people waiting to greet the loving bride and groom and watch them open pres-ents and cut their wedding cake?"

They immediately burst into simultaneous explanations.

"Mother, you don't understand. Brad—"

"Helen, she's being totally unreasonable and won't even listen to me!"

She put up her hand like a policeman stopping traffic. "I don't want to hear it! Thank goodness I no longer have to play referee for the two of you. If you choose to kill each other, you no longer have to explain it to me. Now I want you both to go over to that hall with smiles on your faces and show all those people how happy you are. They expect to see some sort of love and joy in the occasion."

"Love!" Penny repeated contemptuously.

"Joy!" Brad said with a harsh laugh.

Helen opened the door with a decisive turn of her wrist. "Both of you studied acting for years. Surely you have something to show for all the money we invested in your education." She looked at her watch. "I'm going over there and explain that you've been delayed. I'll expect to see your happy, smiling faces in no more than fifteen minutes."

Brad and Penny stared at the closed door for an unnoticed elapse of time after Helen left. Neither of them had any desire to look at the other.

Penny was the first one to break the silence. "What are we going to do?"

He glanced at her, then away, once again walking over to the window. "That's up to you, isn't it?"

"Why up to me?"

"You can go out there and tell everyone that you never intended to marry me."

"I don't understand why somebody didn't say something. I mean, everyone in the wedding party knew I was expecting Gregory to be here today."

"I told them that we talked it over late last night. You discovered that you couldn't marry Gregory after all... because you loved me."

"And they believed you?" she asked incredulously.

"Thanks a lot."

"You know what I mean. As mother just pointed out, you and I fight as much as we're friends."

"Your parents didn't seem to be as surprised as they were pleased."

Remembering their rather strange behavior she asked, "When did you tell them?"

"Early this morning, just as I told my parents. You probably didn't notice, but Dad was my best man."

She shook her head and looked down at the small container she held in her hands. "As you well know, I couldn't see anyone."

"I'm sorry. I had no right to hide your contacts from you."

"At least you admit it!"

"I was only trying to help."

"Fine, Brad. How do you propose to help now, go out there and announce the whole thing was a joke?"

"Hardly. Our marriage was very legal. We have the license to prove it."

"And that's another thing. How did you manage to get a license?"

"Well, one of the benefits of having been raised in a small town is knowing everybody, including the county clerk. It's amazing what people will do when they think they're assisting true love. I explained everything to Reverend Wilder and he made the announcement before the ceremony began, with a few comments about love conquering all.''

So that was what she had heard just before her father escorted her down the aisle.

Penny sat down, feeling as though she were a balloon and someone had suddenly let out all of her air. "So Gregory didn't love me, after all," she said slowly. "He certainly had me fooled.''

Brad heard the pain in her voice and could think of nothing to say.

"I should have known," she said, not even aware she had spoken aloud.

"What do you mean?"

"I hadn't talked to him all week. That isn't like him. Not at all. I kept telling myself he was just busy, but something kept nagging at me, a little voice that refused to shut up.'' She glanced up, then quickly away. "It's funny, really. I was just thinking last night that I wanted to discuss what I was feeling with you, knowing you'd understand.'' Looking down at her hands, she added, "Oh, you understood all right. I just wished you'd explained last night.''

One corner of his mouth lifted in a half grin. "I tried, believe me. But you wouldn't accept what I said. I didn't want to go into all the details, about Gregory calling me and what he said. When I realized that you weren't going to accept what I was saying, I guess I used the situation to my own advantage.''

Penny didn't seem to hear his explanation or apologetic tone of voice. She had dropped her face in her hands. When he stopped speaking she cried, "I can't face all those people out there. I just can't.''

"I could take you home and tell them you aren't feeling well.''

The thought of returning home and trying to explain to her parents what had taken place was just as bad an idea as pretending to be happily married.

She looked over at Brad. "I don't think I'll ever forgive you for this ridiculous situation, but since you got us into this mess, I don't see anything else to do but go out there and pretend we're happy newlyweds."

"Happy?" he repeated sarcastically. "I don't think I'm that good an actor."

"What about me? At least you had a choice."

"So sue me!"

"Don't worry. I intend to just as soon as I know how to go about it."

He looked at her incredulously. "You mean you'd actually take me to court? On what grounds?"

"Don't be ridiculous. I don't want any money from you. I just meant I was going to end the marriage as soon as I know what to do."

"Oh."

She stood and began to brush the wrinkles out of the skirt of her gown. "I'm going to go put my contacts in so I can at least see who's here."

"I'll wait out in the hall for you. We need to arrive together, looking properly blissful."

Every time she thought of Brad's audacity she wanted to throw something at him. How was she going to be able to look at him with a loving smile all afternoon? She shook her head. Acting ability, indeed. It would be the performance of her life.

Penny went into the ladies' restroom and replaced her lenses. Being able to see helped to boost her morale somewhat. She stared at herself in the mirror. Her face was white and strained, her eyes slightly puffy. It was not the face of a typically blushing bride.

Their delay in joining everyone at the reception did not go unnoticed. As soon as they walked into the room everyone started clapping and some of the comments held sly innuendos of Brad's impatience to get her alone.

Oh, no, Penny thought. She'd forgotten all the jokes and teasing that went along with a wedding. The only way she was going to get through the afternoon was by shutting her mind to the fact that she was with the wrong man.

Her mother hurried them over near the table where a three-tiered cake sat waiting for them.

"You can stand here and receive everyone. Then the photographer will start posing you for pictures."

The photographer! Something else Penny had forgotten. She glanced at Brad, and unconsciously did a double take.

She hadn't paid attention to him when she had come out of the ladies' room. It was only now that she saw what he looked like in his tuxedo.

He wore the traditional black and a ruffled shirt. The clothes fit him as if tailored for his tall body with its broad shoulders, lean hips, and long, muscular legs. He looked magnificent. The dark suit enhanced his tan and bright hair. The small bandage gave him a rakish look that made him very appealing.

"Well, if you aren't the sly one, young lady," Mrs. Fielding said, walking up and grabbing Penny's hand in a firm grip. "Letting us think you were marrying Mr. Duncan right up to the last minute. Of course you never fooled me a bit, you know." She winked at Brad. "But your engagement certainly served its purpose. It got Brad to come home so you two could work everything out."

Penny couldn't look at Brad. She couldn't believe the woman and she couldn't think of a thing to say in reply to the outrageous comment.

Brad spoke up, sounding relaxed and nauseatingly pleased with himself. "We're happy you and Mr. Fielding could come today."

"Oh, we wouldn't have missed it for the world, even before we knew of the dramatic denouement," she said archly. "It must have to do with your theatrical background and all."

Penny wondered how much longer she would be able to stand there and smile before she let out a scream.

"It was the most romantic thing I've ever seen," Mrs. Cantrell said when she reached them. "Why, when Reverend Wilder explained how you two suddenly realized how you felt about each other and that nice Mr. Duncan agreed to release you, I thought I would cry. It was better than anything I've ever seen on television!" She leaned over and whispered to Penny, "Even though he seemed a very nice man, I thought Mr. Duncan was too old for you anyway, dear. Isn't it nice how everything worked out so well?"

Penny wondered what all of these people would do if she suddenly started having hysterics? She felt very close to it at the moment. She had an absolutely insane urge to laugh and she knew the tears wouldn't be far behind. Already she could read the write-up in the local paper: "Bridegroom has to slap hysterical bride at wedding reception."

Somehow she managed to get through the next hour without breaking down. Then the photographer took over.

She would have been all right if she hadn't met Brad's eyes during one of the more soulful poses. The dancing light of amusement almost undid her. How many times had she seen the same expression on his face after they'd shared a joke?

Oh, Brad. No matter what, you manage to see the humor in every situation. Nothing in life ever really fazes you. How do you do it?

Then the photographer asked Brad to kiss her. This time the intent look in his eyes held a question. Taking a cue from him and determined not to treat what was happening like some gloomy Greek tragedy, Penny lifted her mouth and closed her eyes.

She felt his arms go around her and pull her tightly against him as his mouth found hers.

This kiss was nothing like the one he'd given her at the altar. As a matter of fact, it was like no other kiss he'd ever given her, and Brad had kissed her often over the years—

friendly kisses, exuberant kisses, teasing kisses, hello kisses, goodbye kisses.

Penny couldn't compare this particular kiss with any of those. She felt a tingle in her body that started in her toes and shot up through her until she felt the top of her head seem to shoot off.

His lips felt firm yet they were also tender. He took his time, as though they had nothing better to do, as if there weren't a roomful of people watching and a photographer whose flash periodically added a fireworks display behind her closed eyelids.

Brad was kissing her the way he kissed the countless women Drew Derek pursued on television. No wonder they kept coming back for more!

Vaguely Penny became aware of the general laughter and a smattering of applause around them and she stiffened. They were making a spectacle of themselves.

She pushed herself away from him and glared up into his smiling face. "You're supposed to look happy," he said just under his breath, never breaking his smile.

Penny flashed him an equally brilliant smile. "You try that again and I will place my knee in the exact spot you instructed me to all those years ago to ward off unwanted advances!"

He flinched in mock horror. Then he laughed—he actually had the nerve to laugh. "To think that you would use my own teachings against me," he said, still too low for anyone to hear.

The photographer interrupted their murmured comments, convinced this was a couple who was counting the minutes until they could be alone. "Okay, now. How about some pictures with you both cutting the cake."

Why not? Penny thought. Maybe I can stuff enough cake into his mouth to choke him. "Bridegroom chokes to death on wedding cake." Then she remembered the previous Sunday's accident coming on the heels of her dire wishes for his early demise. Penny hurriedly explained to the Fates that she didn't really want him to die and to please ignore her last suggestion.

Opening the gifts brought back to her how differently this part of the afternoon would have gone if Gregory had been there instead. Brad seemed to be having a great deal of fun and the onlookers were relishing his reactions and comments.

She had to admit that his quick wit often caught her off guard and she found herself laughing at his humor and antics—until she picked up the envelope that must have fallen off one of the gifts. The envelope was addressed to Brad Crawford.

Very few people could have known that Brad would be there to open gifts. She handed the envelope to him in silence. When he opened it, Brad continued to stare down at the contents, his expression blank.

"Come on, Brad, don't hold out on us," someone yelled. "Somebody give you a million bucks?"

He glanced over at her and she noticed his color had faded.

"What is it?" she whispered.

Without a word he handed her two pieces of paper that looked like airline tickets. They were. She stared down at them in bewilderment. The tickets were for a round trip to Acapulco for Mr. and Mrs. Brad Crawford, leaving that afternoon from the airport nearest Payton, to return the following Saturday.

Penny looked up at Brad in dismay.

"Tell us! Tell us!" several people said, laughing.

Penny cleared her throat. "Well, it's, uh," she glanced at Brad helplessly. Brad looked at her and shrugged. She started again. "It's round-trip tickets to Acapulco, leaving in a few hours."

Her announcement created a great deal of excitement and speculation. "What a wonderful idea! Great wedding gift! Marvelous place for a honeymoon!"

Honeymoon? Penny's heart seemed to sink in her chest. She leaned over and whispered, "We can't use these. Who in the world gave them to us?"

"I don't think you want to know," he said, his expression deliberately noncommittal.

"What do you mean?"

He handed her a note that he had continued to hold. She stiffened when she saw the page with the name Gregory Duncan neatly imprinted at the top. His slashing handwriting read, "You might as well use these since they're paid for. The hotel reservations have been changed to your name." It was signed with Gregory's initials.

The realization of his betrayal seemed to flood over her and for a moment Penny thought she would double over with the pain. Brad must have recognized how she felt because he leaned over and said, "You know, Penny, it might not be a bad idea to take him up on the offer. It would give us time to get away and decide what to do. If we don't go, what then? All these people are just waiting to see us happily depart somewhere or another. Why not Acapulco?"

Acapulco. Gregory had remembered a conversation many months ago when she had commented that she had never been out of the United States. So that's where he'd planned to take her on their honeymoon.

What kind of man would leave his intended bride on the eve of her wedding, then provide the honeymoon trip as a wedding gift when she married someone else?

Penny realized that she didn't know Gregory Duncan at all. Perhaps she never had.

"What do you think?" Brad asked.

The problem was, she could no longer think. About anything. Everything had suddenly piled up on her and she felt that she couldn't deal with another decision. She looked at Brad and said, "I don't care at this point what we do or where we go. Just get me out of here."

Taking her at her word, Brad used the tickets as a reason for their hurried departure. But the well-wishers couldn't let them leave without the traditional spray of rice over them as they dashed for Brad's mother's car.

"My suitcases!" Penny gasped, hurrying down the sidewalk.

"Your dad said he put them into my car this morning."

They got into the car, waving at all the happy, smiling people who had helped them to celebrate their wedding day.

Brad took Penny's hand and squeezed it gently, then placed it on his thigh before driving away. "Well, Mrs. Crawford. We may have the shortest marriage in history, but it looks like we're going to have our honeymoon!"

Chapter Eight

Penny stood on the balcony of the luxury hotel and stared at the sun as it set over the Pacific. She had never seen the ocean before and knew that she should be experiencing all of the excitement of the unknown.

The view below had all the earmarks of a fantasy—white sands, gently swaying palm trees, and the variegated blues of the ocean—a virtual tropical paradise.

Penny felt no excitement, no anticipation, no pleasure. She felt numb.

From the room behind her she heard Brad's voice speaking to the bellhop, but she didn't turn around. She had nothing to say to Brad at the moment. Only questions that needed to be asked eventually, and decisions to discuss. But even the answers to those questions could do little to change the present situation. Nothing could change the fact that she was now officially on her honeymoon—with the wrong man.

Staring out at the panorama spread far below her, Penny

knew when Brad opened the wide sliding glass door and joined her on the balcony. She didn't turn around.

They had spoken very little since leaving the church. By the time they made their connections and were on the plane to Acapulco, Penny felt exhausted. She slept most of the way.

Penny recognized Brad's dispirited mood and no longer believed this was another one of his pranks. During the reception, fleeting memories of their conversation the night before had occurred to her.

Penny realized that the blow to his head hadn't affected him as she had thought at the time. He'd been trying to warn her that Gregory wasn't going to be at the church. One of her questions was how he had known. What could he have said or done to cause Gregory to risk ruining his reputation in Payton rather than marry her? Whatever it was, Penny knew she wasn't quite ready to face Brad's possible treachery.

And that was the cruelest blow of all. That Brad, her childhood friend, her most trusted companion, could be responsible for what had happened.

If that were true, she had not only lost her fiancé but her belief in the integrity of her best friend. How ironic that she was now married to him.

"The view is really something, isn't it?" Brad said quietly.

She could hear the tenseness in his voice. He wasn't feeling any better about the recent turn of events than she was. She supposed that was something they had in common at the moment.

"Yes."

When she didn't say anything more, he asked, "Are you hungry?"

"No."

"Neither am I." Brad pulled out one of the chairs tucked under a small table on the balcony and sat down. "At least we're away from the comments of all the well-wishers," he offered in a gentle voice. "Are you very tired?"

Penny continued to gaze out toward the beach. She hadn't looked at him since he'd joined her. Without turning she said, "Not really. I slept on the plane."

Brad was very aware of that. After she had fallen asleep he had pulled her into his arms so that she slept with her head on his shoulder. What had torn at his heart were the tears she had shed in her sleep.

Why had he ever thought that she would prefer to marry him than be abandoned at the church? Why had Gregory ever suggested it? Unconsciously he rubbed his head. Perhaps that was it—the blow to his head. His brains had been addled. Despite doing everything in his power to prevent it he had managed to hurt her, the very last thing he would ever have wanted.

Penny caught sight of the movement and turned slightly to see Brad massaging his forehead.

"Is your head bothering you?" she asked, suddenly remembering all that he had been through that week. She had been so wrapped up in her own misery she had forgotten what he was going through.

"A little."

"Why don't you take some pain medication and try to rest?"

He looked up at her and smiled ruefully. "Because the stuff is so strong, it puts me out for hours."

Penny found herself smiling for the first time since the wedding reception. "I don't find that such an unfavorable side effect. I wouldn't mind being unconscious for a while, myself."

His eyes met hers in total understanding. They had shared so much over the years. Today was one more experience that strengthened the bond between them. When the challenge of the reception confronted them, they had immediately united and faced the crisis together. Now that it was over, they could fall apart without fear of the other's ridicule.

Brad wondered if Penny had any idea how rare that bond was. Or if she cared.

"Good point," he said, answering her smile. "I may just take your advice." He glanced around, taking in the view from the balcony. "We certainly found a spectacular spot to hide and lick our wounds, wouldn't you say?"

She heard the underlying pain in his voice and she closed her eyes, almost wincing at the sound. Brad looked tired, as though he hadn't slept much in the past twenty-four hours.

His decision must have caused him a great deal of agony, and her accusations hadn't made the situation any easier. She had struck out at him in pain, perhaps unconsciously hoping to ease her own. Why had she placed all the blame on him?

Penny acknowledged that sometimes, when a person is so filled with hurt and the pain takes over, it's hard to recall who administered what particular jab of agony. She had struck out at Brad for some of the pain inflicted by Gregory.

"I'm sorry for all of those hateful things I said to you earlier," Penny said slowly, opening her eyes and meeting his gaze.

His gaze seemed to soften and grow warmer. "Thank you for that, Penny," he replied.

"I think everything will look a little better to us in a few days," Penny said, "once we've had a chance to get used to the idea of what has happened. We don't have to make any decisions today." She walked over to him and softly stroked his forehead. "Why don't you take something for that headache, okay?"

He studied the expression on her face for a long, silent moment. Apparently satisfied with what he saw, Brad nodded. "I think you're right. Without this throbbing in my head, I could probably think a lot more clearly."

Penny watched him walk back into their room. He took off his coat and tie, then opened his suitcase and took out the small bottle of tablets. After disappearing into the bathroom he soon reappeared, sat on the side of the bed and slipped off his shoes.

She could almost feel the groan of relief he gave when he stretched out on the bed and closed his eyes.

Poor Brad.

It was amazing how quickly her perspective changed as soon as she began to think of someone besides herself, Penny thought wryly. She had certainly been enjoying a pity party of her own all day—feeling misused, abused and totally duped.

She needed to look at what the nefarious Brad had done to her. Why, the dastardly fellow had sought her out the night before and attempted to explain that her fiancé had backed out of their engagement at the last minute. When she refused to take him seriously, Brad, being the blackguard he was, had filled in as bridegroom rather than leave her to face a crowded church alone.

Gregory was the one who needed to make explanations. Penny shook her head wearily. What difference did it make? It was much too late to search for answers, but she knew that her mind would busily work to solve the mystery of the disappearing bridegroom.

How well do we ever get to know a person? Penny wondered, leaning against the railing and looking toward the water. No matter how hard we try, there are too many depths to be plumbed in a person to hope that we can ever completely know him.

She probably knew Brad Crawford better than she knew any other living human being. He knew her equally well. He'd once mentioned to her that the knowledge they shared about each other was more significant than she had ever acknowledged.

One thing Penny knew with fierce certainty—Brad would never have done to her what Gregory had done. Never.

She sighed. Today had been the most traumatic day of her life. She was glad to see it end.

Penny slowly entered their room, unsurprised to find Brad asleep. A frown still creased his brow and without thought she reached over to smooth it away with her forefinger.

He muttered something and shifted restlessly on the bed. It sounded as though he had said "Penny." She felt an ache in her chest. It wouldn't be surprising if he were having nightmares with her in the starring role.

Poor Brad. When he had decided to go home to attend a friend's wedding, the last thing he'd expected was to find himself in a featured role.

Penny wandered into the bathroom, a little awed by the luxurious fixtures. "Well, Penny, old girl, it's your wedding night, so how do you intend to spend it?" She reached over and turned on the water in the large tub. A warm soak in the tub sounded like a good way to relax. Too bad she hadn't thought of bringing along a good book to read, she decided whimsically.

And then she'd probably be ready for bed. Bed. She was going to share her bed with Brad. Of course it wouldn't be the first time. But the last time they'd slept together was on a camping trip when the zipper wouldn't work on her sleeping bag and he had offered to share his. As she recalled, she was eight years old at the time.

Somehow she knew that sharing a bed with the adult Brad would be an entirely different experience.

Almost an hour passed before Penny decided that as enjoyable as the water was, there was only so much fun to be had soaking in a tub.

Why was she trying so hard not to think about what this night was supposed to have been? The sooner she came to grips with the reality of her life, and accepted it, the sooner she'd be able to put away her sorrow that the tapestry of dreams she'd woven over the past several months had come unraveled.

After drying herself, Penny remembered that her suitcase still waited to be unpacked. She wrapped the enormous towel around her and grinned. One advantage of being small was that it didn't take much to cover her. This particular towel hung below her knees.

Quietly opening the door she walked into the bedroom. Brad had rolled onto his side and his face had lost its grimness. He was well and truly asleep.

When Penny opened her suitcase she was forcibly reminded of her situation. Her bag was filled with the frothy lingerie and sleepwear she'd received from the numerous showers her friends had given for her. She remembered all the teasing and chuckles regarding the sheerness of the nightgowns and undergarments.

She suddenly yearned for one of her sturdy football jerseys that had kept her company for so many years. Too bad she hadn't had the foresight to pack at least one.

Eventually she found a peach satin gown that was more opaque than any of the others and took it back into the bathroom to put on. When she glanced into the mirror later she wondered why she had thought it would be less revealing.

The satin was cut on the bias and the gown was designed to look like an evening gown from the thirties. Thin straps widened to a well-cupped bodice. An insert of matching peach lace formed a diamond, with a point that nestled just below her breasts, widened at the waist, then made another point on her abdomen. When she moved, the satin slid over her body highlighting each curve and forming shadows at each indentation.

Glancing at her watch, Penny admitted to herself that she had stalled long enough. It was time to go to bed. Turning out the light in the bathroom, she entered the bedroom once again. Only one lamp was on and it was across the room from the bed. She hadn't wanted to wake Brad when she'd come in earlier to find something to sleep in.

She turned back the covers on one side of the bed, thankful of its extra width, then crossed the room and turned off the light. With the room darkened she was drawn to the lighter expanse of the glass door. She peered outside.

The stars seemed so bright she felt she could almost reach up and touch one. Out at sea, she could spot an occasional flash of white where a wave had broken.

What a beautiful spot for a honeymoon.

She returned to the bed and carefully slid in. Oh, how wonderful to lie down at last, was her last conscious thought.

Moonlight pouring through the wide, uncurtained expanse of glass aroused Brad several hours later. He sat up, disoriented. Looking around him he suddenly remembered where he was. Damn! He'd done it again—fallen asleep for too many hours. Thoughtfully he touched his head. At least the headache was gone, he decided.

Penny was curled beside him, although she was underneath the covers. Gingerly he slid off the bed and stood while continuing to gaze at her. She looked so peaceful and serene.

Brad felt as if his heart would explode with the feeling that swelled up inside of him. He had never loved another person as much, and in so many ways, as he loved Penny Blackwell. Penny Crawford, he reminded himself. She was now his wife. His wife!

How many years had he dreamed about someday being married to Penny—making love to her, acting with her, raising children with her... teasing and laughing and enjoying life with her. When had that dream died?

He knew to the minute. The day he'd opened the mail in his New York apartment and found the invitation to her wedding.

He'd felt betrayed. How dare she! He'd been angry and hurt and felt deceived by those he'd most trusted.

All the time he'd been in New York he'd written to her, but Penny was the world's worst correspondent. Even when his mother had written that she was dating a lawyer, he hadn't been terribly concerned. He was dating, as well. Wasn't that the idea? For them to be sure how they felt?

He had been sure. He'd always known, from the time Penny had fallen out of a swing when she was four years old and he'd cried because she cried. He'd felt her pain. She was as much a part of him as his heart or lungs.

How could she possibly not love him in the same way? How could she not know how important they were to each other? The distance had never mattered to him because she had always been in his heart. He could call her up in his mind at will.

He'd studied the invitation and begun to plot. He would go home and put a stop to the whole thing—make her admit that she couldn't possibly love anyone else—that the two of them belonged together.

However, things hadn't quite worked out that way for him. In the first place, he was under contract and couldn't just take off. But he'd started talking to anyone who would listen. He needed some time off. There was a family crisis, one that needed his presence.

Eventually the powers that be had considered the possibility. Then they had needed to prepare new story lines, and that took time, and more time. Only time was quickly running out for Brad.

He'd ended up with a week. One lousy week to try to convince her she was marrying the wrong man. He'd realized as soon as he saw her that his task was going to be tougher than he'd expected.

Penny had changed from the woman he knew so well. That was when he had finally given up hope. He realized he could never do anything that would hurt her, and breaking up an engagement a week before the wedding was inexcusable. He loved her enough to let her go, knowing that nothing in his life would ever be quite so wonderful or joyous or sparkling again. Losing Penny was like losing all the sparkle in champagne. Life would be flat without her.

Somehow he should have known that life would never betray him in such a cold, calculating way. He'd been given another chance to win.

Looking down at her now, he realized he still had a considerable way to go to win her. But what better setting, or more romantic place, could there be to woo the woman that was already his wife?

Brad walked into the bathroom and shut the door. Turning on the shower he adjusted the heat of the water, stripped down and stepped under the invigorating spray.

Did Penny really love him enough to want to continue their marriage? She had told him she loved him, but what did she actually feel? How did a person ever know what another was feeling? Each person had his own conception of what love was, what it felt like, and how he responded to it.

Somehow he had to prove to Penny, as well as to himself, that she loved him and that marrying Brad, instead of Gregory, was the best thing that could have happened to her.

Brad was convinced he wouldn't be able to go back to sleep, not with all he had on his mind, and not with Penny lying so close beside him. He was unaware how quickly he fell asleep after he joined Penny in bed, this time under the covers.

Penny's dream carried her along on a wave of pleasure that she had never before experienced. She was on the boat, out on the lake, and she could feel the warm sunshine and a soft breeze. Brad was there, fussing because she hadn't put on more suntan lotion and insisting she would burn without it.

He was such a nag. She handed him the lotion and suggested that he put it on himself if he didn't like the way she did it. He grinned at her and she could no longer be irritated with him.

Brad began to spread the cream along her back with long, exploring strokes. She loved his touch. He was so gentle and yet his hands were strong, his long fingers sensitive. She could feel the pads of his fingertips softly moving over her.

She shifted to give him better access to her body, wanting him to continue touching her. He responded by sliding his hand from her back, along her arm, down to her waist, then up once again. Those sensitive fingertips lightly drew a line beneath her breasts and Penny wished he wouldn't tease her so. She wanted to feel his hands touching her—Aahh. He cupped her breast with his hand and she was pleased how well it fit his hand. Once again his fingertips caressed her, this time they rubbed gently, back and forth, across her nipple. She thought she would cry out at the unexpected pleasure of his touch.

No man had ever touched her so intimately. Only Brad. She loved Brad, so it was all right. Whatever Brad wanted to do, it was all right. She loved him. She loved . . .

Penny's eyes flew open. She was no longer asleep. No longer dreaming, and yet—she was in Brad's arms.

Her head lay on his shoulder, his arm holding her close to his side. And with his other hand, he was touching and caressing her. And she was letting him.

Her breasts ached with the fullness that his fingers had encouraged. Penny became aware that her legs were intertwined with his, his thigh was nestled between hers. It was as though their bodies knew better than their minds how comfortably they fit together.

Brad shifted, pulling her tighter against him, lifting her chin as he lowered his head to hers. She barely had time to notice that his eyes were closed before his lips touched hers and she forgot everything else.

He was kissing her in the same way he had at the reception, but with even more intimacy. Penny felt devoured. His tongue took possession of her mouth as if by right. He continued to softly brush his hand back and forth across the crest of her breast and Penny felt as though all of her insides were melting.

New sensations shot through her and she became aware of parts of her body that had never drawn her attention before. Her hand seemed to have developed a will of its own and she began to move it over his chest, reveling in the way the rough texture of his chest felt against her palm.

She could feel the heavy vibration of his heart pounding against her. His lungs seemed to be laboring for air but he continued to kiss her without pausing for breath.

Penny was only fleetingly aware that he was sliding the thin strap of her gown off her shoulder. She couldn't find the energy to either help or resist. The dreamlike state she'd been in seemed to continue.

"Oh, Penny," he managed to say when he finally broke away. His breathing was so ragged she could scarcely hear him. "I want you so much," he murmured. "So much."

She didn't need his explanation to know what was happening. Somehow everything that was occurring seemed so natural and right.

Both of them were still more than half-asleep, uninhibitedly responding to their deep-seated, long-standing feelings for each other.

Vaguely Brad knew that he intended to make love to Penny. He loved her, they were married, and he knew of no better way to convince her that he wanted nothing more than to be her passionately loving husband.

But when he stroked his fingers over her abdomen and down, he felt her body stiffen and he paused.

Brad knew he could seduce her. From her reactions he realized she'd never been this aroused before. He knew she wouldn't stop him, if he took his time with her.

The question was, how was she going to feel afterward? There was so much that needed to be said between them. Even though they were legally married, the wedding had been a farce.

Did he really intend to use her sexual response to him to coax her into making a decision that would have lifelong ramifications for both of them?

Brad relaxed his hold on her and lay there, unmoving for a moment.

Penny felt swamped with all of the swirling, unfamiliar emotions she'd been experiencing since she'd awakened. Everything was happening so fast. Her lifelong friend had metamorphosed into a passionate, intriguing stranger whose very touch made her bones melt.

Before she could fully comprehend what was happening, Penny felt Brad move away from her. She watched with bewilderment as Brad tossed the covers back and, clad only in a pair of briefs, disappeared into the bathroom, closing the door behind him.

Chapter Nine

When the bathroom door opened sometime later Brad walked out and casually commented. "I'm sorry I took so long. I guess we'll have to flip a coin each morning to see who gets the use of the bathroom first."

This was the same Brad she'd always known, but Penny discovered she missed the passionate stranger who had shared her bed. She wondered what he would think if he knew how she felt. "That's all right," she said, following his example and entering the other room.

Brad quickly found some clean clothes and, dropping the towel he'd draped modestly around him, got dressed. She won't have any problem with the hot water, he thought wryly. I certainly didn't use much of it.

He was waiting for her when she came out, wrapped in a towel. "I'm sorry about what almost happened this morning," he said tersely. "I have no excuse for losing control like that. I hope you won't add this to the long list you seem to have kept over the years of my iniquities."

Brad stood by the opened door to their balcony, waiting

for her reaction. She could think of nothing to say.

"We need to talk, Penny, the sooner the better. I've discovered I'm not nearly as noble as I thought I was."

After what she had just experienced with him, Penny wasn't at all sure she wanted his nobility. She'd made an astounding discovery since he'd disappeared into the bathroom earlier.

She very much wanted to make love to Brad Crawford. The thought shocked her right down to her toes. If that was what she was feeling for Brad, she'd had no business planning to marry Gregory Duncan.

Another revelation.

She was still reeling from these shocks when Brad greeted her with his apology in a no-nonsense tone of voice. Glancing down at her towel-draped body, she said, "I agree that we need to talk. I'd prefer to be dressed to do it, however."

Brad seemed to find her remark amusing. "I suppose I can understand that. Why don't you go ahead and get ready and I'll meet you downstairs for breakfast. Maybe later we can take a walk along the beach and enjoy some of the atmosphere around here."

"All right." Penny still felt bewildered by her responses to him earlier and her illuminating discovery regarding her feelings for Brad.

She wasted little time finding a sundress to put on, pleased that so much of what she had packed would be appropriate for a honeymoon in Acapulco.

Her honeymoon with Brad.

A conversation she'd had with her mother months ago suddenly flashed into her mind. She had told Helen that Gregory had proposed to her.

Helen had been working in the kitchen at the time so Penny had perched on the step stool nearby.

"Gregory wants to marry you!" Helen repeated in obvious surprise.

"That's what he said," Penny agreed.

"What did you tell him?"

Penny was quiet for a moment. "I told him that I needed time to consider it."

"I should think so!"

"However, I'm fairly sure that I want to marry him, Mom."

Helen turned around and faced her. "Are you, Penny?"

Penny met her mother's look and nodded. "Yes. Gregory offers the type of life I want. He's stable, successful and I know I can always depend on him."

"What about love?"

"That goes without saying, of course."

"Love should never go without being expressed, Penny. Don't mistake compatible and companionable with love. They're necessary to a good relationship, but love is what holds them together."

"I think we're well-suited."

Helen sighed. "I always thought you and Brad would end up together."

"Brad? You must be joking. That man wouldn't know the first thing about making a commitment. He'd run in the opposite direction."

The image of her mother's face dissolved and once again Penny realized where she was—on her honeymoon with Brad.

He'd had every opportunity to run—from the time he'd learned that Gregory wasn't going to marry her—to the day of the wedding and afterward. But he was here. Despite the disruption a sudden marriage would cause in his life and career, Brad Crawford had chosen to commit himself to her and face whatever consequences his actions created.

When Penny returned to the bathroom to put on her makeup she was arrested by the sight of the woman in the mirror. She glowed. There was no other word to describe the look of anticipation on her face. She was a woman in love, there was no denying that expression, the sparkle in her eyes, the slight flush to her cheeks.

Penny couldn't remember the last time she'd faced that woman in a mirror. Gone was the sedate school teacher, the level-headed, sensible woman Gregory Duncan had met and asked to marry. Instead she saw the young girl she'd known years ago, her dreams and fantasies shining like an aura around her.

"I had no idea you even existed," she whispered. Why had she brushed aside this vibrant person who had patiently waited to be recognized? Why had she felt the need to deny the spontaneity that seemed to bubble inside of her?

Here was the woman who had loved Brad Crawford single-mindedly, had followed his lead throughout her childhood, and had played opposite him in most of the plays produced during their high school and college years.

"Where have you been?" she asked, amazed at the transformation.

From the moment she had awakened in Brad's arms to the feel of his touch and the taste of his lips, Penny felt like an entirely different person. She was reminded of one of her favorite stories as a child—the one about Sleeping Beauty, who was awakened by the prince with a kiss.

Her pulse accelerated at the thought that she could have married Gregory, convinced that she loved him, and never known the wonder of what Brad had already revealed to her. She had never been affected by Gregory in such a way. Penny had never known the difference...until now.

She laughed out loud, hurriedly finished applying her lipstick and flicked a comb through her hair. How could she explain what had happened to her when she didn't understand it herself? She cringed with embarrassment at the memory of all that she had accused Brad of the day before. He could have reacted so differently. Gregory would never have tolerated such an outburst from her. Subconsciously she had known that her innermost personality must be kept submerged in order to be acceptable to him.

With Brad, she'd always done and said exactly what she felt at the time. He was so much a part of her that she had never questioned that particular freedom. Nor had she fully appreciated it.

Now he waited for her downstairs, no doubt expecting another childish outburst. His list of iniquities? How about hers? To think that he loved her, despite all her faults. It was up to her to let him know that, for the first time, she fully realized how much he meant to her.

Penny rode the elevator down to the main floor of the hotel, unaware of the smile on her face. Brad noticed her expression as soon as she stepped into the lobby.

"I've seen that particular smile before," he said in a low voice, taking her arm and guiding her into the restaurant. "It bodes ill to someone."

She shook her head. "Not necessarily."

After they were seated and their coffee was poured, he leaned forward slightly and said, "For someone whose life was ruined yesterday, you seem to have made an amazing recovery."

She chuckled, amused by the wariness on his face, "What a difference a day makes, wouldn't you say?"

"That isn't something I find myself muttering very often, as a matter of fact. Actually, you're beginning to make me nervous."

"In what way?"

"I can recall several instances where that particular look in your eye meant trouble for me."

She shook her head with a grin.

"I've got it. You're leaving right after breakfast, flying back home."

"Nope."

"You've made arrangements to rendezvous with a local skin diver?"

She laughed outright. "Don't be silly."

He leaned back and studied her intently. "Oh. Now I understand. You've heard from Gregory."

She sobered. "Why would you say that?"

He shrugged. "Because you look so radiant. Somehow he must have let you know he's sorry and intends to make amends."

"Brad, I haven't heard from Gregory. It wouldn't matter if I had."

"What's that supposed to mean?"

She glanced up as the waiter delivered their breakfast. "Hmm. Doesn't that look wonderful? I can't remember when I've been so hungry, can you?"

For the rest of the meal Penny adroitly avoided anything resembling a serious conversation. She wanted to enjoy these new sensations she'd discovered and to come to terms with the insight she'd gained about herself.

She wondered if this was how a butterfly felt when it first opened its wings—astounded at the myriad of bright colors unfolding. Suddenly she felt free of the restrictions that she'd unknowingly placed on herself.

Today was a brand-new day for her to face the world and adjust to her new life and the person she'd just discovered.

Thank God Brad was a part of her new existence. He was a major part.

They had walked along the beach for some time in silence, watching the swimmers playing in the surf. Finally Brad said, "You're taking this much better than I expected."

"I've had time to think it over."

"And?"

"And what?"

"Have you come to any conclusions as to what you want to do?"

"About what?"

"Us. Our marriage."

He'd been quiet during most of their walk on the beach and she'd known he was thinking. "Some. What about you?" she asked.

"Well," he said after a moment, "I know that I really managed to mess up your life by trying to help out."

"Oh?"

"You might have gone through a few bad days, trying to face everyone when the wedding had to be called off, but then it would have been over, and you could have gone on with your life."

"Yes, I've thought of that."

"Instead, you're now going to have to..." He paused, as though unsure of what to say.

"I'm going to have to...what?"

"You're still going to have to explain why you ended your marriage so quickly."

"You do have a point there. How do we return home and tell everyone that we flunked our honeymoon?"

His head snapped around and he stared at her in surprise. She had an amused expression that added lightness to her teasing comment.

"I think we have our roles reversed here, don't you?" he finally muttered. "I'm the one you're always accusing of never taking anything seriously."

"Yes, that's true. I decided to see if I could become more like you. You've set such an example all these years."

"This isn't exactly the subject I'd use to practice my sense of humor, Penny."

"I don't see why not to use it. The fact is, we are married. To each other. I am very much aware that your vacation plans did not include acquiring a wife. But try to overlook that particular inconvenience and see if you can enjoy your time here," she said, waving her arms at the water, the palm trees and the carefully groomed sand.

Brad had never seen Penny in quite this mood before. Maybe the strain had been too much for her and her nerves had finally snapped. He'd find it difficult to convince anyone of that, however. She looked radiantly healthy and happy. And in love.

Whoa! Wait a minute. That line of thinking was going to get him in trouble. "Are you suggesting we postpone for a few days deciding what we're going to do when we return to the States?''

''Is there anything wrong with that?'' she asked.

Brad thought of the long cold shower he'd endured that morning and almost shuddered. What she suggested wasn't unfair, just humanly impossible for him. Wasn't she affected by sharing a room with him, a bed with him? Hadn't their early morning kiss and caresses warned her of what could happen if they continued to ignore what was between them?

''I don't suppose there is,'' he finally answered.

''Good,'' she said, stopping and looking out at the water. ''We've waited long enough after breakfast for a swim, don't you think?'' she asked.

He glanced at his watch. ''Yes.''

''Then let's go change into our suits. I can hardly wait to find out what it's like to swim in sea water.''

For the next several hours they kept busy, first swimming, then exploring the area, and finally spending a romantic evening watching the divers go off the cliff into the sea below.

Brad had forced himself not to dwell on the night ahead, but as the evening progressed, he had a hard time disciplining himself. He'd never seen Penny more beautiful, enticing, alluring, and yet so unobtainable.

This was his punishment for his sin of coveting her. She was his wife, but he was honor bound not to presume anything regarding their relationship.

By the time they returned to their room, he'd almost decided to fake another headache as an excuse to take more pain medication. At least he could seek oblivion for a few hours.

Penny gathered up her nightclothes and went into the bathroom. She smiled and said, ''I won't be long.''

''That's what I'm afraid of,'' he muttered to himself wondering at his unusual ability to inflict pain upon himself. Wandering out on the balcony he studied the stars and tried to imagine where he would be if the wedding had gone as originally planned.

He felt a gut-wrenching pain at the thought of Penny here with anyone else but him. How could he possibly have borne it, knowing he'd never share this delightful intimacy with her? If that's the case, he thought, then you'd better convince her that the two of you belong together.

To his amazement Brad discovered a few minutes later that he needed to make very little effort.

He turned when he heard the door open and saw her standing there in a thin gown that left very little to the imagination, particularly as she was silhouetted against the bathroom light.

"Penny..." he said, trying to get his tongue unwrapped from around his teeth.

She walked over to him and casually put her hand on his chest. "Thank you for your patience."

There was something in her tone of voice that made him believe she was referring to something other than her use of the bathroom.

Brad could no more stand there and not touch her than he could leap from the balcony and fly. "That's okay. I, uh, think maybe that I'll..."

Penny went up on tiptoe and kissed him softly on the lips, her body relaxing fully against him. If his mind was attempting to resist what was happening, his body obviously did not suffer from similar scruples. It immediately responded to her closeness.

Instead of being repelled, Penny cuddled even closer, if that were possible.

The battle within Brad was intense but short-lived. He might hate himself in the morning, but there was no resisting what he felt tonight.

Penny knew exactly when Brad stopped fighting and gave free rein to what they both wanted to happen. His arms came around her in a grip so fierce she had a fleeting thought as to the safety of her ribs. But it was only a fleeting thought, after all. Having Brad hold her so fiercely was well worth any damage she might accidently suffer.

The kiss he gave her held all the longing that she could possibly want from him and when he paused a moment for them to get their breath she whispered, "Love me, Brad. Please love me."

"Oh, God, Penny. Don't you understand how much I love you?"

"Then show me."

He needed no further encouragment. Brad lifted her in his arms and strode over to the bed. Brushing the covers back, he lowered her onto the pillow.

Brad impatiently stripped out of his clothes, then came down onto the bed beside her. "Oh, love," he muttered as he gathered her in his arms. "Do you have any idea what you've put me through?"

"Not intentionally, Brad. I didn't know," she whispered. "How could I have known?"

Eventually he removed the gown she wore for the express purpose of getting his attention. Penny was more than satisfied with the results.

Brad took his time now that he had accepted the amazing fact that Penny wanted him and was willing to explore the physical side of their multi-faceted relationship.

She willingly followed his silent guidance, imitating each caress. Penny was delighted to see his immediate response to her touch.

By the time he was ready to claim her, she was almost pleading with him to show her the next step in their lovemaking. Yet nothing could have possibly described how wonderful she felt when Brad finally made her his own.

How could they have waited so long to experience something so beautiful, so fulfilling? If only she had known what she had been missing.

And later, just before she drifted off to sleep, Penny reminded herself to ask Brad where he'd learned to be such a gentle, sensitive, and obviously experienced lover!

* * *

They slept late the next morning, content to use the morning hours to catch up on sleep that had been abandoned willingly more than once during the night.

Penny quickly became adept at learning Brad's most vulnerable places. She discovered a great many advantages to knowing a person so well. Sharing a marriage bed became something of an adventure.

Until now, Penny had assumed she was not a particularly sensual individual. In a few short hours, she learned differently.

When she eventually awoke the next morning she saw that Brad was still sleeping. However, since he had an arm and a leg wrapped around her, she realized she wasn't going anywhere until he moved.

"Brad?" she whispered.

"Good grief, Penny," he mumbled. "You're insatiable." His mouth quirked into a mischievous grin.

"Would you kindly let go of me?"

His eyes flew open at her tone. "What's wrong?" he asked with a sinking feeling in the pit of his stomach.

She waited until he edged away from her, then she sat up with a grin. "Nothing. I just have to answer nature's call." Penny fled to the bathroom, laughing, the pillow that followed her barely missing its target.

He lay there for a moment, thinking about the previous night. If Penny intended to dissolve their marriage, she certainly couldn't ask for an annulment. Somehow he doubted her interest in pursuing such a course of action, if her response to him the night before was any indication.

When Brad heard the shower running, he decided to join her.

"What are you doing?" Her startled cry greeted him when he stepped into the shower with her.

"What does it look like?"

"I thought we were going to take turns," she said, suddenly shy with him.

He took the soap from her hand and began to apply it lavishly over her body. "But this is so much more economical, don't you think? We'll be able to get ready that much faster, and look at the water we're saving."

Penny could find nothing to say to refute his statement, so she smiled.

"We still need to talk, you know," he said quietly, after lovingly caressing her all over, then carefully rinsing her off.

"I know."

Penny felt much better prepared to discuss their future together after the night they had just spent. They belonged together, even if they had chosen a rather unorthodox way to achieve that goal. Or to be more precise, *he* had chosen.

They chose to order breakfast sent up so they could enjoy the view from their balcony and not have to dress any more than was necessary to greet the man who delivered their order.

"Are you coming back to New York with me?" Brad finally asked her over coffee.

"I suppose. I guess I haven't really thought about it."

"That's understandable, under the circumstances."

"I really have no desire to stay in Payton. I'm not ready to face Gregory just yet."

Brad could feel his stomach clench at the mention of the other man's name. He took another sip of coffee, not meeting her eyes. "I have to go back on Sunday to be ready to work Monday."

"It seems so strange to be planning to live in New York. Like another world. I'll need to resign my job..." Her voice trailed off.

"You know you don't need to work if you'd rather not," he offered.

"I'd go crazy sitting around all day."

"That's not what I meant. Since we don't need your income, you could take the opportunity to attend auditions and things . . . if you wanted to, of course."

"You mean, try to get a job acting?"

"You've certainly got the credentials for it."

"Oh, Brad, I don't know."

"About what?"

"I just never thought I'd try to act professionally."

He smiled. "Try it. You might decide you like it."

So many things were happening to her in a space of a few days, Penny felt as though a whirlwind had picked her up and swirled her away to another land. A land of endless possibilities.

She gazed at Brad across the table. He looked very relaxed and contented. She couldn't imagine Gregory sitting spinelessly in a chair, with nothing more on than a pair of swimming trunks. They were so different and yet she had been attracted to the one she had felt was more stable.

Her instincts had failed her. But Brad hadn't. She remembered the phrase he'd repeated to her—that's what friends are for.

"Thank you," Penny said with a tender look on her face.

Since Brad couldn't remember anything he'd done that deserved such a comment, he looked at her blankly.

She explained. "Thank you for loving me, for having faith in me, for pushing me until I had to face myself and learn who I really am. I realize now that I would have been miserably bored with Gregory. Thank you for understanding that and doing what you could to save me from my own faulty decisions."

Brad straightened in his chair and stared at her with a look that seemed to radiate happiness. "You mean you're forgiving me for ruining your wedding?"

"You didn't ruin it. You saved it and me."

"I know you still love Gregory, Penny. I can understand and live with that . . ."

She laughed. "I've never heard you sounding so humble, Brad. And it doesn't go with your personality at all. I'm not sure how I feel toward Gregory at the moment. What he did was brutal and inexcusable. Learning that he was capable of such behavior shocked me, because I realized how little I knew him. I'm immensely thankful I didn't marry him." She gazed out over the water. "It never would have worked for us."

"I was very much afraid you'd never see that," Brad said with relief.

Penny got up and trailed around to Brad's side of the table. She sat down on his lap and looked up at him. "There is one thing I have wanted to ask you, though."

Brad tensed. Things were going so well. They hadn't fought since their wedding day. Of course, that had only been two days ago, but he felt they'd made giant strides in learning to live together compatibly.

"What?" he asked warily.

"I've known you all your life," she began softly.

"That's right," he agreed.

"We were always very close, except for those three years you were in New York," she went on.

"Uh-huh."

"Then could you explain how you perfected your technique in bed? I seem to have missed something along the way."

Brad tilted his head back and laughed. Still laughing he picked her up and carried her back into the other room. Since she wore only a negligee that did little to cover her charms, he wasted no time in freeing her of her apparel.

As he lowered her to the bed and stretched out beside her, he said, "Honey, you haven't missed a thing. I intend to teach you all that I know. I told you that not all I learned in college was in the classroom."

There was that devastating grin again, the one that caused women all over America to turn on their television sets every afternoon.

The love in his eyes made it clear that there was only one woman who had his heart. She held him closely, thankful for the chance she'd had to discover just what friends are for.

Epilogue

"Hello," the young secretary said with a smile. "May I help you?"

"I would like to see Mr. Duncan, if possible."

"Do you have an appointment?"

"No, I'm afraid I don't."

The secretary nodded. "I'll see if he has time to see you. Your name, please?"

"Penny Crawford," she said quietly.

While the young woman spoke on the phone, Penny looked around the office. Not much had changed since the last time she'd been there. Everything had a stately, polished look that induced a sense of reassurance and stability.

She heard a door open behind her and she turned around. Gregory Duncan stood in the doorway, staring at her. "Penny! I thought she must have misunderstood—Come in," he said, stepping aside and motioning her into his office.

Penny walked past him, noticing the changes in him since

she'd seen him last. He looked older, which she had expected, but much older than his years. Lines furrowed his
brow and face. Up close she could see the gray in his blond
hair. He looked just what he was—a successful, harried
businessman. She wondered what she'd ever seen in him that
she'd found attractive. The physical resemblance between
Gregory and Brad was barely discernible.

"This is a surprise," he said from behind her. "Won't you
have a seat?"

"I hope you don't mind my dropping in like this," she
said, taking a seat and watching him as he walked behind his
desk and sat down.

"Why, no. It's a pleasure to see you again. It's been a
while."

Her eyes met his. "Yes, it has," she agreed quietly.

They sat there in silence, just looking at each other. Finally Gregory roused himself enough to say, "You're looking wonderful."

She nodded her head. "Thank you."

"Are you in town for long?"

"Just a few days, I'm afraid. We don't get much free time
these days."

He smiled. "I suppose not. How does it feel to be working with your husband on stage?"

"It's been quite an experience. Surprisingly enough, Brad
enjoys it. I was afraid television had spoiled him for the
theater."

"Your reviews have been very good."

"Yes." She paused, searching for the right words. "I
wanted to thank you for the beautiful bouquet you had delivered to me on opening night." Once more her eyes met
his. "I was touched that you remembered me."

"I will always remember you, Penny," he said in a matter-of-fact tone. "As a matter of fact, I was in New York
and caught your opening night."

"You were there?"

He nodded.

"Then why didn't you come backstage?"

"I had intended to. But somehow, when the time came, it seemed inappropriate." He smiled again. "However, I thought you did an outstanding job, for what it's worth. I had no idea you were so talented."

"There was a lot of luck involved there. A case of being in the right place at the right time." She shrugged. "I wish you'd let me know you were there."

"There was no need. Let's say I was appeasing my curiosity." He nodded slightly. "You and Brad work very well together, you know. You seem to be so in tune with each other that the audience can almost see the link."

"I know. We've often remarked on it ourselves."

Gregory picked up a letter opener and began to turn it over, end to end, in his hands. "I suppose your families are pleased to see you," he said.

"Yes. Brad's mother hasn't been well. We thought she might enjoy seeing Stacye, but to be on the safe side, we decided to stay at Mother's. Stacye's energy can wear anyone out. We didn't think Brad's mom needed the extra strain. This way we can let her visit in small doses."

"Do you have any pictures of her?" he asked casually.

Penny laughed. "Of course. I'm a typical doting mother." She dug around in her purse, then pulled out a folder and handed it to him.

Gregory studied the little girl carefully, noting the blond hair and the blue eyes. The smile was very familiar, as was the impish expression. It was her mother's smile, although he had never been exposed to the impish part of her personality.

"She looks a great deal like you, Penny," he said, handing the folder back to her.

"I suppose so. But she has her father's teasing temperament. Those two are a pair." She stopped suddenly, realizing what she was saying, and to whom.

"I don't need to ask if you're happy, Penny. It shows."

"I know, Gregory. That's why I came by to see you." His eyebrow lifted slightly in inquiry. "It took me a while," she went on to say, "but I finally understood what you did and why you did it."

He looked puzzled. "I'm afraid I don't follow you."

"I couldn't understand why you'd refuse to marry me without offering me any explanation, and yet present us with a honeymoon already paid for. On the one hand, one action was brutal, the other sensitive. The two actions didn't fit."

"I'm afraid you're being too generous in ascribing such kind motives to me, Penny," he said. "The truth is that when it came right down to it, I realized I'd been single too long, was too set in my ways to ever accommodate another person in my life. And you were right. I chose a brutal, cowardly way out." He looked down at the letter opener in his hand, as though wondering where it had come from. "As for the honeymoon, I had paid for everything several weeks in advance and would not have gotten the full amount back, even if I'd canceled." His smile was a little forced. "I'm afraid the tickets were a sop to my conscience. Nothing more."

She could feel his embarrassment at being confronted by what he had done. Penny realized that she believed him. He hadn't particularly cared about her feelings, because emotions weren't very high on his list of desirable qualities in himself. He was a practical, pragmatic man. Had she married him, her own emotions would have eventually atrophied from lack of expression.

"Well," she said, coming to her feet, "I wanted to stop by and thank you for the flowers and your good wishes, and to let you know that, just in case you've wondered, you did the right thing when you refused to marry me."

He stood as well. "I've never had any doubts about that," he said with a small smile. He walked around the desk and escorted her to the door. "Thank you for coming in, Penny. I appreciate the gesture."

"Yes, I'm sure by this time tomorrow everyone in town will know I came to see you," she replied with a grin.

His smile was more natural when he said, "I don't know what story you and Brad put about, but I was inundated with unspoken sympathy for weeks after the wedding. Totally undeserved, of course. I felt like something of a fraud."

She laughed. "Since Brad engineered the whole scenario, he was responsible for the story. I didn't know who I was marrying until mid-way through the ceremony."

For once Gregory's face registered emotion. "You mean you didn't know that I wasn't . . ." He couldn't seem to find the words.

"That's right," she said matter-of-factly. "Brad was convinced I would never have married him any other way."

"I had no idea."

She shrugged. "Well, that's Brad. Always being dramatic about something or other. Only the three of us know what actually happened. There was no reason for anyone else to know."

He stood there looking down at her for a long time in silence. Penny didn't feel as if she could turn and walk away from such an intent look.

"Brad must have known the best way to handle you," he said finally, still a little bemused.

"Yes, I guess he does. He's had enough practice." On impulse Penny went up on her toes and kissed his cheek. "Thank you for seeing me, Gregory. I always felt that our relationship had been left hanging, somehow. I needed to tie it off in my mind—to let you know that I've forgiven you for what you did. You did us both a real favor."

Penny's last sight of Gregory was his turning back to his office and his work—his real wife.

When Penny pulled into her parents' driveway, she saw Brad loping toward her from his parents' home. She got out and started toward him. He grabbed her around the waist, his momentum swinging her around.

"What are you doing, you crazy man?" she asked, laughing.

"I missed you. I was coming over to see if your Mother might have left a note that she had heard from you. Where have you been?"

They stood in the middle of the front lawn, their arms companionably wrapped around each other's waist. "I stopped in to see Gregory."

Brad's smile faded slowly. "Why?"

"It's hard to explain. Every once in a while I'd find myself thinking of him, what he was doing, if he'd ever married—that sort of thing."

"Wishing that things had turned out differently?" he asked with a smile. Penny was aware his eyes remained serious.

She went up on tiptoe and kissed him. "Hardly," she said with a grin, "I suppose I needed to see him again, in his own environment, to remind myself how close I came to making the biggest mistake of my life."

He held her close. "Was he surprised to see you?"

"Stunned is a better description. I don't think he ever thought he'd have to face me after what he did."

"So what did he say?"

"Not much. He saw the play the last time he was in New York. Seemed surprised that I could act."

Brad laughed. "He shouldn't have been surprised at all. You were giving him a great performance during your entire engagement."

Penny playfully poked him in the chest. "Not deliberately."

"I know, love," he said soothingly. Now his eyes were filled with mischief.

Brad turned toward the house and wrapped his arm around her shoulders. He glanced down at her with a grin. "Mom asked if Stacye could spend the afternoon with her.

They're busy making cookies, so I said I thought it would be okay."

"Are you sure your mom's up to having such a little chatterbox around?"

He opened the door for them, then guided her up the stairs.

"Oh, I think so. She said the doctor thinks she's well on the road to recovery and that having her one and only granddaughter here was better than anything he could have prescribed." They reached the door to Penny's old room and Brad eased her inside, closing the door unobtrusively.

"Your mom went to town for her art class," he explained. "Said since she'd be late getting home we'd go out for dinner tonight." Brad casually began to unbutton Penny's dress.

"What are you doing?" she asked, suddenly aware of his preoccupation with her clothing.

He pushed her dress off her shoulders and eased it away from her breasts and rounded hips. "I'm rehearsing for a new role," he said with a grin, lifting her and placing her on the bed. Brad quickly discarded his clothes and joined her.

"A new role?" she asked, a little breathless at the sudden turn of events.

"Umm. Isn't this the way to play doctor?"

"I certainly hope not!" she said, looking at his unclothed body with feigned indignation.

"Oh, well. Maybe I just need some tender, loving care, after an afternoon away from you."

She smiled, pulling him closer. "Well, my dear, you certainly came to the right place for that."

"I know," Brad said with a satisfied smile.

* * * * *

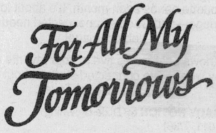

This July, watch for the delivery of...

An exciting new miniseries that appears in a different Silhouette series each month. It's about love, marriage—and Daddy's unexpected need for a baby carriage!

Daddy Knows Last unites five of your favorite authors as they weave five connected stories about baby fever in New Hope, Texas.

- **THE BABY NOTION** by Dixie Browning
  (SD#1011, 7/96)

- **BABY IN A BASKET** by Helen R. Myers
  (SR#1169, 8/96)

- **MARRIED...WITH TWINS!**
  by Jennifer Mikels
  (SSE#1054, 9/96)

- **HOW TO HOOK A HUSBAND (AND A BABY)**
  by Carolyn Zane
  (YT#29, 10/96)

- **DISCOVERED: DADDY** by Marilyn Pappano
  (IM#746, 11/96)

Daddy Knows Last arrives in July...only from

Conveniently Wed

"I do," the bride and groom said…without love
they wed—or so they thought!

Don't miss these six irresistible novels about tying the
knot—and *then* falling in love!

Coming in July, only from

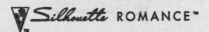

Silhouette ROMANCE™

FORTUNE'S Children™

In July, get to know the Fortune family....

Next month, don't miss the start of Fortune's Children, a fabulous new twelve-book series from Silhouette Books.

Meet the Fortunes—a family whose legacy is greater than riches. Because where there's a will...there's a wedding!

When Kate Fortune's plane crashes in the jungle, her family believes that she's dead. And when her will is read, they discover that Kate's plans for their lives are more interesting than they'd ever suspected.

Look for the first book, *Hired Husband*, by *New York Times* bestselling author **Rebecca Brandewyne**. PLUS, a stunning, perforated bookmark is affixed to *Hired Husband* (and selected other titles in the series), providing a convenient checklist for all twelve titles!

FREE
Keepsake
Bookmark

Launching in July wherever books are sold.

Silhouette®

Who can resist a Texan...or a Calloway?

This September, award-winning author
ANNETTE BROADRICK
returns to Texas, with a brand-new
story about the Calloways...

SONS OF TEXAS

Rogues and Ranchers

CLINT: The brave leader. Used to keeping secrets.

CADE: The Lone Star Stud. Used to having women fall at his feet...

MATT: The family guardian. Used to handling trouble...

They must discover the identity of the mystery woman with Calloway eyes—and uncover a conspiracy that threatens their family....

Look for **SONS OF TEXAS:** Rogues and Ranchers in September 1996!

Only from Silhouette...where passion lives.

Silhouette's recipe for a sizzling summer:

* Take the best-looking cowboy in South Dakota
* Mix in a brilliant bachelor
* Add a sexy, mysterious sheikh
* Combine their stories into one collection and you've got one sensational super-hot read!

Summer Sizzlers

MEN OF Summer

Three short stories by these favorite authors:

Kathleen Eagle
Joan Hohl
Barbara Faith

Available this July wherever
Silhouette books are sold.

Look us up on-line at: http://www.romance.net

Silhouette®

SS96